WITCHING MOON

CRIMSON MOON

EDGE OF THE MOON

KILLING MOON

MOON
SWEPT

REBECCA YORK

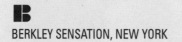

BERKLEY SENSATION, NEW YORK

THE BERKLEY PUBLISHING GROUP
Published by the Penguin Group
Penguin Group (USA) Inc.
375 Hudson Street, New York, New York 10014, USA
Penguin Group (Canada), 90 Eglinton Avenue East, Suite 700, Toronto, Ontario M4P 2Y3, Canada
(a division of Pearson Penguin Canada Inc.)
Penguin Books Ltd., 80 Strand, London WC2R 0RL, England
Penguin Group Ireland, 25 St. Stephen's Green, Dublin 2, Ireland (a division of Penguin Books Ltd.)
Penguin Group (Australia), 250 Camberwell Road, Camberwell, Victoria 3124, Australia
(a division of Pearson Australia Group Pty. Ltd.)
Penguin Books India Pvt. Ltd., 11 Community Centre, Panchsheel Park, New Delhi—110 017, India
Penguin Group (NZ), Cnr. Airborne and Rosedale Roads, Albany, Auckland 1310, New Zealand
(a division of Pearson New Zealand Ltd.)
Penguin Books (South Africa) (Pty.) Ltd., 24 Sturdee Avenue, Rosebank, Johannesburg 2196,
South Africa

Penguin Books Ltd., Registered Offices: 80 Strand, London WC2R 0RL, England

This is a work of fiction. Names, characters, places, and incidents either are the product of the author's imagination or are used fictitiously, and any resemblance to actual persons, living or dead, business establishments, events, or locales is entirely coincidental. The publisher does not have any control over and does not assume any responsibility for author or third-party websites or their content.

PRINTING HISTORY
Witching Moon: Berkley Sensation mass market edition / October 2003
Crimson Moon: Berkley Sensation mass market edition / January 2005
Berkley Sensation omnibus trade paperback edition / November 2006

Library of Congress Cataloging-in-Publication Data

York, Rebecca.
    [Witching moon]
    Moon swept / Rebecca York.
        p. cm.
    Contents: Witching moon — Crimson moon.
    ISBN 0-425-21199-1
    1. Werewolves—Fiction. 2. Botanists—Fiction. 3. Georgia—Fiction. 4. Witches—Fiction. I. York, Rebecca Crimson moon. II. Title. III. Title: Crimson moon.

    PS3575.O6326W58 2006
    813'.54—dc22

                                                                        2006048505

PRINTED IN THE UNITED STATES OF AMERICA

10   9   8   7   6   5   4   3   2   1

CONTENTS

WITCHING MOON

PROLOGUE

SHE woke to the sound of voices and sat up in her narrow bed, rubbing her eyes. The toys on her shelves were only shapes in the darkness. But moonlight peeked in around the edges of the window curtains.

Out in the front room, Momma and Daddy were talking. He wasn't usually here at night, but he came when he could to the little cabin at the edge of the swamp.

He would hug her and tell her she was his special little girl. He would run his fingers through her hair and say it was spun gold.

Maybe he'd have a treat for her. A toy. Or some candy like the last time. Momma didn't approve of candy, but Daddy liked to give her a few pieces—and tell her to enjoy them when Momma wasn't looking.

She started to swing her skinny legs over the side of the bed. Then stopped. Momma and Daddy weren't speaking very loud, and she couldn't make out the actual words. But as she caught the tone of the conversation, the happy sense of anticipation dried up, like the drops of water on the ground in the morning.

Momma and Daddy were worried, the way they'd been that other time when Daddy had said the town was on the warpath. Only nothing bad had happened then. And everything had gone on just the way it always did.

She picked up Mr. Rabbit, her favorite stuffed animal, from the pillow and hugged his limp body to her, as Daddy's footsteps came rapidly across the wooden floor. Flinging the door open, he strode into her room and bent over her bed, scooping her into his arms.

"We have to leave. We don't have much time."

Momma came hurrying after him. "This is my home. I won't let them drive me out."

"You've been taking too many chances."

"No. I've tried to help people."

"And look where it's gotten you. Darlin', you have to listen to me this time."

"If I'd listened to you . . ." Momma's voice trailed off.

Daddy gathered her up and hugged her to him. "Come on little bit, you're going with me."

"No!" Momma protested, almost drowning out the voices in the background. There were people outside, she realized with a sudden spurt of fear. Angry people.

One of Daddy's arms tightened around her; the other reached for Momma. "Jenna, let me get you away from here, before it's too late."

"I can't."

She could feel Daddy's heart pounding, hear his voice rising.

"Oh Lord, don't do this to me, please."

"Come out and show yourself—you damn witch," an unseen voice screamed, making her cower against Daddy. Other voices joined the chorus. "Come out before we burn you out."

Daddy tried to keep hold of Momma's arm, but she wrenched herself away from him and hurried into the front room. "I only tried to help. I've done nothing wrong," Momma called into the darkness beyond the walls of the house. Turning back to Daddy, she said, "I won't let them drive me from my home."

"It's too late." Daddy's warning was swallowed up by a rising babble of voices, like the wind tearing at the tree branches in a storm.

She was afraid of storms because one time a tree had fallen right across the path to the front door. But this was much worse.

She buried her face against her father's shoulder, her free hand clutching Mr. Rabbit. "Don't let them hurt Momma," she whimpered.

"I won't," he answered, starting toward the front of the house.

Before he could reach the living room, the window beside the door shattered, sending glass dancing over the wood floor.

Momma screamed, rooted to the spot where she stood.

Then a smell that was strong and dangerous filled the air—and a strange roaring noise howled through the house.

"Save her. Get her out of here," Momma screamed.

Her father cursed, started forward. But the heat from the front of the house beat him back. Still clasping her to his body, he sprinted across the bedroom, then bent to push up the window sash.

"Daddy! I'm scared, Daddy," she whimpered into the soft fabric of his shirt, trying to breathe through the cloud of smoke choking her nose and throat.

Daddy coughed and staggered, and she thought he was going to fall down, but he kept going.

"It's okay. Everything will be okay," he said. He said it over and over between coughs as he lowered her out the window. When she was standing on the ground, he quickly followed and scooped her up. His body curved over hers, he ran from the cabin. Behind her she heard a sound like thunder. Raising her head, she saw the whole house explode into flames.

"Momma! Where's Momma?"

Daddy put his hand on the back of her head, pressing her face into his shoulder and hunching protectively over her as he ran into the darkness of the swamp.

1

THE last guy who had walked in his shoes was a dead man, Adam Marshall thought as his booted feet sank into the soggy ground of the southern Georgia swamp. But he didn't intend to suffer the same fate. He had advantages that the previous head ranger at Nature's Refuge hadn't possessed.

Still, something was making his skin prickle tonight, Adam silently admitted as he slipped one hand into the pocket of his jeans. Standing very still on the porch of his cabin, he listened to the night sounds around him. The clicking noise of a bullfrog. The buzz of insects. The splash of a predator slipping into the murky waters of the mysterious marshes that the Indians had called Olakompa.

The Indians were long gone, but an aura of otherworldliness remained in this pocket of wetlands, which had managed to withstand the encroachment of civilization. It was a place steeped in superstition, and Adam had heard some pretty wild tales—of people who had been swallowed up by the "trembling earth" and of strange creatures that roamed the backcountry.

In the darkness, he laughed. He'd taken all that with a grain of salt. But maybe he could contribute to the myths while he was here.

This was a very different setting from his previous post in the dry desert country of Big Bend National Park.

He liked the change. Liked the swamp. For now. He never stayed any place too long. It didn't matter where he lived, actually. Just so he had the space he needed to roam free.

He looked up and saw the moon filtering through the branches of the willow oaks and cypress trees. It was huge and yellow and full, and he knew there were people who would think that the large orb in the sky had something to do with his unsettled mood. But it wasn't that.

He dragged in a long breath, detecting a scent that was out of place in the sultry air. Nothing he had ever smelled before, he thought, as he walked into the shadows under the oak trees.

Whatever it was had a strange tang, a pull, an edge of danger that he found disturbing. Of course, he was affected by odors as few people were. And by other things most folks took in stride. Coffee, for example, made him sick. And forget liquor.

Later tonight, he'd probably have a cup of herbal tea. By himself, since he was the only staffer who lived in the park—in the cozy cabin thoughtfully provided by Austen Barnette, who owned this three-hundred-acre corner of the swampland, along with a sizable portion of Wayland, Georgia.

Barnette was the big cheese in the area. And he'd gone to the expense and bother of hiring Adam Marshall away from the U.S. Park Service to show he was serious about running Nature's Refuge as a private enterprise. But there was another reason as well. Adam had a reputation for solving problems.

Most recently, at Big Bend, he had shut down a bunch of drug smugglers who had been bringing their cargoes across the drought-shrunken Rio Grande. He had tracked them to their mountain hideout and scared the shit out of them before turning them over to the border patrol.

He had done a good job, because he always demanded the best from himself as far as his work was concerned. It compensated for the other area of his life where he wasn't quite so effective—personal relationships. But he was damn well going to find out who had killed Ken White, the previous head ranger.

He walked to a spot about a hundred yards from his cabin, a place where he often stopped and contemplated the swamp before going out to prowl the park. It was a good distance from the house, where he was sure nobody would find his clothing.

Standing in the shade of a pine, he sniffed the wind again as his hands went to the front of his shirt. He unbuttoned the garment and dropped it on the ground, then pulled off his shoes and pants, stripping to the buff.

The sultry air felt good on his bare skin, and he stood for a moment, digging his toes into the springy layer of decomposing leaves covering the ground, caught by a push-pull within himself. The man warring with the animal clamoring to run free.

The animal won, as it must. Closing his dark eyes, he called on ancient knowledge, ancient ritual, ancient deities as he gathered his inner strength, steeling himself for familiar pain, even as he said the words that he had learned on his sixteenth birthday—the way his brothers had before him. As far as he knew, the only Marshall boys still alive were himself and Ross. But he didn't know for sure because he hadn't seen his brother in years.

It was when he prepared to change that his thoughts sometimes turned to Ross, but he didn't let those thoughts break his concentration.

"Taranis, Epona, Cerridwen," he intoned, then repeated the same phrase and went on to another.

"Ga. Feart. Cleas. Duais. Aithriocht. Go gcumhdai is dtreorai na deithe thu."

On that night so long ago, the ceremonial words had helped him through the agony of transformation, opened his mind, freed him from the bonds of the human shape. Maybe they were nonsense syllables. He didn't know. Ross had studied the ancient Gaelic language and said he understood what they meant. Adam didn't care about the meaning.

All that mattered was that they blocked some of the blinding pain that always came with transformation.

While the human part of his mind screamed in protest, he felt his jaw elongate, his teeth sharpen, his body contort as muscles and limbs transformed themselves into a different shape that was as familiar to him as his human form.

The first few times he'd done it had been a nightmare of torture and terror. But gradually, he'd learned what to expect, learned to rise above the physical sensations of muscles spasming, bones changing shape, the very structure of his cells mutating from one kind of DNA to another. At least that was how he thought about it, because he didn't understand the science involved. In fact, he was sure modern science would have no explanations for his family heritage.

But the change came upon him nevertheless.

Gray hair formed along his flanks, covering his body in a thick, silver-tipped pelt. The color—the very structure—of his eyes changed as he dropped to all fours. He was no longer a man but an animal far more suited to the natural environment around him.

A wolf. Where no wolves had made their home for decades. But now one had command of Nature's Refuge. It was his. And the night was his.

Once the transformation was complete, a raw, primal joy rippled through him, and he pawed the ground, reveling in the feel of the damp soil under his feet. Raising his head, he sucked in a draft of air, his lungs expanding as his nose drank in the rich scents that were suddenly part of the landscape. To his right an alligator had gone very still. And a bear had stopped and sniffed the wind sensing the presence of a rival.

The large black beast stayed where it was for a moment, then ambled off in the other direction, unwilling to challenge the creature with whom he suddenly shared the swamp.

Adam's lips shaped themselves into a wolfish grin. He wanted to throw back his head and howl at the small victory. But he checked the impulse, because the mind inside his skull still held his human intelligence. And the man understood the need for stealth.

Dragging in a breath, he examined the unfamiliar scent he had picked up. It was nothing that belonged in this natural world. Men had brought something here that was out of place.

The smell was acrid, yet at the same time strangely sweet to his wolf's senses. And it drew him forward.

Still, he moved with caution, setting off in the direction of the odor, feeling the air thicken around him in a strange, unfamiliar way as he padded forward.

Each breath seemed to change his sense of awareness. His mind was usually sharp, but the edges of his thoughts were beginning to blur as though someone had soaked his brain with a bottle of sweet, sticky syrup.

The air stung his eyes now, and he blinked back moisture, then blinked again as he caught his first glimpse of fire.

The flames jolted him out of his lethargy.

Fire! Where no fire should be. Out here in the open—in the middle of the park. The swamp might be wet, but that wouldn't stop a blaze from sweeping through the area, if the flames were hot enough. He'd read as much as he could about the Olakompa in the past few months, and he knew that in the winter of nineteen fifty-five, wildfires had burned eighty percent of the swamp area.

Fires were usually due to lightning igniting the layer of peat buried under some areas of the swamp.

He'd seen no lightning tonight, but it wasn't difficult to imagine a conflagration roaring unchecked through the park. Imagine birds taking flight, animals scattering for safety, the water evaporating in the heat.

His mind fuzzy from the smoke, he kept moving forward, toward the center of the danger. But when he took a second look, he saw that the flames were contained. A bonfire. Deep in the wilderness.

Tall, upright shadows moved around the flames, and in his bleary state, he could make no sense of what he was seeing. Then the wavery images resolved themselves into naked human figures—dancing and gyrating in the glow of the fire.

He shook his head, trying to clear away the fog that seemed to swirl up from the sweet, enticing smoke. For a moment he questioned his own sanity.

He'd heard people describe hallucinations that came from drug trips, heard some pretty strange stuff. Had his mind conjured up these images? Against his will, the circle of fire and the gyrating figures drew him, and he padded forward once more, although caution made his steps slow. He had come upon many strange things in his thirty years of living, but never a scene like this.

He blinked, but nothing changed. The naked men and women were still there, chanting words he didn't understand, dancing around the fire, sometimes alone, sometimes touching and swaying erotically together, sometimes falling to the ground in two- and threesomes—grappling in a sexual frenzy.

The thick, drugging smoke held him in its power, compelling his eyes to fix on the images before him, making the wolf hairs along his back bristle.

Getting high was deliberately outside his experience. He had never tried so much as a joint, although he had been at parties where people had been smoking them. But just the passive smoke had made him sick, and he'd always bailed out, which meant that he was ill-equipped to deal with mind-altering substances. Street drugs were poison to the wolf part of him. He was pretty sure that even some legal drugs could bend his mind so far out of shape that he would never be able to cram it back into his skull.

But the poison smoke had a stranglehold on his senses and on his mind. He was powerless to back away, powerless to stop breathing the choking stuff.

He took a step forward and then another, his eyes focused on the figures dancing in the moonlight. The smoke obscured their features. The smoke and the slashes of red, blue, and yellow paint both the men and women had used to decorate their faces and their bodies. He licked his long pink tongue over his lips and teeth, his eyes focused on sweaty bodies and pumping limbs, his own actions no longer under the control of his brain. Recklessly, he dragged in a deep breath of the tainted air. The fumes obscured the raw scent of the dancers' arousal. But he didn't need scent to understand their frenzy.

He watched a naked man, his cock jutting straight out from his body, reach for a woman's breasts, watched her thrust herself boldly into his hands, watched another woman join them in their sexual play, the three of them dancing and cavorting in unholy delight, the firelight flickering on their sweat-slick bodies.

His gaze cutting through the group of gamboling figures, he kept his heated focus on the threesome. He saw them swaying together, saw them fall to the ground, writhing with an urgency that took his breath away.

His own sexual experience was pretty extensive. But he'd never participated in anything beyond one man/one woman coupling. And some part of his mind was scandalized by the uninhibited orgy. Yet the urge to join the gang-shag was stronger than the shock. He felt as though his skin were cutting off his breath, restraining him like a straitjacket.

He had to escape the wolf. And in his mind, in a kind of desperate rush, the ancient chant came to him, and he reversed the process that had turned him from man to wolf.

"*Taranis, Epona, Cerridwen,*" he silently chanted, the words slurring in his brain.

"*Ga. Feart. Cleas. Duais. Aithriocht. Go gcumhdai is dtreorai na deithe thu.*"

His consciousness was so full of the sweet, sticky smoke that he could barely focus on the syllables that were so much a part of him that he could utter them in his sleep.

But they did their work, and his muscles spasmed as he changed back to human form, the pain greater than any he remembered since his teens.

He stood in the shadows, his breath coming in jagged gulps, his eyes blinking in the flickering light, his hand clawing at the bark of a tree to keep himself upright when his knees threatened to give way. The sudden urgent sounds from the campfire twenty yards away snapped his mind into some kind of hazy focus.

"There! Over there," a man's voice shouted.

"Someone's watching."

"Get him."

"Kill him!"

"Before he rats us out."

The orgy-goers might have stripped off their clothing in the swamp, but they hadn't abandoned the protections of the modern world.

A shot rang out. A bullet whizzed past Adam's head.

Without conscious thought, he turned and ran for his life, heading for the depths of the swamp where either safety or death awaited him.

2

ADAM ran for his life as another shot flashed by, too close for comfort. In some part of his mind, he knew a bullet in the brain would be a kindness, because these people were capable of tearing him limb from limb with their bare hands.

So he ran headlong through the untamed landscape, heedless of anything besides the sounds of the mob behind him.

Nothing mattered except escape. The pungent smell of peat, the sound of insects buzzing in the night, the muck under his feet were a jumbled mixture of sensations.

He might have been running on all fours or on two feet. He didn't know which. He only understood on a deep, instinctive level that staying alive depended on flight. Perhaps he was hallucinating now, but he felt the mob's hot breath on the back of his neck, heard the air hissing in and out of their lungs. He felt hands clawing at him and slipping off his sweat-slick body. Or perhaps that was only the indifferent branches of bramble bushes tearing at his naked flesh.

He splashed through ankle-deep mud, then broke through into water up to his waist as a layer of peat gave way beneath his weight.

Somehow he scrambled to higher ground, where sticky earth sucked at his bare feet.

In the darkness the sounds of pursuit diminished behind him, but still he kept up his frantic flight, his path lighted only by the silvery rays of the full moon.

He ran until he was exhausted, ran until he could run no more. Sinking to his knees, he swayed uncertainly, his hand coming to rest against the trunk of a tree.

As he tried to steady himself, the sickness at the back of his throat welled up in a great wave of nausea.

He leaned forward, retching up the food that remained in his stomach from dinner. The sickness exhausted him, and he rolled to his side, curling into a ball.

Perhaps God had mercy on him that night, because no predators found him as he sank into unconsciousness.

ADAM woke in the gray light of early dawn, to the sound of birds chirping in the trees.

For terrifying heartbeats, he didn't know where he was or even *who* he was. His head felt like a thousand coal miners were working away inside his skull with pickaxes, destroying brain cells as they went. When he tried to move any muscle in his body, the agony increased, so he lay very still, struggling to ride above the pain the way he did when he changed from wolf to man and back again.

Wolf to man.

The fundamental reality of his existence was his secret life as a wolf. Yet somehow he had forgotten all about that as he lay on the damp ground.

Jesus! He was in bad shape.

He closed his eyes, trying to will himself back to normal, although he couldn't exactly say what normal was. He felt as though he were hanging on to sanity by his fingernails.

Wild, disturbing images swirled into his mind. Some came back to him with his wolf's vision. Some were the perceptions of a man.

He saw flickering fire. Smelled a strange acrid smoke that was as sweet as it was pungent.

He squeezed his eyes more tightly shut, feeling the pounding of his heart as his fingers clenched and unclenched in the soft soil where he lay.

Had it all been a dream? A very vivid dream? Brought on by the hallucinogenic smoke?

He took a cautious sniff of the cool morning air. He didn't smell anything strange now. But that proved nothing.

To ground himself, he focused on the sensations of his body. It wasn't just his head that hurt. He ached in a wide variety of places. One spot in particular stung like hell. Opening his eyes, he looked down at the long red scratches that marred the flesh over his ribs. He'd been torn by brambles on his headlong dash through the swamp.

He didn't remember much of that. But he'd heard bullets whiz past his head. And he'd felt the primal anger of the men and women chasing him.

He was thinking about Ken White when he managed to climb to his feet. Ken White, the guy who'd held this job before him, had been found dead out here with a bullet in his brain.

Adam had smugly told himself that he wasn't going to end up that way. Now he contemplated his narrow escape.

He looked back toward the deep swamp, thinking he needed to find the campfire where he'd seen the drug and sex party. But not now. Not when he was naked and vulnerable and covered with grunge. First he was going home to shower, tend his wounds, and dress.

He raised his head, squinting in the early morning sunlight as he got his bearings. He had a good sense of direction, but he was swaying on his feet when he set out for his little cabin. His jaw rigid, he kept moving—hurrying now, wondering what he'd say if the staff found him wandering around naked.

Or if they found the place where he'd left his clothes, he thought, as he picked up his pace and angled toward the spot where he'd undressed.

Although he still wasn't back to normal, his brain was starting to work a little better. In his mind he contemplated the men and women he'd come upon the night before. He didn't know who the hell they were. And finding out was going to be a problem. His wolf's nose wouldn't be able to identify them when he encountered them again.

The smoke had drugged him, fogged his sense of smell and clouded his vision. The body paint had finished the job of hiding the party-goers' features.

A couple of the women had been blondes. At least one of them had been a real blonde he remembered. And the same woman had had big breasts that had bobbed up and down as she'd danced in the flickering light.

He gave a short bark of a laugh. Apparently he'd focused on breasts and female pubic hair. He couldn't recall the details of any cocks he'd seen. But that wasn't really surprising, given his sexual orientation.

He grimaced, thinking that what he knew about the orgy-goers was pitifully small. All his adult life he'd relied on his wolf senses. But now he was as deaf and blind as if he'd been thrown into a witches' cauldron.

TURNING from the water-stained sink, Sara Weston peered at her image in the full-length mirror on the back of the bathroom door, thinking that her rumpled old green pants and faded brown shirt made a kind of fashion statement. They were the perfect outfit for a tramp through the swamp.

She swiped a hand through her blond hair, backed away from the mirror, and walked toward the kitchen of her little rented house, hoping that she might be able to choke down some apricot yogurt for breakfast.

She'd spent most of the night huddled in her bed, sleep an impossibility as she listened to the unfamiliar sounds of the Olakompa. Animals splashing through standing water. Buzzing insects. The occasional passing of a car down the narrow road where her rented house was located.

Along with the sounds came something else. Something she couldn't identify that had drifted toward her on the night air like tainted mist. A mixture of old nightmares and new ones. When she'd finally fallen asleep, she'd dreamed of this house. Not as it was now. The paint on the walls was a darker shade. The furnishings were shabbier. And she'd seen a woman drifting through the rooms, a woman who had turned and held out her hand in invitation. To what? Sara didn't know. She didn't want to know.

She shook her head, denying her dreams. Her two nights in the motel where she'd stayed when she'd first arrived in Wayland had been bad enough. This house on the edge of the Olakompa was worse. The air was different here. Thicker. Enfolding her in an unwelcome embrace that made her feel as though someone had pressed a malicious hand over her nose and mouth.

She tried to banish the unwanted image. But it wouldn't go away. She had always had uncanny judgments. She'd sense that a place or a person was good or bad. And usually those perceptions would turn out to be valid.

It was just one of the things that made her feel different from other people. Different in a way she had never wanted to explore too deeply.

So she kept a lid on the fanciful side of her nature. In her personal life. And her professional life, too.

When she'd been a teenager, she'd had a hard time deciding what she'd wanted to do with her life. She'd been attracted to art. And her high school teachers had encouraged her in that area. She'd been good. Too good, maybe. Because when she'd looked at her drawings and paintings, she'd thought they'd revealed too much about her inner self. And that had made her feel exposed.

So she'd backed away from creative expression. In college she'd taken a lot of science courses. Science was steady and down-to-earth. You dealt with facts and information and numbers. And the numbers didn't give away anything about the person writing them down.

Science had taught her to be measured and methodical. To study each new environment carefully. Before she'd come to Wayland, she'd read about the town. The early residents had raised cotton and tobacco. Then peanuts had become the major cash crop in the area. In the nineteenth and early twentieth century, a weaving factory had provided a lot of employment—until the jobs had gone to countries like Mexico and China where labor costs were lower.

Now tourism was an important part of the economy thanks to Nature's Refuge and the nearby national park that drew visitors to southern Georgia's unique and beautiful Olakompa Swamp.

Many of the same tourists who came to the parks also visited the cute little stores and restaurants along the four block commercial stretch that was now called Historic Downtown Wayland. In fact, the town was getting a reputation for the number and quality of its antique and secondhand shops. As well as the discount mall out near the interstate.

On the surface, Wayland had a good deal of charm—if you didn't poke too closely into the pockets of poverty that she'd seen in some of the outlying areas.

She'd done her homework. And now she would do the job that she'd contracted to do—a research project for Granville Pharmaceuticals. They wanted to find out if any of the plants native to the area had commercial medicinal value. And they'd hired her to conduct a six-month study of the local flora.

This morning, she supposed she should be opening the boxes of lab equipment that had arrived from UPS yesterday afternoon. But she needed to get out of the little house.

So she climbed into the secondhand Toyota, Miss Hester, that Mom had given her when she'd gone off to college in Chapel Hill. Almost eight years later, she was still driving the old rattletrap.

Mom had wanted her to get something better before she headed for Georgia. She'd protested that Miss Hester was just fine.

As she drove, she scanned the highway for the Nature's Refuge access road she'd been instructed to look for, then slowed when she saw the turnoff. Not the paved public drive that led to the front entrance, but the gravel track that skirted the edge of the vast swampland property.

The directions were very precise, and here it was.

Behind her on Route 177 a pickup truck honked, and she jumped, then watched the driver wave his fist in anger as he pulled around her and barreled down the blacktop. He probably was thinking, "stupid woman driver."

Goody for him. Turning off the highway, she came to a stop, peering uncertainly up the road, wishing that this job offer hadn't been so tempting.

Too bad none of the dozens of applications for tenure track teaching had panned out. Apparently, the market for newly minted Ph.D. botanists was depressed.

"Don't worry dear; something will turn up," Mom had said, with that eternal optimism of hers. "You've always loved plants. I know you can do something with your special skills."

Sara smiled to herself. Right, she loved plants. Loved growing them. Loved knowing their names and their uses. But more than that, she'd worked long and hard to earn an advanced degree in botany, which now hadn't seemed worth the effort considering the costs involved.

When she realized her hands were clamped around the steering wheel, she unclenched them. With a sigh, she took her foot off the brake. The car drifted slowly forward as though it had a mind of its own and had somehow acquired information she didn't possess.

Something just out of her grasp.

With a shake of her head, she pressed down on the accelerator, fighting a sense of disquiet as she felt the shadows of giant trees close in on either side of the car.

Really, if you looked at this place objectively, it was beautiful, more beautiful than she'd imagined.

A low area full of water, cattails, duckweed, and water hyacinths ran along the side of the road. In the shallows a blue heron moved slowly away from her, poking its head below the surface, then lifting it gracefully again, and she stopped for a moment to watch its progress. She smiled as she saw a small brown lizard hop onto a floating leaf. There were eleven kinds of lizards in the swamp, and she guessed she was going to see a lot of them while she was here.

Starting up again, she drove a few more yards to a wooden barrier. On a nearby long-leaf pine was a large No Trespassing sign.

She'd been told to expect the gate. Carefully, she looked around, probing the shadows under the trees before grabbing her knapsack and climbing out.

It was early, but she could feel heat rising from the marshy land on either side of the desolate road as she walked toward the barrier.

Still, when a cloud drifted across the sun, she felt a sudden chill. Shaking it off, she walked to the padlocked chain that secured the gate and opened the lock.

With the bar out of the way, she returned to her car and drove through, then swung the wooden pole back into place and snapped the lock closed, thinking that escape was now impossible.

ADAM regarded his haggard face in the bathroom mirror. He looked like he'd been shot out of a cannon and missed the net.

With a grimace, he turned on the shower and stepped under water as hot as he could stand. After washing off the muck, he dabbed antiseptic on his scratches, shaved, and dressed in a clean pair of dark slacks and the green shirt that Nature's Refuge called a uniform.

At least he looked presentable. But his head still felt twice its normal size. Opening the refrigerator, he considered what to eat for breakfast. Nothing appealed to him, but he knew from experience that going without food was bad for his system. So he grabbed some chunks of stew beef and carried them to the table in his small dining room.

He liked the house that came with the job. All he had to do was step out the front door and walk a few hundred yards along a path to the main part of the park complex.

The built-up area of Nature's Refuge consisted of six structures. The largest was the administrative center with offices, a gift shop, and an auditorium where he and the other staffers gave nature talks. They also conducted tours of the swamp, both on foot along well-marked trails and boardwalks and in the trim skiffs moored in the dock area.

Chris Higman and Dwayne Parker had already arrived at the main office by the time he'd washed the meat down with a cup of blackberry tea and two ibuprofen.

Adam stopped inside the office door, automatically dragging in a deep breath, catching his staffers' familiar scent. Under normal circumstances he'd know whether either of these people had been part of last night's orgy. Today, he didn't have a clue. And the lack of knowledge made his chest feel tight.

"You two are always right on time," he commented, trying to sound like his usual chipper self.

"Maybe I'm anglin' for your job," Dwayne joked.

"I'll watch my back," Adam answered, striving for a light tone.

The door banged, and Leroy Hamilton came in. He was slightly older than Chris and Dwayne, and he'd been here a couple of years longer.

In the National Park Service, all the rangers had a college degree in a prescribed set of fields. That certainly wasn't true at Nature's Refuge. When Adam had come to the park, he'd found some of the staffers poorly trained and some of the procedures pretty lax, to put it mildly. But he was getting things into shape.

As he usually did in the morning, he went over the assignments for the day. But it was impossible to turn off his earlier thoughts. He'd established a pretty good relationship with the young men and women who worked for him. Now he couldn't help wondering if any of them had chased him through the swamp last night—intent on murder.

As far as he could see, nobody seemed the worse for wear this morning. But all of them certainly knew what area of the park would be good for an after-hours party.

He stifled a sigh. They looked like clean-cut kids. In fact, he knew they were all fine upstanding members of the local Baptist church, since each of them on separate occasions tried to get him to attend services.

Most of the people around here were churchgoers. So was there some kind of underground cult in town that went completely against the cultural norms?

He snorted inwardly at the sociological jargon. Obviously, he was in a strange mood this morning. Yet the question did bear asking. Had he seen local people out for a night of revelry in the swamp? Or were the trespassers from out of the area? Would they come again? And most of all, were they the same people who had murdered Ken White?

Maybe he'd find some clues when he located the place where they'd made their fire.

Leaning his hips against his desk, he gave the three staffers a serious look. "I thought I smelled smoke out in the park last night."

All eyes riveted to him.

"You hear anything about individuals illegally in the park?"

"No, sir," Leroy said immediately. The others echoed his answer.

"Well, I want to go out there and have a look."

"You want me to go with you?" Dwayne asked immediately.

"No. I'll handle it myself. Send Tim down to the ticket booth at the boat dock when he comes in."

"You got it, boss," Dwayne answered.

Picking up a walkie-talkie from the shelf near the door to the equipment room, Adam headed for the dock where he climbed into one of the motorboats tied up near the main channel. If you knew where you were going, sometimes a boat was the quickest way into the park's interior.

He was thinking about the party-goers again as he started the outboard motor, then settled down in the back of the skiff, his hand on the tiller.

The dark water was smooth as glass, an almost perfect mirror reflecting the trees that hung above the channel. An egret flapped away as the boat rounded a bend, and Adam thought he heard a gator splash into the dark water. Usually he enjoyed the wildlife in the park. This morning he was too preoccupied.

He wasn't sure exactly where he'd encountered the fire the night before, but he had a good idea of the general area, since he'd made it his business to get to know his domain. Fifteen minutes later, he cut the engine and tied the boat to the roots of a dead tree. Climbing out, he scrambled through muck that came several inches up his low boots, then made it onto more solid ground. Pausing again to get his bearings, he headed through the underbrush toward the open area he remembered from the night before, looking for signs of trampled vegetation and seeing none.

Cautiously, he stopped and sniffed the air. When he caught the barest whiff of the smoke, he froze. No way was he going to let that stuff take over his mind again.

For a long moment, he stood absolutely still, breathing shallowly in and out, his perception turned inward. When he'd smelled the stuff last night, he'd started feeling muzzy almost at once. As far as he could tell, nothing like that was happening now. Maybe the residue was at so low a level that it wouldn't hurt him.

Or just the opposite could be happening. Perhaps once you'd been bitten by this particular snake, it only took a little of the venom to wig you out again. And you wouldn't even realize it was happening.

He'd just decided to save his recon mission for later when movement on the other side of the clearing caught his eye, and he went very still. Something was there.

A large animal?

No—a person, dressed in green and brown that blended with the foliage. A guy who knew his way around in the backcountry.

Then the figure stepped out of the shadow of the trees, and he realized it wasn't a guy. Instead, he found himself staring at feminine curves covered by a long-sleeved shirt, cotton pants, and boots similar to his own.

She wasn't aware of him, giving him time to focus on her blond hair, caught at the nape of her neck by a simple band.

He zeroed in on that hair, thinking it was like what he remembered from some of the women last night.

Without moving a muscle, he watched her wander into the clearing. When he saw her kneel, saw her bring something shiny and metal out of the pack she was carrying, he leaped forward.

3

"HOLD it right there!"

The blond woman jerked around to face him, her hand clenched around a clump of sweet flag she was about to dig up with a small trowel.

"You're trespassing on private property," he heard himself say, surprised that his voice sounded normal, because he felt suddenly light-headed as he gazed into wide blue eyes that regarded him warily.

It was the remnants of the smoke affecting him, he thought. It had gotten to him again. He could smell its lingering presence more strongly than he had a few moments earlier, and now he wished he had backed away instead of letting himself be drawn forward into a trap.

But it was already too late, he knew on some deep, buried level. He might have tried to puzzle out what that meant. It was only one of the confused thoughts that swirled in his brain, thoughts that danced away before he could catch onto any one of them long enough to bring it into focus.

Last night the smoke had taken away the sharpness of his senses. Now his reaction was totally different. In the morning sunlight, he was suddenly and totally absorbed by every detail of the woman kneeling before him. His gaze lingered for a moment on a blond strand of hair that had escaped the band at the back of her neck and now curved seductively around her ear. Then he took in the triangle of ivory skin exposed at the throat of her shirt.

But more than the physical impressions, he saw that she was struggling not to show panic as she stared at him with those wide blue eyes.

That panic made his chest tighten. "It's okay," he said, then wasn't sure if the words had reached his lips or only echoed in his mind as he took her in.

What the hell was she doing out here, anyway? Had she returned to the scene of last night's clandestine party? Or was she engaged in some other crime? Like stealing plants from a private park.

He had to admit she didn't look much like a criminal. Her hair was the color of ripe wheat. Her face was heart-shaped and delicately made with beautifully curved lips, high cheekbones, and those blue, blue eyes, framed by dark-tipped lashes.

She was slender. About five five, he guessed. Her breasts were high and very nicely rounded. Probably she thought her hips were too generous, but he liked them the way they were.

He blinked, stood his ground, trying to explain in his mind why he was fixated on this woman. "The smoke," he said, and this time was sure he had spoken aloud, because she dragged in a breath, her nose wrinkling before she answered him.

"What smoke?"

"Don't you smell it? The leftovers from the party."

She tipped her head to the side, looking at him as though he'd lost his mind. Maybe he had. He'd lost it last night and thought he'd found it again in the morning. Now he struggled to remember what they had been talking about.

"You're trespassing," he managed.

She was still kneeling on the ground. Now she reached for a knapsack lying a few feet away, pulled it toward her, and thrust a hand inside. When it emerged, she was holding a small revolver. "Don't come any closer," she said, as she carefully stood up. "Raise your hands."

He'd been feeling spacey, as though his brain and his body belonged to two separate people, and there was no way to bring the two of them back together. The gun did the trick. Suddenly the muzzy feeling was gone. He stood where he was, raised his hands, palms toward her. "Be careful with that thing," he said.

"Who are you? What are you doing here?" she asked.

Had she been the one shooting at him last night? And now was he giving her a free second chance? Too bad he was pretty sure those old legends about werewolves weren't true. You didn't need to load your gun with silver bullets to bring down a member of the species. All you needed was nice hot, conventional lead.

"Who are you?" she asked again, her voice going an octave higher. He heard raw nerves in that voice, which made the situation all the more dangerous. His mind was doing swift calculations now. She didn't look like the kind of woman who was used to handling a gun, but that proved nothing, except that she could shoot him by accident.

"Take it easy," he advised. "You don't want to get arrested for killing the head ranger at Nature's Refuge."

"The head ranger! Don't give me that. The head ranger should be expecting me."

Expecting her? Who the hell was she? Some inspector the park's owner, Austen Barnette, had sent and forgotten to mention to his minions? That wasn't like the old coot. Or was there some information about this woman buried in a pile of junk mail?

"I'm Adam Marshall," he said, his voice calm and steady. "Whom should I be expecting?"

Ignoring his question, she demanded, "Show me some identification."

He watched her eyes, gauging her level of jumpiness. Would she really pull the trigger, or would she hesitate a fraction of a second, giving him time to knock the weapon out of her hand?

Some part of his brain was viewing the confrontation from a distance like a kind of strange out-of-body experience. "Okay, my wallet's in my pocket. Don't drill me when I pull it out," he said, speaking calmly as he reached into his back pocket and extracted the wallet, then carefully opened it to his driver's license, which he held up for her to see.

She peered at the plastic-covered rectangle, then snapped, "That's from Texas."

"Yeah, right. I just took the job here four months ago."

"And you haven't changed your license?"

"I've been busy. If you've been in touch with Austen Barnette, you may recall that the previous head ranger was found shot dead in the park. So pardon me for being a little careful when I meet up with strangers out here."

She winced. After several second's hesitation, she lowered the weapon, and he managed to fill his lungs with air for the first time since the gun had appeared out of her knapsack.

"Thanks," he said, then asked, "So who are you?"

"Sara Weston."

The name was familiar, and he struggled to figure out the context. "The botanist," he finally said. "Working on the drug project for Granville Pharmaceuticals."

"That's right."

"I was expecting a fifty-year-old woman with gray hair pulled back in a bun," he said, feeling foolish as the words came out of his mouth.

She made a face. "You don't have to be an old bat to be interested in the medicinal uses of plants."

"I realize that." He sighed. "But I'd be remiss if I didn't ask *you* for some identification."

She nodded and hunkered down to reach in her pack. As he had done, she pulled out a wallet with her driver's license—and also a letter from Barnette, giving her permission to take plant specimens from the park.

"You looking for a cure for cancer?" he asked.

"I'm looking for plants that native Americans and herbal healers have used successfully. Like this *Acorus calamus*," she said, gesturing toward the plant she'd been about to dig up.

"Sweet flag," he said.

"Yes. *Acorus calamus*. Or sweet flag. Or calamus or sweet root. It's been used to cure various ailments since biblical times. It looks like an iris, but it's actually related to jack-in-the-pulpit and skunk cabbage. The part used medicinally is the root. It shouldn't be peeled, because the active ingredient is right below the surface." She stopped abruptly, maybe because she'd become aware that she was lecturing him.

"Okay," he answered, "you've convinced me of your botanical expertise."

Color spread across her cheeks, and he couldn't stop himself from admiring the effect.

He told himself it wasn't likely that Dr. Sara Weston had been involved with the orgy-goers of the night before. But her turning up in this particular location the next morning was certainly a screaming coincidence.

"So are you just looking for cures for diseases, or are you interested in psychotropic drugs?" he asked.

"That's kind of a strange question. Why do you ask?"

"Because I caught some people having a drug party last night," he said, watching her carefully.

Her eyes widened. "In the park?"

"Yes. Actually right around here. Maybe you can give me your professional opinion on what they were using."

"*Acorus calamus* has no psychotropic qualities as far as I know," she answered.

"But some of the plants here do," he said, "like pearly everlasting or ladies' tobacco, or whatever you want to call it." He tossed the observation over his shoulder. He was already marching past her and toward the clearing where he thought he'd seen the fire.

He waited with his nerves on edge, then relaxed when he heard her following him.

He stopped short when he saw the fire pit. Until that moment he hadn't been absolutely sure he hadn't dreamed it.

Looking around, he half expected to find some discarded article of clothing, but on first glance, there was nothing besides ash and charred wood and a bunch of footprints in the dirt to witness that anyone had been here recently. Apparently the party-goers hadn't been too wasted to take away their personal effects.

The smoke was stronger here. When he drew in a cautious breath, he caught the remnants of the stuff mixed with the unmistakable aroma of stale sex, at least to his werewolf-enhanced senses.

Could she smell that, too? he wondered, giving her a sidewise look. Her posture had turned rigid, and he couldn't shake the feeling that they were sharing a kind of secondhand intimacy.

She walked slowly toward the place where the fire had been, staring down at the cold embers. "Isn't it dangerous—lighting a fire out here?"

"Yeah, but they cleared a fairly large area."

He looked from her to the stone-ringed pit. He had sworn he was going to stay as far away from the smoke as he possibly could. Yet some impulse he couldn't analyze had seized hold of him. He found himself walking forward, picking up a stick, and stirring the cold ashes.

Gray flakes swirled. Caught by a little puff of wind, they rose into the air. The particles gave off the scent of the smoke that had captured him the night before.

Instantly, Adam's mind flashed back to the darkness of the moon-drenched swamp, to the wild movement of naked bodies dancing and coming together in the flickering firelight.

But this time was different. This time, in his imagination, he wasn't an outsider, silent witness to the orgiastic dancing. This time he was one of the participants, writhing and chanting among the press of bodies.

And he wasn't the only one. The pretty blond botanist was back there, too.

The nighttime scene was an overlay on the daytime reality. His gaze riveted to Sara Weston's face—to her body. Her eyes had gone unfocused. Her breath was a shaky gasp. And another flood of color suffused her face.

The remnants of the drug pulsed through his senses, and in that moment of illusion, he saw her as he had seen the dancers the night before. Naked and aroused, her nipples tight, her skin glistening with sweat.

But the smoke-induced hallucination was over before it had time to form into anything solid and real.

She was staring at him, as if she knew what had leaped into his mind.

"What just happened?" he asked.

"Nothing."

"Are you sure?"

"Perfectly."

He shifted his weight from one foot to the other. "What kind of psychotropic drug would use fire and smoke as a delivery system?"

"That's not my field. I don't know." She raised her head, looking at him with assessing eyes. "Why did you stir up the fire?"

"I was making sure it was really out," he answered, wondering if she would call him on the lie. "As you pointed out, a fire here could be dangerous."

She only nodded, then said, "I'm sorry if we got off on the wrong foot. I was planning to stop by your office later today."

On some other morning, he might have accepted her words with a nod. Instead he said, "But you came out here first."

"I was anxious to get started," she answered.

"How did you get onto park property?"

"I have a key to the gate that locks the access road. My car's over that way," she said, waving her hand in the direction of the road that ran along the edge of the refuge and then branched off toward the interior. Probably she was glad for the change of subject. And probably he should bring the conversation back to the drug. Instead, he let it go because he wasn't feeling any more sure of himself than she looked.

"I wouldn't come in here in a car," he said.

"Oh?"

"The ground in the swamp can be wet and slippery. A truck with four-wheel drive is more suitable to the road conditions."

"Too bad I can't afford one," she snapped.

"I could ban you from the park."

"Austen Barnette might have something to say about that."

"You've been in touch with him?"

"It was my understanding that he was in favor of my research. I believe Granville is paying him a fee to allow me to collect specimens here."

"Yeah," Adam conceded. Barnette had told him that he'd worked a deal with Granville Pharmaceuticals. At the time he'd been annoyed, because as far as he was concerned, digging up plants for medicinal purposes in the park was incompatible with the concept of Nature's Refuge. What if Granville found some useful plant that only grew in the swamp? There would be all kinds of people tramping through the place, disturbing the natural environment. He'd wanted to explain that to Barnette, but he'd also been new on the job and unsure of how the owner would take advice from employees. So he'd kept his mouth shut.

Perhaps he was taking out his frustration on Sara when he said, "Do you mind telling me where you were last night?"

"In bed."

"Alone?"

Her face contorted. "Of course I was alone. What are you implying—that I was here at a drug party last night?"

"I have to check out every lead."

Her voice took on a sharp edge. "Well, I don't appreciate you implicating me."

He wasn't going to back down. "The park is pretty big. You have to admit, it's strange that I find a problem in this particular area—then find you here the next morning."

She shrugged. "I'm sorry if it seems odd to you. Perhaps the proximity of the road is a factor."

The urge to keep her talking burned inside him. But he didn't know what else to say. He'd set them up in a confrontational situation, and now he didn't know how to get out of it.

She took care of that problem for him. "I'm sorry. You'll have to excuse me; I must get back to work." She turned and retraced her steps.

He stood watching her. She was acting like she was the only person out here in the swamp, but he knew she had to be aware of his gaze.

She carefully ignored him as she bent to the plant she'd been digging up, looking totally absorbed in the task, except for the rigid set of her shoulders.

He watched her for several more moments, then he went back to the fire circle to look for clues.

This time he was careful not to stir the ashes. He should probably call in the sheriff, Paul Delacorte. As he recalled, there were rules about disturbing a crime scene. But he wanted a crack at the site first. Then he'd see if Delacorte had registered any similar trouble on his radar screen.

He kept his focus pretty much on the area where the orgy had taken place, starting near the fire pit and walking in an ever-widening circle, looking for evidence.

He saw several places where coolers or boxes had been set on the spongy ground. He saw places where he thought the participants might have been writhing together, but that was about all.

Sighing, he continued the visual search and doggedly kept from looking over to where Sara Weston was working.

He saw a stampede of feet where the party-goers had probably taken after the intruder the night before. He followed that trail into the underbrush, but came up with nothing.

Finally, on his way back, he allowed himself to raise his eyes to the spot where he'd last seen the botanist.

She was gone. Somehow, he'd known she would be.

4

STARFLOWER woke and stretched languidly in her bed, the covers drifting down to expose her naked breasts. They were slashed by a line of scratches where one of her lovers had raked his nails across her tender flesh last night.

She fingered the marks now, gently, possessively, bringing back memories of the wild coupling.

She had loved the fire and the smoke and the frantic dancing. When the dancing had turned to touching and kissing and fucking, she had liked that even better.

She had felt her power build while she was with the others. She had felt as though she could do anything. Even though it wasn't quite true.

It was always that way when the clan gathered for a ceremony in the swamp. They were the chosen ones. And they had finally come out of hiding to claim their birthright. Their strength was in their melding together. Falcon had said that would be true. And it looked like their leader was right.

Falcon had told them to pick names from nature. When she'd joined the clan, she had chosen Starflower because she loved the combination of sounds and because the name seemed unusual and elegant.

That wasn't the name she was known by when she went out among the sorry folk who populated Wayland and the area around the town. They thought she was like them. But she had powers they could only dream of.

She sent her thoughts across the room, toward the heavy vase that sat on the shelf below the window. With her mind, she tried to move it. She felt the glass vibrate, but the vase remained where it was.

"Shit!" She had thought that, after the energy flowed into her last night, she could move the damn thing, but it was too frigging heavy. Her gaze darted over the room. A pile of papers sat on the corner of the desk. From where she lay in bed, she was able to riffle them. One flew into the air and drifted downward toward the floor.

She felt a small zing of triumph. She had moved the paper. But it wasn't enough. She had to practice her talent. Falcon had told her to practice. But practicing alone was no fun. And it was hard work.

It was better when she was in the magic circle of the group, feeling their collective power and their sexual energy.

She smiled as she sat up, then pushed back her flowing golden hair. Her fingers caught on a piece of debris, and she plucked it out, holding it up. It was a twig, and she remembered now that her hair had caught on the low hanging branches of a tree as she'd followed the others headlong into the wilds of the park.

Razorback had seen the intruder and sounded the alarm. And she'd had no choice but to join the wild chase.

An outsider had seen them dancing around the fire under the witching moon, and he must be eliminated.

Secretly, she didn't go along with that logic. She had sensed the watcher's presence in the darkness—even as Falcon had played with her breasts and run his hand down her butt crack.

But her mind had reached toward the man beyond the firelight. She had felt his potency. And she had wanted that potency between her legs.

She leaned back against the pillows again, touching her breasts, bringing the nipples to hard, sensitive points as she thought about the guy who had been watching them—watching *her*. Last night she had been sated. But this morning, thinking about the stranger in the darkness brought back her sexual desire.

Eyes closed, she let her hand drift down her body as she thought about the intruder. Falcon said he was dangerous. To the clan. To their plans. He had spied on them for his own purposes. But she had sensed his sexual arousal and his desire to join with them.

Then when the group had attacked him, he had run for his life, because he had no choice.

But he was no coward. She knew that.

The rest of the group might not understand. But she knew he was like them. Well, not exactly like them. But he was no one ordinary. She understood that much. And she would find out who he was and bring him into the clan.

She kept her thoughts on him as she stroked her breasts, pinched the nipples, then slid one hand down her body to her slick, wet sex.

Her finger slipped into the hot, swollen folds. She was sore from the night before, and it hurt to stroke herself. All of the men had had her in the frantic riot of sexual need created by the smoke.

But the pain this morning only added to her pleasure. And when her orgasm rocked her, she heard the vase sway on the shelf and tumble to the floor, where it broke in a shower of glass shards.

SHERIFF Paul Delacorte climbed out of his black-and-white cruiser and stood under the branches of a longleaf pine, looking at the open area near the ranger station at Nature's Refuge. The grounds were well kept, he noted, with plantings of flowers setting off the natural vegetation.

He hadn't been out here in a couple of months. Now he gave his surroundings his usual thorough inspection. As far as he could see, Adam Marshall was doing a right fine job of keeping up the park ambiance. Marshall had come here with a high level of enthusiasm. He had the place shaped up, but it still remained to be seen how far out on a limb he was willing to go to influence policy.

Paul had done some checking and knew that the man had joined the National Park Service right out of college eight years ago. He'd worked for them until accepting the head ranger position in Wayland. Paul wondered how the new head ranger liked the job, now that he'd been here a few months.

The rules at Nature's Refuge weren't quite like the rules that the federal government insisted upon.

Take for example, the large gator that lay sunning himself beside a cabbage palm. The gator's name was Big Jim, and he'd been a fixture at the park for over fifteen years. Paul knew the creatures looked like big scaly slugs, incapable of fast movement. But in reality, when a gator was hungry, it could strike with lightning speed. Big Jim had once snapped up a miniature poodle belonging to a tourist and dragged if off, squealing pitifully, into the swamp. That was back when Paul had first been elected sheriff, and as a black man, he'd been a little reticent about rocking the boat in Wayland. Basically, he'd figured he'd gotten the job because the population expected him to follow his daddy's tradition and not make waves.

He wasn't his daddy, of course. And he'd vowed he wasn't going to be the black lackey of Wayland, Georgia. But he'd also known he couldn't come striding in with his degree from the state university and his top honors at the police academy and euthanize a beloved local icon. So he'd allowed Austen Barnette to persuade him that paying a fine—including a substantial sum to the owner of the poodle—would make up for the loss of the animal. And he'd gotten the assurance of the then head ranger, Ray Thompson, that the gator would be fed large portions of raw meat on a regular basis, to keep him away from the tourist's dogs and children.

Back then Paul was still feeling his way. Now he'd learned that if you were gonna run with the big dogs, you'd better know how to lift your leg in the tall grass.

Straightening his shoulders, he switched his thoughts from himself back to the park. There had been four head rangers since Ray Thompson had retired and migrated south to the Daytona Beach area. Most of them had been good men, except Hank Bradford, who had liked his liquor a little too much.

The face of Ken White flashed into his mind, and he clenched his fists at his sides. Five and a half months ago, Ken had been murdered out in the swamp, and there still weren't any clues about who had done it. Although Paul had his theories.

Which was why he was keeping a close eye on Nature's Refuge. From his position under the pine tree, he caught sight of Adam Marshall coming up the path from the boat dock.

Paul moved to intercept him—noting the man's flash of surprise as he spotted the navy blue uniform. Marshall stopped where he was, waiting for the law to catch up with him.

"What's new?" Paul said.

The ranger gave him an apprising look. "I have the feeling you might already have an idea," he answered.

"Nothing concrete," Paul allowed. It was hard to explain the feeling he'd picked up in town this morning. It wasn't something he could exactly articulate. It was simply a kind of vibration of dark excitement in the air. The kind of murky vibration he'd felt the morning after Ken White's death. Some people might have called it cop's instincts. Maybe that was part of it, but it also made Paul wonder about his own genetic heritage. Over the years, there had been a fair amount of informal interbreeding between the white folks and the blacks in

Wayland. He knew he probably had as much white blood flowing through his veins as black. And he suspected some of his ancestors were involved with the strange doings that had erupted in the area over the years.

"Let me tell the staff I'm back," Marshall was saying. "Then we can go over to my cabin and talk."

"Appreciate it," Paul answered, leaning against a railing at the edge of the parking lot where he could keep an eye on Big Jim.

He was watching a flock of sparrows chattering in the bushes when Marshall returned several minutes later. Had it taken him that long to deal with the staff or was he collecting his thoughts?

Paul eyed the manila folder in Marshall's hand.

"The attendance figures by day of the week and month. I want to see if I need to switch staff schedules around."

"I guess there's a lot of behind-the-scenes management involved with running a place like this," Paul observed, straightening. Together he and Marshall crossed the parking area and stepped into a small grove about a hundred yards from the main complex.

Nestled among the trees were a pair of snug log cabins. They had been used for storage for a number of years. But Ray Thompson had had them cleaned up and turned into living quarters. He and one of his staffers had moved in when the park had had some problems with vandalism. Marshall was living in one of the cabins now. The other was sometimes used for overnight guests.

"You like living out here by yourself?" Paul asked as the ranger opened the door.

"I like my privacy, yeah."

Was that a warning? Paul wondered, as the head ranger led him into a combination living/dining area with a small kitchen off to the side.

Paul looked around unobtrusively, making judgments about the man by the way he kept his personal space. The rooms were military neat, and Marshall hadn't bothered to set out any mementos that would give any clues to his past life. If he were going only by what he observed now, he'd think Marshall was trying to hide his background. But Paul had seen his performance appraisals. They were all good.

"Can I get you something to drink?" Marshall asked, walking toward the kitchen area.

"I remember you don't drink coffee. Or soft drinks."

Marshall laughed. "Yeah, I've got some nice spring water—or some herbal teas."

"Water is fine," Paul said.

The ranger brought a bottle out of the refrigerator and poured two large glasses. "We can sit out back," he said, leading the way to another door that opened onto a small patio shaded by black gum trees.

"Seems like a good place to set a spell," Paul commented as he settled into one of the two Adirondack chairs that looked out toward the natural area beyond.

Marshall took several swallows of water. "You didn't come here to talk about the bucolic scenery, did you?" he asked. "I'd like to know what did bring you out to the park."

"One of my periodic drop-bys to ask if you'd picked up anything on the Ken White case," Paul replied.

ADAM thought about his response as he set down his glass on the low wooden table between the chairs and glanced up into Paul's face, which was the color of English toffee.

"As a matter of fact, something did happen here last night," he finally said. Growing up, he'd developed a healthy disrespect for the law. The attitude came from dear old Dad, who had supplemented his income as an auto mechanic with breaking and entering.

The way kids did, Adam had absorbed some of his old man's attitudes and prejudices. He'd had to learn the hard way that the law wasn't the enemy. And he'd also had to discard some of the racist attitudes his dad had brought into the house. To put it mildly, his father had looked down on anyone whose dark skin color wasn't the result of a nice suntan. It wasn't until Adam had left home that he'd bothered looking at black people any differently. His first boss in the park service, Henry Darter, had been an African American, and with the background of prejudice Adam had absorbed from his father, he'd resented working for Darter—until he'd seen how the man had handled a flash flood in the Big Thompson River valley. Darter had saved a lot of lives that evening, and Adam had come out of the experience with a totally different view of the man.

Adam didn't like to think in stereotypes. But he couldn't help noting that Paul Delacorte was a lot like Henry. He might seem relaxed—even a bit slow, until you saw the intelligence flash in his large brown eyes.

Delacorte got comfortable in his chair. "You plannin' to share the information with me?"

Speaking slowly and deliberately, Adam started with the background of the evening before. "I like to nose around the park at night," he said, liking the double meaning of the verb. "Kind of looking out that everything's the way it should be in my immediate environment, if you know what I mean."

"Like the way I drive around town in my cruiser, just making sure everything's peaceful."

Adam nodded, feeling a sudden current of kinship with the man. Probably that was what Delacorte had intended. "Last night I was out in the swamp, and I smelled something funny."

"Funny—like what?"

"Like smoke. When I got closer, I realized the smoke was hallucinogenic, and the people who had kindled the fire were high."

The sheriff sat forward in his seat. "Oh yeah?"

"As near as I can figure, they came out to the park to have a private sex and drug party."

"With marijuana? Coke?" the lawman asked.

Instead of answering, Adam asked, "You have trouble with any of those in town?"

"Of course we do. Wayland may look like a sleepy little southern burg, but it's not the Garden of Eden before the fall."

Adam laughed. "Yeah. Well, I don't indulge in anything stronger than herbal tea myself."

"Why not?"

"That's a pretty direct question. But I'll answer it—because I don't have anything to hide," he said, vividly conscious of the lie. "I guess you can think of it as an allergy. Or that my system's delicate. Anyway, drugs play havoc with my senses."

Delacorte nodded, and Adam had the feeling the sheriff was taking the disclaimer under advisement.

Adam went back to the original question. "They weren't smoking joints or snorting anything. They were inhaling some kind of stuff that they dumped into the fire. I was trying to get close, and they discovered I was watching them." He gave Delacorte a direct look. "And somebody started shooting at me."

The sheriff's exclamation interrupted his narrative. "Holy Moses." It was a mild curse, but about the strongest he'd heard the man use.

"I was unarmed. My only choice was to get the hell out of there— before I ended up as buzzard feed."

Adam watched the lawman, judging his reaction. He knew that on the face of it, the tale sounded like the head ranger might have been indulging in some of the shit he claimed he never used, yet he could see Delacorte working his way through the story.

"They chased you into the swamp?"

"Yeah."

"And then what?"

"Then I woke up the next morning wondering if I'd dreamed the whole damn thing. Only when I went back to the area, I found their fire pit."

Adam realized his hands were clamped around the water glass. He also realized the sheriff was watching him intently.

"That drugged smoke," he said. "It knocked you out?"

Adam shifted in his seat. "Like I told you, I've never been into mind-altering substances. So, yeah, I couldn't handle the smoke. That's why I can't give you any details about who the party-goers were."

He saw the sheriff nod.

"You've had trouble in the park before?" he asked. "Before Ken White?"

"Yeah."

"So would you mind cluing me in to what Austen Barnette neglected to tell me when he signed me up for this job?"

Now it looked like it was the sheriff's turn to decide what to say. Adam knew he was an outsider. And in a small town like Wayland, it took a while for a newcomer to be accepted.

On the other hand, he'd been willing to take a job in Nature's Refuge, after the last head ranger had died in the line of duty. He figured that should entitle him to the real scoop.

"We've had trouble in the Olakompa over the years," the lawman said.

"Other murders?"

Again, Delacorte hesitated, then said, "About twenty-five years ago. A woman was killed."

"Found in the swamp, like White?"

"She had a cabin about a mile north of here as the crow flies. It's a little longer by road. It happened there."

"Who killed her?"

"The case is still listed on the books as unsolved."

"You weren't the sheriff back then."

"No. It was my daddy."

Adam absorbed that choice bit of information—something everybody in town knew. "The sheriff's job in Wayland is hereditary?" he asked.

"No. I ran for the office and won it."

Adam nodded, considering what Delacorte had chosen to tell him. "Do you think that old murder is connected to Ken White?"

Delacorte hesitated for a moment before saying, "I don't have any evidence to link them."

"What's your gut feeling?" Adam asked.

The sheriff gave him a long look. "I'm reserving my judgment." He stood up. "I think you'd better show me the location where you found the campfire—and the people last night."

Adam set down his glass with a *thunk* and stood as well, certain that the sheriff had decided to end this phase of the interview.

He was pretty sure there was more to tell about Wayland's past problems. He was also pretty sure he wasn't going to hear about them this morning.

"You know the road at the east edge of the park?" he asked, and Delacorte nodded.

"There's a barrier across the lane. The fire pit was about a half mile farther up the road."

"You got the time to carry me up there now?"

"I've got the time. I want to know what the hell's going on in my park."

"I could station a deputy out here at night."

"No!" Adam's answer was instantaneous, and he immediately regretted that he'd spoken so quickly—like a man with something to hide.

Delacorte held up a hand. "Just a suggestion," he said, and Adam knew the sheriff was wondering if he was up to something unsavory at night out here. Like growing marijuana.

Probably he wouldn't like knowing that the head ranger was prowling the park in wolf form at night.

He'd thought that with his wolf senses, he'd be able to figure out what had happened to his predecessor. So far it hadn't turned out that way. But he did know that both Paul Delacorte and Austen Barnette had been expecting trouble. Unfortunately, the park's owner had chosen to withhold that information from his new employee.

"So, you have any choice suggestions for me?" he asked.

The sheriff hesitated for a moment. "Yeah. Don't sit with your back to the window."

5

SARA walked into the kitchen of the small cottage, turned on the tap in the sink, and let it run, waiting for the stream to cool before she drew a glass of water.

She downed it in several gulps, then stood staring out the window at the grove of trees that surrounded her rented house. There were black gum, sweet bay, and an old water oak hung with Spanish moss that must have been hit by lightning at one time. It was split up the middle. But somehow it had survived and grown in a lopsided fashion.

The trees would have been lovely if there had only been a few. But too many had grown up around the little house.

"Darkness at noon," she muttered.

Even in the middle of the day, it was dismal under the canopy of branches, as though the sun had gone into a permanent eclipse. She'd never liked the dark. And here she was in a house where mold and moss grew on the roof and the siding, like insidious unwanted visitors.

A light breeze fluttered through the leaves and the moss hanging on the tree branches. It wasn't enough to do much for the damp, heavy air. But the rustling sound skittered over her skin like insect legs.

As if to ward off a chill, she folded her arms over her chest and rubbed her shoulders. This place gave her the creeps, and she had

learned not to ignore her intuition. She wanted to throw her posses-
sions into the car and flee. But that was not an option. Not when she'd
effectively trapped herself here.

Granville Pharmaceuticals had written her out of the blue and offered her an enormous research grant. She'd been flattered and relieved to get a job. She'd taken a lot of the first payment and sent it
directly to the outfit that held the note on her college loan, because
the idea of being in debt for the next fifteen years made her throat
close.

Of course, she felt that way now—closed in and smothered. And
the sensation had nothing to do with her education loans.

The disquiet came from her immediate surroundings, this cabin
and the wilderness around it. If she could, she would find another
place to live and work. But she suspected that by the time she went
through proper channels to move somewhere else, her stay would be
almost up. So she switched on the kitchen light, then walked around
the little house turning on the lights in every room.

They drove away the darkness but did nothing for the hot, sticky air.

The small dwelling had two bedrooms. She was sleeping in the
larger one. The other was going to be her laboratory.

Granville had already shipped several long worktables, but some
assembly was required, so she'd put that off until later. For the time
being, the plants she'd dug up were resting in boxes on a plastic sheet,
which she'd spread over the narrow bed in her makeshift lab.

She had pretentiously given Adam Marshall the Latin name of
sweet flag. But she was just as conversant with the common names of
the specimens she'd collected.

In addition to the irislike plant, she had lily of the valley, jimsonweed, and male shield fern. All of the latter were poisonous. And the
jimsonweed was reputed to have psychotropic qualities, a fact she
hadn't shared with Marshall.

She sighed, thinking she might as well go into the work room and
start documenting the collection. Maybe she could even make some
extracts from the leaves or the roots or the seeds and start testing
them for antibacterial properties.

But instead of focusing on work, her mind strayed back to the
morning in the swamp—to the moment when she'd met Adam Marshall.

She'd been so intent on the clump of sweet flag that she hadn't even been aware of him until he was almost on top of her. Or maybe it was the way he moved through the swamp, like an animal supremely adapted to the natural environment.

Those first moments had shaken her to her toes. She simply hadn't expected to meet up with anyone else out there in the middle of nowhere.

She'd taken in every detail of the man in those first charged instants. Somehow, when she thought of him, her mind filled with animal images. He was over six feet tall and as dark and dangerous-looking as a hungry bear. His eyes were black and deep set, glittering like the eyes of a bird of prey. He had a blade of a nose, nicely shaped lips, and dark stubble covering his cheeks and chin.

He'd looked like he'd had a hard night. Probably she did, too, she thought, her fingers unconsciously going to her hair.

She was in the act of smoothing back the unruly strands when she stayed her hand. What was she doing? The man wasn't even here, and she was fussing with her hair. Besides, it didn't matter anyway what he thought of her.

Even as the denial surfaced in her mind, she knew it was a lie. Some tender, feminine part of her did care what he thought about the way she looked.

She closed her eyes for a moment, thinking that a twenty-eight-year-old woman should have more experience with men. She'd dated, of course. But it was difficult for her to make connections with people. She'd always felt like there was a barrier between herself and them. A time or two she'd managed to overcome it. But often she hadn't felt like it was worth the effort. So her focus had always been on her studies or the things that interested her, like gardening or her art. And she'd had a good reason to study hard: she was determined to do well and she wanted to make Mom and Dad proud.

Now she was paying the price for her sexual inexperience— getting excited about a guy she met in the woods, a guy so different from the academics who had inhabited her world for the past ten years that she had no point of reference for him, besides the wild animal images she'd conjured up.

Above and beyond those images, she didn't like his manner. He'd practically accused her of being part of some drug cult, cavorting in the park at night. And when he'd stirred the blackened ashes of the campfire, a scene had flashed into her mind.

The darkness, the moon-drenched swamp, the wild gyrating of naked bodies dancing and coming together in the flickering firelight. It had caught and held her for only a moment, but it had shaken her to the core.

Against her will, the image came back to her now, and she squeezed her eyes shut, struggling to make the all-too-vivid picture vanish. She didn't want to see it. Didn't want to know about it. But it held her in its grip. And the most disturbing part was that she had put herself smack in the middle of the scene. She was one of the dancers.

"No!"

She spoke the word aloud trying to drive the nighttime scene from her mind. But the denial did her no good. The world around her disappeared. She was transported to the nighttime swamp. To the campfire with its smoke that clogged her lungs and made her head go muzzy. She heard low, chanted words. Words that stirred her senses.

Unconsciously, she swayed from one foot to the other, no longer feeling the smooth surface of the kitchen floor below her shoes.

Instead, she felt spongy dirt and tree roots under her naked feet.

Dancers moved around her. The smoke obscured their faces. But she saw the sweat gleaming on their bare bodies. And saw that they were aroused. The women's nipples were contracted to tight points. The men were fully erect.

One of them reached for her. With a little moan, she slipped out of his grasp.

Then a man leaped into the firelight. It was Adam Marshall. He was nude and magnificent and aroused.

"Sara." He called her name, called her to his side, and she swayed toward him, craving the feel of his body against hers. He pulled her into his arms, and the contact of naked flesh against naked flesh was glorious.

He drew her away, into the inky blackness beyond the reach of the fire. She knew that they were going to make love—in some dark, leafy place away from the rest of the group where they could have their privacy. And she knew that if she let it happen, her life would change forever.

"No."

"Come with me, Sara. I need you."

"No." Somehow, with strength she didn't even know she pos-

sessed, she wrenched herself away. From him. From the vivid daydream that had hooked its claws into her flesh.

The kitchen blinked back into focus, and she stood there, gasping
for breath, trying to clear the smoke from her lungs.

No, there was no smoke here. She was in the house Granville had
rented for her. She closed her hand over the edge of the counter, feeling the hard surface digging into her palm, fighting a wave of unwanted sexual arousal that held her as she tried to figure out what had
happened to her.

She'd had episodes like this before. Well, not quite like *this*. Nothing remotely sexual. But episodes where she seemed to leave the here
and now and go someplace else.

The daydreams had been vivid. But they had never turned her on.

Lord, what had happened to her?

Adam Marshall had poked at the campfire. Maybe he'd stirred up
some of the hallucinogenic smoke. Maybe the thick, evil stuff was still
affecting her.

She'd felt it last night, too, she silently admitted. Felt some ugly
presence reaching for her from the dark shadows of the swamp.

Now she understood what she'd sensed in the damp humid air beyond her grove of trees when she'd been awake in the dark hours.

Or was she making all that up? Not the feelings. But the images.
Had they come from the overactive imagination she tried so hard to
rein in all her life?

She gripped the kitchen counter more tightly, yet the frightening
perception persisted.

"Stop it," she ordered herself. "You *will not* let your imagination
run away with you."

The order did little to dispel the drowning sensations that threatened to overwhelm her.

Something was waiting for her in Wayland, Georgia— something
she didn't want to meet. Adam Marshall was part of it. But only part.
There was more, and she'd didn't want to find out what it was.

She had been staring out the window unseeing when a flicker of
movement brought her back to the here and now. A figure darting between the trees. A man.

She went very still as her gaze focused on him. Her heart gave a
little lurch when she thought it might be Adam Marshall. Lord, had

she sensed him out there? Was that the reason for the flash of fantasy that had taken hold of her?

It took only seconds to determine that it wasn't his tall, muscular figure she saw. And she breathed out a sigh of relief—and disappointment.

This man was older and more slender.

He must have caught sight of her in the window, because he stopped in his tracks. Across fifty feet of swampland, they stared at each other.

What was he doing here on private property?

She saw then that a wicker basket dangled from one of his hands. And she realized that he must be gathering some kind of food or plants from the area. Which might make him a valuable resource.

He didn't look threatening, yet she had decided not to take any chances. So she turned away from the window and picked up her carry bag where she'd stashed her gun.

Then she headed for the front door. By the time she reached it, the man had taken several steps into what passed for the front yard of the little house.

As she walked onto the porch, he stared at her with wide, surprised eyes.

"Can I help you?" she asked.

The basket in his hand bobbled as he came farther into the yard. "I didn't expect . . ." His voice trailed off. He was staring at her as though she'd dropped from the moon.

"Yes. Well, I'm renting the house for the next few months while I'm here for a research project," she answered. Really, she didn't have to make any explanations. But this was a small town. And people were going to be interested in what she was doing here.

From her position above him, she could see now that his basket was filled with small, dark fruit.

"Blackberries?" she asked.

"Black raspberries. Blackberries don't come into season for a month."

"Oh."

She studied the man. His skin was weathered, but up close he looked more fit than her first impression. Probably he was in his sixties. Probably he made his living in the outdoors.

"Hello," she said, making an effort to sound friendly. "I'm Sara Weston. I'm going to be here for a few months, investigating the medicinal properties of plants found in this area."

"Hal Montgomery," he answered, before backing away. "I'll see you around, Sara Weston."

Moments later he had disappeared into the underbrush, moving as silently as a ghost.

ADAM wiped his feet on the doormat that graced the wide front porch of the red brick mansion, feeling like he had when he'd been out in the woods and about to walk into his mother's kitchen. Well, not exactly the same. The tile floor in front of his mom's sink had been worn through. And the appliances were old and dented—from his dad's kicking them a time or two.

He looked at the gleaming white wood door frame and the leaded glass fan transom above the double doors.

Austen Barnette's southern mansion was a far cry from the modest East Baltimore home where he'd grown up. And a far cry from the two-room cabin that went with the head ranger job.

He'd been here twice before, for his job interview. And then when he'd started work.

The first time the old man had flown him to Jacksonville from southwest Texas and put him up overnight at the Holiday Inn.

The next morning at nine o'clock sharp, a stoop-shouldered old man wearing a dark suit and white shirt had ushered him into Barnette's paneled den with its comfortably worn leather furniture. The lord of the manor had offered him coffee, which he'd declined. He'd settled for a glass of water as Barnette had asked him pointed questions about how he saw the present and future of Nature's Refuge. Apparently he'd passed the test, because a special delivery letter had arrived at his home in Big Bend National Park the next week.

He'd been elated to get the job. Now he was having second—and third—thoughts.

The door was opened by the same servant who had ushered him into the house the first time.

Stepping across the threshold, Adam took a moment to adjust to the dim light as he breathed in the aroma of lemon-scented furniture polish. On the surface, it seemed like nothing had changed since his first visit here five months ago.

"This way, sir." The old man gestured toward the hall.

"I didn't ask your name last time I was here," Adam said.

The butler or whatever he was called looked surprised. "I'm James."

"So what have you heard in town about the goings-on at Nature's Refuge?" Adam asked.

The man's eyes went wide—for just a second, then turned guarded. "Nothing, sir," he answered.

Adam smiled at him and waited a beat before saying, "Well, if you change your mind about talking to me, you know where to find me."

James didn't reply, and Adam didn't push it. He wasn't going to interrogate Austen Barnette's house staff. Not yet, anyway. But maybe after the man thought about it, he might have something to say later.

Adam proceeded down the hall past a parlor where a maid was dusting the furniture. The room was as he remembered it—quietly opulent, with a permanent aura of cigar smoke that grated on his nerve endings. It wasn't the only shock to his system. As always, it was difficult to picture himself, the son of an auto mechanic and burglar, in such a setting.

The mansion's owner was sitting in the same old-fashioned swivel desk chair where he'd been on Adam's last visit. But the man looked like he'd aged a couple of years in the past few months. There was more white in his salt-and-pepper hair and more sag to his wrinkled skin.

"Thank you for seeing me," Adam said.

"Nature's Refuge is important to me. I'm always available to speak to my head ranger."

"I appreciate it."

"Sit down." The old man gestured toward the chair across the room.

Adam sat. Beside it on the table was a silver tray with a cut glass tumbler and a pitcher of water.

Barnette picked up his own beverage of choice, coffee served in a delicate china cup, and took a sip.

"What can I do for you?" he asked, setting down his cup and clasping his hands in his lap.

Adam studied his employer carefully. He seemed composed, yet there was an undercurrent below the surface of that calm. Was he worried about something and unwilling to make the first move? Or was he truly waiting for information about the park?

"The sheriff came to see me this morning," Adam began.

Barnette's raised his eyebrows. "Oh? Did he find out something about Ken White?"

"No. He was just checking in. But it was interesting that he picked this morning to show up." He waited a beat, waiting to see if Barnette would rise to the bait. When the old man remained silent, he continued. "We had an incident last night that I think you ought to know about."

"What?"

"I like to walk through the park at night—just to check on things. Last night, I came across some trespassers." Quickly he gave an account of the strange group who had invaded the park the night before, keeping his description to the drugged smoke and the dancing participants. "When they discovered I was watching them, somebody shot at me," he concluded.

"But you escaped unharmed."

"Yes."

Neither of them spoke for several moments, forcing Adam to direct the conversation once more.

"I got the feeling from Delacorte that you've had problems like this in the park before," he said.

"Not in the park!" Barnette answered.

"Not that anyone told you," Adam answered, giving the old man an out.

His employer nodded.

"Now we might assume that Ken White stumbled onto the same kind of thing I did, but he didn't happen to get away."

"I hired you because you're an excellent park ranger, and you have a reputation for solving crimes. Like that smuggling operation you shut down in Big Bend. And that cattle rustling gang in Montana."

"Yeah, well, it's easier to solve crimes when you have the background to work with. What do you and Delacorte know that I don't?"

Barnette stared at him. "What did the sheriff say to you?"

"Nothing helpful."

"He knows his place in town."

"What's that supposed to mean?"

"It means that his family has lived in Wayland for a long time. They get along here."

Adam looked at his employer, understanding another facet of his personality. He saw Delacorte as a servant—just the way he saw James. Adam's own skin was a different color, but he suspected he fell into the same category. Hired help.

So how to proceed now? He could be a good little servant and go back to the park and watch his back. But watch for what—exactly?

He decided on the direct approach. "Why don't you tell me what I should know about problems in Wayland over the past few decades."

Barnette blinked. "That's a pretty open-ended subject."

"Yes, sir, it is. I'm trying to understand the sociology of the town," he said blandly.

Barnette shifted in his seat. "This is a good Christian community. I don't want outsiders coming in and judging us."

"You wanted an outsider—me—to come in and solve your problems. That's difficult to do when you tie my hands."

The old man thought about that. "I suppose your request is reasonable, but I don't want this discussion going any further than this room."

Adam nodded, thinking that he could agree for now.

"All right. We've had problems with goings-on in the swamp. The trouble . . . uh . . . dates back at least a hundred years."

Adam blinked. "That's a considerable amount of time." He waited for more information. When it wasn't forthcoming, he asked, "What are you talking about exactly?"

"You want to put a label on it? I don't have a label." Barnette stopped and fixed Adam with his stony gaze. "There's magic in the swamp. I'd like to think it's good magic. But sometimes it takes another form."

The revelation was so unexpected that he waited several seconds before asking, "Can you be more explicit?"

"Like what you saw last night."

"That wasn't magic. It was drugs."

"Call it what you want. Did you feel like something strange was going on? Something you didn't understand?"

"Yes."

"Well then."

"I'm not equipped to investigate magic," he said.

"You saw people. Find out who they are."

"How?"

"The same way you identified those drug smugglers in fifty-plus square miles of desolate Texas park."

Adam had no answer for the remark. He wasn't about to explain that he'd been operating last night with a hood over his senses. He needed more clues, and somebody was going to have to give them to him. Apparently, it wasn't going to be his employer.

Barnette gave him a dismissive look.

Adam knew that was his cue to leave. But he stayed where he was. "We should talk about Sara Weston," he said.

"What about her?" Barnette asked, his voice sharpening so that Adam wondered what he'd conveyed in his own tone.

He wasn't sure how he was going to answer until he heard himself saying, "Is she in danger—going into the swamp?"

Barnette's gaze turned inward. "I hope not," he said. "It would look bad for us if something happened to Granville Pharmaceutical's researcher."

"Then why did you allow her to come here—now?"

"What do you mean—why now? Why not now?"

"You had a murder here less than half a year ago."

"I thought it would be all right. I thought with you here, we wouldn't have any more incidents . . ." He let his voice trail off, then asked, "Are you questioning my decision?"

"No," Adam lied.

"If she finds something important in the park, some plant that can cure diseases, then we'll get some great publicity. That will bring more visitors here."

"And if she gets shot by the . . . people I saw last night, that's going to drive the crowds away."

"I'm counting on you to make sure that doesn't happen," Barnette snapped. "You need extra help patrolling the refuge?"

"No."

"I didn't think so. I know you work alone. I know you find clues that other people miss."

If I don't get killed first, Adam thought. Aloud, he said, "I'll do my best."

"Keep me informed on what you find out."

"Yes, sir," he answered, silently reminding himself that if Austen

Barnette could pick and choose what he wanted to reveal, Adam Marshall could damn well do the same.

The meeting had been far from satisfying. It was a relief to leave the old man's private sanctuary and step into the sun again. He stood on the wide front porch, breathing in the fresh air, thinking about why he'd taken this job in the first place. He'd wanted to get out of Texas. He'd wanted a challenge. He'd liked the idea of being in charge of his own park. Now he felt like he'd made his decision with only part of the facts he'd needed.

Across the lawn, he saw a man dressed in a plain white T-shirt and jeans working with a power saw, apparently replacing some of the wood siding on the wall of the detached garage. The guy raised his dark head and looked at him curiously. And he stared back, wondering if they had met.

Something about the workman was familiar, but he didn't know what. Maybe he'd seen him around town. He thought about walking closer. Maybe the guy was curious about the new head ranger out at the park. Maybe if they talked, he could get another perspective on working for Austen Barnette.

But something about the workman's posture kept him standing where he was.

After a long moment, the man lowered his head and went back to the siding, and Adam walked down the steps and back to his SUV, thinking he needed a better source of information about the hidden history of Wayland, Georgia. And he needed something else as well— a gas mask, which he was going to order from the Internet as soon as he got the chance.

6

AMY Ralston looked up from her position behind the boat rental counter and watched her boss's long-legged stride as he came down the mulched path to the dock.

She was pretty sure that the sun shade over the window of the ticket booth hid her face, so she felt free to drink in the view of Adam Marshall. When he drew closer, she lowered her gaze and pretended to be sorting through receipts from recent customers.

It was impossible not to react to the man. He was nothing like the last head ranger. Ken White had been old—in his fifties at least. He'd had thinning hair and a pot belly. She had thought of him like a slightly gruff old uncle. She'd been sad when he'd gotten killed; she hadn't wanted it to happen.

Actually, she'd been more than sad. She'd been frightened by the implications.

After Ken's death, for a while, there hadn't really been anyone in charge at the park. Mr. Barnette had stopped by a time or two, getting driven over in that big black Cadillac of his. But he hadn't known anything about the day-to-day operation of the park. So he'd asked them to carry on with their jobs until he could get a replacement. It had worked fairly well, at least in the short run.

Then their new boss had arrived, and Amy had flipped over him. Not just her. All the female staff had a thing for him.

He knew it, too. But he kept things on a professional level. Unfortunately, because if he made a move toward her, she would be more than willing to do the dirty with him.

He was good-looking, with tanned skin, thick black hair, remarkable dark eyes, and a great body. But it wasn't just his looks that turned her on. There was something about him, something she couldn't define. You could maybe call it charisma.

The guy was a chick magnet.

"How's it going?" he asked, the question casual.

"Fine."

He glanced over at the boats moored in the narrow channel that led to the park's main waterway. "How many tours are out?"

"Dwayne just took a family of four on the hour excursion. Rosie left a half hour ago with another party. And we have a married couple interested."

She consulted her notes. "Mr. and Mrs. Carlton. I explained that we don't want too many boats out there at once. So they're coming back at three for the deluxe tour."

"I'll take them out," he said.

She looked up in surprise. Ken had been very conscious of his position as head ranger. And he'd made it clear that routine stuff was beneath his notice. He'd always given jobs like boat tours to the lesser members of the staff.

"Someone else can do it," Amy offered.

"No. I like to keep in touch with every aspect of the operation." He laughed. "Even feeding Big Jim."

"Yuck." That was definitely one chore Amy tried to avoid. Feeding their "pet" alligator meant handling big chunks of raw meat from the refrigerator.

"PART of the job," Adam said, before moving down the dock and pulling up the engine of a nearby boat to check the propeller for weeds, which were a perennial problem in these nutrient-rich waters.

In addition to feeding Big Jim, he'd already taken care of putting out grain for the waterfowl that the park fed regularly so the birds would be on hand for visitors to look at.

Feeding wildlife went counter to what he'd learned in the U.S. Park Service, of course. The philosophy was that if you gave handouts to animals, you turned them into beggars. He'd abided by the policy when he'd worked for the U.S. government, even when it had meant watching snowbound moose starve. But he also saw no harm in providing food for birds the tourists liked to see around Nature's Refuge.

The simple act of scattering duck feed had given him time to decompress after his conversation with Barnette. And he was hoping that a tour of the waterways would continue the process.

As soon as he'd left the old man's mansion, he'd thought about driving into town and demanding that Paul Delacorte put him in the loop. But he was almost sure he wasn't going to get any more answers from the sheriff than he had from Barnette.

And that wasn't the only reason for heading back to the park. He knew himself pretty well. He knew that going off half-cocked was a bad idea. He needed to calm down. And taking a boat out into the still, dark waters of the swamp was an excellent way to do it.

The tourists arrived at five of three. Barbara and John Carlton were a couple in their late forties, he guessed, from Denver. They had never been to this part of the country before, and they were excited by the prospect of a swamp tour. Adam collected fifty dollars from them, got out life jackets, then helped the couple into the front of the boat, while he sat in back at the tiller and started the engine. Most local residents who took watercraft into the swamp paddled. But that wasn't practical for tourist expeditions because it would add too much time to each trip. So all of the boats at Nature's Refuge were motorized.

They putted slowly away from the dock, then turned into one of the narrow channels that lead into the interior of the preserve. In front of them, the water was still as glass. Rotting peat made it cola dark, creating a natural mirror that reflected the vegetation crowding in on either side of the boat. The effect was like being in a magic tunnel of greenery where you couldn't tell up from down.

Magic. Barnette had used that word. Probably he hadn't been referring to the scenery. But what had he meant?

Adam had thought of the Olakompa as a place that civilization hadn't been able to destroy, a refuge for the birds and animals that lived here. Now he wondered what secrets lurked beneath the dark waters. And really, the dimly lit, mysterious swamp was an easy place to become a believer in the supernatural.

And why not? A werewolf was a kind of supernatural creature. Perhaps his ancestors had sprung from a place very similar to this.

"It's like taking a trip into wonderland," Barbara murmured, her voice hushed. "Is the park all like this?" she asked.

Her husband had gotten out his fancy camera and was busily snapping pictures.

Adam brought his mind back to the tour.

"No," he answered. "We have these narrow channels. But they open up into what are called prairies, kind of water meadows. The higher elevations in the park are dry land. Well, higher is a relative term. We're about a hundred feet above sea level, in a natural depression. Some of the land is also boggy. And we have over seventy islands—I mean in the whole swamp, not just Nature's Refuge. The terrain makes for a variety of plants and animals."

The mention of plants sent his mind zinging back to Sara Weston. He'd met her where the footing was dry. But if she'd come to the swamp, she must be here to collect some of the aquatic specimens like floating heart, arrow arum, pickerelweed, or golden club.

The channels could be confusing, if you didn't know your way around. She'd need a guide. And he was the perfect choice.

He went into a little fantasy, imagining them alone in a boat out in this vast wilderness, pictured himself helping her with her work, the two of them silent but very aware of each other. Sexually aware, like they'd been this morning. But now she wouldn't be wary of him.

She'd want him as much as he wanted her. She'd put her hand on his arm, letting him know. He pictured his gaze locking with hers, before he steered the craft into a shallow waterway where they could reach for each other without worrying about the boat tipping dangerously.

He held the tantalizing image for several heartbeats, then ruthlessly wiped it from his mind. He'd thought that giving a tour would relax him. Instead, he was wound up tighter than a kudzu vine choking the life out of a tree trunk.

Embarrassed, he shifted in his seat, glad that he was sitting behind his passengers and they were looking toward the front of the boat.

His eyes scanning the shoreline. It didn't take too long to spot what he wanted. He cut the engine, drifting toward the bank. "Look at that floating log," he said, pointing.

As the boat eased closer, a small alligator lifted its head out of the water and stared at them.

Barbara started in alarm. John began snapping more shots.

"One of the twelve thousand gators we have in the swamp," he remarked. "Decades ago, a lot of them were turned into shoes and handbags. Now they're protected." He wondered if the couple would also like to know that there were thirty-seven species of snakes in the area, including five poisonous ones.

Probably not, he thought, hiding a grin as he guided the boat around a bend and into one of the more open areas, past clumps of water lilies and tall grass.

He saw a wood stork feeding near the shore and dutifully pointed it out, so John could label his pictures later.

Usually he enjoyed giving these tours. He'd always been interested in wildlife. And he'd done a lot of reading on his own. Maybe he'd been trying to figure out where the werewolf fit into the natural order of things.

He realized he'd been silent for several moments and came up with another piece of nature lore as he guided the boat into another narrow channel. "White-tailed deer come down to the water for a drink."

"Don't the gators get them?" John asked.

"Rarely. They have almost no natural enemies."

"Are there wolves around here?" Barbara asked.

"They were last seen here in the nineteen twenties," Adam said easily. He didn't add that a wolf had been prowling the park for the past four months.

Barbara scanned the shoreline. "I'd like to see the deer."

"Maybe on the way back. They rest during the day, then become more active late in the afternoon."

"It's so amazing that this place survived into the twenty-first century," John mused.

"It almost didn't. The swamp's ecosystem came close to being destroyed in the early nineteen hundreds by a company dedicated to turning cypress trees into telegraph poles and floorboards. They took out four hundred and thirty million board feet of cypress before the easily accessible timber ran out. President Franklin Roosevelt stepped in and converted a large part of the swamp into a wildlife refuge in nineteen thirty-seven."

"He established Nature's Refuge?"

"No. Austen Barnette bought this area much later."

The waterway opened up again, and he steered the skiff through a grove of cypress trees, following a muskrat who swam away from them as quickly as possible.

When he came around a curve, something odd caught his eye. Something that looked as though it didn't belong in the natural environment.

From time to time he found junk floating in the water. Paper cups. Plastic jugs. He always scooped them up and brought them back to throw into the trash.

But this wasn't in the water. It looked like a piece of yellow paper tied to the trunk of a young cypress tree, standing out against the dark bark. It wasn't a bright yellow. It was faded, so that he might have mistaken it for something else. It could have been here for months, he supposed, getting drenched in the rain and baking in the sun. He didn't know for sure because he hadn't been in this particular corner of the swamp recently.

He could feel his heart rate picking up. He wanted to think that he simply didn't like finding something man-made tied to a tree where no human artifacts should be. But he knew it was more than that. Last night he'd encountered drugged smoke and naked people out here. Today there was something strange tied to a tree. Had the party-goers marked their territory?

The Carltons hadn't spotted the thing. He could steer the boat on by, then come back later, when he was alone. Probably that was what he should do, but he wanted to know what the damn thing was—now.

Barbara and John looked in the direction where he was headed and spotted the anomaly.

"What's that?" the husband asked.

"I don't know. It looks like someone left it for a marker," he added, plucking a phrase out of the air.

"Who would do that?"

"Maybe a poacher," he improvised even as his mind clawed for answers. The official entrance to the park was through the front gate, but it was always possible for someone to come in the back way. One of many back ways, actually.

The Olakompa Swamp was over six hundred square miles. Austen Barnette owned only a small corner of the watery real estate, about three hundred acres. That wasn't much in the grand scheme of things. But it was plenty of room for the birds and animals who lived here plus various assorted trespassers.

Like the group last night, he was thinking as he leaned out to examine the object. It wasn't paper, but cloth. In fact, it was a crudely made bag of old fabric, tied together at the top with a piece of rough twine. It looked like there was something inside.

Nothing heavy. But enough material to puff out the yellow fabric.

He pulled the boat as close as he could get, but it wasn't close enough to snag the thing without endangering his passengers, and that would be unforgivable. So he tied up to a cypress knee, then started to climb out.

A scream from Barbara had him leaping back, rocking the boat dangerously.

Both passengers gripped the sides of the craft, and he found himself sitting back down heavily.

When the rocking had stopped, he turned toward Barbara, struggling to keep his expression bland. Really, he wanted to chew her out for startling him, but he knew it was prudent to resist the impulse.

"What's wrong?" he asked.

"Over there. A snake."

He followed her outstretched hand, but if the creature had been real, it had already slithered away.

"Thanks," he said, then took his time inspecting the area before climbing onto the slippery surface of the tree root and finding a handhold on the rough bark. Carefully, he worked his way toward the object.

When he was close enough, he hauled out the penknife he always carried and cut the piece of rough cord that held the bag to the tree.

Moments later, he was back on the aluminum bench, where he stowed the thing at his feet.

John reached for it. Adam kicked it under his seat. "Leave it," he growled.

The other man must have heard the wolf tone in his voice, because he reared back.

"The tour's over," Adam said. "Sorry we have to return early, but I'll refund your money when we get back to the dock."

7

FALCON leaned back in his chair, stretching out his long legs under the table, and crossed his scuffed boots at the ankle as he sipped his Bud Lite. His head had been a little muzzy, but he'd put in most of a day's work.

He was still feeling a nice warm glow from the up close and personal contact with the clan last night.

Of course, he had to steer his mind away from the ending of the night's revelries. But that wasn't difficult. He was the kind of guy who could ignore inconvenient details when he wanted to.

He'd packed up his tools, and now he was relaxing at his favorite little café on Main Street.

Some part of him would have liked to see the core of Wayland shrivel and die like so many of the little southern towns with their boarded-up storefronts, trash blowing down the main drag, and all the action, such as it was, out on the highway in the Wal-Mart parking lot.

But there were some advantages to what the chamber of commerce liked to call Historic Wayland.

The town's core had survived the new development that had come to the cheap land on the outskirts of town. The old business district had transformed itself into a kind of yuppy tourist haven, with a few bright spots for the locals to enjoy.

Like the Good Times Café, with its down-home southern cooking at reasonable prices.

He saw the waitress step out of the kitchen. Her name was Betty Sue, and she was about his age, mid-twenties. She'd lived here all her life. Not like him. His family had left town, suddenly, in the middle of the night. They'd run for their lives and found a place to rent in Jacksonville, where his dad had gotten a job driving a delivery truck.

Daddy had scraped along. It had been better than getting burned up or ripped apart by the nice Christian folks of Wayland.

That had been twenty-five years ago. And now the son was back. And as far as he knew, the good people of the town didn't know who he was. But they were going to find out, and they were going to be sorry for what they had done.

Betty Sue came swishing over to the table and delivered his food. A hamburger and fries, nestled in a napkin-lined plastic basket to save on dishes.

She and the rest of Wayland were in for a surprise when the clan had consolidated their power. Just a few more weeks, and they would be ready to get even for the sins of the past.

He picked up the catsup bottle and shook it over the thick home-cut fries, being careful not to get the napkin soggy.

"Can I get you anything else?" Betty Sue asked.

He considered a suggestive answer, then thought better of it and shook his head as he bit into a fry.

Um, um good.

He had taken a seat by the window, and as he ate his fries and burger, he watched the car and pedestrian traffic. There were a lot of tourists. Which was good for business. But there were a fair number of townspeople out as well.

He watched a woman pushing a baby carriage. A family of four, the parents and kids all licking ice cream cones. An old guy leaning on a cane. An old lady with an ugly dalmatian on a leash.

Wayland looked like such a peaceful little town. Yet the things that had happened here would curl your hair.

Regular witch-hunts. Like in the middle ages. Only now the witches were getting ready to turn the tables.

He chomped off a bite of burger and bun, chewed, and swallowed, his thoughts turning back to the night before. To the smoke, the women, the feeling of strength that he knew came partly from the black waters of the swamp. And the unity of the group. It wasn't just having mind-blowing sex. It was the way they fed each other's power when they joined together. It had been his idea to gather up the descendants of the witches. He'd thought of it after he'd met Willow and found out her parents had run away from Wayland, just like his momma and daddy.

He and Willow had hit it off in bed real well. But he'd recognized the experience as something more profound—as a pooling of energy. And he'd wondered if he could multiply the effect. So he'd set about gathering the clan around himself.

Eyes closed, he relived the scene last night. Relived the orgiastic frenzy and the pleasure like a thousand suns bursting in his brain.

But this time he couldn't ignore the ending. The way everything had all come to a screeching halt in the moment when they sensed that guy watching.

After Ken White, Falcon had been sure nobody else was going to bother them. Then this guy had shown up.

Who the hell was he?

His hand clenched around the glass of beer, and he made a concerted effort to relax.

The guy had been naked. Ready for action.

Falcon gave a soft laugh. He'd also sensed the man's longing for a connection with them.

Maybe and maybe not. He'd decide, after they figured out who he was. Falcon already had a couple of candidates in mind. Actually, by chance, he'd gotten a look at one of them today. With his clothes on, he'd just looked like an ordinary guy.

Of course, Falcon knew that was true of himself, too. But he wasn't ordinary. He had power and the strength of his convictions. And he was going to make damn sure that nobody wrecked his plans. He and the members of the clan had waited too long to get revenge on this town that had killed their parents and their grandparents down through the generations. This time, the hunting and the terror were going the other way.

*   *   *

ADAM was feeling more in control by the time he reached the boat dock. Probably he shouldn't have overreacted to the bag. Or to Sara earlier. But he'd been on edge since the moment he'd opened his eyes.

"Sorry for hurrying you back here," he apologized when he'd tied up and helped the Carltons back onto the planking. "I want to find out what's in this thing."

"No problem," John answered.

It was obvious from the tone of the other man's voice that he'd also like to know what was in the yellow bag. Adam didn't offer to share the information. Really, he would have preferred to have been on his own when he'd found the damn thing. He counted himself lucky that he'd been the one and not someone else on the staff.

Would they have brought it to him? Would they have pitched it in the dark water? Or would they have known what the thing was and hidden it? Ordinarily he wouldn't make that assumption. But he was learning that the town kept the secrets of the swamp to itself.

"I can give you a refund," he said. "Or if you're going to be in the area tomorrow, I can give you another trip into the swamp for free."

The couple exchanged glances.

"A free trip," Barbara said.

"Okay. Good." Free trips weren't something he handed out on a regular basis, because he knew that Barnette could be tight with his money. He wanted an accounting of how much was being spent and how much was being taken in, although he didn't insist that the park make a profit. Sometimes receipts were ahead of expenses and sometimes they weren't. If the operation needed extra cash, the owner had reluctantly supplied it.

But Adam didn't plan to push his luck in that department. He led the way to the service counter, where Amy was staring at them.

Her gaze flicked to the bag, then quickly away.

"You seen anything like this?" he asked.

"No."

He was almost positive she was lying, but he didn't press the point. Instead he asked her to write up a ticket for a courtesy trip for the Carltons. When that was taken care of, he headed back to his cabin. He didn't know exactly why he wanted to be alone when he opened the damn bag. It was just a feeling he had.

Probably it came from his wolf instincts. Subliminal awareness was always stronger when he was a gray shape running free in the darkness of the night.

But he wasn't a wolf at the moment. And he wasn't going to change now, not when someone could come marching up to his cabin and find a dangerous animal inside.

So he set the bag on the kitchen table, then started working at the knotted twine that held the top closed. Of course, he could have slit it with his penknife, but he wanted to keep as much of the artifact intact as possible. And besides, the knot told him something about whoever had left the bag.

It wasn't any kind of expert knot. It was a crude series of ties, probably done in haste.

As he worked, he became aware that the makeshift bag was giving off a pungent odor. Stopping, he took a cautious sniff. The last thing he wanted was to find himself overcome by more drugged fumes like last night.

But this was a clean odor, not like the smoke of the night before. When he'd worked the knot loose, he carefully spread open the cloth. Inside was a collection of leaves and twigs and a few other things, like chicken feathers.

He lifted a sprig of something and sniffed. The unmistakable scent of feverfew filled his nostrils. It was hard to describe. Something like mothballs. But not as unpleasant as moth repellent. The sprig wasn't dried. It had been picked fresh and put into the bag, where it had wilted.

Its condition told him something about the length of time the bag had been there. Only a few days, because the herbs inside hadn't had time to go brittle.

Herbs. Yes. That was a good guess. In addition to the feverfew, he recognized the smell and the small leaves of a thyme sprig. There were others, too. But he wasn't an expert on the subject, so he couldn't be sure what they all were.

He looked at the chicken feathers mixed in with the greenery. They had some thick black stuff on the quill end, stuff he didn't want to examine too closely.

So what the hell was this collection of greenery and feathers and black gunk? A voodoo hex? An Indian medicine bag? A joke? A warning—left for whom and by whom?

That last question sent a shiver traveling over his skin. Not much scared him, but he didn't understand this stuff, and he didn't like it.

He had the feeling Sara Weston could tell him exactly what plants had been included. Maybe she even knew enough old-time lore to tell him what it meant.

Sara. His mind kept zinging back to her every chance it got. The two of them would make a great team, he thought. He loved the natural environment. So did she. She had all the qualifications to be a forest ranger's wife.

That thought stopped him cold. He'd met her exactly once. He didn't know how she'd like living in a cabin in the wilderness. And more to the point, he didn't want a wife. He had never wanted a wife. And the realization that the notion had popped into his head was startling. Even somewhat horrifying.

He fought a sudden impulse to get up and claw off his clothing so he could change into a wolf, leap through the cabin door, and run headlong into the swamp—in a futile effort to outrun his destiny.

Instead, he sat for several moments, dragging air into his lungs, getting a grip on his emotions.

Jesus, everything had been going along just fine. And now, suddenly, he felt like he was losing control of his life.

Too restless to sit, he pushed back his chair and stood, then had to reach for the chair back to keep it from tipping over.

He wasn't going to ask Sara anything. He was going to stay away from her.

He wasn't going to talk about this bag of herbs—to her or anybody else. Yet.

Maybe he'd show it to Delacorte later, if it turned out the lawman was playing straight with him. For all he knew, the sheriff was protecting the murderers cavorting in the swamp. An unsettling notion, but one Adam couldn't dismiss out of hand. For the moment, he was on his own. And his first step was to do some checking in town. Ask some questions and hopefully get some of the answers that he had been seeking since this morning.

But not now. Because he wasn't the kind of manager who just took off when the spirit moved him. So he stuffed the contents back into the bag and put the whole thing into a plastic grocery bag, then into the bottom righthand drawer of his desk.

After that, he checked in at the office, then went on a small inspection tour of the park, asking staff members who had been on water tours if they'd seen anything unusual. Nobody had, which might simply mean that they didn't have his eye for detail. Or they were lying.

He ended up back at the park office and stayed around until closing time, taking care of the usual jobs, then trying to occupy his mind by going back through some park records.

His tour guide spiel on the boat trip into the swamp had gotten him thinking about the history of the park. One thing he hadn't known was exactly when Austen Barnette had acquired Nature's Refuge. Now he saw that the swampland had been purchased twenty-five years ago. So the park wasn't all that old.

Barnette had done pretty well by the natural environment, Adam mused. But opening the park to Granville Pharmaceuticals didn't quite fit the pattern. Why was he inviting big business into Nature's Refuge?

Pulling out the correspondence file, he found the letter Barnette had written him about Sara Weston. When he'd seen it the first time, he hadn't been paying much attention to the details. Now he read it with a lot more interest. She was here for six months. And she was staying right on the east edge of the park, in a cabin that Barnette was renting to the pharmaceutical company.

Not far away. Certainly close enough for a wolf to visit.

So would you like a visit from a wolf? he silently asked Sara.

In his imagination, she smiled. *Yes I would.*

You wouldn't be frightened of me?

She shook her head.

"Yeah, sure," he muttered aloud, banishing another one of his imaginary encounters with Sara from his mind before getting up and stomping back to the filing cabinet.

8

ADAM cleared up after dinner, feeling a kind of leaden fatigue weigh him down. He had thought he'd go into town this evening, but he silently acknowledged that he was in no shape for anything but rest.

The tainted smoke from the night before was getting to him. Not that he was having a flashback or anything. But he knew his body better than most people did.

He needed a good night's sleep. And he needed to think through his next move.

So he stripped off his clothes and crawled into the double bed that had come with the cabin. He lay on the hard mattress for long hours, glancing now and then at the green number of the digital clock. Eleven P.M. Twelve A.M. One A.M.

Against his will, his thoughts went back to the nights of his sixteenth year, when his body was changing from boy to man, and he knew that soon Dad would take him out to the woods for the first time—where he would change into a wolf or die.

He had wanted to talk to Ross about it. Ross had made the change and survived. He had already left home, but Mom knew where to find him. Only he couldn't ask her, because he didn't want her to see his fear.

He thought of Ross now. Some deep, buried impulse made him want to reach out and connect with his brother. But he knew that it would come out badly.

Still . . . back when they'd been friends; they'd made trips to the library together. He'd read about the natural environment.

Ross had read about witches and vampires and werewolves.

Would Ross be able to tell him anything about the bag of herbs? Maybe he'd read something that would be useful.

Longing tightened his chest. He rarely admitted it even to himself, but he missed his family with a very deep and fundamental longing. He missed his brother. And he missed his mother. And in some strange, twisted way, he even missed his dad—the Big Bad Wolf, as Ross had called him.

He wanted to see them. Yet he knew that the old phrase, "You can't go home again," applied to him in spades.

Ross had moved out while he was still in college, after a knockdown fistfight in the kitchen with Dad. Mom had thrown a pan of water on them to break it up, and Adam had watched wide-eyed from the doorway.

He hadn't understood then why Dad was so harsh and why; as soon as his sons grew up, they couldn't get along with him at all.

Then he'd read about wolves in the wild and even watched them. There was always one dominant male, the alpha male, and the others were subservient to him. They had a definite pecking order, with each wolf understanding his place in the pack. Apparently, it wasn't the same with werewolves. Each guy needed to be the alpha male. Nobody was willing to give any ground. So they fought for the top spot. Maybe they didn't even understand what they were doing, but they did it.

So how old was Dad now? In his sixties. Adam could probably go back to Baltimore and wup his hide.

But then what? He'd feel satisfied for a few minutes. Then he'd look into Mom's eyes and feel ashamed.

Mom loved the old bastard. She had no choice; she was the werewolf's mate.

As he lay there in the darkness, he thought about the wild and crazy relationship between his mother and father. They needed each other in a way that had amazed and frightened him ever since he'd been old enough to understand it. The werewolf and his mate. There was a bond between them stronger than the bond between an ordinary man and his wife. He'd heard them making love at night with a passion that had embarrassed him. He supposed no kid liked to imagine his parents making love.

But during the day, it had been so different. His father had dominated his mother. Probably he frightened her. Certainly he hadn't hesitated to raise his hand to her when he'd been angry—which had been frequently.

She could have left him. But she stayed, and she came to him at night like none of the bad stuff had ever happened.

He didn't understand it and he hadn't wanted anything so sick in his own life. Or so intense.

He'd told himself he'd known how to avoid it. He'd had lots of women. It had been easy to attract them ever since his teens, after he'd made that transition from man to wolf and back again.

Girls had flocked to him. He gave a short laugh. Apparently that was an advantage of his animal nature.

And he'd enjoyed playing the field, never getting serious about anyone. That had gotten him in trouble more than once. In fact, he'd been glad to leave Big Bend for Wayland because he'd started to sleep with a woman who, it turned out, was in a serious relationship with someone else.

Of course, he wouldn't have approached her if he'd known she had all but promised to marry another guy. Unfortunately, it had already been too late to make amends when he'd found out. He'd almost gotten himself killed, actually. And he'd vowed to be a lot more careful about his sexual partners in the future.

Wayland had been a new beginning for him. He'd been cautious about getting tangled up with anyone until he knew the town. But there were some women he'd had his eye on. And they'd had their eyes on him. Now the only woman he could think about was Sara Weston.

His right hand clenched and unclenched around a wad of rumpled sheet. He'd met her yesterday morning in the swamp.

Yesterday morning! It seemed like a lifetime.

Yet when he stopped to consider the actual number of hours, he could barely believe the time had been so short. It was easy to imagine her lying in the bed beside him. Easy to imagine her there every night of his existence—so that he could turn to her and make wild, passionate love to her anytime he wanted. He had never thought of another woman permanently in his life. He had only thought of short-term pleasure. And now, suddenly everything felt different.

He reached back and arranged his pillow more comfortably under his head. He had to get some sleep. He had to get Sara Weston out of his mind, he told himself as he closed his eyes.

When he opened them again, the room felt different. There was a vibration in the air. A feeling of expectancy. And the rich, female scent of the woman he had met in the park the day before.

He knew he must be dreaming. But this felt more real than any dream he had experienced before—or could ever have imagined. He had been envisioning Sara in his bed. Longing for her. And his dream had put her there. Slowly, as though he were afraid he was mistaken, he turned his head to look at her.

His breath caught when he saw she was lying next to him. In the park her blond hair had been tied back. Now it was loose and spread across the pillow like a delicate fan. She wore a short cotton gown that covered her hips. His gaze traveled down her body and then back up, pausing to admire her breasts and then rising to her face. She was looking at him as though she couldn't believe she was here.

And she was making the same intimate visual tour. His chest was bare. The lower part of his body was hidden by the wrinkled sheet, and he was thankful for that. He hoped it hid his erection. He didn't move. He was almost afraid to breathe.

He was afraid that if he twitched a muscle, she would disappear. And he was desperate to keep that from happening. He might know he was dreaming, but he didn't want the dream to end.

"What are you doing in my bed?" he asked, hearing the rough, uncertain quality of his own voice.

"You wanted me here," she answered, and he found it reassuring that she looked and sounded as bemused as he felt.

"Yes," he admitted to her dream image.

"What do you want?"

He laughed softly. "What men want with a woman who attracts them. To make love with you."

He saw her swallow. "I don't know you well enough to make love. We just met."

"We can get to know each other real fast."

"You weren't exactly charming yesterday morning. I was pretty sure you didn't like me."

In the waking world, the remark would have made him feel defensive. But this was a dream. He didn't have to be defensive. He could say anything he wanted. "I'm sorry. I was upset. Not with you."

"With those people."

"Yes." He didn't want to talk about those people. Not when he had Sara in his bed. So he said quickly, "I should have said I couldn't believe that a Ph.D. botanist could be so young and beautiful."

One of her beguiling blushes spread across her cheeks. "Thanks. I think."

"You're very beautiful," he murmured. Daring to move his arm the barest little bit, he slid his hand across the surface of the sheet. When his fingers touched hers, she made a small sound, and he went instantly still. But she didn't draw back. Thank God.

They lay there, barely touching. The contact was tentative and also electric. Different from anything he had ever experienced.

His relationships with women had always been hot and sexual. He was hot now. But he felt a kind of sweetness that he had never expected to feel.

Her fingers curled against his, and now he was the one who drew in a quick, sharp breath.

"I want to know about you," she murmured.

He felt tension pulse through him. He wanted her to know him, but he was sure she would run screaming in the other direction if she found out the truth. Yet he knew he couldn't simply remain silent and hope to keep her here.

Scrambling for something to give her, he said, "I love the outdoors."

"The swamp?"

"I've worked all over the country. Like I told you, I was in Texas last. It was dry and hot. But it was majestic. My first post was in Colorado. It was so different from where I lived as a kid. I was at a park high in the Rockies, and it took a couple of months before I could get used to the oxygen level."

"Where did you grow up?"

"Maryland."

"Up north."

"Yeah," he answered, but he didn't want to talk about himself. He was hungry for information about her. "What about you?"

"Wilmington, North Carolina."

"What did you like best?"

"We were really close to the beach. I used to love going down there with my parents. We'd bring back shells and driftwood and other stuff we found."

Eagerly he demanded, "Tell me some more. What else did you love?"

"Barbecue. Playing with my dolls. Building a fort in the woods."

"Did you like school?"

"Yes."

"What subjects?"

She told him about her school days, and he drifted on the sound of her voice, pressing and stroking his fingers against hers, growing more sensual in his touch when she didn't pull away.

It was the bare minimum of contact. Yet that small link of man to woman was the most electric he had ever experienced in his life. Two inches of his flesh and bone against hers, and he knew he was feeling more than he had in any sexual encounter he had ever experienced.

He wanted it to last forever. Yet at the same time, it wasn't sufficient. He wanted more from this woman. Much more.

Slowly, very slowly, he increased the contact, stroking his fingers against hers, all of his being focused on the sliding sensation of his fingers against her. But it wasn't enough. And when he couldn't suppress his physical need for her, he rolled toward her and reached to pull her against his heated body.

"No!"

"Sara . . . please."

In the next moment, she was gone, and he was left on the bed feeling hot and hard and desolate.

Awake now, he lay there breathing raggedly. The dream had seemed so real. Like she'd actually been there with him, exchanging personal information. He couldn't stop himself from reaching to touch the pillow next to him, almost expecting to feel the indentation of her head or the heat of her body The pillow was smooth and flat and cool.

Of course it was! It was just a dream.

Yet the memory of her rich scent seemed to linger in the room like a tantalizing illusion.

He looked over at the clock again. It was after four A.M., and he knew he wasn't exactly in great shape. But perhaps a walk through the Olakompa would help settle him.

He got up and stripped off his briefs. Naked, he padded to the door of the cabin. An owl hooted. Small animals scurried into the underbrush as he walked to a grove of trees and disappeared into the shadows. He stood in the darkness, marshaling his resolve.

He had been sick from the smoke the night before. And that would make the change more difficult. But he longed for the freedom of the wolf.

"*Taranis, Epona, Cerridwen,*" he muttered, almost under his breath, then repeated the same phrase and went on to the next.

"Ga. Feart. Cleas. Duais. Aithriocht. Go gcumhdai is dtreorai na dei-the thu."

Earlier, he had been thinking of the first time he had done this.

Tonight the pain was almost as great, but he knew how to deal with it as he felt his jaw elongate, his teeth sharpen, his body contort. Muscles and limbs transformed themselves into wolf shape while gray hair bloomed on his body. Dropping to all fours, he dragged warm, moist air into his lungs and could detect no trace of the tainted smoke of the night before. After a moment's hesitation, he trotted off toward the east edge of the park, feeling a sense of excitement that he fought to suppress.

He told himself he was simply checking to make sure that Barnette's letter had given him the correct information about where Sara was staying. But he knew deep in his heart that the excuse was only that.

All his senses were on overdrive as he moved like a gray shadow through the park, aware of the incredibly lush environment around him. A wonderful playground for a wolf, he thought, as he skirted the deeper waters of the swamp and the open prairies.

His route led him close to the highway, then through a thick grove of trees to the cabin where Sara was supposed to be living.

He waited in the shadows, listening, sniffing the air with the appreciation of a hunter. Only last night he had been the hunted—and that had counseled caution.

Finally, he made his move, gliding toward the dark shape of the cabin. He couldn't see through the walls, of course. But now he had his full faculties, and he knew she was there. Inside. His nostrils flared as he caught the same incredibly rich scent that had filled his dream. A shiver traveled over his skin, ruffling the hair along his spine.

He had done this before, made the change from man to wolf and visited the homes of women who interested him. A therapist might have called it stalking. He had thought of it as a kind of delicious foreplay that had led to incredibly good sex because it drew out the anticipation.

He appreciated women. He was a good lover. But he always made it clear before he took them to bed that he wasn't looking for a permanent relationship. Maybe they didn't want to believe him, but they couldn't say that he hadn't warned them first.

For a time it didn't matter, because when he finally climbed into bed with his lover of the moment, he devoted himself to her service, turning her on, bringing her to the peak of pleasure again and again.

And then when he left her, he did it gently, regretfully, telling her that it wasn't her fault, that it was some deficiency in himself.

Of course that was true. Only his sexual partners simply didn't understand the magnitude of the problem.

He was a werewolf. And no matter how well he fitted himself into human society, it was just a sham.

Tonight he had made his way to Sara's cabin because a compulsion was on him.

The man would have fought the irresistible impulse. The wolf accepted it.

He moved closer to the house, drawn by her scent and by tantalizing mental images. In his dream he had been ready to make love.

He was ready for that now. He pictured himself changing back to his persona of Adam Marshall, then opening the door, stepping inside, and going to her. In the dream she had said she didn't know him well enough for intimacy. In his supercharged state, he was sure he could change her mind.

They would kiss and touch and cleave together, and it would be incredible. The images swam in his head, blocked out almost all other thought.

But his wolf's awareness finally penetrated the sensual fog. Something wasn't right.

Lifting his head, he sniffed again, and caught another scent. Not an animal who belonged in the still Georgia night, although there were plenty of them around.

He wasn't the only watcher here, he realized. Another man was in the shadows, his gaze tuned toward the house.

9

A surge of anger and possessiveness welled up from the depths of his soul.

The need to protect the woman in the cabin filled his mind, driving out everything else. With no thoughts of guns or bullets, he sprang forward in a rush of fur and fury, his teeth bared, his only goal to bring down the watcher who was out in the darkness where no one should be.

But with his focus entirely on the intruder, the wolf took a misstep in the darkness under the trees. Coming down onto a patch of soggy ground, he stumbled and struggled for several steps to right himself.

The mishap gave the stalker precious seconds. He heard a muffled cry of alarm, then running feet. Moments later a car door slammed, then an engine started.

The car's wheels spun, as the vehicle lurched from its hiding place and then down the road, picking up speed as it went.

The wolf leaped forward, unwilling to abandon the chase. Murderous rage seized him. It was the rage of the werewolf, an anger he couldn't control when it came upon him.

Four strong legs pumped as he tried to keep up with the rapidly departing vehicle. But muscle and bone were no match for the internal combustion engine.

After a quarter of a mile, he was left gasping in a cloud of exhaust fumes that choked his lungs. The man within him snarled a silent curse as he gave up the useless chase, stopping in the middle of the road.

His body was still weakened from the smoke and the mad desperate dash of the night before. And now it was all he could do to stay on his feet.

The boiling anger was still there as he looked down the narrow track where the car was rapidly disappearing. The driver hadn't turned on the exterior lights. Which meant the license plate hadn't been visible, even to a creature with excellent night vision.

The wolf wanted to slake his anger by finding some animal in the park and tearing it to pieces. But the man managed to stay focused on his mission.

He couldn't see who had been watching Sara. But that didn't leave him without resources. The night before, the drugged smoke had confused his senses, made it impossible for him to identify the naked people who had invaded his turf.

Tonight the air had been warm and clean, and he had picked up the intruder's distinctive scent. The man was no one he'd met, but he could search for him in town, follow his trail to his lair. And when they met, he would recognize him.

What had the bastard been doing here? Did he mean Sara harm? Had he simply come to watch her? Or was he here to protect her?

The last thought was as disturbing as the first. Protect her from what?

Turning, the wolf trotted back to the house. Sara must have heard something outside. She had turned on a light, and he could see her standing at the window, peering out into the darkness.

He stayed under the trees where she couldn't see him. He wanted to go to her and find out if she was all right. But he hung back, because he had only two options. He could approach her as a wolf. Or as a naked man.

As soon as he pictured that second tantalizing alternative, it filled his head, driving out all other thoughts. Yes, he could come to her, naked and aroused. And he would mate with her. Complete the promise of the dream.

The vivid picture of the two of them together burned inside his brain. He took a step forward and a twig snapped under his front paw.

Instantly he stopped, shocked at the intensity of his need.

He forced himself to back away. Then he was running, because if he didn't escape from her now, he never would.

He ran headlong into the swamp, the way he had run the night before. But not in fear for his life.

He wasn't sure what drove him. He only knew that he had to get away. Distance from the cabin helped. By the time he had returned home and changed back into human form, rational thought became possible again.

And the fear was under control. He had the perfect excuse for going over to Sara's place in the morning. He had seen a man hanging around her house. He needed to tell her.

But what would he say? If he warned her that someone had been watching her, she would want to know how he knew. What answer could he give her besides that he had been prowling around her cabin himself?

But he couldn't simply ignore the situation. He had scared the intruder off with his wild rush of lupine fur and fury. Maybe that was enough of a warning. Or maybe the wolf would have to come back tomorrow and the next night and the next to make sure that all was well in the little cabin.

THE UPS truck had delivered more lab equipment around nine A.M. Sara had been up and ready to receive it because something had awakened her early in the morning. A car engine starting? Tires grinding on gravel? She wasn't sure if she had imagined that, or if it had been real because separating reality from fantasy was becoming more difficult every moment she remained in Wayland.

To keep herself occupied, she'd started unpacking glassware. She stopped and swiped an arm across her forehead, pretending that she was inspecting a retort when she was really looking out the window. It was the third time in a half hour that she'd checked the outside view. As she had before, she saw no one, but she couldn't shake the feeling that eyes were watching her.

Did they belong to the old man who had come poking around earlier? Or to Adam Marshall?

She could easily imagine Adam coming to her after the vivid dream of the night before. She'd been in his bed, wanting him. But she'd kept the two of them talking because that was the only way she could control the situation.

She made a snorting sound. She'd been desperate for control, yet it had only been a dream. Hadn't it?

Of course it was a dream, although it had seemed very real. She'd awakened hot and needy and feeling like she really had been lying next to Adam, his fingers knit with hers.

No! That was simply the work of her subconscious. Nothing real had happened. Yet it was like the other dreams she'd had since coming here. Too real. Too vivid.

Her lips pressed into a firm line, she reached for another box, then another. They contained more carefully wrapped lab equipment.

Beakers. Measuring cylinders. Retorts. Petri dishes. Each had to be handled carefully. And each had to be washed.

There was no running water in her lab. The kitchen sink would have to do. Carefully she carried the glass items to the washboard, put some liquid detergent into a dishpan and added hot water.

Then, a few at a time, she began immersing the beakers and other items. The chore was soothing and familiar. She could do it without even thinking.

Again she stared out the window into the dark, forbidding landscape. Then, she felt her vision blur. The scene outside seemed to fade and re-form before her eyes. She should have felt a shock of alarm. Instead she felt peaceful. Her mind drifted in a kind of warm haze, and when she focused again, she realized she wasn't staring into the dimness under the spreading branches, but into a scene where more light filtered onto the grass in front of the little house. Because the trees were smaller, she realized.

With a sense of anticipation, she turned and left the sink, crossed the kitchen and the living room, and opened the front door. Smiling, she stepped out into the sunshine.

The scene was different yet so familiar that she felt her heart leap with a kind of unbounded joy.

The air was softer, cooler, and she drew in a deep breath and let it out before walking around the house to the herb garden that she loved so much. It was planted for beauty as well as practicality, with paths wandering among the patches of rosemary and dill, feverfew, tansy, and lavender. She'd lined some of the beds with lamb's ears, and she smiled as she bent down to stroke her fingers over the furry leaves.

Reaching farther into the foliage, she pulled some weeds. There weren't many because she worked in the garden every day. With a feeling of satisfaction, she took the invaders to the compost pile several yards away. Then she came back to gather herbs for a healing tea she had planned to make.

She knew the formula by heart, and she moved among her plants, selecting what she needed until she saw something on the ground nestled in the foliage. A piece of yellow cloth, tied into a bag.

She went absolutely still, her heart pounding. The bag didn't belong here. Not at all. When she bent to reach for the nasty thing, a voice shouted a warning.

"Don't!"

She didn't know whether she heard it with her ears or only in her mind. But she snatched her hand back, then turned to look out across the sunlit field. She expected to see a man watching her. Instead, a wolf was standing in the open area, his gaze fixed on her.

Had he spoken to her?

Impossible. A wolf couldn't speak.

A ripple of fear went through her as he took a step closer and then another. Yet she saw he moved slowly, step by step, perhaps so as not to alarm her.

He was large, about the size of a big German shepherd. The top half of his face was dark gray. The lower half was lighter, except for his black muzzle.

She should run, she knew. He could hurt her. But his beauty rooted her to the spot. Her eyes feasted on him, taking in details. Like his face, the upper part of his body was darker than the bottom. And his pointed ears were an enticing mixture of light and dark fur, framed by a line of black.

Her fingers itched to stroke his shaggy coat and find the softer spot just behind his ears. A strange impulse, she knew, since she had never been particularly attracted to wild animals.

Her gaze was drawn back to his eyes. They were yellow and infused with an unnerving intelligence.

"What do you want?" she asked.

He didn't speak. Could a wolf speak? But he raised his head and the answer echoed in her mind. "You."

"For dinner? Like Red Riding Hood and the wolf?" she asked.

He shook his head, dug with one beautifully formed front paw against the ground.

"Please. Tell me what you want."

His pink tongue flicked out, stroked along his lips, and she watched the movement, feeling it almost as though he had licked her hot skin and not his own flesh.

She raised her arm toward him like an invitation. And he took another step forward, just as the scene around her began to fade.

"No . . . wait," she cried, because she had to know what happened next. But it was no good. There was no way to cling to the strange reality. She didn't possess that power.

The scene snapped to a halt, like a strip of broken movie film. One moment she had been outside in the sunshine. Now she was inside standing in front of the kitchen sink, her hands clamped around a wet measuring cylinder.

She dropped it back into the dishpan, the water cushioning its fall.

Her whole body began to tremble. Lord, what had just happened to her?

She'd been standing here washing lab glassware. In fact, as she looked toward the drainboard, she saw that she'd washed quite a bit of her equipment. Apparently, her hands had kept working. But her mind had drifted off somewhere else.

She'd been standing in the kitchen of this newly rented house. Then she'd gone outside. Craning her neck, she peered out the window. The view was different from what she had just seen in her . . . daydream.

She snatched at the word like a lifeline. That's what had happened! Her vivid imagination had taken over again. Somehow living in this place was bringing out all the fantasy elements of her personality that she'd worked all her life to suppress. It had happened last night, too. She'd put herself in Adam Marshall's bed where they'd had a long, heart-to-heart chat. And just now she'd been having another imaginary conversation. Only this time she'd talked to a wolf.

Her hands were unsteady as she wiped them on the hips of her jeans, then hurried through the kitchen and the living room to the front door. Outside, she charged around the house to the spot where the herb garden had been. She could still see it vividly in her mind. But there was only scrubby grass and weeds where the neatly tended beds had been.

Even when she walked over the area, she could find no sign that a garden had ever been there.

Then her eyes lifted to the shadows under the trees. She was looking for the wolf, but he wasn't there.

Of course he wasn't there!

She didn't want him to be there.

Suddenly wobbly on her feet, she reached out a hand and steadied herself against the side of the house.

She could feel her heart pounding in her chest, feel her breath coming in little jerky puffs.

She wanted to tell herself that nothing like this had ever happened to her before. But she knew it would be a lie. Her mind had drifted off like this before—and into . . . what?

This time she made herself supply an answer—into another person's life. When she'd been little, she'd tried to talk to her parents about it. And they'd let her know it was a bad thing. So, she'd worked hard to make it go away.

She'd gotten good at driving those intrusions out of her mind, because they had frightened her. And because she'd wanted to be a good little girl. But this time she had totally lost control, and she hadn't even known it was happening.

In the past, the episodes had always been brief. Now she didn't even know how many minutes she had lost.

Heart pounding, she looked at her watch. But she hadn't checked it when she'd started washing the lab equipment. So she didn't know.

She didn't know!

And she couldn't even say for sure that she'd been in another person's reality. Some of the thoughts in her head had come from outside herself. But some of them were her own. Or at least that's what it had seemed like.

Closing her eyes, she lowered her head into her hands, trying to sort out what was real and what was fantasy. It seemed like she'd lived in this house years ago when the trees outside had been much smaller.

But what about the wolf?

She felt her stomach clench and knew the reason. She knew the wolf had come to her. Not the woman who had lived here before. *Her*.

And the knowledge was more frightening than the rest of the dream.

Last night when she'd looked out the window, she'd sensed someone out there.

Well, not someone. Something that she didn't understand. Now she was pretty sure that it had been the wolf.

She raised her head and glanced around the kitchen, seeing it as if for the first time. She should pick up and leave this place. The rational part of her that had always stepped back from the strange and the unknown urged her to run away from this place. This house. This town. The vast wilderness that stretched away from her doorstep.

But the other part was silently whispering something entirely different in her ear.

"Stay. Stay and find out."

The scared little girl inside her still wanted to run. But she no longer thought that was possible or even that it would do her any good. Because it seemed that down here in Wayland, Georgia, at the edge of the great Olakompa Swamp, another part of her—the long denied part—had taken control.

ADAM thought about eating dinner in town, at one of the restaurants that were doing reasonably well along Main Street. But then he'd have to explain his eating habits. Mostly he preferred meat and other protein. With only small amounts of fruit or salad or vegetables.

Since the low-carbohydrate craze had come in, he had a pretty good rationale for his requirements. He told people he was on the Atkins diet. But tonight he decided it was simply easier to grab something at home.

He opened the freezer and took out one of the steaks he'd bought on sale at the local Winn-Dixie, "the meat people."

He thawed it in the microwave, then cut it into chunks and ate them, grinning as he thought about Amy's reaction to feeding Big Jim. She might hate handling the alligator's rations. He'd had evil thoughts about snitching some grub for himself. Of course, that might lead to the beast's scarfing up another toy poodle, so he'd restrained himself.

After dinner, he made sure he didn't have any blood on his chin, then strode to his SUV.

Exiting the park, he turned left toward town, slowing as he reached the Reduce Speed sign, since he knew from experience that Sheriff Delacorte or one of his deputies was likely to be hiding in the bushes waiting to hand out a speeding ticket.

Straight from the wide-open spaces of Texas where he could easily push his SUV up to a hundred on the freeway, Adam had been caught in the speed trap the first time he'd come to Wayland. Seeing as he was the new head ranger, Delacorte had let him off with a warning. Since then, he'd vowed to keep from being hauled in.

His destination was an old stone church a block off Main Street that now housed the Wayland Historical Society.

He was always cautious when entering a new situation. So he climbed out of his SUV, closed the door softly and stood looking at the neatly tended graveyard that stretched away to his left, then at the gray stone building with its peaked roof and spire.

From the outside, it still looked just like a house of worship, complete with a rounded stained-glass window over the doorway through which the interior light shone out.

It was pretty, in a stylized sort of way. If you liked that sort of thing.

After climbing the front steps, he paused inside the door and looked around at the interior. The Gothic roofline of the church was accented by high rafters and the old stained-glass windows depicting what he assumed were the usual Christian themes. With no light shining in from outside, it was difficult to make them out.

The Marshall family hadn't gone to church. Sometimes his mother had attended. But his father had seen no use for worshiping in an institution that undoubtedly considered him and his sons an abomination.

Adam had followed his logic. He had been in few churches in his life, although a time or two, a colleague had gotten married and invited him to the ceremony, and he'd gone out of politeness.

He didn't like weddings any more than he liked houses of worship.

Ironic that the historical society was housed in one.

He could see clearly, though, that the pews and podium had been removed, replaced by wooden tables and bookshelves that lined the walls and divided up sections of the large room.

Looking around, he saw only a few people in the building, chiefly a couple of wizened men with their noses buried in books. Not surprisingly historical research appeared to be a pastime of the older generation in Wayland.

He had been standing just inside the door, taking it in, when a woman's voice asked politely, "Can I help you?"

He looked to his right and saw a narrow desk where a white-haired, round-faced woman sat reading a large leather-bound volume. She was probably in her late fifties, he judged. Her name tag identified her as Mrs. Waverly. No first name.

He approached the desk and almost choked on the wave of perfume coming off the librarian. Still, he managed to give her a disarming smile before saying, "I'm the new head ranger at Nature's Refuge."

She raised her head, looking him up and down. "Then you're Adam Marshall. I've heard a lot about you."

He didn't bother to inquire how she'd come by his name. This was a small town, and he'd learned that the new guy in a closed community was always of interest. Particularly if he appeared to be an eligible bachelor.

"I hope what you heard was good, Mrs. Waverly," he answered easily.

A flush came to her cheeks. "Oh yes, certainly." She shuffled the papers on her desk. "What can we do for you?"

"Well, when I start a job in a new area, I like to find out about the local history. I was wondering what reading you'd recommend."

"We have an excellent local history, written by a former member of the society. It was published in nineteen fifty-seven, but it will catch you up on everything up until then."

Nineteen fifty-seven. He stifled an inward groan. Probably some folks thought things here never changed. Still, he responded with another smile.

"Actually, I'd like some more recent history as well."

"We have newspapers and other materials, but they can only be used in the building because often they're one-of-a-kind items."

"Yes, I understand. Can you show me where to find the newspapers?"

"Certainly." She got up from behind the desk and bustled over to an area at the back of the room. He had expected to see a bank of microfilm readers. There was one reader and high shelves stacked with large, black-bound books.

"We have local newspapers dating back to before the War of Northern Aggression," she said.

War of Northern Aggression? Oh, yeah, the Civil War, he mentally translated.

"I don't need to go quite that far back," he allowed.

Mrs. Waverly went into what must be a long-practiced spiel, her voice taking on a sing-song quality. "We started microfilming in nineteen ninety-seven," she said, obviously proud of their modern equipment. "Before that, you'll have to consult bound volumes." She pointed to her right. "You can take them to this table over here."

"Thank you, ma'am," he answered politely.

"Don't put them back because you may file them incorrectly," she added sternly. "The staff will reshelve them after you're finished."

"I understand."

"And we close at nine-thirty sharp."

"Yes, ma'am."

He wasn't sure where to start. But he figured the volumes from twenty-five years ago, the year Austen Barnette had bought Nature's Refuge, might be interesting.

He found January of that year on a low shelf, stooped to gather it up, and brought it to the table that Mrs. Waverly had indicated. It was a hefty volume, and he wondered who carted the heavy stuff around.

Up until the early eighties, the *Wayland Messenger* had come out once a week, so it wasn't difficult to thumb through the entire year. At first he didn't encounter anything beyond births and deaths, routine police reports of robberies and traffic accidents, and feature articles on various people like the owner of the largest peanut farm in the area who had commissioned a batch of peanut recipes and the botany teacher at the local community college who was starting a new course on herbal remedies.

Herbal remedies. That stopped him, and he read the article carefully.

It was interesting, but it told him nothing besides the fact that a local guy was interested in old-time herbs.

He kept looking for additional information. It was in one of the April issues that he found an article cut out of the paper.

What?

He guessed he'd find out because it looked like someone had put it back by folding it up and tucking it into the binding of the volume.

10

THE folded rectangle of paper was brittle, and he opened it carefully. When he had spread it out, he saw that the headline on the article read, "Woman Burned to Death in Cabin."

The story began: "Jenna Foster, a young woman living in a rural area on the old Wayland-Lanconia road, was found burned to death in her ruined cabin early this morning. Although the woman was un-

married, she was reported to have a daughter, Victoria. The girl was
not found."

According to the article, Miss Foster was using a space heater that
exploded, setting the cabin on fire. Sheriff Harold Delacorte claimed
the heater had a faulty cord.

There was more, but no other useful facts. Adam compared the
hole in the paper to the folded article. They did, indeed, match. Then
he thumbed through the rest of the bound volume but found no other
mention of Jenna Foster.

He started to put the large book back, then remembered that visitors weren't trusted to return research material to the shelves. Instead
he got up and fetched the next.

As far as he could see, the fire and her death had been reported, but
then nothing else. He found that startling. The daughter was missing,
but there was no report that she had been found or that she hadn't. He
thought about the media furor that sprang up these days whenever a
youngster went missing. Today, the child's picture would be all over
the national news channels.

And the attention would be even more intense in the local media.
There would be teams of people combing the swamp for her. But ap-
parently that hadn't happened twenty-five years ago in Wayland,
Georgia.

A woman had died, and her little girl hadn't even registered as a
blip on the local radar screens.

Why? Hadn't they cared? Or had some relative come and claimed
her? He could easily picture that happening.

But even if that were true, he would expect the fact that she was
safe and cared for to be reported in the local paper. But there was
nothing.

It was as though someone had decided to erase Jenna Foster and
her daughter from the local records, including cutting out the one
story about her. Then somebody else had rectified the situation.

He looked over toward Mrs. Waverly and found that she was
watching him. When she realized he'd caught her staring, she glanced
quickly down at the papers in front of her.

Getting up, he carried the bound volume and the article to the desk.

"I was hoping you could help me," he said as he set the large
book down.

"Of course."

"I found an article cut out of the paper, then stuffed into the binding."

Her voice turned sharp as she stared down at the volume he'd set before her. "Cut out? How is that possible?" She sounded like she was accusing him of being the one to destroy historical records. Then she focused on the article he'd unfolded.

"Where did you get that?" she demanded.

"Like I said, it was tucked into the binding of the book."

"That's trash," she said, as she snatched it away and put it into her desk drawer. "Why were you looking at this particular volume anyway?"

Her reaction was so out of proportion to what he expected that he considered his answer carefully, then said, "I came to Wayland to work at Nature's Refuge, and I was curious about what was happening in town the year the park was acquired."

"Oh yes. Of course," she agreed, her tone more controlled.

"Naturally I was wondering about the woman and the child."

When Mrs. Waverly simply sat there staring at him, he asked another question, "Did some relatives come and claim the little girl?"

"I don't know anything about that," the librarian said, her tone of voice making it clear that the subject was closed.

Adam took in the shuttered expression on her face. She was looking decidedly less friendly than she had an hour ago.

"Thank you for your help," he murmured.

She had the grace to flush.

After waiting a beat, he turned and exited the building, then stood on the steps staring out at clouds turned pink and lavender by the setting sun.

The natural beauty was a stark contrast to the article he'd been reading. Something ugly had taken place in Wayland, and he wondered what it was, exactly.

Paul Delacorte had told him that a woman had been murdered in her cabin at the edge of the swamp twenty-five years ago.

The newspaper story said that a woman named Jenna Foster had been burned to death in her cabin, the fire started by a faulty space heater. But what if that account wasn't exactly accurate? What if the cause of the fire hadn't been an accident at all?

He thought back, recalling the details that Delacorte had given him. He'd said only that the woman had been killed. He hadn't said how. But he'd been reluctant to talk about the incident, just like Mrs. Waverly had been reluctant to talk about the woman in the newspaper article.

On the face of it, they didn't sound like they had much in common, except the way both Waverly and Delacorte had clammed up. And then there was the startling fact that somebody had cut the article out of the paper—and somebody else had put it back.

Well, he needed to find another source of information about the Jenna Foster death. But now that he knew he was stepping into a pool of swamp mud, he was going to be discreet about asking questions.

STARFLOWER walked into the Road House bar. She didn't have to look around to locate the group. She knew where they were. Not just because they always occupied the back left corner of the room. She could feel their presence because they were part of her, and she was part of them.

And she loved the connection.

In the regular world, she was nobody. A clerk at Great Greetings on Main Street.

But with the clan, she was different. Strong and proud.

She swept back her blond hair and stood in the doorway for a moment. Billy Edwards, one of the guys from town, was watching her. He'd had a yen for her since she'd moved to Wayland. He had a nice new pickup truck and a good job out at the farmer's coop. She might have settled for a guy like him. But that was before Falcon had found her living in Macon and explained why she should come back to the community her parents had fled.

At first she'd been skeptical and afraid, if you wanted to know the truth. She knew that her parents had been run out of Wayland when she was just a baby.

But Falcon had told her it would be different this time. He'd taken her to meet Willow and Grizzly. And he'd brought a couple of gallon jugs of water from the Olakompa Swamp. He'd poured them into a washtub and made everybody join hands and breathe in the rich, rotting scent coming off the water. The water and the connection with the group had made her feel wild and potent.

She'd craved that feeling ever since. Craved being with these people. Craved the power she felt growing within herself.

Falcon looked up, saw her and waved. He wasn't a handsome man. His nose was too big. His eyes were too close together. And teenage acne had pitted his skin. But none of that mattered.

He was a natural leader, and she would follow him where he wanted to take her.

He flashed her his killer smile, and a little frisson went through her as she suddenly remembered the thrill of feeling his even white teeth worry her nipple.

His smile turned knowing, and she wondered if he was sharing the same memory.

"Hey!" he called across the restaurant.

"Hey." She wove her way through the tables and chairs to where the group was sitting.

The entire ten members of the clan only met on prearranged occasions. But six of them were present this evening.

Willow moved over to make room for her on the banquette. Razorback's gaze swept over her, settling for a moment on her breasts, tightening them.

What a sexy bastard. She always made love with him when the group got together for one of their special sessions. And they'd had some fun on their own, a time or two.

Too bad he was always pushing Falcon, making her wonder if the two of them were going to end up fighting it out for the leadership of the clan. That would be exciting. But she hoped they could work out their differences, because she'd hate to see one of them kill the other.

She switched her attention to Falcon. "How's the old homestead comin'?" He was a talented carpenter. When he'd come back to town, he'd found a job that used those skills. And he'd also started rehabbing the house out in the country that his parents had left standing vacant. First he'd made sure the structure was sound and weather tight. Then he'd begun adding rooms. When it was finished it was going to be a palace, where a lot of them could live.

"Great. We've got two of the new bedrooms framed. And we got the spa tub into the new bathroom."

"Wow!"

"Copperhead's a big help."

Copperhead was shy and subdued, good at taking orders. Now he smiled with pleasure at being complimented.

She smiled at him. She was looking forward to moving into the house. The other women might not know it yet, but she was going to be the queen of the place.

"So when are you gonna tell us why you invited us for a drink after work?" Willow asked.

Falcon touched his finger to his brow. "Right now, honey." He paused for dramatic effect. He was good at that. "I spotted a woman in town. Someone who would be an asset to the clan."

Starflower could feel the sudden energy flowing around the table. Being an asset to the clan meant something very particular. It meant that the woman was descended from the same stock as the rest of them, the early English settlers who had developed special powers living in the swamp or at its margin. She didn't know what to call those powers. Falcon had said they were paranormal. He'd given her some books to read, but she wasn't much on book learning. She preferred to think of herself as a modern day witch. And most of the rest of them did, too—when they talked about it among themselves.

They were all here because Falcon had gone to a great deal of trouble, talking to his parents and some of the others who had moved away from Wayland. He'd come up with a list of people who had been shot, hanged, and burned up over the years. From that, he'd gotten a bunch of last names.

"She's from one of the families?" Greenbrier asked, her voice taking on a lilting sound.

"No."

"Then how can she be one of us?"

Before Falcon could answer, the waitress bustled up to ask if Starflower wanted anything to drink and if the others wanted a refill.

The guys ordered more beer. Starflower ordered one, too.

Falcon watched the server leave, then leaned forward and lowered his voice. "She doesn't have to be on my list. We all know there's intermixin' in this town, between their kind and ours."

There were nods of agreement. The famous Jenna Foster was a case in point. As far as anyone knew, she hadn't been married, but she'd had a child. Nobody knew for sure who the father was, but they did know he'd been ashamed to let the town know that he'd been consorting with one of those people. Of course, there was something else about Jenna Foster. She'd been known in the old-time witch community as the woman who had gone over to the other side. She'd shunned her own people. Which had made her a misguided fool.

"The woman you spotted—what's her name?"

"Sara Weston."

Razorback looked Falcon up and down. "I never heard that name around here."

Their leader nodded. "Me neither. But I know the kind of vibrations that are coming off her."

Razorback leaned forward. "Oh yeah? Who is she? Has she been here the whole time? Or did she move back, like us? How old is she?"

Falcon gave an easy laugh. "That's a lot of questions. I can answer some of them. She's in her twenties, I'd guess." He nodded toward Starflower. "She looks a little like you, honey. Maybe she's your long lost sister."

"I don't have a long lost sister."

"You know for sure your daddy didn't sew any wild oats?"

She shifted in her seat and shrugged. Actually, she did know her father had been a ladies' man in his youth.

Falcon was speaking again. "I did a little asking around. She's in Wayland doing a plant research study for one of the big pharmaceutical companies. And get this." He paused, obviously enjoying their eyes on him. "She's living out at the Foster place."

A hush fell over the group. They all knew about the Foster place. It was part of their mythology, a house at the edge of the Olakompa that had taken on the status of a kind of shrine among them, because it was where the very public murder of Jenna Foster had taken place. It didn't matter whose side she had been on. She had been burned to death like an old-time witch. Everybody in town knew about the murder and the cover-up. But nobody talked about it. Least of all that damn sheriff, Paul Delacorte. It was his daddy who had swept the whole thing under the rug, like yesterday's garbage.

"I thought that house burned down," Starflower whispered. "I mean Jenna Foster died in a fire."

"Only part of the house was damaged. A thunderstorm put the fire out. Austen Barnette owned the place then. He still does."

"Do tell," Willow murmured.

"Your boss?" Starflower asked.

"Yeah. The old dude has his fingers in all kinds of pies in town."

"Cow pies?" Razorback smirked.

Everybody laughed.

Falcon waited for them to settle, then continued. "I don't just work out at the estate. I come down here to fix things at a bunch of different shops for him. He's got residential property, too. Like the cabin. He had it built back up so he could rent it out."

Razorback laughed again. "Yeah, to unsuspecting goobers."

"So if that woman is living there, maybe she's . . . she's absorbing some kind of aura from the place. Maybe the house has Jenna Foster's powers."

"Maybe. But there are ways to find out if it's the house or her."

Again the conversation halted while the girl served the drinks.

Razorback took a swig of beer. "Like how?" he demanded.

"I saw her come to town a little while ago. She was doing some shopping on Main Street. We can test my theory tonight."

Starflower felt her nerve endings tingle as a buzz of excitement went around the table.

Falcon lowered his voice and began to describe his plan. It was clever, damn clever. Starflower liked it. Willow seemed excited by the idea.

But Razorback had an objection. "We've never tried anything in town before. It could be dangerous."

Falcon fixed him with a direct look. "Who's going to know?"

AUSTEN Barnette wouldn't have liked knowing that he was the subject of conversation among the witches. In this case, ignorance was bliss. At least for the next few moments.

He was sitting in his study smoking one of his specially imported Cuban cigars when the phone rang. It didn't ring in the office because he always turned it off by eight o'clock.

In this day and age, he could have let an answering machine screen his calls. But he hated many of the devices of the modern world. So, instead, he used James.

The old butler picked up the phone in the kitchen. Then he decided whether it was worth bothering the master of the house.

Austen waited for the verdict. When he heard a knock on the door, he looked up. "Come in."

James shuffled into the doorway. "Mrs. Della Waverly would like to speak to you. Are you available?"

He considered his answer. He had given a very generous donation to the historical society because he believed in keeping the town records in good order. The history of a place was as important as its present and its future. But he was interested in more than historical records. When he'd given the donation, he'd made it clear that the ladies who ran the society would come to him with certain information.

In a way, he'd been waiting for this call. So instead of answering James, he simply picked up the receiver.

"Della," he said in what passed as a jovial voice for him. "What can I do for you?" He and the woman went way back. Not just the two of them, but their families, too. Over the years the Barnettes and the Waverlys had stuck together when the going had been rough. Della's husband had been one of his best friends. Greg had been struck with a heart attack ten years ago when they'd been out on a deer hunt. A good way to pass, he'd always thought. Out with your buddies having fun.

He brought his attention back to Della.

"There was a man in here a few minutes ago going through old newspaper editions," she said, her voice filled with importance.

Austen sat up straighter. "What man?"

"That Adam Marshall."

"My head ranger. Yes."

"He said he was looking for material from the year the park opened."

"And?"

Della heaved a sigh. "You know that article on Jenna Foster? The one we cut out of the paper?"

"Of course!" he snapped.

"Well, somebody put it back."

"How the . . . heck could they do that?" he asked, modifying his intended curse.

"Well, I don't mean it was taped into the paper. But somebody stuffed it into the bound volume."

"I appreciate your telling me," he said.

"I took it away from Marshall. And I didn't tell him anything else."

He kept his voice calm and even. "You did fine, Della. I appreciate your informing me," he said again. "But Marshall won't be any
problem."

"I just wanted to be sure."

"Thank you, Della."

She cleared her throat. "I put the article in my desk drawer. Should
I burn it?"

"Yes," he answered, making the decision for her. Then he let the
old bat prattle on for a few more minutes before extricating himself
from the phone call.

He dragged in more cigar smoke, then blew it out in a heavy
stream.

A long time ago he'd taken care of that article in the historical so-
ciety records. He'd also made sure there wasn't any other mention of
Jenna Foster or her daughter in the newspaper. And he'd made sure
Sheriff Harold Delacorte did the right thing.

He'd thought that the whole incident had gone away, at least in
public. Now he knew somebody had disagreed with that decision.

Who the hell had gone against him?

Well, he had a lot of enemies in town. A lot of people could have
done it.

Of course, the article didn't say anything damaging. But years ago
there had been other materials that could be more of a problem. He'd
had those destroyed, too.

At least he'd assumed so. Now he was thinking it was better to be
safe than sorry. But he couldn't exactly send James down to the historical society. He'd have to go himself. In a couple of days, when his
joints didn't ache so much.

He leaned back in his desk chair, puffing on his cigar, thinking
about the good citizens of Wayland, wondering who had dared to put
that article back into the paper.

11

ADAM walked slowly up the block, pretending interest in the shop windows. But really, he was watching the people going by on the newly bricked sidewalk. It was after nine, and he thought that this was the time when the kind of men and women who had been cavorting around the campfire might be out and about.

Of course, he had no hard evidence of that. It was just a hunch.

He eyed a lanky guy holding hands with his girlfriend, a young woman with medium-brown hair. From where he stood now, either one of them could be part of the group from the other night. But he had no way of knowing, and that set his stomach churning.

He'd relied on his wolf senses for all of his adult life. But they were no help to him in this situation. The smoke had clogged his nostrils, and the paint on the dancers' faces had obscured their features.

Of course, there were bits and pieces he'd focused on. Maybe if the little brunette would take off her tank top, he'd recognize her breasts, he thought with an inward laugh. Or maybe not. Probably he'd been too far gone to recognize anything. And lucky for him he'd been in the shadows, so they wouldn't know who he was either. At least he hoped to hell that was true.

He wandered along toward the Winn-Dixie, thinking that he could pick up a six-pack of bottled water.

After that, he might as well head home, because it was starting to get dark. And he wasn't going to see much without his werewolf's vision. He was halfway to the grocery store when he felt a tingling sensation at the back of his neck.

Stopping in his tracks, he lifted his head. The atmosphere around him had the charged, heavy feel of the air before a storm, yet there was no gathering of dark clouds above the town.

His breath stilled in his lungs. Something was about to happen, but he had no idea what.

As if to give him a better view of the downtown area, the streetlights flicked on. Twenty feet down the sidewalk a woman stepped out of the drugstore, the yellow glow shining down on her blond hair.

One of the women at the campfire had been blond. A real blonde. Was that her? Her height was about right. And her body type. At least he thought so. But he couldn't be sure of anything. Dammit.

She looked like she was waiting to cross the street. When she turned her head to check out the traffic, he knew who she was.

Sara. The woman who had been in his thoughts almost constantly over the past two days. He had only spoken to her once, in real life. But he had dreamed of her, stalked her house, held countless conversations with her in his head.

SARA looked toward the parking lot across Main Street. She'd felt closed in and cut off from the world in her little cabin, so she'd come to town and checked out some of the antique and clothing shops. Her last stop had been the drugstore to pick up a few things she needed, like paper towels and toothpaste.

Pausing on the curb, she opened the zipper of her shoulder bag and fumbled inside to locate her keys.

A woman alone was supposed to have her keys in her hand when she stepped outside a store, especially after dark. She'd started doing it after there had been a rape on the college campus. Probably the advice wasn't so important in a small town like Wayland, but she figured that the habit wasn't a bad one to keep.

With the hard metal keys clutched in her fingers, she stepped between two parked cars and looked both ways up and down Main Street. There were no vehicles coming, so she started across the street. Halfway into the traffic lane, a sudden pain knifed through her head.

It felt like a blast from a ray gun cutting through flesh and bone, slicing into the soft tissue of her brain.

The needle-sharp sensation made her gasp, made her vision blur. For a moment all logical thought completely fled her mind. She didn't know where she was or who she was or even what she was doing. Her whole body had gone rigid, unable to move. Unable to function on any rational level.

She didn't know how long the spell lasted. Just when she thought the unendurable was going to send her to her knees, the intensity lessened. Below the surface of the pain, like bubbles bobbing up through layers of swamp water, she sensed words forming in her mind.

Not her words. Words beamed in from some other consciousness.

Watch out, Sara. You're in danger. Danger. Danger. There's a truck coming. Get out of the street. Watch out Sara. You're in danger, danger, danger. The truck, the truck, the truck.

She raised her hand, pressing her fingers to her forehead as the warning echoed in her mind like vibrations coming off the surface of a drum, sending the words bouncing around the inside of her skull.

It wasn't one voice but a babble of people, men and women, all saying the same things like a Greek chorus.

Watch out, Sara. You're in danger. Danger. Danger.

Her skin had gone clammy. Her heart was pounding wildly in her chest. Somehow through the cotton filling her brain, she knew that she had to bring her thoughts into focus. Danger. She was in danger. But the pain in her head had made it hard to think, impossible to move.

Her fingers clamped around the cold metal of the keys that were still in her purse, deliberately pressing the teeth into her flesh, as she struggled to anchor herself to reality.

Looking to her left, she saw that a black pickup truck had rounded the corner and was coming toward her, as she'd been warned. And she had to get out of the street before it mowed her down.

But she couldn't move. Feeling like an insect caught in amber, she simply stood there, watching the truck bear down on her.

ADAM sprinted down the sidewalk, the scene burned into the tissue of his brain like a flaming brand: Sara in the middle of the street, and a black pickup heading right for her.

He couldn't get there in time. It was all happening much too fast, yet some part of him felt as if he were viewing the scene in slow motion. With no thought for his own safety, he leaped between parked cars, crossing the few feet still separating him from Sara as though his running shoes had sprouted jet propulsion devices.

He grabbed for her, his fingers tangled in her knit top, clutching the fabric as he pulled her away from two tons of metal speeding down the blacktop.

She screamed as his hands dug through her shirt and into her flesh, screamed again as the vehicle whizzed by.

Raising his head, he tried to get a look at the driver. He thought he could make out a large head covered with a cap and shoulders hunched over the wheel. But he only caught a fleeting glimpse through the back window, and he couldn't even be sure if it was a man or a woman.

He lost sight of the driver in the wash from the tailwind. It buffeted them so strongly that he was almost knocked off his feet. Swaying, he braced his hips against the side of a parked car, pulling Sara against himself to prevent the two of them from tumbling to the pavement.

She was safe. And in his arms. His breath wedged in his throat as he folded her close, cradling her slender body protectively against his. She was trembling. Her fingers must have let go of the plastic shopping bag she was holding, because he heard it drop to the ground.

"It's okay. You're safe with me."

"They warned me," she rasped, her fingers closing and unclosing on his arm.

He didn't understand what she was saying. All he knew was that at this moment in time, he needed to shut out the world and simply hold her. Closing his eyes, he wrapped her tightly in his embrace. An inarticulate sound welled in his throat as he lowered his face to the top of her head, unconsciously moving his lips against her golden hair.

In response, she lifted her arms, clinging to him as though they had been separated for a long, long time. And now they were finally together again.

The strength of his emotions made no sense. But as he gathered her against himself, he was filled with an incredible feeling of connection to her, as though the two of them had known each other for a thousand lifetimes. He had never believed in destiny. Yet at this moment, he understood that she was the woman the fates had ordained for him.

And she seemed to understand that, too.

As they stood at the edge of Main Street, clinging to each other, he forgot where they were, forgot why he had folded her into his arms. The feel of her body pressed to his was too overwhelming to leave room in his mind for anything else. He would put her in his car. Take her back to Nature's Refuge, where he could keep her safe. Where he could keep her for himself. She belonged to him as no other woman had ever belonged to him. And he belonged to her in the same way.

A voice snapped him back to reality. "Hey, buddy, you all right?"

He remembered, then, why he was holding Sara and why she was clinging to him.

"You all right?" the voice asked again. It came from somewhere outside the invisible bubble that enclosed himself and the woman in his arms.

He wanted to ignore the intrusion, but he knew that if he didn't answer, the questioner would persist.

"Yeah," he replied, without shifting his attention away from Sara.

"Who was that jerk?" asked the man standing a few feet away.

"I'd like to know," Adam growled, the low, strained quality of his voice coming as much from annoyance with the guy who wouldn't leave him and Sara be as his reaction to the aborted hit-and-run.

But it wasn't just one guy, he suddenly realized. A whole crowd of evening shoppers had gathered on the sidewalk, destroying the private moment.

Lifting his head, he stared at the people who had materialized around them.

"We're fine," he said again, addressing the group at large.

He heard Sara swallow hard. "Yes, fine," she echoed automatically, even though her skin was pale as moonlight, and she was staring up at him with wide, shocked eyes.

Somebody thrust a plastic shopping bag at him, and he took it, then used his shoulders to part the sea of humanity so that he could draw Sara away from the center of attention and into a little courtyard between two buildings.

She was still shaking, and he draped the hand with the shopping bag awkwardly around her shoulder, stroking his other hand up and down her arm. He was waiting for her to pull away from him, but she stayed where she was.

Did she feel what he did? The intensity? The sudden need to caress her mouth with his?

The anticipation of the kiss burned through him like a fire devouring him from the inside out. He knew how it would be. Passionate. Consuming. Branding.

The reality of her overwhelmed him. He was swamped by sensory input: the sweet smell of her hair, the feminine shape of her body, the fine tremor that went through her.

Every instinct urged him to claim her mouth, to claim her for his own. Yet at the same time, he felt as though he had broken through solid ground and was sinking into the black waters of the swamp. In some part of his mind he knew that if he lowered his mouth to hers, there would be no going back. Not ever.

She stared up at him, looking shocked, and he thought maybe she felt the same thing he did. Maybe she knew that they stood on the brink of some discovery that neither one of them was prepared to make.

While emotions roared through him, Sara took the decision out of his hands and pulled away from him.

"Don't," he managed, feeling as though his own flesh were being torn from his body.

Her eyes were wide and round. When she spoke, her voice was barely a whisper. "I have to go."

"Sara." His fingers closed over her arm.

"What do you want?" she asked, her voice a little stronger.

Seconds passed as they both waited for the answer. He couldn't give it because he was afraid to frame the words, even in his mind. All he could say was, "I want you to be careful."

"I will," she told him, then pulled away and fled into the darkness.

FALCON joined the clan where they had gathered in the lot in back of the ice-cream parlor.

Razorback's head swung toward him. "Where did you park, man?"

"A block over."

"What if someone made your license plate?"

"I smeared it with dirt. There was no way to see it."

"Clever!" Copperhead approved.

Razorback kicked his foot against the blacktop.

"So what did you think about the woman?" Starflower asked the group.

"Did you see her go stock still like she'd been drilled with a laser? She got the message we sent her, all right. She knew the truck was coming," Razorback said, his voice emphatic.

"She didn't get out of the way," Grizzly pointed out. "She just stood there in the middle of the street."

"She was spooked. Didn't you see the way she went pale, the way her hand went to her head." Starflower jumped back into the conversation. "We did it too strong. We didn't know it was gonna paralyze her."

"Yeah," Grizzly conceded.

"The way she stood there. That's not proof," Willow argued.

"What do you think?" Starflower asked Falcon.

He spread his hands. "By the time I got there, she looked like a deer caught in the headlights. It's hard to be sure."

Grizzly craned his neck back toward the shopping area. "The street was full of people minding their own business. But it's that one guy who spooked me. The guy who pulled her out of the way. Did you see him zero in on her before he even saw the truck?"

There were exclamations of agreement around the group.

"Who is he?" Grizzly asked sharply.

"He's got . . . power," Starflower murmured, her voice low.

"How do you know?" Grizzly pressed.

"I can feel it. Maybe it's a man-woman thing. Falcon recognized the woman as one of us. And I got something from the guy."

"Yeah," Falcon growled, his eyes narrowing as he stared at the place where the couple had disappeared. It was the guy he had seen the other day at Barnette's house.

He looked at Starflower. "That's the new head ranger of Nature's Refuge."

"Oh, yeah?" Razorback muttered.

"He could be the snoop who was spyin' on us the other night."

That got everybody's attention.

"So we take care of him, like we took care of Ken White?" Grizzly muttered.

"Not necessarily," Starflower said quickly. "Let me find out if he's with us or against us."

"You want to test him? Like Falcon tested her?" Willow asked.

Starflower grinned. "Actually, I have something else in mind."

12

A raccoon appeared at the side of the road, and Sara slowed. The animal hesitated for a moment, then turned and disappeared into the open field at the side of the blacktop.

Sara continued along the darkened highway. She was six miles from downtown Wayland, and the farther she got from Main Street, the more calm she felt.

Strange. She had fled her cabin this evening to get away from the old ghosts who crowded into the small rooms with her.

Now the old ghosts were preferable to the new voices echoing in her mind. The thought brought a trace of her earlier headache, and she gritted her teeth. "No," she said aloud. She wanted it to disappear, along with the memory of what had happened when she'd stepped off the curb. But she couldn't wish the incident away.

Tonight people had called out to her. And she'd felt their words echoing in her brain like the reverberations from a steel drum that had stopped her in her tracks.

They had sounded their alarm moments before the truck had come at her in the street. At the same time, she'd thought she heard them yammering in her head. Now she was able to come up with another explanation that she liked better.

Somebody in town was playing an evil practical joke on the lady from Granville Pharmaceuticals. They knew her name. They'd called out to her, and then one of them had aimed his truck at her.

The scenario wasn't exactly reassuring, but it had the power to make her feel better. Because it put a creepy experience into more normal terms. She clutched it to her breast, even though it didn't fit all the facts.

What about the pain in her head, she asked herself, then came up with another good answer. She had been working hard for the past few days. Too hard. She'd been under a lot of stress. In a new environment. And it was perfectly reasonable to believe that the whole combination of factors had given her a headache.

She breathed out a small sigh, feeling some of her tension evaporate as she drove on into the night.

The voices hadn't been in her mind at all. They had come from people hiding just out of sight. People having some fun with her.

She didn't like it much. And she didn't know why they had picked on her. Or whether they would try something else. But she had given herself an explanation for the truck incident. Which left her free to think about the next part.

Specifically, Adam Marshall.

He had risked his own life to snatch her out of the street when she'd lost the power to move. Afterwards, he had gathered her in his arms as though he were a lover coming back to her after a long absence. And she had clung to him with the same fervor.

The intensity of the encounter had overwhelmed her, replacing the earlier fear. In the real world, she barely knew the man, yet she'd cleaved to him as though . . . as though he were her only salvation.

The idea was absurd.

And scary. Which was why she'd wrenched herself away and run back to the safety of familiar old Miss Hester.

She'd never felt half that much for any other man. Not even the two with whom she'd made love.

And she'd waited months before taking that step with either of them. Adam Marshall was a stranger. So why was she responding to him as though they were two halves of one whole? Why had she met him in a dream that seemed more real than any of her previous bedroom encounters?

She pulled into the parking space in front of her cabin and sat with her eyes squeezed tightly closed, trying to shut out the feelings that had swamped her when he'd pulled her into that courtyard and the two of them had been alone. Banishing the memory was impossible. With a sigh she opened the door and stepped out of the old Toyota, taking a deep breath of the damp air, conscious of how dark it was out here in the middle of nowhere.

When she'd left the little house at the edge of the swamp, it had still been daylight. But she should have thought to turn on the porch light. In the future, she wouldn't forget that.

As she reached for her keys, headlights cut through the inky blackness along the road.

Goose bumps peppered her skin. Whirling, she turned to face the intruder, her arm rising to shade her eyes. But it was impossible to see the vehicle behind the headlights. The only thing she could think was that the guy with the pickup was back.

Earlier, she had frozen in the middle of the street. Determined not to make the same mistake twice, she reversed direction and sprinted for the house, fumbling again for keys in her purse. Her gun was inside the cabin. If the driver or his friends meant her harm, she would defend herself. And call the sheriff.

Should she already have reported the incident? She'd been so muddled up on the way out of town that she hadn't even thought of it.

She heard gravel crunch as she shoved the key into the lock.

"Sara! Wait. It's Adam."

She went dead still. "Adam?" Turning, she saw a tall figure moving toward her across the yard and felt something inside her chest clench. A complex mixture of emotions welled inside her. Joy. Fear. Need.

She had been thinking about him. Puzzling over her feelings for him. And now, here he was, as though she'd called to him, and he'd come to her.

Her lips moved, and she heard her voice quaver as she asked, "What are you doing here?"

WORDS of apology tumbled from his mouth, "I'm sorry. I didn't mean to frighten you. I followed you home to make sure nobody else did. I wanted to be certain you were all right. And I have your shopping bag," he added lamely.

He didn't explain that the need to protect her had sent him bolting for his SUV the moment she'd left him. Or that the feeling of being separated from her after holding her in his arms was intolerable.

"I'm fine," she assured him, the answer sounding like an automatic response.

He reached her as she turned the key in the lock, pushed the door open, and switched on the porch light. Both of them stood blinking in the sudden brightness.

He set down the shopping bag on the worn floorboards, thinking that he shouldn't have gotten out of his car. He should have made sure nobody else was coming along behind her, then driven on past and given her the drugstore purchases another time. But he was here, and the need to reach for her had him pressing his palms against the sides of his jeans.

The pulse pounding in his ears made it difficult to hear what she had said.

"Did you ask me in?"

"Yes."

"I should go."

"I should thank you for snatching me out of the street."

He found himself following her inside. She took several steps into the room. He closed the door, then watched her moving about, turning on a lamp in the corner and one on an end table.

He loved the way the warm light glinted off her blond hair. He loved the grace of her movements. Loved her slender, long-fingered hands.

Pulling his gaze away from her, he focused on the cabin. It was sparsely furnished, yet she'd made it her own in the short time she'd been there. She had set an old metal milk can in one corner and filled it with tall grasses. Indian throws brightened the old sofa and over-stuffed chair. And a piece of old lace covered what was probably the scarred top of the oak chest against one wall.

Set out on the lace was a collection of small boxes, some china, some metallic, some wooden.

"The place looks nice," he said, thinking that the words sounded inane.

"I brought some stuff from home."

"Wilmington."

Her head jerked up. "How did you know that?"

His breath caught. How *did* he know it? "I can guess, from your accent," he answered, because it was the only answer he could come up with.

"Are you an expert on accents?"

He shrugged.

Her gaze pinned him. "Or did you know because I told you in the dream?"

He swallowed hard. "What dream?" he managed to say.

She kept her gaze steady on him. "Did you dream about me last night?"

He clenched and unclenched his hand. "Yes."

"Wouldn't it be . . . strange if we had the same dream."

"How could we?" he asked.

"Was I in your bed?" she challenged.

"Yes. But it's not difficult to figure out why. I've been thinking about you ever since we met in the swamp." He stopped abruptly, realizing he'd given too much away. It was one thing to admit as much in a dream. And quite another to say it in real life. *Change direction.* He added lamely, "And if you were thinking about me . . . it might seem like we met."

She gave a tight nod. "You can explain it that way if you want."

"How do *you* explain it?"

"I can't. And I don't want to. All I know is that strange things have been happening to me since I moved here. Dreams that seem real. Daydreams where I feel like I'm in someone else's head. Then that incident with the truck."

"How do you mean?"

"It's hard to talk about it. Maybe a cup of tea would settle us both down."

He gave her credit for a quick change of subject. "I don't drink tea. Well, not unless it's herbal tea," he said, feeling like he were babbling.

"I have mint. Is that okay?"

"Yes."

She moved to the kitchen and switched on another light. The room was small, and as she turned to snatch the kettle off a burner and fill it, she clanked it against the faucet.

"Sorry," she said as she whirled back to the stove and set the kettle down again.

He was consumed by the urge to go to her, make her face him, and fold her close, but he managed to stay where he was.

"Tell me about the truck," he said.

For long moments, her gaze turned inward, and he thought she wasn't going to speak. Then she sighed. "I've decided the driver didn't really mean to hit me," she said in a rush of words.

"What makes you think so?"

"Someone—a group of people—warned me I was *in danger.*"

He stared at her, struggling to make sense of that. "Warned you? Why? How?"

"They shouted a warning."

"I didn't hear anything or see anybody."

"Maybe they were right near me, where you couldn't see them, but I could hear them. Maybe it just sounded like a shout," she said, acting like she wasn't quite sure. Acting like she was trying out the theory on him.

"Maybe. Why would they do it?"

She shrugged again. "Because they're into mean practical jokes? Because they hate Granville Pharmaceuticals? Because they like to test the nerves of newcomers? Has anyone tried to test your nerves?"

He hesitated. "Well, somebody tried to kill me two nights ago."

She sucked in a strangled breath, raising her head so she could meet his eyes. "The people having the drug party? They tried to kill you?"

"Yes."

"You didn't mention that!"

"I didn't think you needed to know."

"Oh Lord, Adam. What did they do?"

"Chased me like a pack of . . . hyenas. Took a couple of shots at me."

Her hands gripped his arms. "Stay out of the swamp."

"I could say the same to you."

"It's my job."

"Mine, too."

"Did you tell anyone else . . . about what happened?"

"Sheriff Delacorte."

"And he said?"

"That there's been trouble in Wayland. Over the years. Incidents he was reluctant to talk about."

"What kind of trouble?" Sara asked.

"I don't know for sure. But I'm going to find out."

She studied his face, trying to read his expression. He had pulled her out of the truck's path. He had followed her home to make sure she was safe. And now he was telling her things that he could have kept to himself.

Maybe she was testing him—or testing herself—when she said, "I can believe . . . strange things have happened here."

"Why?"

"Because I get feelings about places and people. And my impressions usually turn out to be true. There's evil here. And something else."

When he didn't laugh at her, she went on. "Ever since I came to Wayland, to this cabin, I've felt . . . off balance. Things keep happening. Things I can't explain in any normal terms."

"Such as?"

"What I told you. Dreams. Daydreams. And something that happened just before that truck came flying by."

She watched him carefully to see what he thought about the way she'd put it. When he kept his gaze steady on her, she continued.

"I told you somebody shouted a warning. That's what I'll say if anybody asks about it. But I'm not sure that's what really happened. First I felt like somebody was aiming a ray gun at my skull. Then I heard the voices. But not out loud." She swallowed. "Inside my head. So maybe I'm going crazy."

"No."

"How do you know?"

"I just know. You're not crazy!"

The conviction in his voice warmed her.

"Why not?" she said, the words barely above a whisper.

"Because, like you, I have good instincts about people."

He took a step toward her.

"Adam . . ."

The kettle started to whistle. They both grabbed for it; both drew their hands back. She felt his gaze burning into her as she moved the kettle off the heat, then got out two mugs and two tea bags. She felt her heart racing as she poured the hot water into the mugs.

The sweet pungent aroma of mint filled the kitchen as he reached for her. Maybe he was offering comfort. Or reassurance. Whatever it was, she wanted it.

When he folded her into his arms, she melted against him, letting her head drop to his shoulder.

"What's happening to me? To us?"

"What do you mean . . . to us?" Adam asked.

"Are you going to lie and tell me that nothing . . . important . . . happened . . . after you snatched me out of the path of that truck?"

He had felt the intensity of it all right. But he couldn't talk about it. "We hardly know each other."

"That's usually the woman's line."

"Yeah."

"I'd say what we're feeling has nothing to do with the length of our acquaintance. It's like time has been compressed, like we're living in a speeded-up universe."

As she spoke, she stroked her fingers along his arm. It was only a light touch, but he felt it scorching his skin through the fabric of his shirt.

He'd thought the dream was intense. It was nothing compared to the here and now.

He knew he should step back before it was too late.

Too late for what?

He didn't want to answer the silent question, couldn't answer because his brain had stopped working. But he didn't need words to know what he wanted, what he had wanted since the first time he had seen her.

Instead of backing away, he hauled her closer, allowing a kaleidoscope of sensations to swamp him again. The feel of her slender body that fitted his arms so well. The brush of her soft hair against his cheek as he lowered his head. The rich woman scent that was making him dizzy.

She stood with her head bent to his shoulder. He crooked his hand under her chin, lifting her face to his, his gaze focusing on her beautifully shaped lips.

He ached to kiss her. But he held himself still, because some part of him wanted to hear her tell him "no."

He wanted her to say this was a mistake. He wanted her to be the one to make the decision, so it would be taken out of his hands.

He held his breath, waiting, willing her to pull away as she had on the street. This time she stayed where she was, her lips slightly parted.

But she didn't understand that she was playing with fire. He hardly understood it himself.

And he was helpless to do anything besides lower his head to hers. The first mouth-to-mouth contact was like a lightning strike, deep in the forest, creating a hot, instant blaze that swamped his mind, his body.

He had never tasted anything so rich, so heady as this woman's mouth. And he drank from the sweetness she offered like a man deprived of all sustenance and finally bidden to partake of a feast.

She made a small, needy sound that sent sparks to every nerve ending in his body. He angled his head, first one way and then the other, changing the angle, changing the pressure, changing the very terms of his existence.

With no conscious thought on his part, one of his hands slid down to her hips, pulling her lower body in against his erection, desperate to satisfy his craving for intimate contact with her.

The other hand clasped the top of her, pressing her breasts against his chest.

The drive to mate with her was suddenly an all-consuming purpose. His only purpose. He needed to be on top of her, needed to be deep, deep inside her.

She kissed him as though she felt what he did. And he gloried in her response to him.

Breaking the kiss, he lifted his head, his gaze barely focused as he stared down at her.

He had wished her into his bed the night before. But this was reality. And suddenly he couldn't cope with how much he felt.

"I'm sorry," he managed, knowing that it wasn't an apology for anything he had done.

The desperation of his own need was like a dash of cold water.

Earlier she had fled from him.

Now he was the one who lacked the courage to find out where the heated kiss would lead. He took a step back, then turned and stumbled away, stumbled out of the house. He wasn't even aware that he had climbed into his SUV and started the engine until he realized he was backing away from the house.

ON unsteady legs, Sara crossed the living room and closed the front door, then threw the bolt. She wanted safety where none existed. And in some part of her consciousness, she knew there never would be safety again.

One kiss, and she had wanted Adam Marshall with a force that robbed the breath from her lungs. In her mind, a picture had formed of the two of them, on the kitchen floor, naked, in a fevered embrace.

He had left her shaking. In danger of losing her balance. Physically, emotionally. Mentally. Barely able to stand, she crossed the few steps to the easy chair and sank down.

She had thought they were getting close. Not just sexually close.

Something deeper, more profound. Then he had pulled away, and she could have sworn he was afraid to take it to the next step.

Adam Marshall afraid?

Another image came to her. She saw herself throwing clothing into a suitcase and fleeing the cabin. Fleeing Adam. Fleeing Wayland. Because she was afraid that if she didn't get out of Wayland, she would be sucked under the black waters of the Olakompa—never to be seen again. If not literally, then figuratively.

As that panicked thought surfaced, she knew something even more fundamental. Earlier in the day, she had thought about leaving. She was still here. And now she knew that bailing out would be the worst thing she could do. Fate had brought her here to this place at this time. And turning away from what waited for her was worse than staying. She had to face her worst fear and conquer it or she was surely doomed. She hugged her arms around her shoulders, rubbing her hands up and down her arms, trying to ward off the sudden chill that made her teeth begin to chatter.

ADAM drove into the night, feeling pursued by devils that had always lurked in the darkness. And now they had burst forth.

The raw force of what had happened between himself and Sara astonished him. He knew it had started building on the street in Wayland. Well, before that, really, when he'd first seen her in the park. Alone with her in the kitchen, the need to join with her had gripped him with a savage strength that had shaken him to the core.

He had fled those feelings, and now he didn't know what the hell he was going to do.

Run. He wanted to run. Yet he knew deep in his soul that would do him no good.

If he ran from Sara now, it would be like half his mind and heart had been hacked out of his body. On some deep instinctive level, he understood that. Yet he wasn't able to come to terms with the new reality: He must have this woman or die. Till death do them part.

Although that sounded simple, it wasn't simple at all.

Like, for instance, was she involved with the people who had tried to kill him in the swamp? He didn't want to think so, but he still couldn't be sure. Part of him prayed that she wasn't. And part of him welcomed the theory. Because that would give him an excuse to tear ass out of the state.

Right now his fear was as strong as his need. She had kissed Adam Marshall, the man. What about Adam Marshall, werewolf? Would the wolf send her screaming in terror? He had never worried about that with any of his other women because he hadn't been around long enough for them to find out. He had made love with them. Enjoyed their bodies. Given them pleasure. But none of that added up to a teacup full of real intimacy, the kind of intimacy he wanted, needed with Sara.

His jaw clenched as he imagined her terror.

Jesus. What had his father done about that?

Had Ross faced it?

He dragged in a breath and let it out in a rush. It felt like he had come to some sort of fundamental crossroads in his life. And he couldn't cope with what was happening to him.

When he realized he had almost plowed into the barrier that closed off the main park entrance after hours, he slammed on his brakes.

Unlocking the bar, he drove through into Nature's Refuge, an island of peace in the middle of the great Olakompa Swamp. But not for him. There was no refuge for him. Never again. Not in this world.

13

ADAM spent a restless night, turning the covers into a twisted mass of rope. He told himself he didn't have to make any decisions. He knew he was lying.

He got up early and dressed, prowling the park's public grounds looking for hard manual labor that needed to be done.

There was a place where a path was crumbling into the swamp. The plan was to shore it up with a fieldstone retaining wall. The rocks had been delivered, but the work hadn't started yet because it was going to be a messy job. This morning, Adam put on his grubbiest clothes, then got out a wheelbarrow and started moving loads of stone.

By the time other rangers began arriving, he was covered with sweat, and his arm muscles were protesting. But he had transferred most of the building material from the pile in back of a storage shed to the work area. The staff tried to hide their surprise that the boss was doing the grunt work. Dwayne and Eugene offered to help. He hesitated for a moment. They might take his mind off his problems, but he knew he wasn't fit for human interaction at the moment. So he said he was just getting to the messy part, and he might as well continue by himself.

Eugene looked like he wanted to say something else. But he kept quiet. Adam asked him to check the day's schedule and do any rearranging necessary, as he planned to be here for a few more hours.

Alone again, he marked off the construction area with yellow tape, then figured he'd better get a pair of rubber boots if he didn't want to ruin his shoes. After pulling the boots on, he waded into the water along the path and began evening out the edge in preparation for putting down two layers of stone.

He'd never shied away from hard work. In that way he was like Ross, who had gotten him a couple of construction jobs before he'd left home.

Again, as he had in the past few days, he let himself think about his brother, wonder if he was still alive, even. Werewolves were a violent sort. There were all kinds of things that could have happened to his only remaining sibling.

He bent down, laying the first level of stone in the muck and evening it out, then standing back to judge the length of the wall. The stone was just peeking above the surface of the muddy water, and he figured he'd get his level full of mud if he tried to use the instrument.

He continued, selecting stones that would fit together well, working by feel as much as by eye.

Thinking about Ross kept his mind off Sara. He had been on his own for a long time. What would it hurt to call home and find out where to contact his brother? Or maybe he could even get him through one of those Internet search engines.

He had just set the last rock in the second row when a voice broke through the sounds of chirping birds.

"Seems like you have the makings of a second career, son."

He was glad he'd put down the stone, otherwise he might have dropped it on his foot.

Looking up, he met Paul Delacorte's dark chocolate eyes. "Howdy, Sheriff," he managed.

"You the new field hand at Nature's Refuge?" the black man drawled.

"If I want to be. Rank has its privileges."

"You're right on that one."

"Are you making an inspection tour of the lowlands?" Adam asked.

"I hear you had a little bit of trouble in town last night."

"News travels fast."

"Sure does, in a place like Wayland."

"You're referring to the near miss with the pickup truck?"

"Was there something else?"

"Mrs. Waverly damn near kicked me out of the historical society library."

"Oh . . . well." Paul looked him up and down. "I'd say you could use a break."

"Yeah."

"Why don't we set a spell."

"Sure. Let's go up to my cabin and get a couple of bottles of chilled water out of the refrigerator."

As he climbed up to the path, Adam caught sight of Amy Ralston watching them. Probably she was curious about what Delacorte was doing here, if she didn't already know.

Since the sheriff had heard about the near hit-and-run incident, everybody else probably had, too. On the way to the cabin, he stopped at an outdoor faucet and washed his hands and face—and boots.

He contemplated sticking his whole head under the stream of water but decided that looking like a drowned rat wasn't an advantage when talking to the law.

Delacorte brought only one bottle of water and set it on the table beside Adam's chair. He picked it up and downed half of it in one gulp.

"Hard work, laying stone," the sheriff observed.

"Yeah."

"Ken White would have left it to the staff." The sheriff shifted his weight from one foot to the other. "He went by the philosophy that on a mule team, the scenery is the same for all the mules except the leader."

Adam laughed. "Yeah, well, I like to trade places with the mules in the back. That way I know what's involved in all the jobs."

"A good policy."

"Is that why you lie in wait for speeders?"

"Partly. But I enjoy taking tourists down a peg."

Adam lowered himself into a wire mesh chair and drank more of his water, waiting for the sheriff to make the next move.

The man joined him in the empty chair, crossed his legs comfortably at the ankles, and asked, "Did you recognize the pickup truck or the driver?"

"The driver was hunched over. The truck looked like a hundred others in town. I didn't have time to glance at the license plate."

"It was smeared with mud."

"You saw it?"

"I got a couple of eyewitness accounts."

"So why do you figure someone tried to mow down Sara Weston?"

"You think that's what happened?"

"It looked that way to me. The question is why? You have many incidents like that in Wayland?"

"Not many. It could have been a drunk teenager showing off. Or some guy who had a run-in with her."

"Who would that be?" Adam asked sharply.

"She doesn't know."

"You talked to her?"

"This morning."

Adam leaned forward in his seat. "How was she?"

"A little shook up."

Yeah, he thought. So was he. And not just from the accident.

"She says she's kept pretty much to herself. And she doesn't think she's had time to make any enemies in town," Delacorte continued. "She did advance the theory that somebody might not like Granville Pharmaceuticals."

"Has Granville stuck its nose into town before?"

"No. But they make drugs. If somebody thinks they were harmed by one of the company's products, they could have taken it out on the lady."

Adam ran his finger and thumb up the sweating side of the cold bottle. "That doesn't make a hell of a lot of sense."

"Sometimes crime is like that."

"Yeah."

Adam shifted in his seat. "Since you're here, I'd like to follow up on some research I was doing at the historical society."

"I'm no historian."

"You've been in Wayland all your life. And I'm sure your daddy passed plenty of stories down to you."

The sheriff nodded.

"I was reading an article about a woman whose cabin burned up and her along with it."

Delacorte's shoulders had tensed. *Interesting.* "How did you happen upon that?"

"Funny you should ask. Mrs. Waverly had the same question. What I told her was that I went back to the year that Austen Barnette bought Nature's Refuge. I wanted more information about the park."

"Makes sense."

"So why do you think somebody cut the article about the woman in the burned cabin out of the paper? And somebody else put it back?"

The sheriff shrugged.

Adam watched the man carefully as he continued, "Well, I got to thinking about our earlier talk. You told me about a woman who was murdered around the same time. And I was wondering how many women could die violently around here in a cabin at the edge of the swamp."

Delacorte recrossed his legs again but didn't speak.

"Are they the same case?" Adam asked.

"Yeah. They are."

"So the newspaper article was really about the murder?"

"That's right."

"The story attributed her death to a faulty heater."

"That was the official explanation."

"But?" Adam asked, never taking his attention off the sheriff's face.

"A mob went after her."

"Why?"

"People came to her for herbal remedies. She was said to have special powers with healing. Then a little boy she treated died."

"Oh yeah?"

"Probably he would have died anyway. My guess is he had a heart defect. But the mob blamed this woman."

"Jenna Foster. Her name was in the article. That was about all—besides the faulty heater story—to cover up a murder . . ." Adam qualified, ". . . when your daddy was sheriff."

"That's right." Delacorte's eyes blazed with anger. "He was in the pocket of the white folks that run this town. That was how he made his decisions. I'm not proud of that. And I haven't continued the tradition."

"Probably there are white folks here who expect you to," Adam said, keeping his own voice mild.

"I've already showed them it's not gonna happen. I've made arrests my daddy never would have made. And the legal system has gotten convictions." Delacorte's expression was fierce. "You want the details?"

"I'll take your word for it."

"Appreciate it."

They were both silent for several moments.

It was Adam who spoke first. "Well, you told me right off it was a murder."

"Yeah. And if I knew who killed her, I'd go after him."

"It's a pretty cold case."

Delacorte nodded tightly.

While the lawman was in a talkative mood, Adam pushed for more information. "Did her cabin really burn?"

"Yes. But the owner built it back up again."

"The owner is?"

"Austen Barnette."

The answer sent a tingle of sensation along Adam's arm. "That's interesting."

"He rents the place out." Delacorte paused for emphasis. "Right now Granville Pharmaceuticals has the lease."

As Adam absorbed that, along with the tight lines of the other man's face, his mind made connections. "The cabin where Sara lives?" he asked, his voice low and gritty.

"Yeah. So there could be a couple of other reasons for someone going after her. It could have to do with the location. Or it could have to do with Barnette."

"I thought everybody in town loved Barnette. Didn't he make Nature's Refuge into a major attraction, which brings in wads of tourist dollars?"

"That's true, of course. A lot of folks are grateful to him. But you can't be the big fish in a little pond without gathering some algae. He's had problems over the years. He's done things for the community like build the library and the recreation center. But he insisted on having a say in the staffing of both of them. Some folks don't appreciate that."

"He picked me to run Nature's Refuge," Adam pointed out.

"The difference is, he owns this place."

The silence between the two men stretched again. Adam was thinking that it might not make a difference who owned the park. Some people were probably pissed off that the job of head ranger hadn't gone to a local guy. Like Ken White, for example. Who'd been born and raised in Wayland and knew the Olakompa from childhood.

He pulled his mind away from his own problems and back to the long ago murder. "There was mention of a little girl. What happened to her?"

"She disappeared."

"You think she died in the fire? In the swamp?"

"Her body was never found. My daddy said that someone might have gotten her out of harm's way. Maybe arranged an adoption out of state when the smoke had cleared, so to speak."

"Who would have done that?"

"Jenna Foster wasn't married. But she had a daughter. The child's father could have rescued her."

"And that would be?"

"Whoever he was, he kept it a secret."

Adam absorbed that new detail, his own speculations taking wild leaps. "You think he's still alive?"

"Why do you ask?"

"I told you, I like to walk around the area at night. I was over by Sara's place, and I saw a guy hanging around there."

"A guy. Young? Old?"

"The best I can say is that he was agile. He got away from me."

"I guess I should put some patrols on the house."

"I'd appreciate it."

"Personally?"

"Yeah," Adam answered, his voice tight. He didn't want to talk about his relationship with Sara. If he had a relationship with her. He couldn't be sure of that. He was the one who had walked out the door last night.

Delacorte stood up, and Adam thought the interview might be over. But after walking to a tupelo tree several yards away, he turned and came back to the seating area. He stood rocking on his heals, and Adam felt his heart start to pound. Delacorte had more to say. Something important. But it was obvious he was pretty uncomfortable about spitting it out.

14

ADAM watched the sheriff's throat work. "You look about as comfortable as a long-tailed cat in a room full of rocking chairs," he observed.

Delacorte laughed. "Where did you pick up that country expression, boy?"

"Texas."

"Right. They've got some fine southern traditions in Texas. So do we. Like persecution of people. But I'm not just talkin' about the Ku Klux Klan lynching uppity blacks."

"What are you talking about?"

Delacorte hesitated a beat before answering. "Going after people who have . . . talents that are out of the ordinary."

"I think you're going to have to be a little more direct here," Adam muttered.

"Okay. I'm talking about the line in the bible that says, 'Thou shalt not suffer a witch to live.'"

The way Delacorte said the word made goose bumps rise on Adam's arms. "Witches? Like Wiccans?"

Delacorte stuck out his jaw. "No. Like evil old hags who go off by themselves in the swamp under a witching moon and cast spells that hurt people."

"You don't believe in that stuff, do you?"

"Some people around here do. That's why they burned up the herb lady."

"She was an old hag?"

"No. But she had . . . powers."

Adam made an exasperated sound. "An herb lady. That doesn't sound so unusual."

Delacorte ran a hand over the tight curls that covered his head. "Boy, you're not listening. Right, that doesn't sound so strange. But I heard tell she could lay her hands on you and figure out what was wrong."

"You said they killed her because she made a mistake."

"Look, I'm just telling you the town legends. I never saw any of this stuff myself. One story I heard was about an old man. Old Man Levering. He was supposed to have the evil eye. He could put a hex on you if he didn't like you."

Adam managed a nervous laugh. "You believe that crap?"

"It doesn't matter if I believe it. People in town believed it. And I'm not just talking about the black folks being into powerful superstitions. Everybody talked about Old Man Levering and a woman named Mrs. Gambrills, who had spells, and when she woke up she could tell you stuff that was going to happen. Like if you were going to get yourself eaten by a gator. Her daughter Emily could . . . could make things move without touching them."

Adam stared at the man. It was obvious that he'd heard stories of these people—and other "witches"—since childhood. And he believed them. And at the same time, he was embarrassed to be telling this to a stranger, someone who had lived in Wayland for only a few months. Jesus, suppose he found out that the stranger liked to go off into the swamp and turned himself into a wolf?

He struggled to hold his voice steady as he asked, "You say there used to be people in town who could do this stuff. What happened to them?"

"What usually happens to witches! Like in the middle ages. Or Salem, Massachusetts. Over the years the regular folks would gang up on them and kill them. The last one was the lady who was burned up in her house. The rest of them cleared out."

Adam stared at him, trying to take it in, trying to read between the lines.

"So you're saying that the problems in town now are somehow related to what happened in the past?"

"That's what I'm thinking."

"But the . . . um . . . the witches cleared out."

"I think some of them are back," Delacorte said, his voice going thick with an emotion that sounded pretty close to fear. "And they're angry about what happened to their daddies and mommas."

"And what do you base that on?" Adam demanded.

"To start with . . . Ken White's death."

"He was shot to death."

"That's what people think," the sheriff said.

"And you're saying it's not true?" Adam felt the hairs on the back of his neck stir. "What do you think happened to him?"

"The autopsy report said he died of a heart attack. He was shot after he died."

Adam struggled to take that in. "What are you trying to tell me?"

"That he was scared to death. Or that somebody hexed him to death. I don't know how else to say it."

"Then why shoot him?"

"Hell, I don't know. To make it look like a conventional murder, so they wouldn't be found out? Or maybe the witches thought they weren't strong enough to kill him with mind power, so they brought along a gun."

"Or it was the other way around. He was trying to hex someone to death. And they shot him."

Delacorte looked doubtful.

"You don't think so?"

"I knew Ken White all my life. He was a pretty stick-in-the-mud kind of guy. I don't see him as the witch type."

"He might have been hiding it. According to you, being a witch around here is dangerous."

The sheriff nodded.

Adam was ready with another question. "Why didn't you tell me any of this choice information when I first got to town? Or when we had our little chat the other day?"

Delacorte gave him a direct look. "At first I was thinkin' there was no point in bad-mouthing Wayland unless you were going to stay."

"That comes from loyalty to the town?"

Delacorte scuffed his shoe against the ground. "I was born here. I grew up here. I have a responsibility to these people."

"Including lying to outsiders?"

"I wasn't lying to you."

"Not in so many words, but by omission."

"Well, now I'm telling you what I know. And I expect you to do the same."

"I have. I told you about the sex and drug party in the swamp."

"Uh . . . you mentioned drugs. You didn't say anything about sex."

Now it was Adam's turn to be embarrassed. "Yeah, well that was part of it."

"A witches' sabbath."

"Oh, come on!"

"On the night of the full moon."

"The witches around here did that kind of stuff?"

"Maybe."

"Would they hold a grudge against Sara because she's living in that cabin?"

"Maybe."

"Okay, so the witches could be nosing around her place, because that's where one of them died. Or maybe it's the other way around. Somebody from town is going after people connected with the witches. And since she's in the cabin, she makes a convenient target." He fixed the sheriff with a piercing look. "So, are you going to give me a scorecard?"

"What do you mean?"

"Like who are the families who went after the witches? And who are the witches?"

The sheriff's gaze turned inward. "I'm checking out potential witches. As for the others . . ." He shrugged. "My father didn't keep records on stuff like that."

"Too bad," Adam muttered, wondering if it were true. Delacorte claimed he was coming clean on the "witch problem." But apparently he was only prepared to go so far.

"Are you willing to talk about Barnette?"

"Sure."

"Why do you think he bought Nature's Refuge?"

"I think he wanted to show his faith in the town. I think he wanted to provide a source of income for people around here."

"Or atone for what happened at the cabin, since he owned it?"

"That could be part of it." The sheriff took a step back.

Adam stood up. "I've got one more question before you leave."

Delacorte quirked an eyebrow.

"Something I found in the swamp. Why don't we go inside and have a look at it." He kicked off his muddy boots, then stepped inside. Aware that the sheriff was staying several paces behind him, he went to the dresser where he'd put away the square of fabric with the herbs and chicken feathers and black gunk. The whole thing was inside a plastic bag. He brought it out and set it on the table, then extracted the cloth and the herbs.

When he looked up, he saw Delacorte staring intently at the contents of the bag.

"So, did the witches leave this as a calling card?" he asked. "Does it have something to do with the herb lady who was burned up?"

The sheriff reached out and touched a sage leaf, which crumbled along the edge where his finger brushed it. "That's a charm people used to ward off evil. I remember my granny making something like this," he said, his voice thick.

"Like a voodoo gris-gris?"

Delacorte gave him a considering look. "You know about that stuff?"

"I've read about it."

"I guess this could go back to African traditions."

"But I take it you didn't leave it out in the park?"

Delacorte snorted. "Not likely. I don't protect myself with charms and spells. I don't believe in stuff like that."

But he did believe in the witches. Interesting.

As Delacorte ambled off, Adam propped his shoulder against a pine tree thinking about the campfire in the swamp. The drugging smoke. The naked figures who had come after him with murder in their eyes.

He'd thought they'd shot at him. Had that only been an illusion? What if it hadn't really been a shot fired from a gun. What if it had been some kind of mental energy bolt? And his mind had put it into conventional terms?

He pondered that question for long minutes. It was a strange line of thought. Maybe he could go back to the firepit and look for bullets embedded in trees. Yeah, sure, when he had the time.

He shook his head. Instead of worrying about witches hurling thunderbolts, he'd better go check up on his staff. But first, he'd better get cleaned up before he scared away the tourists.

BY brute force, Sara managed to work most of the morning. Although she spent minutes at a time staring off into space, she was able to make several more plant extracts and start checking their antibacterial properties.

But she'd awakened with a trace of the headache that had stabbed into her brain the evening before. And as the day wore on, it grew steadily worse.

She took an over-the-counter remedy, but it didn't help. Finally, after picking at the salmon salad she'd fixed for lunch, she stuck her bowl in the refrigerator and put the spoons and fork she'd used into a pan of soapy water.

The throbbing in her head had made it impossible to eat. Now it was coming in waves that seemed to beat with the pulse in her temple.

Her fingers clamped onto the edge of the drain board in a death grip. She stood there, unmoving, willing the agony out of her head, picturing it leaving her body and flowing away from her, as if the force of her will could really accomplish that goal.

To her surprise, the technique seemed to work. Thinking she might as well wash the dishes, she lowered her gaze to the pan of water in the bottom of the sink.

What she saw made her gasp. Small waves were rippling across the surface of the water, pulsing like the waves of pain that had been in her head.

She froze in place, staring at the liquid in motion.

Her first thought was that the wind was blowing it. But when she looked at the trees outside the window, they were perfectly still, the Spanish moss hanging limp and gray.

It took a tremendous amount of effort, but she lifted her hand, then thrust it into the water. The waves didn't stop, they beat gently against her skin, each little ripple hitting like a small electric shock as it brushed against her flesh.

The strange feeling raised the fine hair on her arm, the sensation traveling upward to the back of her neck.

She had struggled to force away her headache. It looked, felt like she had thrust it from her body and into the pan of water. Lord, was that possible?

She made a small sound in her throat. She wanted to tell herself that nothing like that had happened to her before. But that would be a lie. She could remember times when she'd done it. Well, she hadn't seen anything like this rippling water. But she remembered willing hurt away. Like the time when she was ten and she'd been riding her bike and hit a patch of gravel. The bike had tipped over, sending her sprawling, her leg badly abraded by the rough surface. She'd known she had to get home. And she'd thought the burning in her leg was so bad that she couldn't walk the three blocks. But she'd gritted her teeth and forced the pain away. Somehow it had worked, at least until she'd staggered into the kitchen and into Mom's arms.

There had been another time, too. When Dad had been driving them home from a movie, and a station wagon had plowed into the rear of the car. She'd been sitting in the back without a seat belt, and she'd been slammed forward so hard that she'd dislocated her shoulder.

The agony had been almost more than she could bear. Even moving a quarter of an inch had made her feel like she was going to faint. But somehow she'd forced the terrible sensation away long enough for the emergency room staff to give her IV painkillers, so they could put the shoulder back into place. She had never really thought much about what she'd done on those occasions.

But now the previous experiences came back to her with a kind of sharp clarity that gave them elevated meaning.

She had done it again—today. But now there was a visual component, too.

The water. The ache had moved from her head into the liquid medium in front of her.

On the face of it, that idea was nonsense. Yet on some deep level of self-awareness, she knew it was true. And the realization was frightening. Her heart was pounding as she reached with both hands, seized the edge of the wash pan and flung it over, sloshing the water onto the wall and into the sink, pouring away the evidence, as it were.

A film of perspiration coated her clammy flesh. She had never fainted in her life, but she had a good idea what the sensation must be like. Taking shallow breaths, she leaned over the sink and squeezed her eyes shut, telling herself a pan of water wasn't evidence of anything—when she knew she was lying to herself.

Finally, she raised her gaze to the window and stared outside, her eyes unfocused. She wasn't sure how long she stood there, trying to make sense of something that she couldn't fathom. Or didn't want to fathom, she silently corrected herself.

Then a stirring in the bushes caught her attention. The movement resolved itself into the figure of a man.

Adam! It flashed into her mind that she'd been unconsciously waiting for him to come back.

When she saw it wasn't him, disappointment and relief surged through her.

Then her mind took another leap to the night before, to the pickup truck and the people who had warned her moments before the truck came bearing down on her.

Were they stalking her here? At the cabin where she lived?

15

SARA blinked as details resolved themselves into a recognizable figure. She was staring at the person she now thought of as the blackberry man, poking around in the bushes. He had his basket with him, but he kept glancing toward the cabin, like he was hoping she would come out. Or that she wouldn't! She couldn't tell which.

Maybe this was his regular berry picking area. He hadn't spoken to her since their first encounter, but she'd seen him lurking in the underbrush several times. What was he doing here? Watching out for her? Or looking for trouble?

She wiped her hands on the thighs of her jeans, glad to have something besides the rippling water or Adam Marshall to occupy her mind. Purposefully, she crossed the small living room, then stepped outside and strode toward the man.

He went still for a moment as he saw her, then pulled himself up straighter. The basket in his hand bobbled. He steadied it, before holding it out toward her. "I brought you a present," he said.

She goggled at him, then shifted her gaze to the plants. She saw hairy, divided leaves, long stems, and knobby rhizomes.

"Cranebill or wild geranium," he said. "The leaves are used as a mild astringent, but it's the rhizomes that have the most potency."

"I know," she murmured, wondering how he had come by the knowledge.

"I thought you might want to use it in your project. And you'd have to go wading through the swamp to get to where it grows."

"I appreciate your bringing it to me," she said, thinking that the words weren't exactly true. This guy made her nervous.

He gave her a small nod. "I can bring you other stuff. Like mock pennyroyal."

She called up her mental files on that member of the mint family. "I thought that only grew in dry soil."

"That's right. So you might not be looking for it around here. But it grows on higher patches, where the water can't reach it."

She nodded, thinking that the stuff was supposed to be good for digestion and headache, although she'd never actually used it.

He thrust the basket toward her, and she took it to prevent an awkward moment.

"How did you get interested in medicinal herbs?" he asked.

She cast her thoughts back, carefully considered the question. Actually, she couldn't remember when plants hadn't been part of her life. Mom had loved gardening, and she'd asked if they could have some herbs. They'd planted them together. Mom had used them for cooking. And she'd treated her dolls with the medicinal ones. Somehow she'd always known that foxglove was for heart problems, and witch hazel was good for insect bites.

Now she shrugged. "I guess I've been interested in them since I was a little girl. Then when I was old enough, I got books out of the library."

He nodded.

"What about you?"

"What do you mean, what about me?"

"You seem to know something about the subject."

"I studied up on them."

He looked like he might say something else. But she heard the sound of a car engine.

Again she thought of the night before. The guy in the pickup had missed her last time, and now he was back. She whirled to see a large black limousine coming majestically up the road.

A limo. Along the edge of the swamp? Some rich guy out slumming? Or picking blackberries?

The windows were dark, and she had no idea who was inside looking out at her.

She expected the vehicle to go on by her modest cabin. But it glided smoothly to a halt.

"Who could that be?" she asked the man she'd been talking to. When he didn't answer, she swivelled to look at him. But he'd slipped silently away.

She scanned the underbrush and thought she caught a flash of his yellow shirt. But it disappeared almost as soon as she saw it.

Behind her, the limo door opened, and she whirled toward the sound.

The driver had gotten out. He was a black man, dressed in a white shirt and a dark suit.

"Dr. Weston?" he asked politely.

"I'm Sara Weston."

"My name is James. I work for Mr. Barnette."

The owner of Nature's Refuge. "What does he want?" she asked.

"He wishes to speak to you," the driver said. He looked pressed and polished, while she was dressed in dirt-streaked jeans and a limp T-shirt.

"When?"

"Now."

Her hands fluttered at her sides. "I can't go like this."

"Mr. Barnette said for me to fetch you."

She glanced back toward the house. "Well, he should have given me some warning."

James shrugged. "Mr. Barnette is used to getting what he wants, when he wants it."

"All right. Give me twenty minutes." She didn't wait for permission. Instead she dashed into the house and skidded to a stop in the bedroom. After grimacing at her reflection, she settled for the fastest shower on record, then gave her naturally wavy hair a quick blow-dry before pulling on one of the few dresses she'd brought to Wayland. It was a simple, black, sleeveless cotton knit, which she topped with a black-and-white camp shirt. She hesitated over panty hose, then shrugged and shoved her feet into a decent pair of sandals. A little lipstick and blusher completed her preparations. In twenty minutes she hadn't exactly turned herself into someone who looked like a Ph.D. botanist. But it was the best she could do.

James was waiting in one of the rustic porch chairs that had come with the house. He climbed quickly to his feet when she came back out. She had her briefcase with her and some of the notes she'd been taking, so at least she could talk about some of the plants she'd started testing.

She'd never ridden in the backseat of a limousine. But she tried to relax as James turned the car around and retraced his path up the narrow road.

Now she was wondering if she should she have paid her respects to Barnette when she first arrived in Wayland. But she hadn't thought he'd necessarily want to be involved with her.

They swung in between brick gateposts and rode up a curving drive through manicured green lawns toward an enormous redbrick mansion with a two-story portico.

It was strange to think that one person lived in a house this big. From the driveway, it looked like her parents' entire house could fit inside the detached four-car garage with room to spare.

The interior was dimly lit and opulent. She didn't know much about fine furniture and fabric, but she suspected that everything here had been purchased with no regard to cost.

James led her down a hall to the back of the house, into a conservatory that would have done the Czar of Russia proud. The floor was flagstones. And the roof was high enough to accommodate several thirty-foot palm and ficus trees.

They crossed a small stream bordered by more tropical foliage and flowering plants to a round patio nestled among pots of blooming azaleas. She'd never seen anything like it except in the Botanical Gardens in Washington, D.C.

If Barnette was trying to impress her with his wealth, he'd done it.

The man himself sat in an old-fashioned wicker rocking chair. She would have guessed his age at somewhere between sixty-five and seventy. He had salt-and-pepper hair, wrinkled skin, and piercing blue eyes. He wore a rust-colored sports coat, a beige button down shirt, khaki slacks, and old-fashioned brown-and-white saddle shoes.

"Forgive me for not getting up," he said, as she stepped onto the patio. "My doctor told me I need a couple of knee replacements, but I figure I can get along with the knees God gave me, if I use them judiciously." He looked her up and down. "Thank you for seeing me at such short notice. I'm Austen Barnette."

"Sara Weston," she replied automatically, although he obviously knew who she was. "I'm sorry I didn't stop by when I got to town," she murmured.

"No need. I wanted to wait a few days before we chatted." He gestured toward the chair that sat across a round table from his own. "Make yourself comfortable. James can bring us some iced tea."

She took the seat opposite the old man, trying not to look overwhelmed.

"How are you settling in?" Barnette asked.

"Very well, thanks," she answered automatically, waiting for a question about her work and wondering what she was going to say.

There must have been a serving area near the conservatory. Before the small talk could continue, James was back carrying a silver tray with a pitcher of tea, glasses, and a plate of cookies.

"Molasses cookies," Barnette said. "My weakness."

"I love them, too. My mother used to make them."

He raised his eyes slowly and looked at her. "Which mother?"

She went very still. "I beg your pardon?"

"You were adopted. Are you referring to your birth mother or the mother who raised you?"

Her heart had suddenly started to pound. "How do you know I'm adopted?" she demanded. "And how could that possibly be relevant to . . . to . . . anything?"

Barnette answered calmly. "Everything is relevant in the grand scheme of things. You joined your family when you were four, I believe."

"What about it?"

"Do you remember anything about your life before coming to live with the Westons?"

"No." She took a quick swallow of tea. She'd thought the cookies looked good. Now the smell of them made her stomach turn because she realized that Barnette had brought her here to ask nosy questions.

"I can see you bonded with your new parents. Your loyalty to them is commendable. But I wouldn't have approved you to work in Nature's Refuge unless I knew your background. I wanted to make sure you were a responsible person who wouldn't go around destroying my property."

She struggled to keep her voice level, but she could hear it rising. "You don't think my educational record was indicative? The references from my professors? The reports from my internships?"

He took a swallow of tea and leaned back in his chair. "I took all of those into consideration, of course. But I've nurtured Nature's Refuge for twenty-five years. I wasn't going to let Granville Pharmaceuticals bring in somebody whose background I didn't know."

Lord, had he sent an investigator to poke into her personal life? She was thinking that he'd given her the perfect excuse to pack up and leave—with the way he'd invaded her privacy. She opened her mouth to say something scathing, then thought better of acting rashly.

"I thought you were perfect for the job," he was saying.

Wondering if she could believe him now, she managed a small nod.

He made a quick change of subject. "I was distressed to hear that you had a bit of trouble in town last night."

"You're referring to the pickup truck that almost plowed into me on Main Street?"

"Yes. And it seems that my head ranger saved the day."

She nodded. Right. All he knew was what people had seen. He didn't know about the voices in her head, and she certainly wasn't going to blab about those.

Or had Adam told him? Was that the reason for this interview—to evaluate her sanity. She fought off a sudden sick feeling in her throat. She had talked to Adam about the incident in confidence. He wouldn't have said anything, she assured herself. He wouldn't go spilling her secrets. Would he? Suddenly, the need to talk to him about her frightened confession last night was like a terrible pressure building up in her chest.

She wanted to stand up and leave. She wanted to go to Adam. But she couldn't simply walk out of here. And she couldn't come across as unstable or impulsive. She reminded herself that Austen Barnette wielded a tremendous amount of power in Wayland. She needed to understand what he wanted from her and deal with it.

"You think somebody wants me out of town?" she asked, keeping her gaze level.

"I hope not," he answered. "Because I'm looking forward to the completion of your research. How is that getting along?

"Very well," she told him, "I was so pleased to find *Impatiens capensis* in the park." With the introduction of the subject, she launched into a long, boring discussion of how an extract from the plant might be the next great cure for poison ivy.

She was pleased to see her companion's eyes glazing over. She loved plants. And she loved nature. But she'd learned in graduate school how to write papers that would satisfy her most pedantic professors. She thought the old man was on the way to falling asleep when he sat up straighter. "I'm glad we had this little chat," he said.

"Oh, so am I," she answered, the words almost sticking in her throat.

"You probably want to get back to work."

"Of course." Recognizing the tone of dismissal, she rose and picked up her briefcase "Thank you for inviting me to tea."

She crossed the conservatory, then walked rapidly into the hall, intending to go straight to Nature's Refuge. To Adam.

Then she remembered that she had come here in a large black limo. No, she'd better go home first and get her own car.

THE day's attendance had been good, Adam thought as he looked at the pile of entrance receipts. There had been over three hundred admission tickets sold. And thirty boat rides into the swamp.

Maybe that wasn't spectacular by Walt Disney standards. But it was quite good for a small natural preserve in rural Georgia.

The crowds had cleared out, because the park closed early on Wednesday. The staff had left, and Adam was filing some forms when he looked up and saw a woman standing in the doorway.

She was blond and nicely shaped, and as she stood backlighted by the afternoon sunlight, he felt his heart leap.

Sara.

Then she stepped into the room, and he realized she was someone else, wearing shorts that hardly reached her crotch and a skinny little knit top with pencil thin straps and a bottom edge that left three inches of skin exposed around her middle. She wasn't wearing a bra, and her nipples were standing up behind the orange knit fabric.

She was dressed to attract male attention, and he responded the way his hormones had programed him to respond. He felt his body tighten as he looked from her long legs to her erect nipples to her carefully painted lips.

"Can I help you?" he asked in a gritty voice.

She slid her own gaze up and down his body with a proprietary air, and he knew she was well aware of the effect she was having on him.

He closed the file drawer and forced himself not to shift his weight from one foot to the other like a sophomore in high school being eyed by one of the "fast" senior girls.

"I'm looking for Adam Marshall."

"The park is closed. Didn't you see the sign?"

"The gate was open."

Oh yeah? Someone on the staff was going to explain that to him tomorrow morning. "I'm Ranger Marshall," he answered, using his title like a sort of shield.

"Well, that's wonderful. I'm so glad I found you. I'm interested in a boat tour."

"I'm sorry. The park is closed," he repeated, keeping his tone even.

She tipped her head to one side and thrust her chest toward him. "Can't you make an exception for me?"

"I'm afraid not. We have our rules," he managed to say.

She wore no perfume, but her scent was strong. It was as though she hadn't washed her crotch that morning. And the heat from her body was wafting the evidence of her arousal toward him. He tried to take shallow breaths, but it wasn't doing much good. Even a normal man would have to react to that raw female scent. And he was no normal man. He was a werewolf, and even in human form he was caught in the sensual web of that tantalizing aroma.

He saw her lips moving, and her words came to him over the buzzing in his brain.

"Oh. That's too bad." She took a step into the room, looking like she wasn't all that upset.

"So this is the Nature's Refuge office. It's a bit primitive, isn't it?" she asked, eyeing the scarred wooden desk and the battered metal filing cabinets.

"We're not going for the designer look," Adam answered as he took in the predatory gleam in her eye. The frank sexual interest.

Most women were more subtle. But he had the feeling she was planning to crowd him into a corner. Crowd him—and more.

And from his vantage point this encounter had the feeling of a trap closing around him.

He didn't know why the trap image sprang to his mind. He only knew it was strong and vivid.

To get out of the confined space, he came around the desk, stepping closer to her so that she'd have to back up. She held her ground.

"I've heard how sexy you are. I thought I'd find out about that for myself."

"I thought you came for a boat ride."

"Well, since that attraction's closed, maybe we can move on to another one."

SARA stopped at the entrance to the park and read the sign that announced the hours. It was ten after five. And the listing said that closing time on Wednesday was five.

The gate was open. But normally, she'd just turn around and go back. Today she needed to talk to Adam, so she drove through and headed toward a cluster of buildings she could see in the distance.

She'd collected some of her plants from the wild, unkempt expanse of the swamp, but she'd never been in the areas that were maintained for the public. When she'd come in the back way, she'd driven over a narrow gravel track. The road leading from the front entrance was two lanes and paved with macadam. To keep it from flooding, it was built up above the level of the swamp.

The drive ended in a rectangular paved area divided into sections by garden ties.

Natural looking, weed-free garden beds bloomed with an assortment of cultivated annuals and perennials interspersed with plants native to the Olakompa. Most of the indigenous plants were labeled with small signs giving their common and Latin names. A nice touch, she thought. The buildings clustered on the other side of the almost empty parking area were either log cabins or simple wood structures painted dark brown.

It was all tidy and well-kept, with a notable absence of trash on the ground. The state of the park spoke well for Adam Marshall. Apparently he ran a tight ship. And he knew how to make a natural area attractive for visitors.

A sign pointed to the office. Getting out of her car, she walked up a short path toward the building—then froze as she saw Adam and a woman standing just inside the door.

THE woman stroked her forefinger along Adam's upper arm, dipping under the edge of his green uniform shirt. The touch of that one finger sent a ripple of reaction through him.

She was well aware of her female power because she smiled and gave him a smoldering look from beneath lowered lashes as she took a step back into the reception area. He followed, pulled toward this uninhibited woman. A buzzing had started in his brain. Probably the result of lack of blood in the upper part of his body.

Last night with Sara, he'd been aroused and achingly ready for sex before he'd wrenched himself away. He'd run from her cabin before he could rip off her clothing and throw her to the floor. Now here was another woman frankly offering herself to him.

"Sugar, we're going to be very, very good together," she purred. "You and me, we're the same kind."

He didn't answer. He didn't understand what she meant. Was she trying to tell him she was a werewolf? His fuzzy brain struggled to wrap itself around that idea. As far as he knew, there were only male werewolves. But maybe she was something new to his experience.

She touched him again. This time her hand stroked across his chest and slipped open one of the uniform buttons so that she could caress the heated flesh beneath.

Plenty of women had come on to him before. But never quite so explicitly, so shamelessly.

She was like a bitch in heat, and the wolf part of his nature was responding with an animal force.

He drew in a sharp, painful breath, and she answered him silently by sliding her tongue across her lower lip.

He watched that erotic pink tongue, mesmerized by the slow, enticing motion. And when she opened her mouth and repeated the provocative action along the edges of her even white teeth, he made a low, helpless sound in his throat.

She reached for his hand, lifting it to her breast, stroking his fingers back and forth across the crest of one taut nipple through the knit fabric of her top. "Harder, do that harder," she whispered.

Somehow the sound of her voice released him from the spell. Or perhaps some dark, primitive god had taken mercy on him. His hand dropped away, and he stood there staring at her. He'd been hard and hot.

Suddenly, he was limp and cold and wondering how he could have thought he wanted to fuck this woman.

There was only one woman he wanted, and it was Sara Weston. "I'm sorry," he muttered.

"You want the same thing I do."

"No."

She took a step back, looking him up and down, taking in his rigid stance and the obvious fact that the erection she'd seen straining behind the fly of his jeans was no longer in evidence.

Perhaps she hadn't believed his verbal denial. But she believed that his body had stopped responding to her.

Anger flared in her eyes as she reached out to stab a stiffened finger into his chest. "You'll be real sorry you turned me down."

"Don't count on it," he shot back.

"Smart ass." Her eyes narrowed, her face contorted, and he felt a sudden pain in the pit of his stomach. It was as if her anger had a physical force that had him grabbing the doorjamb to stay on his feet.

16

ADAM felt Miss Sexpot brush past him, then watched her surge out of the office and march toward the parking lot.

His eyes widened as he saw Sara coming toward her from the parking lot.

The seductress stopped in her tracks, raising her chin defiantly.

"Oh perfect. You! What was I doing, getting him ready to fuck you?" The sharp words rang out in the afternoon silence like a war cry. The fury he'd felt directed at him suddenly had another focus.

"Sara," Adam shouted. "Watch out."

He didn't know what he was warning her about. He only knew

that under that flaming hot exterior, the blonde in Sara's path was dangerous.

There was a charged moment when the two women stood in silence facing each other.

The seductress balled her hands into fists and jammed them against her hips, looking like a street fighter daring a rival to take another step.

Sara went very still, her arms loosely at her sides and her eyes questioning, as though she had no idea what to make of the challenge.

There were several seconds of dead calm. Of utter silence. Even the birds that normally sang in the trees went silent.

Then five doves flapped away, their wings beating the air in a frantic bid to escape. From what?

They had barely cleared the tall pine at the edge of the parking lot when the sky darkened as though a storm were rapidly overtaking them.

Moments ago, Adam had seen no clouds. Now they hung low and ominous over Nature's Refuge. As the sky darkened, the wind suddenly rose, shaking the branches of the trees around the parking area, sending up an eerie clatter as twigs and branches rubbed against each other. Leaves and bits of Spanish moss tore loose, flying through the air.

It felt like something supernatural was happening. And from deep inside Adam's mind came the knowledge that he had to protect Sara, but he couldn't make his arms or legs work.

What happened next was hardly supernatural. He watched in a kind of shocked disbelief as the woman on the path marched up to Sara, drew back her fist, and socked her in the stomach.

As she gasped in pain and surprise, the woman dodged around her and dashed to the parking lot.

Seeing Sara doubled over and swaying on her feet released Adam from his trance. Quickly he crossed the few yards that separated them.

She fell into his arms, and they collapsed together onto the mulch beside the path. He cradled her in his embrace, pulled her onto his lap, folding his body around hers as though he could protect her—when he'd already failed to do any such thing.

Dimly he was aware of an engine roaring to life and a car blasting out of the parking area. But his focus was on Sara.

She was shaking. So was he.

"What happened?" he finally asked.

"I don't know," Sara whispered. "I felt so strange. I can't explain it . . . I thought . . ."

"What?"

"I don't know. I felt like the two of us were going to fight. But not physically. A fight where nobody else could see what was going on. Like with those voices last night." She gave a helpless shrug, lowering her head to his shoulder, pressing her face into the fabric of his uniform shirt.

"Who is she?"

"Hell if I know."

"You two looked pretty friendly."

He made a helpless gesture. "She walked in here and came after me. Maybe somebody dared her to get it on with the new park ranger," he clipped out, hoping Sara would drop the subject. He didn't want to think about the woman who had come here with seduction on her mind. He only wanted to focus on the woman in his arms.

He stroked his hand tenderly over her hair, her shoulders, feeling some of the tension go out of her. Still, when she lifted her head again, the troubled look on her face tore at him. "Okay, forget her. You're sure I'm not going crazy?"

"No!"

"Why not?"

He knew his answer wasn't based on logic, but he gave it anyway. "Because I care about you," he whispered. It was so hard for him to say. Even that much. He'd never told a woman anything that came close to what he'd just said. He'd taken his pleasure with them, and he'd given pleasure in return. But he'd never been compelled to make an emotional connection. Now he felt that compulsion. But he couldn't tell that to Sara. The concept was still too new, too threatening.

She was staring into his eyes, and he was the one who felt stripped naked. If she had secrets, so did he. He couldn't tell her about them, so he rocked her in his arms, his hands soothing up and down her back and across her shoulders.

"You're going to move out here," he heard himself say.

She blinked. "What?"

"I want you where you'll be safe—in the vacant cabin where one of the rangers used to bunk. We keep it ready for visitors, so it's all nice and clean." She opened her mouth, but he rushed on. "I talked to

Delacorte about that damn place where you're living now. A woman was murdered there. She was an herbal healer. A boy she treated died, and a mob went after her."

He heard Sara suck in a sharp breath and let it out before saying, "I think I daydreamed about her."

"About the fire?"

"No. About her living there." She kept her gaze steady on him. "All my life I've felt like I was different. I would . . . see things that weren't really there. And I knew they were true."

"Like what?"

She took another gulping breath. "Sometimes they were things happening in other people's lives. And sometimes I didn't know *what* they were. I didn't want to see them, so I pretended they didn't exist. And finally, they really were hardly there. Or maybe it was that I had trained myself to ignore them. Then . . ." She stopped again and shuddered. "Then I came to Wayland. And right after I moved into that cabin, I went back and stepped into that woman's shoes for a little while. She had a garden. With herbs."

His hands gripped her shoulders. "Yeah, well I don't know why Barnette put you in that damn haunted house, but I want you somewhere else. I feel like you're a tethered goat out there drawing . . . a predator. And I want you where I can keep you safe."

Sara made a small, distressed sound. But he kept talking.

"I'd say there's still a lot of interest in that damn place." He evaluated his options and decided to tell her more of what he knew. Not all of it, but enough. "Delacorte says that the woman who lived there wasn't the only person the town went after. Apparently there were a bunch of people who lived around here, people with strange . . . powers. They were persecuted as witches."

She gasped, "Witches!"

He went on quickly, "Delacorte says most of them left town. Or maybe some of them went underground. I don't know. But he thinks their children have come back to get even with the community. They could be focused on the place."

"Witches," she said again. "Are you sure?"

Adam ran a shaky hand through his hair. "I don't know if it's true. But whether it is or not, there are probably townspeople who think that living in that cabin makes you a bad person."

"What are you trying to say?"

"That I saw someone lurking around your house a couple of nights ago."

"Why didn't you tell me about it?"

"I started to last night. Then we got sidetracked. I'm telling you now. I chased the guy, but he got in his car and drove away. I don't know who he was. But I'll know him if I find him in town."

"How?"

"I . . . picked up his scent."

"His scent," she repeated slowly.

"It's a talent I have." He laughed. "You see ghosts, and I smell out trouble."

"Really?"

"Yeah. Maybe that's why the smoke from that fire in the swamp sent me into a tailspin."

She was watching him, taking it in. There was a lot more he could say, but the idea of telling her the rest made his chest constrict. Not yet. Not when he needed to keep her safe.

"I want you to move out here," he said again.

He saw her wedge her lower lip between her teeth. "The last time we were together . . . we . . . about burned up the floorboards under our feet."

He swallowed around the constriction in his throat. "Yeah."

"If I'm out here . . ."

"I'll behave myself."

"How do I know?"

"Because I want you to trust me. That's important to me."

He leaned toward her and brushed his lips against hers. The touch was light, but it sent heat leaping through him. Yesterday he would have acted on the need to shift her in his arms and press her body to his. Yesterday he might have rolled her to her back and come down on top of her. Today he held himself in check, because he needed to prove something to her—and to himself.

Some inner strength he hadn't known he possessed helped him keep the kiss light. It was a unique experience for him, simply savoring her taste and the contrast between what he felt now and what he had felt when Miss Sexpot had come on to him. He didn't have much experience with restraint, but he could see it had its advantages.

Sara made a small sound, and he pressed his lips more firmly to hers, just for a moment before he lifted his head.

"Sara, I promise you that it's going to be fantastic between us . . . when we're both ready."

She looked dazed. He found that very satisfying.

He helped her up, then turned her to him and held her gently, savoring her, savoring feelings he'd never expected to experience.

"Come see the cabin," he said.

"We have to move all my lab stuff."

"We can use the park truck. And there's another vacant building where you can work."

"Are you sure that will be all right with Barnette?"

"It'd better be!"

He led her along a path in back of the public area. "This is where I live," he said, then showed her the other residence which was about fifty yards farther. He'd had his pick of the two places, and he'd chosen his because it was more to his taste.

The door wasn't locked. Neither was the one to his cabin, and he wondered if that ought to change. Pushing open the door, he stepped aside and let her go in first.

In the living room was a sofa, a rocking chair and a rag rug. White curtains hung at the window. A pine table with two chairs sat in front of a kitchen area along one wall. Someone had draped a quilt across the back of the sofa, a small homey touch.

The cabin's other room had a double bed, a chest of drawers, and an armoire instead of a closet. Besides the toilet and sink, the bathroom was big enough for a stall shower.

Not a very impressive refuge to offer Sara.

"It's smaller than where you're living now," he said, keeping his arms pressed to his sides to stop himself from reaching for her. "But it's comfortable."

She turned back to him, and the breath froze in his lungs as he waited for her to say it wasn't going to work.

What she said was, "You're sure it's okay for me to be here?"

"Perfectly sure. Barnette lets me make the decisions at the park."

"Are you trying to rush me into moving in, before I change my mind?"

"You catch on fast. Come on; let's get your stuff."

He drove the truck to her cabin. She took her own car. On the two-mile drive, he had time to consider what he'd been thinking. The need to protect her had been his primary motivation. But the consequences for him were massive. He wondered how he was going to live near her and keep his hands off her. And he wondered what he was going to do at night, when he needed to roam the park as a wolf. Well, he'd told her he walked around at night. He'd just have to make sure he was deep in the swamp before he changed.

Yeah, but what if she comes into your cabin and finds you eating a hunk of raw meat? How are going to explain that? he asked himself.

STARFLOWER hooked a right onto the dirt road and headed for the meeting place. It was a spot near the swamp where locals sometimes hung out. This evening she could hear rock music blaring from a boom box.

Tonight the music irritated her. But everything had irritated her since the scene at Nature's Refuge.

Adam Marshall had turned her down, despite the power she'd exerted over him—and she'd instantly hated him for that. She could have any man she wanted. But not him. What did he think—that he was too good for her? Then the woman, Sara Weston, had come along and hatred had turned to fear.

Yesterday, when they'd shouted a mental warning at her, Weston had been confused. She'd seemed weak.

But she hadn't been weak today.

The woman had power. Great power. And it looked like she was learning to use it. She'd called up storm clouds and a wind out of nowhere. Apparently she didn't know what to do with them—yet. If she ever found out—God help anyone who was in the way.

When Falcon had brought Starflower into the group, she'd been excited by the contact. Excited at being with others of her kind. But she'd discovered that wasn't enough.

Falcon was the leader. The strongest man. And so far she was the strongest woman. She liked that position, at the top of the heap. And she didn't want anyone around who could challenge her. Like Sara Weston. Which meant pretty little Dr. Weston had to be eliminated. Her and her boyfriend, Adam Marshall.

He was dangerous, too. And totally expendable, as far as she was concerned. He'd rejected a good thing a few hours ago. And he was going to find out the consequences of that.

Starflower climbed out of her car and eyed the portable CD player.

She wanted to tell Falcon to turn off the damn music, but that would give away her mood.

So she kept her simmering hostility to herself.

Her gaze zeroed in on the six-packs of beer sitting in a tub of ice. Tonight she needed a couple.

She'd spent the past several hours thinking of how to put the best possible face on what had happened at Nature's Refuge. She'd worked out a good story, and she was sticking to it. And really, most of it was true. There were just a few little details that she'd changed.

Usually she liked being the center of attention. Not this evening.

"How did it go?" Willow asked, taking in the scanty shorts and top she was wearing.

"Not exactly the way we planned," Starflower tossed off as she walked toward the beer, snatched a can out of the ice and flipped it open. She took several swallows before she turned to face the group.

"He didn't want to get it on with you?" Grizzly asked.

"Of course he did. Then that Sara Weston came along and interrupted us."

"Interrupted how?"

"I had him ready, willing, and able. Then she showed up, and he was embarrassed about getting caught with me."

Of course, that wasn't exactly how it had happened. But she was pretty sure none of the other participants was going to get a chance to revise the story.

In the light from the camp flashlight, she could see Falcon watching her closely. She kept her gaze trained on him.

"So are you saying the park ranger is fixated on her?" he asked.

"Yes. And she's fixated on him, too. She lashed out with her mind and called up a storm when she caught me fooling with him. She was going to fight me for him. Only she didn't quite know how to do it, because she doesn't have anybody to teach her how to use her powers."

"We could teach her," Willow said.

"No!" Starflower caught Falcon's piercing gaze and lowered her voice. "I mean. She's strong. And dangerous. I felt it. Together they make a dangerous pair."

"So how do we deal with them?" Falcon asked.

"I don't think either one of them would work out in the group."

Razorback had been silent until now. "Because she's a rival?" he asked with a knowing smirk.

The question hit too close to home. "Because neither one of them is going to go along with our plans. Because both of them are too locked into the . . . the world of the regular folks in Wayland. They fit into the system. They don't have anything to gain by joining us," she answered. She wasn't going to admit that she'd developed an intense hatred for Sara Weston and Adam Marshall. She wasn't going to explain that her personal plans included making sure they both ended up dead. At least not yet.

Falcon gave her a considering look. "Let's not do anything hasty. I think we ought to wait and see how things develop."

"Just don't wait too long," she said, making the warning low key because she could see that pursuing the subject was only going to reveal too much of her own feelings.

"Let's get back to the fun stuff. I've been waiting to tell you what I have in mind for later this evening. A little raiding party in town that I think you're going to like. But we need to wait until after midnight."

Starflower was only half listening to the plotting session. She couldn't stop thinking about Sara Weston and Adam Marshall. Falcon might want to put off making a decision about them, but the matter was of more urgency to her. The sooner they were eliminated from the face of the earth, the better she was going to feel.

17

ADAM spent a long restless night, unable to sleep. He knew that a satisfying run into the wild, untamed acres of the park would settle him down. He needed to turn off his human thoughts and submerge his personality into a simpler, more primitive being. He wanted to be a wolf—his only object to stalk prey and satisfy his craving for warm flesh and blood.

But he kept picturing Sara waking up early in the morning and going outside. Sara coming upon a wolf tearing apart a deer, and the image made his blood run cold.

So he tossed in his double bed, and got up early, thinking that running as a man would work off some of his excess energy. It wasn't the same, he conceded as he sped down the access road to the park entrance; then he did another couple of miles along the highway before heading home.

Back in his cabin, he pulled a beef roast out of the refrigerator and hacked off several slices, which he ate raw.

He was in the office early, waiting for the others to arrive, looking at each of his fresh-faced rangers with new eyes. When all the full-time staff had reported in, he called a meeting. The office was too small, so he used the room where they did nature programs for school kids. Moving aside an alligator jaw, he leaned back against the table at the front of the room.

"I want to talk about security," he began, looking at each of the men and women sitting on wooden chairs ranged around him.

"Because there's been some trouble in town?" Rosie Morgan asked.

"You're referring to the truck incident?" Adam responded.

"And the break-in at the historical society," Dwayne Parker added.

"When? What break-in?" Eugene Brody and Lisa Hardin asked, speaking at the same time.

"Last night," Dwayne answered. It was obvious he'd enjoyed dropping that bombshell. "I found out about it because my mom is tight with Mrs. Waverly," he said importantly.

Adam saw Amy Ralston shift in her seat. "Why would anyone break into the historical society?" she asked.

"Who knows? They don't keep any money there."

"Just old books and papers," Rosie said. There were nods of agreement around the room.

"Okay. I didn't know about that," Adam said, thinking he was damn well going to find out what he could—later. "But I am concerned with a breech of security at this facility. Last night, someone came through the gate after hours claiming it was unlocked." He looked toward Eugene, who had the duty of closing up the night before.

He saw the boy blanch. "I locked it," he said.

"Are you sure?"

"Yes."

Adam gave a tight nod. He was inclined to believe the kid. Eugene was a good worker. He was smart and conscientious. And he wanted to get ahead. Adam had been thinking that when he eventually moved on, Eugene would be a good choice to run the park.

"So then we have to assume that someone unlocked the gate after you left." He looked at each of his staffers in turn, thinking that they all had keys to the padlock. Amy was the one who looked the most uncomfortable. What did she have to gain by letting Miss Sexpot onto the grounds?

"If anyone has something to tell me, we can speak in private," he said. "Meanwhile, I have something else to discuss with you."

The staffers waited for what he was going to say.

"I'm sure you're aware that Nature's Refuge is the site of a project being conducted by Dr. Sara Weston for Granville Pharmaceuticals."

There were nods of agreement.

"She's been living and working at a cabin near the back entrance to the grounds."

"The witch house," Rosie murmured.

"What do you know about it?" Adam asked sharply.

She looked down at her hands. "Most people know about it. I mean that's what people call it."

"You know it burned down," he asked, putting the question in pretty bland terms, considering what had happened there.

"Yes."

"So should I assume that everybody in greater Wayland knows about that except Dr. Weston and me?"

"Pretty much everybody," Dwayne answered. "It's hard to rent the place, you know."

"Yeah, well, considering its history, I've determined that living there might not be good for Dr. Weston's health. So I asked her if she wanted to move into the vacant cabin here on the grounds. She accepted the offer. And she's using the old workshop next to the cabin for her plant experiments. So you'll probably see her around. She's got the run of the facility."

"Sure. Okay," Dwayne answered for the group.

Adam went on to discuss work schedules, then went back to his office, closed the door, and made a phone call.

The sheriff picked up on the second ring. "Delacorte here."

"I hear you've had some more trouble in town. At the historical society."

"News travels fast."

"What was taken?"

"I've got Mrs. Waverly working on that. So far, she hasn't told me about anything that sounds valuable."

"Interesting. So what do you think it means?"

"I'd like to know."

They talked for a few more minutes before hanging up. Adam rocked back in his chair, thinking that a wolf he knew was going to pay the society a visit after it got dark.

He thought about going over to Sara's cabin to tell her what had happened downstairs. Then he stopped himself. He wasn't going to charge over there this morning. He was going to give her time to settle in.

SARA knew that Adam was deliberately staying away from her. Did he regret his impulsive invitation to move her to the main grounds of Nature's Refuge? Or was he simply giving her space? she wondered as she arranged her petri dishes on the long tables in the workroom.

She'd spent the morning giving the place a good scrubbing. It was dusty from disuse, but really it was a better place to work than the old cabin.

There was even a utility sink with running water.

As she arranged her equipment, she saw various staffers going about their duties. But they—and Adam—kept their distance.

In a way she was grateful. At the same time, she was disappointed.

But she held the disappointment in check while she considered her reasons for coming here. Fear had been one of her motivators. She'd never been comfortable at the cabin.

The dark foreboding atmosphere had played a part in that. And now she knew that people were watching the place. She'd felt it, hovering in the background of her consciousness. Adam had confirmed her subliminal impression.

Of course, it could be that the man he'd seen lurking around had only been the blackberry man. But she couldn't count on that. She couldn't even assume that the blackberry man wasn't going to turn from mild to aggressive. If it was him, what was he doing down there at night?

The danger had been a good reason for letting herself be persuaded to move onto the grounds of Nature's Refuge.

But she knew that wasn't her only motivation. The admission brought her back to Adam. She'd wanted to be near him. She'd welcomed the excuse. Even if she wasn't going to tell him.

THE phone rang in the Nature's Refuge office at two in the afternoon.

"This is Austen Barnette," the testy voice on the other end of the line announced.

"Yes, sir." Adam's hand tightened on the phone receiver. He'd been expecting the call, and now he had to deal with it.

"I didn't authorize you to move Sara Weston into a cabin on the park grounds."

"Do you disagree with the decision?" Adam asked, keeping his own tone mild.

"That's not the point. What did she do, come running to you right after she left my house yesterday?"

"I wasn't aware that she was at your home."

"She's in Wayland because Granville approached me about using the park as a research site. I invited her over to find out how she was settling in. She seemed upset about the incident with the pickup truck."

"Almost getting run over could do that to you," Adam answered blandly.

"Why is she at your place?"

"She's not at my place. She's in the vacant cabin on the grounds."

"That's what I meant," the old man snapped.

"She was concerned about the history of the cabin where she was living," Adam said. "And I was concerned, too."

"What do you know about that?" the sharp voice on the other end of the line demanded.

"I know a mob killed a woman there."

"That was years ago!" Barnette said, emphasizing each word.

"Uh huh. But I discovered someone lurking around the place this week."

After several seconds of utter silence, the old man spoke, putting his retroactive stamp of approval on the action Adam had already taken. "You have my permission to do what you think best."

"Thank you, sir," he answered. "Can I do anything else for you?"

"Keep me informed of what's going on at the park."

"Yes, sir. In my monthly report." Adam hung up, wondering how long he was going to hold his present position.

"DR. Weston?"

Sara looked up from her worktable to see a young, dark-haired woman wearing khaki pants and a ranger shirt standing in the doorway of the shed.

"Yes?"

"I'm Rosie Morgan. Mr. Marshall sent me over to see how you were doing."

"I'm fine. Thanks."

"Do you need anything?"

"No. But I appreciate your asking. This is an excellent work space."

The young woman lingered.

"I love the way the park looks," Sara offered. "The grounds are so well kept. And those plant identification signs are a nice touch."

"Yes. We've had them for a few years. But a lot of them were missing. Mr. Marshall had a bunch of new ones made."

Sara nodded.

"Did you hear about the robbery at the historical society?"

Sara set down the beaker she was holding with a clunk. "No. I didn't know about it."

"Somebody smashed a basement window and got in. But they don't know what was taken."

"Oh. Thanks for telling me," she answered.

"We talked about it at the meeting this morning. And the break-in here, too."

"The break-in?" she echoed, feeling her chest tighten.

"Well, Mr. Marshall said somebody came in after hours."

Sara nodded, pretty sure she knew who that was.

The young woman glanced over her shoulder, then back at Sara. "There's a lot of bad stuff going on in town. Mr. Marshall said that probably everybody in town knew about it, everyone but you and him."

"Like what?"

Rosie lowered her voice. "Like, some people think the witches are back! There are old-time stories about them. But now people are talking like they're real."

Sara felt the air freeze in her lungs, but she managed to say, "I'd like to hear more about them."

Rosie examined her fingernails. "I shouldn't talk about it. I just thought you ought to know."

"Know what exactly?"

The woman shrugged. "It's good that you're out here now. It's safer here than at that cabin."

Before Sara could ask another question, the woman turned and hurried away. Leaving Sara standing with her heart pounding and wondering why the park staffer had said so much.

IT was after one in the morning, which was perfect for Adam's purposes as he drove through downtown Wayland.

Leaving the business district, he headed for a house he knew was vacant. After pulling around the back of the garage, he cut the engine, then climbed out and sniffed the wind, sniffed for danger.

He was taking a chance. But he wanted to know who had been at the historical society. Slowly he took off his clothing and stood naked in the starlight. After stepping into the darker shadows cast by the house, he began the ancient chant that had been such a familiar part of his life since his teenage years.

The change from man to wolf was painful as always. It would be nice if there were some way to make it easy, he thought as muscles and bones contorted and transformed.

Still, he felt the old familiar exhilaration as he came down on all fours and looked around, sniffing the wind again. He had been born for this. It was his destiny.

He was a creature of the night. At home in his familiar surroundings, he breathed more deeply, suddenly excited by the prospects of the environment. The scents were richer now, more distinct. There was a squirrel in a tree several yards away. Fresh meat.

A very small meal. Hardly worth the effort. And food wasn't his primary concern tonight. He was hunting men. Not to eat them, but to sort them out.

Down the block, a dog suddenly howled. Apparently it had caught the scent of wolf. He trotted off in the opposite direction, keeping to the shadows and heading for the historical society.

* * *

SARA looked through the darkness toward Adam's cabin. Earlier there had been a light on inside. Now the place was dark. She'd thought about inviting him to dinner, then decided that was being too forward.

After that, she'd waited for him to come over and see how she was doing. He'd stayed away.

Now he'd probably gone to bed.

The sudden image of herself walking over there in only her nightgown flashed into her mind.

She pressed her shoulders against the back of the chair where she was sitting. Where had that come from? She wasn't the kind of woman to throw herself at a man.

But then, it wouldn't exactly be throwing herself. Adam wanted her. That was pretty clear. Yet he'd backed off. And now maybe he was waiting for her to be the one to make the big move.

Well, she had a good reason for going to his cabin. She wanted to talk to him about the conversation she'd had with Rosie. The woman had brought up the subject of the witches, then run away like she was sorry she'd mentioned it.

That was something she and Adam should discuss. But at one in the morning? she asked herself, unable to hold back a shaky laugh. The laugh turned to a groan. Talking wasn't the real reason she wanted to see him.

The image of herself and Adam alone in the cabin came back to her, sending a hot tremor of chills over her skin. There was no point in lying to herself. She wanted him, the way she'd wanted no other man she could remember. He'd said it would be good between them. She knew it would be. But still, she knew on some instinctual level that she'd be playing with fire. He'd brought her here to keep her out of danger. Danger outside the park. But he was the danger close at hand.

ADAM waited a long time before emerging from behind a monument in the cemetery next to the old church that now housed the historical society. Most of his wolf expeditions had been in open country. Being surrounded by the trappings of civilization made him nervous.

Probably he was responding to some primitive animal instinct, he thought as he moved from gravestone to gravestone, then slowly approached the building. He'd heard that the break-in had been through a basement window. He stopped when he got to the boarded up rectangle and drank in a long draft of air.

There were many human scents mingled together. He could distinguish men and women. The men smelled more raw. The women had a dainty aura that always called to him. Some were people he had met in town. Others he didn't recognize.

He got a near-choking draft of Mrs. Waverly's perfume. What had the woman done—crawled through the window on an inspection mission? Or was she the one who had broken into her own precious building, to make it look like something had been stolen?

SARA had just changed into her nightgown when a sense of overwhelming danger closed in on her, choking off her breath. She staggered back, hitting her shoulder against the bedroom armoire, then sprang away, gasping, trying to fill her lungs with air.

Something bad was outside in the night. But it wasn't coming for her. Somehow she knew Adam was in danger.

Not here at the park, but in Wayland. Downtown. Outside an old stone building that shimmered in the vision of her mind. A church that looked dark and forbidding. And ominous.

She reached out and grabbed the bathroom door frame, her fingers digging into the vertical surface. Somehow she was able to ground herself, to ease the tight, sick feeling in her chest. Just a little. Just enough to keep herself from fainting.

A flicker of movement at the edge of his vision startled the wolf, and he whirled. But there was nothing there.

Well, not exactly nothing. He caught the ghost of a shadow image just below the level of his vision. A shadow he could see and yet couldn't see at all. It was something completely beyond the realm of his experience. A phantom image with no scent. No substance. Yet it raised the wolf hairs along his spine.

Not *it*.

Them. Watching him.

He went very still, trying to bring them into focus. But he simply couldn't do it. And then he didn't know if he had made the whole thing up because he already felt like he was treading on broken glass.

He shook his head. This was no illusion. He felt something at the edge of his consciousness where he couldn't reach it.

He didn't like the sensation. And the wolf in him wanted to turn and run away before it was too late. But the man inside the wolf forced him to stay where he was and gather what information he could. He went back to what he was able to detect with his sense of smell.

Paul Delacorte had been here. Of course, the sheriff had been investigating the break-in. And a whole crowd had apparently come by to goggle at the broken window.

Another individual leaped out at him. Miss Sexpot, the woman who had appeared yesterday at the park office and tried to get into his pants. He'd been halfway toward fucking her when thoughts of Sara had stopped him.

Her scent was mixed with a bunch of others, male and female. Because he had been so intimately involved with her, she stood out to him, although her presence here proved nothing. She could be one of the curious or one of the people who had broken in. But he had no way of knowing.

SARA blinked. The image of the church stayed lodged in her mind. But she saw something else as well. Big booted feet stealthily crossing a patch of gravel. She didn't know who the man was or why he was there.

She tried to get a better look at him. Her view expanded enough for her to see a gun in his hand. A dark-skinned hand.

She still didn't know who he was. All she knew was that the gun was pointed at Adam.

Panic seized her.

"Adam!" she screamed. "Adam, watch out."

She couldn't see him. She didn't know where he was in the midnight picture wavering in her mind. And that was as terrifying as anything else.

ADAM was pawing at the edge of the window frame when a voice rang out in his head.

Sara's voice.

"Adam!" she screamed. "Adam, watch out."

He whirled around, smelling the strong scent of man. A very familiar scent. Not from earlier in the day.

Now. He strained his eyes into the night and caught a man-shaped shadow standing out against the darkness around him.

He had been so intent on his mission that he hadn't heard the crunch of shoes on gravel.

But Sara's voice had cut through the focus of his concentration.

He leaped back as the beam of a flashlight hit the spot where he had been standing.

"Holy Moses!" a voice rang out in the blackness behind the light. A glint of metal flashed in the man's hand. He knew that voice. Knew the scent. It was Paul Delacorte, probably prowling around for the same reason that Adam was here himself. He was hoping to find out who had broken in.

Only the sheriff was armed with a gun, and the wolf had only his teeth and claws.

Would the lawman risk a shot here?

Adam didn't wait around to find out. He turned and fled into the night, dodging through the cemetery, expecting the hot pain of a bullet slamming into his flesh.

18

SARA'S hand clamped into a fist. She pressed the fist against her lips, trying to hold back a scream—or a sob.

Adam was in danger. Terrible danger. Being stalked by a man with a gun.

She had seen that much, along with the bulk of a large stone church. And something else. Something that raised goose bumps on her bare arms. In the background were flickering shadows. People-shaped shadows. Not solid. She could see through them, like ghosts.

She made a little moaning sound. Could they be the witches?

Adam had told her about them. So had Rosie. And she'd started wondering if they were the people who had shouted at her. Now she was
seeing them. Well, not exactly. They had been at that place. But they
weren't there now. Somehow she was picking up their afterimages.
And those images rocked her to her soul. Just like their voices echoing
in her mind.

Their forms were blurred, indistinct.

And she hadn't seen Adam. Just a blur of motion like an animal
running from danger. And she didn't understand why that fitted into
the warning reverberating in her head.

The whole ghostly vision began to dissolve. She tried to clutch
onto it, but it was suddenly gone, and she saw only the bedroom of
her little house. She had been standing by the bathroom door. Now
she found herself sitting on the edge of the bed.

Seconds ticked by. Then endless minutes. She waited for something else to happen. The past few minutes had left her cold and shaking. She should get dressed, she thought vaguely. But she didn't have
the energy for that.

All her strength was focused on trying to bring back the mental
picture she'd just seen. But it wouldn't come!

For a lifetime she had ruthlessly shoved such visions out of her
consciousness. In Wayland that had been impossible because she
didn't seem to have any control over the images that came into her
mind. Or the images that faded away, either, leaving her weak and
shaking. Now she wanted desperately to find out what had happened
with the man and the gun, but she couldn't make the dark scene come
into her mind again.

Chills rippled over her skin. Wandering into the living room, she
snatched up the quilt from the sofa, opened it up, and wrapped it
around her shoulders like a large shawl as she moved to the window
and stared out into the darkness.

She didn't know how long she stood there before the headlights of
a vehicle cut their twin beams through the night.

It was Adam. Or it was Delacorte. Or someone else official coming
to give her bad news.

Clutching the quilt around her shoulders, she opened the door and
dashed into the night, her bare feet pounding the mulched path to the
parking lot.

A vehicle's door slammed. She headed for the sound and saw a man standing beside an SUV parked at the edge of the lot. One of the over-head lights shone down on him, and she could see his face.

"Adam! Thank God. Adam." She ran toward him as he started to-ward her. They met on a soft bed of pine needles under a cluster of trees.

The quilt fell from her shoulders as she lifted her arms and reached for him.

ADAM reached for her at the same time. He had been longing to come back to her, yet all the way home he had been dreading the re-union. He had heard her voice shout a warning to the wolf. But she hadn't been there. Not physically.

He heard her breath come out in a gasp as he pulled her toward him, then stopped with his hands on her shoulders.

"You called out to me!" he said, hearing his voice rasp like sandpa-per on rough tree bark.

"You were in danger."

His hands tightened on her shoulders. "How did you know? How did you warn me?"

"I . . . I don't know." She stopped, closed her eyes for a moment, then started again. "I had . . . had . . . one of those visions that I hate. But this time, I knew you were in trouble."

He dragged in a painful breath and let it out in a rush. He had to struggle to keep his fingers from digging into her shoulders. "You saw me?"

She stared up into the harsh lines of his face, looking confused. "No. That was the strangest part."

"What did you see?" he demanded.

"Not you. I saw another man's feet. I saw his boots. And I saw he had a gun."

"Delacorte."

"Oh!"

"But you didn't see me?" he pressed.

"No."

He felt like a condemned prisoner given a stay of execution. On a sigh, he pulled her to him, his arms closing around her.

"Do you believe me?" she whispered.

"Oh yes." If she had seen him, she wouldn't be in his arms now. Would she?

She lifted her face to his, her eyes troubled. "I told you I've been having strange experiences . . . strange perceptions since I came here. That dream we had. When I was in your bed. We both had it. It was real. Somehow, it was real. And what happened tonight. That was real, too." Her fingers dug into his shoulders. "Adam, what's happening to me?"

"I don't know. We'll figure it out," he promised, because he didn't know what else to say.

"Having . . . visions is wrong."

"What do you mean—wrong? Was it wrong to keep me from getting shot?"

She went on as though she hadn't heard him. "My parents thought it was a bad thing. They didn't like it . . . so I made it stop."

"Jesus! What did they do, beat you?"

"Of course not. They would never have beaten me. They adopted me because they loved me."

"You're adopted?"

"Yes. But that doesn't make a difference." She looked like she was on the edge of tears. "They just made me understand that it made them uncomfortable."

He swore again. "Don't tell me anything you do is wrong," he clipped out. "And certainly not tonight. You saved my life!"

"I wanted to help you," she murmured. "But I didn't even know where you were. Were you outside a church?"

"A church building. The historical society took it over. I was trying to figure out who broke in there last night."

"And Delacorte thought you were one of the witches come back to the scene of the crime."

A bolt of tension went through him. "The witches? How do you know it was the witches?" he asked, hearing the strain in his voice.

"I saw them," she whispered. "I mean . . ." She stopped and started again. "I don't know what else it could be. I saw that they had been there. Last night I guess, when they broke in. They were like ghosts, flickering in the darkness."

"Yeah."

"You saw them, too?"

"Not exactly. I could *almost* see them. And I felt . . . something strange. I didn't know what it was. I think you just told me."

She wrapped her arms around his waist, pulling herself tightly against him. "Adam, I was so scared for you. And scared for myself, too. I don't like this."

She was trembling in his arms, and at the same time running her hands over his back, his shoulders, her touch telling him how relieved she was to have him safely home.

The need to soothe away the remnants of her fear was like a deep, primal longing that seemed to envelop him and at the same time wrap the two of them in a curtain of silk that sealed them away from the world and sealed him to her.

After the heat of their first kiss, he had vowed to take things slowly with her. But her touch and the warm look in her eyes was making that impossible.

He was aroused. And while he'd been holding her, arousal had passed beyond pleasure to pain. It felt as if he had been turned on for days. Turned on since he had first come across her in the swamp and known that she was his destiny. He had raged against that destiny. Some part of him was still trying to outrun it. But how could he fight his own need when she was in his embrace, silently telling him that she wanted the same thing he did?

A thick fog of sensuality was rapidly obliterating his ability to think. Her face was turned upward toward him, and he drank in the honey and sunshine scent of her mouth, feeling each exhalation of her breath drawing him toward her. He didn't make a conscious decision to lower his mouth to hers. It simply happened.

And that first touch of their lips was like a jolt of molten intensity that sizzled its way to every one of his nerve endings.

He drank from her like a man who had crawled out of the desert and found a cool, clear pond waiting in a shaded oasis.

She made a needy sound, her mouth opening to give him better access, and he knew that this time if he didn't make love with her, he would lose his sanity.

He should have warned her to run for her life, but he was beyond warnings. His hand slid down to her hips, reveling in the feel of her silken skin beneath the thin fabric of her gown.

Under the protective canopy of the tree branches, he stepped back long enough to drag the gown up and over her head.

Now there was nothing between the wonderful curves of her body and his hands and lips.

He stroked his fingers over her back, down her flanks, pulling her against his aching erection.

When she made a whimpering sound and rubbed against him, he felt as if his body was going to ignite and set the grove of trees on fire.

He reached up to take her breasts in his hands, his thumbs stroking over the hardened tips, bringing another whimper to her lips.

He needed to get rid of his clothing. She made a sound of protest as he stepped back.

But when he pulled his T-shirt over his head, her hands went to the waistband of the sweatpants he had worn so he could get in and out of his clothing quickly.

He kicked off his shoes, then helped her scrape the pants down his hips.

Naked, he pulled her in against himself, desperate for intimate contact. His cock nestled against her belly; his hands stroked over the rounded curve of her bottom.

He needed to be on top of her. Inside her. Here. Now. He looked down at the pine needles under his bare feet and blinked when he saw a quilt lying on the ground.

Sara followed the direction of his gaze.

She laughed. "It must have fallen off my shoulders. How convenient for us."

They both knelt, spreading out the quilt. Then he pulled her back into his arms, tumbling her to the makeshift bed on its soft mattress of pine needles.

Their bodies crushed the needles, flooding the air with the pungent aroma of pine mingled with the dark, rich scents of the night.

It seemed right that he was making love with her for the first time out here, the wind a light caress on their naked bodies.

He clasped her to him, hot and hard and needy. He had never wanted a woman more. Yet his own satisfaction was only a small part of what he craved. He ached to give her pleasure, ached to bring her to the same peak of satisfaction that waited for him.

"Sara," he murmured through trembling lips.

Lowering his head, he caressed her breasts with his face, then turned his head so that he could take one pebble-hard nipple into his mouth, sucking on her, teasing her with his tongue and teeth while he used his thumb and finger on the other nipple.

She arched into the caress, her fingers winnowing through his dark hair. He shifted so he could trail one hand down her body, finding the hot, slick core of her.

When he dipped his finger between the silken folds, she made a low, needy sound and pressed her hips upward, telling him silently that she craved more.

She was ready for him. Thank God, because he knew that he was too close to the edge to wait.

Positioning himself between her legs, he entered her in one swift stroke.

She cried out at the joining of their flesh, circled his shoulders with her arms as he began to move within her in a fast, hard rhythm.

She matched him stroke for stroke, her nails digging into his back, the intensity quickly building to flash point. He felt her inner muscles tighten around him, the contractions like small electric shocks jolting his nervous system. And while orgasm still gripped her body, his own release grabbed him and spun him into a whirlwind of sensation that left him gasping.

He had never felt anything as profound, not with any other woman. Shaken to the depths of his soul, he collapsed against her, his head drifting to her shoulder, and she reached to soothe her fingers through his hair, turning her head so that she could stroke her lips along the line where his hair met his cheek.

They lay there for long moments. On the verge of sleep, he finally roused himself with visions of the staff arriving in the morning to find them lying naked on a quilt under the pine trees.

"We can't stay here," he murmured.

"A bed might be warmer," she conceded.

Which bed, he wondered, as he thought about protecting her reputation. He didn't want people in town gossiping that he'd asked her to stay at Nature's Refuge and invited her into his bed the next night.

"Your place," he said in a gruff voice. "So I can get back to my own cabin before anybody else shows up."

She nodded against his shoulder, then roused herself. Together they collected clothing from the ground around them. She picked up the quilt and put it back where it had been, over her shoulders. He put an arm around her waist, holding her close as they made their way back to her cabin.

In her bedroom, he lifted and pushed aside the covers for her, then stretched out beside her and took her in his arms.

He'd dreamed of this. But the reality was better than any dream. Sara, warm and pliant in his arms.

He was still shaken by what he was feeling. Still unable to put it into words. But as he gathered her close, fear was one of the elements circling painfully in his brain.

He had asked her what she'd seen. She had seen Delacorte. But not the wolf. Earlier, he'd been relieved.

Now—

Now he felt his chest constrict so painfully that it was difficult to draw a full breath. She had made love with a man named Adam Marshall. Would she run screaming from the werewolf? And what would he do if she turned away from him after giving herself to him?

His arms tightened around her, and she snuggled into his warmth. But she didn't speak.

What was she thinking now? He was afraid to ask.

But he needed to talk to someone who had faced this crisis. Had his brother, Ross, dealt with this? And what had he done about it?

The questions tore at him. In the warmth of Sara's bed, he made an effort to unclench his jaw.

He closed his eyes, thinking he would just lie here holding her. But the night's activities had worn him out.

Sometime before dawn, he drifted into sleep.

And sometime after the sun had come up, he woke with a start. The bed was cold. He was alone. Sitting up, he fought a wave of dizzying fear as he staggered through the cabin looking for her.

She wasn't there. And when he got to the dining area, he found a folded note waiting for him on the table. With a shaking hand, he reached out to pick it up.

19

WAS she a coward? Sara asked herself as she headed north in Miss Hester, her rattletrap Toyota.

She'd snuck around the cabin, throwing a few things into an overnight bag because she hadn't been able to face Adam in the morning. Not because of anything he'd done.

A warm flush heated her whole body. Making love with him had been more wonderful than anything she could have imagined. She'd given herself to him with a joy she'd never known before.

Last night she had been swept along on a tide of passion, and then in the morning, reality had set in. Her world had turned upside down since she'd arrived in Wayland. Not just by Adam Marshall. Something was happening within herself, and she needed to understand what it was.

It had borne fruit in Wayland. But she knew that the roots went much further back. To the time before she'd come to live with Barbara and Raymond Weston.

Last night she'd talked a little to Adam about her parents. They'd loved her. But they'd let her know that they wanted her to be a "normal" little girl. She'd done her best. And for a while, it looked as if it had worked. But now she felt like the fabric of her life was unraveling. There were things she needed to understand. Things that only Mom could tell her.

She knew the Westons hadn't been able to have children of their own. And they'd been in their late forties when she'd come to them. Probably it hadn't been an adoption through an agency. Probably they'd worked through a lawyer or something like that. They'd never talked about how they'd gotten her.

She'd loved her parents. And they'd loved her. They'd given her a good foundation for going out into the world. When Dad had died of a heart attack five years ago, she'd mourned his loss.

But she'd come to understand that they were people with rather rigid and traditional values, people who didn't know how to cope with a child who saw things that weren't there.

Had they done her a favor? Certainly they'd helped her fit in to the conventional world. But their upbringing hadn't prepared her for what had happened after she'd come to Wayland.

Come back to Wayland, she thought now. Because the minute she'd driven into town, the place had seemed familiar. She hadn't wanted to admit that then. Today she had to.

As she pulled into the driveway, she stood looking at the house. Dad had taken care of the home maintenance. But since his death, there hadn't been anyone to do the work. And Mom couldn't afford to hire out.

That was one of the things Sara hoped to remedy. When she got a steady job, she was going to take out a loan and get the house back into shape.

Even Mom's beautiful garden was a little less polished than in previous years. There were fewer annuals among the perennials. And she saw weeds poking up in the unmulched beds.

Mom was in the kitchen when Sara knocked at the back door. Her mother dropped the colander she was holding into the sink and rushed to the door.

"Sara! What are you doing here? Is something wrong?"

With a shake of her head, she hurried to reassure her mother. "No. Nothing's wrong. I just got a little homesick," she answered, thinking that was just a bit far from the truth. But she wasn't going to come bursting through the door complaining about her problems—or making demands.

"But you drove all this way!"

"It's not so far." She crossed to her mother, and they gave each other a tight hug. Once again she was back in the warm, sheltered environment of her childhood.

"You should have warned me, and I would have fixed extra for lunch. I've only got my spaghetti."

"I love your spaghetti."

"We can stretch it out with a salad."

"Wonderful. And I want some of your iced tea."

"There's a pitcher already in the refrigerator."

She and her mother fell into the familiar rhythm of putting together a meal. Twenty minutes later, they sat down at the dining room table with the place mats and flowered china she remembered so well.

Mom watched her from across the table.

She forked up some spaghetti and sauce, chewed, and swallowed. "This is so good. I missed your cooking."

"If I'd known you were coming, I would have made chocolate chip cookies."

"We can make them together after lunch," she answered, thinking that if they were both busy it might be easier to talk. She still wasn't sure what she was going to say. The only thing she was sure of was that she wasn't going to chicken out.

ADAM sat at his desk pretending to go over a list of books he was considering for the gift shop. But his mind was on Sara. She had gone to her mother's. She said in the note that their lovemaking had been wonderful. But she had some issues to resolve about her own background.

He made a snorting noise. She might think *she* had issues. But how was she going to react to the tooth and claw monster watching over their shoulders?

He wanted to know if she would run screaming from the wolf. He *had* to know. He wasn't going to be able to think about anything else until she came back.

A knock at the office door made him jump.

He looked up to see Delacorte standing in the doorway carrying a large cardboard box. "You got a package from UPS," the sheriff said.

Adam's hand froze on the paper he was holding, and he had to force his fingers to unclamp.

Without asking permission, the large black man came into the office and closed the door, setting down the box beside the desk.

Adam gestured toward one of the wooden chairs across from him. "Have a seat."

Delacorte accepted the invitation.

"What can I do for you?"

"Since you asked about the break-in at the historical society, I thought I'd keep you posted on . . . developments. I've been keeping an eye on the place."

Adam managed a steady gaze and an even voice. "After the break-in? Isn't that like locking the barn door after the horse has escaped?"

"You can put it that way if you want. I think of it as seeing whether the witches come back to the scene of the crime."

"The witches! You think it was them?"

"I did some pondering on it. Who else would steal a devil's lot of old history records?

"An interesting way to put it. Was it a whole bunch of stuff?"

"I was speaking figuratively. Mrs. Waverly claims she doesn't know exactly what was taken. But I think she's lying. I think the witches were looking for evidence of who did what to whom in Wayland in the past."

"You think they got what they wanted?"

"I reckon we'll find out."

Adam shifted in his seat, hoping the sheriff couldn't detect the wild pounding of his pulse.

"When I was a little pitcher, I had pretty big ears. I listened to all the old tales about the witches. Some of them had more holes than a screen door at an orphanage."

"Yeah. I'll bet."

"But they all followed a kind of pattern. And I think I encountered a new wrinkle last night. I was down at the historical society after midnight, and I saw what looked like a wolf."

Adam raised an eyebrow. "A wolf? Are there wolves in this area?"

"Not that I know of." The sheriff shifted in his seat, tension crackling through him. "I came over here to try out a theory on you."

Adam's mouth was so dry that he could hardly speak. But he managed to say, "Okay. Shoot."

"Keep an open mind. I don't want you to get the notion that I'm crazy."

Adam nodded, thinking that the sheriff and Sara appeared to be having similar doubts. Delacorte seemed to relax a notch. "Like I said, I've heard the old spine-tinglers since I was a kid. About stuff the witches could do. But I never heard tell of a werewolf."

The word Adam had been dreading was out in the open. He sat very still, half expecting the sheriff to draw his gun. But he only ran a hand over his short-cropped hair.

"What if the witches have developed a new talent?"

"Are you talking about shape-shifting?"

"It's not impossible."

"It sounds like a stretch to me," Adam managed to say. "Why would they add something new?"

"Because they're growing and evolving. They're getting stronger."

"You sure are into this paranormal stuff."

"When I was a kid, I didn't really believe it. It was just stories the bigger boys and old men told to scare you. But now that I'm in the middle of it, it looks kind of different."

"Yeah," Adam muttered. "But that doesn't mean you saw a werewolf. You said it was last night, right? Why wasn't it just an ordinary wolf?"

"You would have had to be there," the sheriff answered. "He wasn't just trotting around town. He was sniffing around the exact place where they broke into the historical society. He was pawing at the plywood tacked over the broken window. He was acting intelligent. Like he had a purpose."

"What did you do?"

Delacorte laughed. "I panicked. I pulled my gun. And he ran like hell."

Adam wished he could share the humor. In a tight voice he asked, "Would you have shot him?"

"I would have last night. Now I think that would have been a mistake."

Adam sighed. Well, that was something anyway. He pretended to be carefully considering what Delacorte had said, pretended that his heart wasn't threatening to beat its way through the wall of his chest.

"You think I've gone off the deep end," the lawman finally said.

"No. I'm thinking about what you said. Let's agree for the sake of argument. Suppose you saw a werewolf. If he was part of the witch group, why would he have gone back there? What would have been his purpose? I mean, you're assuming he has human intelligence. What would he have to gain by sniffing around the place where his friends broke in?"

Delacorte rocked back in his chair. "I don't know."

"Well, since we're getting into the twilight zone, let me try a theory on you. You think that a . . . uh . . . coven of witches has come back to town to get revenge. Suppose there's another faction. Suppose somebody with . . . um . . . psychic powers is fighting the witches. And the werewolf is part of that other faction. So he was down there . . . investigating."

The sheriff's brows knit together. "That's an interesting hypothesis. I suppose it's a possibility. But who would it be?"

"Folks who were never friends with the witches?" Adam suggested. "Folks who have figured out what they're doing and want to stop them."

"Yeah. But folks with . . . powers."

"Superman!" Adam said, cutting through the tension.

"More like wolfman."

Adam leaned back in his chair and dredged up a laugh that he hoped didn't sound like he had a throat full of ground glass. "So the wolf got away. How are you coming on tracking down the witches?"

"I'm compiling a list of new people in town. Including Sara Weston."

Adam had told himself he was starting to relax. "Not Sara," he said.

"She arrived just when you tangled with that group dancing around a drugged campfire."

"Not Sara," he said again, flashing on what had happened last night. Not the lovemaking. Before. When she'd told him she'd had a vision of him in trouble.

Delacorte was watching him carefully, and he wondered what showed on his face.

"You're telling me you've gotten to know her pretty well," the sheriff said.

"Yes," he answered, speaking around the lump that clogged his throat.

"You're sure you know what kind of person she is?"

"Yes," Adam answered, hoping that he was telling the truth. Shifting in his seat, he said, "If you're looking at new people in Wayland, what about me?"

"I thought about you," Delacorte said. "And I checked into your background. You're from Baltimore. You've got no connection to this town."

"Sara's from Wilmington, North Carolina."

"Sara's adopted," the sheriff said.

Adam sat forward. "How do you know that?"

"Barnette did a background check on her. She's about the same age as that little girl whose momma burned up in that cabin. If she's that little girl, that would sure give her reason to hate the fine upstanding people of Wayland."

THEY were washing the dishes, when Sara screwed up her courage. "I'm not sure I ever told you how lucky I feel to have found a home with you and Dad."

"Why thank you, dear."

Sara finished soaping a plate and set it in the tub of rinse water. "We never talked about my real background. From before I came to live here."

A glass slipped out of her mother's hand and bobbed back into the tub of water.

"Can you tell me where I came from originally?"

"I don't really know. Why are you asking? I mean, why now?"

Sara listened to the quaver in her mother's voice. It sounded like she was either lying or worried about telling Sara the answer to the question.

She cleared her throat. "I met a man. I think we might be right for each other. But . . . that got me thinking about my . . . genetic heritage, you know," she stumbled through the plausible explanation she'd thought of on the way up from Wayland. "I mean, what if I were in danger of passing something . . . bad to my children? Or what if . . . um . . . it turned out that I could develop some genetic disease? Like Huntington's chorea."

"Oh no, Sara. I'm sure there's nothing like that in your background."

"Why not? What about that stuff that used to happen to me? When I'd hear and see things that weren't there."

Her mother sucked in a sharp breath. "I don't want to talk about that."

"But just because you don't want to talk about it doesn't mean that it will go away."

"It did go away! Long ago."

"Yes, Mom. You and Dad made sure of that," she said, hearing the strident note in her own voice.

Her mother's face had tightened. "You were little and scared. We did what we thought was best for you."

Sara made an effort to soften her tone. "I know that, Mom. I know you had my best interests at heart. But I'm grown up now. And I need to know about my background. I'm hoping you'll help me."

FALCON watched Starflower working on the drywall joints of the new addition to the house. He liked seeing her rounded bottom when she leaned over to get more mud out of the plastic tub. Even though she wasn't much of a worker, she had other attributes. Basically, she was a sex magnet. But she needed to learn a little discipline.

She was going to be the mother of his children when they got this house finished and set up their commune. As far as anybody in town would know, they'd be a bunch of retro hippies living in the country and getting back to nature with their brood of kids running naked in the bushes.

The image pleased him. A nice freewheeling commune was the perfect camouflage for the clan. There was a lot of land here. They'd build other houses when they got this one finished. Then they'd get money out of some of the low lifes in town who had tormented their parents. Before they killed the sorry bastards.

He came up to Starflower and ran his hand down her back from her shoulder to the nice rounded curve of her butt.

"You might as well take a break from the finishing work. You're not getting much done."

She gave him a saucy grin. "I was hoping you'd notice."

"You and Willow and Water Lily can start dinner."

Her face fell. "I'm not the chief cook and bottle washer."

"But we all pull our weight here. And you're a good cook." That wasn't exactly true. But she was getting better.

She gave him a little nod. "Can we have some fun later and use that cool smoke?"

"You like that, do you?"

She swayed against him. "You know I like it a lot. You know I'd love to get high and have a nice hard cock inside me. Yours especially."

The suggestion made him instantly hard. "You know, we can't use the smoke too much. The more you use it, the less effect you feel."

"But it's still a lot of fun."

"Yeah." He stroked his hand over her right breast, feeling her pebbled nipple. With his thumb and forefinger, he gave her a nice hard squeeze, and she sucked in a sharp breath. Another woman might have yelped in pain. But she liked that. Liked it rough. And he was more than willing to accommodate her. He liked fucking her fast and sharp. And he liked being the leader of the clan. He liked making the decisions about when they had group sex.

They could break off into couples if they wanted. But the group gropes and fucks were important—and not just for fun. Arousal increased their powers. So it wasn't just having a hot time. They needed to be together in a group. They needed to practice with the power they generated.

He glanced over his shoulder. The others were outside clearing away construction debris. It had piled up for a couple of weeks, and he was afraid somebody was going to end up stepping on a nail.

"We'll have a party tonight," he said.

"Good." She shifted her weight from one foot to the other. "Something you should know."

"About tonight? You're having your period?"

"No. About Sara Weston. My spy at Nature's Refuge told me she went out of town."

"Oh yeah."

"But she's coming back. She left all her stuff. And everybody in town knows she's working for Granville Pharmaceuticals. She's got a fancy-ass research grant, and she left her science experiments, so she can't be away long."

"And? What's your point?"

"We can set a trap for her. Like we did before. Only this time, she's toast."

Falcon gave Starflower a long look. "You hate her, don't you?"

She took her lower lip between her teeth. "I'm only trying to protect us. She's dangerous. She's got powers. And if she learns how to use them, she can hurt us."

He gave a tight nod. "What kind of trap did you have in mind?"

She smiled and he saw some of the tension go out of her. "I've been thinking about what kind of death would work for the scum who hunted down our parents. We want to kill them, but we don't want anyone to know we had a hand in it. What do you think about a one-car auto accident?"

"Tell me more."

She started outlining a very well-developed plan, and he realized she'd probably been thinking about it since the afternoon Adam Marshall had rejected her. And Sara Weston had scared the shit out of her.

The rejection was minor in the grand scheme of things. But Sara Weston was another matter. At first it had looked like she might be an asset to the group.

But he trusted Starflower's judgment. Dr. Weston was dangerous. She had the power to challenge their plans and disrupt the clan.

So she had to be eliminated. And Marshall, too. Because he had gone to the trouble of protecting her, by moving her into Nature's Refuge. He cared about her. Which meant that if he found out the clan had offed her, he'd come after them.

20

AFTER the sheriff's visit, Adam couldn't even pretend he was focused on paperwork.

Thinking about Sara being in danger from Delacorte made his insides ache. He couldn't deal with that. Yet he couldn't put Sara out of his mind. She crept into every empty space in his thoughts like fresh air seeping into the hard crevices of a dark cave. His mind zinged back to the morning—when he'd awakened in bed alone. He had made a frantic search of her room. Most of her clothing was there. And the lab was still set up in the shed.

She was coming back.

She had to be coming back, because he couldn't deal with the alternative.

Closing his eyes, he let his thoughts drift back to that first morning in the swamp, feeling again the primal burst of attraction between them. He had wanted her then. Wanted her every moment since. Last night he had made love with her. Binding her to him for all time, the werewolf and his mate. The way his father had told him it would be.

And instead of waking up next to her, he found she had fled.

From him? Or was she telling the truth about going home to talk to her mother about her background.

She'd told him she was adopted. And Delacorte had wondered if she was Jenna Foster's daughter. The woman would be about the same age as Sara. What if they were the same person? That was hard to believe. A real coincidence. But what if it wasn't a coincidence at all? What if somebody had brought her back to town? Back to that cabin where her mother had died.

With a tight feeling in his throat, Adam got up and wandered back to the cabin where Sara was living now. For a long time, he simply sat in the front room, breathing in her scent. If he closed his eyes, he could picture her walking through the door. Picture himself reaching for her. Picture her melting into his embrace. But she wasn't there. And he could torture himself only so long.

Heaving himself out of the chair, he walked stiffly down to the supply shed, where he got out a bag of feed for the deer that frequented the park.

He measured out the day's portion, then headed out to the area where the animals had been coming for their handout.

After spreading the pellets around, he stood staring for a long time at a pair of sandhill cranes poking through a marshy area. He knew from his reading about the swamp that old-timers in the area had mistaken them for whooping cranes. But they'd gotten the species wrong.

He managed to occupy his mind with bird lore for another five minutes, then sighed and headed back to the shed with the empty plastic container. Sensing that someone was watching him, he looked up. A tall, fit-looking man was leaning against the corner of the wooden building watching Adam's progress up the path.

He froze in his tracks, feeling like he'd been punched in the pit of the stomach.

The man was standing with his arms casually at his sides. Maybe he was trying to look calm. But the tension radiating off of him was like heat radiating off molten lava.

After finding Sara gone and then his meeting with Delacorte,

Adam's own stress level had already shot through the roof. He had little control left, and the first words that came out of his mouth were, "What the hell are *you* doing here?"

The man gave a bark of a laugh. "That's quite a warm greeting for your long lost brother."

Adam swallowed. "Sorry, Ross. You have to admit it's a bit of a surprise seeing you here. How did you find me?"

"I'm a private detective. I'm good at locating people. I've been following your moves around the country."

"And now you're in Wayland, Georgia. Why now, after all these years?"

"I know you're investigating Ken White's death."

"Oh yeah, well I don't need your help."

Ross Marshall sighed. "I figured you wouldn't."

Adam shoved his hands into his pockets, trying to rein in the emotions warring inside him. Some deep buried part of him wanted to stride across the space between them and embrace his brother.

But Ross had taken him by surprise. And there was a more urgent need than that of physical contact. He wanted to protect his turf. This patch of Georgia was his. And another werewolf was invading his territory.

He knew that was a knee-jerk reaction, the animal inside him acting on instinct, and he struggled to curb it. It appeared as if Ross had come in friendship. But was friendship between two adult werewolves really possible?

Ross was watching him with keen, dark eyes. "I figured you were probably struggling with some personal stuff now."

Adam's breath was shallow in his chest, but he gave a small shrug.

"Can we go somewhere and talk?"

"What's wrong with right here?"

"Okay. This is your dominion. You call the shots." Ross shifted his weight from one foot to the other again. "You're the right age to be looking for a mate."

When Adam didn't speak, his brother went on. "I guess the most important thing I came down here to tell you is that I'm happily married. I met a wonderful woman. Her name is Megan. And the miracle isn't just that she can put up with a husband with my . . ." He stopped and looked around, mindful that they were standing outside where anyone could come upon them. "With my wild nature."

"Congratulations," Adam said.

"The best part is that she's a medical doctor. A geneticist. She's done some research into our . . . problem. We have an extra chromosome that causes our genetic aberration. It's a sex-linked trait. I can give you more details if you want. The bottom line is that she's working on how to keep boys from dying when they . . . reach puberty. She's got a few years to do that. Our son, Jonah, is two and a half. And she's pregnant with our daughter."

"A girl!"

"It's okay," Ross said quickly. "She's fixed it so she doesn't have the fatal genetic problem our sisters had."

Adam nodded tightly, fighting against the lump that had formed in his chest. He remembered all those babies who had died at birth. And all the brothers who hadn't survived into adulthood because being a werewolf's child carried a heavy chance of mortality.

So he understood the importance of what Ross was telling him. He hadn't been thinking about his terrible heritage when he'd been pursuing Sara. He should have been, he realized. But he'd only been focused on his own selfish needs. His own overwhelming drive to mate with her.

"I came down here to tell you that if you find the woman you can't run away from, Megan can help you avoid the tragedy of our parents' life."

Ross paused and studied Adam, who could imagine what he looked like. Ragged around the edges. Strung out. Sick.

"You've already found her, haven't you?"

"I'm not discussing that with you!"

"Right. You're too uptight to get personal with me. And I understand that. We haven't seen each other in eight years. Maybe I should have sent you an e-mail. But once I decided to get in touch with you, I wanted to do it in person. I wanted to let you know it's possible for us to get along with each other."

"You really think so?" Adam asked, unable to keep the note of scorn out of his voice.

Ross sighed. "If you want it as much as I do, we can work it out. Violence was a big part of my adult life. I guess you've had some of the same problems. I'm going to raise my sons a lot differently from the way the Big Bad Wolf raised us."

"The Big Bad Wolf! I haven't heard that in years. That's right. That's what you used to call him." He found himself asking, "Is the old bastard still alive?"

"Yes. And Mom, too. She'd love to see you, if you ever get up to Baltimore."

"But not him."

"He'd probably like to see you, too. For about five minutes. He might not want to be in the same room with you for long, but he'd be proud of how well you've done."

Adam gave a harsh laugh. "Proud or jealous."

They stood facing one another, each caught in his own thoughts. Each remembering the dysfunctional home life at the Marshall house. His mother had tried her best. But the Big Bad Wolf had dominated the family. And his idea of dinner table ambience had been a cuff on the ear for any little boy who annoyed him.

Ross spoke first, in a firm, level voice. "I know what you went through as a kid because I went through it, too. I'm going to make sure I get along with my sons when they grow up. If I can do it with them, I can do it with you."

"How are you planning to accomplish that?"

"I see a shrink once a week. He's helping me cope with my aggressions."

Adam could literally feel his jaw drop open. When he'd closed it, he said, "You're kidding. Right?"

"I've never been more serious. It doesn't hurt as much as you think."

"I'll take your word for it."

Ross took a step back. "I came down here to make contact with you. I wanted to make sure you were all right. You can call it curiosity if you want. I call it caring about my brother. But I'm not going to push you into anything you can't handle. I just wanted to let you know that I'd like to keep in touch. And I'm here to help you any way I can."

"Okay. Thanks," Adam answered because he couldn't think of anything better to say.

"I know seeing me is a shock. So I'll back off. I'm in Maryland. Howard County. I've got a nice patch of woods where I can roam at night. And a family I care about. You're welcome to visit us anytime you want."

"Okay."

Ross turned away. Then he was gone. Adam wanted to run after him. But he stayed where he was. He had enough problems right now without trying to figure out how he felt about his long lost brother.

SWALLOWING her frustration, Sara wandered out into the garden, looking toward the spot where her swing set had stood. Dad had taken it down when she'd been in her teens and replaced the old play area with a slate patio with some wrought iron furniture. Along the border were beds of tall annual phlox in white pink and lavender. They were at their peak and lovely. But the furniture was covered with dried leaves and other debris. In the utility room she found an old T-shirt, which she used to wipe off the chaise longue. The long cushion was in the garage. She brought it out and laid it on the metal frame. After sweeping off the patio, she lay down in the late afternoon sun.

It had been a long time since she'd relaxed out here. Memories came back to her. Some good. Some bad. She had played hard in this sheltered garden by herself and with the neighborhood kids. She had helped her mother pull weeds and plant flowers.

But there was a strong memory that dominated all the others. Out here was where she'd had her first strange experience when she was five years old.

She'd been playing on the swing. And suddenly her head had started to pound. Like the headaches she'd had since coming to Wayland.

The scene around her had disappeared. And she was someone else. Timmy. She was inside her childhood friend Timmy's head.

She didn't know where he was. All she knew was that he was in a box where the lights were flickering. Then they went off, and it was dark and scary and closed in, and she felt like she couldn't breathe.

She heard Timmy crying. Or was it herself crying? She didn't know, and she didn't want to be there. Terrified, she yanked her mind back to herself. In the process, her hands lost their grip on the metal chains that held the swing, and she fell onto the ground, knocking the breath out of her lungs.

The sensation left her shaking. When she could get up, she ran to the house, weeping.

"Daddy! Daddy! I was scared. I couldn't get out."

Daddy caught her in his arms.

"What is it? What happened, sweetheart? Did you skin your knee?"

"I was there! In the dark. I . . . I was inside Timmy's head!"

She had felt her father go very still. Over his shoulder, she saw Mommy looking down at her with a strange expression on her face.

Daddy was saying. "You're here with us. Right here. Everything's okay." His gaze burned down into hers, and he gave her a little shake. "You're right here with us. Right here. Nowhere else."

He frightened her then with his eyes drilling into hers and his voice as hard as bricks. She wanted to please him. She was afraid that she might be sent away.

So she clamped her lips shut and fought away the image behind her closed eyelids. And later, when she saw Timmy in the park, and he told her how scared he'd been when he'd gotten stuck in an elevator downtown at his doctor's office, she listened like she didn't already know about it.

The next time something like that started to happen, she clenched her fists and squeezed her eyes shut, and somehow she fought it off. Because she would do anything to please her new parents. Anything including suppressing a part of herself that had always struggled to break out. She'd understood that part of her was bad. That it wasn't normal. And she'd understood that her parents wanted a normal little girl.

So here she was, in the spot where she'd had that first frightening psychic experience. Because she was all grown up, she knew what to call it. And she finally understood that repressing part of herself over the years had taken its toll. It had made her closed-up. Made her play it safe.

Now, whatever the cost, she had to embrace her own uniqueness. And since this was where she'd first shut away part of her personality, this was where she'd come to bring it into focus.

The trouble was, she wasn't really sure how to invite it back.

She made a frustrated sound. Then she thought of the pain that had drilled into her head when she'd stepped into the street before the truck came rushing toward her.

She remembered the intensity of the headache. And she didn't want to feel it again. But maybe she had to. Leaning back, she closed her eyes and focused on the sensation of a blast from a ray gun drilling into her head.

As she tried to open herself to whatever would come next, a terrible sense of guilt clutched at her. She had been taught that this was wrong. And she had tried her best to do whatever would gain Mommy and Daddy's approval. It was hard not to feel like she was betraying them.

"No!" she said aloud. She wasn't betraying them. She was an adult, and she was reaching for her true heritage.

She'd pleased her parents with her denial. She had tried to be normal. For a while it seemed to have worked. She'd been successful in school. She'd made a life for herself. But she'd never really gotten close to anyone.

Then she had come to Wayland, Georgia, and everything had changed. And she realized she had never felt normal. Not deep down.

She squeezed her eyes more tightly shut, trying to open herself to what she had always known was forbidden. It had happened in Wayland without her permission. It could happen here just as well. It had to happen here.

Need was greater than fear. She wasn't sure what she was doing, except that she was reaching out with some kind of mental hook and pulling something dangerous toward her.

And suddenly, her consciousness was no longer in the garden. She was somewhere else. In a child's narrow bed. In the dark. In a nightmare.

She didn't want to be there! Not there. And she tried with desperation born of fear to escape from the terrifying place where she found herself.

21

BUT it was too late for Sara to flee. She was trapped in a nightmare. In the cabin at the edge of the swamp. The same cabin, but different.

In the front room, she could hear Daddy and Momma talking. Not the Daddy and Momma who lived in the house in Wilmington, North Carolina. The other Momma and Daddy.

She wasn't Sara. She was Victoria, and she started to swing her small legs over the side of the bed. Then she heard something scary in the sound of Daddy's voice—and his words.

"Come on, we have to leave. We don't have much time."

As one of Daddy's arms tightened around her, he reached for Momma with the other. "Come on. Let me get you away from here, before it's too late."

Outside, above the babble of voices, she heard a man shout, "Come out and show yourself—you damn witch."

"Yeah, you can't hide from us," another man joined in. "You and the rest of your damn tribe."

"No. I'm not one of them," Momma screamed from the front room.

"Don't lie to us," the man who had spoken first shouted.

Others joined the chorus. "Come out before we burn you out."

Victoria buried her face against her father's shoulder, her free hand clutching Mr. Rabbit.

Daddy started to go after Momma in the front room, but before he reached her, the window beside the door shattered, sending glass spraying across the wood floor.

Momma screamed. Then a strong, dangerous smell filled the air. All at once, Victoria could hear a strange roaring noise.

"Save her! Save her!" Momma screamed.

Her father cursed, trying to get to the front of the house. But the heat beat him back. Turning with Victoria in his arms, he sprinted across the bedroom, then bent to push up the window sash.

"Daddy! I'm scared, Daddy," she whimpered, trying to breathe through the cloud of smoke choking her nose and throat.

"It's okay. Everything will be okay," he said between coughs. "I'll get you out of here."

After lowering her out the window, he quickly followed. With his body bent over hers, he ran into the darkness of the swamp, carrying her past the old crooked tree where she'd liked to play.

Behind her Victoria heard a sound like thunder. Raising her head, she saw the whole house explode into flames.

"Momma! Where's Momma?"

SARA'S eyes blinked open. Her breath was coming in painful gasps. Her heart was threatening to explode.

She folded her arms across her chest, trying to ward off the sudden chill that gripped her body.

She had been there. Been right in the middle of it. And now she knew what had happened.

She had lived in the cabin at the edge of the swamp long ago. With Momma. And a mob of townspeople had killed her mother. Townspeople from Wayland. There was no shred of doubt in her mind about what had happened. In the waking nightmare, she'd seen the old bent tree. The same tree that was still there.

The woman who had been killed in the little cabin, Jenna Foster, had been her mother. The witch had been her mother!

And what did that make her?

She squeezed her eyes closed, trying to drive away the answer. But it had lodged in her brain like shards of glass.

The scared little girl part of her wanted to escape—into madness, if that was her only option. But the woman she had made herself into—the scientist—stood back and approached the subject with cool logic.

She might have died in that cabin. But she had survived. And now, twenty-five years later, someone had brought her back to Wayland. To the scene of the crime.

But she was in Wilmington now. At her adopted mother's house. And she had to find out what Barbara Weston knew about it. Because there were details the little girl would never be able to learn unless someone could fill in more of the puzzle pieces.

On shaky legs she went back to the house to confront the woman she had called mother for most of her life.

Mom was sitting on the living room sofa, a magazine spread on her lap, but she wasn't reading. She was pleating the edge of a page in her fingers.

As soon as Sara entered the room, her mother's gray head came up. Her gaze was questioning and troubled.

Sara stood in the doorway, unsure of what to say. She'd come charging into the house, bent on confrontation. But now she saw how small and old her mother looked. Her face was pale, and her lips trembled as she stared at her daughter.

Sara crossed the room and sat down on the couch. "It's okay, Mom," she murmured.

To her horror, tears welled in the older woman's eyes.

The hard shell Sara had tried to erect around her heart instantly melted. "Mom . . . don't . . ." Sara whispered. "What's wrong?"

Her mother brushed the back of her hand under her eyes. "I knew . . . when you came home . . . when . . . when I saw the look on your face."

"What look?"

"Determined." She sighed. "That determination you taught yourself."

"Did I?"

"Yes. Then when you started asking about your background, I got scared."

"It's been on my mind a lot lately."

Her mother's head bobbed. "I told Raymond this would happen!"

"What?"

"That it would all come back to haunt us eventually." Her mother swallowed hard. "When you first came to us, I wanted you to . . . to be yourself. He thought that you'd be happier if you forgot about your past. If you were like all the other little children."

"Oh!" She'd never realized that her parents hadn't agreed on how to bring her up.

"I promised him I'd keep the secret."

Sara felt shivers slither over her skin. "What secret?"

"About your mother."

"I know who she was. She was a woman named Jenna Foster, wasn't she? And I was her little girl, Victoria."

Mrs. Weston moaned softly. "Was that her name? We never knew."

Sara nodded, trying to put herself in her parents' situation all those years ago. She covered her mother's wrinkled hand with her own. "I had a good childhood. But . . . I can't function as an adult like this. I have to know what you can tell me. Did you know I came from Wayland?"

"Wayland? Where you have that research job?"

"Yes."

Her mother made a small, distressed sound. "We never knew the town where you lived. We only knew it was somewhere south of here."

"How did you know that?"

"Because the money always came from down south."

Sara's eyes widened. "What money?"

"He would send us money orders. From different banks and from different towns."

"Who?"

"Your real father."

"You knew my father? How did you adopt me?"

Her mother stared across the room, her gaze unfocused. "We were too old to get a child through an agency. So we put an advertisement in several newspapers saying that we wanted to provide a loving home for a baby or a toddler. For months we didn't get any response, and we were thinking it wouldn't work. Then we got a phone call asking if we wanted a little girl. Of course we did. A man arranged to meet us down at the Big Boy restaurant. He had you with him. We had lunch and talked. Then the next day he came to our house. You were so quiet. You stayed right by his side all the time. It seemed like you were in shock."

Sara nodded, picturing the little girl who had just lived through a terrible experience. At the same time, she tried to imagine the situation. Raymond and Barbara Weston had taken in a child they didn't know. A child who was obviously traumatized.

"You were taking a chance on adopting me, weren't you?"

"We didn't think about it that way. You were so sweet. So fragile. And we just gave our hearts to you."

Sara squeezed her mother's hand. "And I gave my heart to you."

"When you went off to the bathroom, he told us there had been some trouble, that your mother had died. The man said he was your father, and he couldn't take care of you. And he wanted to find a good home for you with people who would love you. He made it a condition of the adoption that we not know his name. The legal details were handled by a lawyer."

Sara tried to process everything she'd heard. "If you didn't know where I came from and you didn't know the identity of my father— how did you know about the murder?"

"You had nightmares. You told us about the night your mother was killed."

Sara gasped. "It came from me?"

"Yes. And we would comfort you and tell you the best thing was to forget all about it. And we thought the bad stuff had gone away. But I was always afraid that it would somehow come back."

Sara looked down at her and her mother's joined hands. "I understand," she murmured.

"Do you forgive me?"

"Yes," she said, then reached to hug the woman who had raised her with love, a simple woman who, understandably, hadn't wanted to deal with a child with psychic powers.

They sat together on the sofa for a long time. Then Sara stirred herself. She had to get back to Wayland. But first she had to make sure that Mom was okay.

"So, are we going to make those chocolate chip cookies?" she asked.

"Oh yes!" her mother answered, relief flooding her voice.

BY four in the afternoon, Sara was too keyed up to stay any longer. So she hugged her mother good-bye and started back to Wayland to face her past and to face Adam. Making love to him had been like nothing she had ever expected to experience in her life. It had been like something out of a romance novel. Like a man and a woman finding their soul mates.

Yet how could a man be soul mate with a witch?

Her hands clamped around the steering wheel. Part of her wished that she had never come back to Wayland, because coming home had awakened that deep, buried component of her psyche. The part she had always feared. Yet if she hadn't come back to the town where she was born, she never would have met Adam.

But she was the wrong woman for him. Her mother had been a witch. She was a witch. And being with a witch could be dangerous for so many reasons.

She wanted to turn the car in the other direction and flee. But she couldn't make herself do it.

Her mind was a disordered jumble as she drove through the late afternoon and into the night. So many pieces of her personal puzzle had fallen into place. She had been having psychic experiences ever since she'd arrived at that damn cabin. But they didn't just come from the cabin. They came from within her. And some of them had to do with Adam.

"Oh Lord, Adam. I'm sorry," she said into the darkness of the car.

Adam had told her about the witches. He'd told her that their children had come back to town to get even.

Witches with an evil purpose.

Her mind made another jump. They had attacked her. She knew that now. They had sent pain shooting into her head, then warned her that a truck was speeding toward her. So what had they been doing, testing her because they knew she was like them?

A cold chill traveled from her hairline down her spine.

Why had they hurt her? Was she some kind of threat to them? And what about her own psychic power? The power she could feel developing within herself. She didn't think she would use it to hurt Adam or anyone else. But how could she know for sure?

There was so much to think about. Herself. Adam. And her natural father.

He had saved her from the fire. But he had given her up. Then he had sent money to the Westons.

"So who are you, Daddy dearest?" she asked into the closed compartment of the car. "Are you still in Wayland? Are you even still alive? Did you somehow arrange for me to come back to the little cabin beside the swamp?"

That certainly seemed like a radical step. And if he'd done it, what did he hope to gain?

As she drove on through the darkness, her mind spun back to her interview with Austen Barnette. He owned the cabin. He'd had it rebuilt. He was connected to her past. Did that mean he was connected to her? Was *he* her father?

She kept thinking about him as she drove south. But as she drew closer to Nature's Refuge, her thoughts went back to Adam.

She longed to see him, yet she was afraid, too. Thinking about him made her heart pound and her mouth go dry. Then all at once, she realized that wasn't the only reason she felt like her nerves were rising to the surface of her skin.

She tried to analyze the sensation.

Maybe it came from her witch's instinct.

She shuddered. Something was going to happen. Something vibrating in the background of her mind. Something bad.

Pain shot through her head. The same kind of pain she'd felt just before Adam had snatched her out of the way of the pickup truck.

22

SARA'S heart leaped into her throat as a car shot straight toward her out of the darkness, its lights off, and she knew it wasn't some driver losing control. Last time the witches had been playing game with her. But this was no game. This was for real. They were trying to kill her. Fear might have paralyzed her. But anger and determination were stronger. She was damned if she was going to let herself get run off the road along a deserted stretch of highway. She wasn't going to have a fatal accident here. She was going to see Adam again. She had to see Adam again!

Without conscious thought, her mind called out to him, even as she yanked the wheel to the right.

Luckily she had already slowed her speed. Still she whizzed along the shoulder, bumping over potholes, grazing tree trunks, hearing metal tear off of poor old Miss Hester as she pressed on the brake. She threw up her arm to shield her face as the car bashed into a tree branch, then lurched to a halt against the trunk of another tree.

The impact sent her flying forward. Then the seat belt caught and pulled her back again.

She sat behind the wheel, dazed, struggling to drag in a full breath, thankful that nothing worse had happened. Looking over her shoulder, she tried to find the car that had come out of the darkness and crossed the double yellow line, barreling toward her. But it was gone.

With a shaking hand, she unbuckled the seat belt and leaned back against the headrest, trying to bring her emotions under control. Miss Hester's engine had stopped, and she doubted it would start again. And even if it would, driving would probably not be such a great idea.

The danger was over. It should be over. But it didn't feel that way. Through the windshield, she peered into the darkness. Too bad she didn't have a cell phone, because she was alone on this deserted stretch of rural highway, and there was no one to help her.

But she was pretty sure she was only a quarter of a mile from Nature's Refuge. That would be an easy walk.

Her fingers closed around the door handle, but some deeply felt instinct kept her from getting out of the car.

Out in the darkness, she felt eyes were watching her. And she knew who they were.

The bad witches. The ones who wanted to hurt her, and she didn't even know why.

Her chest tightened with apprehension, and she reached to snap the door locks shut. But how much protection would that be?

Oh God, Adam. Adam, help me, her mind screamed—although she didn't know where he was or what he could do.

But he had pulled her out of the street the first time the witches had attacked her. And she clung to that memory, clung even harder as another terrible pain arrowed into her head.

They were doing it. She felt them, even though she could see nothing as she stared into the darkness. Mist rose from the surface of the road now. It spread beyond the blacktop, obliterating underbrush and tree trunks, turning the landscape into a strange, forbidding place. A place of terror and black magic where anything could happen.

Through the car windows, she strained to see into the darkness and caught a flicker of movement, forms gliding through the trees. People. Like apparitions in a horror movie.

They were coming toward her slowly, slowly, ghosts moving through a graveyard, the horror movie effect magnified by their black-hooded cloaks. But it wasn't their physical bodies that threatened her.

Ahead of them, they were sending a wave of pain that filled her brain, swamped her senses.

Her hands clenched. The pressure inside her skull was too much. She was going to die. Right here in the car along this fog-shrouded stretch of road. And everybody would think that the auto accident had killed her.

That thought brought a wave of anger pounding through her. Those bastards! They had made her crash. But they weren't going to kill her.

She roused herself. Leaning forward, she sent back her own wave of energy, instinctively fighting the pack of witches with their own paranormal weapon. She saw them pause, saw their hooded heads turn toward one another. One woman raised a hand toward her face.

Sara had momentarily stopped them. But her feeble weapon wasn't enough. The coven started moving forward again, and Sara felt an invisible noose was closing around her neck, choking off her breath.

She struggled to send another energy burst. And she managed some kind of power surge. But it was like trying to put out a forest fire with a garden hose.

She was still choking, still gasping. Still on the verge of passing out, when suddenly the pressure lifted. She struggled for breath, sitting forward and peering out of the windshield, trying to figure out what had happened.

Through the fog she saw a gray shape charging at the black-hooded figures. An animal. She saw it leap on one and then another, knocking them down, sending high-pitched screams through the group as they flailed at the marauder with their arms and kicked at it with their legs.

The animal looked like a large dog. Or a wolf.

And in that moment of recognition, she knew she had seen that wolf before. In a daydream. A daydream that had overtaken her after she had arrived in Wayland. She'd been standing at the kitchen sink. And her mind had gone back in time. She'd stepped into her mother's life. She knew that now.

But it hadn't just been her mother. The wolf had been there, too. Warning her of danger.

She was pulled back to the present by the screams of the witches echoing through the night as they scattered into the swamp. She watched the wolf chase one of the men, nipping at his legs, almost knocking him to the ground.

The coven was in full flight. Probably the wolf could have killed at least one of them.

Instead he turned and raced back toward the car. He reached her door, standing with the mist swirling around him, staring up at her through the window. And she would have sworn that he was begging her to tell him she was all right.

She should have been terrified. He had savagely attacked the people who had come to hurt her. But she felt a kind of awesome calm settle over her. In her heightened state of awareness—her witch's state of awareness—she knew who he was.

It made no sense. But she knew the wolf was Adam, and that he had come in response to her call for help, come to her with no regard to what might befall him.

Last night, the reverse had happened. She had known he was in danger. And she had been terrified. Then she had seen the sheriff's boots and called out a warning. But she hadn't seen Adam. Now she knew why. He had been a gray wolf in the darkness, and her mind had rejected that vision.

Tonight it was impossible to turn away from the knowledge of the wolf. Man and animal were the same. She was staring down at him through the glass when flashing lights in the rearview mirror suddenly captured her attention.

A police car. The wolf saw it, too.

He waited for a few more seconds, then turned and dashed away, disappearing into the fog. And she was left sitting in the car, breathing hard, trying to deal with the unthinkable.

Paul Delacorte stepped out of the police car and came toward her car, shining his light through her window.

She raised her hand to shield her face, and he directed the beam away from her.

"Dr. Weston? Are you all right?"

She opened the door. "Yes. I . . . I had an accident."

"Are you all right?" he repeated.

"I'm all right," she assured him, trying to keep her voice steady.

"Please get out of the car."

She did, wanting him to know that she hadn't been driving under the influence. As he shined the light on her, she started shivering.

He moved the beam away from her and inspected the damage. "What happened? Did you fall asleep?"

"No."

He played the beam around the bottom of the car, then at the trees along the side of the road, then onto the blacktop.

"Did you swerve to avoid an animal?"

"No."

He made a more thorough inspection of the area, then came back to her.

"I always call for an ambulance. But it looks like you don't need one."

"No, I don't."

She waited while he spoke into the microphone clipped to his collar, canceling the emergency vehicle.

She was debating what else to say to him, when more headlights cut through the night.

A surge of fear shot through her. She was sure Delacorte caught her contorted features. Then he turned toward the newcomer pulling up in back of the police car.

It couldn't be the witches coming back, she told herself. Not now. Not when the sheriff was here. But logic had nothing to do with the sudden chattering of her teeth.

She cringed against the car, then breathed out a small sigh as she saw who it was—Adam, looking disheveled, as though he'd just thrown on his clothing.

A feeling of unreality seized her as she stared at him. He had been here only a few minutes earlier. He had come to her rescue. But the last time she had seen him, he had been a wolf.

She fought off a jolt of hysterical laughter. If she thought he had been a wolf, she had another reason to doubt her own sanity. Yet she knew it was true.

He ran across the road, his eyes fixed on her, yet he stopped a few yards away, and she knew that he was hesitant to approach her, now that she'd seen the wolf in action. Then another thought struck her. She hadn't said anything to him. He didn't even know for sure if she had recognized him.

Yet she felt unspoken messages passing between them.

A sane person would be afraid to get near him now. But she wasn't frightened of him. Really, she was more afraid of herself.

"Adam." She raised her hand toward him, and he closed the distance between them, taking her in his arms.

"Are you all right?" he asked, and she felt the question rumbling deep in his chest.

"Yes."

"Thank God." He pulled her tightly to him, and she leaned into his warmth. He was here. He had come to her again. Even when he didn't know if she was going to run screaming from him.

His hands stroked up and down her back, and she knew he must feel the fine tremors of her body.

Behind her Delacorte was speaking. "I was trying to find out what happened."

She turned to face the sheriff, letting Adam hold her against his body. "I . . . I . . ." She stopped and started again. "A car was coming toward me. I swerved off the road to avoid it."

The lawman looked around. "I don't see another car."

"It managed to keep from hitting me. I guess . . ." She stopped, wondering what to say.

Adam filled in the gap. "What I think is that the witches were lying in wait for her. They forced her off the road. Then they came to finish her off."

Her head swung toward him. Then to Delacorte. Then back.

FALCON gripped the arms of the easy chair.

"What the fuck are you doing? Trying to burn my skin off?"

"I'm trying to disinfect this bite," Willow answered as she dabbed antiseptic on his mangled flesh. "You don't want to end up in the hospital, do you?"

Falcon gritted his teeth as she slopped more of the stuff on the places where sharp teeth had punctured his skin. He had a bunch of deep bites on his legs.

So did the rest of the clan. They were gathered in the living room of the house where a big plastic sheet hung between them and the construction mess.

Until a few days ago, the addition had still been open. Now he was profoundly glad that the house was secure and that the wolf or dog or whatever it had been couldn't get in.

"What was that thing?" Razorback asked, echoing his thoughts.

"I don't know. But it was something strange," Starflower answered.

"It was a dog gone mad," Razorback said.

"And it came streaking out of the night and started tearing at us just when Sara Weston needed help," Starflower said. "Don't you think that's a little convenient for her?"

"What are you saying?" Falcon demanded.

"Maybe she's the kind of witch who has a familiar. In fairy tales, it's a cat. But maybe she's got a damn wolf."

"Oh yeah, right," Razorback said, trying to sound sarcastic and not quite pulling it off.

"If it's true, it's another reason we have to get rid of her. Because next time, that wolf of hers could rip us to pieces."

* * *

"WHY would the witches be after her?" Delacorte asked Adam in a slow, careful voice.

Adam watched Sara drag in a breath. He thought she was going to speak, but she evidently changed her mind and closed her mouth. He pulled her closer and filled the silence by saying, "I think they're afraid of her."

"Why?"

"She's some kind of threat to them. They didn't just drive her off the road. They came after her with their psychic powers! The way they came after me that night in the swamp."

The sheriff was watching him closely. "How do you figure that?"

His own tension level was so high that he didn't have to fake a show of emotion. He ran a hand through his hair in a good imitation of a man who was thoroughly perplexed. "Maybe I've got a little of their . . . their powers. All I know is that I sensed that Sara was in trouble out here—from them. And I came running. Or rather driving."

Which left out the part when he *had* come running. But he wasn't going to bring that up. He was pretty sure Sara wouldn't, either—if she'd understood what had happened. He didn't even know that much.

He kept his gaze fixed on Delacorte, to see how the explanation had gone over. The sheriff nodded as if the answer didn't really surprise him. "I've got a theory about that," he muttered.

"Oh yeah?"

"It's the Olakompa. There's something in the swamp that seeps into your system. From the water. Or the rotting vegetation. And if you've got the right receptors in your brain, it acts like a drug to . . . to . . . give you psychic power."

Adam tried not to gape at him. Obviously the man had been mulling over this rationale for Wayland's supernatural troubles for quite some time. The lawman focused on Sara. "Have you found any plants that might be involved?"

"There are plants that cause hallucinations. I . . . I don't know about ones that . . . that increase psychic power," she stammered.

Adam tipped his head to one side, torn between this fascinating discussion and his need to be alone with Sara. "That's a pretty enlightened point of view from a small-town sheriff."

"I've lived in Wayland all my life. I grew up with the witch tales.

I've had a lot of time to think about what's happened here over the years."

Adam nodded.

"If you've got a better hypothesis, I'd like to hear it," Delacorte said.

"I don't. And I'm not going to stand on the side of the road speculating about it," he added, finally unable to control his own emotions a moment longer. He could feel Sara leaning more heavily on him, and he suddenly wondered how she was managing to stay on her feet at all. Probably she'd had an emotionally draining experience at her parents' house. And she'd come home to *this*. Now she must be beyond exhausted.

"I'm going to take this woman home," he said, hearing the tightness in his own voice. "We can arrange for towing tomorrow. Unless you need her for something else."

Delacorte looked at the wrecked vehicle. "I'll call a truck and have the car towed to Jerry's Garage in town, if that's agreeable with you."

"Yes, thank you," Sara murmured.

When Adam started to shepherd her toward his SUV, the sheriff shook his head. "Before you leave, I need some basic information from you."

"Like what?" Adam demanded.

"Dr. Weston sideswiped a tree. I have to fill out an accident report, and for that I need her driver's license, vehicle registration, insurance card, home address, phone number—that kind of information."

Adam nodded tightly, stepping back so Sara could comply with the request. She had to call him back, though, to ask for the phone number at the park.

He waited for Delacorte to finish, listening to Sara's even voice, trying not to look like a pressure steam valve was about to burst in his chest.

When the sheriff had taken the basics, he put away his notepad. "Did you recognize any of the . . . witches?"

Sara shook her head. "They were all wearing black capes with hoods."

"Okay." Delacorte didn't write it down. Obviously the witch part wasn't going into the official report.

"Are we done?" Adam asked.

"Yes."

Adam silently led Sara to his vehicle, opened the passenger door for her, and then closed it after she climbed in.

He had been desperate to be alone with her. Now he walked slowly around the car, putting off the moment. But finally there was nothing left to do besides slip behind the wheel.

He looked back, seeing Delacorte watching them. The sheriff had already seen him pull Sara into his arms and hug her, so he knew something was going on between them. But it could be over in the next few moments.

So instead of dragging her close and hanging on to her, he started the engine, then headed back to the safety of Nature's Refuge.

Taking his eyes from the road, he glanced at Sara. She didn't speak. His voice was gritty as he asked, "So, what about the wolf?"

23

ADAM had dropped the question into a deafening silence. He clamped his hands on the steering wheel, thinking that he'd made a terrible mistake.

But he wasn't going to take it back. He risked a glance at Sara. She had knit her hands in her lap so tightly that her knuckles were white.

Instead of answering his question, she said, "We were talking about the witches like some science fiction movie we'd seen! But it's not a science fiction movie. I'm one of them."

"Jesus! That's not true!"

"What am I?"

"A woman with . . . with some special talents."

She twisted her hands in her lap. "I told you I was going home to find out about my background. While I was there, I had one of my old *daymares*. Only this time, it made better sense. It was the one about the little girl and her mother in the cabin. I put some of it together, and I made my adoptive mother tell me some of it. I'm Jenna Foster's little girl. My mother was the witch they killed. My father was there

that night. He got me out of the cabin, then found adoptive parents
for me."

She let that settle into the darkness before demanding, "Say
something."

"I was starting to wonder if you were her daughter. Delacorte
was, too."

"You talked about that? About me?" she demanded.

"That's not how the conversation started. He dropped by while
you were away to talk about the wolf he'd seen downtown at the historical society building. The wolf he almost shot."

She made a low, moaning noise.

"So, yeah, we were having a pretty . . . intense conversation. And
you came into it. I told him that even if you were Jenna Foster's
daughter, you hadn't come back to town to get revenge on Wayland.
You weren't one of them."

"It doesn't worry you that I'm her daughter?"

"That didn't bother your natural father when he was having a relationship with your mother."

"Oh, I think you're wrong. He was ashamed of his liaison with her.
He kept it hidden from everyone in town. After she died, he took me
to North Carolina and found a childless couple to adopt me."

"It didn't have to have anything to do with the damn witch thing.
He could have been married, for all you know."

He saw her taking that in and went on quickly. "But he loved you.
He didn't let you down. He found good parents to bring you up."

"Far away from Wayland where nobody would know who I was."

He made an exasperated sound. "Maybe he sent you far away to
keep you out of danger."

She shot him an astonished look. "I didn't think about it that way.
But it doesn't change anything. I'm still worried about my . . . background. When I was driving back here, I kept wondering how I was
going to face you."

He started to speak, but she waved him to silence.

"Let me finish! The closer I got to Wayland tonight, the more I felt
the world closing in on me. I kept thinking, What happens when he
finds out the real truth about the woman he made love with? I kept
thinking, The witches are after me. And they could hurt Adam. Or I
could hurt him. Somehow, something bad could happen."

"No!"

She kept talking, staring straight ahead, as though he hadn't spoken. "Then . . . then they forced me off the road, and they started that stuff with me that they did the other day. Only it was worse. They had on those damn hoods. And they were using their minds to attack me. Sending mental energy bolts at me. And you know what I did? I fought back the same way!"

"Good."

"You can accept what I'm telling you . . . just like that?"

"Yes."

"Why?"

He thought about the answer for a moment, recognizing the importance of what he told her—to both of them. "I guess because my whole life has been lived knowing there were things in the world that would scare the . . . the spit out of ordinary people. If there are men who change themselves into wolves and roam the woods at night, who knows what the hell else is lurking in the genetic heritage of humankind."

As they'd been talking, he had been driving, going on automatic pilot, going home. When he looked up, he saw that he was in the parking lot of Nature's Refuge. He'd left the gate open when he'd come tearing down the road in his car.

He'd driven inside the park grounds without even thinking about what he was doing.

Sara sat staring straight ahead. "The witches would have finished me off except that the wolf came along and started tearing into them. He could have gotten hurt. Or killed."

"The wolf did what he had to do! The problem is that he *is* a wolf."

She had avoided looking at him. Now she turned and met his eyes. "I saw the wolf before tonight. Not in real life. In a daydream about the past. When it started off, I was my mother, living in that cabin. Then I looked up and saw the wolf. I didn't know his identity. But I knew he had come . . . for me."

"Were you afraid of that?"

"Yes."

"And now?" he asked, hardly daring to breathe.

Instead of answering the question, Sara asked one of her own. "Why aren't you running screaming from a woman you know is a witch?"

"Because I love her!" he fairly shouted, then realized what he'd said.

* * *

AFTER Adam and Sara drove away, Paul Delacorte focused on routine tasks, like drawing a quick sketch of the scene. Then he took some measurements, triangulating the vehicle to a big tupelo tree, so three or four years later, he could place the car in the exact position where it had come to rest—in case there was going to be a trial for some reason. Next he took some flash pictures of the Toyota and the road surface and a couple of comprehensive shots covering the scene from different angles.

Finally, he looked around for any evidence he might have missed: drugs, alcohol, anything that might have been thrown out of the car. But he found nothing. So he drove to a nice quiet spot on a side road and began writing up the accident report. When he'd first come upon Sara Weston's battered Toyota at the side of the road, he'd wondered if he'd come upon a case of falling asleep at the wheel or DWHUA, driving with head up ass. Swerving to avoid a porcupine or a raccoon fell into that category, and she looked like the tender-hearted type who wouldn't want to hurt a small animal. Instead, she'd come up with the story about another vehicle that had vanished into the night.

She'd been shaken. And she'd been trying to figure out what to say. Unfortunately, Adam Marshall had driven up and started speaking for her.

Marshall blamed the accident on the witches. But there was more to it than that. Stuff that neither he nor Weston was saying. Paul had been a cop for too long not to recognize evasive answers when he heard them. They were leaving something out, and he was going to find out what it was.

Was Sara Weston involved with the people he'd come to think of as the bad witches?

Adam had said it wasn't true. Paul was still waiting for the rest of the chickens to come home to roost. And he had a lot of questions. Like, for example, he wanted to know how Adam Marshall had gotten there so fast. Did he really have some psychic power that had drawn him to the accident site?

He sighed. That was the least of his problems. At the moment, he had to figure out how to write up his report. Because he sure as hell wasn't going to mention anything paranormal. Not hardly.

* * *

ADAM heard Sara's indrawn breath. "Is love enough?" she asked.

"What the hell do you mean—is love enough?"

"It's a fair question."

"The hell it is!"

"Adam, I'm scared."

"Of me?"

"Not of you. Of . . . of . . ." Her hands fluttered. "Of what's happening. Of the witches. Of myself. Didn't you hear what I said? When they hurled thunderbolts at me, I started fighting back the same way. Adam . . . I'm frightened of what I am. Of what I can do."

"But not of a man who changes into a wolf and roams the woods at night?" he asked, putting the question in the most stark terms he dared.

"Not of you!"

"In that case, we'll make it work," he growled, unhooking his seat belt, then unhooking hers so he could haul her across the console and into his arms.

He cupped the back of her head with one hand, bringing her mouth to his in a kiss that started as a desperate attempt to show her what she meant to him. What they meant to each other.

The other hand dragged her closer so he could feel her beautifully rounded breasts pressed more firmly to his chest.

The contact delivered a jolt of sexual need that drove everything from his mind except the feel of her, the wonderful taste that he had discovered so recently.

She might have resisted, but her fingers kneaded his shoulders, moved to his upper arms, and back again, her touch questing and erotic.

He had driven home as though he were traveling through a dream landscape. He was still in a fog. He had forgotten where they were. Forgotten everything but the enticing woman in his arms.

With a jerky motion, he released the lever and pushed back the seat to its maximum extension. Lifting her up, he pulled her skirt out of the way and settled her in his lap, positioning her so that she was facing him, her legs straddling his.

He accomplished all that without lifting his mouth from hers.

When he had her where he wanted her, he pushed up her knit top, then reached around to unhook her bra so that he could take her breasts in his hands.

She moaned into his mouth, moaned again as he played with her nipples, the feel of those hard pebbles against his fingers driving him close to insanity.

Her hips moved restlessly against his, and her lips were soft, warm, and open, silently begging him for more. He obliged, deepening the kiss, using his tongue and his teeth and his lips in all the ways he'd learned to please a woman.

It wasn't enough, and he realized that he had moved her onto his lap too quickly. The layers of clothing separating them were driving him beyond the point of madness. And when she made a frustrated, whimpering sound of agreement, the blood in his veins turned to molten lava.

Somehow he kept himself from screaming in protest when she pushed away from him—until he saw that she was trying to struggle out of her panties. He ripped the fabric and tore them free of her body, so that he could dip his fingers into her throbbing center. She was hot and wet, and the stroking touch of his fingers seemed to make her whole body pulse and tremble.

Her fingers scrabbled at the snap of his jeans, then the zipper. And when she took him in her hand, he thought he would self-destruct.

"Sara," he gasped. "Don't. I want to come inside you."

"God, yes!" As she spoke, she lowered her body, bringing him into her with a sure, swift motion that robbed them both of breath.

He brought his mouth back to hers, caressing her breasts as she moved frantically above and around him, her moans of pleasure mingling with his.

They climaxed in an explosion of passion that felt to him like a rocket blasting off into outer space.

She wilted against him, her face damp, her breath ragged.

He kissed her cheeks, her lips, his hands stroking possessively over the silky skin of her back.

For long moments, neither one of them moved.

He was the one who spoke first. "Don't give this up because you're afraid of the future."

"There's more to working out our relationship than great sex."

"Was it?"

She reached up and gave a tug at his hair. "You know damn well it was!"

He laughed, a low rumble in his chest. "Yeah." Laughing felt good. She felt good, her body covering his, clasping him. He kissed her again, slowly, tenderly, then with more urgency as he felt himself getting hard a second time, still inside her.

She raised her head, looking down at him, smiling. The smile turned to a small gasp as he found her breasts again.

"Good, that's so good," he whispered.

"Yes."

They kissed and touched, arousing each other more slowly now that the urgency was sated. This time they enjoyed the delight of being together. Of giving and receiving pleasure, of working their way from peak to peak until climax overwhelmed them once more.

When they could finally move again, he helped her up, and she flopped into the passenger seat.

He stepped out of the car, pulled on his jeans, then circled around to her door. Helping her out, he stuffed the ruined panties into his pocket, then swung her up into his arms and carried her along the path to his cabin, determined to keep her safe no matter what the cost.

24

IT was too early in the morning for a business meeting. But Paul Delacorte was responding to a summons from the most powerful man in Wayland. The message had been on his voice mail when he'd arrived at the office. He'd figured that he might as well get the interview over with.

James Lucas had apparently been waiting for him. The two men met outside the front door of the mansion next to one of the variegated ivy topiaries that flanked the wide entrance.

They eyed each other gravely. They weren't really friends. But they weren't enemies, either. Their skin color made them allies. Although they were of two different generations, they were both African

American men who had done very well for themselves in the small town of Wayland, Georgia. Each was conscious of his position in the community.

They were both wearing uniforms that proclaimed their status. James, who was in his late fifties, was dressed in the neatly pressed black suit and crisp white shirt that his employer required him to wear. There were folks in the black section of town who thought that suit was a badge of oppression. He ignored them and had survived bigotry from both the black and white communities with grace and determination and an ability to keep his mouth shut when faced with stupidity from either race.

Paul, who was in his early thirties, wore the crisp navy blue police uniform and plain black trooper boots provided by the Wayland taxpayers. He and James had grown up in a different world. James had come from a generation where Negroes were considered to be inferior to whites for a variety of racist reasons, ranging from skull thickness to body odor. Paul had been born into a world where equality was supposed to be within reach, if you trod carefully among the tar pits and quicksand traps of life in a small southern town.

Ironically, each thought the other had gone too far in bowing to the subtle and not so subtle pressures that the white folks imposed on them. But neither of them would ever have voiced that opinion. They were allies in a struggle that remained on the collective radar screens of the African American community.

Paul might be the sheriff, but as the younger of the two men, he allowed James to take control of the conversation.

"I got a summons to the big house this morning. What's up?" he asked.

James lowered his voice but spoke in tones dripping with sarcasm. "The massa's scared," he said, mocking a term of respect once used in slavery days.

"The field hands are rebelling?" Paul asked.

"Naw. I hear tell the witches have a grudge against him."

"You got any idea why?"

"He don't confide in me."

"Yeah, well, maybe I can get the straight story out of him."

"Good luck."

Paul had been summoned to the mansion a few times in the past. The last occasion had been when Barnette had wanted a police back-

ground check on the farm manager he was considering hiring. Paul
had seen no harm in earning some brownie points by doing the town
benefactor a favor. It had turned out the guy had a slew of DWI convictions, and Barnette had hired someone else.

"Where is he holding this audience, in the study or the conservatory?"

"Neither. You're in the front parlor."

"Well, well. The black folks is comin' up in the world," Paul muttered as he followed James inside.

The butler squared his shoulders and stood up straighter when he
led the way down the hall to the house's main sitting room.

"Sheriff Delacorte, sir," he intoned, as though he were announcing
an important courtier to an eighteenth-century English monarch.

Paul strode through the doorway, then stopped and studied the
man sitting in a carved wooden chair that might have been a throne.
It had been almost a year since their last face time. The patriarch of
Wayland, Georgia, looked older and on edge, despite his studied casual air.

"I appreciate your coming," Barnette said.

"Yes, sir," Paul answered, hating the way he'd added that *sir*. But
it seemed to come automatically out of his mouth when he was in this
house.

"Have a seat," Barnette invited.

Paul looked around at the uncomfortable furniture and selected a
Chippendale chair about five feet from the master's throne, waiting
for the man to say what was on his mind.

"I understand we have a situation in town," he began.

"A situation?"

"Newcomers moving into the area and making trouble."

"What trouble?"

"I expect you know what I'm talking about!"

"I'd like your perception, sir."

Barnette permitted long seconds to stretch before allowing, "You
know that over the years, we've had some unfortunate . . . incidents."

He paused, but Paul remained silent and remained sitting quietly
in his chair, although his pulse rate had picked up. He knew very well
what the last unfortunate incident had been. It was decidedly different
from what was happening now. Did Barnette recognize the difference?

The old man spoke again. "Things have been quiet for a while. But we both know there have been people in town who . . ." He stopped and cleared his throat. "Whose behavior doesn't conform to the community norm. Or any other norm. I expect that you're alert to that?"

"Yes, sir," he answered, sorry that they were still tiptoeing around the subject.

"Down through the years, there's been a history of incidents involving those people and the rest of us."

Paul nodded, thinking that what Barnette meant was that homicide had been committed here. Out of fear and hatred.

Barnette rocked in his seat. "What happened was . . . documented."

Paul blinked. "You mean murder? You mean somebody was stupid enough to write it down?"

Barnette's face contorted. "We're talking about papers that were supposed to be destroyed. Apparently, they ended up in a locked safe at the historical society."

"Is that what the break-ins were all about?"

"Yes. And I wouldn't call it murder."

"What would you call it?"

"Self-preservation."

"We have a different interpretation of the term."

"I believe your daddy and I saw things the same way," the old man snapped.

"I'm not my father," Paul said in a low but firm voice. "I don't sweep homicide under the rug because that's what the white folks want me to do."

A flush spread across Barnette's wrinkled face. "That's not what I'm asking."

"What *are* you asking?" he inquired, keeping his voice low and even.

"First, that you recover the stolen property."

"I'm doing my best. But we have no leads."

"You know as well as I do who took those records."

"Do I?"

"Troublemakers who have moved into the area. New people who . . . who are connected with families that might have lived here at some earlier time. I want them brought to justice."

"I don't have much to go on," Paul repeated.

"You have employment applications. Real estate transactions. Phone records. Credit receipts. All kinds of information."

"I've made a start on that. But I don't have the resources to go through months of random civil records with little hope of finding anything useful."

Barnette snorted. "I can provide the resources."

Paul raised an eyebrow.

"A special grant to the sheriff's department. More money for additional personnel. You run the department with eight deputies. That's not much manpower."

So the old man was paying attention to things like staff numbers. What else was he into? "The offer of additional money is very generous of you, sir. But we can't hire personnel off the streets. Officers must have special training for their jobs. According to our charter, we can only take candidates who have graduated from the state police academy or who have been working in law enforcement."

"I thought you'd give me some excuse like that!"

"I'm willing to hire suitable candidates after a thorough background check."

"Which means it will take months."

"I'm afraid that's so. When sheriff's departments skip that step, they can wind up with felons on the payroll. That happened in Dade County, Florida, not too long ago."

Barnette's eyes narrowed. "Well, I don't intend to make myself a sitting duck. I'm hiring a private security company. I'm starting with two men right here."

"At your estate?"

"Yes."

"Do you have some reason to worry about your personal safety?"

"No more than any other normal citizen of Wayland." He made a throat clearing noise. "I'd appreciate your keeping me informed on what you find out about any troublemakers in town."

"I'm afraid I'm not authorized to do that, sir."

"Yes, well, perhaps we should elect a sheriff who's more cooperative. When are you up for reelection?"

"Next year."

Barnette stroked his chin thoughtfully. "That soon."

Paul ignored the implied threat and stood. "If there's nothing else, I need to get back to work."

"Of course." Barnette gave a dismissive wave of his hand, as if he was sending away one of the house slaves.

Paul pressed his palm against the side of his uniform pants, thinking that it was a good thing he was getting out of here before he lost his cool and said or did something that would make his daddy roll over in his grave.

As he left, James appeared in the hallway. They walked silently toward the front door, then exited onto the porch.

"Well?"

Paul looked around, wondering if the portico was bugged. He made a quick negative gesture with his head, then walked slowly down the steps. James followed.

"You're right. He's actin' like a cat on a hot tin roof. He wants me to find out who broke into the historical society."

"I guess that old lady, Mrs. Waverly, has her skirt in a twist."

"It's more than that. What I got out of the conversation is that somebody kept some notes on who did what to whom over the years."

"You're kidding."

"No. Barnette thought they'd been destroyed. Apparently, he was wrong!"

USUALLY Adam was up early. But exhaustion kept him asleep until long after the sun had risen.

He woke with a feeling of disorientation, followed immediately by a terrible tightness in his chest. The tightness eased when he found that Sara was still in bed with him. She was sleeping on her back. The covers had slipped partway down her chest, revealing the tops of her creamy breasts. He wanted to reach out and slide the sheet the rest of the way down so he could see more of her. But he held himself still, thinking he should be content with what the morning had given him.

Really, he thanked God for the morning's gift because he had been secretly afraid that Sara was going to disappear again.

They had cleared that hurdle. Now all he had to do was make sure he woke up next to her every morning for the rest of his life.

His right arm was in an uncomfortable position. But he was afraid to move, afraid to wake her. So he feasted on what he could see. The mass of blond hair spread across her pillow entranced him. So did the curl of her ear and the curve of her eyebrow.

Long moments later, he saw her lashes flutter, and his breath

stilled. Her eyes opened, and he caught her momentary sense of confusion. Then she turned her head and looked at him.

"Good morning," he whispered, shifting to ease the cramp in his
arm and hearing the gritty quality of his own voice.

She gave a small nod.

"Thank you for being here."

"I'm not going to run away again."

The sense of relief was profound, followed by the need to pull her
into his arms then, and make love to her all over again. But her next
words stopped him.

"That isn't a promise that I'll stay forever."

"What is it?" he managed to ask as he sat up and plumped his pillow behind him, giving himself something to do so he wouldn't have
to meet her eyes.

She looked at him, then slid up carefully, pulling the sheet with
her to cover her breasts. Then she took several moments to arrange her
own pillow.

"A promise that I'm going to try and act like an adult, not a scared
little girl."

"Good." He wasn't sure what else to say. What else to do. But he
couldn't stop himself from reaching for her hand and holding on. He
had gone to sleep wondering what he could say to influence her
thinking. And he'd known it would have to be the truth. But the
speech that had sounded so plausible as he'd silently rehearsed it last
night now rang hollow in his mind. Still, he had to try and make her
understand.

"I was always a very happy bachelor. I loved playing the field. I
loved having a good time with a lot of different women. Those kinds
of times are over, because now the only woman I can think about making love to is you."

"Making love with you is wonderful," she breathed.

He shifted his hand and knit his fingers with hers, then couldn't
stop himself from leaning over and brushing his lips against the tender place where her cheek met her hair. He ached to hear her tell him
she loved him. But there was no way to force her response or her feelings. She had made discoveries at her parents' house that he knew had
jolted her. Then she'd come home to an attack from the witches. And
to the wolf. He knew she was still grappling with the aftershocks. All

he could do was hold on to her and hope that she'd come to feel about him the way he felt about her.

"I'm not very experienced with men," she murmured.

"Is that supposed to be a negative?"

"Isn't it?"

"No. But at least this morning you're worrying about man-woman stuff. Not witch stuff."

"I'm still worried about witch stuff."

"Okay. But let's demolish the man-woman problem first. At least from my point of view. I knew the moment I saw you that you were the right woman for me. But that scared me. I tried to run away from it. I tried to tell myself it wasn't true. None of that did me any good. I kept thinking about how much I wanted you . . . needed you. Don't tell me you didn't feel something . . . significant that morning in the swamp!"

"Are you trying to get me to say I felt an instant attraction to you?"

"Did you?"

She heaved a little sigh. "Yes."

"So it wasn't all one-sided. That's a relief."

"You know it wasn't all one-sided."

"Yeah. But I like hearing you say it."

"And do you like hearing me say that I pick up information from your brain?"

He kept himself steady, knowing that she was trying to get a reaction out of him. "Like what?"

"Like your watching the witches that night in the swamp. I saw it in your mind."

"You tapped into my consciousness because something . . . bad had happened to me. Then you did it again, when you thought Delacorte was going to shoot me."

"You can call it what you like. I say we're right back to the witch stuff."

He wanted to physically shake the negative thinking out of her. Instead he turned and reached for her, pulling her close against him. "All my adult life I've run from real intimacy. But you are the woman who completes me. Maybe all my life I was waiting for a witch."

She laughed, then quickly sobered again. "Living with me isn't going to be easy."

"Then I guess we're even." He swallowed hard. There were still things he didn't want to tell her. He wanted some time to show her how good they could be together before he had to get into the really bad stuff. But Ross had given him hope that life with a werewolf wasn't going to be the total disaster of his parents' marriage.

He was desperate to make her understand how he felt, yet at the same time, something else teased at the back of his mind. Something important. Perhaps she felt his sudden tension, because she drew back and asked, "What?"

"Something . . ." He closed his eyes, trying to bring a scent into focus. And when he did, his body jerked.

"What? What's wrong?"

"Her smell!"

"Whose smell? Who are you talking about?"

He tried to make his muddled thoughts clear. "I was thinking that when the woman came to my office and tried to seduce me, I didn't respond, because the only woman I wanted was you. Then I started thinking about the way that other woman smelled."

"Good? Bad?"

"That's not the point. The point is that her distinctive scent wasn't masked then. Later, I picked it up down at the historical society building. Her and a lot of other people. Too many people for me to sort them all out. Then last night in the mist, there were only five witches. I couldn't see their faces. But I could distinguish their scents. Including that woman. She was there. Lord, maybe I should have figured out before that she's one of them."

Sara shuddered, her gaze turning inward. "Maybe I should have. That woman hates me," she whispered. "I saw it in her eyes the afternoon when she came on to you. She's so sure of her womanly power. But you turned her down. In front of me. Then last night, she tried to kill me. It was her. She was the one driving it. I know that know."

Adam felt a wave of cold sweep his skin. "She'd kill you because I want *you* instead of *her*?"

"Well, not just that. I think she's afraid of me. And I think she hates both of us, because we didn't give her what she wanted. And she always gets what she wants."

"Jesus." He turned and grasped her by the shoulders. "Maybe you're right. Maybe she's the motivating force. But whatever it is, I want you to promise me to stay in the Refuge where you're safe. Promise to stay here!"

She gave a tight nod.

"And I want you to do something else. Practice."

She looked puzzled. "Practice what—my plant experiments?"

"No, your witchcraft."

"What . . . ?" she gasped.

"You said that they hit you with mental thunderbolts. And you hit them back. But they were stronger than you. So practice doing it."

Her voice rose in panic. "I don't know how! I don't know what I did. I don't even know where to start."

"Figure it out, because they tried to kill you once, and they're going to come back looking for you."

His words had been harsh. The look of terror on her face tore at him. He reached for her, held her tightly, rocking her gently in his arms. "I'm sorry," he murmured as he skimmed his lips against the side of her face and her silky hair on the top of her head. "I hate to scare you."

"I know why . . . why you did it. I have to face facts."

He nodded against the top of her head. "Yes. We both do. Tonight I'm going to go out looking for the bastards. I don't need to see their faces, like I told you . . ." He still couldn't say the word *werewolf*, so he put it in third person terms. "The thing about the wolf is that he has a fantastic sense of smell. And tonight, he's got something to work with."

"Adam, for God's sake, be careful. Last night, you hurt them. I could feel their fear and their anger. It's not just her now. The whole coven is out to get you."

"Yeah, but I'll bet they don't know that the wolf is me."

"Don't count on it."

"Okay, and I'll be careful," he growled, because it was the answer she wanted—needed—to hear. And he would do anything to keep her happy while he tracked down the Satan's spawn who had tried to kill her.

25

AMY Ralston was in the office down at the boat dock when her cell phone rang. The number on the screen brought a kind of sick feeling to the pit of her stomach. Furtively, she looked around. No one was in the immediate vicinity, so she pressed the Receive button.

"Hello?" she said in a lowered voice.

"What's up?"

"Nothing."

"Where's Marshall?"

"At the office."

"And where's Weston?" The voice took on an ugly ring as the speaker said the woman's name.

"She's in that shed, working with her laboratory stuff."

"Tell me if either one of them leaves the park."

"I'm only here till dark. It will look funny if I stay after hours."

"I know that! Just do your best. Try to get some extra evening hours. And one more thing, if you take any tourists out into the back-country, see if you can spot any more of those cloth bags."

"I hate those things."

"Somebody put them out in the swamp to warn us away. I want to know if there are any more."

"Okay," Amy whispered.

The line clicked, and she was left listening to dead air. She wanted to turn off her phone, but she left it on because she didn't want to get into trouble.

Brenda had hurt her once, given her a terrible pain in the head. And her cousin could do it again if she wanted.

But that wasn't the only reason why she'd agreed to be Brenda's spy at Nature's Refuge. She had been surprised when her cousin had come to town and looked her up. She had heard stories about some of the people in her family. Her great-great grandfather had been killed by a mob. And her uncle and aunt had gotten out of town after an-other woman had been killed.

Brenda had come back with a group of friends. Friends like herself, she said.

Amy wasn't exactly sure what that meant. Her own family had never had any of the problems of Brenda's parents. And she knew she was pretty ordinary.

But Brenda was special. At first, Amy had been excited about that. Now she was afraid of Brenda and her friends. Especially that spooky guy who was fixing up his parents' old house outside of town. She didn't like him or the others. She wished Brenda wouldn't hang around with them. But Amy knew she wasn't going to stop her. And she knew that if she didn't do what Brenda said, she could get hurt— real bad. So she'd tell her when Adam Marshall or Sara Weston left the park. And she'd look for some more of those yucky bags in the swamp.

ADAM knew Sara had spent the day in her laboratory. He suspected she hadn't gotten much done. But he wasn't going to press her for details, because he was trying to show her that he could give her space. If that was an issue.

Still, he could only stay away from her for so long. When he went off duty, he invited her to his cabin for dinner. Steaks on the grill and salad. A nice normal meal. Only his steak was almost raw and he went easy on the salad.

She didn't comment on his dietary habits. And he did his best to steer the conversation to her work and his stewardship of the park, because those were safe topics.

But she had a way of turning everything back to the subject that was uppermost in her mind. He watched her playing with the wax that had dripped down one of the candles he'd set on the dining room table for atmosphere. He knew how to set the stage for physical intimacy. He had a lot less experience with sharing his thoughts.

"I was thinking about why I went into botany," she said.

"Why?"

"Probably I have some of the same interests as my mother."

He nodded, admiring what the candlelight did to her pale skin.

"But science is so . . . logical. There are reasons for everything . . . even if you don't know what they are. That appealed to me. I think I was looking for control and structure."

"Would you have liked some other field better?"

"I don't know. Maybe I'll give up plants and become an artist."

"What kind of artist?"

"I loved working with oil and acrylic paint. I think I'd be good at painting the swamp. The birds and animals. The vegetation. Land-scapes." Her voice had taken on an excited glow.

He covered her hand and lightly stroked it. "You should do what makes you happy."

"And does your job make you happy?"

"You probably know I picked it so I could be outside. Close to nature."

"Yes."

"But I was never exactly happy. Until you walked into my life."

"Adam . . ."

"Sorry. I'm not trying to force you into anything," he lied.

Finally he reached for his plate, intent on carrying it to the sink.

"Let me do the cleaning up," she said.

"You don't have to."

"You cooked. I'll clean."

"Okay," he answered, thinking that being with her, sharing chores with her felt natural. Simple. But nothing in their lives was really simple, was it?

He cleared his throat. "I'm going out. Will you wait here for me?"

"Yes."

He wanted to add, *in my bed*. But he didn't press his luck.

"Are you driving into town?"

He had debated about that. He could travel faster in his car. But he wasn't taking any chances on the witches watching the park entrance. He wanted them to think he was here guarding Sara. "I'm going the back way."

He let that statement settle in the candlelit room. The back way. Through the swamp.

She nodded, then reached toward him. That was all the invitation he needed to pull her into a tight embrace.

"Be careful," she murmured.

"I will. And you lock the door as soon as I'm gone." He bent and kissed her. Just one undemanding kiss that made him instantly hard as one of the candle shafts. Before he lost his resolve, he turned and walked through the front door, feeling her gaze follow him as he strode into the wilderness.

*   *   *

SARA stood quietly by the window watching Adam disappear down one of the nature trails. Then she locked the door, feeling reassured by the rasp of metal against metal. But as she seated herself on the couch, she knew that a locked door only provided a false security. Anyone who wanted to get in here could break a window. Unless she stopped them. The gun she'd brought to Wayland was in her purse which was resting on the floor near her feet.

She had boldly pulled out the weapon that first time in the swamp with Adam when she hadn't known who he was. And before that, she'd had several sessions at a practice range to make sure she knew how to use the gun and how to take care of it. But she still wasn't certain if she could actually shoot anyone.

There was something so awful about pulling the trigger when you were facing a person, not a paper target.

And even if she could do it, what if a whole group of people attacked the house, the way they'd done with Jenna Foster.

The thought brought a clogged feeling to her throat. She had brought the gun for security, but it might not do her much good. Adam was right. She needed another form of protection. The power that she'd inherited from her birth mother.

Strangely, she didn't feel the same reluctance as when she thought about a gun. A gun was a mechanical device. The skills Adam had told her to cultivate came from within her.

But how did she call them up? She'd flailed out in response to the witches' attack. But what guarantee did she have that she could do it again?

Had her mother tried to save herself on that terrible night? Sara didn't think so. Her mother had been a gentle woman. A woman oriented toward healing. That had been her special talent, and maybe she hadn't even known there was a way to defend herself.

Sara sighed, feeling weighed down with a deep sorrow. Jenna Foster had died so young. Lord, she probably hadn't been as old as Sara was herself. And not only that, she'd borne a child by a man who couldn't even admit their relationship to the world.

Adam was different. He had told her he loved her, blurted it out when he'd been trying to make her understand why he wasn't afraid of her.

She was sure he wanted her for his wife, although he was being careful not to press her. Was she the right wife for him? She still wasn't sure. But the idea of living without the man she loved made a cold knot form in her stomach.

The man she loved. She knew it was true, even if she'd been afraid to say it to him.

Her hands clenched and unclenched. Fear seemed to rule her life. And she hated that.

When she felt her nails digging into her palms, she deliberately tried to relax. Tried to open herself. Tried to bring back the feeling of power that had seized her when the witches had come hunting for her.

WHEN Adam was deep in the swamp, he took off his clothing and changed, then headed toward Wayland, sticking to the paths through the wilderness, moving quickly, intent on staying out of human sight.

The thought of going into town made his steps falter. A wolf was made for the natural environment, with trees or open sky overhead and soft dirt under his feet, not hard pavement lined with buildings.

More than that, the town was dangerous, now that Delacorte was on the lookout for a werewolf. Every minute he spent on the streets was a minute too long. But he had no alternative. It wouldn't do him any good to simply pick up the trail of a witch. He needed to trace it back to the man or woman's house.

His thoughts flashed to his brother. Ross had offered to help him. And if he couldn't find the damn witches in a reasonable amount of time, he might have to ask for help. Two noses would certainly be more efficient than one.

He had reached the residential area and began moving more cautiously. At the edge of the downtown, he stopped dead and sniffed the air, hoping he wasn't going to pick up the strong scent of Paul Delacorte.

He didn't. But that proved nothing. The sheriff could be in his cruiser, metal and glass between himself and the outside air.

The wolf moved cautiously from building to building, a gray shadow gliding down back alleys when he could, cataloging the odors he encountered.

Garbage. Marijuana. Roses. And in one of the houses he passed, fresh baked bread and a pot of beef and vegetable soup slowly cooking.

Once or twice he stopped. The witch woman's scent was strong outside a Main Street shop that sold greeting cards. He stopped and dragged in a deep breath. She had been here. He was certain of that. But the trail ended in the parking area. Did she work in the store? He could come back during the day and find out.

No. He could only come back at night until the witches were put out of action. The minute they knew he was off the park property, they might go after Sara. And he couldn't take that chance. They knew where to find her, and he was the only thing that would keep them away.

IN the warm glow of the table lamps, Sara looked around the small room where she waited for her man to return. It was rustic and simple, but she liked it. Maybe because it was where Adam lived. She felt his presence here, even when there wasn't much to see of his personality in the room. He hadn't set out any family photos. Or mementos of his assignments. Probably he'd lived in a lot of parks around the country. But you couldn't tell it from looking at his house. He was a man who had lived a solitary life. And now he was reaching out to her. More than that, he had totally changed her perception of herself. He accepted her for who she was. What she was. And she hadn't really thanked him for that, she realized.

"Adam." She murmured his name, partly because it filled the silence of the room. She supposed she could put on the television set or the radio. But she wanted neither distraction.

Leaning back, she closed her eyes, opening herself to something that came from within. Inviting psychic energy to bubble up in her mind. It was a strange task, because she had no idea what she was doing. She didn't have one shred of control over her special abilities. Long ago, she had worked hard to shut a door in her mind. She had taken her father's word that the visions from her past or her flashes of insight into the present were strange or abnormal, bad elements to be rooted out of her life. And now Adam was telling her they weren't bad. He was telling her they might even be the key to her survival.

She tried to imagine where he might be. He had walked away from the cabin on two legs. He hadn't exactly said so, but she was pretty sure it was the wolf who had gone into Wayland.

A little frisson went through her. Going into town as a wolf was dangerous. But he had done it for her.

She tried to imagine him now, a gray shadow moving through the darkened streets. A clear image formed in her mind. But she was still unsure of herself. The image was just as likely her imagination as anything real.

ADAM waited at the entrance to an alley, his gaze darting up and down Main Street, probing the darkness between the overhead lights, his ears tuned to danger.

No one moved on the street, and he trotted forward again, then stopped short as he caught another familiar smell.

It was the hidden watcher he had spotted outside Sara's house. One of the witches! It had to be.

The man's distinctive essence filled his head. It started outside one of the shops. The dry cleaners.

That night at the cabin, the guy had escaped in his car. But now Adam had picked up his trail in town. Did he work at that shop? Or had he just been dropping off or picking up his cleaning?

Riveted to the man's odor, intent on the hunt, Adam followed the trail down the sidewalk, praying that the guy lived nearby, praying that he hadn't gotten into a car and driven away, leaving another dead end. He trotted along one block, then another, his breath burning in his lungs from the tension of not knowing. Three blocks from the dry cleaners he came to a small house, a bungalow walled off by a low boxwood hedge.

He went past, and the scent was less sharp. Turning back he stepped onto the front walk, breathing deeply.

The guy lived here. Or he had spent a lot of time here.

It wasn't what Adam would have pictured for a witch's lair. It was an ordinary house. But very well kept, he decided as he looked up at the porch which sat three steps above the walk. His gaze skimmed the white wicker furniture and the pots of impatiens. The wide porch roof was supported by massive stone pillars. The siding was yellow clapboard and looked newly painted. Stepping back, he took in the grounds. Even in the darkness, he saw that every inch of the front yard was planted with neatly mulched beds of flowers and vegetables set among paths of natural wood rounds.

He made out beds of daylilies. Some yellow flowers he'd seen before but couldn't name, tomato plants. Green bean vines. Hydrangeas.

The front of the house was dark. He stepped around the side. Through a lighted window, he saw a man sitting in a leather recliner.

He was totally focused on his quest, so intent on his purpose that the rest of the world had ceased to exist. A dangerous situation for a wolf on the streets of Wayland.

26

SARA felt a shudder go through her. Once before when Adam had prowled the dark streets of Wayland, she had warned him to run.

Now it seemed like she was there with him again. Only the scene was more vivid. More real. This time it felt like she was standing right next to the wolf.

He was in the side yard of a small house, looking up toward a lighted room.

Someone was inside. And a shock of recognition went through her as she took in the man's face.

At any other time, he would have commanded her total attention. But she knew there was something else more important in the scene.

She had caught a glimpse of the street in front of the house where a police car was gliding slowly and silently forward.

It must be Delacorte. Or one of his deputies. And he must have seen the wolf.

"Adam—Watch out!"

She was sitting alone in the living room of the cabin. But her vision was focused on the garden of a house miles away. In that scene, she saw the wolf's body go rigid, saw him raise his head and look around.

"Run," she shouted again into the empty living room. "Use the alley and not the street. Delacorte's out there."

Her body was back at the cabin, but her mind was somewhere else. With Adam. With the wolf. At least part of her mind.

A split second later, he faded back into shadows, then trotted off into the backyard and hurried through the alley.

She saw the sheriff stop the car and get out, shining his light into the bushes and up and down the street. But the gray shape had made his escape. And all Sara could do was sit there on the couch, her arms wrapped around her shoulders, waiting for Adam to return.

AS Adam turned the knob on the front door, he saw Sara through the glass. She was huddled on the sofa, her shoulders hunched and her eyes closed. When he'd left, he'd pictured her in his bed. Now he was glad that she was still up and dressed.

The slight noise had her gaze shooting in his direction, and she was off the sofa and throwing the door open before he could get out his key.

She flung herself into his arms, pressing herself to him, her hands locking over his shoulders. "Are you all right?"

"Yes." He waited a beat. "Because you warned me again."

He stepped through the open door and closed it behind himself, leaning back against the solid surface as he hugged her to him.

"I was trying to do what you told me, trying to . . . to hook into . . . my powers. And then I saw you. Only I didn't know if it was real. But . . . it . . . it felt real. And when I saw the police car, I knew you had to get out of there." The words were high and shaky, and he realized she was near to hysteria. "Then I couldn't tell if it had worked, if you'd gotten away."

"It's all right. It's all right," he whispered, his fingers kneading the tense muscles of her neck and shoulders.

He had come rushing back here to tell her something important. But now that she was in his arms, all he could do was hold on to her. She was the one who eased away so that she could meet his eyes. "Before Delacorte came, you saw the Blackberry Man," she gulped out. "Inside the house."

He tipped his head to one side, trying to make sense of her words. "Who?"

"Well, that's the name I gave him. I saw him in the woods a few times near my cabin."

"I think he's one of the witches."

"He's not!"

"How do you know?"

"I . . ." She stopped, made a helpless gesture. "I don't know. I just think you're wrong. He was always friendly."

"Yeah, he'd have to act friendly, wouldn't he, if he didn't want to seem like a threat? But we're going to find out."

She goggled at him. "How?"

"We're going back to his house. I'd like to confront him on my own, but I'm not going to leave you in the park without protection."

She glanced from him to the darkness out the window, then back again. "You mean we're going now?"

"Yeah, now."

She gave him a panicked look, and he knew she was frightened. He could have told her that he'd rip the guy's throat out if he tried to hurt her. But he kept that insight to himself.

"Wouldn't . . . wouldn't it be better to wait until the morning?" she stammered.

He shook his head. "This is the perfect time. It's so late that the witches may not be watching the park entrance. I think the guy's alone in the house. I want to confront him while he's not with his buddies."

"But what . . . what if you're right about him? What if he attacks us?" she gasped out.

"I'm hoping he keeps up the pretense that he's friendly. And if he doesn't, we can handle him together," he said, projecting confidence because that was the only way to deal with the situation.

He hurried her into the car before she could marshal another protest. Then, as a precaution, he took the alternate route out of the park, using the road where she'd come in that first day. It was only a quarter mile from the main entrance, but it might fool the witches.

He drove with his headlights off down the narrow gravel lane and didn't switch them on until he was a mile down the highway. As far as he could see, there was nobody following them. But, of course, the coven, or whatever they called themselves, could be using the same tactics that he was employing, driving in the dark with their lights off.

Sara sat rigidly in her seat, and he wished to hell he didn't have to drag her to this confrontation. But leaving her alone was not an option. A few minutes later, he pulled up in front of the small house, then went around to open the passenger door.

She stepped out, and they both stood on the sidewalk, staring at the residence.

"It looks so normal," she whispered.

"Yeah."

When a flash of movement caught his attention, he turned his head and saw a police cruiser rolling to a stop beside them.

Shit! He should have driven around the block, looking for the cops. He should have realized that if Delacorte had been here earlier, he might have staked the place out, checking to see if the wolf came back. Unfortunately, his mind had been focused on the guy Sara called the Blackberry Man.

Now they were going to have some explaining to do.

The lawman got out, walking stiffly toward them.

Adam cursed again under his breath.

"What's up?" Delacorte asked.

He stuck with a version of the truth. "The guy who lives here was the man I saw lurking around Sara's house. I want to talk to him, but I don't think it's safe to leave Sara by herself. So I brought her along."

"How do you know it's the guy?"

It was then that Adam knew he'd made another bad mistake. What reason could he give now, a reason that wouldn't tie him to the werewolf?

He was a good talker. But he'd jumped in with an explanation before his brain was fully engaged.

He realized Sara was speaking. "I asked him to bring me here," she said.

Delacorte's attention focused on her with the intensity of a laser beam. "And why is that?" he asked.

He saw her swallow, wondered what in the hell she was going to say. "The other night you asked why the witches might be after me. I didn't want to tell you then because . . . because it was too personal." She dragged in a breath and let it out in a rush. "What I didn't want to tell you then was that I'm Jenna Foster's daughter."

The sheriff gave a tight nod. "I was wondering if that might be true."

"Why?"

"Because you're the right age. Because it looked like somebody wanted you back in that house."

Adam moved to Sara's side and put his arm around her. "You don't have to tell him any more," he muttered.

She turned to him briefly. "I think I do." Addressing the sheriff again, she said, "When I moved into the cabin, I started having memory flashbacks. I didn't know what was happening to me, so I went back to my adopted parents' house and made my mother tell me some things she's kept hidden all these years. That was last night. I was on my way back to the park to talk to Adam about it when the witches forced me off the road."

"And when she told me about the guy hanging around her house, I figured he was one of them," Adam jumped back into the conversation.

Delacorte looked doubtful. "The man who lives here?"

"Yes," Adam answered, hoping the sheriff wasn't going to question the logic gap in their explanation.

"I'll be surprised if he's one of them," Delacorte said.

THE clan gathered in the shadows under the trees. Falcon and his band of followers. Willow. Water Lily. Grizzly. Razorback. Copperhead. Raven's Claw. Greenbriar. Water Buffalo. And Starflower. He was glad the rest of them were here. He needed to feel their presence. They had become part of him in a way that he couldn't explain. All of them. But the one he needed the most was Starflower.

She was the strongest of the women. Almost his equal. And she would play a key role tonight.

They were all naked—except for loincloths. And they would shed those later.

All of them except Starflower were wearing bright designs of paint in streaks and circles all over their bodies, the way they'd been on the nights of the ceremony. Because tonight was another special occasion. This was a crucial test of their power. And a time for celebration, because they were finally turning the tables on one of their enemies. More than one if everything worked out the way it should.

They came through the swamp, drifting like brightly painted birds through the fog that rose from the cooling ground.

A large bulk loomed in the background. The house. But Falcon knew his way around. Which was why he headed for one of the guest houses. Through the window, he saw a man sitting in an easy chair.

"Go get him," he said to Starflower.

She smiled, thrusting out her magnificent naked breasts before she stepped up to the door and knocked.

* * *

ADAM shifted his weight from one foot to the other. "If you don't think the man who lives here is one of the witches, then who is he?"

"Dr. Montgomery didn't just move to town. I remember him when I was a little kid."

Sara looked stunned. "He told me his name. He didn't say he was Dr. Montgomery."

"Well, he was the botany teacher at the community college until he retired a few years ago."

Adam felt a shiver travel down his spine as he remembered an item from the newspaper he'd seen. "The botany teacher . . ." he repeated. "Back in the year Barnette bought the land for Nature's Refuge, Dr. Montgomery was starting a course on herbal remedies at the community college."

THE night air was cool, but Sara felt beads of sweat break out on her skin. She backed away from the two men and darted quickly up the walk. Before she could give herself time to think, she rang the bell. She was aware of Adam and the sheriff climbing the stairs behind her, but all her attention was focused on the slim man with salt-and-pepper hair who had turned on the porch light and was peering through the front window.

When he saw her, his wrinkled face went pale.

But she wasn't seeing him exactly as he was. She was seeing his face without lines. Seeing him with dark hair. Seeing him come striding toward the cabin with a jaunty step, like he was escaping from his everyday existence into a world of magic.

The lock clicked and he opened the door, his eyes fixed on her.

Something she couldn't name passed between them, and in that moment she was sure.

"You figured it out," he said in a raspy voice.

"Yes. You're my father."

He stepped back, and she followed him inside. Adam and Delacorte were behind her, but she didn't take her gaze from the old man.

"How do you know?" he asked.

"I guess I was a little slow. But I finally got it."

He nodded, studying her face. "You look just like your mother, you know. I saw you at the cabin that first time, and for a few moments, I thought it was her, come back from the dead. I've missed her every day since that night. I've missed you."

She fought a choking sensation. It was hard to keep standing in front of this man who had betrayed her and had chosen to keep lying to her. "You abandoned me."

"What choice did I have?"

"You could have taken me to live with you!" Somehow she managed not to shout the words.

"I found you a good home. I sent you money."

"Money. Yes, money," she whispered, her eyes blazing. "Did that help salve your conscience? Did that make up for your being ashamed of me and my mother?"

"I wasn't ashamed of you!"

"You only came to our house when you could sneak away from town."

"You don't understand how it was."

"Why don't you tell me?" she shot back, unable to keep the sarcasm out of her voice.

He looked at her pleadingly. "I used to go off into the swamp gathering plants, just like I do now. That's where I met your mother. She was a ray of sunshine in my life. I couldn't believe that someone so sweet and beautiful could be interested in me."

"So you seduced her. Why didn't you marry her?"

"I would have, if I could. But I was already married!"

Sara struggled to assimilate the information. She'd made certain assumptions, assumptions that weren't quite right.

"Dora, my wife, was sickly. She couldn't give me children. She couldn't give me much of anything. My life was a wasteland. Then I met Jenna and fell in love with her. But I couldn't give up my responsibility. I couldn't leave a sick woman on her own."

She could only stare at him, trying to take it in, her mind forced to reject old assumptions. If he was telling the truth.

From behind her, Delacorte cleared his throat, and she turned briefly to look at him. She'd forgotten that anyone else was in the room with her and her father. "You're the one who got the child out of the cabin," he said.

"Yes."

"You saved her life."

Sara's head was swimming as she listened to the conversation.

Adam stepped toward the man who he'd thought was one of the witches. That was the biggest irony of all, Sara thought. He was no witch. He was her father.

"Do you have something to do with Sara's coming back to town?" Adam demanded.

Montgomery gave a tight nod.

"What?"

He dragged in a breath and let it out. Addressing himself to Sara, he said, "I funded the grant to Granville Pharmaceuticals. I made sure they contacted you. I convinced Austen Barnette it would be good for the town to let you work in the park. And, of course, he liked the idea of making some money by renting Granville that cabin nobody in town wanted." When he finished he looked relieved, like he'd finally gotten a burden off his chest.

"You?" Sara breathed.

"I wanted the association kept secret."

"Why did you bring me back here—to that house?"

He lifted his hand toward her, then let it fall back to his side. "So you could realize your full potential. I knew you had your mother's heritage. I kept pretty close tabs on you. As close as I could. The Westons were good for you. But I was afraid they had failed you in one important way. I was pretty sure they had made you turn away from . . . from your special abilities. So I arranged a job that would bring you to Wayland—to the cabin—because there's something in the swamp— something that brings out the paranormal powers in people who have them."

Delacorte made a sound of agreement.

Adam jumped back into the conversation. "So you wanted her back here. But you picked the wrong time. Others, with a similar heritage, have come back, too. To get revenge on the town. And she's caught in the middle of it."

The old man blanched. "No!"

Delacorte faced the old man. "If you know who they are, I want you to tell us."

Her father—she was still having trouble thinking of him in those terms—looked helpless. "I don't know anything about that."

"The only one of . . . the people with power you knew was Jenna?" Delacorte asked.

"Yes," he answered in a shaky voice. "She kept to herself. She didn't like them. Then, when she was killed, there was only that one little article in the paper. And some bastard cut it out of the volume down at the historical society. But I put it back. I wasn't going to let them wipe her out of existence."

Suddenly, it was all too much for Sara to take in. She felt no affection for this old man. He had never acknowledged her. He had given her up for adoption years ago. Then he had brought her back to town and spied on her, without telling her who he was.

"I need to get out of here," she whispered, turning and stumbling out the door.

ADAM followed her, hurrying to catch up, drawing her close, as she paused at the end of the front walk.

Shivering, she leaned into his warmth.

He wondered exactly what to say. "It must have been a shock, meeting him."

"He brought me back here, but he still couldn't be straight with me."

"He was trying to do what he thought was best."

"Are you defending him?"

"I feel sorry for him."

"Why?"

Adam's voice was raspy now. "He lost the woman he loved. And he gave up his child. He thought that was for the best."

"For his best," Sara answered, pulling away because she needed to be alone now. "Take me back to the park."

"Yes."

Delacorte came out.

"Did you get any more out of him?" Adam asked.

"No."

"Keep us posted if he comes up with any more information."

"You do the same if you find out anything more about . . . the situation."

They both nodded, and Adam helped Sara into the car.

The sky was lightening as they drove back to Nature's Refuge. Adam was thinking that tomorrow was going to be a hell of a day. Maybe he could snatch a nap sometime in the afternoon. Otherwise, he was going to be wasted by closing time.

In the gray light, he shot Sara a glance. She sat rigidly in the front seat, her hands clasped in her lap, unable to rid herself of the tension that was coursing through her.

A few miles out of town, both of them sat forward in their seats as they spotted a figure stumbling along the shoulder of the road.

It was a man running toward them, waving at them to stop.

27

ADAM slowed, staring at the wild man. He was black, dressed in a dark suit and shiny dress shoes, totally inappropriate for an early morning jog, and it took only moments to realize who he was.

"It's James," he said, pressing on the brakes, his mind scrambling for explanations. What the hell was Austen Barnette's butler doing looking like a wild man out here?

"Yes. I remember him from the other day, from that command performance with Barnette."

Adam screeched to a stop on the shoulder, and Austen Barnette's butler came staggering toward them. He stopped beside the SUV, his eyes wild, his breath coming in gasps. His mouth working for several moments before he was able to speak.

"Praise the Lord it's you! They got Mr. Barnette." James sounded frantic. "They drug him off into the swamp."

"Did you call the police?" Adam asked, climbing out of the SUV and going to the man's side.

James shook his head violently. "No. They said they'd kill him if I did." He went on breathlessly. "They cut the phone lines. They did something to my car," he puffed. "I had to come down here to the road. Cars went by, but nobody would stop. Black and white, both. Damn them."

The man looked like he was on the verge of having a heart attack. Adam opened the back door of the SUV and helped him in. The butler flopped onto the seat, leaning his head back for several moments before sitting up straighter.

Adam squatted beside the open door. Sara knelt in the front seat and turned around so that she was facing James.

"Okay, take your time. Tell me what happened," Adam said.

"I was in my little room off the kitchen, where I relax in the evenings waiting for when Mr. Barnette calls. I didn't know anything was happenin'." He stopped and swallowed. "I looked up, and outside the window I saw . . ." He glanced at Sara.

"Tell me what you saw," she encouraged.

In the illumination from the dome light, his dark skin turned ruddy. "A . . . a naked woman. With war paint all over her body."

Sara kept her gaze steady.

Adam felt a jolt of recognition. Naked people with war paint. That sounded a lot like the witches in the swamp. "A white woman?" he asked.

"I only got a flash . . . you know." He stopped and cleared his throat. "But, yes, she was white under all that paint. Then somebody came in and hit me over the head." He reached up to gingerly touch the back of his head. "I guess I was out cold for a while. I came to all hog-tied—lyin' on the floor."

"What about the security guards?" Adam asked.

"Dead."

"Oh, God," Sara breathed.

"How long ago did this happen?" Adam asked.

"An hour ago, I reckon. It took me a while to get free of the ropes. Then I ran around the estate looking for the guards." He stopped and swung his gaze from Adam to Sara and back again. "What am I going to do?"

"Call the sheriff."

James jolted upright. "No! I told you. They'll kill him if we call the law."

"They told you that?"

"They left a note on the table in the front hall." His gaze focused on Adam, and he blinked. "Inside it was addressed to you, but I had to read it!"

Adam touched his shoulder. "Of course you did."

"They said that if you called the police, they would kill Mr. Barnette. They said they wanted half a million dollars. They said you should handle it."

"Let me see it!"

James pulled a folded piece of paper out of his pocket, and Adam snatched it away. "Why me?" he asked.

"Maybe 'cause you run the park for him."

He still didn't know why he'd been singled out, but he scanned the message quickly. "Money?" he muttered, wondering what the hell was going on. Were these people planning to collect a ransom and leave town? It didn't fit in with the image he had of them. He had been assuming they'd come to Wayland to make the old-time residents miserable. But he supposed he could have gotten it all wrong. They could have been planning to disappear and live high on the hog off Austen Barnette's money.

"I picked up the note, and then I didn't know what to do," James was saying. "I jumped in the car, but it wouldn't start. So I ran down the drive."

"We can't keep this a secret. We have to call the cops."

He could see James's teeth chattering. "They'll kill him."

"They may kill him anyway!"

"How can we take the chance?" the butler demanded.

Adam didn't know. He saw Sara reach back and put her hand on James's arm. Softly she said, "They took Mr. Barnette off somewhere. They won't know we called the sheriff. They were just saying that to give themselves a free hand to do what they want."

"You think so?"

"Yes."

Adam looked at James. "I'm going to make the call. Okay?"

"Don't put it off on me," James muttered. "The note was addressed to you. You take the responsibility."

Adam felt his throat tighten. But he knew that they couldn't handle this by themselves. And he was pretty sure Mrs. Waverly down at the historical society wasn't going to be much help. Pulling out his cell phone, he dialed the number that Delacorte had given him. The sheriff answered on the second ring.

"Delacorte here."

"This is Adam Marshall. I just picked up James Lucas along the road. He says that Barnette has been kidnapped. Taken into the swamp."

"The swamp. Jumping Moses! Where are you?"

"About a quarter mile from the estate. And I took the responsibility of calling you. The kidnappers left a note addressed to me, saying they'd kill Barnette if the police got involved. They said they want money, but I don't know if it's true. So maybe you'd better come in some kind of unmarked car. And we'd better meet you up at the house, so we can get James off the road."

"I'll be there as quick as I can."

"Good." Adam turned to James. "He's coming in an unmarked car."

Starting the SUV, Adam headed up the road, then turned into the private drive that led to the house. There were dead men up there, and he didn't want Sara to see them. But he needed to know what had happened, and he couldn't leave her down on the road.

They pulled up in front of the house. "Anything inside that Sara shouldn't see?" Adam asked.

James caught his meaning immediately. "The house is okay."

They all went in. James showed them where he'd been sitting. The remnants of his rope bonds lay on the floor. It looked like the kidnappers had done a half-assed job of tying him up. Apparently, they'd just wanted it to last long enough to give themselves a head start.

Down the hall in the master's den, there were signs of a struggle. Small items from the desk were scattered across the floor, and the desk chair was overturned.

Adam heard a car engine outside and tensed. "Stay here," he ordered.

When he saw a pickup truck pull up in front of the house, he looked around for a weapon. But the man who climbed out was the sheriff, wearing jeans and a flannel shirt. A baseball cap was pulled down over his eyes. Adam glanced toward the tree line. If somebody was spying on them, it wouldn't look like the law had arrived.

Delacorte jumped out and trotted toward Adam. "Lucky your coming along and finding James Lucas," he said.

Adam wondered if there was some kind of hidden meaning in the comment. He chose to answer with a tight nod.

"What do you think happened here?" Delacorte asked.

"Barnette's gone." Adam hesitated for a moment, then gave his theory. "I think the witches kidnapped him."

"The witches? Why the witches?"

"James saw one of them through the window. He described a naked white woman with war paint. That's a pretty good description of the group I saw in the swamp the night they came after me."

Delacorte nodded. "It could be somebody imitating them."

"Could be. But who would do that? Who would know enough to do it?"

Delacorte shrugged. "If it's the witches, what do they want with him?"

"Well, they asked for a ransom. But that doesn't fit what we've discussed about them."

Delacorte nodded again. "Anything else you want to tell me before I talk to James?"

"He says the security guards are dead. He says one's out on the grounds. The other is in the guest house where they were living."

"Hard to get the jump on guys like that."

Adam nodded.

"Okay. I'll get some deputies up here to secure the area." He spoke into the microphone attached to his collar as he followed Adam into the house, then down the hall to the sitting room, a location that the witches didn't seem to have invaded.

Stepping back, he listened to the sheriff question the butler. James recounted the same story that he'd given them. Under Delacorte's careful questioning, a few more details emerged.

Barnette had been nervous that evening. He hadn't been out of the house for several days. He had called his lawyer for some kind of consultation. James had gotten the impression he was making a change in his will.

"For what?" Delacorte demanded.

"I have no idea, sir," James answered with dignity.

"It sounds like he was afraid something was going to happen to him," Adam muttered.

As they spoke, two deputies arrived, also dressed like the sheriff. They fanned out to search the area.

"Does Barnette have any relatives nearby?" Delacorte asked.

James shook his head. "No. But he's got a sister in Atlanta."

"Are they close?"

"No, sir."

Delacorte scowled. "Then there's probably no point in getting her all riled. But we need to set up recording equipment, so we can monitor the phone if they call with a location for dropping the ransom. And it looks like it will have to be here. I'll leave two deputies with you. That's all I can spare."

"They won't know the phone is tapped?" James asked.

"No." Delacorte answered, then gave him some instructions for what to say if he received a call. "Try to keep them on the line as long as possible. Try to get them to let you talk to Barnette. Tell them you want to make sure he's okay."

Adam listened, growing increasingly restless as the conversation progressed, because he didn't really think the ransom was the point.

He was pacing back and forth across the room when he finally reached the end of his patience.

"The longer we wait, the less chance there is that we find Barnette alive. I'd say we can risk two guys in the swamp if they look like they were out there for a nature walk or something." He nodded toward Delacorte. "You and me. Your clothing is good. But a green shirt would work better. Or a camouflage outfit. I'll wear something similar."

The sheriff considered the plan, then bobbed his head. "Okay, we'll use cell phones. If one of us finds Barnette or one of the . . ." He stopped short and started again. "If one of us finds the kidnappers, he calls the line I'll have set up for information. But it's a lot of territory for two guys to cover."

"Not that far. They're limited to the distance Barnette can walk. Or they can carry him."

"What about by boat? They could go to one of the islands."

"Let's assume they aren't into boats. They didn't use them the other night. I think they're not comfortable deep in the swamp, that they'll stick to the fringes."

Adam turned and focused on James. "I work for Mr. Barnette. I want to help find him. But I can't go looking for him unless I know Sara is safe. I think the people who took Barnette have been threatening her, as well. Are there some relatives of yours in town where you can take her? That's the last place where the kidnappers would look for her."

James blinked. "You went to take Dr. Weston down to the east end of town?" he said, referring to the black community.

"I'd be honored to go there," Sara said.

Delacorte looked thoughtful. "Yeah, it's a good idea."

FALCON stepped back and looked at the old man whose hands were tied around the back of a tree. Austen Barnette pressed his shoulders against the trunk and stared wide-eyed at the group of naked, painted

figures around him, then brought his gaze back to Falcon. He was trying to keep his voice steady as he said, "Your name is John Ringell.
You work for me. How dare you do this." The words were imperious,
but the tone was faltering.

Falcon laughed, conscious of the clan members in back of him.
"You're not the lord of the manor out here. Yeah. I go by that name
sometimes. But not today. Today you can call me Falcon."

The captive stared at him, trying to take in what was happening.
"Why are you doing this?"

Falcon lifted one shoulder. "You killed Jenna Foster."

The wrinkled face contorted with fear. "No!"

Falcon kept his voice mild. "Of course you did. It's all written
down in those secret records from the historical society. The ones you
thought were locked up. But I know how to open a safe. Pretty stupid
of you to keep that stuff around. What, do you have a death wish or
something?"

"I thought . . ."

"What?"

"Those records were supposed to be . . . gone."

Falcon snorted, "Well, it's too bad for you they were in that safe—
big as life and twice as plain. Maybe you weren't the one who tossed
that firebomb into her cabin. But you were the one who stirred people
up against her."

"No!"

It was time to make this man face the consequences of his actions.
Falcon stepped forward and gave him a good slap across the face.

"Don't lie to me! You were the leader of the God-fearing people in
town. You rented her that cabin so you could keep an eye on her. And
when you decided she had done evil, you whipped up the town
against her."

Barnette goggled at him.

"You killed her, and you and your good buddies drove the others
like her out of town. That's how you got the land for your damn park.
I always wondered why my uncle sold that property. But I've put two
and two together—and they add up to over three hundred acres he let
you practically steal, so he'd have money to move his family. That's
true, isn't it?"

The old man moaned.

"Say it!"

"Yes. It's true. I wanted that land to benefit the good people in town. I opened the park to bring money to the area."

"How much other stuff like that did you pull?"

"Nothing."

"Sure."

Barnette's eyes filled with tears. "Let me go," he pleaded. "I can pay you."

"How much?"

"A million dollars."

"That's very generous of you, but money's not the point. We don't want your damn money."

"But I heard you say you were leaving a ransom note."

"That was the story we wanted James to believe. But we knew Adam Marshall wouldn't fall for it. We knew he'd come out here looking for you. And when he does, we'll be ready for him."

He turned to Razorback. "Light the fire."

The old man cringed. "Are you going to burn me?"

Falcon laughed. "You burned her up. Maybe that would be poetic justice; but actually, we have other plans for you."

28

WHEN the fire was blazing, Falcon nodded toward Starflower. She brought a long stick with a wad of cloth at the end, cloth that had been soaked in a drugged solution.

Everyone in the clan watched eagerly as she thrust it into the fire, watching it smolder.

The first hints of aromatic smoke drifted toward him, and he took a breath, smiling as he looked over at Barnette. The smoke didn't work quite so well for them now as it had the first few times. The effect was less, and they were going to have to find a way to boost the pleasure. But it was still potent, and he knew that it would hit the old man hard because this was his first time.

"You'll like this," he murmured.

"What is it?" the captive quavered.

Falcon laughed. "Something to put you in the right frame of mind for the festivities."

"No. Please."

"Don't waste your breath," Falcon growled, then turned away.

Starflower brought the brand toward her face, inhaling deeply. Her eyes took on a dreamy look as she held out the offering to the rest of them.

Each in turn, they leaned over to drink in the smoke.

Falcon was last. After he had taken his first portion, he turned and walked toward Barnette, thrusting the brand into his face, forcing him to breathe the smoke.

Starflower had come up behind Falcon, caressing the bare skin of his back, trailing her hand down to his hips and then his buttocks. He felt himself getting hard and looked back toward her.

"Later. We'll have fun later. But business before pleasure."

She made a pouting face but took her hand off his body.

Falcon turned his attention back to the old man who coughed and swivelled his head away. But there was no escape from the inevitable. All Falcon had to do was move the stick so it was in his face again. He watched with satisfaction as the old man's eyes glazed over.

With a smile, he picked up the knife that he'd left on the ground near the tree. "I think you're overdressed for this party, don't you?" he asked, inserting his knife into the fabric of Barnette's shirt and ripping it open.

SARA listened to the men talking about their rescue plans. She was confident she'd be safe with James's sister, but she wasn't so sure about Adam. He'd done enough already. She wanted to beg him to stay out of the swamp today. But she imagined he wouldn't listen to her.

She turned to face him. "I want to talk to you about this."

"About what?" he demanded.

"Can we have some privacy?"

"I'd like the sheriff to be in on the discussion," he answered, his tone brusque.

She swung her gaze to Delacorte. There were reasons why she wanted to keep the conversation with Adam private. Like, was he going into the swamp as a wolf or a man? But how could he go as a wolf, if he was supposed to be staying in communication by cell phone.

It struck her then how much her thinking had changed over the past few days. She had accepted the wolf because the wolf was part of Adam.

She studied him now, convinced that he was deliberately making sure she couldn't talk him out of looking for Barnette. She sighed. "Okay. Did you talk to the sheriff about what happened the last time you encountered those people in the swamp?"

"Yes."

"So he knows that they were having some kind of ceremony using drugged smoke. He knows that the smoke made you high. He knows that they chased you through the underbrush and almost killed you."

From the corner of her eye, she saw James's eyes bug out, as he took in the exchange.

Adam's gaze had narrowed. "I told him what happened. The smoke was a problem, but I don't think it will be a problem now."

"Why not?"

She saw him hesitate for a second before going on, and she wanted to challenge that hesitation. But he was already answering the question.

"Because they have a kidnap victim. It's not like the last time when they were having a party."

His reasoning made sense, but she wanted to tell him she was still worried. She wanted to beg him to keep out of it. But she knew that he wasn't just going after the people who had abducted Barnette. He was also going after the people who had tried to harm her. Probably the sheriff knew that, too.

She gave a tight nod, feeling like she had no choice but to agree. And once she said the word, the plans proceeded with lightning speed.

James called his sister, and after a few minutes conversation, she offered to take Sara in.

As James put down the phone, Sara looked at Adam, wanting more than ever to be alone with him. "Can you drive me down there?" she asked.

Delacorte shook his head. "It would be better if I did it. That way you'll be introduced to Tyreen by a neighbor."

"Who happens to be the sheriff," Adam pointed out.

Sara nodded, understanding the wisdom of that approach. Still she didn't like the look of relief on Adam's face. He didn't want her to beg him to stay out of danger.

"We'd better go," Delacorte said.

"I wish I could change my clothes," Sara murmured. "I've been dressed in this outfit since . . ." She stopped short, unwilling to give away that she had been waiting up for Adam to come home from his spying trip into town.

Lord, it seemed like a thousand years ago since he'd tracked her father to his house.

She glanced at Delacorte. He was waiting for her. Letting him wait for another few moments, she crossed to Adam and reached for him. He went still for several heartbeats, then he raised his arms and hugged her to him.

She wiped their audience from her mind, focusing only on Adam as she tipped her head up and pressed her mouth to his. He looked shocked, then settled into the kiss. And she felt the familiar consuming passion that she always felt when they came together.

But he only allowed himself a few seconds of the intimate contact before he raised his head.

"Be careful," she ordered.

"I will," he said, the answer sounding automatic.

"Adam. I mean it. I don't know what I'll do if anything happens to you."

His face took on a look of sudden intensity. She felt him clench his hands on her arms before asking, "Does that mean you'll marry me when I come back?"

Totally unprepared for the question, she gasped. "That's not playing fair!"

"I want it settled before I go. I want to be thinking about how much I'll appreciate coming back to you."

She knew what he was doing—manipulating her. Yet she was willing to be manipulated because the crisis had done wonders to clarify her thinking. "Yes," she breathed.

He hugged her tighter with a kind of savage triumph, almost crushing the breath out of her. When he released her, she felt momentarily dizzy. Then the world snapped back into focus. A few feet away, she heard two men shuffling their feet and clearing their throats.

She looked around and blinked, seeing the bemused expression on Delacorte's face.

"Good going, son," he said with a note of awe in his voice.

Her own face flamed. "Let's go," she muttered, marching toward the door.

"You go on out," he said, "I want to have a word with the sheriff."

She glared at him. "You don't want to be alone with me. But you want to talk to him in private?"

"Yes."

SARA had left the house angry, angry with Adam for keeping secrets, even if he thought it was for her own good.

She sat tensely in the front seat of the sheriff's pickup truck. But as they rode toward town, fatigue won out over tension. She'd been up all night, and now she slumped against the passenger door. One moment she had closed her eyes. In the next, she felt the truck come to a stop.

Looking up, she saw she was in a driveway between a beat-up station wagon and a large, fenced backyard where two dogs barked and jumped at the chain links. One was a shepherd. The other some kind of standard poodle mix. To her right, Sara saw a small woman with skin the color of coffee with a nice dollop of cream. She looked to be in her mid-thirties. Dressed in jeans and a baggy red sweater, she was standing inside the fence on the back porch of the two-story clapboard house.

That must be Tyreen Vincent, James's sister, she thought.

Delacorte looked around, then turned to Sara. "Best you get into the house quickly. I don't want the neighbors wondering what you're doing here."

What a white lady is doing here, she silently edited his statement. But she kept the observation to herself.

Tyreen was looking down at them, an uncertain expression on her face. The sheriff had told Sara that she lived there with her husband, Noah, and her children, Trinity and Isaac.

More than a bit uncomfortable, Sara took a tentative step forward. She was imposing on these people. And she didn't even know how long she would have to stay. Would someone be able to get her a change of clothing from Nature's Refuge? She hoped so.

The yard had been turned into a dirt patch by the dogs. They were still barking and jumping, and Sara eyed them uncertainly.

"Amos and Andy won't hurt you," Tyreen said as she hurried down the back walk.

"Amos and Andy!" Despite the circumstances, Sara grinned, glad that she'd landed with someone who had a sense of humor. She reached to open the gate, then stepped inside, staggering back as one of the big dogs leaped up, put its paws on her shoulders and licked her face.

"Amos! Mind you manners," Tyreen called out as she pulled at the dog's collar.

"It's okay. I love dogs," Sara told her as Amos detached himself from her shoulders. "And I love your names, boys." She continued talking to the dogs, partly because she did like animals, and partly because she knew that they were helping to break the ice with their owner.

"Let's get inside," Delacorte said.

"Yes. Right."

Leaving the canines outside, they stepped into a country kitchen with pine cabinets, a vinyl tile floor, and a long trestle table over at one side.

"I'm sorry for imposing on you," Sara said.

"No. This is fine. I know James wouldn't ask if it weren't important."

Delacorte nodded. "I told you over the phone that this visit has to be kept confidential for the time being. We're in the middle of a kidnapping case. And Dr. Weston—"

"Sara. Please call me Sara," she interjected quickly. "You must be Tyreen. I appreciate your letting me stay here. I don't want to be any trouble to you." She held out her hand, and the other woman shook it.

"The kids are going to be home from school at three-thirty. They're going to tell their friends that a white lady is staying at our house."

"We don't want the kidnappers to know that the police are involved," Delacorte broke in. "Maybe she can hide out in one of the bedrooms for a while. She's been up for hours, and she fell asleep on the ride over."

"If that wouldn't be too much trouble," Sara said quickly.

"It's a good solution. I can take you up to the guest bedroom, and tell the kids we've got some unexpected company. After you come down, I'll keep them inside."

"Yes. Thanks."

Delacorte shifted his weight from one foot to the other. "I'd best be going."

As he turned to leave, Sara reached out and put a hand on his arm. "Call me the minute you know something."

"I will."

Her hand dropped away, and he opened the door, leaving her alone with this woman she had just met. A woman who was taking in a stranger out of kindness and probably a sense of duty.

"So, can you tell me what's going on?" she asked.

There was curiosity, too, Sara amended her assessment. She swallowed. "I wish I could. But the bottom line for me is that the man I love is going off with Sheriff Delacorte to look for the kidnappers. And I could put him in more danger than he's already in by talking about the situation."

The black woman's face contorted. "Oh, you poor thing."

"I'd like to be alone for a while. Then, later I can help you get dinner ready."

"There's no need for that."

"I don't want to be any extra work."

Tyreen led the way upstairs to a small room that was dominated by a double bed. "It's not very plush," she said.

"It's perfect. Just let me borrow your bathroom, and I'll flop into bed and get some sleep."

ADAM stood at the edge of a patch of brackish ground and shifted the knapsack on his shoulder. Sara was safe. He couldn't have come here without being sure of that. The knowledge that she was out of danger gave him the freedom to concentrate on what he had to do now.

He and Delacorte had left as soon as the sheriff had gotten back from stashing Sara. Before moving out, they discussed where to look. Delacorte had chosen the area where the campfire had been that first time. Probably he thought that was the most likely place to find the witches. Adam didn't agree. He was pretty sure they would be somewhere else, somewhere less obvious.

He had a cell phone with him, and he had promised to use it. But getting help would depend on his being able to describe his location, which might be a problem deep in the swamp.

He would have liked to go on this hunting expedition as a wolf. But that was out of the question.

He sniffed the wind and caught a scent he had smelled before. The smoke that had turned his head muzzy. In front of Sara, he had told the others that he didn't expect it was going to be a problem.

Actually, he'd been thinking that the witches might well use the stuff. And if they did, it would lead him to them. But at the same time, he'd have to be damn careful. The fumes had overpowered him last time. This time it wasn't going to happen, because he'd come prepared. He hoped.

First he took a quick breath to tell him the direction the poisoned fumes were coming from. It was still far away, its tendrils reaching toward him, pulling at him.

The effect was dangerous. Not just because it muddled his mind. It was addictive, and he was more susceptible than most, because of his physiology.

Too damn bad.

Before the probing tendrils could choke off his rational thoughts, he took a gas mask out of his knapsack and pulled it over his head, adjusting the nosepiece and the straps so it was comfortable.

Just before they'd left the mansion, he'd told the sheriff it might be a good idea to bring along a mask. He hadn't wanted to talk about that in front of Sara because he hadn't wanted to alarm her.

He'd thought he was being clever by thinking of the protective gear. He'd read a lot about gas masks on the Internet before he'd bought one. In fact, it had been in the package Delacorte had brought into his office a couple of days ago.

It was a good model. At least the reviews said it was good.

But he'd never used one before. A surge of claustrophobia made him grit his teeth like when he tried the thing on. But it hadn't been quite so bad.

Stop it, he ordered himself. This isn't any worse than a snorkeling mask. You've snorkeled on a couple of vacations.

Yeah, he'd snorkeled plenty of times. And this wasn't anything like the same sensation.

A snorkeling mask only fits over the front of the face. This thing enclosed a lot more of his head.

He took a breath, fighting a choking sensation.

"Stop it," he ordered again, this time speaking the words aloud because he needed to hear them, as he plunged into the swamp.

29

SARA hesitated for a few moments. She needed to lie down, but she wanted to be ready to leave the moment she found out Adam was safe.

So she kicked off her shoes, then folded back the spread on the double bed and lay down. As she closed her eyes, she told herself she had to relax, despite the pain pounding in her head.

Adam had come back to her safe and sound when he'd gone into town to look for the witches. But now he had marched off into danger again and she'd wanted to beg him to stay out of the line of fire. Especially when he was risking his life for a man who might not be worth it.

Unable to lie still, she sat up and fluffed the pillows behind her head. Her eyes stared unfocused at the striped wallpaper on the wall.

She hadn't liked Austen Barnette when she'd met him. Despite how she felt about him, she knew he was in a horrible situation. Unfortunately, that situation had put Adam in danger.

Pressing her fist to her mouth, she struggled not to scream out her fear and frustration.

She had to stop thinking about Adam, had to stop worrying about him.

So she focused again on her father. She still hadn't gotten over the shock of finding out his identity. And she still didn't know how she felt about him. He'd abandoned her all those years ago.

Well, not abandoned, exactly. But it had felt like that to the little girl he'd left to the kindness of strangers.

She'd grown to love those strangers. They had given her a warm, supportive home. A good foundation in life. But she'd always known a piece of her heritage was missing.

She'd met her father tonight, and she'd walked away from him because she'd been in shock. Could she forgive him? She didn't know. But he had brought her back to Wayland. He had made contact with her, although he hadn't said who he was.

Maybe he'd been afraid she'd reject him, which was what it looked like she *had* done. But when she thought about it more objectively, she could see it would be a terrible shame if she never got to know him as an adult.

Her mind made another leap back to the Olakompa. Adam and the sheriff were out there somewhere. She kept picturing the vast wilderness area. The trees blocking out the light. An alligator sliding into dark water.

Then she was seeing a group of naked men and women, their bodies painted with bright slashes and circles, dancing wildly. This time the campfire wasn't the only focus. This time, as they gyrated, they also circled around a tree. And tied to the trunk was a naked man, his face a mask of terror.

She gasped when she saw it was Barnette.

There was no way to know if the image was real or if she had made it up. But it stayed firmly in her brain like a piece of festering shrapnel.

THE dancing stopped, and a hush fell over the group. Falcon stepped up to the old man who was sagging against the bonds that held him.

He struggled to stand up straighter as the leader of the clan approached him. Falcon counted that as a mark of respect—for all the good it would do the old bastard.

"Listen up," he said.

Barnette tried to focus on him. The smoke had whacked him out some, but not completely.

"You didn't give Jenna Foster a chance," Falcon said. "But we're going to give you one. We're going to let you loose. We'll give you a head start. And if you can keep us from finding you until it gets dark, we'll let you go."

Barnette struggled to keep his eyes in focus.

With the delicacy of a surgeon, Falcon cut the old man's bonds and pulled the rope away.

"Go on. Git!" he ordered.

Barnette wavered on his feet as he looked around at the circle of faces.

Then he made a moaning sound and staggered off into the underbrush.

"How long do we give him?" Copperhead asked.

"It won't be any fun if we go after him right away."

"We could lose him," Razorback muttered.

"You think so? I think he's going to leave a trail an elephant would envy."

The rest of the clan snickered. Razorback flushed and clamped his teeth together.

PAUL Delacorte kicked at the cold ashes of the campfire. He had been sure the witches would be here again. But he had been wrong. And now he had no idea where to look for them.

He removed the phone from the holder on his belt and dialed the private line that would connect him to Adam.

After several rings, the park ranger answered. "I can't stay on long," he said.

"What's up?"

"I had to take my gas mask off to talk to you. And I have to put it back on pretty soon."

"You're using it?"

"Yeah. There's drugged smoke here."

"Where?"

"Near that cabin where Sara was living. You'll know by the fumes. Gotta go."

The line went dead.

Paul sucked in a deep breath. He smelled something strange. Something evil. He remembered Adam's description of the stuff. It was nasty.

Unpacking his gas mask, he pulled it over his head.

ADAM wavered on his feet and shot out a hand to steady himself against a tree trunk. He'd had the mask partially off for less than a minute, and his head was swimming.

Shit. He shouldn't have answered the phone. But he'd had to do it in case Delacorte had some important information.

Now his brain felt like cottage cheese. He sat down heavily, staring off into the distance, trying to remember where he was and why he was here. And the damn Halloween mask over his face was choking off his breath. What he needed was air.

He reached up to free his nose and mouth. Then he stayed his hand.

The thing that felt like it was cutting off his oxygen was a gas mask. He'd put it on because of the drugged smoke. And he'd gotten a couple breaths of the stuff just then. Only a few breaths, and his brain had gone mushy. Because it was worse for him than for other people. It took only a little bit to turn him into a space cadet.

He closed his eyes and leaned his head back against the tree trunk, thinking of Sara. Thinking about how much he wanted to be with her. To be holding her in his arms.

She should be here with him. She'd like the smoke. It made him feel really good. She would feel good, too. The witches had used it for sex. That sounded like fun.

He blinked. Not good. Bad. This stuff was bad, and he wasn't responding normally.

He hadn't gotten too much of it. Just a little. He was going to be okay if he just sat here for a few minutes.

SARA'S body jerked, then went rigid. Another picture leaped into her mind. Once again she saw the wild, natural landscape of the Olakompa. But the dancers were gone.

The scene was calm. Still.

She recognized the location because it was right near her cabin. Well, not the cabin where she was living now. The cabin that belonged to Austen Barnette.

In the center of the mental picture was a figure sitting with his back propped against a tree trunk. A man, wearing a camouflage shirt and pants. But his face . . . his face was so strange: elongated like an animal's muzzle, but with the features obscured.

She made a small, strangled noise. Her head pounded as if someone were using it for a drum set. Her vision blurred, but she struggled to understand what she was seeing.

Was it Adam—his face turning to that of a wolf? No. That was no wolf. As she tried to take in more details, she focused on the man's hair. Black hair. Cut just a little too long.

It *was* Adam. Or someone who looked just like him from the forehead up.

And there was something over his face. Something she'd seen before in a movie or on television.

She wasn't sure what it was. Some kind of protection? Then the answer leaped into her mind. It was a gas mask, attached by straps that went over the top and sides of his head.

She watched another figure appear in the scene. A naked man staggering out of the swamp, staggering toward Adam, screaming something she couldn't hear.

Mud coated his feet and legs. Long scratches ran down his thighs and across his chest. His gray hair was matted to his head. His features were contorted with terror and pain. But she knew who it was: Austen Barnette.

She had seen him with the witches. Now he was fleeing through the swamp. Naked as the day he was born. Had he somehow gotten away?

He ran up to Adam, clutching at him, clawing at the mask that obscured his face.

Adam raised his hands, but they seemed to move in slow motion. She watched as the mask came off his face so that she could see his reddened skin and the wide, vacant look in his eyes.

She was out of bed and pulling on her shoes before she knew what she was going to do.

RAZORBACK poured water on the fire.

"What the hell are you doing?" Falcon demanded.

"Getting rid of the damn smoke."

"Why?" the leader of the clan demanded.

"'Cause I was thinkin' we need to be on top of the situation here. People could be looking for Barnette. What if they find us, and we're all wasted?"

"There's no *they*. There's only Marshall."

"He could have figured out we don't give a shit about the money. He could have gotten help."

Some of the clan murmured their agreement. Falcon's eyes narrowed. Razorback was challenging his authority. And that was bad. Bad for him. Bad for the group. But maybe the guy was right. Maybe they'd had enough of the smoke.

"Come on, we've given Barnette enough time. Let's go find out if a gator's got him. Or if we need to finish him off ourselves."

There were shouts of agreement from the clan. Falcon had them back in hand. But over Starflower's head, his gaze met Razorback's eyes, and he knew this wasn't the end of the rebellion.

* * *

SARA came pounding down the stairs and into the kitchen, her eyes wide. Tyreen must have been keeping a lookout for her, or maybe she'd simply heard the heavy footsteps, because she came running toward the back of the house.

"Honey, what's wrong?" she asked.

Sara dragged in a shuddering breath. "Adam is in trouble!"

"I didn't hear the phone ring. Did you get a call on your cell phone?"

Sara swallowed, thinking about what she could possibly say that wasn't going to sound completely crazy. "I . . . I had a dream . . ." she said.

"You dreamed something bad?"

"Yes. But I know it's true! Adam is in trouble. I have to go to him."

When the woman only stared at her, Sara blurted, "My . . . my dreams can be about things that are really happening."

Tyreen spoke gently. "Honey, you need to calm yourself. You're under a lot of pressure right now. And your imagination is working overtime."

Sara clenched her hands at her sides. She *knew* that Adam was in terrible danger. She also knew with absolute certainty that there wasn't going to be any way to convince Tyreen of that.

Sara's gaze flicked to the black purse sitting on the kitchen counter—and the key ring next to it—before she brought her attention back to Tyreen. "I . . . I'm really worried . . ." she murmured. "Could you call Sheriff Delacorte and find out what's happening?"

"We don't want to bother him when he's out on a kidnapping investigation."

"Please. Call him!"

Sara waited with her heart pounding, waited to see if the other woman would do what she asked.

30

TYREEN gave a small nod. "All right. I know you have to be jumpin' out of your skin. If it will make you feel better, I'll call the sheriff. But I left his card in the den."

Sara spoke around the knot in her throat. "Okay."

Waiting until Tyreen had disappeared from sight, Sara grabbed the keys and exited the kitchen, closing the door quietly behind her. She'd never stolen anything in her life. And she wouldn't be starting now. But she needed the woman's car. Because she had to get to Adam before it was too late.

As soon as she was out of the house, the dogs ran toward her, and she stopped to speak to them in a soothing voice. Then she ran to the car. Climbing in, she locked the door behind her and inspected the keys. When she found a standard ignition key, she jammed it into the slot and turned. The car shuddered, but finally the engine caught, sending a puff of black smoke shooting from the exhaust pipe.

Sara was backing out of the driveway when she heard Tyreen shouting at her. "Wait! Come back. What do you think you're doing?"

Sara stepped on the brake, needs and emotions warring inside her. Then she rolled down the window and stuck her head out. "I'm sorry. I need the car. Tell Sheriff Delacorte that I've gone to my old house. That's where they are. In the swamp near my old house."

She thrust her head back. Then, teeth clenched, she pulled onto the road, hearing the tires squeal as she reversed direction and sped away. She hated what she was doing. But she saw no other option. Adam was in trouble and she had to go to him.

But now it was hard to drive, hard to see what she was doing, because of the phantom scenes flashing before her eyes, scenes of what was happening in the swamp.

*   *   *

THERE was no problem following the old man's trail. As Falcon had predicted, he had crashed through the underbrush with the grace of a wounded ox.

They splashed through shallow water, then came out onto a wide, dry stretch of ground. Across the clearing, the old man's skinny white body was crouched beside a tree trunk.

It took several moments for Falcon to figure out what he was seeing. Another man dressed in fatigue pants and a shirt sat propped against the tree.

He must have caught a flicker of movement from their direction because he looked up.

Falcon and the clan stared at him.

"It's Adam Marshall," Starflower crowed. "I told you he'd come looking for the old bastard. Kill him."

"Wait." Falcon pointed toward the seated figure. "Look at him. He's not moving. I think he's in no shape to fight us."

"You're taking a chance," Razorback muttered.

"I want to do the old man first. Give him what he deserves for leading that gang of townspeople against Jenna Foster because he branded her a witch, then running my uncle out of town and grabbing his land for that damn park. When we're through with him, we can take care of Marshall." He glanced at the figure slumped against the tree. "He's not going anywhere."

Barnette must have heard them because he turned and screamed, then staggered away. Falcon captured Starflower's hand. The others saw what he was doing and reached for the hand of someone next to them.

He waited until they were centered, until the clan was working together in harmony. Then he stretched out his free arm toward Barnette. The group's power flowed through him, through his mind as he hurled an invisible thunderbolt at the pitiful, naked figure.

He felt like the god Thor, raining destruction down from heaven. Barnette cried out and fell to his side, then lay still.

"Make sure he's dead," Falcon said to Water Buffalo. The other man loped over to the huddled body while Falcon strode toward Marshall.

The ranger raised his head and blinked, staring at them with dull eyes.

                                    *   *   *

PAUL was in the pickup speeding toward the back entrance to the park when his cell phone rang.

"Delacorte here," he answered as he pressed the Receive button.

"This is Tyreen. That crazy woman you left here stole my car."

Paul's hands clenched on the wheel. "Why? What happened?"

"She came tear-assing downstairs, saying that she knew her man was in trouble. I asked her how she knew, and she said she'd dreamed it. Sure! Then she tricked me into going and calling you. While I was looking for your number, I heard my car start." Tyreen stopped and made a huffing sound. "She yelled a message out the window before she took off."

"What message?"

"She said to tell Sheriff Delacorte, 'I've gone to my old house. That's where they are. In the swamp near my old house.' "

"Okay. Thanks!"

"Paul what the hell is going on?"

"Tell you later." He hung up and tried to get Adam on the line.

FALCON walked toward Adam Marshall. "Good of you to join the party," he said to the ranger in a conversational tone. Before he could say anything else, a ringing noise made him start. A cell phone. Marshall tipped his head to one side, listening. Then, slowly he reached into his pocket and brought it out.

Falcon snatched it away from him and threw it into a pool of water where the ringing cut off as it sank from view.

"Any other toys on you that we ought to know about?" he asked.

Marshall's lips moved, but no sound came out.

"Like the smoke, do you?" Falcon asked.

Razorback stooped and picked up something black and rubbery on the ground. "He was wearing a gas mask. Lucky for us he took it off."

Falcon lifted the mask from the other man's hand and tossed it away before turning his attention back to Marshall. "He's overdressed for the party. Strip him."

"I want him dead," another voice rose from behind him. The speaker was Starflower. "Once he's dead, we can get Weston, too."

"Not yet. I want to know what he knows." He turned to Razor-back. "Go back and get the rope. I want him secured."

Marshall said something, but it sounded like gibberish.

"Send one of the women!" Razorback challenged.

"I told you to do it."

There was a moment of silence while the two men stared at each other. Then Razorback shrugged and started back to the campfire.

Falcon bent over the ranger. "I'm the leader of this clan. You can call me Falcon," he said. "If you can talk. You can beg me for mercy."

SARA sped past the cabin and continued down the road, then turned off onto a side trail. Her teeth were clamped together to keep herself from screaming.

She pulled to a halt just before the trail disappeared into a flat stretch of black water and started running into the swamp.

Jumbled images were still coming to her.

Austen Barnette lay crumpled on the ground. Unmoving. Probably dead.

Adam still sat propped against the tree trunk, the group of painted witches standing over him.

She watched them kneel down, watched them tearing at his clothing.

God, what were they going to do to him?

She ran toward the clearing where the scene was happening. The last time she'd confronted these people, they'd been wearing hoods over their heads. Now they were wearing nothing. Just as she reached the campfire, a figure loomed in front of her. One of the naked, painted men. One of the people who had hurt her.

Only now he was alone.

He stopped short, staring at her with malevolent, glittering eyes. Before she could react, he attacked—not physically but with one of those thunderbolts that made the inside of her skull feel like she'd been strapped into the electric chair and someone had pulled the switch.

She struggled to stay on her feet. Struggled to find a way to protect herself from him. Because if she couldn't do it, he would kill her.

*   *   *

ADAM lay on the ground, forcing himself not to react to Falcon's goading words, or to the feel of hands moving roughly over him, stripping the clothing from his body, tearing fabric and popping buttons.

They had killed Barnette, and there had been nothing he could do about it. They planned to kill him, too. They had used Barnette to lure him out here. And he had walked right into the trap.

He recognized two of them. One was the workman he'd seen that afternoon at Barnette's house, the one who called himself Falcon. The other was the sexpot who had come to the park and tried to get into his pants. Falcon had addressed her as Starflower.

She was tearing at his pants now. But her motives were a bit different. She wanted him naked and vulnerable.

He concentrated on keeping his body limp. For a while there, his mind had been filled with the smoke. Thoughts had floated in a cloud of cotton wool. But the drug had drifted away, and now he was only a little impaired. At least he hoped so.

He kept his lids lowered and his mouth slack as they tore off his shirt and pants. Then his undershorts and shoes and socks.

By the time they had finished, he was already chanting, his voice low, barely audible.

"*Taranis. Epona. Cerridwen.*" He tried to repeat the phrase as one of them pushed him onto his back and kicked him in the midsection.

The chant turned into a groan of pain. He lost his place and had to start all over again, wondering if he was going to manage the change under these circumstances.

Another of the bastards aimed a kick at his head, and he somehow ducked away from the blow.

Hands clenched against the pain, he focused on getting the words out.

"*Ga. Feart. Cleas. Duais. Aithriocht. Go gcumhdai is dtreorai na deithe thu.*"

The crowd of people had sprung into savage action, flailing at him with hands and feet, making it all but impossible for him to focus.

"What the hell are you saying?" one of them shouted.

He didn't answer. He was beyond speech. The change was on him now. His vocal cords would no longer form human sounds.

One of the women screamed. Then another. All of them jumped back as his body jerked and contorted. Wolf hair sprouted on his skin, covering his body in a thick, silver-tipped pelt. The color and structure of his eyes changed as he rolled over so he could stand on all fours. He was no longer a man but an animal, far more suited to the swamp than the crowd of painted, naked people who surrounded him.

"Jesus Christ! He's the wolf who went after us. He's the damn wolf!" one of them shouted.

"Run!"

Yes he screamed in his mind. *Yes, you bastards. Run.*

Howling his rage aloud, he sprang at the man who had kicked him, tearing at a naked thigh, finding that he wasn't in quite as good shape as he'd thought. His movements were slower, more sluggish than they should be.

He could hear someone shouting, but he was too absorbed in the chase to pay attention to the words.

People were scattering, screaming. He charged a woman and brought her to the ground, slashing at her arm and leg. Then he rounded on a man, dragging him to his knees.

He was slashing the man's naked back when something hit him. A blow to the back of his head that sent him sprawling.

He thought at first that one of them had thrown a rock at him. But it wasn't something physical, he realized. It was like a mental jolt to his brain. Like what Sara had described. Like when he'd thought they were shooting at him. Only now he knew for sure that had just been an illusion his mind had manufactured to cope with what it hadn't understood.

He turned and faced the enemy. Three of them were holding hands, their eyes bright with concentration. It was the workman guy, Miss Sexpot, and another one of the women.

He felt another invisible blow slam into him and fell back, gasping with the pain.

He had watched them kill Barnette like this. They were going to do the same thing to him, because teeth and claws weren't going to cut it against their thunderbolts. His only hope was to get them before they got him. But he couldn't do it. When he tried to stagger toward them, he couldn't make his legs cooperate.

He sank to the ground, panting, trying to keep his brain from dissolving under the force of the pain. He was going to die here in this patch of swamp, because the hatred radiating from these people was going to destroy him.

He longed to disappear into unconsciousness to make the pain go away. But he knew that the moment he let go, he was giving in to death. So he focused all of his energy on keeping hold of consciousness. It was all he could do. He knew that it wasn't nearly enough.

31

BY some miracle, the agony suddenly lessened. Somehow Adam managed to raise his head in time to see the three witches jolt as though they'd been hit by rifle bullets. The woman he didn't recognize fell to her knees. The workman and the sexpot whirled around, as if to face another enemy. Had Delacorte found him?

Not the sheriff. Adam's heart stopped, then started pounding hard as he saw Sara standing beside a large tree, her eyes focused on the group.

The sky had been a clear blue moments earlier. Now storm clouds swirled over her, turning the whole scene dark and ominous. Trees swayed as the wind picked up bits of plant material and sent them flying through the air.

He wanted to howl in fear and frustration.

Sara was here! He'd made sure she was safe. He'd counted on that. But now she'd rushed into danger to help him.

She must be fighting the witches. And whatever she'd done had broken their hold on him. The pain still pounded in his head. But he could move now.

He saw Sara sag against the tree, saw the witches move from their frozen positions. The two still on their feet, Falcon and Starflower, bent to the other woman and pulled her up, pulled her toward Sara.

Lightning flashed in the clouds above them. He heard Sara gasp and knew they had hit her with another one of their mental artillery shells.

Anger surged through him. With a savage snarl, he gathered his remaining strength and sprang, taking down the one named Falcon, clawing at his back, biting at his shoulders, mauling for no other purpose than to inflict pain on the bastard who was hurting Sara.

The man screamed. The unknown woman fell to the ground again, drew up her knees, and folded her hands protectively over her head, no longer in the fight.

The man's body went limp, and Adam instantly backed off, planning to go after Starflower.

He made a low, growling sound when he saw all of her attention was focused on Sara.

His body coiled as he prepared to spring at her. But a voice in his head rang out, "NO!"

It was Sara. Warning him off. Warning him to stay out of it. There was a charged moment when the two women faced each other, and he knew that only one of them would come out of the confrontation alive.

The clouds turned darker. The wind roared through the trees, sending leaves flying like small guided missiles.

Energy seemed to crackle in the air. Deadly energy. Sara squared her shoulders, her whole body rigid with concentration.

Then Starflower's body jerked, and he thought she would go down. But she stiffened her legs and thrust her head forward as though every cell of her mind and body were focused on her enemy: Sara.

The struggle was one he could only imagine.

Sara had warned him to stay clear. But when he heard her scream and saw her knees buckle, he went mad, leaping at the woman.

As his teeth closed around her arm, a bolt of electricity seared through his body, but he held on, bringing her to the ground, aware in some part of his mind that she was already as limp as a dead bird. That she was already defeated.

He might have ripped out the bitch's throat just for the satisfaction of it, but he head Sara shout again, "No. Don't do it!"

Lifting his head, he watched her stagger forward. Watched the clouds above her float away in the howling wind, leaving the sky as blue as it had been a few minutes earlier.

"Adam, Adam," she shouted above the roaring in his ears. "It's over."

He raised his head and stared at her, dragging himself on all fours across the ground toward her. She looked pale. Deep purple streaks marred the tender skin under her eyes, making them appear bruised. But she was moving under her own power.

They met at the edge of the clearing. She knelt beside him, and he turned his face, rubbing it against the parts of her he could reach, her leg, her hand. He was hurting and bone weary, but he scooted closer, needing the contact, needing to know she was all right.

She curved her body around his, running her fingers over his head and his silky ears, then lower to the thick hairs that ringed his neck.

He sighed with pleasure at the contact, then shifted so that he could meet her eyes.

"Are you all right?" she asked urgently.

He gave a small nod, his gaze intense on her face, because as a wolf, there was no way he could ask the questions he urgently needed answered.

But she seemed to understand what he wanted. "I'm okay," she whispered, circling him with her arms, pressing close, stroking her hand along the length of his back, her touch soothing and sensual at the same time.

Long moments passed. Long moments when all he wanted to do was nestle in her arms, feeling her magic touch. But before he had his fill of her, she made an effort to rouse herself.

"Delacorte is coming. You have to get out of here. You have to change before he sees you."

He kept his gaze on hers, asking a silent question in his mind. What good would it do to slink away now? The damage was already done.

"Don't worry about the damn witches. They won't remember the wolf. They won't remember much of anything. I figured out how to hurt them. I . . . I put up some kind of shield in my mind. It sent their nasty little guided missiles back at them. And I think it fried their damn brains."

Was she right? Well, they'd find out.

"Go on. Go! Hurry."

He gathered his last small bits of energy, then heaved himself to his feet and staggered away from the clearing and into the underbrush. He was beyond fatigue. Almost beyond remembering what Sara had said. All he wanted to do was sink into the ground and sleep.

But she had told him to change. And he had something else he must do, also. He raked the claws of his right paw down his left side, fighting off the jolt of pain. Then he turned his head and bit into his right front leg. The pain helped to concentrate his mind. With his remaining strength, he changed back to his human form, then lost consciousness.

Voices woke him.

Sara and Delacorte talking.

He pushed himself to a sitting position and dragged shaky fingers through his hair. His arm hurt. And so did his side. He looked down and saw the long scratches and the bite he'd inflicted. He also saw he was naked. But so was almost everybody else out there in the clearing. And he wasn't the one who had torn off his clothing, he reminded himself.

It took a considerable effort to make it to his feet. When he did, he staggered toward Sara.

She looked up when she saw him, then ran to him and embraced him.

"Adam! Are you all right? Where were you?"

He hugged her to him. She'd seen the wolf at his savage worst. But she wasn't running in the other direction. She was still letting him hold her. For that he was profoundly grateful. "I'm all right."

Delacorte strode toward him. "What happened here?"

He shifted Sara so that she was standing at his side, his arm still around her. "I'm not sure. The smoke did something wacky to my brain. I remember Barnette staggering out of the swamp, terrified and naked. I was already kind of out of it because I had to take off the mask to talk to you. I'd put it back on, but Barnette clawed it off again.

"Then this gang of painted savages came after Barnette. I know it doesn't make a whole lot of sense, but I think they did something with their minds that killed him." He turned and looked at the men and women sprawled around on the ground. "I mean, they used some kind of mental weapon on him. After that, I remember them tearing my clothing off." He stopped and looked around again. "I'd like to put my pants on, if you don't mind—if they aren't ripped up."

He made his way to the tree where he'd been sitting and found his clothing. The trousers were torn but wearable. One half of the hook at the waistband was torn away. But he pulled up the zipper, which more or less kept them on. Getting partially dressed gave him a chance to plan what he was going to say next.

Turning back to Delacorte, he said, "Whatever they were doing to Barnette, I think they were trying to do to me. It felt like they were sending flaming arrows into my head. It hurt like hell. It must have screwed up my memory, because that's the last thing I remember."

"Lucky it didn't kill you, too."

"I'm younger and stronger than he was."

"Some of them are clawed up and bitten," the sheriff said in a tight voice.

He could see Sara's eyes on him. He opened his mouth and said, "Maybe a bear or some other big animal came out of the swamp and attacked them. Maybe the smoke made him crazy. It looks like the thing attacked me, too." He pointed to the scratches on his side and to the bite on his leg. "But I honestly don't remember any of it."

The sheriff peered at him. "Yeah, you're kind of mauled up. You'd better get some antiseptic on those wounds."

"I will." He looked toward the witches. "Are they dead?" he asked.

"One woman is dead."

Sara held herself steady. He assumed the dead woman was Starflower. He assumed she had died in the battle with Sara. But he wasn't going to ask about that now.

"The rest of them are alive," Delacorte was saying. "But none of them is making sense. It's like their brains are cooked. I'd like to know what happened to them."

Adam gave him a steady look. "Maybe this is a case of a bunch of druggies poisoning themselves. Maybe they got too much of that smoke, and it killed too many of their brain cells. It was pretty potent stuff. Or maybe it made them so crazy that they turned their death rays on each other. It couldn't happen to a nicer group."

Delacorte took in the explanations. After a moment, he nodded.

Adam wondered if the sheriff believed any of it. Maybe and maybe not. But at least the drugged smoke and the big animal gave him something to put in his police report. It played better than the real scenario: the werewolf and his mate fighting off the evil witches.

Adam looked back at the naked men and women sprawled on the ground and added, "One of them told me his name was Falcon. He said he was the leader of the clan. I guess they had names they used among themselves. I recognized him. He was a workman at Barnette's place."

"Yeah." The sheriff looked from him to the casualties and back again. "It won't be hard to get his real name. I suppose the same ought to be true for the others. I've seen some of them around. The dead woman worked at the card shop on Main Street."

"I heard them say they were going to kill Barnette because he was the one who led the mob against Jenna Foster. Then apparently he grabbed the land of one of the witches he ran out of town."

Delacorte looked startled.

"He did?" Sara gasped.

"I don't know if it's true," Adam answered.

"Maybe the part about Jenna Foster was in those historical records that got stolen."

"Why would Barnette want them saved?"

"Hell, I don't know," Delacorte answered, his language stronger than Adam had ever heard it. "Maybe he felt guilty all those years. Maybe in some twisted way, he wanted to be punished."

"Or maybe he didn't know the dippy lady down at the historical society wasn't much for housecleaning," Adam gave another plausible explanation.

In the distance, a siren wailed. "I sent for the paramedics," Delacorte said. "And my deputies."

"That smoke and the thunderbolts about did me in," Adam said, speaking the truth. "I know you want to question me some more. But there's not much I can tell you."

Sara moved closer to him. "Adam's in pretty bad shape. Can I take him home?" she asked.

"In the car you stole?" Delacorte asked.

She flushed scarlet. "Oh Lord, I did, didn't I."

"How did you know that Adam was in trouble?" the sheriff asked.

She took her bottom lip between her teeth, then let it go before she started to speak. "A . . . a vision. I saw it in a vision. Images . . . pictures have been coming into my mind since I got to Wayland. Dreams that turned out to be real. I knew Adam was in trouble, and I jumped up in a panic and ran down to tell Tyreen. But I knew right away she didn't believe me. So I . . . I took her car. I'm sorry, but I had to do it."

The sheriff nodded.

Sara looked toward the men and women lying on the ground. "I . . . I hope you don't think I'm like them. I hope you know it's possible to have . . . psychic powers and not be . . . evil."

Delacorte gave her a long look. "The way I heard it, your momma was a good woman who was in the wrong place at the wrong time."

She swallowed. "Yes."

"You go on. I'll square the car with Tyreen. You're going back to the park?"

"Yes."

"Then I guess I'll know where to find you. I'll send someone out there to pick up the vehicle."

Sara nodded, then turned to Adam. Reaching for his hand, she led him back in the direction from which she'd come. He held tight to her, waiting until they were in the vehicle before he pulled her into his arms, crushed her against himself, and kissed her.

She kissed him with equal passion. When she lifted her head, it was to say, "Adam, don't ever put yourself in danger like that again."

"Funny, I was going to say the same thing to you. I only agreed to look for Barnette because I knew you'd be safe. Then it was like a nightmare when you showed up."

Her eyes shone into his. "But I had to come here, because I love you. Because I couldn't lose you."

He made a strangled sound and clasped her tightly again. "Sara, Sara," he murmured. "I love you so much. I need you so much."

"Yes."

"You can make a life with a man who turns into a wolf so he can tear his enemies to bits?" he found himself asking, because he needed to know it was true.

"Well, it looks like you scratched and bit yourself, too. That was a clever move."

"Yeah. I thought so!"

She dragged in a breath and let it out in a rush. "I can make a life with you, if you can make a life with a woman who hurls thunderbolts when she's pissed off."

He managed a small laugh. "More like majorly pissed off. More like your life was in danger."

"And yours."

He hugged her tightly, overwhelmed with the feel of her in his arms. Moments ago he had barely been able to stand. Now he might have made love to her right there in the station wagon if he hadn't realized that they were no longer alone. Men in uniform were hurrying past the station wagon, some of them wheeling stretchers.

"Let's get out of here," he said.

"Yes. Let's go home so I can tend to those self-inflicted bites and scratches. And then I'll tuck you into a nice warm bed."

He grinned. "Only if you tuck yourself in with me."

"How did you know what I was thinking?"

"Maybe I'm learning to read your mind."

EPILOGUE

ADAM stopped the car at the edge of the meadow and stared at the modern wood and timber house where his brother lived. It looked like Ross had done pretty well for himself.

He was glad he had come here. But he was also nervous. Two adult male werewolves were going to try to stay in the same room for more than five minutes without getting into a fight.

But he figured if Ross could keep his cool, so could he. He had to because the need for a connection with his family was greater than the need to assert his dominance over his brother.

He and Ross had been exchanging e-mails for the past month. And then phone calls. And Adam had finally convinced himself he was ready to make the trip to Maryland—with Sara beside him.

They were getting married soon. Her mother was fluttering around in Wilmington, making arrangements. And he was going to stand up in front of a minister and fifty other people and say the words. Sara said she wanted a minister. A judge would have done it for him. But he decided he didn't object to having a man of God join a witch and a werewolf in holy matrimony. If that's what it took to make sure he kept Sara for the rest of his life.

They'd talked about the wedding. And he thought Sara was probably going to invite her father, too. She had been so confused about her feelings and so angry at the man. But now it looked like she was coming around to acceptance and understanding. And Adam was glad of that, because he wanted as much joy in her life as she could gather up.

He reached for her hand.

"Nervous?" she asked.

"Yeah."

"If he attacks you, I'll hurl a thunderbolt at him."

He laughed. "I hope you're kidding."

"Well, just a little one."

He pressed on the gas pedal, and the car started again with a jerk.

They crossed the meadow and pulled up in the parking area, next to an SUV that looked a lot like his.

The front door opened, and Ross came out. Followed by a pretty blond woman holding the hand of a little boy. His wife, Megan, and his son, Jonah. Megan looked like she was five or six months pregnant.

Adam climbed out of the car, then went around to Sara's door, to give himself a few more moments.

Ross had stopped several yards away. But Megan had given him the care of the little boy and came forward.

Holding out her arms, she said, "Adam! Ross has talked so much about you. I feel like I know you already." She gave him a hug, then turned to Sara and hugged her, too.

Stepping back, she said, "If Adam is anything like Ross, you're a lucky woman to have hooked up with him."

"I know."

Turning, she held out her arm to Ross, and he came slowly forward.

"I'm glad you're here," he said to both of them.

"An historic occasion," Adam answered around the lump that had formed in his throat.

"The two werewolves and the witch," Sara said.

"You must have been waiting for hours to deliver that line," Adam muttered.

She grinned. "Days, actually."

"Let's go in," Megan said. "I've made a big pot of blackberry tea. And some oatmeal cookies." Then she looked at Adam. "Your mother's recipe."

"I remember those cookies!"

"I'll get the recipe from Megan," Sara said.

It sounded so normal. So normal that it made him feel dazed. He had never dreamed of anything like this. But here he was at his brother's house. Meeting his brother's wife and son. And bringing the woman he was going to marry.

They all went inside. The boy stuck close to his parents while they got the refreshments. It was so strange seeing Ross and Megan work together, Adam thought. His dad had sat back and let his wife do the "women's work." Ross was obviously different.

They all settled down in the great room, with its huge windows that looked out over the woods and the meadow.

"So what did you decide to do?" Ross asked.

Adam turned his mug in his hand. To his shock, just before Austen Barnette had been kidnapped and killed by the witches, Barnette had changed his will and left Nature's Refuge to him—along with a trust fund to keep the place running—and an endowment to give the head ranger a very nice income. Maybe he'd had a premonition that something was going to happen to him.

There had been another change at Nature's Refuge, too. Amy Ralston had quit. He'd wondered if she'd had something to do with the witches. Like was she the one who had left the gate open? He'd found out that Brenda from the card shop, who called herself Starflower, was Amy's cousin. But he wasn't going to pursue the matter.

Now he looked at Sara. "We're talking about staying. The park is the perfect environment for me, of course. All that land where I can roam free. And Sara wants to try and find some of the other witch families. She's thinking we can have a little werewolf and witch colony down there."

"A refuge where we can live in safety," Sara clarified. "One thing I hope I can do is save children with my heritage from growing up feeling like they're different from everybody else. We know it's not all going to be smooth sailing. We know there could be problems with some of the people in town. But we think it will be worth the effort," she added.

"Sounds like a plan," Ross answered. "Just be cautious about who you invite to join you."

"I will," she answered solemnly.

Ross began to speak again. "And I want you to know there are people who don't have our . . . special genetic heritage who can still accept us. Tomorrow I want to introduce you to Jack and Kathryn Thornton. I met Jack through my P.I. work. He's a police detective, and he knows what I am. Once he even saw the wolf in action. But we're still friends."

Adam was watching him intently. "He saw what . . . ?"

Ross glanced at his son. "I'll tell you about it later."

"Yeah, right."

Sara looked at the little family seated across from her. How did you deal with a child who would grow up to be a werewolf? Well, she'd find out. She was almost sure she was pregnant, although she hadn't said anything yet.

She would tell Adam soon. But she also wanted to talk to Megan about the genetic research she was doing. Research that Adam had told her would make it a lot more likely that the children of a werewolf would survive.

Sara knit her fingers with Adam's, then looked up and saw Megan watching her. She smiled. The two of them had talked on the phone several times. She already thought of Megan as a friend. Which felt so good. She hadn't had many real friends in her life.

Ross broke the silence. "We're in this together," he said, his gaze moving from his wife to Adam and Sara.

Megan tipped her head toward her husband. "You've come a long way toward accepting yourself."

He answered with a small shrug, obviously uncomfortable with the subject. He was like Adam in that way. Quick to question the wolf part of his heritage. But Sara understood that. She'd had the same kind of worries. She still had them. And maybe if Adam had been a different person, she would have left him, at least for a time, until she was more sure of herself. But there was no question of separating herself from Adam Marshall. He was as necessary to her as the air she breathed. And she knew it went both ways.

He'd opened up with her in the weeks since the witches had kidnapped and killed Barnette. Many of the things he'd told her about his family had made her sad. His father had been a tyrant who insisted on obedience from his wife and sons. They'd lived on the edge of poverty because he'd been an uneducated man who relied too heavily on his werewolf skills. But probably he'd only been doing what he'd learned from his own father.

Adam would be different. He was her lover. Her partner. Her companion in a journey she'd never thought she'd take.

She looked up and saw Ross watching them. "I'm glad you found Adam," she told him.

"I wasn't so sure at first," Adam muttered. "Now I'm damn glad."

She knew how hard it was for him to say that. Her hand squeezed his tightly.

He was no ordinary man. But then, she was no ordinary woman. She had tried to be one, but she had failed. And then fate had brought her Adam Marshall. And her whole world had turned into an adventure. A lifelong adventure.

It wouldn't always be easy. She knew that. They were two people who didn't quite fit into twenty-first century life. But they had found a place where they could live and thrive. Near the black waters of the Olakompa swamp. Where she had learned that anything was possible.

PROLOGUE

IF I'm dead, why does it hurt so much?

The question echoed in his mind as he lay on the hard slab. His eyes blinked open, or as open as the swelling would allow. A field of white covered his face. Clouds? A sheet?

Every square inch of his body throbbed from punches and kicks. He shifted slightly, testing. Ribs and kidneys screamed in agony.

That wasn't the worst. Memories flitted in and out of his brain. The beer. The knockdown, drag-out fight. He'd tried to match the bikers drink for drink. That had been a bad mistake. Not his first.

A loudspeaker crackled to life. An urgent voice assaulted his ears.

"Dr. Pearson to ER. Stat. Dr. Pearson to ER. Stat."

He was in a hospital. But why was his face covered? Why was the bed so hard and the air so cold?

Out in the hall, running feet. Voices. He caught snatches of conversation.

". . . three-car pileup."

"We've got all those busted-up bikers, too."

"Triage."

He tried to hang on to consciousness. It slipped away.

Sometime later, he woke again. This time he remembered the babble of excited voices he'd heard as he lay bleeding on the barroom floor.

"Jesus! Roy's dead."

"What happened?"

"Looks like he hit his head on a table when he went down."

More voices, punctuated by loud exclamations of dismay.

"What the hell are we gonna do?"

"Shit, I don't know!"

"Tell the cops the Marshall kid did it. Serves him right for bringing his sorry ass in here."

"Yeah." A boot kicked at his ribs, but he couldn't muster the effort to groan in pain. "He can't say otherwise."

"You think he's dead?"

"What does it matter? We all give the cops the same story, he's dogmeat."

Satisfied laughter.

And now the hard table.

Inching a hand upward, he pulled the sheet off his face. He was lying in a dark room.

In the distance, an ambulance siren wailed.

Had he heard that before? He didn't know. His brain was too bruised.

Cautiously he tried to sit up and gasped as agony caught him in an iron grip. But he was tough. Too tough, maybe. He'd dedicated the first twenty-two years of his life to screwing himself up.

Somewhere in the recesses of his addled brain, through the fogging pain, he saw an opportunity to escape—for good.

Teeth gritted, he managed to lower himself to the cold tile floor and passed out.

Later, his eyes snapped open again. It was still dark. The hospital loudspeaker crackled again.

The staff was busy.

Could he stand the pain of transformation? He must.

He had lost one shoe. It took centuries to work the other one off, then struggle out of jeans and T-shirt caked with dried blood. Centuries to crawl naked to the door, then raise his arm high enough to turn the knob and push the door open a crack. The effort sapped most of his strength, and he sat with his head thrown back against the wall and cold air rasping in and out of his lungs.

But he couldn't stay here long. Eyes closed, he gathered his inner resources, calling on rituals passed from father to son back to the time before written records.

He had learned the words on his sixteenth birthday—the way his brothers had before him. Only two of them were still alive. The ones who were tough enough to survive.

"*Taranis, Epona, Cerridwen,*" he whispered through split, swollen lips, then repeated the same phrase and went on to another.

"*Ga. Feart. Cleas. Duais. Aithriocht. Go gcumhdai is dtreorai na deithe thu.*"

Pain flashed like lightning in his brain. As bad as the first time.

No—worse, because his body was too battered to abide the change. He forced himself to endure the agony because he must.

As they had throughout his adult life, the ancient words helped him through the torture of transformation, opened his mind, freed him from the bonds of his human shape. His brother, Ross, had told him the words were Gaelic. An appeal to Druid deities for powers no man should possess. He didn't care what they were—so long as they helped center his being.

The human part of his mind screamed in protest when he felt his jaw elongate, his teeth sharpen, his body jerk as limbs and muscles transformed into a different shape that, still, was as familiar to him as his human form. Gray hair formed along his flanks, covering his body in a thick, silver-tipped pelt. The color and structure of his eyes changed. And when he forced himself to stand, he was on all fours.

He had been a man. Now he was an animal.

A wolf.

If anybody saw him, maybe they'd think he was a big dog. Or maybe they'd be too busy to notice him. If he was lucky.

The pain was almost too much to bear, but he forced himself to hang onto consciousness. Forced himself to poke his head out the door and reconnoiter in the hallway. He could see an open doorway, where the ambulances unloaded the injured and the dying.

Mustering every ounce of resolve he possessed, he staggered toward the exit.

Someone behind him shouted. "What the hell?"

He kept going, into the night. Into the woods.

HE holed up in an old shed until he was strong enough to hunt. With deer meat in his belly and only a vague plan in mind, he transformed back to his human persona. He stole a car and drove west, changing his name, courtesy of a convenient gravestone in a cemetery in Canton, Ohio. He vowed to stay out of trouble from now on.

Thirty miles west of Denver, he detoured onto a narrow mountain road, drawn by the majestic scenery, so different from the rolling countryside around Baltimore. At the edge of a pine forest, he stopped to stretch his legs. Or perhaps, fate had tapped him on the shoulder.

As he stood in the sun-dappled forest, he realized something was badly wrong. No birds chirped in the trees. The small animals he expected to hear in the underbrush were strangely quiet. Even the insects seemed to have abandoned the area. The only sound was that of water gurgling over rocks.

A hundred yards from the road, goose bumps rose on his arms when he found a she-wolf and her pups, sheltered by a small cave of rock—all dead. The pups nestled against their mother's belly fur as she lay on her side, her eyes closed. The little family looked as if they were sleeping. Still, he knew the smell of death, knew they would never get up and run free, breathing in the scent of pine and earth and game.

His vision blurred as a profound sense of loss washed over him. Was it for the lifeless wolves—or for himself?

As he dragged in a draft of the forest air, he knew the wolf and her pups were not the only dead creatures here. There were others—too many to count.

Some disaster had befallen the land, as if an evil magician had put the forest under a spell.

Which, he reminded himself, was none of his business, even if it were true. He looked back toward the old Chevy he had liberated from Jack's back lot of half-dead wrecks. He had left his own problems behind. He didn't need anyone else's. Still, something compelled him to walk farther into the shade of the tall pines, feeling their needles crunch under his feet. Sheltered by the forest, he probed for danger, but he knew he was alone. And he knew he wasn't going to leave until he found out what had happened.

Swiftly, he removed all of his clothing. Then, in the light shifting through the tree branches, he ran his hand down his ribs. His body was healing. He could see taut skin and firm muscles, although various parts of his anatomy were still marred by yellow bruises. He'd stopped peeing blood, though. The cut on his forehead, covered by a lock of dark hair, was healing, as was his split upper lip. He was damned lucky he hadn't lost any teeth.

For the first time since leaving Baltimore, he uttered the words that brought the change upon him. Unlike the last time when he'd barely been able to speak, his voice was strong and sure as he rode above the pain.

Transformed, he stood and sniffed the air. Usually in the woods, he felt a raw, primal joy at his change from man to wolf. Today that pleasure was tainted by the air around him. Something raw and ugly wafted from the surface of the water where it splashed over the rocks.

Poison, his sharp sense of smell told him. His human intellect wondered why the she-wolf had drunk the water. Maybe the smell had changed gradually, so she hadn't known what was happening. Maybe a sudden discharge of chemicals had taken her by surprise. Or perhaps she simply hadn't recognized the danger.

The animal in him wanted to flee from the evil that hung like tainted fog over the landscape. The man he was overrode that instinct and forced the wolf to stay, forced him to follow the creek upstream.

He was hardly aware of time and distance passing as he traveled through a nightmare landscape. Everywhere he looked, he saw evidence of man's obscenity, illuminated by the rays of the setting sun. Death and destruction followed the creek.

A doe tried to run from him and floundered on legs that wouldn't hold her weight. A raccoon stared with glazed eyes. He found fish floating in the water and a family of dead foxes. As he picked his way along the riverbank, heading upstream, the water changed. It had been clear, but it began to have a brown tinge. Farther on, scum clung to the rocks, and farther still, the smell of poison began to clog his nostrils.

Then, in the distance, he saw a scar on the face of the land. Smoke belched from a tall chimney, where a mining or logging operation defiled the land.

A sign warned: PRIVATE PROPERTY, KEEP OUT.

He ignored the admonition, but he never got close enough to discover what man-made nightmare was changing the pristine forest into a charnel house.

He sniffed the scent of a man on the wind at the same instant a sound like a firecracker split the air, and something plowed into the trunk of a nearby tree. A bullet.

The wolf was no fool. He turned and ran for his life. But he knew he would come back. If not in person, then in spirit.

1

A uniformed rent-a-cop directed Sam Morgan to a grassy parking spot beside the curving driveway. He pulled his sleek Jaguar next to a boxy Volvo, then got out and clicked the remote control lock. It was a precaution he always took, although he was probably the only thief attending the Wilson Woodlock party.

He'd garnered an invitation to the Montecito, California, mansion through one of the tony organizations he belonged to for the purpose of mingling with the well-to-do, especially the ones who raped the earth for their own gain. The ones who killed animals and savaged forests. The ones who poisoned water and air and earth. Liberating some of their ill-gotten wealth was his chosen profession, as well as one of his chief pleasures.

His next target was Wilson Woodlock, whose company was currently denuding a stand of timber in Washington State with the enthusiasm of a termite nest on steroids. Woodlock. It should be Woodkiller.

"Enjoy your evening, sir," the rent-a-cop said as Sam strolled up the driveway.

"I certainly will," he answered, with the right touch of enthusiasm.

A middle-aged couple in evening dress joined him on the curved drive, and the perfume wafting off the woman almost knocked him to the blacktop. Holding his breath, he dropped several paces behind them, pretending to admire the scenery.

The house sat in the middle of a walled park big enough to swallow a good-sized townhouse development. Instead of cookie-cutter dwellings for the masses, wide lawns with artfully naturalized plantings stretched into the darkness.

A blaze of lights and the buzz of conversation at the end of the driveway announced the mansion. The structure was typical of the upscale southern California neighborhood—Spanish grandee, with wrought-iron balustrades and a red tile roof.

As Sam stepped into the entrance hall, a waiter immediately approached with graceful flutes on a silver tray.

"Champagne."

"No, thanks," he answered politely. He hadn't touched a drop of alcohol since the long-ago disaster in the Baltimore bikers' bar. Back then he'd been rough and tumble Johnny Marshall wearing a black T-shirt and an attitude. Now he was Sam Morgan who felt as much at home in a tuxedo as he did in his wolf's skin.

From saloon to salon in eight years. It was amazing how easily he'd taken on the veneer of civilization—once he'd put his mind to it.

Johnny would have been intimidated by the size of the house and covered his discomfort with a derisive sneer. But Sam fit easily into the posh surroundings. He didn't have to prove anything—to himself or anyone else.

And he silently complimented his host on the small engraved sign at the front of the hallway: THANK YOU FOR NOT SMOKING. At least Woodlock shared one of his values. Like alcohol, cigarettes were on his Don't-even-think-about-it list. Smoke made him sick, even secondhand.

At the bar in the conservatory, he requested his usual: "Soda water with lime." Then, drink in hand, he wove his way through the party-goers. He recognized many of the faces—some from *Newsweek* or the California papers. Others were from households he'd robbed. But why not? A man with Woodlock's environmental record would have friends of the same persuasion.

He greeted a few acquaintances but kept moving. When he felt the hair on the back of his neck prickle, he went still. Casually he stopped to look at a Picasso print hanging over a Bombay chest. Then, just as casually, he turned. When he saw no one staring at him, he continued on his way.

He encountered his host in the dining room. The lumber baron, a balding sixty-five-year-old man with a shallow chest and stooped shoulders, was propped against a sideboard, talking to several cronies. He seemed almost inert, except for his eyes, which were bright. Too bright. It looked like the guy had fortified himself with something potent in order to withstand his own party.

When Woodlock looked in his direction, Sam pasted a smile on his face and came forward. "I'm pleased to have this chance to meet you," he said, holding out his hand. "I'm Sam Morgan."

"Oh, yes. From the Glendora Fund list. So glad you could come."

The other man's palm was damp and pudgy against his, and Sam had to work to keep a look of disgust off his face. They chatted for a few minutes; then Sam said he'd like to see his host's famous pre-Columbian art collection, the one that had been written up recently in *Smithsonian Magazine.*

The man flushed with pride and directed him toward the back of the house, leaving him to find his own way while he kept up his host's duties.

Sam easily found the small gallery. It was full of glass display cases that held a wealth of miniature carved and sculpted figures, produced by skilled artisans before the arrival of Columbus in the New World. He bent to look at a woman with large breasts and exaggerated sex organs, then studied the alarm system on the case. When he'd seen what he needed to see, he moved on to other figures—a man riding a llama and a mountain cat, ready to spring. Sixteen little gems were exquisitely rendered. And all were too distinctive to sell on the open market. But he wasn't interested in their cash value. Simply depriving Woodlock of his fabulously expensive tchotchkes would be enough of a reward.

He switched his attention from the art objects to the room itself, looking for a control panel for the alarm system. Although he saw nothing, he'd studied the house plans and had made an educated guess. As he'd hoped, the keypad was in a closet that backed up to the gallery. Once inside, he turned on the small flashlight he'd brought. Taking a piece of special paper from a case in his pocket, he carefully laid it over the keys, then replaced it and slipped the case into his pocket again.

His task completed, he strode to the buffet table and enjoyed a slice of rare roast beef on a cocktail bun. But the crush of people was starting to oppress him. There were too many bodies. Too much heat and noise. Too many smells. If somebody on the other side of the room farted, he knew it.

When he found a closed door, he opened it and stepped into the family room, where he could be alone for a few minutes of decompression.

The shelves behind the boxy chenille sofa were filled with an interesting assortment of books and knickknacks. Mentally he noted a couple of figurines he was pretty sure were Limoges. Nice, but probably not worth his time and trouble.

French doors at the side of the room led to a terrace. He thought he might step outside and give the back of the house a quick inspection. Before he could open the door, however, the swish of a silk skirt stopped him.

"So what do you think of Romberg's chances in the primary?" a woman asked.

He was about to say that he thought the man would be the Republican candidate for governor, but the words froze in his throat as he turned to gaze into the most extraordinary pair of green eyes he had ever seen. Automatically his mind catalogued other details. She was about five foot six, slender, with delicate features and long golden brown hair swept back from her face and held by antique platinum clips studded with tiny diamonds. A matching pendant hung from a slender chain around her throat, dipping toward the cleavage just visible at the top of the softly draped bodice of her ice-blue cocktail dress.

"Very nice," he murmured.

When she gave him a quizzical look, he realized his response hadn't exactly meshed with her question.

He cleared his throat and tried not to sound like a tongue-tied teenager. "Romberg is going to get the votes of people who are worried about raising taxes."

She played with a strand of her hair. "He can't run on one issue."

Sam wanted to say something intelligent. But the woman's enticing scent wafted toward him—not perfume but her own delicious essence, wrapping him in a seductive embrace. He felt her green eyes stripping away his carefully cultivated veneer, and he couldn't help wondering if she saw all the way down to the wolf lurking deep inside.

Impossible. Nobody could detect the wolf—unless he wanted them to.

He knew who she was. He'd been intrigued enough to dig up every scrap of information on her that he could find.

Some people photographed well. She was just the opposite. As they stood face-to-face, he saw that all the cameras pointed her way had failed her utterly. None had managed to capture her subtle beauty.

Before he could speak, she filled the silence. "I don't think we've met. I'm Olivia Woodlock."

"Sam Morgan," he answered, then heard himself asking, "Were you following me around?"

Did a little flash of guilt cross her features? Before he could analyze her expression, she dipped her head and looked up at him through a screen of lashes.

Her voice turned flirtatious. "You caught my attention."

"I try to blend into the woodwork," he answered.

"You couldn't."

Her tone sent a little jolt along his nerve endings, which he tried to ignore. Starting anything with Woodlock's daughter would be insane. His best option was to put some distance between them, but she took a step closer, moving so that she was facing him.

"I'm glad you stopped by," she murmured.

"Why?"

"I get tired of the same old faces, the same conversations. Do you live nearby?"

"I drove down for the evening," he answered easily.

"From where?"

He almost told her where he lived before quashing the impulse. "North," he said, and left it at that.

It was difficult to keep his focus on her face. He wanted to look at the place where that diamond pendant decorated her cleavage.

He should excuse himself and blend back in to the crowd. He and Olivia Woodlock were standing too close, getting too involved. He didn't want to be attracted to Wilson Woodlock's daughter. And he didn't want her to remember him later.

Too late for that. They were reacting on too basic a level—a very sexual level.

Below the surface of the conversation, he was feeling his own guilt, since his purpose in her home wasn't exactly honorable. Then he reminded himself sternly that she had been brought up in solitary splendor in a house that hundreds of people would be happy to share. Her bedroom alone could probably house three families.

Her bedroom. If he asked her to go up there with him, would she accept the invitation?

The outrageous thought shocked him. Since the bad old days in Baltimore, he'd learned caution. He'd learned to focus on what was important at each moment of his existence. Olivia Woodlock was muddying his brain, tempting him to break the ironclad rules he'd made for himself. He knew by the tension crackling between them that he wasn't the only one sexually interested.

"Do you often play with fire?" he asked, hearing the thickness in his own voice.

"Never."

"Then what are we doing now?"

She licked her lips, and his gaze followed the movement of her tongue.

"We're getting to know each other."

"And then what?"

He waited for a snappy rejoinder. Before she had a chance to continue the conversation, a loud thumping noise and a shout from somewhere outside the room made her eyes go wide.

The blood drained from her face. Pushing past him, she rushed out the door.

2

OLIVIA bolted from the room, her pulse pounding in her throat, her high heels clicking on the Mexican tiles as she rushed down the hall.

She sensed Sam Morgan behind her but didn't spare him a glance. Several partygoers turned in astonishment, and she rudely shouldered past, tossing out a perfunctory "sorry" as she made for the front hall. When she saw a crowd of people facing the bottom of the steps, her heart stopped, then started again in double time.

"Let it be a waiter who spilled a tray of hors d'oeuvres," she whispered, without much hope.

As she reached the front of the crowd, she caught a glimpse of dress shoes and black trouser legs halfway down the stairs.

"Oh, Colin," she breathed.

Her brother didn't have the brains God had given a hamster—at least when it came to common sense, she amended quickly. He was brilliant with computers; the guest list for the party would have been somewhat different if it hadn't been for his research. But he'd gotten sick and had to go to bed. Still, she'd been afraid he'd try to come down, anyway.

Following the pants legs upward, she saw he had lost his footing somewhere between the landing and the middle of the flight. His partner, Brice, was bending over him, looking as worried as she felt.

Scrambling up the steps, she dropped to her knees beside her brother. "Are you all right?" she asked urgently.

Colin's eyes went from Brice to her. "I'm fine." With his jaw clenched, he pushed himself up, then flushed as he glanced at the onlookers.

She cupped her hand over his shoulder. "You're hurting."

"Not much. Just my ankle." He dragged in a breath, then grabbed the banister and tried to stand. But his leg crumpled beneath him, and he sat down heavily again. From the corner of her eye, she saw her father hugging the wall, probably too embarrassed to step out of the crowd. For him, appearance was everything. The sight of his son sprawled on the stairs did not make a pretty picture. Particularly with Colin's male lover leaning over him like an anxious wife.

Inclining her head toward the onlookers, she raised her voice. "My brother is fine. He has a touch of the flu, and he got dizzy on the stairs." As she spoke, she was thinking how good she'd become at telling lies. Smiling, she added, "I'll be with you shortly."

"Yes, yes. Nothing to get excited about," her father finally chimed in as he ushered some of his guests back toward the bar. "Just an unfortunate mishap. Come, have a drink."

To her relief, the gawkers began to clear the hall—all but one. Sam Morgan, of all people, came up the stairs toward them. As he climbed, he stopped and picked up Colin's glasses, which she hadn't noticed and might well have trampled.

"Let me help you," he said, handing the glasses to Colin, who put them back on to stare at the newcomer.

She watched recognition dawn in his eyes. He hid it quickly, clearing his throat and asking, "Do I know you?"

"Sam Morgan."

Olivia tried to interrupt. "We can manage."

But Morgan was already pushing up Colin's pants leg to look at his ankle. "It's swollen. Either it's sprained or broken," he said.

"Sprained," Colin answered instantly.

"You should have it X-rayed," Morgan said.

"I think ice will take care of it," her brother answered as he turned to Brice. "Could you get me some in a plastic bag?"

"Of course." Brice scurried off, probably glad to be useful.

She wanted to tell Morgan to join the other guests. He was too aggressive, too distracting. She couldn't prevent her response to him, even when her full attention should be on Colin. She was aware of Morgan's every movement and his indisputable masculinity. Aware of the clean, woodsy scent of his body, his strength, his assessing dark gaze, the nearly black hair that needed a trim . . . the mouth that hinted of carnal knowledge.

She blinked, chagrined that her mind was wandering down such paths at a time like this.

Morgan helped her brother stand, then steadied him when he wavered. Colin hobbled slowly up the steps, leaning heavily on the other man.

"Which way?" Morgan asked.

Colin hesitated for a split second. "Right."

The computer room. The last place she'd have taken him.

She bit back a protest, as she followed them down the hall and into the room, her gaze darting immediately to the piles of printouts. Some of them might be papers Sam Morgan shouldn't see.

Colin sighed in relief as he dropped onto the leather couch. Brice arrived with the ice pack in time to help him get settled, with his leg propped on the glass and brass coffee table, a pillow beneath it and the ice pack placed carefully over it.

While Brice was fussing over her brother, Olivia scanned the papers on the desk and decided they were safe.

Then, turning, she crossed to the sofa and inspected her brother's outstretched leg, making a critical assessment of his condition, thinking how much their roles had changed. After their mother had left, he'd been the one who'd cleaned her scraped knees and administered first aid for bee stings. Now she was tending to him. He looked shaken, and perspiration filmed his forehead. She wanted to shout at him that he should be taking better care of himself. But she wasn't going to do it in front of Morgan.

Colin and Brice exchanged a very private glance.

The warmth in that look sent a stab of envy through Olivia. Not that she begrudged her brother the comfort of the relationship. It was just that no one had ever looked at her like that. Maybe no one ever would. If her father had his way, she was doomed to a loveless marriage.

Well, she and Colin were going to do something about Dad's cowardly plans. Of course, she could get herself killed in the process. But she'd decided that would be better than ending up as the wife of a man who wanted only to wield his power over her.

Her brother interrupted her dark thoughts, and she realized he was speaking to Morgan.

"Thank you for your help." He laughed. "Although I would have picked a less dramatic way to meet."

"Glad I was here," Morgan replied.

"I should introduce you to my very good friend, Brice Brayman."

"Nice to meet you."

Olivia watched them shake, aware that they were assessing each other. Undoubtedly, Morgan had picked up on Colin and Brice's relationship, but he wasn't going to pass judgment, at least not overtly. Brice joined his partner on the couch, reaching for his hand and knitting their fingers together. "Morgan's right. Maybe you should get that X-rayed," he murmured.

"If the swelling doesn't go down," Colin answered grudgingly.

Maybe Morgan was embarrassed to be intruding on the family scene, because he turned away and stared at the long desk, taking in the computer, the various peripherals and the custom-sized screen that helped compensate for Colin's reduced vision.

"Quite a setup you have."

Colin grinned. "It keeps me in touch with the world."

"Yeah." To Olivia's relief, Morgan added, "I should be going."

"You don't need to rush off," Colin countered, and she wanted to take him by the shoulders and shake some sense into him.

But Morgan was already heading toward the door. When Olivia started after him, he shook his head. "I can find my own way out."

His broad back disappeared down the hall.

Olivia waited several beats before asking, "I don't suppose you pulled that falling down the steps act on purpose?"

"Oh, come on. I twisted my ankle *on purpose*?"

"Maybe that part was an accident."

"You think I'd risk having Dad furious at me? You know damn

well he's going to come charging up here later and chew the hell out of me."

"Yes," she answered, quietly. She didn't envy Colin. Years ago he would have gotten lashed with a riding crop. Now it would simply be a tongue lashing.

Surprising herself with her calm voice, she gave Brice instructions for the cold pack. "You're supposed to alternate twenty minutes on and twenty minutes off with the ice."

"I will."

She wanted to stay and make sure Colin was all right. He was getting sicker more quickly than any of them had expected.

He caught the look in her eye and probably knew what she was thinking. He said only, "I'll be fine."

"I hope so," she answered with sincerity.

He gave her a mischievous look. "You go on down and act like nothing happened. You're good at that."

She wanted to protest that she hated playacting. Instead she left the room.

In the hallway, she started for the steps, then stopped short when she felt a sudden wave of dizziness. Clenching her teeth, she braced her hand against the wall to steady herself and stood with the world swaying around her.

"No. Stop it this minute!" she ordered herself.

Standing in the hall, she waited until she was feeling almost normal. The dizzy episode lasted only a moment, but it was an excellent reminder of why she'd persuaded Colin to help her embark on the biggest lie of her life. Still, it felt as if she and her brother had set a doomsday machine streaking down a mountainside. All they could do was make the best of the ride and hope they didn't crash-land at the bottom.

Once she'd rejoined the guests, she wove her way among them, her progress slowed by frequent questions about her brother. She gave them all the flu story again, but her eyes scanned the crowd, searching for the man she had encountered in the family room.

He wasn't there, nor did she find him anywhere else. She fought a mixture of relief and disappointment. It seemed he had left, and she couldn't shake the disturbing feeling that he had taken some part of her with him.

3

FIGHTING the restless rush of blood through her veins, Olivia stood in the dining room, watching people from the catering company help Irene and Jefferies clean up after the party.

Her gaze wandered to a Marc Chagall lithograph in the small gallery collection over the buffet. It showed an exuberant man flying through the air toward his beloved, his neck at an odd angle and a bouquet of flowers in his hand. In an art history class she'd taken at the University of California at Santa Barbara, the professor had explained that Chagall was depicting his wildly ebullient feelings for the woman he would marry, that he often painted a fantasy representation of life. Years ago, her father had liked that quality in the artist. Probably he walked past the picture now without seeing it. For her, the unbridled joy of the man in the painting was a reminder that the Woodlock family no longer possessed the joie de vivre it once had.

"Is there anything I can do for you, Miss Olivia?" Jefferies asked. He was lean and gray-haired now. And his features had aged over the years. But his face was still the one she pictured when she needed warmth and comfort.

She quickly rearranged her own features. "Oh, no. Thank you." Olivia still felt uncomfortable being called "Miss" by a man who had been her substitute parent when she was a child, but she knew she would only embarrass him by trying to put the two of them on a more familiar basis.

"We have some of that raspberry chocolate mousse cake left. It's one of Mr. Colin's favorites," he said.

"Yes. Thanks. I'll take him a piece."

She followed Jefferies into the kitchen, where he put a generous slice of cake onto a dessert plate. She knew he was as upset about her brother as she was.

When their parents had been out of town or out for the evening, Jefferies was the man who had played Monopoly and Clue with them and taken them to riding and tennis lessons. It was he who had bought her sanitary pads and told her what she would need them for. They'd both been embarrassed, but he'd done it because he knew nobody else would.

She touched his arm. "Thank you."

"I'm glad there's some left."

The exchange was warm but brief. She didn't want to linger because he needed to finish up, so he could get some sleep. And she could see Irene, the maid, waiting to ask him a question.

Plate in hand, Olivia headed upstairs. In the upper hall, she could see a flickering light from what had once been a bedroom—until Brice had taken it over.

Drawn to the doorway, she looked at the fat candles set in holders on three carved chests that had been in the attic for years. A golden Buddhist altar stood between the heavily curtained windows. On it, several sticks of incense burned in shallow dishes. An antique rug that had probably adorned a desert nomad's tent covered the floor.

Colin sprawled against several of the pillows, his ice-draped ankle resting on a bolster.

"How do you feel?" she asked.

"Fine."

She wanted to say, "Sure," but she kept the sarcastic comment to herself. Brice, still wearing his tuxedo minus the tie, reclined against another bunch of the rich pillows. Between the men, a square Hermés scarf with a pattern in mauve, gold, and red drew attention to a selection of small objects arranged on top of it.

She knew Brice was propitiating the gods. Or calling on the realm of magic. Or perhaps both.

"Is it okay for Colin to eat a piece of cake in here?" she asked.

Brice looked torn. Probably, eating didn't fit in with his idea of the room's ceremonial purpose. On the other hand, he wanted his partner to get some nourishment. After several seconds hesitation, he nodded his acquiescence.

She handed Colin the plate, collected her own mound of pillows, and took a seat between the two men, her knees tucked up to accommodate the skirt of the cocktail dress.

Brice had set out a strange collection of objects on the scarf. One was a lifelike rendition of a human eye in white and blue glass—an amulet to ward off evil. She knew he'd bought it in Los Angeles, from a shop in the community of Middle Eastern immigrants.

Next to it was a sixteenth-century ornamental brass padlock from China. Brice had told her it was meant to be hung from a child's neck to lock up the youngster's soul and protect it from harm.

He had borrowed a small Aztec statuette from the museum downstairs—a figure of Tlazolteotl, goddess of sexual pleasure, giving birth to the maize god. She sat next to a carved Indonesian male figure with a huge penis and testicles. An ivory Buddha from Burma faced them. And there was something she hadn't seen before—a paperback novel called *Guards! Guards!* by Terry Pratchett.

"What's this doing here?" she asked.

"It's for inspiration," Brice explained.

"Like how?" Olivia asked, aware that he appreciated the interest in his projects.

"It starts with a group of ordinary men who come together to create magic," Brice said. "They each bring objects that might have a little bit of power. And the aggregate adds up to more than the sum of its parts."

"What did they do?"

"Summoned a fire-breathing dragon."

Colin chewed and swallowed a forkful of cake. "I read the book. Unfortunately, the guys couldn't control the dragon. It flew around the city incinerating citizens."

Brice shot him an annoyed look.

"What does it matter?" she couldn't stop herself from saying. "It's just a story, isn't it?"

"Sometimes fiction can be an entrée into all-embracing truth," Brice told her, his voice low and serious.

She didn't argue. She knew how much he wanted it to be true. He thought that divine intervention might be the way to save Colin. But being Brice, he hadn't simply gone to a Christian church and prayed to the Holy Trinity or, maybe, asked the Blessed Virgin to intercede with Jesus for Colin's sake. He'd come up with his own method of asking for supernatural assistance.

She picked up the lock and turned it in her hand before returning it to the altar. Brice immediately moved the talisman back into the position he'd decided was important.

"So you think you can work magic with these objects?" she inquired.

"Well, I asked the gods to bring you into our circle. And you came. Three is a magic number, you know."

She restrained herself from saying the flickering candles had drawn her to the room. Nor did she point out how bizarre it seemed for the three of them, all dressed to the nines, to be lounging on the floor in front of a makeshift altar full of a bunch of spiritual and secular objects—all laid out on a Hermés scarf.

Colin set aside the half-finished cake, so they could join hands. When Brice nodded his approval, she gave him a small smile. He was so serious. So beyond her experience. And he was totally devoted to Colin.

He was going to be devastated when Colin died.

She cancelled that thought. Colin was going to make it. He had to. And if this magic ceremony could help, she was willing to give it a try.

Brice began to speak in a low, steady voice. "On this winter night, we ask the guidance of the gods who watch over the universe. We ask for protection. And we ask for special favors for a man who has done no wrong, yet terrible tortures have fallen on his shoulders."

Olivia closed her eyes, trying to convince herself that they could make something real happen.

"As the candles flicker, his life flickers. As the world turns, his fate hangs in the balance. But the gods or the fates have the power to set him on a new course. Do not deny him the chance. Let your love and mercy shine down on him all the days of his long life."

As Brice continued to speak, she tried to coax a kind of hopeful anticipation into her being. Magic was real. If you could just find the key to using it.

Please, she silently begged. *Please let it happen.*

As Brice's prayer wafted over her, she glanced at him, then at Colin, from under lowered lashes. Involuntarily, her hand tightened on her brother's.

They'd both been raised to fulfill certain roles in life. She'd balked at the restrictions. She'd been intimidated by the obligations. Then she'd been angry that the responsibilities weren't going to fall equally on her brother's shoulders.

But her anger had been nothing compared to the wrath of Big Daddy Woodlock when his only son had picked the family's Thanksgiving dinner to announce that he was gay.

Then and there, her father had called his only son every insulting name he could dredge up—from fag to nancy boy to queer. Later, he'd threatened to disinherit him. And Colin had coolly told him that he could make a very good living as a stock market analyst.

Olivia wondered if Colin secretly wished he were the son their father wanted. She knew she wished he hadn't focused on her as the only hope of carrying on the Woodlock line.

Brice stopped talking, and the room was suddenly silent. "I can tell that neither one of you is taking this seriously," he complained.

"I'm trying," Olivia murmured.

"Maybe if you tried harder, it would work."

"We all know what would work," she shot back. When she realized they were still holding hands, she detached herself from the two men.

Colin shifted against the pillows, making himself more comfortable. Silence filled the room. She was wondering what to say, when her brother asked, "So what did you think of Sam Morgan?"

Olivia felt a dart of warmth spear through her. She wasn't going to tell Colin that Morgan turned her on. Instead she allowed, "He's too sure of himself."

"He's been very successful at his chosen profession. It's made him very rich."

Brice picked up the evil eye and turned it around in his hand. "He exudes sexuality."

"You would notice that," Colin muttered.

"You didn't?"

"Yeah, but I also noticed he's as straight as a knight's lance."

"A nice phallic image."

Olivia listened to the two men banter. Once she had resented Brice. Now she accepted him as one of the family—and trusted him implicitly.

"We can control him," Colin said with the confidence that sometimes drove her crazy.

"With magic?" she asked, then gave a shaky laugh.

"I think you've got a better way to control Sam Morgan."

She blanched. "What do you expect me to do?"

"As much as you want. By all accounts, he's very good in bed."

"Colin!"

"I saw the sparks leaping back and forth between you two," her brother murmured.

She sighed. "You don't miss much. Even when you're in pain."

"I know you pretty well. I like seeing you come alive."

"You won't like trying to work with Morgan. He does what he wants, when he wants, and for his own reasons," Olivia answered, rubbing her hands on the suddenly prickly flesh of her bare arms. In one of their late-night strategy sessions, she had come up with the idea of getting help to steal back their family heritage from Luther Ethridge, the man who had snatched it from them.

Colin had eagerly begun looking for the right candidate. Sam Morgan stood head and shoulders above the others he'd found.

Had sexual attraction swayed her judgment? She'd been obsessing over Sam Morgan since she'd first read Colin's biography of the man and looked at his photograph. Really, she should have stayed away from him tonight, but she hadn't been able to resist following him into the family room.

Realizing the two men were looking at her, she deliberately lowered her hands. Colin thought they'd hit the jackpot with Sam Morgan, but she wasn't so sure it was going to work out the way anybody expected.

She was savvy enough to recognize that Morgan had stirred something hot and sensual inside her. Too bad she couldn't whip up a witch's spell that would keep him under control.

A sudden noise made her head jerk toward the door. An instant later, her dad came blasting through it. He'd taken another hit of coke, or whatever he was using now, and his eyes were manic.

UNCONTROLLABLE anger surged through Wilson as he charged into the room. They were in there again. Doing one of their fake magic ceremonies. And the thought of Woodlocks sinking so low made his blood froth.

He was the head of this family. And they were defying him. A few years ago nobody would have dared. But now they had no shame.

"What the hell is going on?" he demanded, because he wanted to hear their half-baked answer.

Colin blanched, but he kept his voice even. "An after-party conversation."

"Fuck this! Stop this crap. Stop it, do you hear!"

With some part of his mind, he watched himself. And there was still enough rationality left in him to be appalled at his own behavior.

But once the anger took him, it was in control. Striding across the room, he grabbed Brice by the arm and yanked him to his feet. "Get out. Go on, git. I want to talk to my son without his fag lover and chief wizard hovering around."

Anger gathered on Brice's face. But a warning look from Colin had him stalking out of the room like the good little lapdog that he was.

With the fag lover gone, Wilson focused on Olivia. "I expected better of you."

"Sorry," she whispered.

"Sorry isn't good enough." To keep from striking her, he paced to the window, then whirled and faced Colin again, almost knocking over one of the candles.

Olivia reached to steady it, as Wilson let loose with a torrent of words. "If you'd married Demeter Ethridge, the family wouldn't be in this mess," he shouted at his son.

"Demeter Ethridge has the IQ of a stalagmite," Colin shot back.

"You didn't have to discuss quantum physics with her. You just had to fuck her," he shouted.

"I didn't want to fuck her, as you so delicately put it."

The boy's insolence only fired his rage. "Didn't *want* to? Or *couldn't* get it up for a woman? Couldn't you just pretend she was a boy, and that you were fucking her in the ass?"

"Are we going through all this again?" Colin asked in a weary voice.

"Don't smart-mouth me, sonny. You may beat me out on an IQ test, but I was still in charge of this family, the last time I looked." Unable to stop himself, he charged across the room, this time scattering the magic objects spread on the scarf.

He felt Olivia grab his arm and try to yank him away.

He could hear her voice buzzing in his ears, "Get off! Get off him!" she shouted, pounding on his shoulders with her fists. Though he paid no attention to her, the exertion was too much for him. Unable to support his own weight, he sank down heavily in a nest of pillows, panting, watching Colin fall back against the wall.

Olivia's first words were for Colin.

"Are you all right?" she asked urgently.

"Yes," he answered, reaching to shove his glasses back into place.

Only then did she turn to her father—the man who should have been her first concern. "Dad, you need to rest."

He felt tears stinging the backs of his eyes, and he fought to keep his children from seeing them. Somewhere deep inside himself, he hated his behavior, hated his weakness, hated the way he'd lost control of himself and his family.

He'd been holding everything together. Doing his best for himself and for his children. Suddenly, it was all slipping away.

And he was too tired to do anything about it. When Olivia took his arm, he let her help him up. Trying not to lean on her too heavily, he allowed his daughter to help him toward the door.

Still, he needed to make something clear. "I need one of you to do your duty," he growled. "If not Colin, then you."

"My marrying Luther Ethridge won't accomplish what you think it will."

"He'll give us what we need."

She sighed. "He'll enslave me and kill you and Colin and Uncle Darwin."

"No," he said. He'd thought of that. He'd thought of a way to keep it from happening. But now he couldn't remember what it was.

"Come on. Let's get you to bed," she said.

LUTHER Ethridge was sweating. But it was a good sweat. He'd spent a half hour on the stair climber and was two minutes away from finishing his hour on the weight machines that occupied the spacious gym on the lower level of his home.

The house—well, no, it was a castle, really, with a front designed to resemble a medieval fortress and stone walls reinforced against earthquakes—was built into a mountain overlooking La Jolla. Long ago, he'd bought himself the home and almost everything else that he deserved. All through his childhood, he'd been held by his parents to standards set by the Woodlocks, and he'd always rated second best. Well, he wasn't second best to anyone now. The Woodlocks' fate was in his hands, and he planned to keep it that way. Through the floor-to-ceiling, bulletproof windows of the gym, he looked out at the lights of the city and the black vista beyond, which would metamorphose into an expanse of the Pacific Ocean as the sun rose. He was waiting for his contact at the Woodlock house to call. He knew it might be hours before his spy could slip away, but that knowledge didn't curb his impatience. This was a big night for Wilson. The old man had scheduled a formal party, and Luther was eager to know how it had gone.

After wiping his face on a butter-yellow towel, he snatched the portable phone from the chrome-and-steel credenza and strode into the dressing room. With efficient movements, he pulled off his damp shorts and shirt and carefully stowed them in the wicker hamper. Naked, he stood in front of the mirror, inspecting his body. At forty, he was in excellent shape and worked with single-minded intensity to keep it that way.

For just a moment, another image flickered in his mind: the scrawny kid who had been the butt of practical jokes at the exclusive Dickensen Preparatory School for Boys.

"Go away," he muttered, angry that the persona he'd obliterated long ago still had the power to leap into his mind when he least expected it.

Once again he was a ten-year-old kid, his heart pounding as he walked into the hushed entrance foyer of the school where the Woodlock boys had gone for generations. He'd thought Dickensen Prep would change his life.

He laughed, an angry, grating sound. It had done that, all right.

He'd been weedy and awkward then—the last guy picked for any team. The kid nobody wanted for a roommate. The butt of countless jokes and insults. His first six years at Dickensen had been a living hell. But over the summer before his junior year, when his body had metamorphosed from boy to man, he'd seen an opportunity to change his life. He'd vowed to turn himself into a guy nobody would dare mess with, and he'd started working out in the gym, determined to return to school in the fall with new muscles and a new attitude. He'd accomplished those goals. And he'd been working his ass off ever since—in the gym and in every other venue where he could excel. He was strong and competent, in control. A millionaire many times over. He was proud of what he'd accomplished in life all by himself. He'd learned the value of hard work. The value of instilling fear. The value of focusing on a goal and doing whatever it took to get what he wanted.

He made a small face as he patted his abdomen. No matter how many hours he spent in the gym, he couldn't rid himself of the little paunch below his waist. But he could fix that easily. Time for a trip to Dr. Tomaso in Tijuana. The town had a bad reputation as a tourist trap, but he wasn't going there for painted pottery or jai alai. The city across the border from San Diego was also the perfect location for the luxury clinic that his favorite plastic surgeon ran. Dr. Tomaso was a very talented man. Luther had been there half a dozen times for minor procedures. Like the chin implant and liposuction that had given his face a more masculine profile. And the neat little operation that had lowered the interior shaft of his penis so that two more inches hung down. The kids at school had teased him about his small dick. Well, the hell with them. He looked fine now. Potent. Masculine. Although, another two inches would be even better. Too bad those pills and patches he kept seeing ads for on the Internet were dangerous.

Tomorrow he'd get his secretary to schedule a quick session to take care of his midsection. He'd be in and out of the clinic in twenty-four hours, tops.

Reaching into the large shower stall, he turned on the water and adjusted the temperature, then stepped in, enjoying the feel of the six sprays hitting his body. Afterward, he toweled dry and turned to the closet where he selected Yves Saint Laurent jeans, a soft baby blue knit silk pullover by Armani, and a pair of alligator loafers he had had made at a small factory in Genoa.

The phone rang as he was fixing a health drink.

"Yes?"

"I can't talk long."

"Understood."

"The party was a success. Except for the unfortunate incident where Colin fell down the steps."

"Did he?" Luther chuckled. "The poor boy. What about the others?"

"Wilson is maintaining himself on stimulants."

"And Uncle Darwin?"

"He's showing definite signs of mental instability."

"Good."

"After the party, Wilson gave Colin hell for not agreeing to marry your sister."

"Leave her out of this!"

"Yes, sir."

"And get me the guest list. I mean those who actually attended."

"Yes, sir."

He rang off, thinking that his plan was going very well. Soon he'd have the Woodlocks exactly where he wanted them. Especially Olivia.

He wanted her in bed—under him, on her back, on her stomach, any and all ways he could think of.

But meanwhile, it was time to go have some fun with the special visitor in his tower room.

4

THE dress rehearsals were over. If he was going to change his mind, now was the time.

In wolf form, Sam approached the Woodlock estate from the mountains above the property, wending his way easily down the steep slope that would be difficult for a man to navigate. In the shadow of a small grove of trees, he sniffed the chilly night air, searching for anything that might threaten him in the immediate environment. Many animals had been here—raccoons, magpies, sparrows, deer—but no other human had visited this patch of ground in the past few weeks.

A car passed on a nearby road, its headlights cutting through the early morning darkness. The gray wolf waited until he was alone in the blackness again. Then, in the shadows under the trees, he silently said the ancient chant that would change him from wolf to man.

With the transformation complete, the wind sent a shiver over his bare skin. Quickly he scooped up the layer of pine needles covering a newly dug hole in the ground, then brought out a large plastic trash bag with his clothing and equipment.

Minutes later, dressed in black sweats, he slung a knapsack over his shoulder and crossed the hundred yards to the back wall of the estate. There, he threw a grappling hook attached to a rope to the top of the wall and climbed over.

On the other side, he lowered himself to the ground and cautiously approached the mansion, skirting the pavilion that housed the swimming pool. From under the branches of an oak tree, he studied the house as he had on so many nights. At two in the morning, it was dark and still. But that didn't guarantee all of the occupants were tucked in their beds. Colin had trouble sleeping. So did Wilson. Other people lived here, too: Wilson's brother and three servants. A big crowd for a house that Sam planned to rob.

His eyes darted to Olivia's window. Sometimes she stood in the darkness, looking out, as though searching for something. He wanted to believe she was looking for him. She wasn't visible in her window, but the thought that he might see her if he waited long enough made him suddenly breathless. Was it she, not the little figurines in the art gallery, who drew him back here night after night?

He tried in vain to stomp out the question and the even more useless train of thought. He was here to rob the place, dammit.

Yet Olivia continued to invade his mind. Vivid pictures danced in his head: the two of them, naked and aroused. It was easy to conjure the scene he had dreamed so many times since the party, where he'd first laid eyes on her. In his fantasy, he leaned back against a solid stone wall and splayed his legs, equalizing their heights as he gathered her in, so that there was no space between his body and hers. Yet she inched closer, pressing her breasts tightly against his chest and her belly against his groin, his erection nestled in the cleft at the top of her legs. In his imagination, he swayed her body in his arms, cupped her bottom so he could rub her sex against his aching cock, at the same time he angled his head to feast from her mouth.

Five tortured minutes later, he was hot and hard and cursing himself for a fool. He dragged in air and let it out in a rush. When he was sure his attention was focused where it belonged, he looked at the mansion again. On some deep, instinctive level, he sensed that bailing out of the Woodlock job would be a good idea. But somewhere along the line, it had become more personal than any other heist he'd undertaken, and not only because of Olivia. The further he'd dug into Wilson Woodlock's business dealings, the more he despised the man. He'd traveled north and seen the Woodlock logging business for himself. It was destroying a habitat where thousands of animals lived, and nobody was doing anything to stop it—especially not the government.

Of course, robbing the man's estate wouldn't stop the destruction. Maybe Greenpeace or the Sierra Club could get the EPA to act against Woodlock Industries. He'd given both of them large sums of money—and he would give them more—designating the contributions to fight the wholesale leasing of public lands to logging operations. He hoped the money, combined with the organizations' political clout, would be enough to take care of Woodlock.

Meanwhile, Sam wanted the lumber baron to feel a sense of violation akin to his violation of the land. And ravaging his priceless collection of pre-Columbian artifacts would certainly do the trick.

Sam strained his eyes and ears toward the house. As far as he could tell, no one was on the first floor. "Let's roll," he muttered under his breath, then slipped through the shrubbery at the edge of the wide lawn, heading for the patio.

He was operating by the book he'd written. First, he checked to make sure that the motion detectors were off. Then, he stood for a long time, listening for sounds of movement. Everything inside was as still as a tomb.

He was prepared to cut the glass on the patio door, but it was unlocked. All he had to do was walk inside and close the door silently behind him.

In the family room, he sorted out the scents of the various people. Wilson, the son, his lover, the uncle, servants. Above all, Olivia. Her scent wafted around him, sending a dart of arousal through him. She had been in the room recently.

He was here to steal artifacts. Instead, he pictured himself going up the stairs and searching out her room. It was easy to imagine slipping into her bed and folding her close.

With a grimace he canceled the heated scene. What the hell was wrong with him?

His jaw clenched, he made his way down the hall to the art gallery, went past, and stepped into the closet that housed the control panel. The paper he'd employed on his last visit to blot up body oil showed him which keys were touched frequently.

Taking out a small computer designed by a very specialized electronics shop, he activated it and waited while it made connections to the keypad and simulated various combinations of punches. He didn't need to know the access code. The processor would figure it out for him. Still, this was always the part that made him the most nervous. He hated standing around while the computer did its work. In five minutes, his patience was rewarded. With a small electronic beep, the computer turned off the alarm on the cases holding the artifacts.

His night vision allowed him to work without switching on the

light. He had just unscrewed the glass panel on the side of a case when
a noise from the doorway announced that he wasn't alone.

Whirling, he saw a figure standing in the darkness.

"Put your hands in the air," a cool voice said.

5

OLIVIA stood in the gallery doorway, her heart blocking her throat as
she kept the revolver in her hand trained on the shadowed form she
knew was Sam Morgan.

Reaching for the wall switch, she turned on the light. He stood casually beside a display case, and as they regarded each other across ten
feet of charged space, she knew he was trying to decide what to do:
rush her and damn the consequences—or bide his time.

She tried to keep her expression neutral, but it was difficult, given
the mixture of emotions roiling through her. Before the party, Sam
Morgan's bio and picture had intrigued and attracted her. After their
meeting, thoughts of him had filled her mind, both awake and in her
dreams.

Still, she'd been sure she was prepared to see him again. As he casually studied her, she knew she had been a fool.

He spoke first, in a maddeningly controlled voice. "I take it you
knew I was coming back."

She might have denied the obvious. Instead, she gave a small nod.

"Me, specifically? Or just some random thief?"

"You, specifically."

He tipped his head to one side, studying her. "How did you know
this was the big night?"

"There are sensors installed under the rug," she answered, because
it was easier to focus on small details than on the big picture.

"And your brother dreamed up an elaborate plan to trap me?"

She raised one shoulder. "You don't think I could lure you here by
myself?"

A smile flickered on his well-shaped lips. "Not with pre-Columbian artifacts."

The wolfish way he was looking at her sent a shiver over her skin, and she silently cursed herself for reacting to him.

"So was your father in on it, too?" he asked.

She felt her facial muscles go rigid. "Dad's going to . . . hit the roof when he gets the news."

"The news about what, exactly?"

She was the one with the gun. She had the advantage, she told herself, as she moved out of the doorway and into the room. "The news that Colin and I have hired you for a job."

His eyes widened briefly before he could hide his surprise. "I hate to mention it," he said evenly, "but I haven't accepted. I don't even know the job specs." His gaze went pointedly to the gun. "Is that my reward if I decline?"

She licked her dry lips, watching him take in the small movement. He had picked a very bad night for his invasion, but she'd simply have to make the best of it and hope that nothing went wrong. "I can turn you over to the police. But I don't want to do that. I'd rather have you on our side."

"That's an interesting suggestion," he said, and she had the distinct feeling he wasn't afraid of her or the gun or the cops. "What's in it for me?" he added.

"The thrill of pulling off the biggest heist of your life," she answered, giving him the line she'd rehearsed. Even to her own ears, it sounded stilted.

"You mean, I walk away with a lot of money?"

"Not from the job, exactly."

"Then what?" he pressed.

"If we get back the family jewels, then I'm sure Dad will pay you a handsome sum."

His calm façade cracked open. "The hell he will!" he spat. "I wouldn't take his money if he stuffed it in his mouth and crawled over broken glass to hand it to me."

"I believe you said the wrong thing, my dear." Colin's maddeningly rational voice came from over her left shoulder.

She fought a mixture of relief and annoyance as her brother stepped into the room. She'd told him she could handle this, knowing he was probably going to butt in, anyway. As her gaze flicked to him, she saw from his expression that there had been an unfortunate development upstairs.

"What?" she asked.

He gave a small shake of his head, and all she could do was hope everything was under control.

When he spoke, he addressed her, not Morgan. "Daddy's money means nothing to him—unless he steals it. He thinks he's Robin Hood, with a modern twist. His mission is to screw the nasty bastards who rape the land, then give the loot to the environmentalists."

She'd argued that couldn't be Morgan's primary motive, but the sudden hard look in his eyes told her that Colin had him nailed.

Her brother moved farther into the room and sat down in the easy chair in the corner. His health had been a little better recently. Maybe Brice's magic ceremonies had done some good. Or maybe it had been the herbal concoctions Brice kept whipping up in the blender and making Colin drink. Still, she knew her brother needed to conserve his strength.

Morgan addressed his next comment to Colin. "Let's cut to the chase. Stop playing the grand puppeteer, and tell me what's really going on."

Her brother spread his hands. "We're not playing anything. A thief of your caliber seemed like the perfect solution to our problem. But given the nature of your profession, we didn't think we could call you up on the phone and ask you to steal something for us."

"You've got that right." Morgan shifted his weight from one foot to the other. "Okay. What's so insanely valuable that you hatched this elaborate plot to get me here?"

Considering the stakes, Olivia thought Colin sounded surprisingly calm as he replied, "Something . . . important to our family. We want it back."

"Your sister just called it the 'family jewels.'" Morgan cocked an eyebrow. "I assume she didn't mean it in the usual sense. So what is it?"

"A valuable artifact," Olivia elaborated.

"So how did you decide I was the guy to come to your rescue? I'm not exactly a knight on a white horse."

"Colin is a computer genius," she answered.

Morgan cocked an inquisitive eyebrow at her brother. "Congratulations. Um . . . pardon my rudeness, but so what?"

"Olivia exaggerates my talents," Colin clarified. "I know how to tease facts out of the Web. I know how to calculate probabilities and make correlations, and to put information from one source together with completely different data. We went looking for a master thief. I saw a pattern of difficult robberies, and I began assembling known facts. They led me to you. So we made sure you knew about Daddy's prized collection."

Morgan waited a few beats before saying, "Well, if *you* figured all that out, maybe the police are about to scoop me up."

"I doubt they have the resources to produce the kind of statistical probabilities I can generate," Colin answered, and she heard the touch of pride he couldn't conceal.

Morgan nodded and leaned casually against the display case, silently telling her that he wasn't worried. What did he know that they didn't?

"I think you'd better tell me more about your employment specifications. But first"—he cocked an eyebrow at her—"put down that gun, before somebody gets hurt."

In truth, the damn revolver had been weighing down her hand. After a quick glance at Colin, she set the weapon on the cabinet near the door, then cleared her throat. "The Woodlocks have been feuding with the Ethridge family for years," she said. "Luther Ethridge has stolen something important from us. It's heavily guarded, and we can't get it back without help."

"What is it?" Morgan demanded.

"A priceless ancient box that's been in the family for years," she answered.

Morgan studied her face, as though he knew very well she wasn't telling the whole truth. "A box. Uh-huh. What's in it?"

"Maybe nothing," Colin tossed out, his voice dismissive.

Olivia couldn't stop herself from shooting him a shocked look. "Don't say that!" She looked from her brother to Morgan. "It's something valuable—but not to anyone but us." Right. Only a matter of life and death.

"Then why does this guy named Luther Ethridge think it's worth stealing—and keeping?"

"To hurt us," Colin answered for her. "It's a revenge thing."

Morgan folded his arms across his chest. "What did you do to him?"

"Our families have been . . . associated for decades. We've been more successful, and he can't stand that."

"That's a start. Now let's have the truth—not a bunch of crap that sounds like you lifted it from a bad spy movie." Morgan gave them both a disgusted look. "You're not hiring me to steal a box."

Colin spread his hands. "This isn't like any movie. It's more like a fairy tale."

"Ah. Well, then, I beg your pardon," Morgan answered, sarcasm coloring his voice.

Ignoring the editorial comment, Olivia added, "There's an ancient legend handed down through the years that we must keep the box safe or our family will . . . come to ruin."

Morgan studied her, and she felt naked under his gaze. "And you believe that?" he asked sharply.

"My father does. Luther does," she whispered. "And as long as they think it's true, it is. You studied my dad's environmental record. It was a lot better five years ago before Luther took away . . ." She stopped and started again. "Before Dad lost confidence in his own judgment, and his business started failing."

"So, now you're telling me I should save your family—for the sake of the spotted owl?"

"I can't tell you any more, not until I know I can trust you." Even as she uttered the phrase, Olivia silently admitted the lie. She could never tell him the truth. And even if she did, he wouldn't believe it.

But maybe she'd piqued his curiosity.

Colin began speaking again. "If you need another incentive, there's always saving yourself. I've documented your criminal history. I could send the information to the cops."

She gave her brother a pitying look. Apparently he still thought he could operate on a logical level with this man. That was Colin— tied to logic and numbers and probabilities.

Morgan kept his gaze fixed on her. "Let's assume for the sake of argument that I buy into your grand scheme."

"Okay."

"First, you and I have to talk—alone. Otherwise, no deal."

She looked at Colin. "I guess you'd better clear out."

"I don't like that idea. He's dangerous."

She wanted to shout that she'd known that all along. Instead, she simply answered, "You said he's never killed anyone."

"Yet."

"If you want my cooperation, I get some private time with Olivia," Morgan reiterated.

Her brother's only response was to stand up and leave the room.

When he was gone, Morgan looked around. "Come outside, where it's less likely that someone is going to be listening in on the conversation."

"Are you implying the room is bugged?" she snapped.

"Now, why would I think a room with sensors under the rug might be bugged?"

She made a dismissive sound but did as he asked, leading him down the hall to the room where they'd first talked. He opened the door to the patio, then gestured for her to step outside.

She would have preferred to stay in the house, but she gave him a defiant look as she strolled onto the patio. The moon allowed her to see only a little in the darkness, and she concluded that his night vision must be better than hers when, as she shivered, he came up and put an arm around her shoulder.

She stiffened. "Don't."

"Why not?"

"You make me nervous," she admitted, hating the quaver in her own voice.

"But you want me to work . . . with you," he said.

"For me."

"I don't work *for* anyone."

Yet he was still here. Standing close, with his arm around her.

The cold air should have helped clear her brain, but it didn't. She had thought of him night after night. And she couldn't fool herself about his motives. Olivia knew he'd come back to the house where she lived because he wanted—no, needed—to be with her again. As much as she needed to be with him.

He made an angry sound.

"What?" she asked, alarm lacing her voice.

He took her by the shoulders and turned her to face him, staring down into her upturned face. "Maybe you picked the wrong guy. Maybe I'm too ruthless to deal with," he said, and she caught something unexpected below his words. He was as wary of her as she was of him.

That gave her the courage to insist, "You're not the wrong guy."

"You're sure you haven't made a bad mistake, luring me here?"

"It wasn't a mistake." She could hear the desperation in her tone as she begged, "Please, can't we just make this simple. I need your help. I'll make it worth your while."

He laughed. "I'm afraid you've caught a tiger by the tail. Are you smart enough to realize that?"

"Yes," she whispered into the darkness.

"You mentioned fairy tales. Don't you remember that the man who saves the kingdom ends up with the king's daughter?"

Her mouth was almost too dry for speech. But she managed to say, "In this case, that's impossible."

He didn't answer with words, only stared at her mouth. For a charged moment, neither of them moved, but she was aware of the silent messages passing between them.

I want to kiss you.

I know. But you can't. I can't.

You can. Because I have to do this. Just this once . . .

Before she could back away, he lowered his head. As his lips touched down on hers, a conflagration crackled to life, heat blazing through her, startling and all-consuming in its intensity.

She was instantly ready for sex, and she made a small, shocked sound deep in her throat, because nothing in her experience had prepared her for the speed or intensity of her response. Until this moment, she'd been able to fool herself into thinking she could handle Sam Morgan. Now she didn't even know if she could handle herself.

His lips had looked so hard when they'd been talking in the gallery. But they weren't hard at all. They felt soft and yielding against hers, as though he was caught by the same wild sexual need that had swallowed her whole.

She forgot about how she and Colin had tricked him into coming here. Forgot about the desperate reason why they needed his help. Her only reality was the strong, intense man who held her in his arms. She felt her heart slamming against the inside of her chest as he gathered her into a possessive embrace. Or maybe it was his heartbeat she felt.

Every danger signal urged her to pull away. Some rational part of her mind was issuing warnings—demanding that she end the kiss before it was too late, insisting that she tear herself out of his arms and run away into the darkness.

Instead, she opened her mouth for him, begging him to deepen the kiss. He gladly accepted the invitation, angling his head for better contact, devouring her with his lips, his tongue, his teeth.

He tasted of dark, mysterious forests and ancient legends. He tasted of the magic that she had so desperately sought. She didn't know how it could be so, but without doubt, it was. With a gruff sound, he gathered her even closer, holding her firmly against his hard-muscled body, as though the intimate contact were as necessary to him as the air he breathed.

Suddenly a wind sprang up, disturbing the still night, shaking tree branches and whipping around them. When she swayed on her feet, his hands slipped to her hips, cradling her bottom and anchoring her more firmly against his erection, showing her in no uncertain terms that one simple kiss had made him ready to drive himself into her.

She answered with a small sound that might have begun as a protest. Instead, she knew it only revealed her own sharp and powerful needs. In the tiny corner of her mind that could still deal with concepts, she recognized him as the man ordained for her since the beginning of time. But the part of her that had to live in the world shoved the knowledge aside. She simply couldn't deal with such thoughts. Not now. Not ever.

Yet the sensations he was arousing inside her were too powerful to ignore. She wanted him. This instant. On the damp grass, if they couldn't make it to some place more comfortable in the next five seconds. And from the way he clung to her, swaying on unsteady legs, she gathered that the feeling was mutual. The knowledge gave her a sense of power.

In the next instant, that power, along with all else, was shattered by the sound of a gunshot cracking the night air.

6

THE sound of a gun firing was like a bolt of lightning lancing through Sam's brain. It had come from inside the house, but the shooter could come charging out the door at any minute.

"Get down!" In one swift motion, he pushed Olivia toward the shelter of the back wall. Following her to the ground, he covered her body with his, offering her what protection he could.

Instead of cooperating, she struggled against him.

"Stay down," he snapped. "Do you know who's shooting?" The thought of her in danger was like a garrote tightening around his throat, and he tried to hold onto her, even as a gust of wind seemed to be bent on tearing her away.

And she wasn't helping. "Let me up. I have to—"

Colin dashed onto the patio, breathing hard as his gaze darted around, finding them and instantly taking in Sam's protective position. "It's . . . Darwin," he said between gasps for air.

A blast of wind roared across the patio, as though punctuating the words.

"Where is he?" Sam demanded.

"He ran onto the sun porch and locked the door," Colin answered, pitching his voice above the roar of the wind.

"Upstairs?"

"Yes."

Sam helped Olivia to her feet, then guided her toward the overhang where the second story sheltered the patio.

She pushed her hair back, drawing Colin's attention, and Sam wondered if it was obvious what he and Olivia had been doing before the shot rang out.

But, hell, who cared? Compared to being shot at, it hardly mattered that he'd been about to ravage the fairy-tale princess.

Colin took a deep breath and seemed to gather his wits. "Darwin must have come down and found the gun in the gallery."

Olivia's skin had gone pale as bleached bone.

She opened her mouth, but Colin spoke first.

"I should have been thinking about him," her brother said. "I knew . . ." He trailed off when his sister shook her head.

"What the hell is going on?" Sam cut in. "Is anybody hurt?"

"Uncle Darwin's having mental problems," Olivia said, raising her voice above the moaning of the wind.

Before Sam could comment, another shot split the darkness, the bullet whizzing past his shoulder.

"I think you'd better call the cops," Sam growled as he herded Olivia and Colin through the door, fighting to close it as gusts of wind tried to tear it from his hands. Finally, he slammed it shut, and the noise level dropped abruptly.

"No police," Colin answered.

When Brice appeared in the family room, an anxious look passed between the two men.

"Are you all right?" Brice asked.

"Yes."

The discussion broke off abruptly when Wilson Woodlock came puffing into the room. He stopped short when he spotted a stranger in the middle of the family group.

"Who the fuck are you?" he demanded.

Olivia answered quickly. "He's Sam Morgan. You met him at the party. Remember?"

"What's he doing here—tonight?"

"He's going to help us."

"How? By taking Darwin off to the funny farm?" her father snapped.

"Of course not."

Sam stepped between father and daughter. "I understand your brother is holed up on the sun porch. Maybe you'd better make sure he stays there."

"Thurston is watching the door."

"Is he armed?" Sam asked.

"Yes."

"And what's he going to do if Darwin decides to come out? Shoot him?"

Wilson took the point. "Maybe I can talk Darwin into putting down his weapon. He might listen to me."

"That would be helpful," Sam muttered under his breath as the old man hurried off. He'd watched the house for weeks. It had seemed relatively normal, considering the massive wealth of the occupants. Who knew it was an insane asylum? Giving Colin a sideways glance, he suggested, "Maybe it's time to get some professional help for your psychotic uncle."

"He's not psychotic," Olivia broke in.

Instead of arguing with her, he said, "Okay, we'll discuss abnormal psych later. Tell me about the sunroom and the roof." He hadn't studied that area in detail because he hadn't planned to go anywhere near it. Stupid—and he knew better. He should have been thorough. "How do you get into the sunroom without going in through the hall? Are there windows? What else? What about a door to the roof?"

Realizing he'd hit them with a lot of questions at once, he added, "Maybe you'd better draw me a diagram."

Colin sat down at the desk in the corner and pulled out a sheet of paper and a pencil. With great precision, he began drawing a picture. The room was rectangular, with long, wide windows. One door opened to the end of a hallway. French doors opened onto a roof deck.

"The door to the hallway is solid? I mean, all wood—with no glass?" Sam asked.

"Yes."

"And it's closed?"

"Yes."

Sam studied the layout, wondering if he could climb up without getting shot, particularly with the wind blowing. "Let me have a look at the wall," he said. "Maybe I can get up there."

Olivia put a hand on his arm. "What if he comes outside with the gun again?"

"You'll lose your draftee thief," he said dryly.

She looked torn. "You think you can get the gun away from him?" she asked.

"First things first." His gaze swung from Olivia to Colin and Brice. "Listen carefully. If I do this, I need to handle it my way. I want that door"—he pointed to the sun porch door on Colin's diagram—"to stay closed until I say it's okay to open it. Do you understand?"

"Yes," they all answered, but he wondered, anyway, if somebody would come bursting into the room at the wrong time. They'd get a nasty surprise if they did.

"I'd better go up," Olivia said and started for the door.

Sam grabbed her arm. "Be careful."

She turned and looked into his eyes. "I will," she answered, and he knew from her expression that there was a lot more she wanted to say to him. Personal things. But not in front of an audience. And not in the middle of a crisis.

When she had left the room, Sam turned to Colin. "Your uncle—a couple of years older than your father, five foot ten, a hundred and eighty pounds, practically bald, pasty complexion. Right?"

"Yes," Colin answered. "I'll probably end up looking like him—if I live that long."

"You're going to be all right," Brice said fiercely.

Sam wanted to ask what was wrong with Colin, but this wasn't the time to satisfy his curiosity. Gripping the handle of one French door, he held it tightly against the wind as he opened it and stepped outside. What was with this damned wind, anyway? He'd checked the weather reports—standard procedure for break-in nights. The forecast had been for clear skies with hardly a breeze. Yet as he wormed his way past a line of tall shrubs whose long branches were wildly thrashing, he thought a hurricane must have blown in out of nowhere.

He finally spotted the second-floor balcony. As he looked up, he saw a vine-covered drainpipe along the wall, but he had the feeling that neither the vine nor the pipe would hold his weight. He circled the other way around the house, stopping where he'd dropped his knapsack. Squatting, he pulled out the coiled rope and grappling hook he'd used to scale the wall encircling the estate. Olivia and her family might as well reap the benefits of his having come prepared.

The situation had a certain irony, he thought as he hurried back to the balcony, throwing an arm in front of his face to ward off a flapping branch. To get a view of the sunroom, he took a dozen steps away from the house. As far as he could see in the moonlight, the homicidal uncle had gone back inside—or he was lurking in the shadows, waiting for someone to attack him.

Hoping the latter wasn't the case, Sam judged the range. As he calculated the amount of swing he'd need for the rope, he asked himself why he was leaping into danger to help the Woodlock family. They'd given him the perfect opportunity to slip away. He could go over the wall, then call 911 and tell the police there was a crisis in progress at the millionaire's estate.

But he knew he wasn't going to do that. The choice he'd made to help had a lot to do with Olivia, but she wasn't the only reason. It seemed he'd stumbled into a nice little mystery, and his curiosity had gotten the better of him.

Let's hope curiosity doesn't kill the wolf. Compensating for the wind, he managed to connect with the metal railing, the hook clanging like a church bell. He tensed, then breathed out a sigh when no wild-eyed bald guy with a gun in his hand bent over the edge of the balcony to see what was going on.

In fact, the sound of furniture breaking somewhere above seemed to suggest that Uncle D was busy elsewhere.

Since success in his profession depended as much on his physical as his mental power, Sam kept himself in good shape. The climb to the second floor normally would have taken him less than a minute, but the wind kept blowing him back and forth as he clung to the rope. By the time he swung onto the tiled balcony surface, he was breathing hard.

He waited until his breathing had returned to normal, then quietly crossed the eight-foot-wide balcony. Careful not to step into the light pouring from the open doorway, he looked through the window. He saw wicker furniture, a variety of flowering plants, and a hulking bald man standing with his back to the open French doors. Uncle Darwin, Sam presumed. He was wearing dark slacks and a dress shirt that was plastered to his body by perspiration. Waving the gun, he was shouting words Sam couldn't make out—doubtless, at someone on the other side of the hallway door.

As he watched through the window, he thought about the best way to take the guy down. He considered going in as a wolf, since that was his most natural fighting mode. But a wolf couldn't subdue a man without inflicting serious damage.

So he pushed the door open a crack, relieved that Darwin was still focused on whoever was in the hall. Obviously upset, he waved his arms and shouted, "If you won't join me in the good fight, go away! The demons of war are on us."

Demons? What the hell . . . ?

"Darwin, let me help you," came Wilson's voice, muffled by the closed door but sounding far calmer and more reasonable than he had downstairs.

"Help me how?"

"Let me in. Everything's going to be all right if you just put down the gun."

"How can you say that, you fool, you . . . you dupe of the Old Ones? We are doomed! The demons have stolen the breath of life! And now they are coming to finish us off!"

"No. Darwin, listen to me. You're sick. There are no demons."

"What's wrong with you? Can't you feel their hot breath on your face? On your neck?"

"Darwin, let me in. You'll feel better if you take your medicine."

"You lie! The demons have corrupted your thoughts! They have put false images in your mind!"

"Please, don't do this."

The conversation between the brothers was fascinating. Darwin was obviously delusional, but something—an intuitive feeling he couldn't define—made Sam wonder if there was some grain of truth in the old man's ravings. He wanted to keep listening, but when Darwin pointed the gun at the door, Sam acted swiftly.

Sprinting across the room, he leaped onto Uncle Darwin's back, intending to grab the gun and bring him down.

The weapon discharged, the bullet hitting the floor. And a shout came from the other side of the door. "What's going on?"

When the door rattled, Sam yelled, "It's okay. Stay back."

He didn't have time or breath for more conversation. Hoping Wilson was smart enough to remain where he was, Sam banged Darwin's gun hand against the floor. But old Uncle D was stronger than he looked. Or perhaps he had the ferocity of the insane. Regardless, he wouldn't let go of the weapon, even when Sam banged his hand repeatedly against the floor.

Darwin had a hundred pounds on him, and before Sam could stop him, the lunatic wrenched away, rolled over, and pointed the gun at his attacker.

Instinct took over. The ancient chant came to Sam's lips without conscious thought.

"*Taranis, Epona, Cerridwen,*" he growled, fighting danger in the way his ancestors had fought since they had emerged from the forests of ancient Britain. He was still fully dressed, but he felt himself changing, felt the gray hair sprout on his face and hands, felt his features re-form themselves.

His vision blurred as the world around him changed in shape and texture. But Darwin Woodlock was very close, and Sam had no trouble seeing the look of utter horror suffusing the man's features.

7

DARWIN made a low, anguished sound, part fear and part pain, then scuttled across the floor like a crab looking for a hiding place. As if tuned to his fear, the wind still raging outside strengthened even more, rattling the windows as it howled. Dropping the gun, he cradled his arms over his head.

The wolf had served his purpose and was of no further use to Sam. He broke off the chant in mid-syllable. The pain was terrible as he stopped in the early stages of transformation. He could barely think. Barely breathe. Barely keep a scream of agony locked in his throat. When the door burst open, all he could do was look up stupidly at the figure charging into the room.

"The demon. The demon," Darwin shouted, pointing toward Sam.

A muscular man who looked like a bodyguard or a bouncer gave him a hurried glance, and Sam braced for some kind of violent reaction. But he assumed he must have returned to acceptable human parameters because the newcomer hurtled past, heading for Darwin, with Wilson following more slowly behind him.

The bodyguard dropped to his knees beside the old man. In his hand was a hypodermic needle. He looked back at Wilson, clearly asking for permission.

"Give me a moment," Wilson answered, then took a step closer to his brother and hunkered down beside the bodyguard. They looked like they were getting ready to pray for Uncle D's salvation.

"Darwin, you're all right. Everything's all right," Wilson soothed.

The man on the floor fixed his eyes on Sam and shrank back against the wall. "He's a demon! With wolf's teeth and claws! Kill him! Kill him!"

Sam winced.

"No, we're not going to kill him. Everything's under control now."

"Get him away from me!" He kicked out at the bodyguard.

Wilson gave a short, frustrated sigh. "We'd better do him."

They worked as an efficient team, probably because they'd done this before. Wilson grasped his brother's shoulders, and the other man plunged the needle into a pudgy arm. Uncle D struggled and screamed, then went still.

A third guy came in. He, Wilson, and the bodyguard picked up Darwin and lugged him out.

Sam climbed to his feet. All attention was focused elsewhere, which gave him the opportunity to slip out of the room and down a set of back stairs. Outside, he dragged in lungfuls of the night air, trying to clear his head. Some part of his mind noted the utter calm around him. The wind had died, leaving the night air still and cool.

So what about Darwin? He'd seen enough to know there was something pretty strange about Sam Morgan. With luck, nobody would believe him. After all, he'd already been babbling about demons.

Sam sighed. He'd jumped right in and tried to subdue the mental patient. Now that he was thinking a little more clearly, he wondered why he was still here.

Olivia and Colin had set a trap for him—baited with pre-Columbian artifacts. He'd told himself he was coming to steal them. So . . . why not take them now, while everybody was busy dealing with Uncle D?

Because he didn't really want the damn little figurines enough to bother. He'd come because he couldn't stay away from Olivia, and he had made a serious mistake. Without giving himself time for a big mental debate, he walked outside and picked up his pack. Then he took off across the lawn, climbed the wall, and headed for the grove of trees where he'd changed from man to wolf. He hesitated for a moment, then decided not to risk another transformation tonight. He picked his way up the hill, which took twice as long on two legs as it would have on four.

TWO hours after he'd arrived at the estate, he was in his Lexus and on his way home.

It wasn't a long trip. He lived in the mountains south of Lompoc, on a ranch that he'd purchased from a dedicated old environmentalist who wanted any potential buyer to sign a contract saying he wouldn't subdivide the property. The conditions suited Sam just fine. The whole point of buying a ranch was to make sure he didn't have any neighbors besides deer and coyotes.

He'd lived in the ranch house for a couple of years, while he'd constructed the dwelling he wanted, bringing in skilled tradesmen for the jobs he couldn't do himself. The new house was built into the side of a hill, with a window wall overlooking the valley and an interior courtyard lit by a skylight. It was a wolf's den, basically. But that was what he loved about it. It was wonderful to step into his lair and lock out the world. The den wasn't a trap. He had an escape hatch, if he needed it—a tunnel in the back that led to an exit on the other side of the hill.

By the time he pulled into the parking area, he was emotionally and physically exhausted. Not too exhausted, however, to realize he'd made a miraculous escape. He'd been damned lucky to get away alive and unharmed.

The darkened house was a blur around him as he strode to the bedroom and threw himself onto the king-sized bed.

He went to sleep almost at once and, soon afterward, began to dream. In his dream, he was a wolf, running through the hills, reveling in his freedom beneath the moon and stars shining down from a velvet dome of sky.

A tantalizing scent blew toward him on the wind, but he turned away from it to hunt game. He brought down a mule deer and filled his belly with fresh meat, then drank from a stream that rushed down the mountain in the rainy season.

He trotted on, traveling farther and faster than whatever would be possible except in a dream. Still, the scent he'd sniffed on the wind followed him, pulling at him. All at once, he recognized it—the tantalizing woman scent of Olivia Woodlock. It wrapped itself around him, calling him. And finally there was no way he could deny his need for her.

In the dream, he turned toward home, racing now, an impossible blur of motion in the darkness. His steps were sure and steady until he reached the bluff above his home. There, he faltered to a stop, looking at the magnificent sight that awaited him on his patio: Olivia Woodlock, dressed in a white silk shirt and slacks. He had fled her, but she had followed him home, because the two of them were bound together by invisible cords.

She sensed him, as he had sensed her. Raising her head, she met his gaze, her eyes asking him silently to make love with her.

The cords between them tightened as he walked down the hill.

Take off your clothes. Let me see you. The wolf couldn't speak, of course. But he knew she heard him in her mind when she smiled, then began to unbutton her blouse.

He came eagerly to her, his eyes never leaving her as she opened the garment, then tossed it onto the flagstones. She'd worn nothing beneath it, and he watched transfixed as she lifted her beautiful breasts in her hands, offering them to him.

Stroke your fingers over the tips. Make them hard.

She did as he asked, giving him a smoldering look that made his blood run hot and fast in his veins.

He stood ten paces from her as she pulled off her slacks. Again she was wearing nothing underneath. Naked, she faced him, so that he could take in every detail of her body. The high breasts, the inward curve of her waist. Her flat belly and sensually rounded hips. The tantalizing dark triangle of hair covering her mound.

Suddenly, the patio table and chairs were replaced by a wide bed, and she lay down upon it, her gaze still locked on his. He climbed onto the mattress and pressed his flank against hers. She reached for him, circling his neck with her arms, kissing his ruff, the side of his face, his muzzle.

He moved his head so that he stroked his face against her breasts, then circled them with his tongue, taking them delicately between his wolf's teeth.

She made soft, aroused sounds that incited him further, her body writhing as he kissed and licked his way down to the hot, swollen core of her, lapping up her luscious nectar as he gave her pleasure.

"Please . . . please, don't make me wait," she cried.

Then, suddenly, he was a man, aching and trembling with white-hot need for her. His body covered hers, and he plunged his hard cock into her, claiming her, making her his. His hips moved in a frantic rhythm that she met thrust for thrust, excitement and need and sheer, unadulterated pleasure swirling around them until the very air turned white with it, and all that existed was that hot, wet, throbbing place where their bodies joined.

He felt the signs of impending climax only seconds before it took hold of him. He gave himself up to it entirely, crying out as it washed through him and out of him and into her, leaving him weak and shaking and replete. . . .

Sam blinked awake and knew immediately that he was alone in his own bed. The sheets were tangled around him, and his body was slick with sweat and the sticky evidence of ejaculation.

"Christ . . ."

He couldn't remember the last time he'd had a wet dream. Hell, he'd never had one like it. He had left the Woodlock estate last night, convinced that he had put the whole insane family behind him. But the dream had made a liar of him. He had brought Olivia with him—to his bed.

"Christ," he said again, shaken to the core.

He had never invited a woman to his home. Nor had he ever come to a woman in wolf form, although he had fantasized about it. But none of those fantasies had been as arousing or vivid—or as real—as the one his subconscious had just conjured. What struck him most about it, though, wasn't the almost blinding sexual excitement he'd experienced. More telling was that Olivia had accepted him for what he was.

"Oh, sure. Right."

He climbed out of bed to stand on unsteady legs. Cursing again, he strode down the hall and stood staring out the front windows at the brown hills. It was late afternoon. He had slept for hours.

He clenched his hands at his sides, struggling for calm. When he felt more in control, he thawed a steak from the freezer and brought the meat outside to the patio, to his normal table and chairs, not the bed where he and Olivia had ravaged each other.

It had been a dream. Just a dream. Just a very male response to a very attractive woman.

He sat eating the meat, looking out at the scraggly vegetation on the hills, the live oaks, and the clumps of pampas grass he'd planted along the creek, struggling to keep his mind in neutral.

Later he tried to work. But he couldn't keep his attention on any of the jobs he had started planning. As the sun dipped low, he left the house and walked over the hill, into the brown landscape. When he was certain no other human being could see him, he took off his clothing and laid it on the ground. Then he raised his face to the wind and began the chant he had started in the Woodlock sunroom.

This time it wasn't an emergency. This time he was doing something he wanted—needed—for himself.

"Taranis, Epona, Cerridwen," he said in a clear, loud voice that car-

ried across the hillside. He repeated the phrase, then went on to the next. *"Ga. Feart. Cleas. Duais. Aithriocht. Go gcumhdai is dtreorai na deithe thu."*

The transformation didn't come without penalty. There was always pain, like needles stabbing into his brain, into his muscles. But the ancient words helped free him from the bonds of his human shape.

He was a creature of the natural world now. A wolf. His life was easy. Uncomplicated. But as he leaped into the dry grass and started off across the mountains the way he had in the dream, he knew in his heart that he was trying to outrun kismet.

His father had told him years ago that this would happen to him around the age of thirty. Every man in his family was destined to find his mate—the one woman who would complete him. And he would be helpless to resist her.

He had been away from his family for so long that he had stopped believing the old myth—until he had felt someone's eyes drilling into his back. There, standing in a house he'd planned to burglarize, he had turned around and found himself facing Olivia Woodlock.

The daughter of a man he despised.

She couldn't be his mate. He wouldn't let it be true. He would take control of his life. He would break the ancient magic and find another woman. Someone who shared his values. Someone who hadn't been raised like an exotic flower in a temperature-controlled hothouse.

He was safe here, in his own realm. He had saved himself by coming home. The dream was just a fantasy. Nothing to worry about.

Of course, there were other things he might consider a tad worrisome. Olivia and Colin knew he was a master thief, and they could send the cops after him—if they even knew where he lived. Which he doubted, because he had kept his home a secret from the world.

If they sicced the law on him, he was pretty sure their "evidence" wouldn't hold up in court. But they could certainly add a harassment factor to his life.

Still, he didn't think they would do it, if only because he could harass them right back—starting with a report to the Environmental

Protection Agency detailing the Woodlock record in Oregon and ending with a visit from Uncle Darwin's "demon."

LUTHER Ethridge stood in his tasteful beige and brown living room,
looking out over the lights of the city.

He was one step closer to his goal, and the thought made his lips
curve in a satisfied smile. Too bad his toxic parents hadn't lived long
enough to see his triumph. They had been in awe of old Abner
Woodlock—Wilson's father. They'd sent their son to the tony prep
school where the Woodlock sons had gone for generations. And when
they'd paid his college tuition, they'd told him he was preparing for a
career with the Woodlocks.

But Luther had had other plans for himself. When he'd gotten
tired of arguing with his parents about his future, he'd broken off contact with them.

He'd taken the money that had come to him on his eighteenth
birthday and started a business, delivering fast food to the dorm
rooms of the students at U.C. San Diego. He'd made money and in-
vested in several other businesses, always improving his financial position. And when his big opportunity to buy dot-com stock had come
along, he'd jumped into the world of Web enterprise— but had had
sense enough to get out before the bubble burst.

Today he was doing a lot better than any of the Woodlocks. And
he had ensured that he would do better still.

The report of Darwin Woodlock going on a psychotic rampage
warmed his heart. "Old man, you'll be dead soon," he said into the
darkness beyond the window. "And if you're in shit shape, Wilson
can't be far behind. Or Colin."

A prickle of uneasiness nipped at him when he put Olivia into the
picture. But she would come to her senses. Or he would force her to
see that he was her only choice. Either way, he'd have her.

Of course, he did still wonder who the wild card in the mix had
been that night. Some guy named Morgan had been meeting with
Olivia and Colin and had helped subdue the wigged-out old man.
Luther's informant didn't know what Morgan had been doing there or
even how he'd arrived. Or, for that matter, how he'd left. In the confusion after Darwin's outburst, Morgan had somehow slipped away.

But that had been three weeks ago, and as far as Luther could see, nothing of note had resulted from Morgan's brief appearance on the scene. As a precaution, he had told his informant to keep an eye out for the man, but his intuition told him that nothing would come of it. Nothing was going to spoil his project. If it took a little more time, well, he was an expert at waiting. That was one of the lessons drummed into him at Dickensen Prep.

A smile flickered on his thin lips. It was amazing what you could pick up at a top prep school, along with math and English. He'd discovered that even if it took six months or a year or two years, he could find a way to get even with each of the boys who had tormented and humiliated him. He had cultivated the art of making elaborate plans. And he had learned that you could often get what you wanted by paying someone else to do the dirty work.

Like when poor Sid Howard had come down with that nasty case of food poisoning, after a smidgen of shit had gotten onto those chocolate chip cookies his mom had sent him.

Or when Ryan Underwood had gotten expelled after someone had alerted his teacher that he'd bought a term paper from a "scholastic service." That one had been easy because a lot of the boys had hated smug, cheating Ryan.

But the victories at Dickensen had been schoolboy stuff. Now he was playing for the highest possible stakes.

He had no doubt that his plans would eventually come to fruition. Until they did . . . well, he would continue to entertain himself with the reluctant houseguest who had moved in a few months ago. In fact, he'd pay a visit this very evening.

But first, he thought he might go down to the security vault. Not because there was a problem. He just liked to admire his treasure.

The security was state of the art, updated every few years. The basement alarm system was on at all times, except when he was in personal attendance in the secure area.

Luther punched in the code on the keypad, then opened the heavy door, and started down the steps. Anybody who disarmed the lock and came down here thinking he was safe was in for a nasty surprise. Before he reached the bottom of the stairs, Luther stopped and opened another panel on the wall. Inside was a second keypad into which he pressed another code.

A click told him that the automatic weapon emplacement at the bottom of the stairs had also been disarmed. Still, he never passed it without a slight shiver running through him. It was cold in the windowless chamber because, for security reasons, the heating system did not run down to this level. Nor did the plumbing.

There was no furniture. Only a tasteful Oriental rug warmed the floor in front of the vault. The whole enclosure, including the vault, had been blasted out of the solid rock of the mountain. There were no windows or doors besides the one he had come through.

The natural stone walls called to mind a dungeon, as did the vault door, which had been specially made of reinforced steel. Like a bank vault, you could unlock the door manually, the old-fashioned way. But unless it was done with the remote control scanner, the outer chamber would flood with knockout gas.

He punched in the scanner code, then waited for the click to signal that the door had opened.

As always, his chest tightened painfully as he turned the handle on the door and stepped over the threshold. The room beyond was like a vault but with a very high ceiling so no one could reach the spy camera high above. Inside there was one piece of furniture: an ornate antique table about four feet square, carved from a single block of mahogany.

Sitting in the middle of the table was an even more ornate box. It, too, was made from a solid block, although this one was semiprecious stone—white jade barely tinged with green. A stylized flower was carved into the middle of the lid, with the roots spreading from the base of its stem in all directions, over the top and down the sides. The hinges were also carved from the jade and so was the catch.

Luther stared at the box for a moment, then crossed to the table and lifted the lid. His breath caught, as it always did, as he looked down into crimson liquid shimmering in the bottom of the box. He estimated there had been three inches of the precious substance when he'd stolen the Woodlock family legacy. It now appeared more like two. Some of the fluid had evaporated even with the lid closed, even in the climate-controlled atmosphere of the locked room.

Luther swore softly under his breath. He hadn't expected the elixir to evaporate. But each time he checked it, he saw less liquid. Which meant that he had less time than he had assumed he would.

But that wasn't going to be a problem, he assured himself. He was going to bring about a resolution within the next few weeks.

He stared at the shimmering red elixir, wondering if the amount would make a difference to him—personally. Maybe less was actually better where he was concerned. He kept his hands at his sides, willing himself not to reach out. He had done it before and been very sorry. Still, he kept coming back, hoping something had changed. Intellectually, he knew it hadn't, but for a moment, desire and need overcame rational thought, and he simply could not prevent his hand from reaching into the box, almost as if someone else were moving his muscles.

The instant his finger touched the surface of the glistening liquid, he came to his senses, screaming. It was like sticking his flesh inside a furnace filled with molten glass. He yanked his hand back and staggered to the wall. There, he slumped, cradling his hand and breathing hard, cursing himself and the Woodlocks and the whole damned universe.

THE wolf trotted over the crest of the hill and stopped short. It was early in the morning, and he was going home to his lair to sleep off the night's hunt.

But as he looked down toward the parking area in front of his house, he saw a car that didn't belong there. Next to his Lexus sat a sporty little silver Jaguar. As if sensing she was no longer alone, Olivia opened the car door and climbed gracefully out, stretching her arms over her head and shaking her rich golden brown hair over her shoulders.

Finding her there was so much like his dream that for an instant he felt disoriented, as though he wasn't certain if what he was seeing was real. It helped him to put things into perspective. She wasn't wearing the same white blouse and slacks she'd worn in his dream. Her nononsense denim skirt and long-sleeved blue sweater weren't designed with seduction in mind.

It did appear, though, that she was alone, unless someone was hiding on the floor of the car, which was highly unlikely, given its size.

Sam watched her, his heart pounding hard and fast. Every deep breath of the mountain air he dragged in was filled with her scent, carried on the early morning breeze. And he had to wonder how the hell he had managed to keep on living these past few weeks as though nothing cataclysmic had happened to him.

She stood back, looking at the unique house he'd designed for himself, then walked to the front entrance and knocked on the door. Of course, she got no answer. After a minute, she knocked again, and when no response was forthcoming, she cupped her hands to the window beside the door and looked in at his warm and cozy den.

A couple of seconds later, she turned away from the window and stood staring out across the hillside, her arms wrapped around her shoulders.

Over the past weeks when he was awake and rational, he had told himself he was better off without her. He had told himself she couldn't be the werewolf's mate. He had even convinced himself that he believed it. But as he stood struggling to draw breath into his lungs, utterly mesmerized by the sight of her, he couldn't remember any of his reasoning.

She hadn't spotted him. He still had a choice. He could still turn and fade into the mountain landscape.

Right, a choice. Stop kidding yourself.

Yet even if he had run headlong into what his father had claimed was his fate—and he still wasn't entirely ready to acknowledge that he had—what was her excuse? Why was she here? She must have gone to considerable trouble to track him down. He never listed his home address on any written communications. In fact, only an unnamed gravel track leading into the mountains marked his ranch. He picked up his mail at a post office box in Lompoc. So she'd had to do some serious sleuthing to find him.

No, not her. Her brother. Colin Woodlock, whatever else he might be, seemed to be a persistent bastard, and Sam realized he must have sent Olivia looking for the master thief. After all, she was the one who'd do a better job of making their pitch. He sighed, then opted for honesty. He didn't care why she was here. He was simply delighted to see her. In fact, if he were a normal man, he would have pulled out all the stops and set about courting her.

Courting? If his vocal cords could have formed the sound, he would have laughed.

He couldn't picture his parents doing anything so mundane. He had always assumed that when his father had known his mother was the one woman for him, he had carried her off to a cabin in the woods and fucked her eyeballs out until there was no way she could deny the bond that had formed between them. Then he'd broken the news that he was a werewolf. He didn't doubt that the shocking revelation had completely freaked her out.

Olivia was a lot more sophisticated and more complicated than his mother. But would that make it more or less likely that she would lose it when she learned the truth about him?

When.

He had progressed from if to when.

Walking at a steady but unrushed pace, he started down the hill, wondering if he were moving of his own volition or being drawn by the invisible cords he had first sensed in his dreams, the cords that connected his soul to hers. He might have admired the fanciful imagery, if his pulse hadn't been pounding so hard in his ears that all he heard was the roaring of his own blood.

When she raised her head, he stopped. He knew from the sudden tension in her shoulders that she had seen him moving through the brown grass.

If life were like his dreams, this was the place where she would hold out her arms to him.

Instead, she took a careful step toward her car, reached for the door handle, and opened the door. Yet she didn't climb into the car. Maybe, deep in her heart, she knew the truth, too.

Forcing himself to walk slowly, wanting very much not to frighten her, he descended through the scrubby grass and brush to the edge of the parking area. But he came no closer. From twenty feet away, he stood looking at her, every cell of his attention focused on her.

As the wind ruffled the fur on his back and played with the strands of her hair, he felt as though the currents of air were pulling them together. Dream images mixed with reality. Olivia naked. Holding out her arms. Gathering the wolf to her.

He wasn't sure how long they stood in front of the house, gazes locked in mutual fascination. But finally some inner voice told him it was enough—they'd gone as far as they should go. For now.

He moved one leg, then another. Not toward her, but away. The movement released him from his trance, and he turned quickly. Circling around to the back of the house, he headed into the hills again.

8

THE wolf had disappeared. Or maybe it had been a dog, but she didn't think so. Either way, with the animal gone, Olivia suddenly felt as though her legs had turned to limp ropes. Stumbling to the patio, she flattened her hand against the top of the table, then sat down heavily in one of the comfortable chairs.

There were two chairs, one on either side of the table. With part of her mind, she wondered who might have sat here with Sam Morgan. Or did he have the two merely for symmetry? As isolated as he was—and as hard as it had been to find out where he lived—she wondered if anyone besides him had ever seen the place.

But those were only stray thoughts weaving in and out of the whirlpool of information in her brain.

When the dog or wolf or whatever it was had come toward her, she had been terrified. But he'd stopped far enough away that her fear had ebbed slightly—enough to keep her from jumping into her car and slamming the door. The beast had simply stood there, staring at her with intelligent eyes, as though he knew very well what was going through her mind. At the same time, she had felt a connection to him that she was at a loss to explain. It was as if she knew him. As if she could trust him. Impossible notions. She had never laid eyes on the animal before.

While she was still trying to figure out what had happened, a flicker of movement at the top of the hill caught her attention.

Her head jerked up, and she prepared to meet *canis lupus—familiaris* or not—again.

Instead, she saw a man. Sam. He was dressed in sweatpants, a T-shirt, and running shoes. Obviously he had been out for an early morning run.

Relieved, she watched him descend the hill. He came toward her just the way the animal had come—slowly, as though he were afraid she might jump up and leave. The comparison between the animal and the man was so strong that her throat tightened, and for just a second she felt as if she were experiencing the supernatural.

Clenching her hands, she forced herself to look as if her nerves weren't screaming.

She and Sam regarded each other across fifteen feet of charged space. When he remained silent, she cleared her throat.

"Your dog scared me," she said.

"He's a wolf," Sam answered promptly, his gaze unnerving, as though he expected her to object.

"He belongs to you?"

He hesitated for a moment, then finally said, "As much as a wolf can belong to a man. He's part of my early warning system."

"He seemed intelligent."

"He is."

She wanted to ask more about the wolf, but she sensed that the subject made him uncomfortable. Actually, there was nothing comfortable about this whole reunion.

He shoved his hands into his pockets. "I notice you didn't sic the police on me."

"I never intended to."

"That's not what you said."

She kept her eyes focused on his face. "At the time, I didn't think I had a choice. I was taking Colin's advice."

"So you follow your brother's lead?" he said, making it sound like an insult.

She raised her chin. "I had the idea of looking for a master thief. He came up with several candidates, and I picked you."

"Oh yeah? So you started off thinking you would use someone."

"I wouldn't call it that."

"You mean you don't want to call it that."

She sighed. "Okay. Make it sound as bad as you like. We were desperate. We still are."

She wanted to look away. Instead, she kept her chin up and her gaze fixed on him as he slowly crossed the patio and lowered himself into the chair across from hers.

"I told you, I don't work for anyone but myself," he said.

She ignored his statement and went on. "We still need your help." She paused and licked her lips. "And I realize you need to know why I'm desperate."

He leaned back in his chair and stretched out his legs, but she knew he wasn't relaxed.

Before she lost her nerve, she said, "There's a genetic problem in my family. Colin, my dad, and my uncle are all sick from it."

That got his attention. "What is it?"

"It doesn't have a name. Call it Woodlocks' Disease. I don't know anybody else who has it."

He was still listening with unnerving attention, and she had to look down at her hands as she said the next part. She hoped he would think she was only embarrassed about revealing intimate family details. "It causes various symptoms. You had a nice demonstration of what it's done to Uncle Darwin—attacked his brain. It affects Colin's muscles and, I guess, his nervous system. He doesn't talk much about it to me. But it kills me to see him fall down the stairs or trip for no apparent reason or drop things."

She took her bottom lip between her teeth, wondering if she'd made any real dent in the harsh assumptions he'd made about her family.

She raised her gaze once more to find him still watching her with unblinking intensity.

"Your dad seemed in pretty good shape," he said. "At the party—and then when your uncle wigged out."

His almost casual tone made her want to scream at him. She wanted to ask how he'd like seeing the members of his family slowly die.

Instead, she spoke calmly. "I know you don't think much of my father. I feel like anything I say will be wrong. But maybe telling you things I shouldn't will make a difference."

He answered with a small shrug.

"I'm speaking in strictest confidence. Dad is a lot sicker than he looks, but he takes drugs to keep himself going. I mean stimulants. Medications he can get from a doctor who's willing to treat his symptoms. And sometimes cocaine. The drugs keep him functioning. But he knows they will shorten his life. He's made that trade-off because he can't stand to be weak and sick."

Sam's expression gave no hint of his reaction. He simply went on staring at her.

Quickly, she added, "My dad is rich, as you know. The disease has plagued our family off and on for generations. This . . . this is the first time so many of the men have it at the same time. So Dad hired a researcher to work on a cure. Dr. Regario did find something that seemed to help. He called it Astravor."

Sam's eyebrow quirked upward briefly. "Weird name. So that's what's in the box?"

"Yes."

"If you had the sickness for years, why are you just now developing a cure?"

Olivia realized she hadn't thought that through very well. Damn! She hoped she didn't look like she was lying when she said, "We had a folk remedy. Modern medicine is obviously better. But we never broke the tradition of using the ancient box.

"And before you ask—the folk remedy doesn't seem to be very effective anymore. Or maybe it never was. Or maybe the sickness has mutated . . . But the Astravor was a godsend for us. I guess the doctor made up some combination of syllables for the name. Or it's a foreign word," she said carefully, then hurried on. "Dr. Regario was in a fatal car accident. When we went to his lab, we found all of the doctor's notes had disappeared. We think Luther Ethridge took them when he stole the Astravor."

"All that because he hates your family?"

Olivia sucked in a steadying breath, then let it out in a rush. "There are several factors. I think his parents urged him to be like us. They even sent him to the school Dad and Uncle Darwin had attended. He was a social outcast there. It was a miserable experience for him. I think that's part of the reason he hates us."

"Part?"

"He wanted to unite the families. He wanted his sister to marry Colin."

"Who flat out refused."

"Yes." She swallowed hard. "And he wanted to marry me. I couldn't stand the idea of his laying a hand on me."

She kept her gaze steady on him. "The bottom line is that if we can't get what my dad refers to as 'the elixir' back, he and Colin and Uncle Darwin will die."

There was more to it than that, of course. But she had revealed enough about their personal tragedy.

Sam's gaze turned inward. "Can you strike a deal with Ethridge?" he asked. "He's proved that he can bring you to your knees. Maybe now he's willing to take your money."

Olivia shook her head. "We tried that. He's not interested in money. He's already very rich."

"And you're not lying about this . . . this elixir?" Sam asked bluntly, his gaze still trained unwaveringly on her face.

"No!" she insisted, holding that piercing gaze, knowing he couldn't possibly detect any lie in either her tone or expression, because it was the truth she spoke. "It's a matter of life and death for us."

"And this, uh, family disease . . . you're not talking about some thing that's . . . catching?"

"No," she said, fudging the truth a bit. At least, it wasn't "catching" in the literal sense.

9

SAM studied the woman sitting across from him. She certainly looked as if she had run out of options and was willing to throw herself on his mercy. Her eyes were huge and impossibly green. They would have been beautiful except that the dark circles below them spoiled the effect. The marks were like purple bruises on skin that was otherwise so pale it was almost transparent. In the bright sunlight, he could see fine lines at the corners of her eyes that he hadn't noticed before.

The last time they'd talked about what she wanted him to steal, she'd given him a cock-and-bull story about an old box. She was still lying—or, at least, holding back. Oh, he believed her about the men in her family being sick. But there was something else . . . something she wasn't saying.

"What's Dr. Regario's first name?" he asked.

"Henry," she answered promptly.

He'd check that out later. Meanwhile, he wanted to leap out of his chair, take her by the arms, and tell her she had to trust him if she wanted his help. He wanted to ask if her uncle's ravings about demons had any basis in truth. Was her family really haunted by malevolent creatures?

Sam knew all too well that there were things ordinary mortals dismissed as myth and fairy tale that were, in fact, as real as the sunshine beating down on them from above. Still, he didn't want his own experience—his very existence—to cloud his vision of the obvious. A genetic defect that was so rare as to be unique to one family sounded pretty far-fetched. Even his own genetic anomaly wasn't *that* uncommon. There were werewolves other than those in his immediate family—or so he'd been taught as a child. He hadn't met any of them besides his father and brothers because of an unfortunate werewolf trait: all of them were Alpha males. Once they reached adulthood, they fought for dominance, which was why he'd moved out of his father's house as soon as he'd been old enough to get a job working for a landscape company.

As he took in Olivia's shuttered expression, he could see he wasn't going to get any closer to the truth by grilling her further about the so-called Woodlocks' Disease.

Besides, grilling her was the last thing he wanted to do. He ached to hold her and tell her that everything would be fine, to fold her close and stroke her soothingly. . . . Well, okay, more than stroke, and quite a lot more than soothingly.

For a moment he was caught up in the vivid memories from his dreams. As he sat across from her, he pictured her falling into his arms, begging for his help. And he imagined telling her that they'd talk about it—after they made love.

Instead, he came back to the truth buried beneath his wild, erotic fantasies. This woman was his mate. She didn't know it yet, but these were the first moments of their future together. He wasn't going to start off by dragging her, either by physical force or coercion, into his bed.

So he sat where he was, struggling to hold his carnal impulses in check while he pretended they were discussing his terms of employment, since she still apparently thought she'd come up here to hire him for a job.

"Let's back up to the way your father runs his business," he said. "It's unacceptable from an environmental standpoint. If I agree to help your family, I want him to sign a statement saying that he'll discontinue all practices that are poisoning the water and the land."

She stood up and walked to the edge of the patio, her restlessness proclaiming her tension. When she turned to face him, her face was grim. "He won't."

"If he wants my help, he will."

"He doesn't think he needs your help. Colin and I have to change his mind. So starting off with an ultimatum will just scotch this whole deal."

"What do you suggest?"

"Colin and I will work on the company's environmental practices."

"Who runs the company?"

"Dad has been relying on managers. We'll meet with them."

He wanted to push for more, but he was a realist. He nodded and watched some of the tension ease out of her shoulders.

Lifting her chin, she said, "We need something from you, too."

He waited while she seemed to screw up the courage to continue.

Finally, in a rush, she said, "We need you to be at the estate, so we can be on top of everything you're doing."

"I always work alone," he shot back.

She shook her head. "We have to be in on your plans."

"I don't like the 'we' concept. I'll deal with one person—you," he countered, then watched color creep into her pale face.

"Why me?" she asked in a thin voice.

He stood, facing her squarely. "Who else would you suggest? Certainly not your father. And not Colin. Not your uncle. And not that guy Thurston—the one who's probably the head of your father's security detail."

She blinked, as though she were surprised he'd picked up on the goon's function around the estate.

He waited for her answer, his breath shallow. "Okay," she finally said.

"Good." He couldn't stop himself from pushing her a little farther. "And your mom's not in the picture because she left your father fifteen years ago?"

Her head jerked toward him. "How do you know that?"

"I research everything about places I plan to rob."

"And why was that particular piece of information helpful?" she demanded.

"It established how many people live in your house."

He saw her lips compress into a grim line. "We don't need to talk about my family."

"I disagree. If I'm going to live with you, I need to know what kind of atmosphere I'm stepping into. Are there any other surprises like Uncle Darwin?"

"No."

Even as she answered the question, his mind was streaking off in another direction.

"So you want me to live with you."

"Not *me*. Us."

He let it slide. "What am I supposed to be doing at your estate?"

"You could be working for my father."

He laughed. "Nobody will buy it that I'm working for your old man. We need something more believable."

"Like what?"

"Like I've moved onto the estate because you and I are getting married."

Her dumbstruck expression wasn't particularly flattering.

"What? You can't bear the idea of getting hitched to a thief?"

"It's not that." She flapped a hand in a searching gesture. "I just . . . I'm not sure . . ."

But he'd reached his limit on calm discussion.

"I am," he said, rising to his feet and circling the table. "And we'd better be able to convince anybody watching us," he added, as he pulled her out of her chair and into his arms, "that we're comfortable with each . . . other." He spoke the last word an instant before his lips covered hers.

He had kissed her once before, and the meeting of his mouth with hers had torn through his body like a smoldering forest fire bursting into flames. He was prepared for something similar. Or perhaps he wanted to prove to himself that he could handle his response, that he could manage his lust until the time was right for them to make love.

Either way, he'd been a fool.

Control evaporated like water escaping a steam valve. He made a sound that was half gasp, half growl as his lips brushed hers, then all at once his mouth was locked to hers, the essence of her making his head spin. She tasted of warmth and spice and some indefinable quality he had craved all his life without knowing it—until the night he'd kissed her on her patio. It had taken hold of him then, worked its way into every fiber of his being, and he knew as surely as he knew his own real name that he'd never again be satisfied without it.

He could tell himself any damn lie he wanted—like he was conducting a private test of his self-control. The experiment was over before it had begun. He was caught in a trap of his own making.

Helpless to do anything else, he went on kissing her with lips and teeth and tongue. The small sounds she made in her throat gripped him like iron bands, binding him to her even more tightly. Her hands moved restlessly up and down his back and over his shoulders before she twined her arms around his neck and tangled her fingers in his hair.

"Yes," he growled into her mouth. "Yes."

Reaching downward, he slid his hands under her bottom and pulled her against him, nestling his aching cock against her belly, his hips rotating slowly, rhythmically, increasing the pleasure and the pain. They were standing outside, under the sparkling dome of the blue sky, but that didn't stop him from slipping his hand under her knit top to cover her breast. Through the silky fabric of her bra, it felt soft and at the same time heavy in his hand, and the hardened tip pressing into his palm stabbed at his nerve endings.

"Oh!" she cried out as he rubbed his hand back and forth, torturing himself with the feel of that hard bud and imagining it inside his mouth.

Imagining wasn't enough. Not nearly enough.

With both hands, he dragged her top and her bra up, freeing her breasts, then held the quivering mounds in his hands. They fit perfectly, neither too big nor small, exactly as if they'd been made just for him to hold. And they had—again, the truth hammered home. Taking the pebbled nipples between his thumbs and fingertips, he pulled and twisted gently, hearing her breath accelerate.

When he tore his mouth from hers and lowered his head to swirl his tongue around one taut nipple, she went absolutely still. And when he drew it into his mouth and sucked, she made a low, sobbing sound, her hands cradling the back of his head, holding him against her.

The need for her was like a fire in his blood. Now. The wolf would claim his mate now, in the morning sunlight.

But not in the scrubby grass that would scratch her tender flesh.

He picked her up and set her on the table with her legs dangling, then pushed her skirt up and out of the way. Her panties were a flimsy barrier. He ripped out the crotch, exposing her most intimate flesh to his questing fingers. She was wet and swollen for him, and she made low, pleading sounds as he stroked her slick folds. Her woman's scent wafted toward him like musky perfume, fueling his need.

He wanted to taste her. But as he bent his knees, anticipating that delicious goal, far above them a jet plane screeched through the sky, splitting the silence of the hillside. He could have ignored it—could have ignored anything at that point, short of World War Three—but the noise clearly shocked her, brought her back to the real world. He saw her eyes blink open in alarm, watched her stiffen.

Scrambling off the table, she struggled to put her clothing back into place.

He could have reached for her and stopped her frantic efforts. Instead he dug his nails into his palms and did nothing. He absolutely was not going to force her in any way.

She spoke in a high quavering voice as she reached under her shirt to rehook her bra. "You . . . you made me forget myself."

"And that's a bad thing?"

"Yes. I have to remember why we can't do this."

"And why is that? You want me. You know damn well I want you."

She dragged in a shaky breath. "But I can't trade sex for your cooperation."

He shook his head. "You're not."

"Then what am I doing?"

"Admitting that there's a lot more between us than a business deal."

Again she paused to draw a breath. When she looked at him, her eyes were haunted. "Sam, what I feel for you frightens me."

"Why?" he asked softly.

She hesitated, seeming to debate what answer to give him. Finally she settled on, "Because being a Woodlock comes with obligations. You think of my family as . . . well, as out for whatever we can get. I was raised to believe that I had a responsibility to the Woodlocks."

"Like what?"

"Like marriage as a way of cementing an alliance with another powerful clan."

His reaction was swift and angry. "That's medieval!"

"Yes," she agreed in a tight voice.

"With Luther Ethridge?"

"No! And we're going to change the subject now."

He watched her breath turn shallow as she waited for his answer. He knew she was asking him to play a very dangerous game. If he wanted to come out of it in one piece, he had to make her lay more of the Woodlock cards on the table. But right now he had the luxury of time.

"All right," he agreed. "Let's talk about what the scenario will be when I get to your place."

"What do you mean?"

"Well, for starters, if I'm your fiancé, how did we meet? And, uh, what do I do for a living?"

She blinked. "So . . . what *do* you do for a living?"

"I manage my investments. Anyone who checks into my background will find I have more than enough legitimate resources to account for my lifestyle. But, of course, I'm not as rich as the Woodlocks appear to be. So maybe I'm a gold digger who wants to marry the tycoon's daughter for her money."

He'd spoken off the top of his head. Now he paused to collect his thoughts. "Yeah, I met you at some of the charity events you attend, and I ingratiated myself to you. I've made a point of going to other events where you would be present. But mostly we've been carrying on our courtship by phone and E-mail. The high point was those two visits to your house—the first time at the party and the second, when I came at night to see you and got caught in that flap with your uncle."

"You came up with all that in the last five seconds?" she asked.

"I'm a quick study," he answered, unwilling to admit that his fantasies had suddenly turned into reality. Before she could ask another question, he fired off one of his own. "What computer do you use for E-mail?"

"We have a wireless network in the house. My laptop is hooked up to it."

"Is it password protected?"

"No."

"Too bad. Because if anyone has been checking up on you, they'd see that we haven't been sending messages."

"Who would do that?"

He shrugged. "Your father, for all I know."

"He's too busy for that."

"Good. Does your maid snoop?"

"Irene? Of course not!"

"How many maids do you have?"

"Until my family got sick we had day staff come in. But now it's more convenient to have live-in help."

"Okay. But I'd like to have a trail of correspondence. I can manipulate the date on my computer so that if anybody goes back and checks your E-mail, he'll see that we've been writing to each other."

"What were we writing?"

"Love letters."

She tipped her head to one side in a skeptical look. "You're going to manufacture a bunch of love letters, just like that?"

He hesitated fractionally. "No, I'm going to copy some posts from a blog site I came across—and alter the contents so it looks more personal." He was not going to tell her that he'd already written her love letters, when the pressure of his feelings for her had clamored for release.

Instead, he said, "I've got a lot of things to do in the short term. So perhaps I'd better agree to meet you at your house three days from now."

Her eyes widened. "Three days! We need to get started right away."

"You waited this long for me to come and claim my bride. I'm afraid you're going to have to wait a little longer."

10

THE woman in the high tower room looked through the barred window at the lights of the city spread below her. It was a beautiful view. A rich man's view. But she took no pleasure in it.

To keep her hands from trembling, she clasped them in front of her. She was in a hell of a fix, and she had no clue how to get out of it.

My name is Barbara Andres. She made the proclamation in her head because she didn't dare utter the words aloud. The room was bugged, and she had been punished in the past for daring to speak her own name. Standing with her back to the room, she raised one hand and gently touched her face. The skin felt smooth. Her nose was small and straight. But it wasn't the nose she had been born with. A Mexican doctor had changed the shape—and more. He had carved new lines into her features. Now that the scars had healed, she looked so much like another woman that the change took her breath away. She looked whole and healthy. Because no one could see the mental scars.

She fought to keep them hidden, because that was the safest course.

Turning, she glanced at the clock. It was after six, and her captor would unlock the door and come in all too soon. He would test her on her lessons, and if she failed the test, he would punish her.

First she turned to the DVD player and played the disk again. It showed several people. But the focus was on a young woman who looked a lot like she now looked.

She watched the woman smile. Holding up a mirror, she imitated that smile. After watching the woman walk, Barbara took a trip across her room, gliding with the same elegant motion. Next, she got out the sheets of paper she was supposed to memorize by that evening. The questions today were all about food.

She sat at the small desk beside her bed and laid the paper in front of her. Covering the right side of it with one hand, she murmured the answers. "My favorite breakfast food is scones with blackberry jam because the cook used to fix them when I was little. My second favorite jam is strawberry. A long time ago, my mother would take me and my brother to a farm, where we picked our own berries. We loved to pick them. And we loved to help Momma make jam."

She gave another quick glance at the paper and went on. "I like my steak medium-well. I like sweet potatoes with orange and spices, never marshmallows. I like lobster bisque and onion soup with lots of cheese on top."

She paused and took a breath. "I hate eggplant, snails, and coconut cream pie. I love chocolate mint ice cream. When I was a little girl, I always asked for a chocolate birthday cake."

She glanced down and saw the word "nuts."

"Oh, right. I love pecans, but I hate walnuts. And I joke that peanuts are for elephants."

She wanted to shout to the hidden microphones that she couldn't be someone else. It was stupid. Impossible. But she remembered what her captor had done to her when she'd refused.

I'm Barbara, Barbara Andres, she silently insisted, but this time she couldn't repress a small shudder. She was trapped in this nightmare. He had said he would let her go when she had done what he asked. But she didn't believe it. She had to get herself out of this trap. If she was given a chance to escape, she had to take it—even if she risked her life to do it. Because fulfilling her role was a death sentence. She knew too much about him to be allowed to live when he had finished with her.

Fear made her chest tighten. Willing herself to steadiness, she wiped her sweaty palm on her slacks. Then her eyes darted to the clock on the bedside table. She didn't have much time left before he arrived. She'd better make sure she had memorized the list of facts. Grimly, she went back to the paper. Yet, as she paced alongside the queen-sized bed with its damask spread, the thought of seeing her captor this evening set her heart to pounding and made it almost impossible to concentrate. Memorizing facts from another woman's life was bad enough. But not as bad as the rest of it. The way he treated her. The way he touched her. The way he wanted her to act with him.

She thought of slapping his face and of the satisfaction that would give her. Then she thought of what he did to her when he was angry, and a sick feeling rose in her throat.

With renewed determination, she sat down once more at the desk and applied herself to memorizing the list.

11

OLIVIA tried to project an appearance of calm as she waited nervously in the living room. She paced to the front window several times before forcing herself to sit on the burgundy-colored sofa that she hated.

In fact, she hated the whole room. Once it had welcomed her with light, delicate colors. But after Momma had walked away from the family, Dad had gone on a rampage, wiping out every trace of her presence. He'd brought in a trash bin for her clothing and anything else that was personal. Well, not her fine jewelry, of course. She'd taken a lot of the good pieces with her. What she'd left was in a safe in one of the guest bedrooms.

After pitching out Momma's things, Daddy had hired a profes-

sional decorator to redo the house—starting with the master bedroom, which was now dark and masculine.

Before the trash company had picked up the bin, Olivia had risked
her father's wrath and secretly climbed inside. Rooting through the
mess, she'd taken out a few precious things. A beaded evening bag
that had always fascinated her. A Mardi Gras mask with the blue and
green feathers. A gold pen and pencil set that she and Colin had given
Momma one year for a birthday present. The ivory cup she'd used in
the bathroom.

Olivia squeezed her eyes shut, trying to force the painful memories back into the locked corner of her psyche where they usually
resided. They'd popped out because she was nervous about seeing Sam
again, after the mind-blowing encounter on his patio. And after the
letters he'd sent. Eighteen of them had appeared in her E-mail files, in
groups of three or four, spaced out as though they had arrived over the
past six months. She'd read—and reread—every word. They were
very personal. Too personal to be copies of anything. Besides that, the
words sounded so much like him that, as she read them, she heard his
voice echoing in her head.

He'd started by establishing a history for the two of them.

"It was great to meet you at the Paper Products Expo. I enjoyed
our talk about the spotted owl. . . ."

Despite herself, that had made her smile. He'd managed to work
the environment into the letter.

"I would love to see you again, but I do understand that your
family duties keep you busy. You mentioned the dinner being
given by the California Business Association in Santa Barbara on
the fifteenth. I'm looking forward to meeting up with you
there. . . ."

And so the early letters had gone on—merely friendly in tone, a
man who didn't want to be too forward with a woman he'd recently
met. But as the supposed months of their relationship progressed, the
tone changed, and he began to sound more like a lover than a friend.
She could almost believe that she was reading the history of a de-

veloping romance. One of the last letters in particular had burned itself into her brain.

"I miss you so much. I will be counting the hours until I can hold
you in my arms again. Your kisses were so sweet the other night.
You taste like a field of flowers or the pure water of a stream high
in the mountains. And your body is like no other woman's. I can't
stop thinking about the feel of your breasts in my hands, of your
nipples beaded against my palms, telling me that you want me as
much as I want you."

She made a sound low in her throat. They had done those things
together—and more—only a few days ago. She remembered it all in
vivid detail. And so must he, if he could write about it in such explicit
detail. He sounded too poetic for a thief—not that she knew how a
thief should sound. But she did know that Sam's words had the power
to make her burn with arousal.

And he was going to be living in this house. He'd be here in the
morning when she woke up and at night when she went to bed. And
she had no idea how on earth she was going to cope with having him
so close.

She shook her head, wishing she could shake off the restless frustration she felt thinking about Sam Morgan and their kiss . . . and his
hands on her bare skin, his fingers rubbing her nipples, stroking the
inside of . . .

Ruthlessly, she quashed the heat rising in her belly by turning her
mind to a relationship gone wrong—her parents. Had they ever loved
each other? Had there been kindness and tenderness and passion between them once, even though theirs had been an arranged marriage,
like the one her father wanted for her?

She couldn't ask her father about his love life any more than she
could ask about his destructive business practices.

She'd told Sam those practices had started after Luther had stolen
the elixir and the family fortune had gone downhill. In truth, she
didn't even know if that was true.

The sound of tires on the driveway made her head whip around.
Hurrying to the window, she saw the car that had been parked in
front of Sam's house.

He was here.

Swiftly, she crossed the living room and the front hall and threw open the door. As he lifted a suitcase from the trunk of his car, she had a moment to admire his dark good looks. He had been devastating in a tuxedo and drop-dead sexy in his burglar outfit. Today his mahogany-colored hair was cut to a conventional business length, and he had dressed neatly in a black golf shirt and gray slacks. The perfect outfit for meeting his fiancé's father, she thought.

Closing the trunk, he picked up his bag and turned toward the door. When he saw her in the doorway, a smile of such warmth and intimacy spread across his face that it was easy to believe he had come to stay for no other purpose than to see the woman he loved.

She barely had time for an answering smile before he surged across the driveway and pulled her into his embrace. He held her as though he planned to never let her go. Although that should alarm her, she could do little more than cling to him. He was so solid and warm and strong. But she had to keep remembering that trusting him completely was too dangerous to risk.

"Olivia, I missed you," he said in a voice meant to carry inside the front hall.

"Yes."

They were playing the parts he'd dreamed up for them, she told herself as he lowered his mouth to hers.

She had lain in bed at night, hot and wanting and anticipating the heat of this kiss. The heat of his hands on all the intimate places he had touched before. But the contact was over almost as soon as his lips touched down. Before she had time to melt against him, he was putting his hand on her shoulders and setting her away from him. Despite all the warnings to herself, she couldn't hold back a spurt of disappointment.

"Let me feast my eyes on you," he said, then added tenderly, "You look fantastic."

It had to be a lie, of course. She knew her worry and uncertainty were etching themselves into her face.

He stroked the corner of her mouth with his thumb. "But I do detect a little stress."

"Well, I was anxious for you to get here," she managed.

"Mmm, me, too."

She looked up and saw their butler and maid hovering in the doorway. "Jefferies, Irene, this is my fiancé, Sam Morgan," she said, hoping they would attribute the quaver in her voice to engagement jitters. "He was here a few weeks ago. And he'll be staying with us for a while."

"I've gotten the room next to yours ready, the way you asked me to do," Irene answered.

"Thank you." She turned to Jefferies. "Would you see to it that his things are put there, please?"

"Of course."

In fact, she would have put Sam down the hall from her room, but he had suggested in an E-mail that it should look as if she wanted him close by. She had seen the logic in that—and also the danger. The closer he was, the more tempted she would be.

"Nice to meet you," Sam told Irene and Jefferies, then he took Olivia's hand. "Let's go for a walk."

"All right."

He guided her around the house and into the back garden, confidently leading the way as if he had been there many times before. Probably he had. Before the night in the gallery, she'd sensed him— watching the house, watching her.

They walked down a path that ended in a little arbor where bright purple bougainvillea climbed up a white trellis.

His demeanor in front of Jefferies and Irene had been confident, assured of his position, but her sideways glances told her that the farther from the house they walked, the more uncertain he seemed to be.

"What?" she murmured, suddenly afraid he was going to tell her that he'd changed his mind about getting involved in her family's problems. When he reached into the pocket of his slacks and pulled out a small black velvet box, her eyes widened in shock and she felt suddenly light-headed.

With a hand that wasn't quite steady, he held it out to her.

"Sam?"

"Open it," he whispered.

Her heart was thumping as she took it from him and lifted the lid. Inside was a square-cut diamond, at least two carats, set in white gold with baguettes on either side of it.

When she drew in a sharp breath, he spoke quickly. "Don't worry, I paid cash for it."

"I . . . I can't accept this," she stammered. Seeing the ring over-whelmed and confused her. Sam Morgan was a hard case. A man who lived on the edge. Was he letting her see his softer side? Or was this some kind of trick to make her drop her guard?

When he spoke, his voice gave no clue to his real intentions. "Of course you can accept it. We're engaged."

"But . . ."

He lifted the box from her grasp, took out the ring and cupped her icy hand in his while he slid the ring onto her finger.

Her pulse pounded even harder as she stared down at the token of his invented love for her. The ring fit perfectly. But it felt all wrong on her hand. He had no business acting as if this were a real engagement. Yet what was he supposed to do? She had agreed to the charade because she couldn't think of a better reason for him to be living with her family. Suddenly, she was trapped into making it look plausible.

When she stole a glance at him, the anxious look on his face made her heart ache.

Questions bubbled inside her, but all she could manage was, "Sam?"

His Adam's apple bobbed.

Determined to find out what was really going on, she raised her arms to his neck. This time when they kissed, it didn't end before it got started. And she couldn't stop thinking of where else his mouth had been on her body.

Remembered intimacy fed into the kiss. At the same time, she was caught in a moment that was real and passionate and brimming with unspoken emotions. He opened his mouth, drinking her in as his arms drew her close, holding her against the hard length of his body. She wanted more. So much more. Not just for this moment, though, but for the whole of their lives. Things she couldn't have, she frantically tried to remind herself. But it was impossible to hang on to her doubts as his hands skimmed up and down her ribs and the sides of her breasts, arousing her through her bra and silk blouse.

She spoke his name with her mouth against his, then passed beyond speech as his tongue stroked inside of her lips. Her tongue glided against his, sending vibrations throughout her body. She knew he felt her response as he drew her deeper into the shadows of the private bower.

"I missed you," he growled.

"Yes."

When his hand cupped her breast and his fingers skimmed over the nipple, she felt the heat of his touch.

"Lord, Olivia. Let me . . ."

"Yes." Again, she gave him the only answer that made sense.

They were fast progressing to more frantic activities when the sound of someone clearing his throat made them both go rigid.

In alarm she looked around and found Colin standing eight feet away, just outside the arbor, watching them.

"How long have you been there?" she demanded at the same time Sam muttered a curse and turned to hide her body with his as he lowered his hand to her waist.

"Not long."

"You could have given us some privacy."

"Yeah, well, congratulations on your engagement," he said, his tone somewhat wry.

"Thank you," Sam answered, sounding a lot less flustered than she was certain he must feel.

"Father has been eager to see you," Colin said to him.

"Give me a minute." He stayed facing her, and she knew he was trying to will away his erection.

She couldn't help thinking that her own arousal was probably equally obvious, and she smothered the impulse to look down at her nipples. They ached, and she knew they were probably standing out against the thin fabric of her blouse.

Three days ago, on the way back from Lompoc, she'd thrown her torn panties away in the ladies' room of a rest stop. After arriving home, she'd showered and changed her clothes before seeking out her brother. But she knew she hadn't been able to hide her emotional state then. Colin had known that something heated and personal had taken place at Sam's house. Today he could see the evidence for himself.

Colin confirmed her assumption with his next words. "So, this is a little more than a business relationship."

"Yeah, it is," Sam answered. "Do you want to make something of that?"

"I'm not my father. I want my sister to be happy."

"I appreciate your pragmatic attitude," Sam answered.

She kept her expression as neutral as possible—and shifted her attention away from herself, as she did so often.

Hoping she didn't look obvious, she gave Colin a quick inspection. He'd been spending the afternoons in bed for the past few days, and she would have suggested that he conserve his strength now. But she knew he wanted to be in on the meeting, to show that they were in this together.

"Your father knows I'm coming?" Sam asked.

"We figured we'd better make him part of the plan."

"How did he take it?"

"With the predictable explosion."

12

SAM strove to keep his face impassive as they walked back through the garden.

"The ring is a nice touch," Colin said.

"It adds verisimilitude," he answered evenly. The ring had started as an expensive impulse. Then he'd decided he liked the idea of putting his brand on Olivia.

As they crossed the lawn a jagged bolt of lightning slashed horizontally through the clouds billowing over the house. Looking up, he was surprised to see how dark the sky had grown. It had been perfectly clear when he'd arrived.

Sam watched Colin and Olivia exchange nervous glances.

"Better get inside," Colin muttered.

They all walked quickly to the terrace, and Sam couldn't help feeling that the weather was pushing him toward the coming confrontation.

Inside, Colin led the way toward the home office complex, then knocked on a closed door.

"Come in," a gruff voice called out.

They stepped into a room that was a movie set designer's idea of a man's retreat, with dark wood wainscoting, a matching desk as big as New Jersey, and Leroy Neiman horse-race paintings on the walls, along with photos of Wilson Woodlock shaking hands with a dozen notable men.

The patriarch of the Woodlock clan sat in the power position, in a high-backed leather chair behind the wide desk.

At first Wilson ignored them while he scratched some notations on the papers in front of him.

As they all stood waiting, Sam ordered himself to stay cool, but he couldn't stop his stomach from knotting. Deliberately, he used the time to size up the enemy. Woodlock might want to project the appearance of power, but the tightness around his mouth gave away his tension. Finally he looked up, his gaze flickering over his son and daughter before fixing on Sam.

"So, you're a thief," he said, getting right to the point.

Sam slipped a hand into his pocket. "Yes. And a very good one."

"You fit right in at my party several months ago. You looked and sounded as if you came from a good family. Yet there's no record of you before you appeared out of nowhere in California eight years ago."

"I value my privacy."

"Who were you before you were Sam Morgan?"

He kept his gaze steady. "You don't expect me to answer that question, do you?"

"Not really," Woodlock conceded. "I guess the most important thing about you is that my children think you can get into Luther Ethridge's fortress and steal back the . . . medicine that's going to save our lives."

"That's right." Without being invited, Sam walked to one of the guest chairs and sat down. After a moment's hesitation, Olivia took the chair next to him. Colin retreated to the easy chair in the corner.

Woodlock glared at Sam. "I don't like a stranger knowing . . . sensitive family business."

"I'm sure you don't," Sam answered quietly. "But what alternative do you have?"

"I always have alternatives," Woodlock shot back. His gaze jumped to his daughter—where it lingered.

In less than a heartbeat, the man's condescending expression hardened and a red stain spread rapidly across his face. Jesus, was he going to have a stroke right there in front of them all?

"What the hell is that?" Wilson demanded.

Olivia looked startled. "What?"

"On your finger! What the hell is that on your finger? Let me have a better look."

She held up her hand, keeping her voice even as she answered the sharp question. "My engagement ring. It's lovely, isn't it?"

"Don't get smart with me. That ring is carrying your charade one step too far. I forbid you to wear the accursed thing."

"Not a good idea," Sam interjected as calmly as he could, considering his pulse was now pounding in his temples.

"That's not your call," Woodlock snapped. "Or did you suggest this whole farce thinking you could use it to persuade my daughter to marry you?"

The man's perception rattled him a little. Still, Sam kept his tone even as he replied, "Olivia and I are supposed to be getting married. You're a rich man. It would look very strange if your daughter were engaged to someone who couldn't afford to give her an impressive ring."

Woodlock shifted in his seat. "Did you buy it or steal it?"

"Bought it. Do you want to see the receipt and the appraisal?"

"No!" He fixed Sam with a menacing glare. "I expect results—in the thievery department—from you!"

"You'll get them," he promised, projecting confidence when he didn't even know the specs of the job.

"It would be a good idea if we all had dinner together," Colin said from the corner of the room, and Sam realized he had forgotten all about him.

"I'll be working late," Wilson snapped.

"I think we need to establish a friendly tone for Sam's stay here," Colin added.

"You go ahead and do that for me," his father muttered. "And now, I need to get back to business."

"Thank you for giving us so much of your time," Sam said as he stood.

Woodlock's eyes narrowed. "Are you being sarcastic?"

"I wouldn't dream of it." Turning, he walked toward the door, followed by Olivia and Colin.

In the hall, Colin said, "If he kicks you out, we'll have to go to Plan B."

"I wasn't aware there was a Plan B," Sam said, suddenly wary.

"There isn't. But I'll think of something," Colin replied with a twisted smile.

Despite his tension, Sam laughed. "I guess you didn't inherit your old man's rigidity."

"I prefer to alter my opinions—and my plans—to fit the facts."

"Good," Sam answered, thinking that under other circumstances he and Colin could have been friends. "I liked the way you kept out of the conversation."

"I used to be in Dad's face all the time. It wasted energy, his and mine."

"Smart decision."

The butler approached them in the front hall. "Will the family be eating in the dining room?"

Colin answered, "We're going up to get a little better acquainted. Send something light up in a couple of hours—for me, Olivia, Sam, and Brice."

"Would you like some of Cook's quesadillas?"

Not exactly wolf food, Sam thought. "I'd like steak—or burgers, if it isn't too much trouble," he said.

"Certainly, sir."

Olivia gave him a look that suggested she didn't like having him make requests of her staff. But she only nodded to the butler.

WILSON sat behind his desk, his shoulders rigid, eyes fixed on the papers that he'd picked up when he'd made it clear to the conspirators that the interview was over. The text was a blur before his eyes.

He had sent his children and the interloper away because he couldn't stand the sight of Sam Morgan. But the three of them were out there talking about him. Making plans. Scheming. And Brice would be in on it, too. Let's not forget his son's sycophantic lover.

Some part of his mind recognized the thoughts as paranoid. His children were doing what they thought was right. But he didn't have to like it. He just had to let them think he was going along with them.

"Sam Morgan," he muttered. He didn't like the name. It was too short. Too common. A name the man had made up, and he couldn't even pick something distinctive.

He didn't like working with a common thief. Corporate theft was one thing. This was completely different.

He didn't like having Morgan living under his Spanish tile roof. And he didn't like the sexual energy sparking back and forth between the man and his daughter. There was something dangerous going on there. Something more than a business arrangement, and he was going to find out exactly what.

But the big question was—did he get rid of Morgan now or later?

He leaned back, smiling, allowing himself the pleasure of considering some delicious choices.

WHEN Sam and the others reached the upper floor, they found Brice standing in the hall, looking anxious. "How did it go?"

"He didn't kick me out—yet," Sam answered.

Brice nodded his approval, but it was clear most of his attention was focused on Colin. "Okay, you made it to the meeting. But you haven't been so great for the past few days. You need to rest," he said.

"I'm fine!"

Brice flicked a glance at Sam again. "He shouldn't be involved in this!"

Sam put a hand on Brice's arm. "Let's go into the computer room," he said, just as a nearby door opened.

A burly man in a white coat stepped out. Beyond him, another man dressed in burgundy pajamas was sitting on a bed. It was Uncle Darwin, his round face cradled in his hands and his sparse hair sticking up in tufts. As he looked up and stared at Sam, recognition bloomed in his eyes.

Horror contorted his face, and he reared back. "The devil," he screamed. "The wolf devil! He wants to drag me to hell! Get him away! Away!"

The attendant swore and bolted back into the room. After throwing a quick look at Sam, he knelt beside the patient. "Calm down. It's all right. Everything's all right."

"No! He's the devil! The devil, I tell you! Come here in the shape of a wolf!" Outside, thunder rumbled, punctuating his words.

"Oh, great," Sam muttered.

The attendant gave them an apologetic look and shut the door. But Uncle Darwin's voice continued to reverberate through the hall.

Sam stood where he was, until Olivia took his arm and steered him down the hall.

"Sorry," she said.

"Is he worse?" Sam asked.

"No worse physically. But he keeps talking about you."

"Should I be flattered?"

"Apparently you made an impression on him."

Sam could have told her why but didn't. All in good time.

He followed her into the computer room which was as much up-stairs lounge area as work space. When they were all inside, he closed the door, then turned to face them. "I hope you haven't been talking openly about your burglary plans. The fewer people who know about this, the better."

"Only in the privacy of our bedroom," Brice answered.

Colin chose to make a point. "You're in on our little conspiracy be-cause we need your expertise. Brice is in on it because he and I are a couple. You can consider that anything I know, he knows."

"Okay. But my comment about keeping this close to our vests wasn't just a random crack. The more people who know our plans, the more likely they are to fail."

"There's no one here but family and trusted servants," Colin an-swered.

"I hope so."

Olivia glanced at Sam, then started to sit in one of the easy chairs. He steered her toward the sofa.

"I . . ."

"You want to sit with your fiancé, so anybody who happens in here can see how happy we are," he finished for her, linking his fingers with hers and feeling a slight tremor go through her hand.

"You were fantastic with your father," he murmured.

"I've had practice," she said, detaching herself.

He could have insisted on the contact, but he gave her the space she was asking for. And gave himself space, too. Just sitting next to her was arousing enough. Touching her was a big distraction.

Colin cleared his throat, then went back to Brice's original ques-tion. "I need to be in on this meeting," he said to his partner. "Sam's doing this for me. The least I can do is support him."

"I thought you agreed that Olivia was going to work with Mor-gan," Brice said.

"Call me Sam. I'm going to be one of the family, after all."

Brice nodded. "Okay."

Sam turned to Colin. "Are you up to briefing me on Ethridge's home and security?"

"Yes." Crossing to the computer, he sat down and tapped a key. A screen saver sprang to life. It was a view of Michelangelo's David in the Academy art gallery in Florence. With another keystroke, he replaced the picture with a directory. "I have exterior and interior shots of the Ethridge house. I have the architect's plans, specs from the security company that Ethridge hired, and interviews with some former employees. And I have several pictures of Ethridge."

"That's pretty thorough."

"We're trying to give you as much information as possible."

"Where does he keep the . . . elixir?"

"In a basement vault. I'll tell you what I know about the security."

"Have you been able to talk to anyone who works there now?"

"He has no live-in help. Various people come in during the day. If one of his people talked to us, that person's life wouldn't be worth much."

The way he said it made the hairs on the back of Sam's neck prickle. His gaze fixed on Colin, he asked, "You have proof that he's killed somebody?"

13

COLIN slowly turned toward Sam. After casting a quick glance at his sister, he said, "Yes, as a matter of fact."

Sam fought to keep his voice even. "Who?"

"A couple of young women he stalked."

Olivia made a strangled sound. Apparently she hadn't heard about this part of Colin's research.

Sam clasped her hand as he asked, "And the police didn't arrest him?"

"They didn't have enough evidence to link him to the victims. There were no bodies."

"But you know he killed them?"

"I don't need the same standards of proof as a court of law. I deal in probabilities. And I know two women who got mixed up with him disappeared."

"You have names?"

"Yes. Alana Holz and Barbara Andres. Alana was a ditz-brain

health club instructor who went missing on a camping trip in the
mountains. Barbara was a graduate student, a woman with no family
and no boyfriend. Ethridge was careful to make sure he didn't create a
pattern—and careful to make it appear that he couldn't possibly be
involved."

Sam fixed Colin with a dark look. "You knew this, but you with-
held the information until you'd roped me into working with you."

"I didn't rope you in." Colin's gaze shot briefly to Olivia, then
back to him. "You made the decision on your own."

Olivia's brother knew why he was here, all right. Sam gave her
hand a gentle squeeze, and when she returned the pressure, he felt his
throat tighten.

The family illness, whatever the hell it was, weighed heavily on her.
If he could ease that burden and make a difference in the way Woodlock
Industries was run, it would be worth a few risks. But he'd be damned
if he was going to get himself killed *only* to save the male Woodlocks.

"Okay, show me the house," he said.

Colin brought up a picture of a castle, a forbidding pile of stone
clinging to the side of a mountain.

"Hmph. The hall of the mountain troll," Sam muttered.

"Yeah," Colin agreed, zooming in on the front. "Notice how the
door is recessed, so an invader can be trapped and killed before he gets
inside."

He switched to the rear elevation, where the building presented a
sheer wall.

There were several more exterior views, then some interior shots.

"How did you get them?" Sam asked.

"We bribed workmen with large enough sums to make them willing to risk their lives. Here's the stairway leading to the vault."

Sam leaned forward to inspect the photo. "I assume there's only
one way down there?"

"As far as we know."

"Maybe we can tunnel under the structure," he murmured.

"You're kidding, right?"

"Right."

"I'll show you what we have from one of the security companies."

"He has more than one?"

"He's switched several times."

"Because he wants to make sure that we can't get the elixir back," Olivia interjected.

"How did he get it in the first place?"

Olivia and Colin both went tense. She was the one who finally spoke. "My dad thought, since it was of no use to anyone but us, nobody was going to steal it."

"So he just left it lying around?" Sam asked, astonished.

"Of course not!" she said, indignant. "It was locked up. But he should have beefed up his security precautions."

Sam saw plainly in both Olivia's and Colin's expressions—hers, chagrin hiding behind indignation; his, carefully blank—that there was more to the story. He also saw that he wasn't going to get it out of them. Not yet, anyway.

With an inward sigh, he said, "Okay, tell me about the security companies he's used. Who are they?"

They spent the next two hours focusing on the recovery operation, mostly going over information Colin had collected. After a short break for dinner, delivered by Irene, they went back to work. But it wasn't long before it was clear that Colin needed to rest.

"Print out everything you have for me, including the pictures of Ethridge," Sam suggested. "I can go over some of this stuff on paper. Then we'll talk again."

"Yeah," Colin agreed. "But it will take a while."

"I'll handle that," Brice said, then turned to Sam. "You can come back and get it later."

"Thanks." He inclined his head toward Olivia. "Why don't you show me my room?"

"Okay."

He gave her a closer inspection. She looked worn out, too. He rather hoped it was because she'd spent the last few nights tossing in bed, thinking about him as he'd been thinking about her.

She led him down the hall to a spacious room with a view of the back garden. He would have liked to fall with her onto the large, comfortable bed, but he had work to do that required privacy.

"I don't know about you," he said to her, "but I'm beat. I think I'll take a nap."

She looked a little surprised—but also, he noted ruefully, relieved. "Sure. I'll, uh . . . well, come and find me later, if you want." And before he could change his mind, she stepped into the hall and closed the door, leaving him alone.

Sighing, Sam opened his overnight bag and took out what looked like a travel alarm clock, but was really a high-tech device designed to detect hidden cameras and microphones. With the "clock" in hand, he walked around the room, checking the antique furnishings, the knickknacks, the spectacular Oriental rug, and the marble tiles in the bathroom. He hated to think that his hosts would bug him, but he wouldn't put it past them.

He didn't find a camera, but he unearthed a small microphone in the base of a ceramic lamp. His lips quirked as he thought about who might have put it there. Wilson Woodlock, wanting to know if his daughter was being screwed by a thief? Colin, being obsessively thorough in obtaining every last fact he could learn about the burglar he'd hired?

Or could it have been Olivia—and what would her motive have been? He didn't know and didn't want to think about it.

One thing was certain. If he destroyed the damn thing, whoever had planted it would know he'd searched the room. He decided to leave it where he'd found it and make sure nobody heard anything interesting from it.

He looked around the opulent room, wondering what it would have been like to grow up in a house where the bedspreads and drapes were real silk and the bed and cabinet pieces were English antiques. Sam Morgan didn't belong here. But for the time being he was trapped.

He considered lying down with his shoes on, just to show the maid how uncouth he was. Instead he slipped the shoes off, pulled the pillows from under the spread and lay down, intending to relax for twenty minutes.

When his eyes blinked open and he looked at the clock on the bedside table, he saw that two hours had passed.

Well, at least the printing should be finished. After using the bathroom and washing his hands and face, he went back to the computer room. No one was there, but papers were stacked beside the printer. On top was a sealed envelope. Inside, a typed message said: "I need to talk to you. And I don't feel comfortable doing it in the house. Could you meet me outside? If you go out the patio door and walk straight back, you'll see a dead tree near the back wall. I'll be out there at seven, and I'll wait for you."

The signature, Olivia, was scrawled across the bottom.

So, did that mean she knew about the bug in his room? Or was she just being cautious?

He glanced at his watch and saw that it was already a little after seven. Quickly he grabbed a light jacket from his duffel bag, pulling it on to ward off the chilly Southern California evening as he headed downstairs.

He saw no one as he hurried through the family room, then out the French doors into inky darkness. As he crossed the patio, he breathed in the night air. It smelled of rain and damp earth. Somewhere not far overhead he heard a bat's wings flap.

As he started across the grass, a chilly wind riffled his hair. The temperature had dropped a few degrees, and several steps farther on, he felt splatters of light rain hit him.

He wanted to call to Olivia, but ingrained caution kept him silent as he continued across the lawn. The bare trunk and branches of the tree loomed in the darkness.

Suddenly, he saw blue denim fabric flapping on the other side of the trunk. It looked like the skirt she'd worn when she came to his house.

"Olivia?"

She didn't answer, and a sudden spurt of panic made him hurry forward, his eyes fixed on the patch of fabric.

"Olivia, are you all right?"

As he rushed toward her, the smell of damp earth intensified. But, fixed on his goal and worried, he didn't note it as a warning and, so, was totally unprepared when the ground disappeared beneath his feet.

14

BY the time Sam realized what had happened, he was plunging downward into an open shaft of some sort.

"Shit," he cursed as he tried to stop his fall, arms and legs bashing against jagged rocks.

Frantically he grabbed at them, scrambling for purchase. When his left foot collided with something solid, he instinctively stiffened his leg to keep it there while grabbing with both hands for another anchor. His left hand pulled away a chunk of rock, but his right found a crevice. The broken-edged surface was slimy with something that smelled of mold and algae and mud. But his fingers gripped it, and he flattened himself against the wall, checking his descent.

Heart pounding, he clung precariously to his perch and tried not to do anything that might cause him to lose his hold on the slippery surface beneath his right hand and left foot. For several muscle-straining minutes, he remained perfectly still, feeling dampness wafting upward, toward him.

In the darkness, he could see nothing beyond the rough surface, a few inches from his face, that could have been either rock or brick.

Cautiously he shifted his right foot, gently probing the surface until he found another rocky protrusion that might serve as a second foothold. The instant he attempted to put any weight on it, though, it crumbled. A few seconds later, he heard a series of splashes, telling him that the chunks had landed in water.

Great. He'd fallen into the shaft of an old well. And from its eroded condition, he guessed the walls had been damaged in an earthquake. Lucky for him. For as painful as those sharp-toothed walls had been during his fall, if they were smooth, he'd be treading water right now. Now that he was in here, he remembered noting an old well on the Woodlock property. It had been securely covered. But how recently? Had someone removed the cover and planted Olivia's skirt as a lure? Then left him the note?

He'd deal with that later. Right now he had to figure out how to get out of here.

Another careful search with his right foot located a fairly large crevice, and when he tested it, it held. He performed the same operation with his left hand but found no other spot for it but the one his right hand was occupying. To relieve his burning muscles, he very slowly switched hands.

Then, being careful not to follow the pieces of the wall down the shaft, he tilted his head back and looked upward. He could see the wide circle of the well mouth and a patch of cloud-covered sky. He judged he was down only about six or seven feet, but without more

light, he couldn't see any other footholds that would bear his
weight—if there even were any.

He was contemplating the possibility of having to remain in his
current strained and very unstable position until daylight when a
high, urgent voice floated toward him from above.

"Sam?"

"Olivia?" His voice boomed upward, echoing off the walls of the
well that surrounded him.

"Sam, where are you?"

"In a damn well."

"Oh, Lord, are you all right?"

"At the moment."

Her head appeared over the rim. "Oh, Lord," she said again.
"What happened to the cover?"

"You tell me," he growled.

"I . . . I don't know."

"Yeah, well, I'd like to get out of here. The shaft's too wide for me
to reach from one side to the other, but I could shimmy my way up.
Do you have a rope?"

"I . . . Hang on a sec."

It was more like twenty seconds before something dark came dangling down toward him. Cautiously, Sam reached out and grabbed
what he realized instantly was the leg of a pair of jeans. He gave her
high marks for quick thinking and inventiveness, but he knew she'd
never be able to support his weight.

"Can you tie the other end on something up there?" he asked.

"There's nothing close . . . wait. Maybe this will . . ." He heard her
moving around, and a minute later, she looked over the rim again. "I
tied a knot in the leg, then wedged it into a crack in the bricks."

He pulled carefully, and the connection felt solid. It would do—as
long as the wall didn't crumble away from the knot. Supporting some
of his weight on the pants leg, he braced his feet against the wall.
When that didn't bring a pile of bricks down on his head, he let the
makeshift rope take all his weight and began to inch upward.

It was slippery going in the old shaft. He'd climbed only about
two feet when a section of brick gave way under his foot and plunged
into the water below.

Above him, Olivia gasped. "Sam! Are you okay?"

"Yeah," he clipped out, unable to spare more breath for explanations.

She must have realized that talking was a bad idea, because she kept quiet, even when he slipped again, cursing loudly. Still, he kept moving upward, and as he approached the top, he could hear her breath sawing in and out of her lungs—like his. He realized then that she didn't just have the pants leg wedged between the bricks. She was holding on to it—insurance against the possibility of the wall disintegrating.

About fifteen inches from the rim, the pants leg began to rip. Olivia screamed as he fell back, one leg dangling into space.

Sam lashed out with an arm and caught the rim of the well. Pain shot through his hand, but he hung on because it was the only option.

Teeth gritted, he let go of the pants leg, transferring his other hand to the rim, then began hauling himself up and over it.

When Olivia leaned into the opening, his heart leaped into his throat as he imagined the lip of the well crumbling under her weight. "Get back!"

Ignoring the warning, she reached under his arms and tugged him toward her. With her help, he was able to pull himself over the edge. Flopping onto the damp ground, he lay panting.

Olivia crouched over him, her breath as labored as his. "Sam . . . Sam . . ." she gasped. "Are you all right?"

"Yes," he answered automatically. As he looked up at her, he saw she was half naked and shivering. He reached for her, pulling her down so that she sprawled on top of his body.

She melted against him, and he clasped her fervently. In the process of almost getting killed, he had found out something important. She cared about him—a lot, it seemed. Enough to risk her own safety.

"Thank you," he whispered.

She wrapped her arms around him and hung on. "I was so scared."

With a growl low in his throat, he caught the back of her head, bringing her mouth down to his in a wild, desperate kiss that had him instantly hard and aching. He wanted her with a fury that frightened him. And she returned the kiss with the same mindless need.

The near-death experience made him reach out for life on the most basic level. And life had become Olivia.

He gathered her against himself, his mouth ravaging hers. His hands roamed over her body, moving her so that her cleft cradled his rigid cock, then cupping her bottom to increase the pressure for both of them. When she moaned and squirmed against him, his hands dove under her blouse, stroking across the silky flesh of her back.

There was no doubt in his mind what they would do next. He would tear off her clothing and his, then roll on top of her, and plunge his aching cock deep inside her. He would finally slake the hot lust that had consumed him since the night they had first met.

But even as those tempting images danced in his mind, even as he fumbled for the catch at the back of her bra, he recognized that she was shivering in his arms. And he knew he couldn't make love to her here. He had to get her out of the wind . . . Christ, and the rain. It hadn't even registered in his brain that the few splattering drops he'd felt earlier had now turned into a steady drizzle.

Pulling his hands from under her blouse, he shifted to his side, then gathered her up and helped her to her feet. "You're cold," he said, his voice gritty.

She blinked, then murmured, "No. I'm hot."

He allowed himself the luxury of a laugh. "We both are. But we can't make love out here." Or now, he realized as intellect began to conquer emotion.

Someone had tried and failed to kill him. How soon would they try again?

He pulled off his jacket and wrapped it around her legs like a skirt, tying the arms at her waist, keeping her close as he led her to the side yard, avoiding the direct route to the house.

"Doesn't that damn well have a top?" he asked.

Olivia looked back over her shoulder into the darkness. "It should. Sam, I was . . . so scared you were going to . . . to fall to the bottom. . . ."

"I know. But it's all right now," he said, his arm tightening around her waist in a gentle squeeze as he steered her onto the patio. "Where can we talk—where it'll be private?" he asked. "I mean, not my room," he clarified. "There's a hidden microphone in there."

Olivia stared at him, genuinely astonished. "What?" she breathed.

"Someone put a bug in my lamp. And I don't mean a grasshopper."

She felt a frown flicker across her brow. "How . . . how do you know?"

"I don't take my surroundings for granted. Did Colin feel that he needed to keep tabs on me?"

"No!" she objected immediately.

"What about your father?"

She took her lower lip between her teeth, not quite so certain. "I . . . I don't know."

"We can't stay out here. Where can we talk?" he asked again.

She thought for a moment before leading him to the left side of the yard, to the glass-enclosed pavilion that housed the swimming pool. Rain drummed on the glass roof. But inside, the air was warm and heavy with the odor of chlorine. After switching on a small lamp in the bar area, she turned to face him.

He shut the door behind them, keeping his gaze on her, and she wondered if she looked as frightened and fragile as she felt.

Unable to look him in the eye, she studied the azure water of the pool, trying to find her equilibrium. It amazed her that she had almost made love with Sam out there on the lawn. She had been terrified for him. When he had pulled her on top of him, the only thought in her mind had been getting as close to him as she could. She would have let him do anything he wanted. But he was the one who had stopped. Now he was deliberately keeping several feet of space between them as he studied her face. Pulling a sheet of paper from his pocket, he unfolded it and thrust it toward her.

After scanning the type, she raised her head and finally looked into his eyes. "Do you think I wrote that?"

"No," he answered, his voice harsh and grating. "I figured out you didn't, but not until after I ended up on my way down to Hades."

"The signature looks a little like mine. But it's not."

"Yeah, well, if we go back out there, we'll find some fabric attached to the tree. I thought it was your skirt. Somebody went to a lot of trouble to take the top off the well, then lure me out there—so I'd fall into the shaft and drown, if I didn't break my neck on the way down."

She sucked in a sharp breath but didn't contradict him.

"How did you know where I was?" he demanded.

"I . . . I was standing at the window. I saw you and wondered where you were going."

"Lucky for me."

He took her by the shoulders, his fingers digging through her sweater. "Who wants me dead?"

"I don't know."

He sighed. "Okay. We can go over the list of suspects later. Pack some clothes. You and I are going somewhere safe."

"What?" she managed.

His voice turned low and dangerous. "Don't you get it? I've been at your house for less than ten hours, and somebody's already trying to get me out of the picture. If I stay, they're going to make another attempt. And another. I'm not going to play sitting duck. And if you want to keep working with me, you're going with me."

"Where?"

"I'm not going to talk about that while we're still on Woodlock property."

"I can't just leave," she objected.

"I'm clearing out. You can come with me or stay here."

It sounded as if he were offering her a choice, but she had already discarded the illusion of choice.

She raised her chin. "Are you trying to get me off alone so you can . . . have me?"

"I wouldn't put it in those terms."

"What terms would you use?" she asked in a shaky voice, knowing what she wanted to hear, yet at the same time dreading it.

"I'd call it making love. And you wouldn't have stopped me out there on the lawn—would you?"

She swallowed. "No."

"At least you're being honest about that."

She ignored a twinge of guilt and plowed on. "But now I'm thinking straight again. And we both know . . . intimacy . . . is more likely if we're off somewhere by ourselves."

He gave her a crooked grin. "If you say so."

She knit her hands together in front of her. "I was trying to avoid . . . getting involved with you . . . sexually."

"Why?"

"Because we have to stick to business."

"Oh, yeah?" He crossed the space between them and pulled her to him, leaning down to nuzzle his lips against her neck, her jawline, and she knew he felt her instant response. "We're already involved sexually. We just haven't taken the final step. Yet."

His words and the feel of his body against hers sent heat leaping between them. A familiar heat that only he could generate. "I should be afraid of you," she whispered.

"Why?"

"You're a violent man. I didn't really know what I was getting into when I hired you."

"Yeah, I can be violent. But I would never hurt you, Olivia. I swear it, on my life."

"I think I know that, too," she answered, marveling that they were speaking so frankly, yet not quite frankly enough. "But you might hurt my father. Or my brother."

"Only if I found out they'd done something . . . underhanded to me."

"We're all working together."

"You and Colin. But not necessarily your father."

"He wouldn't try to kill you." Even as she mouthed the protest, she couldn't be completely sure. And she knew he sensed her uncertainty.

"Unfortunately, I can't take your word for that."

"Doesn't it create a problem for you—wanting me and hating my father?" She asked the question that neither one of them had addressed until now.

"Yes," he said with a catch in his voice. "But we're getting off track. Let's go."

"I have to let Colin know we're leaving."

"No. We're not talking to him or anyone else right now. We're simply disappearing," he said, making it clear that he was setting the rules. Stepping back, he gave her a critical look. "Put on my jacket. It's big. It will hide the fact that you're walking around with your butt hanging out." Before she could object, he untied the jacket from her waist and handed it back to her. Feeling trapped, she shrugged into it and let him usher her out of the pool enclosure and toward the house. Unfortunately, almost as soon as they stepped inside, they ran into Jefferies.

"Miss Olivia! What happened?" he asked, his gaze taking in her appearance.

"We had a little run-in with the well," Sam answered, watching the man's face.

To Olivia's relief, he looked shocked and confused. "The well? What . . . ? Oh! You mean that old well the previous owners used before the waterlines were laid?"

"Yes."

"We're just going to clean up," Sam said brusquely, and without further explanation, he took Olivia's arm and urged her toward the stairs.

They quickly headed up to her room. Once inside, he closed the door behind them. "Pack a few things," he said tersely.

She didn't want to leave the safety of the house. Except it had suddenly ceased to be a refuge.

"I'm going to get my stuff," he said, then left the room.

As soon as he was out of the room, she started scribbling a hasty note. But he came back in less than a minute and snatched the message out of her hand and read it.

"Dear Colin, Sam says he and I have to leave. I've agreed. I'll talk to you later."

He might have crumpled it up, but he allowed her to write a few more lines. "Ask him to see if he can find out who took the cover off the well."

"Okay."

She wrote that down, then packed. On their way out, she slipped the note under Colin and Brice's door.

Fifteen minutes after they'd gone upstairs, they were in his car and heading for Route 101.

"Now are you going to tell me where we're going?" she asked.

"Actually, not until I make sure that there isn't a bug in the car. Or a transponder, with someone sitting on the receiver end, tracking our movements."

"That sounds kind of paranoid."

He grunted. "Do you blame me?"

"I guess not."

"We're going south?"

"Yes. We might as well end up a little closer to Ethridge's house. I'll decide where, after we put some distance between us and your place."

She slid him a sideways glance. His face was set in harsh lines. She wanted to reach out and make physical contact with him, but she kept her hands locked in her lap. He was such a study in contradictions. He could be tender, angry, sexy.

Somehow, without even realizing it was happening, she had formed a strong emotional bond with this man. Of all the times in her life when she'd been frightened—and there had been more than a few of them—one of the worst was finding Sam dangling by his fingernails in the well.

After several miles of silence, he said, "Tell me about the people who live in the house. Is there anyone besides the ones I've met—your father, Colin, Brice, Darwin, Jefferies, Irene, Thurston."

"Mrs. Leon, our cook, comes in during the day. We have several trained attendants taking care of Uncle Darwin now. Ralph Patrick." She thought for a moment. "George Swift. Will Murphy."

"And everyone knew your fiancé was going to be staying with you."

"Yes. Well, maybe not the part-time staff."

"Which ones of them were at the house today?"

"We had a four-man crew from Arbor Gardening Service."

"Oh, great. Four more suspects." He turned his head toward her. "Maybe someone asked them to remove the cover from the well."

"Why would anyone want to do that?"

"I don't know. But someone arranged for it to disappear. Or maybe a big wind blew it off?" he muttered. "And then one of your skirts blew off the clothesline you don't have and got stuck on the back of the tree trunk."

He was watching her from the corner of his eye. Deliberately she tried to relax her grip on her own hands. "Obviously, someone did it," she whispered.

He took an exit off the freeway and drove into Carpinteria. When he found an all-night gas station with a car wash, he drove into one of the stalls.

"What are you doing?" she asked.

"Looking for transponders and bugs."

He got out, inspected the undercarriage of the car, then the bumpers, before going over the interior thoroughly. When he found nothing, he drove them through the car wash, then gassed up, and headed back to the freeway.

"I'm sorry," she said as they merged onto the road.

"About what, exactly?" he asked cautiously.

"About putting you in danger."

"You did that the minute you asked me to steal back that Astravor stuff from Luther Ethridge."

"Yes. But you chose to be a thief. That's the main thing I knew about you. And I . . . I didn't know I was going to get . . . involved with you." She had used the word "sexual" before. Now she gulped and said, "Emotionally, I mean."

His gaze shot to her before he focused on the road again. "Would you like to elaborate on that a little bit?"

She hesitated, then drew a steadying breath and spoke the truth. "I don't know you very well. I shouldn't care what happens to you. But I do. I care a lot."

He reached over and laid his palm gently against her cheek. She drew comfort from the contact, but that didn't stop her from wondering how far she could trust him.

LUTHER was waiting by the phone. When it rang, he snatched up the receiver.

"Where have you been?" he demanded.

"Busy. I can't get away anytime I want, you know."

He did know, but he wasn't going to give an inch.

"The fiancé arrived this afternoon," his informant said.

Luther bit back a snarl. The very idea that Olivia could be seeing anyone made his blood boil. Who the hell was Sam Morgan? And how had she met him, anyway?

He'd done a great deal of research on the man, picking up every scrap of information available. Morgan seemed to be wealthy, although he could be living beyond his means. Which might mean he was after Olivia for her fortune.

Morgan spent money generously on liberal causes—and also gave some bucks to conservative ones. He liked his privacy. There wasn't much on record about him. Most interesting of all, he had little history. Eight years ago, it appeared as if the well-built, dark-haired man had simply blinked into existence. Before that, there were no credit card bills for Sam Morgan, California resident. No medical, dental or school records. No mortgage loans or apartment rentals.

The earliest information Luther could find about Morgan showed he had lived in a cheap apartment in Isla Vista near the University of California, Santa Barbara, and that he had worked as a golf caddy. He'd moved several times since then, always to better digs. Five years ago he'd bought a home in Ojai. Then a ranch near Lompoc. It looked as if he'd connected with Olivia at some of the charity functions they'd both attended.

Luther clenched his fingers around the receiver. Olivia belonged to him. And he wasn't going to allow some mystery fiancé to get in the way.

"What about the well?" he demanded.

"He took the bait."

"And?"

"He fell in."

Luther's thin lips curved into a smile. "Good."

His informant waited a beat before delivering the bad news. "And somehow he got himself out."

"Fuck! How?"

"I don't know. They came back to the house together after stopping in at the pool house. Unfortunately, I don't have a bug in there."

"She was outside—with him?"

"Yes."

He swore again. "Why?"

"I don't know."

"Then what?" Luther demanded.

"Then he hustled her upstairs, and they both packed."

"What are you saying?"

"They've left."

"Jesus Christ! Where did they go?"

"I don't know."

"Find out! Damn you. Find out."

"If I can, I will."

Luther shouted obscenities into the phone. The informant waited through the barrage, then asked for further instructions.

"Do your damn job," Luther snarled, then slammed down the receiver.

Seething, he paced back and forth in his office, his blood pounding in his temples. Images of Olivia in another man's arms filled his mind until he thought his head would explode with fury. He couldn't stand it, couldn't bear to think about it. Yet he couldn't think about anything else.

But he had to. If he didn't keep a clear head, everything he'd worked and planned for would be lost. And he wouldn't be able to bear that, either.

He needed to get himself back under control. Find something else to focus on for a while. Not exercise—that would engage his body but not his mind. He needed something mentally distracting. But something soothing and pleasant . . .

A visit to the woman upstairs.

He stopped pacing, and gradually, as he considered his guest, who would do anything he asked because she had no other choice, he began to feel calmer. She really was quite lovely.

And as he pictured her familiar face, he couldn't stop a little fantasy from playing in his head. What if she were eager to see him? What if his loving wife were waiting for him upstairs? What would that be like?

Deeply buried needs stirred inside him.

He clenched his fists, willing away the tender feelings.

The desire for intimate human contact was only a weakness. He had learned long ago that he could trust no one but himself. Love no one but himself. No matter how much he might long to let down his guard, he could never do it again. He had done that once at school. He'd thought he could trust his secret fears and longings with another kid who was as miserable as he was at Dickensen Prep. He'd thought Teddy Branson was his friend. But the little snot had gone running to the bigger boys. He'd used his new knowledge as a way to curry favor, and he made things a whole lot worse for Luther Ethridge.

He made a low sound that was part pain and part anger. He'd trusted Teddy with his most private thoughts. And that had been a big mistake. He'd made the mistake one more time in his life. Maybe he was a slow learner. But he'd let himself be vulnerable again, this time with a woman. He'd been willing to give her the world. And she'd flat out rejected him.

Well, never again. He'd grown stronger for it. Too strong for anyone to hurt him.

A few minutes later, with a smile on his face, Luther headed upstairs to spend some quality time with his unwillingly cooperative houseguest.

IN her prison, Barbara heard the sound she feared most—the sound of gas hissing into the room.

Her fingers clutched at the neck of her robe, echoing the sick dread that clutched her throat.

Her gaze darted to the wall, to the metal stems of the gas jets. She had tried to twist them off or stuff them up with washcloths, but to no avail. He had only increased the pressure, blowing away her makeshift barriers.

As she stared in terror at those shiny protrusions, she dragged in a lungful of clear air, then held her breath, even though she knew it would do no good. When her lungs felt like they were going to burst, she would be forced to gasp in a choking breath.

He had done this before—too many times. The bastard. And she had no defense against him.

The vapor filled the room, filled her mind with swirling clouds, and made her body heavy. She swayed on her feet, then dropped to her knees. With the last of her strength, she lowered herself to the carpet.

She wanted to close her eyes. But it was too hard to work the muscles. She wanted to scream for help, but she knew that no one would hear her. So she lay on the rug, unable to fight the sick, scared feeling that made her limbs tremble.

The trembling increased when she heard the pump that evacuated the vapor from the room and made it safe for Ethridge to come in. The gas had made her groggy. It had done its work. And now he was coming in to claim her. She longed to lash out at the man who held her captive. But all she could do was lie there, waiting for him with her pulse pounding.

Then he was in the room, looking down at her. Bending, he hauled her up and tossed her onto the bed, where she bounced like a rag doll.

"It's useless to defy me, Olivia," he said in an even voice, putting special emphasis on the name.

She wanted to scream that she wasn't Olivia. But he had hired a plastic surgeon to change her face, and he had turned her into a woman named Olivia Woodlock. A woman he wanted. A woman he apparently couldn't have. So he had created a substitute.

He stood above her, watching her as he slowly took off his clothing. She saw his hairless chest and his muscular arms. And as he sat beside her on the bed, she saw his disgusting penis, red and swollen, jutting toward her.

A smile played on his lips as he opened the buttons of the robe. It was the only garment he allowed her to wear. He spread the placket apart, baring the front of her body for his inspection. And there was nothing she could do about it, because the gas had made it impossible to move.

But not impossible to feel.

She wanted to scream at him to stop as he tenderly began to stroke her. First the column of her neck, then her breasts. She was helpless to prevent his touch. He delicately circled her nipples, creating the illusion of arousal as he made them pucker.

"I love the way you get excited for me, Olivia," he murmured.

She wanted to shout at him. She wanted to tell him he was mistaken. She wasn't excited—only disgusted. But speech was beyond her.

He squeezed her nipples too hard, knowing there was no need for gentleness. He opened the drawer of her bedside table and took out lotion, pouring it on his fingers before slipping them inside her vagina, pretending he had made her wet.

"How do you want it tonight, sweet Olivia," he asked in a silky voice as he fondled her. "How many times can you come?"

None, she silently cried out.

She ached to tell him she wasn't Olivia and that all she wanted was for him to leave her alone. Instead she said a silent prayer that he would finish with her quickly and leave her alone. And that he wouldn't hurt her too much.

15

AS they drove into the night, Olivia slouched, sound asleep, in her seat, her head resting against the window. Sam knew she must be both emotionally and physically exhausted, so he let her be. But he kept glancing at her, admiring the shape of her lips or the way her dark lashes lay like raven's wings against her cheek. She was beautiful, although she looked fragile, too.

Was she the reason someone had gone after him? Did someone opposed to their engagement want him out of the way?

Or was the attack designed to keep the Woodlocks from getting back their magic elixir? If that were the case, the person who'd tried to kill him had to be someone who knew why Olivia had hired him.

He decided against turning off the highway again until he knew that he was too tired to keep driving with any degree of safety.

As he approached Tarzana, he took a secondary road, heading into the mountains. He'd stayed at the Burroughs Motel a few times, but he didn't want to go where he was known. He drove to another place he'd seen before—the Rustic Lodge. Each room was a separate cabin, and the wooded grounds backed onto a state park, the ideal place for a wolf to roam.

Olivia's eyes blinked open when he cut the engine. Sitting up, she peered at the unfamiliar scenery. "Where are we?"

"A little east of Tarzana. I'll get us a room."

"With two beds."

"If they have any left."

He woke a clerk who had nodded off and signed in, using an alternate identity that he'd kept up over the past few years. Sam Lucien.

After ushering Olivia into cabin fifteen—with two double beds— he went to get their luggage. When he returned to the room, she was in the bathroom. As she came out, her gaze found him.

"You wouldn't try anything I didn't want you to do—correct?"

"Correct," he answered. It was the truth, as far as it went, although he was sure that if he started kissing her, he could bring her around to his point of view pretty quickly. But he wasn't going to try anything now. She looked too washed out. When they made love for the first time, he wanted it to be as good for both of them as he could make it.

Turning her back to him, she pulled off her jeans. Still wearing the T-shirt, bra, and panties she'd put on earlier that evening, she climbed into one of the beds and rearranged the pillows before snuggling down.

He was tempted almost beyond endurance by the need to strip off his clothes, climb into bed with her, and take her in his arms. He grew hard as he stood looking at her. Before she could open her eyes and see his state of arousal, he turned away.

In the bathroom, he took a cold shower, then pulled on clean briefs and a T-shirt.

When he crossed the room again, he could tell from her even

breathing that she'd fallen asleep. Either she was too exhausted to keep her eyes open or she trusted him enough to let herself go—or both.

He thought about going outside, changing to wolf form and running through the park. But he was tired, too. So he slipped into the other bed.

He woke early, as soon as he heard her stirring. When he opened his eyes, she was looking across at him.

Unable to stop himself, he climbed out of bed and slipped under the covers beside her. He felt her body stiffen, but he only slung his arm around her and stroked his hands through her wonderful hair as he cradled her head against his shoulder. He wanted her with a force that shook him. He knew he was going to make love with her soon. But maybe he was savoring the anticipation as much as the act. That was a new experience for him. Bending his head, he kissed the tender place where her hair met her temple.

"How are you this morning?" he asked.

She stirred against him. "Wondering why I let you convince me to leave home.

"It's safer."

She turned her head and looked at him. "That depends on your point of view."

"The point of view of my not getting killed," he answered immediately.

"There's that."

He kept stroking her hair. "I took all the papers that Colin printed out. I'll study the material he's got on the Ethridge house. Then I should drive down to La Jolla and have a look around."

"I'm going with you."

"I don't want you near the place."

She sat up and looked at him. "I mean, when you break in, I'm going with you."

"The hell you are. It's too dangerous."

"I know it's dangerous. But . . ." She stopped and sucked in a breath. "I'm the one who knows what the elixir looks like."

He sat up and returned her direct look. "You can tell me about it."

She kept her gaze steady. "No."

As they glared at each other, his mind scrambled for a good way to keep her out of danger. "Taking you could be the thing that sinks the mission."

"Why?"

"Because I work alone. Because you could be more of a liability than a help."

"I have to go." The fierceness in her voice told him that he wasn't going to argue her out of it. Not this morning.

"I won't take you along unless I know your capacities," he said, keeping his voice even.

"What does that mean—exactly?"

Thinking fast, he said, "We go on another job first."

"As in rob someone else?" she clarified.

"Jackpot."

"I'm not going to participate in anything like that."

"Then we're not going to Luther Ethridge's."

She swallowed hard. "Who were you planning to rob?" she asked.

He thought over the next project he'd been scouting out. He liked to do a lot of research, contemplate his subject for months before going in. "A man named Harold Reese," he finally said. "He's got mining operations all over the west. His father was responsible for giving hundreds of miners radiation-related diseases and asbestosis. Instead of paying their medical bills and compensating their families, he spent millions fighting their claims. Harold has continued in the same pattern." He climbed out of bed, pulled his duffel bag to the top of the dresser, extracted a folder he'd brought with him, and tossed it on the bed.

Before she could continue the conversation, he picked up the duffel bag again and carried it and clean clothing into the bathroom. He kept his expression calm until the door was closed. Then he clenched his teeth so hard he could have bitten through an iron bar. He wanted to stamp back into the bedroom and give Olivia hell. He'd never conjured up pictures of the woman who might be his mate. But in a million years, it wouldn't have been rich Miss Olivia Woodlock. Who was it—F. Scott Fitzgerald?—who had said "the very rich are different from you and me"? Fitzgerald had been right. And now Sam was stuck with one of them. A modern princess who insisted on getting her way.

He hadn't thought he could fall for a woman like Olivia. He hadn't thought he'd be forced to cooperate with her. He couldn't even be sure if he could trust her. And now he was wondering about his motives for leaving her estate so quickly. Sure, he wanted to keep his hide intact. But hadn't he been secretly relieved by the excuse to de-camp because he didn't feel comfortable living in a house where he fell over servants every time he turned around?

When he came out, Olivia was sitting up in bed reading the dossier on Reese like she was studying for an exam.

"Well?" he asked, struggling to keep any hint of temper out of his voice.

"He sounds like a person who doesn't care about anything besides himself and his money."

"Right."

"But he's just a side issue."

"Not for me."

They glared at each other.

"I'm hungry," he finally said. "There's a fast-food restaurant up the road where we can buy breakfast. I know it's not what Jefferies would serve in the dining room. But you can get pancakes or some kind of breakfast sandwich."

"What are you getting?"

"A couple of sausage sandwiches."

"I'll have pancakes," she said.

Leaving Olivia alone in the cabin, Sam climbed into his car, drove to the restaurant, and pulled into the drive-in line.

OLIVIA stared at the closed door, then at the phone sitting on a table in the cabin. She had only moments to make a decision. As she pic-tured Colin's worried face, she chose loyalty to her family.

Picking up the receiver, she dialed her brother's private number. He answered on the first ring.

"Where in the hell are you?"

The curse and Colin's tone of voice told her he was worried out of his mind.

"I can't tell you, but I don't want you to worry," she tried to reas-sure him.

"Come home!" he demanded.

"I can't."

"Why did you leave?"

"Because somebody tried to kill Sam. Was it you?"

"How could you even ask a question like that?"

"Because you've lost control of the situation. And you hate that. Maybe you even hate him."

"Stop trying to analyze me."

She sighed. "Colin, I have to get off. I just called to tell you I'm okay."

"No! Wait! He's taking you on a job—right?"

She sucked in a sharp breath. "What are you talking about?"

"You told him you wanted to go to Ethridge's with him. He said he wouldn't take you unless you proved you were up to the challenge. Now he's going to drag you on a burglary."

"How do you know?"

He answered with a sardonic laugh. "I'm the boy genius, remember. Who are you going to rob?"

"You know I can't tell you that!"

"Then tell me the town where you'll be."

"Why?"

"So I can check the news to make sure you're not in jail."

"Carmel." Her head jerked up. "He's back. Got to go."

Before he could ask any more questions, she hung up, then stood and looked at her reflection in the dresser mirror, trying to wipe away the trapped, guilty look. When she couldn't manage it, she went into the bathroom and splashed cold water on her face.

SAM walked into the cabin. For a panicked moment, he thought Olivia had fled. Then he heard the toilet flush.

When she came out of the bathroom, he studied her expression. After setting down the sacks of food, he said, "I guess it's not safe to leave you alone. Who did you call?"

Instead of denying it, she asked, "How do you know I called anyone?"

"It's plastered all over your face."

"I was hoping it wouldn't show."

"Well, either you called Colin, or you called the cops to come arrest me."

Taking a shallow breath, she let it out and said, "I knew Colin would be worried. I only wanted to reassure him."

He gave her a long look, then walked to the bathroom, collected his toiletries, and packed them in his duffel bag. "We're leaving."

"Why?"

"We're not safe here."

"I didn't tell Colin where we were."

"But somebody could trace the call." He went on quickly, "You trust Jefferies with your life? Or Thurston? Or that maid? Or the men taking care of your uncle?"

"I . . ." She stopped, probably because no one had put it in those terms.

"You've got five minutes to get your stuff together."

"I haven't showered."

"Take two minutes for that."

Apparently she felt guilty enough to do what he asked without arguing.

He had planned to stay put for several days, relaxing and studying the Ethridge material. Instead, once they'd stowed their gear in the car, he drove to the office and settled the bill.

In the car, he fished into one of the fast-food bags, pulled out a cup of water, and took a small sip as he headed onto the highway.

"Why are we going north?" she asked.

"Because Reese's house is our next stop. When we're through there, we'll go back to La Jolla."

Her head swiveled toward him. "You're not just testing my resolve?"

"No. I'm going to find out how you react under stress—and how well you think when you're under pressure." He set the water in the cup holder and glanced at her. "Well, I guess I know how you react. You call your brother."

She sank down into her seat and turned her head away, watching the scenery.

"Eat your breakfast."

"I'm not hungry."

"Too bad. You put me in charge of this operation. And Master Sergeant Morgan says you're going to take care of yourself and eat."

"Why aren't you a general?"

"I didn't go to college. I can't be a commissioned officer."

Sighing, she fished a pancake out of her bag and nibbled on the edge.

"Hand me a sandwich. And take off the top layer of bread," he said.

"You're on the Atkins diet?"

"The what?"

"Low-carbs. You know."

"Yeah. That."

Neither of them ate much as he drove.

"It's not fair to say I call my brother because I'm under stress," she finally said.

"He called you?"

"You know he didn't. But Colin and I are close." She sighed. "We grew up in difficult circumstances."

"Such as?"

"When I was little, my parents didn't have a lot of time for us. Dad was at work most of the time. Or that's what he said. Momma had a lot of obligations—parties, charity committees."

He let her keep talking. He'd thought she'd grown up getting anything and everything she wanted. He had a sinking feeling his assumptions had been dead wrong.

"My mother hated having so much to do outside of the house, but my dad wanted her to have a public presence. Or maybe he wanted to keep her busy. If anyone raised us, it was Jefferies. When he was busy, Colin and I turned to each other."

When she didn't continue, he cast her a quick glance. "Go on. I'm listening."

She gave him a look that said she wasn't worried about his listening but about his feelings about the Woodlocks. "Our family life built up to a big crisis. My mother realized Dad wasn't working every minute—he was sleeping with a lot of women." She swallowed hard. "She told Dad he had to change, or she was getting a divorce. He refused to live his life any differently. I don't know if it was a matter of principle for him or . . . or if he didn't really love her. Maybe he just married her because she was beautiful and smart, and he wanted beautiful and smart children."

"You're both of those," he said, softly.

"You think I was stupid to call Colin."

"You haven't been in this situation before." He reached over to take her hand and give it a squeeze.

"No, I haven't," she replied.

A sideways glance told him she was staring at his hand covering hers. He kept the contact until a curve in the road required both hands on the wheel.

"What about your parents?" she said suddenly.

He felt a sharp pang of homesickness. "They have a strange marriage—but it's solid."

"They're both still alive?"

"Yes. I check up on them from time to time."

"Could you elaborate on the 'strange' part?"

"My dad insists on ruling the roost. But he and Mom want to be together," he said, keeping it brief. The knowledge that he would eventually have to spill everything made his stomach knot.

He wondered if his anxiety showed when she spoke again. Her voice had softened—a gentle, sympathetic sound, as if she actually cared. "Do you go home for visits?" she asked.

"No. They think I'm dead."

She drew in a sharp breath. "Dead? Why?"

He hadn't planned to tell her so much so soon, but he heard himself saying, "I left home when the members of a biker gang pinned a murder on me." After spitting out the confession, he spared her a quick look to see how she was taking that.

She was focused on his face, and he found it difficult to breathe while he waited for her verdict. "You didn't kill the person," she said, making it more of a statement than a question.

"No. But I cut my losses and split." He made a self-deprecating sound. "You come from money. My dad didn't make enough as an auto mechanic to support his wife and kids. So he supplemented his income by burglarizing houses." He managed a sharp laugh. "That's how I picked my profession—family tradition."

She tipped her head to one side. "I get the feeling he wasn't as methodical as you are."

"No. But before I left home, I wasn't the same guy, either. Back then, I was running wild—out of control, you might say."

"Tell me about the murder," she asked softly.

"There was a fight in a bar, and one guy ended up dead. Maybe one of his friends used the excuse to do him. But none of them was going to take the rap. They thought I was unconscious and agreed to pin it on me."

"You were hurt?"

"Yes."

"How did you get away?"

"They took a lot of guys to the hospital. It was mass confusion.

Then a bunch of victims came in from a big car crash. The emergency room physician thought I was dead. Or maybe I *was* dead—and God gave me another chance." He laughed. "Maybe God decided to let me come back as Super Thief because he let me slip out of the morgue."

She gave a quiet snort.

"Anyway, I'm here."

"So you made up a new identity," she concluded.

"Yes."

"With your background, how did you learn to . . . fit in with the rich and famous?"

"You mean, how did I acquire some polish?" he clarified.

"Yes."

"First, I got a job as a caddy at a tony golf club. I studied the men . . ."

"And you furthered your education in the women's beds."

His head snapped toward her, then back to the road as a truck approached. "How do you know?"

"You're sexy and very appealing. And you're pragmatic."

"And I learned from a whole string of women who were older than me how to be a good lover," he added. She might as well know the whole ugly truth.

They were both silent for several moments.

"Married women?" she finally asked.

"No. Divorcées and widows."

"Did they pay you?" she whispered.

"For sex?"

She gave a small nod.

"Some of them wanted to. I was too proud for that." He sighed. "I've always had principles. Sort of." He'd let them buy him a few presents. Not many, though. "And I was already supplementing my income with some B and E."

They fell silent again.

"How did you get to be an environmental Robin Hood?" she finally asked.

"I've always had a love of nature. That was something positive my father taught us."

"Aren't you lonely? I mean, don't you miss your family?"

"Enough about me," he said brusquely. "What sports do you play?"

"Why?"

"I'm trying to assess your burglarly skills."

She hesitated for a moment, then launched into a recitation. "I took gymnastics when I was a kid. I was on my school's swim team. I'm a good tennis player. I've been rock climbing a few times. And my Girl Scout troop went on a lot of camping trips that involved hiking, backpacking, canoeing, sailing, and skiing. I've tried to keep up with some of them now and then, especially skiing, which I enjoy a lot."

"Impressive."

"Thank you."

"What about guns? Can you really shoot? Or was that revolver in the gallery just for show."

"I can shoot."

"That was on the curriculum at Miss Worthington's?"

"No. My father wanted to be sure both Colin and I could defend ourselves."

"He couldn't eat dinner with you, but he had time to teach you to shoot?"

"No. Thurston's predecessor had that job."

"Okay. We'll stop somewhere it's safe to engage in a little target practice."

"You have a gun with you?"

"A Sig." He turned and looked at her. "Target practice is one thing. Have you ever shot a man?"

"Of course not. Have you?"

"No."

"But you think you could kill?"

"Yes." The violence of the wolf was part of him. If he were cornered or provoked, he didn't even have to question that he would be capable of killing.

"I guess I saw that in you."

"What else did you see?" he asked, not certain he wanted to hear the answer.

"You're a man who rarely tells the truth," she said, the insight too close to home.

"Truth is an occupational hazard for me," he tossed back.

"But you've made it clear you want a relationship with me. What are you going to base it on—mutual lust?"

"That's a good start." He hoped the flip response disguised his growing tension.

"But it's not enough. You're going to have to trust me."

"Or what?"

"Or I walk away from you when this is over."

He didn't argue. Let her think she had the option. He knew she was only kidding herself—or engaging in wishful thinking. At least, that was what he wanted to believe.

16

SAM drove to a vacant ranch near his home. He'd thought about buying it, so he'd inspected the property.

Kids had set up a target range in the shelter of a hill. He had no trouble picking up pop and beer bottles lying around on the ground.

After setting up some targets, he handed her the Sig Sauer that he kept in a locked box under the front seat and watched her check it out.

He didn't have to tell her what to do. She took the gun in a two-handed grip and fired at the first bottle, shattering it. Then she went on to the rest, missing only one.

He felt a surge of pride. His woman could defend herself.

His woman. It felt startlingly good to think of her in those terms.

"Okay, we know you can shoot," he said in a thick voice.

She gave him a surprised look, probably wondering why he was getting all choked up about guns. "I told you," she murmured.

He made his tone businesslike. "Tonight when we stop, you can read more on Harold Reese."

"I'll do some more as soon as we get back on the road."

When they were finished with target practice, they headed back to the car. There Sam dug the folder out of his luggage again and handed it to Olivia. She scanned the pages as they drove north, or maybe she was only pretending to read so she could put some distance between them. He mostly kept his eyes on the road. But every so often he cast glances at her.

They were going to be spending another night together. And he could make love with her. That's what he ached to do. If she was any other woman, he'd reach for her the moment they were alone in the motel bedroom. But he had a feeling he was going to let her escape again.

WHEN they pulled off the highway, Olivia raised her head and blinked, aware of their surroundings for the first time in several hours. Not far away she could hear surf pounding against sand.

"Where are we?"

"Pismo Beach."

"I've never been here. But I always thought the name sounded funny."

"It's a variation of the Chumash Indian word for tar. *Pismu*. They got it from a nearby canyon and used it to seal their canoes."

"You looked that up?"

"Yeah."

"I never heard of a Chumash Indian."

"That's because so many of them were wiped out by the Spaniards. Not in wars. They caught our diseases and died."

"Sad. And infuriating," she murmured.

"They were here a long time. Nine thousand years. And the white man swept them off the face of the earth in a few decades. Just another example of the benefits of civilization."

Taking in her gloomy expression, he lightened his tone. "I won't blame the disaster on Woodlock Industries."

That won him a little smile. "Thanks."

"The white man's town started as a seaport, then got into tourism. They still have some motels right on the ocean. It's a nice environment."

"Do you know every nature-oriented place to stay up and down the California coast?"

"I know a lot of them," he allowed as he pulled in at a motel with a VACANCY sign. "Wait here while I get us a room."

"Two beds," she said automatically.

Several minutes later, he emerged with a key. Their room was around the back, less than eighty yards from the shoreline. The place was smaller than the cabin where they'd spent the previous night, and he watched her looking around nervously. Well, too bad. She'd have to earn his trust before he let her have her own space.

COLIN was using his laptop. Dressed in jeans and a sweatshirt to keep his arms warm, he sat propped up in bed. The table lamp was turned low, as he checked some of the Web community where he lurked. You never knew when Out of the Closet or the American Philatelic Exchange was going to come up with something interesting. And if he was scanning messages, he didn't have to worry about Olivia.

A movement from the doorway had him glancing up.

"You should be sleeping," Brice said.

"I'm resting."

"You're restless."

Colin took off his glasses and rubbed the bridge of his nose. "Yeah."

"Since you're not sleeping, anyway, come down to the family chapel."

"To pray for the favor of gods?" Colin asked.

"Yes. And we wouldn't want to forget the goddesses."

Colin swung his legs over the side of the bed. Brice offered his hand, and he let the other man pull him to his feet. It wasn't something he allowed many people to see, but in the privacy of his bedroom, he didn't have to worry about family or servants evaluating his lack of muscle tone.

Brice pulled him close, and he rested his head on his partner's shoulder. They stood embracing for a long moment. When Brice stroked his hand down his back, then over his butt, Colin felt a surge of regret.

"Sorry I haven't been thinking much about making love lately," he murmured.

"You will, when you're feeling better." Brice found his hand and squeezed hard. "Come see what I've set up in the chapel."

They walked hand in hand down the hall, then stepped into the magical realm of flickering candlelight, soft textures, and carefully selected icons. Colin lowered himself to the carpet and gathered a comfortable pile of pillows to lean on, then studied the arrangement of talismans, which were now lying on a square of the highest quality Thai silk.

As Brice settled opposite him, Colin picked up the Indonesian male figure with the huge penis and testicles, turning it one way and then the other for a good view of the outsized equipment. "Are you praying to get me well enough for some fun?"

Brice laughed. "That's one reason for including him. But also, he projects a sense of power."

"Yeah. Like her." He picked up the Aztec fertility goddess and held her in his other hand, then put both statues down.

There were new objects on the scarf, including a small carved totem pole and a four-leaf clover encased in plastic.

Colin touched the clover and raised an eyebrow.

"I go by instinct. There's no point in excluding something because it's too modern."

Colin nodded, then pick up a small gray-green jade figure of a wolf. "I understand the symbolism of the clover. What's this for?"

Brice gave him a direct look. "It felt . . . important."

Colin nodded. He'd always paid attention to his partner's hunches. Brice's mystical side was one of the things that had attracted him in the first place.

Brice cleared his throat. "Have you been listening to Uncle Darwin lately?"

"He's so loud, you can't miss him."

"He was talking about demons. Now that includes wolves. One wolf in particular. Sam Morgan."

"Yeah."

"So . . . did he see something we haven't?"

"How?"

"Sam was in the sunroom with your uncle for a few minutes before Thurston broke in. I've tried to talk to Uncle D about that. When he's calm enough to hold a conversation, he says he saw Morgan turn into a wolf. Well, not completely. He was half wolf and half man."

Colin shivered. Still, he felt compelled to offer a counterargument. "We both know that since Darwin's mind started turning to oatmeal, he's seen plenty of things that weren't there."

Brice gave a small nod.

"But you think there could be something to it this time?" Colin pressed.

"Maybe." Brice cleared his throat, shifted against the pillows. "Do you believe in werewolves?"

"More than most people would, I guess." But even as he said it, he felt a spark of alarm igniting in his gut. They were talking about the guy who had spirited his sister away from the safety of the estate. "Damn," Colin muttered.

"What?"

"If it wasn't for me, she would never have met him. I got them together—for criminal purposes."

"You didn't know he was dangerous."

"I should have seen . . . something."

"Maybe I'm way off base."

"I hope so," he whispered, his mind going down some interesting pathways. Before he could get too far, Brice hit him with another zinger.

"Do you think perhaps we should talk about the weather?" he asked.

"You mean the thunderstorms that come out of nowhere?"

"Yeah. Those. And the windstorms."

SAM lay in the bed next to Olivia's, his nerves too taut for sleep. The blood ran hot and fierce through his veins, and he gathered up a fistful of sheet to keep from rising out of bed and going to her. He'd been with her all day, repressing his need for her. In the darkened motel room, he felt on the brink of madness.

Yet he understood that taking the final step would change his life forever, and not only because of who he was. Olivia Woodlock was no ordinary woman. She was a member of the powerful Woodlock family. More than that, there was a quality about her that he couldn't name that had something to do with presence or . . . maybe power. Given time, he'd figure it out. Given time, he'd uncover all her secrets.

He turned his head on the pillow and looked toward her. He knew she was no more relaxed than he was, but exhaustion had apparently kicked in because she was asleep.

Good. He could leave the confines of the room for a while and run along the beach.

Climbing quietly out of bed, he padded barefoot across the room and carefully opened the door. Then he slipped into the night, closing the door behind him.

He was the only person out and about so early in the morning. Once on the beach, he headed for the darkness under a clump of palm trees. After checking the area to make absolutely sure he was alone, he pulled off his T-shirt and sweatpants and said the chant.

The change started with the familiar pain and ended with the sense of freedom that always suffused the wolf spirit within him. Raising his head, he drank in the night air, catching the familiar scent of deer not far away. He needed to hunt. Needed to run wild and sing the song of the wolf. But he didn't want to return to the motel room, to Olivia, with deer blood in his mouth. So he raced down the beach, drinking in the salt air, listening to the crash of the surf. Stopping to dash into the waves and cavort as only an animal could.

An hour later, he turned and retraced his steps, toward the motel, hoping the wolf had calmed him enough to slip back into bed and get a few hours of sleep.

IT was four in the morning by the clock on the nightstand when Olivia's eyes snapped open. Something had awakened her. Swiveling her head toward the other bed, she didn't see Sam. And he wasn't in the bathroom either.

Panic gripped her at the thought that he might have left her. She had hired the man because he was a skilled burglar. In the beginning, she had told herself that his profession meant she was better than he was. But she had never really believed that. She believed it less every moment she spent with him.

He had overcome a childhood she could only imagine. He had made his own life. And he had a moral code that was as strict as it was unconventional.

She felt a surge of relief when she saw his duffel bag. He must have waited until she was sleeping, then climbed out of bed and gone for a walk. Probably to get away from her—because proximity and sexual frustration were driving them both crazy.

Wide awake now, she was too keyed up to lie in bed, wondering when he was coming back. Instead, she crossed to the door, opened it, and made sure it wouldn't lock behind her. Then she stepped outside. It was still dark, but several overhead lights illuminated the motel grounds.

Standing by the door, she scanned the area, then took a few steps toward the ocean. Her body went rigid when she spotted something moving along the beach. Too low to the ground to be a person. Had to be an animal—a dog or . . .

A wolf.

She had seen a wolf less than a week ago. Sam's wolf. He hadn't brought the animal with them, and it was simply impossible that the animal could have followed them and kept up.

But what was a wolf doing loping along a beach on the crowded California coast?

All this ran through her mind in an instant, the same instant in which she drew in a startled breath. Clearly hearing her, the animal raised its head and pinned her with a glowing yellow gaze. As he regarded her, she felt a shiver stir the hairs on the back of her neck and travel down her spine.

He was coming for her. She knew it. She should dash back into the motel and lock the door. But Sam was outside. She couldn't lock him out—not with a wolf on the prowl.

How the devil had the creature gotten here? Was he even real? Or was she caught in the grip of a dream brought on by worry and stress and, yes, sexual frustration?

She scraped her bare foot a couple of inches against the edge of the concrete strip, feeling it firm and solid and rough against her flesh. But that proved nothing. She could make any rules she wanted in a dream.

While she was trying to work her way back to reality, the wolf faded into the shadows under a clump of palm trees. And she was left with her pulse pounding in her temples.

Released from indecision, she started to back up—until another dart of movement grabbed her attention, and her heart leaped into her throat.

Then she saw it was Sam, running across the sand, wearing only a pair of sweatpants. His chest was bare and so were his feet.

"Sam, thank God!"

"Is something wrong?" he asked in a careful voice.

"I saw a wolf! He was here!"

"Forget about the wolf," he said, his voice low and thick.

As he came toward her, she felt the same panic she had felt moments earlier when she'd seen the yellow-eyed creature approaching her.

Sam fought to think logically, his head spinning. The one thing he knew was that he had to make Olivia forget about the animal she had seen outside the motel room.

Closing the distance between them, he folded her into his arms and lowered his mouth to hers. Fierce emotions roiled through him. She clung to his shoulders, anchoring herself to him, returning his kiss with a passion that turned his blood molten. When he finally broke the kiss, they were both breathing in great gasps.

Her vulnerability showed in her eyes as she looked up at him. "This time you're not going to stop, are you?" she asked.

"No."

"Thank God."

His gaze burned down into hers. "You wanted separate beds."

She swept her hand down his back, stopping at his buttocks, pulling him more tightly against herself. "I was afraid."

"And now?"

"I can't fight the pull. The power. The . . . oh, Lord, Sam, I can't help it. I just want you so much." Lowering her head, she pressed her lips against his shoulder.

The feel of her form molded against his sent waves of arousal crashing through him. Hardly able to catch his breath, he held her cradled against him, feeling the world tip and sway beneath his feet. She spoke of power and fear and desire. And yet it was more than any of that. Much more. Deep down he had feared the potency of this moment. Maybe that was why he had drawn back every time. But finally he knew that he had no choice.

No choice at all.

She was the one who stirred. "We'd better go in."

"Yes."

Locking his fingers with hers, he led her back to the room, feeling her hand tremble, and he silently vowed that he would wipe away her fear and replace it with ecstasy. His and hers.

The moment they were inside, he slammed the door closed with his foot, then fumbled behind him to snap the lock before bending to ravage her mouth again as he dragged her T-shirt up and pushed her bra out of the way so that he could take her breasts in his hands. When he circled her nipples, then caught them between thumbs and forefingers, he heard a sob break from her lips.

"Sam. Oh, Sam," was all she managed as he skimmed her panties down her legs, then stroked his hands along the strong line of her back, over her bare bottom and between her thighs, his own hands shaking all the while.

She was hot and wet and aroused, moving restlessly against him. He had almost made love with her outside his house. Then he'd nearly taken her on the lawn beside the well. He was grateful that he had waited until they were in a bedroom, where he could love her with some finesse. Wanting a horizontal surface under them, he swept back the covers on the nearest bed and laid her down.

Never taking his eyes off her, he tugged down his sweatpants, then kicked them away. Naked and on fire, he turned on one of the bedside lamps, then swept his gaze over her. She lay with her arms stiffly at her sides, and the look of raw nerves on her face made his heart ache.

"You look so beautiful—and so vulnerable. But I would never hurt you."

She swallowed. "I know. But standing over me like that, you are a little intimidating. Well, not just intimidating. Magnificent," she added.

He gave her a crooked grin. "Concentrate on the second part, and I'll work on being a little more, uh . . . approachable."

In truth, the flames lapping at him made it difficult to think. But he knew tonight would set the tone for the rest of their lives together, so he moved slowly as he came down beside her and gathered her into his arms, awed by the feel of her naked body against his.

She stroked her hand over his shoulder, through his hair. "Sam, I have to tell you something."

He reached to touch his thumb to her cheek, then trace the curve of her lips. "You want to tell me what you like when you make love?"

"I . . . want to tell you that I haven't had much experience doing this."

The little tremble in her words made him go very still. "How much experience, exactly?"

Her breath hitched. "None."

17

FOR an instant, the world stood still around him as the single word she'd spoken, and its implications, filtered into his brain.

His voice, when he finally managed to speak, was little more than a raspy whisper. "You're a virgin?"

She buried her face against his shoulder and nodded. "I told you I wasn't into casual sex. I didn't . . . well, it just never felt . . . right."

He lifted her face with a finger beneath her chin, then bent forward to kiss her cheek. "And it does with me?"

"You know it does."

Yes, he did. And maybe he should feel energized, he thought, as his fingers stroked, barely moving over the silky skin of her shoulder. Like those terrorist martyrs who thought they were going to heaven with eighty-seven virgins, or whatever the number was. If you took a virgin to bed, she didn't have anyone to compare you to and, so, wouldn't know how badly you'd failed if you didn't satisfy her. Only that wasn't the way he was thinking about it at all.

He had wanted her since the night he had first met her. No, not just wanted. He hadn't thought of another woman since, and he'd never thought of any woman the way he'd thought about her. Yet he felt nearly overwhelmed with the responsibility she had just handed him.

"I guess I've given you something to worry about."

He nuzzled his lips against the tender place where her cheek met her hair. "Yeah. A little," he admitted. Well, a lot, actually.

Her fingers played nervously across his chest, winnowing into his thick dark hair. They found one nipple and drew a circle around it, sending a cascade of reaction through his body.

"You've got that part right," he whispered.

"I figured if it felt good to me, it would feel good to you, too," she answered. He saw her cheeks redden. "And . . . uh . . . in the interest of full disclosure, I should admit that I know what an orgasm feels like."

"Oh, yeah?" He watched her color deepen. "I appreciate your sharing that with me," he added, thinking about what he wasn't yet ready to disclose.

This time, when he kissed her, it was a tender exploration, his lips moving against hers, his tongue stroking the sensitive tissue just inside her lips, then playing with the edges of her teeth. His mouth moved to her jawline, then the curve of her ear, making a leisurely tour that traveled to her collarbone and back to her mouth.

"Thank you for trusting me," he murmured, knowing she still wasn't entirely sure about him. He planned to do everything he could to wipe the uncertainty out of her mind, once and for all.

He set himself to fueling her pleasure as he brought his attention to her breasts, his fingers plucking at one peaked nipple while he drew its mate into his mouth, swirling his tongue around the crest, then taking it delicately between his teeth. He was rewarded by the small sounds of wanting she made.

He was so hard he thought he might self-destruct, but he was determined to keep his focus on her. Then her hand slipped between them, finding his cock and closing around him.

His indrawn breath brought an answering murmur of satisfaction from her.

"I guess we can't call you a . . . shy virgin," he managed.

"I want to be an active participant."

For a few moments, he let himself enjoy her caresses, tentative at first but incredibly talented—indeed, almost uncanny in how she seemed to know exactly what felt good to him. Then, when he couldn't take any more, he lifted her hand and brought her fingers to his mouth for a quick kiss.

"Better stop. I'm already so turned on, I could come in about a minute flat. And I want this to last awhile. But turnabout is fair play, don't you think?"

His hand slid down her body, paused to play with the dark curls at the top of her legs, then delved lower between the slick folds of her sex, taking one long stroke and then another, barely dipping inside her before traveling upward to her clit. She made a sound low in her throat, then showed him what she liked, covering his fingers with hers, increasing the pressure of his touch as she rocked her hips against his hand.

He leaned to stroke his tongue around the curve of her ear, then whispered, "Do you want me to make you come, love?"

"Yes. But not this way."

He had never wanted a woman more in his life. And at the same time, he hesitated to take the next step. "I don't want to hurt you."

"Maybe you can't avoid it." Again she reached for his erection, sensuously stroking her fingers up and down his shaft, wringing a sharp exclamation from him.

"Open your legs for me," he gasped, gathering her to him, moving against her but not trying to penetrate her yet. He was so close to the edge that he knew if he put even the first inch of his cock inside her, it would all be over. She was slick and wet, and he slid his shaft back and forth, stroking her as he had with his hand. Determined to make her first time something she remembered with pleasure, he kept up the sweet torture and listened to her breath come faster and faster as she climbed toward climax.

"God, yes. Come for me. Show me how good it feels," he crooned. When she cried out in pleasure and her body shuddered in his arms, he felt a surge of triumph. She clung to him as the spasms shook her, and he kept stroking until he felt her settling down to earth.

Then, changing the angle of his thrusts, he warned her, "Now, love," and plunged into her. He did it fast, in one decisive stroke, while she was limp and relaxed with the force of her orgasm. Still, she made a strangled sound and dug her nails into his shoulders as he broke through the barrier of her virginity.

"Olivia . . . Oh, love . . . I'm sorry," he gasped. But he was caught in a whirlwind of need, his hips moving, his cock stroking in and out of her, and he came quickly—as he knew he would.

He collapsed on top of her, his breath coming in great gasps. Raising his head, he looked down, his eyes meeting hers. "Are you okay?" he asked urgently.

She reached to kiss his cheek, then she stroked back a lock of damp hair from his forehead. "More than okay."

Staying inside her, he rolled to his side, holding her in his arms, kissing and caressing her, keeping her with him as he began to build her pleasure—and his—again.

She clung to him, returning his kisses, trailing her fingers over his back and shoulders and down to his buttocks, pressing him into her as they rocked together, caught again in their spiraling need.

"Good, that's so good," she whispered.

"God, yes."

He felt the exquisite pleasure of her inner muscles contracting around his penis as he brought them both back to full arousal. This time he made the pleasure last, barely moving inside her until she was thrashing against him, silently begging for release.

He slipped his hand between them, finding her clit, stroking with his hand as he moved in and out of her—holding back until she convulsed in his arms, moaning. While the aftershocks of her climax still rippled over him, he let go and poured himself into her.

As his heart rate came back to normal, he felt her stir against him.

"I didn't know how wonderful that would be," she whispered against his neck. "It's not just physical release. It's so much more."

"Only with you, love."

Her breath caught. "You're telling me the truth?"

"Oh, yeah. I've never felt anything like that," he answered, because it was the truth.

He held her for a few more minutes, then slipped out of bed and went into the bathroom. It was past dawn, and by the light from the window, he could see her blood on his body. He used a washcloth to clean himself, then warmed another cloth under the faucet and wrung it out.

Her gaze fixed on him when he came back to bed with the cloth and a towel.

"What are you planning?"

"A little TLC," he answered as he eased onto the bed and gently moved her legs apart so he could clean her inner thighs and her still-wet and swollen folds.

"I should be embarrassed."

"Nothing we can do together is ever going to be embarrassing," he said, meaning it.

When he had washed the blood from her body and dried her with the towel, he came back to bed and gathered her in his arms.

"I was afraid of you," she whispered. "I never knew you could be so gentle."

"You make me gentle," he answered, meaning that, too. "I just wish it could always be true."

He had been balanced on a knife blade of sexual obsession for days—weeks. Finally he could relax, holding her in his arms as he slept.

When he opened his eyes hours later, he found her studying him.

"Second thoughts?" he asked, hearing his own tension.

"Of course."

"You belong to me now."

"In the caveman sense?" she asked, the edge in her voice warning him that the statement had been a bit too aggressive. So he struggled to frame his feelings differently.

"No. You said you weren't into casual sex. That wasn't casual for either one of us."

"What was it for you, exactly?"

He wanted to duck away from her penetrating gaze. Instead, he held it with his own as he told her the stark truth. "It was the most important night of my life."

Her eyes widened a little. "Why?" she breathed.

"Because I knew that if we made love, we would be . . ." He stopped and fumbled for words. "Making a commitment."

The look in her eyes told him she didn't want to think in those terms.

He had to stifle the sudden urge to let the caveman take over. Before he could say something else he regretted, he rolled out of bed and got out clean clothing, then ducked into the shower.

Later, while she dressed, he walked down to the beach, raising his face to the salt wind. He had to tell her about the wolf—soon. But not yet. Not until he was sure she wouldn't run from him. Because he had to keep her with him now. Whether she understood it yet or not, she was the wolf's mate.

When she was showered and dressed, he took her to one of the restaurants in town for an enormous breakfast.

She ordered coffee. He got his standard herbal tea.

"You don't drink coffee?" she asked.

"No. Or liquor. And I don't smoke, either." He laughed. "I'm into clean living."

She glanced over her shoulder to make sure they were alone. "Except for your profession."

"Yeah."

"So, are you going to let me off the hook with that Mr. R?" she asked as she forked into a huge stack of pancakes.

"I will, if you agree to stay home when I visit Mr. E."

"That's not negotiable," she answered.

"Then neither is Mr. R."

They sat looking at each other across the Formica table. Had his mother ever defied his father like this? He didn't think so.

But Olivia Woodlock was her own woman. And he'd sure as hell better remember that.

FROM his mountaintop haven, Luther Ethridge sat in a comfortable chair by the window, looking out at the magnificent view spread out below him.

It was early in the morning, and as he watched fluffy white clouds drifting across the blue sky, he felt like a king surveying his domain. He was rich enough to be a king. And when he had the Woodlocks begging for mercy, his satisfaction would be complete.

It was easy to imagine what that would be like, because he was already well along in the process.

His mind went into a little fantasy about the woman in his tower room. The woman who looked so much like Olivia that even he couldn't tell the difference. Jesus, that gas he pumped into the room was wonderful. He could do any damn thing with her that he wanted. Just thinking about what he was going to do next made him hard as a rock.

Leaning back in the chair, he unzipped the fly of his slacks and reached inside, stroking his fingers against his enormous boner.

Then the phone rang.

"Fuck."

He didn't want to be interrupted. He wanted to enjoy his fantasy. Then he looked at the number on the Caller ID and a new surge of excitement coursed through his veins.

Snatching up the phone, he demanded, "What do you have for me?"

"I think I know where Olivia and the fiancé are going."

"You think?"

"She didn't say. But Colin has been trying to track them. I know from what he's been doing on the computer."

"You got into his files?"

"He left some notes beside the machine. I copied down the important information." The voice on the other end of the line began reeling out facts.

"Not so fast. Let me write it down." He jumped up, forgot his pants were unzipped, and had to pull himself back together as he wedged the phone between his ear and his shoulder, then grabbed a notepad from the drawer in the drum table beside the sofa.

"Okay. Give it to me slowly," he ordered.

"I don't have much time," the person on the other end of the line complained.

"That's your problem, not mine." He took down the information. It didn't make a lot of sense, but his informant had never been wrong.

"How's Colin's health?" he asked when he had the gist of the material.

"His energy level is dropping. He's spending more time in bed."

"Good."

"I have to go. Sorry."

The connection went dead.

"Shit!" Luther stared at the receiver, longing to dial back and demand some explanations. Instead, he settled for staring at his notes as his mind formulated new plans.

SAM sat in an Adirondack chair, looking longingly at the woods. He would have liked to strip off his clothing, transform, and run free. But until he told Olivia his secret, he had to keep the wolf in check.

She opened the door and cooking smells wafted from the kitchen. They were in a rental house in Monterey—a short-term lease. The real estate agent didn't know it was for less than a week—since he'd paid for a month.

"I have the salad and the potatoes done," she said.

"Then let me put the steaks on."

They'd been sharing the simple cooking duties because he wanted it that way. He wasn't going to make her do all the work, the way his father had done with his mother. And he'd make sure they got someone in during the day to help with the kids.

Hell, who was he kidding? He was picturing married life in terms of his parents. In a tiny house stuffed full of scrappy little boys. Would a woman who had been raised like Olivia stand for less than a mansion staffed by a butler, a maid, and a full-time nanny?

Well, that wouldn't be possible when the daddy was a werewolf! He'd have to make that damn clear.

He took a deep breath. He was getting way ahead of himself—he hoped. The first night they'd made love, he'd been too overwhelmed by need even to think about birth control—another sign that she was his true mate. Because he'd never forgotten about that little detail with the women in his past. Since then, however, he'd gotten a supply of condoms. He hoped to hell it wasn't a case of locking the zoo cage after the tiger had escaped.

As he laid the steaks on the grill, he thought about why they were on the Monterey peninsula. He'd been excited about the Reese job months ago. The guy had some stunning old German snuffboxes and some Chinese jade pieces from the Chang Dynasty. Scooping them up had totally lost its appeal, because it clashed with his need to keep

Olivia safe. But he couldn't let her off the hook if she was going to Ethridge's with him.

He took his steak off the grill, then cooked hers a few minutes longer.

When he stepped into the dining room, she raised her head and gave him a direct look. "How about tonight?"

He knew immediately that she wasn't talking about making love, which they'd done every night since Pismo Beach.

"Unless you've changed your mind," she added.

"I haven't changed my mind," he clipped out.

"Then we'll eat quickly so we can get some sleep before we have to leave."

SAM woke Olivia at two in the morning, then watched her eyes blink open and focus on him. She looked fragile. Worn out. Because he'd been keeping her up for hours every night. Every night but this one. And during the days, he'd been testing her physical abilities.

"We don't have to go now," he muttered.

She climbed out of bed, wavering a little as she headed toward the bathroom. "I want to get it over with." When they met in the front hall a few minutes later, she seemed okay. He gave her last-minute instructions as they drove to Carmel, to a side road off the beach. Leaving her in the car, he made a final reconnaissance trip to the Reese house. He knew the owner was in Europe, but he carefully checked the exterior, including the hookup to the security system. The setup looked perfect. There were a few lights on around the grounds, but the lot was large and well-screened by trees. Still, he waited for almost half an hour, making sure everything looked okay.

It did. But he couldn't banish the tight feeling in his chest. Because he hated this whole deal, he told himself. He'd rather be home in bed making love with his mate.

She jumped when he leaned down toward her car window.

"What are you trying to do, scare me into wimping out?"

"It's a plan."

Ignoring the comment, she asked, "Are we all set?"

"Unfortunately."

At least he was gratified to see a flash of pure nerves on her face as she stepped onto the gravel road surface.

Shrugging into his pack, he adjusted it for comfort, then turned and started up the coast, listening for the sound of her running shoes crunching behind him.

He would have preferred to go in as a wolf. But since he hadn't dredged up the courage to break the bad news to Olivia, he led her up the coast, glad that the darkness hid his grim expression.

Silently he willed her to back out. He longed to hear her say that she'd changed her mind about starting a career as a burglar. But she followed him to the back of the house, which had been built before underground utilities.

He put on climbing spikes, went up the electric pole, and disconnected the system at the power source, so that the security company would think the electricity was off.

Then he came back down.

Next he walked to a small double-hung window in back and jiggled the top part until it came free of the lock.

"I'm ready," Olivia said.

Since Reese was out of town, they had agreed that she would go in first, then come around and unlock the back door for him. He didn't like that much. But it was part of the test he'd told himself it was important to administer.

Making his hands into a step, he hoisted her up. She slithered inside, then disappeared.

Quickly he walked to the back door. He was always calm and methodical on a job. But his heart was drumming inside his chest, and his hands squeezed into fists as he waited for her to let him in.

It was taking too long. Where in the hell was she?

He dragged in a thankful breath as he saw her pull aside the curtains, then reach to unlock the door.

"Where were you?" he growled.

Her eyes were large and round. "Come in, and I'll tell you," she whispered.

The look on her face made him hesitate. Something was wrong, but he didn't know what.

Then a voice behind her cut through the pounding of his pulse in his ears.

"Drop your pack. Raise your hands and come inside, or I'll drill a very messy hole in Miss Woodlock's back."

18

SILENTLY, Sam raised his hands and stepped inside the darkened house. Standing directly behind Olivia was a hard-bitten man with stringy hair sticking below a baseball cap. He had a gun in his hand.

The gunman's expression was something between smirking and grim. "Thanks for finally showing up," he gloated.

Sam kept his voice steady as he worked his way through the implications. "You're not Reese."

"This isn't about Reese."

"Then what?"

"That's for me to know. And you to find out." He stepped back, then gestured with his gun. "This way."

Olivia kept her hopeful gaze on Sam. For the moment he was clean out of options.

Their captor led them down the hall, then into a small room that had apparently been prepared for their arrival. It was empty except for several pairs of handcuffs on the floor.

The gunman turned to Sam first. "Sit down. With your hands behind your back."

Sam sat.

The man turned to Olivia. "Cuff him," he ordered. "Wrists and ankles."

She gave Sam a miserable look, and he tried to tell her with his eyes that he'd get them out of this. At least he hoped to hell he would.

After she'd done as their captor ordered, he made her slip the cuffs onto her own ankles before he snapped them closed and secured her wrists. She was cuffed with her hands in front. Which could be an advantage. But he wasn't going to ask her to take any chances. "Back soon," the gunman said, sounding pleased with himself as he slammed the door.

The moment they were alone, sitting on the floor in the almost pitch-black room, Sam leaned forward.

"Did he hurt you?" he asked urgently.

"No."

He heard the edge of tears in her voice, and he wanted to scoot across the floor and comfort her. That would have to wait until later.

"He knew who we were. He was waiting for us," he said in a grim voice.

"I know," she agreed, sounding miserable.

Confronting his worst fear, he demanded, "Did you tell anyone where we were going?"

"No. I swear I didn't." She stopped and swallowed. "Well, after Colin guessed you'd be testing me, I told him what city we were going to."

"Shit! And Mr. Computer figured out the rest. Then he ratted us out."

"No!"

"Okay. We don't have time to argue about it. The main point is that we walked into a trap. And when that guy comes back, things are going to get worse."

"What are we going to do?" she asked, and he heard the fear in her voice.

So much for hoping he could break the news to her gently. The only saving grace was the darkness; she wouldn't be able to see a helluva lot of anything.

He took a deep breath and let it out in a rush. "You remember that wolf you saw at my place—and the one you saw at the motel?"

"Yes," she answered in a shaky voice.

"Same wolf. He's going to get us out of here."

A couple of seconds of silence passed.

"How . . . what do you mean?" she whispered.

Ignoring the question, he plowed on. "We don't have much time, so listen closely. The wolf can't talk. And when he's here, I won't be. I'm going to get out of my cuffs. I can't get you free until later. Move as far into the corner as you can. *The wolf will not hurt you,*" he said, punching out the words. "But it could get a little dangerous in here when our captor comes back with his gun. So stay out of the action."

He pressed his ear against the wall. "He's out there, talking on the phone. Someone's coming to get . . . you."

"Get me? What about you?"

"Apparently, I'm expendable."

"Oh, my God," she breathed.

"I'm not going to let any of it happen," he said, praying it was true. "So let me do what I have to—and stay out of the way. Now, move!"

His night vision was good enough for him to see her scooting across the floor. He did the same, moving as far away from Olivia as possible. The knowledge of what came next made his stomach curdle, but he knew it was their only chance.

Thankful again that the darkness would hide him, he began chanting.

"Taranis, Epona, Cerridwen."

"Sam? What is that?" she cried out, her voice high and edgy.

Ignoring her, he repeated, *"Taranis, Epona, Cerridwen."*

"Sam. You're scaring me."

"Ga. Feart. Cleas. Duais. Aithriocht. Go gcumhdai is dtreorai na dei-the thu."

Long ago, his father had been with him when he spoke the chant for the first time in a clearing in the woods. Later, he and Dad had changed together a few times. No one else had ever heard him say the words of transformation. But he stopped thinking about either the past or the present danger as he felt the change take him, contorting his body, transmuting skin and bone into a different shape. The cuffs had bound the man's hands, and their position would have been agony for the wolf. But even as he changed, he yanked his front paws from the metal bracelets. When they were free, he used his teeth to hold the other set of cuffs steady as he pulled his back paws from them.

He was still hampered by his clothing, but long ago, he had practiced undressing post-transformation. He tugged at the sweatpants with his teeth, pulling them down and over his legs, ripping the fabric in his haste.

"Sam?" Olivia's voice quivered in the darkness. "Sam?"

He stayed away from her, working feverishly to get himself ready. But he ran out of time when he heard footsteps returning.

Quickly he yanked his paws from the sweatpant legs. He was still wearing the T-shirt, which now hung on his lean wolf's body. But it didn't restrict his movements.

Footsteps stopped outside the room. Flattened against the wall behind the door, he tensed as the lock clicked. Then the door opened. The guy had set a battery-powered light on the floor. The first thing

Sam saw in the shaft of light was a hand holding a gun. He sprang, sinking his teeth into flesh and bone.

The gun discharged. The man screamed. And so did Olivia.

Sam felt his insides twist, but he couldn't let go of the man to see if she was all right—or neither of them would get out of this mess.

Their captor went on bellowing as Sam crunched down on his hand. When the gun finally dropped, Sam sprang forward and knocked the man to the floor. The baseball cap flew off the man's head as he went down. The violence of the wolf was on Sam. He wanted to rip out their captor's throat. The guy was scum. But he stopped himself from making the kill. Olivia had already seen enough for one night.

The last thing he wanted to do was leave her alone with their captor. But when he pawed at the guy, he didn't move.

Unwilling to make eye contact with Olivia, Sam dashed into the hall. As he moved, he was already saying the chant again in his head, hurrying through the words. The transformation seemed to take forever. But he knew it was less than a minute before he was a man again—naked except for his black T-shirt.

Ignoring the strange picture he must make, he sprinted back into the room.

Olivia was sitting with her back to the wall, looking dazed.

"Are you all right?" he asked urgently.

She stared at him, and the wounded look in her eyes nearly destroyed him. Slowly, he came closer. She was very pale and still. Worse, blood had plastered her shirt sleeve to her arm.

"Shit. Your arm. You're hit."

Following his gaze, she looked down at her arm, her eyes widening into a look of horror.

He bent, inspecting the wound.

"It's not bad. It's not bad," he tried to reassure her.

She gave a small nod, but her face said that she didn't believe him. He ached to gather her close. But they couldn't stay here.

Quickly, he turned back to examine their former captor, who lay unmoving on the floor, his body limp and his jaw slack. Sam checked to make sure the man was breathing, then riffled through his pockets and found the key to the cuffs.

When he swung toward Olivia again, she hadn't moved a centimeter and still looked as if she were in shock. His heart was pounding as he freed her hands and feet, then spared the time to pull on the pants and shoes he'd discarded, ignoring the rips up and down the pant legs where the wolf's teeth had bitten through the fabric.

After grabbing the gun, he carefully helped Olivia to her feet.

"Can you walk?"

"Yes."

She moved slowly, and they were barely out of the house when he saw headlights cutting through the darkness, coming up the long drive.

"Shit!" he muttered again, pulling her into the shrubbery as the lights approached. "We've got to split."

Stuffing the gun into the pocket of his sweatpants, he picked her up and slung her over his shoulder like a sack of rice, then ran back the way they'd come.

"Don't," she protested, her voice weak.

"We have to get the hell out of here."

Without sparing any more energy on explanations, he headed for the beach, keeping in the shadows as much as possible as he made for where he'd parked the car.

By the time he reached their sheltered parking spot, he was breathing hard.

Trying not to sound like a wounded elk, he opened the passenger door and set Olivia in the front seat, then turned and ripped away the sleeve of her shirt.

She made a small sound as he used the flashlight in the glove compartment to examine the wound. As far as he could see, the bullet had cut across the skin of her arm, and the wound had already stopped bleeding.

Glad that he had parked facing the highway, he looked toward the Reese house. When he saw no traffic, he pulled out and headed in the opposite direction, deliberately keeping below the speed limit when he wanted to floor the accelerator.

He didn't want to get stopped for speeding, but at the same time, he kept picturing a car full of thugs coming after them. He watched the rearview mirror as much as he watched the road ahead. When he was sure nobody was behind them, he headed toward the house they'd rented.

She had seen the wolf in action. And they needed to talk about it—despite the fact that he would have liked to avoid the topic for the next hundred years. Luckily, it would have to wait, since he had other urgent business.

"I want some straight answers from you. Did you tell Colin where we're staying?"

"No!"

He sighed. "Okay."

"You think I'd lie about something like that?"

"I hope not."

"Right, like you wouldn't lie about that damn wolf," she tossed at him.

He wanted to look away, but he kept his gaze steady. "I haven't lied to you except by omission—not telling you all there is to tell. As we both know, you're guilty of the same thing. Trust doesn't seem to come easy for either one of us."

She dropped her gaze, a frown flickering over her brow.

He turned back to the road. He knew it wasn't the best time for hard questions, but he also knew he had to ask, "Do you want me to take you home?"

From the corner of his eye, he saw her head jerk toward him. "And leave me there?" she asked as he pulled into the driveway of their rental.

His mouth was so dry that he could only nod.

Centuries passed before she whispered, "No."

Because you know it's dangerous, or because you want to stay with me? He couldn't make himself ask the question. For now, it was enough that she wasn't running away.

"I'd better take care of your arm," he muttered.

Opening her door, he scooped her up again, hugging her against his chest as he carried her into the house and into the bathroom.

Neither of them spoke, and he could feel his heart thumping as he bent his head and brushed his lips against her. She didn't respond in any way, and she remained silent while he set her on the toilet, then ran warm water in the sink.

He cleaned the wound in her arm, then inspected it carefully, giving it his full attention. Looking up, he found her watching him, and his heart leaped into his throat at the soft, tender look in her beautiful eyes. He'd expected anger—and revulsion. "I'm sorry," she whispered.

"For what?"

"Making you take me there."

"It was my idea," he muttered.

She sighed. "We both know why."

"We'll talk about that later," he answered, then moved to catch her as she lost her balance and slipped to the side.

"You need to lie down." When she seemed steadier, he fumbled in the medicine cabinet, finding alcohol. He would have preferred something she wouldn't feel, but it was the only antiseptic they had. He slopped some onto a hand towel, the fumes almost choking him. "This is going to sting."

When she winced, he clenched his teeth. She endured the procedure silently. Then he tore open a sterile gauze pad, covered the wound with it, and wrapped more gauze around her arm to hold it on.

"Let's get you to bed," he said, kneeling to pull off her shoes and socks before carrying her to the bedroom.

He should leave her alone. She needed to sleep. But he stayed beside the bed. Swallowing hard, he asked, "Can I lie in bed with you?"

Again, centuries passed before she gave another small nod, looking as if it took her last grain of strength to do it.

His movements were jerky as he crossed to the dresser, found a clean pair of sweatpants and pulled them on. Then he dragged off his T-shirt and climbed in beside her.

Taking her gently in his arms, he cradled her against himself, stroking her hair and grazing his lips against the side of her face. And when she stayed in his arms, he allowed himself a spurt of hope.

She had seen the wolf attack a man, and she was still here.

As he held her, he mentally went over the list of people living at the Woodlock estate—starting with her brother and his boyfriend. Were they trying to help? Had they hatched a plan to get Colin's sister out of the clutches of the nasty burglar?

Or was there a more sinister explanation?

He had no way of knowing and no proof of any theory.

He tried to stay awake, because he wanted to be there if Olivia needed him. But the events of the very long day had left him exhausted. His eyes closed, and despite his raw nerves, he slept.

* * *

HIS face a mask of anger, Luther Ethridge paced back and forth across the length of his elegant living room.

He had been so close. So close. And now . . .

He'd been gleefully anticipating a cheerful call from the men he'd hired to kill Sam Morgan and bring Olivia to him. But it had gone completely wrong.

Nobody had known exactly when Olivia and Morgan would show up at the Reese house. So it seemed that only one of the thugs—a man he knew as John Smith—had been on the scene when Morgan and Olivia arrived. He'd had complete confidence in the team he'd hired. Well, he'd been confident that the men wanted to do the job and collect their pay.

But somehow they had screwed up. It sounded like Smith had gone off the deep end. He was babbling about being attacked by an animal with teeth and claws that leaped out of the empty storage room where he'd locked Olivia and Morgan.

It was ludicrous, of course. There was no other entrance to the room besides the locked door, and no animal could have gotten in there. Obviously, the man was handing him some load of bullshit to cover his own mistake. Maybe he'd been drunk—or high. Or maybe he'd scrambled his brain when he hit his head fighting with Morgan.

Smith's cohorts didn't know. They claimed they'd been in town picking up food—at three in the morning. *Damned unlikely,* Luther thought. Still, there were all-night stores, so he couldn't prove they were lying. Regardless of where they'd been, they had told Smith they'd come straight back when he called them to say he'd apprehended the would-be burglars. But the captives were gone when they arrived, and Smith was staggering around babbling nonsense.

The other men had found a trail of footprints—human, not animal—on the beach. One set, not far from the house. Luther guessed that Morgan had to have been carrying Olivia. But why? Was she hurt? Or sick? His chest tightened at the thought.

He'd plotted everything out so carefully, but one thing after another was going wrong. Swiping a hand angrily through his hair, he acknowledged that he'd probably never know the truth of what had happened at the Reese house.

But dammit! He needed to know what the devil was going on up there in Carmel. And right now, it looked like there was no way of getting reliable information.

"Fuck!" He hated hired help who failed. He could easily arrange for their punishment. But that left the problem of Olivia.

Again he couldn't hold back a curse. He wanted badly to know what had happened to her and if she was all right.

Maybe Morgan would take her back to the Woodlock estate. Then his informant could give him an update.

SOMETIME later, Sam's eyes snapped open.

Enough light filtered in around the curtains for him to get a good look at Olivia. What he saw made fear leap inside him.

Her eyes were closed. Her skin was clammy, and sweat had broken out on her forehead. Her head moved back and forth on the pillow, and her arms struck out at him.

"Olivia. Wake up. Olivia." He shook her shoulders, and she moaned, but it took several moments before her eyes opened and focused on him.

He braced for her to shrink away from the wolf locked inside him. But she stayed where she was, her breathing ragged.

He swallowed hard. "What? What were you dreaming?"

"It's . . . all my fault," she cried out.

"What?"

"Ethridge . . ." She broke off, moaned again.

"How?" he asked urgently.

"Ethridge. He was . . ."

He gathered her close, rocking her in his arms.

"Sam . . ." The pressure of her hand against his chest made him shift his grip. Looking down at her, he saw her face was contorted. Her lips were working, but it took several seconds before she managed to speak again. "He was . . . holding it out to me. Teasing . . . me. But he wouldn't let me have it. And I was getting so sick. So sick."

"It's okay. I won't let him get you. It's okay."

"No. You don't understand." She gulped, then started to cough. When she raised her head, her face was bleak with tension and sadness. "I lied to you."

19

A curse sprang from Sam's suddenly dry lips. "Christ! What the hell did you lie about? Is your father going to show up here? Or are you communicating with Ethridge? Is that it? You've been cluing him in all the time."

Her face turned frantic. "No! Not that . . . never him!"

"Then what?"

She swallowed and squeezed her eyes closed, as though she couldn't stand to face him.

Her skin was as pale and fragile-looking as skim milk. And a pulse was beating at her throat.

"What did you lie about?" he growled, making an effort not to shout. Before she could answer, she gasped and pressed her palm to her forehead. Then a moan of agony contorted her features.

He went from anger to fear in a heartbeat. "Olivia, love? What?" Self-reproach clawed at his throat.

He wanted to reach for her, but holding her might block off her oxygen. So he kept his hands at his sides.

Her whole body jerked and began to shake. From her throat came a low, anguished sound of pain that raised the hairs on the back of his neck.

Against his will, his mind flashed back to the night that her uncle had gone berserk and started shooting at anyone in sight. He had sounded a lot like Olivia did now.

"What is it. What's wrong?"

She tried to answer, but she could only gasp for breath, her eyes wide with terror.

He couldn't sit there doing nothing. Gathering her up, he carried her into the bathroom. When he'd been a little boy, he'd had breathing problems a few times. And his mother had filled the bathroom with steam.

He did that now, setting her on the toilet seat while he turned on the hot water in the shower full blast.

Then he lifted her up again, taking the seat and gathering her onto his lap, cradling her against his chest as he stroked her damp hair.

The water heated, the room turned hot and steamy. Maybe it helped. He didn't know. But as he stroked her hair and shoulders, feeling tremors wrack her body, he knew that if he could have taken them into his own body and spared her, he would have done it.

Through a swirl of steam, he watched her open her eyes and tip her head toward him. He watched her trying to get control of herself.

"You . . . have to . . . call Colin . . . or . . . my father," she gasped out.

He had been prepared for disaster. But not that. Her plea was the last thing he wanted to hear. Managing not to shout, he said, "You know I can't do that. Let me get you to the hospital."

The suggestion made fear leap in her eyes. "No! Doctors don't . . . know"—she stopped, dragged in a breath, and let it out—"die . . . in hospital."

His own terror made him grip her shoulders. This time he couldn't keep his voice steady when he demanded, "What do you mean? What the hell is going on? You have to tell me!"

"I have . . . it."

"What?"

"Like . . . Colin . . . my uncle. My family . . ."

He felt as though a knife blade had sliced through his chest. "Jesus. No. Why the hell didn't you tell me?"

"First time . . . I . . . like this." She tried to say more. Her lips moved, but no sound came out. Then her body went limp against his chest.

His heart blocked his windpipe as he felt the pulse in her neck. It was thready, and her breath came in gasps.

"Olivia, what is it? What's wrong? Jesus Christ, tell me!"

But she didn't answer. And when he tipped her head up again, he saw that she had slipped into unconsciousness. He gathered her to him, thinking that he would carry her to the car and take her to the nearest emergency room. She looked like she'd die if he kept her here. But she had said she would die if he did the logical thing. Could her warning possibly be true? Or was she delirious—like her uncle?

He tried to force that idea out of his head. But it came bouncing back. She had told him to call Colin. And he was sure Colin was responsible for their getting caught at Harold Reese's house.

He stroked Olivia's damp hair again, willing her to wake up and tell him what the hell to do for her. But she lay against his chest, still as death, and terror constricted his throat and chest.

He felt as if his own life were in the balance as he stared down at her. Standing, he turned off the shower, then carried her back to the bedroom and laid her back on the sheet. After grabbing his cell phone from the dresser, he eased back onto the bed, clasping Olivia's hand as he dialed the number that he knew from his research was Colin's private line. It rang once, twice, three times.

To his everlasting horror, Brice answered.

"Hello."

Sam almost stabbed the OFF button, but then he looked over at Olivia's pale face and he knew he had to continue with what he'd started.

"This is Morgan," he said tersely. "Let me speak to Colin."

"Where are you?"

"Let me speak to Colin."

"I can't do that."

Unable to control his anger, he shouted, "Well, this is a matter of life and death, you jerk."

There was a long pause before the other man said, "Just a minute."

Sam waited with his heart pounding while the boyfriend went away. The longer they stayed on the line, the more likely it was that someone could trace the call. Was Brice setting up a trace? Sam clenched and unclenched his hand around the phone, wanting to hang up. But he couldn't.

COLIN snatched up the phone. "Morgan? What the hell is going on? What have you done to Olivia? Where are you?"

"Never mind where I am. I have to talk to you alone. Get your boyfriend out of there."

"Brice and I . . ."

Sam cut him off before he could finish. "Somebody just tried to kill me—at the Reese house. And that's your fucking fault, isn't it?"

Sick horror constricted Colin's throat. "How can you say that?" he managed.

"You figured out where we were going. And if you didn't turn us in, somebody else did. But that's not what I have to talk about now. Olivia just collapsed."

"No!"

Ignoring the exclamation, Sam plowed ahead. "Before she went unconscious, she said she has the same sickness you do. I need to talk to you about that. Now!"

He sounded like he was at the edge of his control.

Colin put his hand over the phone, and looked at Brice. "Give me a minute," he murmured.

Brice must have seen the agony on his face. After a short hesitation, he stepped out of the room.

"Okay. I'm alone," he said.

"I can't stay on the phone long—in case somebody is tracing this call."

"They're not!"

"How the hell do you know? Somebody there arranged for an armed reception at the Reese house. Who knows what kind of technology they're using."

"Let me talk to Olivia," Colin demanded.

"You can't. She's unconscious."

"Oh, Christ!"

"Shut up and listen," Sam snapped. "I need information. Before she passed out, she said that if I took her to the hospital, it would kill her. Is that right?"

"Yes," Colin managed to answer.

"Why?"

He struggled to keep his voice from shaking as he thought about his sister lying in bed, sick and unconscious. "Because we don't respond the way the doctors expect. Her blood pressure and her heart rate will be low. They'll give her stimulants. And that will kill her. As far as we can figure out, that's what happened to my Uncle Randolph."

"You lying bastard. Your damn father takes stimulants."

"Now. But not in the early stages. This is the first attack?"

"As far as I know."

"She could have been hiding the symptoms."

"Wonderful," Sam snapped.

"Was she injured?"

"Yes. A tough guy with a gun was waiting for us. When I was trying to get us out of there, she got shot."

Colin gasped. "How bad is it?"

"The bullet grazed her arm. I treated the wound and put her to bed. She was having a nightmare. When I woke her up . . . she started shaking—and babbling."

"She should be all right in a few hours. Or . . . she won't be," Colin heard himself answer.

"What the hell does that mean?"

"The first time . . . it can go either way."

"I'm taking her to the hospital."

"Don't do it," Colin shouted. Struggling to sound coherent, he cleared his throat. "Bring her home where we can take care of her. We've had experience with this."

"How many of you are sick?"

He gulped in air and let it out in a rush. "All of us. When we reach our late twenties."

"So it's not just the men."

"Of course not!"

"You want me to bring her home—so somebody there can make sure she doesn't recover?"

"She'll be better off here. You have to trust us," he pleaded.

Morgan answered with a bitter laugh. "Trust you? I can't trust any of you—including Olivia. Since one of the last things she said was that she lied to me. If you're not the one who blew us out of the water, then put your energy into finding out who did."

"How?"

"Oh, for Christ's sake! You're the computer genius. Figure it out." Morgan sighed, then spoke more calmly. "No. Wait, we'll have to do it together. Set a trap. I'll e-mail you later. Just tell me what to do for Olivia now."

"Keep her warm."

"With blankets?"

"Yes."

"What else?"

"That's all you can do."

"Oh, that's just great." Morgan slammed down the phone, and Colin replaced the receiver, then lowered his head into his hands.

He'd thought he'd known what he was doing. Now he wondered what the hell he had set in motion.

* * *

SAM wanted to scream in frustration. Was that really all he could do for his mate? Keep her warm? He wanted to call the brother back and drag out every fact that Colin could dredge up about the family illness and the elixir, Astravor, that saved their lives. This was the time to do it, while Colin was still grappling with the shock of his sister's attack.

But Sam couldn't take the chance that he would lead the bad guys straight to them. And he needed to focus on Olivia.

Razor wire twisted in his gut as he looked at her, lying on the bed, so still and lifeless.

He found the pulse in her throat, counted the beats. Forty. Her heart was beating slowly. At least Colin had told him the truth about that.

After pulling the comforter up to her chin, he got off the bed, took the spare blanket from the top shelf of the closet, and folded it in half before placing it over her.

As he stared down at her, he clenched and unclenched his fists. Her brother had been through this. Other people in the family had been through it, too. Some of them had died.

"Not you, love. Not you," he whispered. "I need you to live. Olivia, do that for me. Get well. Please, get well."

He didn't know if he believed in God. But that hadn't stopped him from praying once—long ago, the night before his dad was going to take him out to the woods so he could change to wolf form the first time.

Four of his six older brothers had died trying to get through that damn change. Only Ross and Adam had survived. He'd been scared shitless and worked hard not to show it.

He was scared shitless now.

"Please, God, don't let her die," he begged. "You can save her. She's a good woman. Brave. Loyal to her family. She didn't ask for this. Please save her."

The prayer sounded hollow—coming from a man like Sam Morgan. But it was the best he could do.

20

THE neck of Sam's T-shirt felt like it was strangling him. He pulled at the knit band, but it retracted back into place. Finally, when he couldn't stand the constricted feeling, he pulled the shirt over his head and tossed it away.

It helped. But not enough. His wild nature clamored for open space. He needed to run through the woods, howling his fear and his anger. But there was no way he could leave Olivia. He had to be here when she woke up. He had to be here if she needed him.

The concept was a strange one to him. Had anyone ever needed him?

Like all kids, he'd been dependent on his parents when he was little. His mother had nurtured him, shielded him from the wrath of the Big Bad Wolf, as his brother Ross had called their dad.

But his father had done the one essential job bred into his genes. He had taught his sons the ancient ritual and coached them through the first awful transformation from man to wolf. Some had lived. Others had died.

Johnny Marshall had needed his father then. But nobody had ever needed the man he had become—Sam Morgan.

Well, he thought with a start, that wasn't exactly true. Olivia had needed him to break into Luther Ethridge's house. She'd said it was to save her family. Now he was pretty sure it was to save herself as well. But she hadn't told him that. She'd hidden that part from him.

He wanted to pick up the lamp and hurl it across the room. If she'd just confided that she had the family illness, he would have played this differently. He certainly wouldn't have fucked her brains out every night—and worked her hard every day.

He wanted to blame the whole mess on her. But he recognized the self-protective impulse. She had kept her secrets. He had kept his.

She knew the worst about him. He still didn't know what else she was hiding from him. Somehow he stopped himself from pounding his fists against the wall. He ached to do something that would help his mate. But all he could do was keep her warm, for God's sake.

Getting up, he returned with first aid supplies. Carefully he took the bandage off her arm and examined the wound. It looked like it was healing normally, so he put on a fresh gauze pad.

As he finished, he felt her stir.

Her eyes stayed closed, but her lips moved. Bending over, he heard her whisper his name. "Sam."

"Right here, love. Did I hurt you?"

"No."

He couldn't stop himself from pulling aside the covers so he could slip underneath and take her in his arms.

She moved her head against his naked shoulder. "Yes . . . hold me."

He stroked his lips against her cheek and the tender place beside her ear.

"Have to . . . sleep . . . sorry," she murmured without opening her eyes, and he fought a fresh spurt of panic as she drifted off again. But unlike earlier, her respiration seemed normal. And when he laid his hand over her heart, he felt the strong steady beat. Counting, he found it was up to sixty.

All of which proved that she was going to recover, didn't it? He wanted that to be true so badly that he could barely breathe. But he didn't know the progress of the attack. His fingers itched to pick up the phone and call Colin. If her brother wasn't the one who had betrayed them, he was probably suffering—waiting for news. But every contact with the Woodlock mansion was taking a big risk. So he kept one arm firmly around Olivia and gathered up a fist-ful of sheet with the other.

Again, the waiting was agony. The next time she stirred, she looked more like herself. And he fought a mixture of relief and nerves.

She ducked her head and eased away from him.

"Got to go . . . to the bathroom," she said.

"Probably a good sign," he answered. When he would have scooped her into his arms, she shook her head. "Let me walk."

"Okay," he agreed, but kept his arm around her as she made her slow way down the hall, leaning against him. She stepped into the bathroom and shut the door, and he propped his shoulder against the wall, waiting for her to emerge.

After he'd helped her back into bed, he asked, "Do you want some food?"

She thought for a minute. "The proverbial tea and toast."

"Okay."

He knew they were both postponing a frank conversation as he went into the kitchen, started the kettle and toasted wheat bread, then added a little butter and blackberry jam.

He put a mug of sweetened tea and the plate of toast on a tray for her, then added a mug of cranberry tea for himself.

When he came back to the bedroom, he saw she'd combed her hair and changed into a fresh T-shirt.

"I'd say you shouldn't be up. But I have no idea what I should be advising," he said.

"The way we do it is to see what we can manage," she murmured.

He set the tray on the bedside table near her, then took his own mug. "How do you feel?"

She considered the answer. "Weak. But I'm recovering."

"How long before you get sick again?" he asked, unable to keep the harshness out of his voice.

"I don't know," she said in a low voice.

He muttered a curse under his breath.

She watched him set down his mug on the nightstand, then said in a conversational tone, "I thought maybe you didn't drink alcohol or tea because you were a straight arrow. Now I guess it's a werewolf trait."

He was glad he hadn't taken a sip of the hot liquid, because he might have choked. "Yeah, our sense of smell and taste are too acute. And we overreact to drugs," he managed, then plumped up the pillows before sitting down beside her.

She took a bite of toast and washed it down with tea before saying, "I would have appreciated knowing your . . . special talent before you seduced me."

His hands clenched on his mug. "Like I would have appreciated knowing you had the family illness before I dragged you on a risky mission. Why the hell didn't you tell me?"

"Because I knew you wouldn't take me," she shot back, then looked down at the bandage on her arm. "I think I would have avoided the attack, if I hadn't gotten shot."

"Your brother asked if you'd been injured."

"You talked to Colin?"

"Yes."

He saw alarm flash in her eyes. "What else did he say?"

"What else are you hiding?" he shot back.

"Nothing!"

He regarded her carefully. "I know that look. You're avoiding something. Some crucial fact I need to know to keep your butt out of the wringer!"

When she didn't deny it, his anger flared again. He wanted to ask her about the dream she'd had just before she'd gotten really sick. She'd woken up saying this was all her fault. What was she talking about? He wanted to know, but he was going to have to wait on that.

Instead he said, "Colin said you could have died if I'd taken you to the hospital. I was scared enough to do it. I would have, if I hadn't talked to him."

"I'm sorry," she whispered, then leaned back against the pillows and closed her eyes. "This is wearing me out."

"Or you're using it as an excuse not to continue the conversation."

"That, too," she admitted in a small voice.

He sighed. "I'll let you rest. For now."

She sank down lower against the pillows. Seconds later, she was sleeping.

Gently, he took the plate off her lap and set it on the table.

Because he was still afraid to leave Olivia alone, he brought his laptop computer into the bedroom and booted up. For a long moment he stared at the screen. Then he connected to the phone line and opened a Web browser. There was something that didn't add up. Something that he had meant to check out and had never gotten around to. He might not be as good a researcher as Colin Woodlock. But he was pretty proficient. When he put Dr. Henry Regario into several search engines, he came up with no one who could have produced the elixir that Olivia had told him about.

He brooded about that for a while. Then he opened the e-mail he rarely used.

After deleting the accumulated junk, he looked over toward his mate. She was still sleeping, so he typed in an address from memory. An address he had looked up but never used. Rmarsh@asl.com.

Simply staring at his brother's name made him feel light-headed. When he'd run away from that hospital morgue in Baltimore, he'd let his family think he was dead. Now there was a reason to contact them. He needed a better understanding of what the future held for him and Olivia.

Yet what the hell was he going to say? Ross was five years older— a big gap in their ages when they'd been young. Ross had always been a real straight arrow. He'd gone to the University of Maryland, worked two jobs, and basically bought into solid citizenship, at least as solid as a man could be who turned into a wolf at night and roamed the woods, probably helping to thin the deer population.

That image gave him the courage to write:

"I guess if you're at the computer, you're sitting down. I know that eight years ago you thought Johnny Marshall's body got lost in the shuffle after that bar fight. That's what he wanted you and everybody else to think. He woke up in the hospital and remembered the bikers from the bar talking about how they were going to pin a murder rap on him. So he decided it was dumb to stick around and try to defend himself when a dozen witnesses were going to say he did it. Being the sophisticated guy you remember, he stole a car and got the hell out of Dodge. On the way to California, where he lives now, he changed his name—to Sam Morgan. That's me."

He stopped and read the message, made a few changes, and considered his next words. Ross might revert to the violence of the werewolf when he was alone in the woods. But when he was a man, he was a private detective, which probably meant he was in favor of law and order. The minute he found out his youngest brother wasn't dead, he was going to do some checking up on him. And probably he'd come to the conclusion that his sources of income weren't entirely legal. Would he rat on him? Or would he be glad to hear that his kid brother wasn't dead after all?

He thought about pressing the DELETE button. Then he reminded himself why he was taking this step and went on:

"After I got out of Baltimore, I decided it was better just to live my own life, considering how well the Marshall guys get along. But I need to find out some things. I've checked up on you. I know you married a doctor who's a genetics specialist. Did she figure out anything that would give your children a better chance at survival?"

He broke off again, because his chest had tightened painfully. Before he could change his mind, he sighed the message, "Your brother, Sam Morgan."

After clicking the SEND button, he looked up and saw Olivia was awake and watching him warily. "What are you doing? E-mailing Luther Ethridge?" she asked in a shaky voice.

"Of course not! What makes you think so?"

"The look on your face."

"Which is?"

"Tense. Guilty. You look like a kid taking the loose change your dad left on the dresser."

He sighed. "I was e-mailing my brother."

"The one you haven't talked to in eight years?"

"Yeah."

"Why?"

He scrubbed a hand over his face. "I need advice."

"About what?"

He had a split second to come up with an answer. He settled for a half-truth. "Married life."

He saw her complexion go a shade paler. "Who said I was going to marry you?"

"Will you?" he asked, because he had been thinking about it for weeks.

"I don't know. Don't you think you should have told me the truth about the wolf before we got locked in that storage room?"

"Yes. You know why I didn't. But the way you found out doesn't change anything between us."

Her eyes narrowed. "I wouldn't count on it."

He kept his own gaze steady. "One thing about the sexually mature young werewolf—he can have any woman he wants."

"That's pretty arrogant."

"Yeah, but it's true. Until the happy-go-lucky werewolf hits his thirties, and he meets the woman who is going to be his mate. When that happens, the two of them bond." He swallowed. "The moment I met you, I knew you were that woman. I tried to fight the attraction because I didn't like the idea of being tied to anyone, especially the daughter of Wilson Woodlock."

She raised her chin. "I don't like the idea either. And I'm not going to be your ordained mate because you think it's written in the stars."

21

SAM ached to set her straight. Instead, he dragged in a breath and let it out, before forcing himself to say, "Okay. One thing at a time. Stay with me until I get the elixir—the Astravor—that will keep you alive. Then you can walk away from me if you want."

Her face contorted. "You're not playing fair."

"What do you suggest? Or did you give up the idea of my helping you?"

She looked down at her hands, then back up at him. "No. I didn't give that up. I knew instantly that you were the right person for the job." She clamped her fingers together. "And that was way before I knew your special talents."

She had given him the opening to say, "Well, that's something we have to talk about. I mean, you've got your secrets, and I have mine. I'd appreciate it if you kept the wolf to yourself."

"What do I tell my family about how you got me free?"

"It was dark. I'm Houdini. And I don't give away my secret methods."

She licked her lips. "Okay."

He eyed her cold toast. "You need to eat. At least, I think you do. I don't know much about your family illness, Woodlocks' Disease."

She looked relieved at the change of subject. "Yes. I'm hungry."

He went back to the kitchen, brought more toast and tea. And a small glass of orange juice, in case she could handle that. He also made a quick roast beef sandwich for himself because he had gone without food for hours.

The few minutes he was away gave them both time to cool off.

"Thank you," she said politely when he returned with the food. He delivered hers to the bed, then sat back down at the desk, turning his chair so he could look at her. They both ate in silence for several minutes, and he didn't push her to talk because he wanted to judge how she was feeling.

When she had finished the toast and taken several sips of tea, she asked, "What did Colin tell you about the family sickness?"

"Not much. It was a short conversation since somebody at your house told the guy waiting at Reese's that we were coming. So who is the stool pigeon working for? Your father?" he pressed.

Her head jerked up. The look of fear that flashed in her eyes told him that he'd hit a nerve.

"Why him?" she asked in a shaky voice.

"He wants you back, and he's got plenty of money to spend. He could have arranged for a reception committee. And I think he's ruthless enough to want me eliminated if he thought that was the best thing for you."

"I know you have a low opinion of him. But I can't believe he'd have you murdered."

He sighed. "Let's put that aside and go back to Woodlocks' Disease. You told me a little about it. I need to know more."

She swallowed and looked away, and he wondered if her next words would be truth or fiction.

"Nobody develops symptoms until after age twenty-six or so. Then the elixir keeps it in check. It's worse for some of us than for others. I thought . . ." She stopped and huffed out a breath. "I didn't get sick right away. And I thought I would be okay for a while longer." She made a snorting sound. "Maybe I was counting on how healthy I'd always been. Dad and Colin would rather die than exercise. I always made the gym part of my life."

"You're better now. But for how long?" he asked, digging relentlessly for information.

"I don't know." She kept her gaze steady. "I've survived the first full-blown attack. It can be fatal."

"Colin told me that. It scared me shitless."

"Oh, Sam. I . . . I'm so sorry I did that to you." She held out her arm, and he went to her, folding her close. "I can be okay for weeks or months," she whispered. "But sooner or later, I'll get sick again. And there's no way of knowing what it will do to me. It could attack my body. My brain." Raising her head, she looked at him. "How would you deal with that?"

"I'm going to get you that elixir. And I understand why you didn't tell me. Believe me, I know about family secrets. The Marshalls had a lot to hide."

"Marshall—was that your name?"

"Yes. You're the only person in the world who knows that Johnny Marshall is Sam Morgan, at least until Ross gets my e-mail. I'm being honest with you," he said, thinking that he had no choice. And he didn't want to give her one, either. "Get used to being honest with me."

"I am."

He gave her a narrow-eyed look. "Then let's talk about Astravor. You said a researcher developed it, a Dr. Regario."

"Yes," she said carefully.

"That's a lie, isn't it?" he said quietly.

He watched her expression turn uncertain. "How do you know?" she asked.

"In the first place, you're not talking about it like it's a new discovery. It sounds like it's been around for generations—like it's that 'folk remedy' you mentioned. Only it was always effective. And in the second place, I looked up Dr. Henry Regario. He didn't work for your father, did he?"

"No," she finally whispered.

"Why did you lie about that?"

"Colin and I thought it sounded more plausible than telling you that Astravor has been part of my family heritage back into ancient times." She swallowed. "The legend is that a pagan goddess gave it to us to save us from an enemy. My ancestor accepted the bargain. And that tied him and his descendants to the Astravor for all time. I mean, how many people are going to believe that?"

He laughed. "A man with an ancestor who asked the Druid gods for special powers and doomed himself and his descendants to be werewolves."

"I didn't know that at the time."

"You do now."

"Yes."

"So what else are you hiding about Astravor?"

She swallowed but said nothing.

"Can I assume you're not concealing something that would be dangerous to me?"

"Yes," she whispered.

"Maybe when we get the elixir back, you'll trust me."

"Sam . . ."

"Did the goddess give your ancestor the Astravor to fight demons?"

She blanched. "Why do you ask?"

"Because the first time I met Darwin, he was raving about them."

She gave a small nod. "Yes. That's part of the legend. I never took it literally until Luther Ethridge stole the Astravor. Then I started wondering if it was a metaphor for the enemies of my family."

"Yeah," he agreed, sensing he had pushed her as far as he could on the subject of Astravor for now. Clearing his throat, he asked, "Are you feeling well enough to travel?"

"Yes."

"And well enough to help me set a trap for the spy at the estate?"

She firmed her lips. "Yes."

"And you'd stake your life on it not being Colin or Brice?"

"Yes!"

Could he trust that? Not completely. But he answered, "Okay. First, I want you to get dressed. I want to see if you're steady on your feet."

"I am," she said again, then eased away from him and got out of bed. He watched her rummaging in her suitcase for clean clothing, watched her head for the bathroom. While she was gone, he sent an e-mail to Colin.

ALONE in the bathroom, Olivia leaned toward the mirror and inspected her face. She had been feeling sick off and on for the past few months. But she'd tried to ignore that.

It hadn't done her any good. The illness had grabbed her by the throat anyway. And that wasn't her only problem. Sam had told her she was going to be a werewolf's wife! How did you prepare yourself for that? Or did you run? If you did, would it do you any good?

When she came out, she saw Sam was lying comfortably on the bed. Well, he looked comfortable with the pillows bolstered, his hands stacked behind his head. But he couldn't hide his tension from her.

Watching her carefully, he said, "Last time Colin and I talked, it was on his personal line. I've just e-mailed him and gotten an answer. And he's erased the messages. I told him you'd call in a little while. He's agreed that this time we'll use the house line, keep him on the phone for a while, and hope that our spy is listening in." He went on to give her instructions, then handed her the phone.

Olivia looked from the small instrument back to Sam. "Thank you for trusting me," she whispered, then sat down in the chair by the window.

He stood in the doorway, watching her—making her nervous, if she was honest.

Without looking at him, she made the call. Jefferies answered, and her stomach clenched. It could be him. He could be the traitor. She didn't want it to be him. She didn't want it to be anyone in the house.

"Can I speak to Colin?" she said.

"Miss Olivia. We've been so worried about you. Where are you?"

"I can't talk about that now. I need to speak to my brother."

"Of course. I didn't mean to overstep."

"I know you didn't."

He was away for several moments. Then Colin came on the line. "Olivia?"

"Yes."

"Thank God. How are you?"

"Okay," she said around the lump that had formed in her throat. "I have to tell you some things. Important information."

"What?"

"I can't do it over the phone." She stopped and took a breath. "Sam is out. If he comes back, I'll have to hang up right away." She wanted to add, you know that's a lie, don't you? But she could only think it.

"What would he do if he caught you?" Colin asked.

She raised her head and looked at Sam. "Beat me within an inch of my life."

"The bastard," Colin said. "I take it he's treating you pretty badly."

"Yes," she answered, knowing that he understood she was putting on a show for whoever might be listening. "I'm going to try and get away from him. He has to sleep sometime. If I can get home, I'll drive straight through. I'll meet you at the old well out back—where we had that earlier incident. You know where I mean?"

"Yes."

"Where are you?"

"I'd rather not say. But I'll do my best to be home by midnight. If

I can't make it by then, wait for me." She paused. "And keep it secret. I feel like such a fool for going off with him. I don't want everybody there to think I'm a fool."

"They won't!"

"Promise you'll come alone, so we can work out some kind of story. Like we did when we were kids, getting around Dad."

"I'll be alone."

She looked up and saw Sam scribbling something on a piece of notepaper which he handed to her. Quickly she read the message and nodded. "Repeat back to me where we're meeting."

"We're meeting at the old well. Out back. At midnight. Or later, if you can't make it by then."

"Yes. Thanks. I love you."

"Love you. Be careful, Olivia."

"I will."

She hung up and glanced at Sam. "How was I?"

"Perfect. Anybody listening would think you hate me."

The look on his face made her heart squeeze. "I don't," she whispered.

"But you're not entirely sure how you feel," he said in a gritty voice.

He had told her to be honest. The best she could say was, "I'm still confused." Maybe it was the safest answer.

WHILE Olivia got some sleep, Sam took the computer into the den. He might go days without checking his e-mail, because there wasn't anyone he wanted to communicate with. Now he connected to the phone line again and opened his mailbox.

When he saw a message from Rmarsh@asl.com, he sat staring at the subject line for several moments. It said, "Thank you for contacting me."

Wondering exactly why Ross welcomed the contact, he pushed the ENTER button and watched the message flash on the screen.

"Sam, I'm so glad to hear from you. I've been hoping and praying for years that I would. I investigated the bar murder. I knew you didn't do it. But I couldn't be sure the cops would believe me."

With a feeling of unreality, Sam stared at the words. Ross had believed in him all those years ago.

"I also investigated the hospital morgue. I knew there was a chance you'd slipped away. But I knew you didn't want to be found. So whenever I talked about you or even thought about you, I acted like you were dead. Because that was my only option."

He rocked back in the deck chair, stunned by what he was reading.

"Sam, I'm so thankful you pressed the SEND button. And I have a pretty good idea why. You're thirty. And I'd guess that you've met your lifemate. If so, I have some good news for you. As you know, my wife Megan is a doctor with a specialty in genetics. She's been able to figure out that we have an extra chromosome that's responsible for our . . . special qualities. It's sex-linked, which is why only male children survived. But she's been able to overcome that. She and I have a son and a daughter, if you can believe that. Adam, who runs a private nature park in Georgia, is married and has a son. And Megan thinks she has the hormone problem figured out—so that none of our sons will have to face the risks we did when they reach puberty. She thinks we can make sure they make it through the change."

Stunned, Sam had to stop reading again and simply focus on his breathing. Then he went back to the text.

"So I'm here to give you any help you need in that department. I know you're probably blown away by the information I've just given you. And there's so much more I want to say. But the bottom line is that Adam and I are friends. And we've even made contact with our cousin, Grant Marshall. I know you're thinking about the way we used to fight with Dad. But if you understand how to work it, you can control the impulse to dominate. I guess the big point is that the guy who's on his home turf gets to call the shots. I'm telling you so you'll consider coming back for a visit—with your mate. I won't give away your secret. But I know Mom would be thrilled to see you. And so would Dad, for about twenty minutes. No, maybe longer. We're slowly bringing him into the twenty-first century.

"So now the ball is back in your court. Your brother, Ross."

Blinking back the moisture in his eyes, Sam reread the e-mail, then read it again, then pressed REPLY.

His hands weren't quite steady as he typed:

"Thanks for getting back to me so fast. Yes, I'm blown away. And relieved. And I'll contact you again after I've absorbed some of that."

After sending the message, he sat staring at the computer screen. He'd just gotten more than he bargained for. The part about the children was a shock. A good shock. But there was still the problem of his profession.

Or did Ross already know his brother was a thief? Was he keeping silent on that point because he wanted to establish better communications first?

THREE hours later, he woke Olivia. In the dimly lit room, he slid her a quick look. They had gone into the Reese project feeling uneasy about each other. Their relationship still wasn't exactly on what he'd call normal footing. Yet something had changed.

Together, they packed efficiently, got in the car, and left Monterey. She dozed on the way down the coast, then woke as they approached the northern suburbs of Santa Barbara.

Watching her stretch, he asked, "How are you feeling?"

"Not bad. You can drop me off, then park the car nearby so it won't take too long for you to get into the backyard." She rummaged in her purse and pulled out a key ring. "There's a door in the front wall—about twenty feet to the left of the driveway. It's covered by ivy, and most people have forgotten about it. Nobody would be expecting me to come in that way."

"I don't like us getting separated. And I don't like using you as bait."

"I know. But it's the best way."

They rode in silence for another ten minutes, before he cleared his throat and managed to relate the news, "My brother sent back a message."

"I'll bet he was happy to hear from you," she said instantly.

"Yeah." Sam's hands tightened on the wheel. "When we were teenagers, we all had to face . . . the first time we changed."

"I guess it was frightening," she said in a strained voice that made him think she might have some understanding of what it was like.

"A lot of us didn't make it. I mean . . . some of my older brothers died in the process."

Her gaze shot to him. "It's dangerous?"

"Yes. But Ross married a doctor who specializes in genetics. She thinks she has a solution."

"Good."

He wanted to add "for our children." But he couldn't go quite that far. So he said, "Another thing my parents had to face. In our family, the only children born alive were boys."

When she sucked in a sharp breath, he went on quickly. "But Ross's wife has solved that problem, too. They have a daughter and a son." He glanced at her to see how she'd taken the information.

"Will the daughter be . . . like you?"

"I don't know. I don't think so."

They had arrived in Montecito. He stopped down the road from the estate and put the car into park. When she turned toward the door, he dragged her back and wrapped her in his arms.

"If I didn't think I'd scare off the traitor, I'd be there with you," he said.

"I know, but I'll be fine," Olivia answered. The reassurance was as much for herself as for him.

With one hand, Sam reached toward the glove compartment, opened the latch, and got out the gun she'd practiced with and a set of handcuffs that he also carried with him. "Take these. If you catch the spy before I get there, get Colin to cuff him."

She eyed the gun. "Why didn't you bring that to the Reese house?" she asked.

He laughed. "Habit. A wolf doesn't need a gun. And a burglar who gets caught with a weapon is in a lot more trouble than one who's unarmed."

"So taking me to target practice was just one of your ploys to get me to back off."

"Pretty much, yeah," he admitted.

"Thanks for leveling with me."

He cupped his hand over her shoulder. "Olivia, everything between us is on the level—as far as I'm concerned."

She looked down at the weapon, hefting its weight in her hand, wishing she could say the same thing to him. But that was still impossible.

After slipping the gun into the compartment in the door, she hugged him tightly. "You be careful."

"I will."

She gave him one more fierce embrace, then took the gun, and got out.

WHEN Olivia disappeared from sight, Sam felt a surge of panic. He had come up with this plan to trap the spy. But now that they were in the middle of it, he had to force himself not to go after her.

With his jaw clenched, he drove to the next cross street, then to the end of the block.

Quickly he got out and retrieved his small pack from the back. After methodically checking the contents, he hooked the pack over one shoulder and headed for the grove of pine trees where he'd changed before. Hanging the pack on a low branch, he took off his clothing, feeling the cold wind whip against his body. It was uncomfortable, but it also helped sharpen his senses as he said the ancient chant that changed him from man to wolf.

After dropping to all fours, he sniffed the wind before wiggling into the pack that dangled low enough for him to reach easily. Then, because he knew Olivia was feeling alone and scared, he raised his head and howled—calling out to his mate.

THE hair on the back of Olivia's neck prickled as she heard the sound of a wolf howl. There was only one wolf around here. At least she hoped so.

"Sam," she whispered, knowing that he was calling to her, telling her that he would be there soon.

Quietly she opened the door in the wall and slipped inside. For a long moment, she stared into the darkness beyond the glow of the floodlights. Then she stiffened her knees and walked around the house, holding the gun down beside her right leg.

The moon came out from behind a cloud, turning the garden into a place of magic. She had always thought of it like that. The Woodlocks' magic realm.

Tonight the silvery light and the smell of the flowers enveloped her like a familiar caress. Still, she felt goose bumps pepper her arms as she crossed the open space between the house and the well.

It was impossible to shake off the notion that somebody was standing in the shadow of a tree or bush, watching her progress as she walked toward the wall at the back of the property.

She kept her pace steady, struggling not to show the lingering effects of her recent illness. She knew how hard Colin worked not to let the family curse interfere with his life. If he could do that, so could she, particularly since he was probably watching her.

In fact, he was already at the spot where they had agreed to meet, leaning against a tree.

When she softly called his name, he raised his head, and she speeded up, rushing toward him.

"Thank God, you're all right," he whispered. "I've been worried about you."

"I'm fine."

He lowered his voice to a whisper. "Sam said you were sick."

She swallowed. "I thought I was going to escape the family curse. I guess not."

"I was hoping you would."

"We'll fix it!" she said, then stopped suddenly as the sound of leaves crackling told her that someone had followed her from the direction of the house.

The spy.

Whirling, she strained her eyes into the shadows beyond the moonlight. When she saw Brice coming out of the darkness, a grim look on his face, her heart leaped into her throat.

Oh, God. Not Brice.

22

OLIVIA fought for breath. She was so unprepared to see Colin's partner that she didn't know what to do. Raise the gun? What?

"We were worried about you. Are you all right?" he asked in a tense voice.

"Yes," she managed.

Colin stepped forward, looking as sick and conflicted as she felt. "What the hell are you doing here?" he demanded.

Olivia's head swung toward him, aching with sorrow for her brother.

Brice raised his chin and addressed himself to Colin. "We're in this together, in case you've forgotten. I knew something was going on. Something to do with Olivia and Sam, and I wasn't going to let you deal with it alone."

Lord, was he telling the truth? Or was he an excellent liar? Either way, he had just thrown a wild card into this rendezvous.

"There are some things I have to deal with on my own, family things," Colin snapped.

As she turned toward her brother, the feeling of being watched from the shadows made the hairs on the back of her neck straighten.

Someone or something was edging closer to the three of them, concealed by a screen of shrubbery.

The wolf? He had said he would change back before they confronted the spy. But everything was happening too fast now.

Brice moved, dashing into the bushes, pulling someone out into the moonlight. Again Olivia couldn't stifle a feeling of disorientation. It was Irene Speller, the maid who had helped Jefferies run their household for the past five years.

Brice stayed close to the woman. Colin stared at her, looking as shocked as Olivia felt. "Irene? What . . . what are you doing here?" he demanded.

"I was out for a walk," the maid answered, with just a hint of nerves in her voice. "I'm sorry if I intruded."

Colin wedged his fists on his hips. "I don't think so—not at this time of night. Not when I've been tripping over you every time I turn around. You were in the hall when I came out of my room after I was talking to Olivia. You were spying on me. Why?"

"No," she said, but she couldn't quite hold her voice steady.

"You'd better stay right here until we sort this out," Olivia said as she raised the gun, pointing it at the maid.

Irene glanced at the weapon, then took a step back.

"Stop right there," Olivia warned.

The maid raised her chin. "Or what?"

"Or . . . I'll shoot you," Olivia answered.

"You don't have the guts." Irene turned and ran, heading for the house.

"Don't shoot," Brice shouted. Tearing after Irene, he caught her in a football tackle, bringing her down on the grass.

Olivia and Colin rushed forward. Brice kept his hand on the maid's arm, pulling her to her feet.

"Why do you want to hurt us?" Colin whispered.

"I don't!"

"Stop lying," Colin ordered.

"I'm not," Irene insisted, but her eyes darted nervously to the side. Brice shook her. "Talk!"

"Get your hands off me," she shrieked, apparently cracking under the stress.

Olivia stepped forward. "I know you're scared. Let us help you."

"Oh yeah. Sure. You're just like everybody else in your filthy rich family." Fear and anger must have given the woman strength because she wrenched away from Brice, leaping at Olivia, who screamed as Irene knocked her to the ground and tried to snatch the weapon away.

THE wolf had reached the exterior of the garden wall when he heard Olivia scream.

Oh, Lord, no! He had sent his mate into danger. And now she was in trouble.

He wanted to howl in anger. Instead, he crouched down and sprang upward, making it to the top of the wall in one bound. Pausing only an instant to catch his balance, he plunged down the other side and bounded forward, spotting the maid named Irene on top of Olivia.

The wolf sprinted forward and leaped onto the woman's back, making her screech in terror as he yanked her away and tossed her like a dirty rag onto the grass.

He could hurt her badly. The wolf part of him ached to leave some tooth or claw marks on her.

But someone was shouting at him. It was Olivia. "Don't, S—" She started to say his name and changed her mind. "Don't! Please, don't!"

Raising his head, he saw the pleading look in her eyes and the stunned expressions on the faces of the two men.

OLIVIA pushed herself up. Leaving the gun where it had fallen on the ground, she pulled out the handcuffs that Sam had given her and knelt beside the maid, cuffing her wrists behind her back, the way Sam had been secured at the Reese house only days before.

When she was finished, Olivia scrambled over to the wolf, throwing her arm over his back as she looked up to face her brother and Brice.

The two men both stared at her as though struggling to take in what they were seeing.

Olivia gave them a fierce look. "My new guard dog," she clipped out, hoping that her voice and her expression conveyed that she wasn't going to go into any more explanations in front of the woman who had been spying on them for months—maybe years.

"Let's get Irene back to the house," Brice suggested.

"No, I want to know what she was doing here," Olivia answered. She hadn't been able to shoot an unarmed woman in cold blood. But Irene wasn't going to escape anytime soon. And she was pretty sure Sam would want to press their advantage right now. When she turned toward the wolf for confirmation, he gave her a small nod, then pawed at the woman, who whimpered, the fight gone out of her now.

Olivia found the gun and handed it to Brice. "Keep her covered. But don't shoot her unless you have to."

Brice moved closer to Irene, keeping the weapon trained on her. "Unlike you, I will kill her if I have to," he muttered.

The wolf stayed where he was, standing guard.

Olivia yanked Irene to a sitting position. Part of her was standing back, watching in amazement as she grabbed the maid's hair and tipped her head up. "I'll have my dog tear you to pieces," she said, "unless you tell me who you're working for."

"Please. Let me go," Irene begged, her eyes fixed on the "dog."

"Tell me why you informed someone where Sam Morgan and I were going."

The wolf growled and bared his teeth, and the maid shrank back. When the animal took a step toward her, she moaned, looking like she might have a heart attack on the spot. "Please, get him away from me."

"Who are you working for?" Olivia snapped, giving the maid's head a shake.

When she refused to speak, the wolf took her shoulder in his teeth. Olivia could see he was acting with restraint, but Irene didn't know that.

She moaned. "No. Don't! Make him stop."

"I will, if you tell me who paid you to spy on us," Olivia answered, then held her breath as she waited for the worst.

"Luther Ethridge," Irene whispered.

A wave of relief washed over Olivia. Not her father! At least it wasn't her father who had tried to kill Sam. Still, the confirmation that a trusted household member had been feeding information to Ethridge made something inside Olivia go sick and cold. "You work for us," she said. "How could you work for him, too?"

When Irene raised her head, her eyes were cold. "Do you have any idea what it's like to work for Wilson Woodlock?" she spat out. "He wants value for money! That means he wants you to work eighteen hours a day, seven days a week. And he wants to pay you shit. Just think of all the staffers who have quit because they couldn't take it! I was going to leave a couple of years ago. Then Ethridge made me a very nice offer. And I decided to collect double pay. More than double."

Olivia sucked in a shaky breath, hardly knowing what to say. She raised her eyes to Colin, and he looked as sick as she felt.

"We'll take her inside," Brice said, "then figure out what to do."

"Yes," Olivia agreed. When she turned her head, the wolf had faded back into the shadows.

She tugged on Irene's arm, pulling her erect. "Come on."

As they crossed the lawn, Sam joined them, dressed in a different shirt and pants than he'd been wearing earlier, and she realized they must have been in the small pack he'd had strapped to his back.

The whole group stopped in their tracks, shrinking back from him.

Olivia looked at Colin and Brice, giving a small shake of her head when Brice opened his mouth.

"It looks like you missed the excitement," she said to Sam.

Sam gave her an approving look, noting the relieved expressions on the men's faces. He didn't know if they bought her explanation. But he'd bet they wanted to believe it.

Moving next to Olivia, he slung an arm around her shoulder, the way she had embraced the wolf. "I gather you did fine without me. I'm sorry I wasn't here to help."

When they were almost to the house, Wilson Woodlock stepped out onto the terrace, his hair uncombed and his white shirt only partially buttoned.

"What the hell is going on?" he demanded.

"Your maid has been feeding information to Luther Ethridge," Sam answered.

Woodlock's gaze riveted to Irene. "I don't believe it!"

"We just set a trap for her, and she walked into it," Olivia added. "Then she confessed."

"But you can't prove anything," Irene pointed out, speaking for the first time since the interrogation.

"You told us you were working for Luther Ethridge," Colin clipped out.

"I lied."

Colin snorted. "Now that we have you in custody, I can prove you didn't."

Irene glared at him.

Ignoring her, Colin addressed the group. "What are we going to do with her?"

"Get her out of here! Turn her over to the cops," Brice bit out.

Woodlock's head whipped toward him. "We don't deal with the police," he snapped.

For once, he and Sam were on the same side.

"But that doesn't solve the problem. We can't keep her prisoner," Olivia pointed out.

"I think we can, until we discuss some other matters," Woodlock answered. "Bring her inside."

Brice and Sam each took one of the woman's arms and marched her into the house. They halted in the family room while Woodlock con-

sidered their next move. Finally, he led her to an interior bathroom
that had a bar lock on the door. Sam unsnapped the cuffs before ushering her inside.

As the door lock clicked, Irene started to whimper.

Sam took Olivia's arm and led her away. "How come you have a
bar on the outside of a bathroom door?"

"We actually did have a dog for a few years before Daddy got tired
of having him mess up the furniture. He got locked in here for punishment," Olivia answered.

"Charming," Sam murmured, then took a good look at her. "You
need to sit down." When she didn't argue, he put his arm around her
and guided her back to the family room, where she dropped heavily
onto the sofa.

He followed her down, clasping her hand in his. "Are you all right?"

"Well, it's been a strenuous evening," she answered, moving closer
to him.

He wanted to order her upstairs to rest. But he'd already figured
out that she didn't take orders real well.

He looked up to see the rest of the group watching them. Before
anyone could make a comment, Thurston came around the corner.

"Irene's locked in the bathroom crying. What's going on?"

"We had a little problem," Sam answered. "But it's under control."

Woodlock was breathing heavily. After slowly crossing the room,
he dropped into one of the recliners.

Brice and Colin sat down on the other sofa. Thurston remained
standing in the doorway.

Sam studied the crowd. As far as he was concerned, the fewer people who knew his personal business, the better. But there were a lot of
questions floating around now. They had to at least cover the basics,
but he didn't know how much each of these people knew.

He looked at Thurston. "You're in charge of security here?"

"Yes."

"Well, you'll want to know that Irene Speller has been feeding information to Luther Ethridge."

Thurston's head swiveled toward Woodlock. "Is that true?"

Woodlock sighed. "It appears so," he answered.

"You knew that Olivia and I were on a . . . secret mission?" Sam
asked, feeling as if he'd slipped into the spy mode.

Thurston nodded.

"Olivia spoke to Colin, and he figured out where we were going. Irene snooped around and got our exact location, then told Ethridge. A hired gun was waiting for us."

"Sam got us out of there," Olivia jumped in. "Otherwise, he'd be dead. And I assume I'd be on my way to Ethridge's house." As she said that last part, she glanced at her father.

Colin made a strangled exclamation. "I am so sorry," he said, giving Olivia and Sam an apologetic look. "I started figuring the odds on where you'd go—and came up with your most likely target. With ninety-seven percent probability."

"Yes," Olivia whispered.

"Luckily, we made it back here alive," Sam added, pausing to let the observation sink in. It had been touch and go. "And now we know what happened. But it's been a long day, and Olivia and I need to sleep. We can talk later about what to do with Irene."

He stood, tugging on her hand. "Come on."

Without looking at anyone else in the room, he led her into the hall before she could object. But he was aware that Colin was following them up the stairs.

Sam opened the bedroom door and waited for Olivia to go inside, then turned to face her brother. "I take it you have some concerns?"

"You've convinced me it's better not to speak in the hall."

"Yes."

They stepped into the room Sam had used on his last visit to the house. Crossing the carpet, Sam picked up the lamp where he'd found the bug, removed it, and crushed it between his fingers.

"What was that?" Colin demanded.

"A microphone. I'd like to assume Irene left it in here. But I can't be sure."

"Good Lord!"

"I'll check the rest of the house later."

Crossing the rug, he propped his hips against the dresser. Although he was pretty sure he knew what Colin wanted to talk about, he looked at the other man questioningly.

Colin cleared his throat. "First, I want to thank you for getting my sister out of a bad situation—and taking care of her when she got sick."

"You know damn well I'm going to take care of her." Sam shifted his weight against the dresser, then looked up as Olivia stepped through the connecting bathroom.

"You're supposed to be lying down," Sam said.

"I know. But I saw Colin follow us, and I have an excellent idea of what's on his mind." When she crossed to Sam's side and slipped her arm around his waist, he dared to let out the breath he hadn't known he was holding.

Colin looked from Olivia to Sam. "Dad may be too sick to ask the right questions, but I have to."

Sam struggled to keep his expression neutral. "Okay."

"Darwin has been babbling about wolves for weeks. Not just wolves . . ." He stopped and swallowed. "Wolves and—you."

Olivia tightened her grip on Sam. "And what did you make of that?" she asked.

"Brice thought the connection between you and the wolf was . . . an interesting possibility. You know I've always been open-minded. In public I'm willing to go along with your guard dog story. But in private, I'd say that we got a pretty good demonstration tonight of what an intelligent wolf can do."

Turning his head, Sam watched Olivia give her brother a fierce look. "He heard me scream. So he came leaping over the wall to rescue me."

"So you're admitting that was him—and you knew it."

Olivia glared at him. "Of course I know!"

"When did you find out?"

"The night Ethridge's goons caught us at the Reese house. That's how he saved us!"

Colin winced.

"I'd appreciate it if you don't say anything to Dad about his special abilities. He's got enough to worry about. Deal?" she asked.

Again Sam held his breath, waiting for the answer.

Colin's full attention was on his sister. "You have to admit that it's a little unsettling knowing your sister is involved with a werewolf, but I'll bow to your judgment," he finally said.

Once again, Sam was able to breathe. "I appreciate it."

"The two of you have had a pretty traumatic couple of days," Colin muttered.

"Yeah."

"So get some sleep. We can talk again in the morning."

When Colin had gone, Sam turned to Olivia. "Thanks for getting him off my back."

"It was the least I could do—after everything you've done for me."

She walked through the bathroom to her own bedroom, and he listened to the sounds of her getting ready for bed. He waited until she was quiet before using the bathroom and taking a quick shower. Then there was nothing to do besides lie down in the guest room and stare at the shadows on the ceiling.

Until Olivia, relationships had been easy—and pleasant—for him. If he'd said the words, he could have married several different super-rich women. But he had never met "the one" until Olivia. Now he had no clue about how to get her to feel committed.

He lay awake for a long time, aching to climb into her bed and make her moan with ecstasy. But she needed to get her strength back. So he stayed where he was and finally closed his eyes.

His sleep was marred by nightmares. In his dreams he'd be holding Olivia in his arms. Then someone would snatch her away from him. Sometimes it was Wilson Woodlock who shouted that he would never let a werewolf fuck his daughter. Sometimes it was Colin who protested that it was his duty to protect his sister. And sometimes it was another man: Luther Ethridge, whom he recognized from the pictures he'd seen.

Sam shook off the dream, then couldn't stop himself from tiptoeing to the door of Olivia's room to see if she was safe in her bed. She was there. Breathing slowly and evenly, so he returned to his room and fell into his sweat-drenched bed.

He woke again before dawn, instantly alert, knowing something was wrong downstairs.

Leaping out of bed and pulling on the sweatpants he'd draped over the chair, he headed for the stairs.

23

SAM reached the first floor, then followed the sound of raised voices.

Thurston was standing in the front hall, struggling with Uncle Darwin. He was dressed in pajamas and a robe. His gray hair was wild, and he was muttering curses.

The security chief was obviously trying not to harm a family member and was consequently taking a beating from the man's large flailing fists.

"Need some help?" Sam asked, pretty sure that the mere sound of his voice would affect the outcome of the altercation.

He had guessed right. Darwin whirled. Wide-eyed, he cowered back against the man he had been fighting only moments before. "You! Get away from me," he wailed.

Thurston was able to grab the older man's arms and hold them behind his back.

Darwin kept his gaze fixed on Sam. "It's him. It's the wolf demon. Get him away from me."

"I won't hurt you," Sam soothed, moving slowly forward.

Darwin began to whimper.

Sam pulled Darwin's belt free of his robe. "Turn him around," he said to Thurston, who apparently agreed with the strategy.

As Darwin shivered and buried his face against the security man's shoulder, Sam tied his hands, listening to the sound of more footsteps.

Aware that they now had an audience, he raised his head. Colin, Olivia, and Brice were ranged along the upper balcony, looking down with expressions ranging from nervous to alarmed. Jefferies had come around the other way and was in back of Thurston and Darwin, his face a study in perplexity. And Wilson Woodlock was on the stairs, his complexion red with anger.

"What is the meaning of this?" he bellowed. "What's all this uproar? Take your hands off Darwin."

"I can't do that, sir," Thurston answered quickly. "I came down and found Mr. Darwin wandering around. I also found the door to the bathroom unlocked. It looks like he helped the prisoner escape."

"Christ!" Sam shouldered his way past Thurston and Darwin. When he came to the open bathroom door, he cursed again.

Hurrying back, he gave Thurston a sharp look. "Wasn't Darwin confined to his room?"

"Yes," the security man answered smartly.

"Doesn't he have round-the-clock attendants?"

"The man who was supposed to be here this evening didn't show up."

"And somebody took advantage of that to let him out," Sam said.

"Or he got loose on his own," Wilson countered.

"How likely is that?" Sam snapped.

"Impossible," Thurston muttered in a voice that didn't carry very far.

"The main point is that Irene got away," Sam answered. "How long has she been gone?" he asked Thurston.

"Hard to say," the security chief answered. "I found Mr. Darwin about ten minutes ago. But I don't know how long he was down here."

"On the off chance that Irene is still in the neighborhood, we'd better look for her," Sam said, heading for the backyard as Wilson ushered Darwin upstairs. In the shadows, he tore off his clothes and changed once more.

He'd picked up the maid's scent in the bathroom. Rounding the house, he caught it again at the front door, then followed down the driveway—where it stopped abruptly. Obviously she'd gotten into a vehicle. Had someone been waiting for her? Or had she called someone to pick her up?

When he returned, human once more, the other men had gone out to search in cars and on foot.

"Well?" Olivia said as he joined her in the family room.

"She got into a vehicle at the end of the drive."

"You're sure?"

"Unfortunately, yes. Her trail ends abruptly."

The others drifted back, reporting they had found nothing.

"Three guesses where she's gone," Sam muttered as they assembled in the family room an hour later.

LUTHER Ethridge sat in the easy chair in his comfortable den, a snifter of brandy in his hand.

A lesser man might need the alcohol to steady his nerves. Luther was simply having an afternoon drink after a little bit of an exertion. He'd just thrown Irene Speller's body into the deep well that had originally supplied his mountaintop property with water. Despite his anger, he liked the irony. Irene had taken the cover off the old well on the Woodlock property, then lured Sam Morgan outside.

Sam had escaped the trap. Now Irene was the one in the well.

She'd arrived in a cab that morning—following the instructions he'd given her long ago. "If you get into trouble at the Woodlock house, come to me. Take a cab if you have to. I'll pay for it."

Unfortunately, she didn't know who had helped her escape. They'd unlocked the door and run away. He'd gotten all the information he could out of her, then terminated her with extreme prejudice, as the spooks liked to say—at least in spy novels.

Her story had been unsettling. A big dog had figured in the scenario. Was it the same dog that had leaped out at Mr. Smith in the Reese house? That couldn't be a coincidence. But what did it mean?

That Sam Morgan seemed to have a very well-trained dog or dogs at his disposal? Or that he had strong hypnotic powers? Maybe that was it. He made you think you were being attacked by an animal, which allowed him to get the drop on you.

Luther didn't much like that hypothesis. But either it was true or the beast was real. Which made Sam Morgan a continuing problem and one he wouldn't tolerate.

SAM spent the morning checking the estate for hidden microphones, paying particular attention to the computer room. He found listening devices in Colin and Brice's room—much to Olivia's brother's chagrin. And one in the dining room.

By noon, Sam felt like he had to get out of the Woodlock Asylum, so he hunted up Olivia.

"I'll be out for the rest of the day," he informed her.

"Where are you going?"

"I'd like to tell you. But under the circumstances, it's probably better to just say I'll be back around six."

She answered with a quick nod, and the look of uncertainty on her face tore at him. So he pulled her close, to reassure her—and because he needed to hold her for just a moment before leaving.

Then he drove back to his own house to collect some more of his clothing and check his mail. The moment he was in his own place, he felt more at ease. Just being confined at the Woodlock estate set his nerves on edge.

On some deep, instinctive level, he knew he didn't belong there. Or he didn't want to be there. And he wasn't sure what he was going to do about it. Olivia was his mate. But she was tied to her family in a way he couldn't even understand. When he thought about how they were going to work out the details of their lives together, he came up against a blank wall.

Now that he was away from the Woodlock home again, he wanted
to stay away. And that was as disturbing as anything else. But he
knew he had to go back. Olivia was sick and in danger. And he belonged at her side.

So, around five, he started back.

When he stepped into the front hall, he saw a padded manila envelope sitting on the ornate side table. It hadn't been delivered by the
U.S. Post Office.

There was no stamp. Only the words "Sam Morgan, Personal and
Confidential," written in bold black marker on the front.

Sam's hands were suddenly damp. He wiped them on the legs of
his jeans, but he didn't pick the envelope up. Instead he went to find
Jefferies.

"When did that package arrive?" he asked.

"Just an hour ago. A messenger delivered it to the front entrance."

"Did you ask who hired him?"

"He works for a delivery company that the Woodlocks have used
in the past."

"So somebody in the family could have sent me this package?"

"Yes, sir."

"Okay. Thanks."

Sam's heart was pounding as he returned to the hall, picked up the
envelope, and sniffed it carefully. If it contained any explosives, he
couldn't smell them—and he was pretty sure he wouldn't miss something like that.

He wanted to plunge the envelope, into a bucket of water, just to
be on the safe side. Instead, he went into the kitchen and set it on the
counter. Then, using a sharp knife to slit the wrong end, he spread the
sides of the cut apart before reaching inside and extracting a plastic
DVD case.

A bright orange note stuck to the case said: "Dear Sam, here's
something for your viewing enjoyment."

He held the case in his hand, pretty sure that he wasn't going to
enjoy it. He'd seen a DVD player in the family room. But he didn't
want an audience. So he carried it to his room, set his laptop on the
desk, and booted the computer.

After inserting the disk in the player in the side of the machine, he
leaned back in the padded desk chair to watch.

The image that flickered on the screen made his whole body go rigid. It was Olivia. She was lying naked on a bed in a room he didn't recognize. A very opulent room.

He didn't want to see any more of the DVD. But his hand refused to obey when he ordered himself to turn it off.

Gripping the arms of the desk chair, he kept staring at the computer screen.

The image was sharp. Olivia's face looked so familiar that he could barely breathe.

Her eyes were closed, and as he watched, they flickered open and looked toward the camera. The expression on her face was dreamy as she moved her head on the pillow.

Then a man stepped smartly into the scene. Like the woman on the bed, he was naked. His shoulders were broad. His hips lean. He obviously took care of his body. It was tall and hard.

Turning, he favored the camera with a satisfied grin.

Sam felt sickness rise in his throat. He recognized the man from the pictures he'd seen. It was Luther Ethridge. And his erect dick was standing out from his body like a flagpole. He stroked his erection slowly, as if displaying himself for the viewer.

Then he turned back to Olivia, and the camera angle changed so that the view was from the other side of the room, giving Sam a clear picture of both Ethridge and Olivia.

He said something Sam couldn't hear. But the sound didn't matter. It was the images on the screen that made bile rise in Sam's throat.

Ethridge sat down beside Olivia, leaning forward as he stroked her face, her neck, and down to her breasts, lifting and shaping them in his hands before taking her nipples between his thumbs and fingers, pulling and twisting them—hard.

Olivia made a sound that was lost on the tape. Had he hurt her? Or did she like it rough? He didn't want to watch any more of this home movie. But he couldn't drag his eyes away as Ethridge leaned down to take one nipple between his teeth, biting down on one as he used his fingers on the other one.

Sam wanted to gag when he saw one of Luther's hands slide down Olivia's body, separating her legs, sliding into the folds of her sex. As he caressed her, she moaned. From pleasure? Or pain?

He kept stroking—one hand playing with her breast, the other at her vulva. Then the view was partially blocked, and he couldn't tell if the bastard had brought her to climax.

He tasted blood in his mouth. A familiar taste for a werewolf. Only he knew that he had bitten into his own lip as he'd watched the man and woman on the bed.

The man on the DVD must know the effect he was having on the viewer. He looked directly at the camera, grinning again. Then he shoved Olivia's legs wider, his hands working her clit, his fingers dipping into her vagina to slather moisture on himself. Then he covered her body with his and plunged his swollen dick into her, pulling far enough out with his first few strokes so Sam could see exactly what he was doing.

When he climaxed, he turned his face toward the camera again, silently shouting out his triumph.

A gasp from the doorway told Sam that he wasn't alone. Looking up, he saw Olivia watching the picture, a hand pressed to her mouth, her features contorted into a mask of horror as she watched herself being fucked on the screen.

24

THROUGH a red haze of anger, Sam watched Olivia—the real woman, not the image on the screen. In a voice that sounded surprisingly calm to his own ears, he said, "I know that wasn't shot anytime in the past few days, since you've been cozied up with me. How did you manage to convince me you were a virgin?"

"I was a virgin. Until we made love."

"Oh, right. So how do you explain that?" His arm shot out as he gestured toward the computer screen.

Her gaze swung back to the damning image. He was amazed she could keep her tone level as she asked, "Where did you get that fascinating piece of trash?"

"Special messenger," he spit out. "A surprise from your ex-boyfriend. Maybe you'd like to finally stop the goddamn lying, and tell me what's really going on."

She closed the door, then crossed the room, and laid her hands on his shoulders, making him flinch. Making him want to smack her across the face.

He knew she felt the violence in him, but she spoke with only a small quaver. "Luther Ethridge has never been my boyfriend. And that woman is not me."

"I wish to holy hell you were telling the truth," he said through parched lips.

He wanted to run from the room before he hurt her. He wanted to flee from all the lying and the pretending that filled this house. He had sensed there was something very wrong here. Now he knew what it was. He could have broken Olivia's hold on his shoulders. He was stronger than she was. But her slender grasp kept him where he was.

"You've lied to me from the first. I knew you were still lying about something. Now we both know what's really going on."

Her hands were trembling now. They should be!

Yet her next words sounded strangely calm. "That woman isn't me," she said again. "Try and be objective. Go back to some part where you can get a good look at the person lying on the bed. Freeze the image, and you'll see what I mean."

"Why not? You missed most of the show, didn't you? We might as well enjoy the whole thing together," he growled.

She lifted her hands away from him. With jerky movements, he clicked back to the first track where she was lying on the bed alone. Then he froze the picture on the screen.

Olivia was moving around behind him. He heard the door lock click. When he looked up, she was standing with a deadened expression on her face as she took off her clothing.

"What the hell are you doing, trying to get me to fuck you and forget about Ethridge?"

"No."

She had already kicked off her shoes, skirt, and panties. As he watched, she tossed her blouse onto the floor, then her bra.

Naked, she walked over to the bed in Sam's room. After arranging the pillows the way they were on the screen, she raised her head toward him, and he saw that all the color had drained from her face. Then, staring straight ahead, she lay down on the bed with her arms at her sides.

As though she were delivering a seminar paper, she said, "I know you were too upset to look for important details. But what you saw in that video is some kind of trick. Look at the screen and look at me. Her face is a lot like mine, I'll give you that. Almost identical. But it's not my body. Not at all. Her hips are narrower and her thighs are smaller. Her breasts are bigger. Her hands are all wrong. And so are her feet, for that matter. Look at the body parts—if you can still think rationally. Do that for me," she added in a voice that suddenly dropped to a whisper.

If she could lie there naked when she knew he wanted to rip out her throat, he could do as she asked. It was easiest to start with the hands. He looked at the screen, then back at Olivia's hands. He drew in a breath as he saw that they were narrower than those of the woman on the video, with longer fingers. Next he looked at her feet. Then back at the screen. They were different, too. Olivia's toes were longer and her entire foot was shorter.

His heart was pounding as he dragged his gaze a little higher up the frozen image. Now that she'd forced him from emotion to logic, he saw a lot of differences.

When he finally lifted his gaze to her face, he saw that her eyes were large and staring, and tears were slipping silently down her cheeks.

With a low sound in his throat, he sprang out of the chair, surged to her side.

"Oh, Christ. I am so sorry, love. So sorry."

OLIVIA had lain very still, forcing herself not to clench her fists or cover her body with the sheet. Now that Sam was beside her, she lost control. Suddenly it was impossible to stop a sob, then another, from wracking her body. She had held herself together long enough to prove that the woman in the video wasn't her. But his words were somehow too much. When he reached for her, she tried to roll away, but he wouldn't let her go. Stretching out beside her on the bed, he gathered her close, rocking and stroking her body and whispering urgently to her.

"I'm sorry. So sorry, love," he repeated over and over. Lifting her hand to his lips he kissed her palm, her fingers. "I never should have doubted you. I couldn't stop myself from reacting the way he wanted me to react. Forgive me for that. Please forgive me."

She nodded against his shoulder, trying to stop crying because she hated letting him see her weak and helpless. But now that she had started sobbing, it was so hard to gain control again. And she knew it wasn't just because Sam had doubted her. She had been through so much in the past few weeks. Then the video and his reaction had been like an anvil falling on her, delivering a crushing blow.

But finally, finally she conquered the tears.

When Sam reached for a tissue on the bedside table and handed it to her, she blew her nose, then tipped her face toward him.

"You know that woman isn't me?" she asked, needing to hear him say it.

He must have understood, because his Adam's apple bobbed. Then he said, "I know that woman isn't you."

"I don't know how he did it. I just know it's some kind of very nasty trick. You said he sent the DVD to you?"

"Yes. By messenger," he repeated.

"So I guess Irene ran to him and talked about what happened last night. She must have told him you and I were close, and he wanted to drive a wedge between us."

"And he would have. I would have walked away from you, if you hadn't brought me back to my senses," Sam admitted in a gritty voice.

Her eyes questioned his. "All the things you've been proclaiming about a werewolf and his mate. Now you're saying you could walk away from me?"

He swallowed hard. "I didn't think so. But I was sure you had betrayed me. I was angry and wounded enough to run away. I don't know what would have happened after that."

She was cold now, icy cold. When she started shivering, he pulled the covers aside for her. As she slipped under, he got up and pulled off his jeans and shoes, then climbed in beside her.

She needed the warmth of his body, but it wasn't enough to stop the shivering.

"I think I got a little taste of how a rape victim feels," she whispered.

"Oh, Lord, Olivia. I am so sorry. I should have turned the damn thing off. But I had to keep watching."

"So did I."

"How much did you see?"

"Enough to almost throw up." She stopped and knit her fingers with his, holding on tight. "You went out. You were gone for a long time, and I was waiting for you to come home. When I heard you come in, I needed to be with you. So I came up here—and got treated to the horrible picture on the screen."

He played his fingers through her hair, gathered her close.

Trying to hold her voice steady, she said what she should have admitted out loud a long time ago. "Sam, this is all my fault."

"Of course it's not."

He said that now. He hadn't heard her story yet. "Let me get this off my chest . . . finally."

She could feel his muscles stiffen, but he said nothing.

To moisten her dry throat, she swallowed. "When Luther Ethridge turned thirty, he threw himself a big party to celebrate his birthday and the millions he'd made. We were invited, and my father said we had to go. I could tell he was proud of Luther. His family and the Ethridges had been close. We all got together a few times a year. So we knew each other. And I knew that Luther . . . liked me. But he always gave me the creeps."

Sam stroked his hand up and down her arm.

"Dad had let him think it might work out, if he made himself worthy of me. And now I think he had decided Luther had done well enough for himself."

"Jesus."

She wanted to look away, but she kept her gaze steady. "Luther had always been . . . diffident . . . with me. But my father's reaction must have given him the message that things had changed. He got me off in one of the private rooms of his house. Not the castle where he lives now. He hadn't bought that yet."

"What did he do to you?" Sam growled.

"Not much. I mean, he started talking about how he had always admired me. And how he thought we would make a good team. He kept telling me his plans for the future. His plans for *us*. And then he tried to kiss me. Only I was grossed out . . . and scared spitless. I panicked and shoved him away. Then I ran out of the room." She closed her eyes, then opened them again. "And after that, he was cold and angry. And I knew . . . I knew . . ."

"How old were you when that happened?"

"Seventeen."

"And he was . . ."

"Thirty."

"Jesus! He was a grown man. And you were in high school. You think the incident was your fault?"

"It was—to his way of thinking. He wanted me to love him. Or at least respect him and acknowledge we were a good match. And when I rejected him so dramatically, he found another way to get me—to get us."

"The sick bastard. You were a kid and he was an adult." Sam's gaze bored into hers. "And you've carried that guilt around all these years?"

"Yes," she whispered.

"You're not responsible for Luther Ethridge's delusions. Don't ever think that."

"I should have told you sooner. But I felt like it was a deep dark secret I needed to keep. I didn't even tell my father the details."

"It never should have happened. *You were not responsible,*" he said, punching out the words. "And stop letting your father make you think otherwise."

She took in his tone, his expression, his reassuring touch. She had felt guilty for so long. And alone, even in the midst of her family. Her father had been furious that she'd rejected Ethridge. Now, miraculously, Sam had helped her sort out reality and guilt.

When she reached for him, he lowered his mouth to hers for a quick, savage kiss that meant more to her than she could ever tell him in words.

As he raised his head, she looked into his eyes. "I need you to make love with me."

"You were just sick. I . . ."

She reversed their positions and gazed down at him. "I need to tell you I love you."

He looked stunned. "I thought I would never hear you say that."

"I've been thinking it, but I've been afraid to say the words out loud. Now I'm afraid not to. I want you to know that I would never betray you. Never. Not with Luther Ethridge or anyone else."

"I know that! I should never have doubted you."

She went on, because she had to finish. "I belong with you. Only you."

"Olivia. Olivia. I think I knew you were the woman meant for me before we ever met."

"It was the same for me. As soon as Colin told me about you, I asked for every scrap of information I could get on you. There wasn't much. When you came to the party, I had to get close to you—even though I had told myself I'd keep my distance."

He made a rough sound. "That night, when I first saw you, it felt like the earth dropped out from under my feet. I'd been intrigued by you. But your pictures didn't do you justice. You are so, so beautiful."

She flushed. "I'm not."

"Of course you are! And so much more. But I didn't want to be in love with Wilson Woodlock's daughter. Then I stopped kidding myself. I knew there was no fighting what I felt for you."

"Yes. Oh, yes." She lowered her mouth for a deep, hot kiss, a kiss that left them both panting.

Coming back for more, she drank from him, trying to tell him how much she needed him, how much she loved him.

"I love you," he said, thrilling her with the words as he gathered her to him, taking and giving, just as she did.

The kiss flared from hot to white hot, igniting a depth of feeling she had only imagined before. With a low growl, he angled his head, his mouth greedy and soothing at the same time as he gathered her to him, urging her body to his.

Finally she understood what it meant to be the werewolf's mate. Powerful and weak at the same time. And she surrendered to that knowledge, because her only hope of survival lay in clinging to this man. And everything that had come before was only preparation for this vivid, golden moment in time—this moment when their lives together really began.

Surrender was sweet. So was conquering.

She shivered as his tongue took possession of her mouth, then felt him tremble in turn as she returned the pleasure.

She knew why the images on the screen had cut him like a dull saw blade. He had made a commitment to her long before she had the courage to do the same. She had been afraid of the ultimate intimacy. Not just giving him her body. But her heart and soul.

Tonight she silently offered him everything she had the power to bestow. "I need you naked," she murmured. "I need to feel your skin against mine. All of you."

"God, yes!" He eased away long enough to tear off the rest of his clothing before wrapping her in his arms, and she sighed as she absorbed the rough feel of his hairy chest against her breasts, his lean hips pressed to hers, his erection nestled in the cradle at the top of her legs.

He lowered his mouth to hers again, nibbling and sipping by turns as his hands stroked up and down her back and buttocks, rocking her against him, increasing their pleasure.

When he pulled back, she reached for him.

"Lie still," he growled, moving his lips against her cheek as he spoke.

She did as he asked. And he kissed her mouth again. Then slid his lips to her chin, her neck, her collarbone, then lower.

He paused at her breasts, stiffening his tongue and flicking it at her nipples, then drawing each in turn into his mouth, wringing low whimpers from her.

She wanted more. And he knew that. He took one pebble-hard tip between his fingers, playing with it as he kissed his way down her body, pausing to dip his tongue into her navel. She was so hot and wanting that when he gently ran his hands up her inner thighs, she arched her hips, begging for more intimate contact.

He looked up and smiled at her.

"Sam. Please."

"You are so beautiful. So ready for me," he murmured, then lowered his head and made an exploratory foray with his tongue, stroking upward, ending by circling her clit.

He had kissed her intimately before. But he had never brought her to climax this way. Now when he slipped two fingers inside her and stroked them in and out, she knew his intentions.

She closed her eyes, focusing on the sensation of his lips and tongue on her, his fingers adding to her pleasure with their erotic rhythm. In seconds, she was helpless to stop her hips from rising and falling in tune with the sweet torture.

She reached down to tangle her fingers in his dark hair. She was close to orgasm, very close. And when he added a sucking pressure on her clit, her movements turned frantic as she strove for release. She came then, in a wave of ecstasy that lifted her up and over the sun, suspended above the earth.

When he felt the aftershocks subside, he withdrew his fingers and lifted his head.

"Sam, Sam," she cried out, holding out her arms.

"Olivia." He slid up and over her body, covering her, kissing her mouth as he plunged his penis inside her. Then he began to move with the same frantic rhythm that had driven her.

He was her mate, and she wanted to give him pleasure, every way she could. She angled her hips so he could drive deep into her, her hands stroked over his back, down to his buttocks, urging him closer. He moved with her—in her—hard and fast. Then he shouted out his satisfaction as his body went rigid and he poured himself into her.

"My love. My only love," he whispered, turning his face to nuzzle her ear.

"Stay with me," she murmured.

"Yes. Straighten your legs."

She did, and he hugged her close, rolling to his side, taking her with him. Still joined to her, he kissed her deeply, as he swept his hands up and down her back in long, luxurious strokes. And she felt the wonderful sensation of his penis hardening inside her again.

"I read some books about sex," she murmured as her hands played with the curve of his buttocks.

"Oh yeah? What did you learn?" he asked, amusement in his voice.

"That most men can't get hard this fast after climaxing."

"A werewolf has special . . . gifts. To please his mate. And himself." He moved his hips, just enough to demonstrate.

She closed her eyes, drifting on the sweet sensations of arousal. Then, as he nibbled at her ear, an erotic but shocking idea made her inner muscles tighten around him.

"Nice," he murmured.

"I thought of something."

"Um?"

"Something that's not in any books I read." She gulped in a breath, then let it out before asking, "Does a werewolf ever come to his mate when he's a wolf?" she whispered.

Sam went very still. Then his Adam's apple bobbed. "How would you feel about that?"

"Turned on."

She felt him grow harder inside her. "You want to do that with me?"

"I want to do everything with you," she answered, her own blood running hotter.

"Up at my ranch. Out in the hills," he said, his voice thick. "Me tracking you. Following your wonderful scent. Catching you."

"When?" she asked in a breathy whisper. He stroked his lips against her cheek. "Not until we get the elixir back." He slid his mouth to hers, found the hardened crests of her breasts with one hand, making her moan as he brought her to climax again.

Finally, exhausted, she slept, more content than she had ever been in her life.

WHEN she woke, she knew instantly that Sam was not in the bed with her. Then, in the darkened room, she saw the glow from the computer screen—and went rigid.

He must have heard her stir. "I'm e-mailing my brother," he said in a low voice.

"Oh."

"I've progressed from hiding my identity to telling him a little about our problems. He's offered to help us. Would you object to that?"

"No," she said instantly. "Because I trust your judgment."

"But you were worried I might be looking at that DVD again."

"Yes," she admitted.

"I might, if I thought it would give me insight into Luther Ethridge. Would that upset you?"

"Yes. But I think I can handle it." As she spoke, she got out of bed, turned on a lamp, and found the clothing she'd discarded. When she'd pulled on her skirt and shirt she crossed to Sam, reached for his hand, and held on tightly.

"How are you?" he asked.

"Good."

Sam swiveled around to study her. "You don't exactly look relaxed. Are you really okay with my hooking up with Ross?"

"Yes." She cleared her throat. Then before she lost her nerve, she said in a rush, "We have to talk to Colin about the DVD. If anyone can figure out how Ethridge pulled off that video, it's him."

He nodded. "But you hate the idea."

"Yes."

25

"MAYBE Colin doesn't need to actually see the DVD," Sam offered.

"The moment you tell him, he'll insist. He'll want to try and figure out the technology. And he can't do that sitting behind a screen, having you describe the action."

Despite the situation, that image made Sam laugh.

"It's not funny," she murmured.

"Actually it's a good reminder that we need to keep our life as normal as possible."

This time, she was the one who laughed. "Normal! A tree hugger werewolf and the daughter of an environmental rapist."

"If you put it that way, I see the problem. But you know what I mean. Like . . . when was the last time you ate?"

"This morning."

"Same here. So let's get some food," he said, glad that he could make the suggestion for both of them instead of mentioning his real concern: her health.

"Okay. I guess I can manage a bowl of lobster bisque."

"You have lobster bisque on tap?"

"No. But I've liked it ever since I was a kid. So I have packs from a gourmet Web site in the freezer."

"Then lobster bisque it is," he said, thinking she'd just jolted him back to the real world Woodlock-style. When he'd been a kid, his favorite food had been a McDonald's hamburger.

While she heated her soup, he thawed a steak in the microwave.

She'd eaten half her soup when Colin walked in. As the brother eyed his cold steak, Sam forced himself not to drape his arm around his plate.

"Raw flesh?" Colin asked.

"Yeah, steak tartare. Like in the best restaurants," he answered. Then, seeing that the blood had drained from Olivia's face, he abruptly shifted the focus from himself.

"I can handle talking to your brother," he said. "You don't even have to be involved."

"I can't just put it off on you," she answered, her voice strained, her eyes haunted.

"What are you talking about?" Colin asked.

"Let's discuss it in private," Sam answered.

The three of them went up to the computer room.

When they had settled on the sofa, Colin closed the door and asked, "So what was on the DVD?"

"A personalized sex show," Sam answered.

"What the hell is that supposed to mean?"

"To be blunt, a woman is lying naked on a bed. Ethridge comes into the bedroom—also naked—fondles her, then screws her."

Colin's features were suffused with tension. "And why do you think he sent that particular video clip to you? He wants you to marvel at his virility?"

"Maybe. But I think he had another motive as well, since the woman on the bed looks almost exactly like Olivia."

Sam watched Colin whirl on his sister, his face flushed and his body rigid. "Did you go to him? Let him fuck you? And then he didn't let you have the Astravor anyway? Is that what this is about?"

"No!"

"I want to see the video," Colin demanded.

"You don't need to," Sam heard himself saying. "Not to verify the woman's identity. Or rather her non-identity. It's not your sister. I can guarantee that."

Colin stood with his hands on his hips as he glared down at Olivia. "She could have done it—for the wrong reasons."

Olivia glared back at Colin. "You're worse than Sam!"

"Why?"

"Because you're supposed to be logical. Use your famous probability method. You can be one hundred percent certain that Ethridge wouldn't have needed to try and capture me in Carmel if I'd been with him. All he'd have to do was offer me the Astravor again."

After several tense seconds, her brother dropped into the computer chair and Olivia continued, "Ethridge wasn't counting on someone like Sam coming along to rescue us. And I think that one purpose of the DVD was to make everyone think he's 'got' me. It worked with you—and you haven't even seen it."

Colin looked abashed. Taking off his glasses, he polished them on his shirttail.

"You're not the only one who jumped to the wrong conclusion," Sam admitted stiffly. "I thought she had been playing mind games with me all along. Then she made me see that the woman wasn't her. I mean, the face is very close to hers. But not the individual body parts."

Colin blew out air. "I'm sorry. I guess you're right. He wanted us to react, and I did."

Sam looked over at Olivia. She was sitting with her lower lip between her teeth. When their eyes met, she said, "It's more than that. I think the home movie represents his fantasy of getting even. Of doing whatever he wants with me. Somehow he put all that on a DVD." She pressed herself close to Sam as she gazed across at her brother. "I'd rather be dead than let that man touch me. But I could only make that decision for myself. Refusing Ethridge has meant condemning the rest of my family. In the end, I have always felt I was going to have to give in."

As Sam clasped his mate more firmly, he was thinking that he understood this whole mess better. But not completely. "I've been getting this chronicle in bits and pieces. I think this might be a good time for the whole saga, whatever it is," he said quietly, but with steel in his voice.

OLIVIA kept her focus on her brother. "Colin?" she murmured.

He glared at her. "If you're asking me to give you permission, you're not going to get it."

"Sam has let us in on his deep dark family secret."

"Not because he wanted to," her brother shot back. "Because a wolf came bounding into the backyard—and we all knew it was him."

"He heard me scream," Olivia reminded him. "And he risked everything to save me. So I think we need to tell him that the elixir does more than simply keep us alive."

"We only tell a husband or wife after we're married," Colin said. "Maybe never."

"Are you saying you haven't told Brice everything?" Olivia asked carefully.

His expression revealed that he had.

"Well, Sam and I are as 'married' as you and Brice. We can go down to the courthouse and get a license, if that will make you feel better. But we're having a crisis now."

The silence in the room lengthened. Finally Colin gave her a small nod.

She answered with a grateful look, yet she couldn't help glancing anxiously at the door, imagining her father suddenly swooping down with fire in his eyes.

He didn't magically appear, and she knew that he was too sick now to be making decisions for the family.

Moving so she could look Sam in the eye, she cleared her throat. "I told you about the family illness. I told you that we have a genetic problem. An illness that's peculiar to us. If we don't take the elixir, starting in our mid-twenties, we gradually—and painfully—die. But that's only part of the truth." She paused for a gulp of air, then went on.

"In your family, you and your brothers have the ability to change your form. In our family, the elixir gives us special powers, too. Powers we hide from the world—just as you do."

She watched Sam's eyes widen as he took that in. "Shape-shifting? Are you telling me that you're like me?"

She had locked his hand in a death grip and didn't seem to be able to let go.

"No. It would have been a lot easier to tell you that!" She sighed. "Just to make things confusing, we have a grab bag of psychic powers. It's not exactly the same with each of us. Just like the illness doesn't run the same course in each of us. My father could see into the future. Which, as you can imagine, was a big help in building the Woodlock financial empire. That's why he's so frustrated now. And it's why the business has been in trouble since Ethridge stole the Astravor."

"Yeah, I can imagine," Sam muttered. "But if what you're telling me is true, how did your father let Ethridge steal the stuff? I'd like to know exactly how he let that happen."

"Liquor impaired his psychic abilities," Colin snapped. "And he was arrogant enough to think the security here was good enough." He clenched his teeth before relaxing his jaw and going on. "Then he was in an automobile accident and ended up in intensive care with a concussion. Probably Ethridge was responsible because while we were all at the hospital, he broke into the house and took the elixir."

"So it wasn't Dr. Regario whose car crashed. It was your father's car," Sam clarified.

"Yes."

"And suddenly Ethridge had all of you by the short hairs."

"Yes. Without the elixir, our psychic talents faded away, along with our health," Colin added.

"What talents, exactly?"

"My uncle who died could move objects without touching them. It was more of a party trick than anything else," Colin answered.

"Did you get some doses of the elixir?" Sam asked.

"Yes." Colin laughed. "I could . . . um . . . put my hand through walls. Maybe if I'd gotten more of the stuff, I could have walked through them. But I think I'm not destined to be the most powerful member of the family when it comes to psychic talents. I think it's because my brain is too straightforward and logical for the supernatural. Uncle Darwin was more down to earth. Or maybe that's the wrong way to put it. When he was angry, he could summon a thunderstorm. Or a hailstorm, if he was really pissed off. I think he hasn't completely lost that power. I think he's still affecting the weather around here, maybe because he's the oldest, and he got the most elixir."

Sam nodded again, taking it in.

Olivia was still holding on to him tightly, still desperately needing the contact. "So that's our big secret," she murmured. "To be guarded at all costs. Is it freaking you out?"

He pulled her close to his side. "It might, if I didn't have my own strange family history."

Clearing his throat, he asked, "I guess you don't know what you can do because you never got the elixir."

"Right," she said in a small voice.

Colin jumped back into the conversation. "But once every few generations, one of us comes along who has multiple talents. We're hoping it's Olivia."

"Which is why I have to go with you when you get the Astravor," she said. "I may need to take a dose of the stuff, then use whatever power it gives me to fight Ethridge."

"If it's such a big secret, how does he know what the Astravor really does?"

"Because, like I told you, young people in his family often married into our family." She sighed. "It was a big honor, which is part of the reason he wanted me. Like his cousin who married Uncle Randolph."

"What happened to her?"

"She's in seclusion somewhere," Olivia murmured. "Under Luther's protection."

"Did they have any children?"

"No. It's always worked out that only one line is fertile. There aren't many of us. Maybe because the Astravor can only support a limited number of people."

She watched Sam take it all in, seeing wheels turning in his head. He might not have the benefit of a college education, but he was a very intelligent man. "Let's get back to you," he suggested. "What you're not saying is that going in to steal the Astravor and trying to use it all in one fell swoop could be dangerous, right? Because you're going to use psychic abilities that you haven't tested and you don't know how to control?"

SAM saw a host of emotions flicker on Olivia's features. She was so used to playing fast and loose with the truth that this interview must be pretty difficult for her. But finally she looked at him and sighed. "Yes," she admitted.

"And I get to put you in that position?"

"I'm sorry. Yes."

He had known the answer, but he couldn't hold back his reaction. "Shit!"

"I don't like it any better than you do," she insisted, tightening her grip on his hand.

"I have another question. Why did you need me? Ethridge was going to give you the stuff anyway—right? You could let him do it, then zap him."

"I don't know for sure that I can zap him, as you put it. Also, he understands that allowing me to develop my powers would be dangerous to him. I think he was only planning to let me have a little of the elixir, just enough to keep me alive. Not enough for me to work any . . . psychic tricks."

"Giving her only a small amount could ultimately kill her any-way," Colin added.

"Nice guy," Sam muttered. After a few moments of thought, he came to a decision. "I'm going to take Ross up on his offer."

"Who is Ross?" Colin asked.

"My brother. It looks like you're going to get two wolves for the price of one."

"You approve?" Colin asked his sister.

"If we're going up against Ethridge, I think we need all the help we can get," she answered. "We know he's ready to use any dirty trick he can think of. We should have the same privileges."

Sam could see that Colin didn't like the idea of inviting another werewolf into the sheep pen. Probably there were a lot of things he didn't like. Maybe he'd wanted the special powers that turned up every generation or so. He'd lost the lottery, and he was forced to root for his sister. That couldn't be easy for him. So—was he on Olivia's side only until they got the elixir? Then was he going to stab her in the back? Sam didn't want to think so, but he wasn't going to relax his guard, either.

"My brother Ross and I have been in touch by e-mail," he said. "But I haven't seen him since I left home eight years ago." He looked at Olivia. "You need to get some rest."

"I'm fine."

"No, you're not. You need to do everything you can to guard your health."

He watched her stop fighting him, stop struggling with her own pride. "Okay. I'll go lie down."

"I'll be up in a minute," he told her, walking her to the door. "I want to finish that steak."

When she had left the room, Colin said, "You're not really hungry, are you?"

"No. We need to talk about that DVD."

"Yes."

"Olivia hates the idea of your seeing it. And I certainly understand why. I hope you'll be gentlemanly enough to skip the nasty part. The beginning gives you the best view of the woman. I want you to tell me if the image is computer-generated. Or did he find some woman who looks like Olivia's twin?"

"I think I can do that."

"I'll meet you in the computer room."

Sam hurried up the steps and ducked into his bedroom. Quickly he removed the DVD, put it in the case, then carried it down the hall. Colin was waiting for him.

He sat down, slid the disk into the slot, and began to play it. When the image of the woman flashed on the screen, he swore, then swore again as a naked Ethridge stepped into the picture. "That bastard. I understand why he enjoyed sending this to you."

"Yes," Sam said through his teeth.

"Well, now that I've talked to you, I think I can keep my cool. I told Brice I would be busy. You go get some rest. I'll get back to you when I know something."

Sam scuffed his shoe against the rug. "You were sick. How are you feeling?"

"I'm in remission. Or whatever you call it. Keep your fingers crossed."

"I will." His gaze bored into the back of Colin's neck. "What about Olivia?"

Her brother turned to him. "There is no way to predict the course of this damn disease. Which is why we need to get that elixir."

Sam fought not to clench his teeth. "Okay. If I'm sleeping when you finish with the DVD, wake me up."

When he came back to his room, Olivia was in his bed under the covers, dressed in a T-shirt, but he could tell from the rhythm of her breathing that she was awake.

She lay very still while he pulled off his shirt and pants and climbed into bed. When he was beside her, she found his hand and knit her fingers with his, then whispered, "There weren't many times when I defied my father. But I felt a terrible urgency about not hooking up with Ethridge." In the darkness her breath hitched. "I think now that I was waiting for you."

His heart swelled. "I'm thankful you did," he answered, gathering her to him.

She snuggled down beside him, her body warming his.

He was relieved when he felt her drift into sleep. But he lay awake, staring into the darkness. He had found his mate. But nothing with her was ever going to be simple. Before he'd met her, he had thought of her as a spoiled rich princess. Then he'd found out she had problems he hadn't even dreamed of. When he'd come to live with her, he'd realized the difference in their backgrounds was going to make things difficult. Tonight she had let him in on the big family secret, and everything had shifted under his feet again.

Suddenly, it was hard to catch his breath. Olivia had called him because she needed him. In some ways she was dependent on him now. She needed the elixir to live. But when she got it, would their relationship change in ways he couldn't handle?

He just wanted everything to be normal. Well, as normal as a werewolf's life could be. But he was pretty sure he'd have to be prepared for the unexpected again.

Finally, he slept. Some time later, a sharp rap at the door made his eyes snap open. Glancing at the bedside clock, he saw that it was six in the morning.

Quickly he slipped from under the covers and reached for the sweatpants he'd draped over the back of a chair. When his head swung toward Olivia, he saw that her eyes were open.

"Go back to sleep," he said, then strode toward the door.

A rumpled-looking Colin was standing in the hall, a mixture of triumph and disgust on his face.

26

SAM studied Colin's expression. "I guess you figured it out," he said.

"I think so."

"And you don't like what you found."

"Exactly," Colin answered, but now he was looking past Sam and into the room.

Turning, Sam watched Olivia climb out of bed. She was wearing shorts under her T-shirt, the outfit telling him that she'd been prepared all along to sit in on any upcoming information sessions—and he'd be wasting his breath by objecting.

He expected her to follow him down the hall. When she didn't, he felt his chest tighten. He knew she had hidden an oxygen tank in the dressing room. He knew she was sneaking breaths from it. But he wasn't going to say anything until she did.

Her color looked better when she joined him in the computer room.

Colin strode to the sideboard and filled his mug from a quarter-empty glass coffeepot.

The idea of someone dumping that much caffeine into his body made Sam wince. But he made no comment as Colin took a sip and hunched toward the computer screen.

"Did you look at the video?" Olivia demanded.

He took off his glasses and wiped them on his shirttail, then put them back on his face. "For about five seconds. I know it's not you."

"Is it a real person—or a computer projection?" Sam asked.

"Real."

Olivia made a low, anguished sound. "How do you know?"

"Ethridge isn't shooting *The Lord of the Rings*. His capacity for special effects is limited."

"If she's a real person, tell me who she is," Olivia demanded.

To Sam's surprise, Colin answered. "With ninety-nine percent probability, a woman named Barbara Andres."

"Wait—didn't you tell us she was dead?" Sam asked.

Colin glanced at Olivia, then back to Sam. "That's what I thought. I told you two women who knew him disappeared. Apparently, with the first one, he was practicing his hunting skills—and his ability to foil the police. He killed Alana Holtz. I think he kidnapped Barbara and held her captive. She was a graduate student at UCSD with her own apartment in San Diego. Her parents died and left her enough money to live on while she went to school. No siblings. And it looks like she didn't have many social contacts. She spent a lot of time in chat rooms, which is where he picked her up. So she wouldn't be missed by too many people. She disappeared five months ago."

"He's had her for that long?" Olivia breathed. "Oh Lord, I wonder if she's still sane."

"I hope so," Sam muttered. "What about her apartment?"

"The rent's still being paid," Colin answered. "For all I know, Ethridge has the refrigerator stocked with groceries and then has them cleaned out again."

Colin worked the mouse, and a picture flashed onto the screen. It was a woman with delicate features, large green eyes, and golden brown hair.

"That's her?" Sam asked, studying her face. She was Olivia's type, but that was as far as the resemblance went. "What did he do to change her face?"

"Well, let's look at the records of the Tomaso Clinic in Tijuana." Colin brought up another file. It was a medical form, showing a photograph of the woman named Barbara Andres, only now she was listed just by a number—597.

Colin scrolled through the file. It detailed what had been done to her, complete with before and after pictures.

Sam stared at the transformation, then at Olivia. Her jaw had literally dropped as she looked at the woman who had gone from family resemblance to twin.

"I wouldn't believe it unless I'd seen it," Sam muttered. "How did you get these pictures?"

"I hacked my way into the clinic records," Colin said.

"But how did you get to the clinic in the first place?" Sam asked.

"Digging! And some luck. I've been sifting through every scrap of information I had on Ethridge—then looked for more. Four hours ago, I found a record of a prescription for pain medication for Luther Ethridge, written by a Doctor Hernando Tomaso and filled in Tijuana. Then I asked myself, what was Ethridge doing down there? Buying recreational drugs? Or something else? When I found out that Dr. Tomaso was a plastic surgeon, I figured that perhaps he'd done some work on Ethridge."

"Did he?"

"Oh yeah. Ethridge has had his eyelids lifted. His chin liposuctioned. His penis lengthened."

"How the hell do you do that?" Sam asked.

"The top of the shaft is apparently inside the body. It can be dropped down."

Sam winced. "Sounds painful."

"I wouldn't want to do it. But with him, image is important. I've just given you the highlights."

"How do we get from Ethridge's plastic surgery to Barbara?" Sam asked.

"Well, from Ethridge's correspondence with Tomaso, I assume he's got something on the doctor. And he used the leverage to get his co-operation to operate on Barbara Andres."

"All that's interesting," Olivia snapped. "But we need to get that woman out of there as soon as possible! I told Sam I felt like a rape victim. She *is* one."

"Let's look at the house plans again," Sam suggested. "And see if we can figure out where she is."

The conversation was interrupted by a loud voice from the doorway. "What the hell are you all talking about? What is this, some kind of conspiracy?" They all jerked around to see Wilson Woodlock, dressed in a rumpled silk robe, glaring at them.

Sam had never seen him looking so sick. His complexion was gray and moist. His eyes were red-rimmed, and he was swaying on his feet. In the past few days, his condition had obviously gone downhill quickly. The implications for Olivia made his throat tighten. Then he told himself that she was younger and stronger, and she hadn't put herself on a course of powerful self-medication.

Woodlock raised his hand. The sick old man was holding a gun. It swung unsteadily toward Sam.

God, another crazy Woodlock with a weapon. *I guess this is what they do when they've had magic powers, and now they can't use them.*

Colin's voice cut through the sudden silence in the room. "Put that down," he said, speaking slowly and deliberately. When he took a step forward, the weapon swung toward him.

"Stay where you are, you worthless piece of shit."

The color rose in Colin's face, but he stopped in his tracks.

"That's right," Woodlock said. He propped his shoulder against the doorjamb, apparently too sick to stand on his own.

"Please, Dad. You're not well. You need to lie down," Olivia whispered.

Her father answered by pointing the gun toward her, and Sam's heart leaped into his throat.

Woodlock was breathing heavily. "I'm tired of this farce. I want Morgan out of here. I want you to do your duty." He dragged in air and let it out in a rush. "Can't you see I'm going to die? And it's your fault. Call Ethridge. Tell him that you'll give yourself to him."

"She already has," Sam said, making his voice low and angry, hoping he sounded convincing, because he wanted this to end without any violence—to Woodlock or anyone else in the room.

The old man focused on him with narrowed eyes. "If you expect me to believe that, you've got the brains of a jackass. We both know she hates Ethridge. She said she'd never marry him. That's why we're in deep shit."

Sam didn't bother to point out that Olivia wasn't the one who had let the elixir slip from her grasp. Instead, he said in a grating voice, "But little Miss Goody Goody decided you were right after all. So she went to him. I can show you."

"How?"

"Ethridge sent us a tape to prove it," Sam answered, knowing he had everyone's full attention. "That's why we're up so early."

"You're lying," Woodlock gasped.

"I wish I were. Have a look for yourself."

Wondering if he was going to end up with a bullet in his back, Sam crossed to the computer and brought up the directory.

"Don't," Olivia shouted, still trying to protect the damn image on the DVD.

But it was too late. Sam switched to the DVD drive and began to play the video that Ethridge had sent the day before.

Woodlock's eyes riveted to the screen as he saw a woman he thought was his daughter lying naked on the bed. Then Ethridge entered the scene. As he sat down beside the woman and began to touch her, tears glistened again in Olivia's eyes.

"He doesn't have to see that," she moaned. The old man spared her a glance, then swung back to the screen. As he focused on the man-woman action, Sam moved slowly and cautiously behind him.

"Get down," he shouted to the group as he wrested the weapon away from the sick man. Thurston darted in from the doorway and helped subdue his employer.

Woodlock sobbed in frustration, then turned to the security man, screaming. "Do your duty. Arrest them! Arrest them!"

Sam held his breath, wondering what would happen next.

"Sorry, sir, I can't do that."

"You work for me," Woodlock sobbed out.

"I work for the family. And I have to take your best interests to heart."

Olivia had stepped in front of the computer screen. Still blocking the image, she turned off the picture, then joined Colin at her father's side.

"I'd love to tell the bastard how we just used the DVD he sent me," Sam growled. "Maybe I'll get a chance."

WILSON lay in bed, listening to the voices in the hall. The door was open, and he could hear his daughter talking to Jefferies.

"How is he?" she asked.

"He's calmed down," the butler said.

"Is he sedated?"

"He was. He's due for another dose."

"Don't give it to him yet."

"Why?"

"I need to talk to him."

Jefferies stuck his head into the room, then disappeared again. "I wouldn't recommend it. He's very unpredictable at the moment."

Wilson wanted to bellow, "You're fired." But he didn't waste the energy. This was his chance to escape. If he could just get out of the damn bed.

Olivia was blathering again. "I understand. But I need to speak to him about something important."

Yes, send her in. I'll give her some important advice.

"He may not be able to help you."

"Jefferies, you've been with us a long time."

"Yes."

"So you know how vital it is that we get the elixir back."

Yeah. He knows it keeps them alive. He doesn't know it gives them magic powers. Nobody except people in the family knows about the powers.

"If you need to speak to your father about it, I'll come in with you."

Wilson waited, every muscle in his body tensing.

"No. I have to be alone with him."

When Olivia stepped into the room without Jefferies, Wilson let out the breath he was holding.

He lay with his eyes closed, a light blanket over him. He could feel the perspiration making his cotton pajamas stick to his body.

He longed to surge off the bed and give his daughter the shock of her life. He found he couldn't muster the energy. But when she bent over him, he was able to shoot out a hand and grasp her wrist.

She gasped, and he opened his eyes in satisfaction. He could still frighten his little girl. And he could still demand obedience.

"Why aren't you with Luther?"

She looked him in the eye and said, "I will be soon."

"That's a lie."

"Believe what you want."

"You're a . . . disobedient daughter," he said, his voice hoarse.

"No. I'm trying to save your life," she corrected him.

"You're . . . selfish. Go back to Ethridge." He pulled himself up, glaring at her, then felt confused for a moment before his thoughts cleared. "What . . . are you doing here?" he asked, hating the way the question came out as a quaver.

But he kept his fingers clamped on her arm, knowing he was inflicting pain. "Dad, please listen. Ethridge wants me. But he doesn't want you or Colin. You're a danger to him. Do you really think he'll give the Astravor to anyone besides me? Do you really think he'll give me enough to tap into my psychic abilities?"

He felt a moment of uncertainty. Then his lips firmed. "You can . . . force him."

"Tell me how! Tell me how to use the Astravor. How to use it to fight him."

His mind drifted back to his young manhood. "You don't have much control at first. You have to wait for it to develop."

"I'm only going to get one chance," she whispered. "Help me. Tell me how. What did you do when you used it?"

Memories crowded in on him. Good memories. He had been powerful, and his lips curled into a smile.

"You feel like a god," he murmured. "It's wonderful. Better than any drug." He looked at her urgently. "But it's not free. It comes with responsibility."

"I know that," she whispered.

"You know nothing! You must learn to control it. That takes practice. It doesn't work all at once."

"Yes, but if you had to learn fast—how would you do it?" she asked.

He had used up all his energy. His lids drifted closed.

He felt her hand grasping his shoulder, shaking him. "Dad, please. Tell me what talents I can expect?"

He mustered the resources to look at her again. He had been angry with her. But he felt pride, too. "You may have . . . strong powers. . . . Nobody has had . . . the great power in generations."

"Maybe it's gone. Maybe that's why."

He was speaking to her, but to himself also. "Get it back for us. One way or another, get it back. Let it into your mind," he whispered. "Let it fill you. Then take control. You have to . . . fight the fear."

"How?"

He felt himself falling, falling into darkness. And he knew that he didn't have much time left.

27

SAM paced back and forth in the family room, trying not to keep his gaze fixed on Olivia. It was only thirty-six hours after Woodlock had come at them with murder in his eyes. Now, he was locked in his bedroom, like his brother. A very visible sign that things were going rapidly downhill at the mansion.

But the two elder Woodlock men weren't Sam's primary concern. Fear such as he had never known in his life threatened to steal his sanity. The possibility of Olivia ending up like her father or her uncle clawed at his gut.

He tried to focus on his plans for going into Ethridge's house. One thing he knew; they sure as hell better do it right. But he kept losing his train of thought because he was listening for the sound of the doorbell as he paced back and forth. Even so, when he heard the chimes, he literally jumped a few inches off the carpet.

Olivia stood and moved quickly to his side. He took her hand as much to steady himself as to reassure her.

Striding into the front hall, he threw the door open and stared at the tall, dark-haired man standing under the front balcony's overhang. Suddenly he felt like a kid again, the kid who had fled Baltimore because it was the only way out of the mess he was in.

Ross Marshall stepped forward, set down his duffel bag in the hall, and caught him in a bear hug.

"Sam," he said in a gritty voice. "I'll have to get used to calling you Sam."

The black sheep of the Marshall family clung to his brother for a long moment. His flesh and blood. He had thought he would never see this man again. But as soon as Ross learned what was happening in California, he'd started making arrangements to get on a plane and come out here to help.

Stepping back, Ross looked him up and down. "You've grown up," he said, his voice edged with emotion.

Sam swallowed around the lump in his throat. "I hope so."

Ross's gaze swung to Olivia. "And you've found . . . "

"A mate," she answered for him. "We just have to get through this rough patch before we can settle down."

Ross nodded.

"Thank you for coming to help us," she said.

"I'm glad to be here. I was afraid I'd never see . . . Sam again. Just tell me what you need."

"Thank you," she answered, holding out her arms. Ross gave her a hug, then stepped back.

"My brother, Colin, and his partner, Brice, are anxious to meet you," she said. "But I'm sure you want some private time with Sam."

As she walked upstairs, Sam stiffened. He wasn't sure if he wanted to be alone with another adult male werewolf, given the stories he'd heard, the father-son brawls he'd witnessed, and his own violent tendencies.

To buy himself some time, he said, "Let's go up to the computer room."

Ross followed him up the stairs and down the hall.

After Sam had closed the door, his brother lowered himself into an easy chair; Sam was too restless to sit.

Ross raised his head. "The first thing I want you to know is that you're in charge. I'll make suggestions, if I have something to contribute, but you call the shots."

Sam answered with a tight nod.

"Getting along takes a little practice. But it's worth it. The way Adam and Grant and I handle it, the guy on his own turf is the leader," he said, restating his previous assurance.

Sam thought about it for a few seconds and decided the idea had merit. "Okay," he said. "Makes sense."

"So what do you need?" Ross asked.

"Is breaking and entering against your code of ethics?"

Ross laughed. "Are you trying to start off this reunion by getting me into a moral argument?"

"Maybe I am," Sam admitted.

"Well, the way most PIs operate, breaking and entering is part of the job description. And other stuff I won't brag about in public. But I'm ready to do what it takes to bring down Luther Ethridge. Or, to put it another way, it's against my code of ethics for the bastard to withhold the medicine my brother's mate needs to live. And holding an innocent woman captive against her will is also against my code of ethics. So I think we're on the same page."

"Good," Sam answered. He had longed to see Ross, but he hoped they could take the relationship in easy steps. "Let me get the others," he said.

"Right," Ross answered, probably because he understood the need to take the personal stuff slowly.

Sam walked back into the hall where he found Olivia looking anxiously in his direction. "Is everything okay?" she asked.

"Yes. Go get the rest of the troops."

She hurried to Colin's bedroom.

Five minutes later, Colin, Brice, Olivia, Sam, Ross, and Thurston were assembled in the computer room. Olivia made the introductions, and Ross shook hands with the others.

Sam had filled him in on everyone's background—and who knew who their special talents. They were still keeping that secret in the family. In fact, while Thurston and Jefferies knew the elixir was imperative to the family's health, they didn't know it gave the Woodlocks special abilities.

When they had all taken a seat, Ross turned to Sam. "Why don't you tell us what you have planned."

Sam fought the impulse to clasp his hands together in his lap. He wasn't used to sharing his private business—or used to public speaking. He had made a virtue of being self-sufficient. But he'd learned enough about Luther Ethridge to know that he couldn't go up against the man without help. And he was counting on the assembled group to give him any assistance they could.

After clearing his throat, he began. "We have two missions to accomplish at the Ethridge castle: to rescue Barbara Andres and to take back the elixir that Luther Ethridge is holding hostage. I think the best way would be to do both at once."

"What kind of time frame are you looking at?" Ross asked.

"As soon as possible," Olivia answered, then looked embarrassed to have jumped in.

He turned his head toward her. "I know you're in a hurry," he said, keeping his voice even so that he wouldn't broadcast his fears to everyone in the room. "But we have to proceed carefully. We're dealing with a man who is absolutely ruthless. A man who won't hesitate to kill Barbara—or us—if he thinks he's cornered. So let me outline what I have in mind."

28

A cloud drifted across the gibbous moon, and the night turned inky black. In silence, two wolves trotted up the lower slopes of the mountain.

Despite the dangerous circumstances, this was a strange and marvelous occasion, Sam thought. He'd never dreamed of having his brother with him out here among the scrubby Southern California vegetation and rocky landscape. But Ross was right beside him, and he had to fight to keep his vision from swimming when he thought about the implications.

This might be the first time two werewolves had worked together in all the years since their misguided ancestor had asked for powers no man should possess.

The thought that they might learn to cooperate on a long-term basis made his throat tighten. But first, he had to live through the next hour. So for now, it was enough that they hunted together.

Sam looked up at the solid walls towering above them like manmade cliffs. Ethridge had constructed a fortress, a medieval castle designed to repel an invading army. With modern additions, like the video cameras scanning the immediate area.

Sam pawed the ground, and they both took a step back, well out of what they assumed was the range of the cameras. If Ethridge was watching he would see only two wolves. But there was no point in attracting his interest.

Since the meeting three days ago, they'd kept watch on the road to his property, and he hadn't stepped out of his castle. So he was certainly in there, protected by the booby traps Colin had uncovered.

The camera scanned the grounds. The only alarms appeared to be on the doors and windows, and Sam already had a plan to deal with them and the other security devices.

Beside him Ross made a low sound, and Sam turned his head. They had talked before they had changed from man to wolf. Now they could only convey the simplest ideas.

They had both seen a light go on in the tower room high above them, but there was no way to know if Ross had picked up the detail that Sam saw: the grillwork that he'd noted in the video. No other window had the same protection. So, unless Ethridge had moved his captive for some reason, that was the room in which they'd seen Barbara Andres on the DVD. Sam switched his gaze back to the sheer walls. They were built of rough stones which offered some opportunity for foot and handholds. At least for a man.

He wanted to say, "What do you think? Should we do it tonight?" But he couldn't speak. He could only take his brother's nod for silent agreement with his thoughts.

They were obviously operating on the same wavelength because they both turned and started down the hill to where Olivia was supposed to be waiting in an SUV screened by brush.

Only she wasn't inside the vehicle. She was standing in the darkness, looking up the hill.

He had to repress a growl. He'd told her specifically to stay out of sight until they gave the all clear. But she hadn't followed orders, which was typical. Although he wanted to give her a lecture, he wouldn't do that. Not when he had watched her stumble on the stairs. Or when he had seen her secretly going into her closet to take a hit from her oxygen tank.

Ross disappeared into the bushes.

Sam lingered for a moment, his gaze sweeping over Olivia, assessing her fitness for the evening's activity, before he joined his brother.

Ross was already pulling on his shirt when Sam made the transformation from wolf to man.

"What do you think?" he asked.

"There's no wind. I'd say this is as good a night as any. And we have surprise on our side," Ross answered.

"I hope," Sam muttered. He knew that no matter how carefully they planned, this was the most dangerous job he had ever attempted. He was sure they were going to encounter some surprises. He just prayed they weren't fatal surprises. When they were both dressed in black sweats, they returned to Olivia, who was wearing a similar outfit.

"You didn't spot any extra security?" she asked anxiously.

"No. Only what we were expecting."

"Then you're going ahead with Plan A?"

Sam sighed. "Yes," he confirmed, then gave her a hard look. "You're not going to try anything foolish on your own, right? Because this operation only works if the timing is right."

"I know that," she answered coolly. Yet he saw from the rigid lines of her profile that she wasn't as calm as she sounded. Worse, she was as likely to make her own decisions as follow orders.

She was her own woman, and always would be, werewolf's mate or not.

But she was getting sicker faster than anyone had anticipated. She needed the elixir.

Turning toward the SUV, Sam helped Ross get out the backpacks with the equipment they needed, plus the long roll of canvas Colin had provided.

Then he got one more thing from the back of the SUV.

Olivia eyed the small oxygen tank. "What's that for?"

"For you."

"I don't need it."

"Let's not waste our breath arguing. We're going to climb up a hill that will have us all puffing. You haven't got the strength we have."

She nodded fractionally, and they started up the hill, moving more slowly than before.

Sam carried the oxygen, then made Olivia stop and take several breaths of it.

They paused four more times until they reached the spot where they'd stopped before; then they stepped out of camera range again. At least it was out of range, if Colin was right. And his judgment was critical to their success.

Sam set down his pack. Then he got out the pieces of tent poles he'd brought along and snapped them together to make uprights. While Ross and Olivia attached the six-and-a-half-foot high canvas to the uprights, Sam stretched out on the ground, making his profile as low as possible as he hammered in spikes with hollow tops, then set the poles into the holders.

The side of the canvas facing them was blank. On the other side was a computer-generated landscape that mimicked the scene from the windows—based on Colin's computer projection of what the view should be.

After making sure the canvas screen was stable, Sam looked at Ross and Olivia. She nodded tightly.

Behind the screen of the canvas, he retrieved the rope from his pack. During the past two days, he had practiced this maneuver, using several abandoned warehouses as a substitute for Ethridge's tower. He'd kept at it until he could hit the high window on the first try.

Now that he was faced with the real thing, he found that it was harder to work on a slope rather than a level area. Judging the range, he swung the rope, and held his breath as it sailed upward into the air—toward the window. The grappling hook attached to the end hit the window grill with a clank. But the connectors failed to catch, and the rope fell toward the ground.

LUTHER Ethridge sat up in bed. He'd been restless all evening. Before settling down, he'd thumbed through several decorating magazines, collecting ideas for when he redid the living room. Now something outside had awakened him.

Without turning on the light, he got out of bed and looked out the back window. The moon was behind a cloud, and the view toward the city looked as peaceful as ever. Had some animal come tramping across his property? He knew there were deer in the hills and smaller animals.

He saw nothing, but the unsettled feeling wouldn't go away. So he pulled on his pants and a shirt, thinking he could go down to the kitchen. He'd laid in a nice supply of lobster bisque. He served it to his guest almost every evening, because he liked to watch her eating it. But he'd developed a taste for it himself. He could get a packet out of the freezer, heat it in the microwave, and eat it while he took a look at the view from the TV monitor screens in the den.

*   *   *

SAM held back a curse.

He and the others stared up at the window. When a face appeared, he caught his breath.

It took a frantic second for him to register that it wasn't Ethridge. It was the woman, and she looked out over the landscape.

They couldn't shout to her. They couldn't tell her they had come to spring her.

All Sam could do was stand there with his heart pounding as she tried to figure out what had hit the grill over the window. Finally she stepped away.

His jaw tight, Sam tried again. This time, the hook caught. Almost immediately, the woman was back and staring down.

Sam wished he could see the expression on her face. But they were too far away to judge her emotions.

"She's not going to warn him," Ross whispered. "If she's smart, she'll get the idea."

Sam hoped it was true, as he watched his brother step around the canvas and sprint to the wall.

LUTHER tore the top off the plastic bag, then poured the contents into one of the large, wide-mouthed mugs that he liked to use.

Selecting some imported French crackers to go with the soup, he placed the small meal on a tray and carried it across the hall. After setting the tray on the Chinese inlaid end table, he opened the walnut doors that covered the surveillance monitors.

Sometimes he didn't look at the tapes for days at a time. Now he felt the compulsion to make sure all was right with his world.

Settling on the leather couch, he took a sip of soup, then activated the six screens. They showed various views around the interior of the castle and outside. But because there were twelve security cameras, the view varied unless he chose to focus on one scene.

As he looked up from another sip of soup, he saw a flash of movement on the upper right hand screen.

A little jolt sizzled along his nerve endings. Quickly he brought back the scene. It was a view of the rear of the castle, but as he leaned forward and stared at the screen, all he could see was the peaceful view of the valley below his wall.

For a long moment, his gaze stayed riveted to the screen, searching for something that shouldn't be there.

Then, because he saw nothing, he pressed the replay button and went back about forty minutes. Watching the picture closely, he ran the tape forward again.

When another shadow flickered on the monitor, he stopped and ran the tape slowly forward, then froze the frame.

What he saw made goose bumps pop up on his arms. Two large gray animals. German shepherds. Or wolves. Like his man at the Reese house had been babbling about. And Irene. Now they had appeared on his property.

He tried and failed to draw in a deep breath.

What the hell was going on?

He started the tape again, expecting them to approach the house. Instead they both took a step back, out of camera range, and he was left with a heavy feeling in his chest.

For a long time he sat paralyzed, his gaze riveted to the screen. Then he began slowly searching the tape again.

SAM looked across the fifteen feet that now separated him from Ross. His brother hugged the side of the stone wall where the camera couldn't pick him up. At least, that's what they were praying was true. If Ethridge figured someone was going in to rescue his prisoner, Ross would be left dangling from a rope, twisting in the wind.

But that wasn't the most dangerous job. Sam and Olivia were the ones going in the front door—then down to the vault. But the timing had to work with split-second precision.

Sam wanted to make sure his brother would be all right. But he needed to be in position for the next phase of the operation. So he and Olivia moved back down the hill, then circled around the house.

They had studied the security system. Sam was sure that all the elements on the stairs and in the vault area would be armed. But he knew from experience that few people kept the front door alarm on when they were in the house—since remembering to turn it off when opening the door was a major inconvenience. Was Ethridge paranoid enough to have the alarm on while he was in the house? Sam expected to find out pretty quickly.

BARBARA'S heart was thumping so hard that she thought it might bang its way through the wall of her chest. As she looked down from the tower room, she saw a man climbing up a rope. What should she do now? Was this some elaborate test that Ethridge was pulling on her? He'd come up with nasty surprises before. And he could do it again.

She glanced over her shoulder at the signal bell near the bed. Almost against her will, she took several steps toward the bed. She could use the bell to call her captor. If he had arranged this surprise and she didn't alert him, he would be angry, and he would hurt her.

On the other hand, what if what she had been praying for had happened? What if against all odds, someone had figured out she was here, and they had come to rescue her?

But then, why hadn't they simply called the police?

Her mind spun in so many different directions that she wavered on her feet.

Should she press the bell? Go to the window? What?

A man's head appeared over the sill. And she gasped.

He looked at her. Then he silently pulled something from the pack on his back. It was a sign with letters printed from a computer—in large type:

I AM A FRIEND.
I WILL GET YOU OUT OF HERE.

It could still be a trick. She couldn't take the sign at face value.

In terror, she watched as he got out a socket wrench and began to work on what must be the fastenings of the grillwork. Backing away, she took a step toward the buzzer.

29

A sudden vibration made Sam jump. Then he realized it was the silent buzzer on his phone. Looking at the number on the screen, he saw Ross was signaling him to get ready.

He glanced at Olivia and caught the look of stark terror in her eyes. "Ross?" she mouthed.

He gave her a tight nod. He'd thought about pulling a fast one on her. Letting her think she was going in with him, then giving her knockout gas or something at the last minute.

He wanted her outside. Out of danger. He could go in, get the damn magic potion and bring it to her.

Ross already had spirited the woman named Barbara Andres out of the tower room. And the two of them were down the hill by the car. So no matter how this came out, his brother was out of danger. Ross had volunteered for this job. But he had a wife and family back home in Maryland, and Sam was glad he was almost out of the action.

He would keep Andres safe until they had the elixir and were in the clear.

Inside the house, the phone rang. And Sam hoped to hell the call wasn't someone selling home equity loans.

LUTHER picked up on the first ring.

"Hello?"

"Is this Luther Ethridge?"

"Yes. How did you get my number?"

"I found it hidden in Irene Speller's room."

"Who the hell is this?" Luther demanded.

"Eric Thurston. As you probably know, I work in the Woodlock household."

"What is this, some kind of trick?" Luther snapped.

"No. I'm applying for a job."

"As what?"

"I want to take over where Irene left off. She did a lousy job of informing you of what's going on at the Woodlock household. I can do better. And I can prove it."

"I'm listening," Luther said cautiously. This could be a trick, but he wasn't going to hang up without trying to find out what the man really wanted.

"The Woodlocks are planning a raid on your stronghold."

"I'm ready for them."

"Not ready for what they have in mind. Sending that DVD to Morgan was a mistake. He and Colin figured out that you're holding a woman named Barbara Andres in your tower room. They're coming there tonight to get her out."

"I don't believe you," he shouted. Yet this man knew some inconvenient facts. Like his prisoner's name.

"It may already be too late. Check your security camera."

Luther looked up at the screen that would show Barbara's room. At present, it held a view of the front hall, and he quickly switched the picture. The room was empty. Or maybe this was some kind of trick. Maybe Barbara was hiding.

"Is the grillwork gone from the window?" Thurston asked.

Luther's gaze shot to the window. "Fuck!"

Slamming down the phone, he dashed for the stairs, taking them two at a time as he headed for the tower room.

SAM strained his ears. From inside the house he heard a loud curse, followed by feet pounding up the stairs.

As soon as the racing footsteps were out of earshot, Sam sprinted forward, a set of picks in his hand. The camera was still on, of course. But presumably Ethridge was too busy to be watching it. And when he stepped into the tower bedroom, he'd have a nasty surprise. Barbara would be gone, and a booby trap would go off in his face.

At least, Sam was praying there were no screwups in the tower.

By hacking into the security company computer, Colin had gotten the specifications for the front door lock, and Sam had practiced working on a similar model, just as he'd practiced with the rope. He was good at this part of his profession, and he had the lock open in under a minute. Olivia was right in back of him.

When she tried to rush through the opening, he blocked her way.

"Wait," he whispered. Before crossing the threshold, he took the Sig from his pack and held it in a two-handed grip, then stepped inside. The front hall was empty. But, as he looked into the room to the right, he could see six monitor screens glowing in the darkness.

That was a little worrisome. Apparently, even before the phone call, Ethridge had suspected something was up. Or maybe that's how he relaxed when he couldn't sleep. The mug of something on the end table confirmed the latter theory.

Sam took in the details in an instant, then ushered Olivia into the hall. They both knew where to find the stairs to the vault. And they both knew the security precautions.

LUTHER reached the top of the tower landing, two flights above the main floor, and skidded to a stop. The door to Barbara's room was still closed. But Thurston—if it was Thurston—had said someone had come in through the window. Luther's first impulse was to unlock the door and rush into the room. But now that he was here, he was thinking that might not be such a wonderful idea.

What if someone had taken his prisoner and left a little surprise in the room? Or what if Thurston was lying? But for what reason?

Luther paced back and forth on the landing, trying to figure out what to do.

Usually he referred to the woman inside as Olivia. Tonight he used her real name. "Barbara?" he called out. "Barbara, are you in there?"

There was no answer.

"When I come in, I'm going to punish you," he growled, thinking of the things he was going to do to her. She didn't have long to live anyway. Soon he would have the real Olivia. Then he wouldn't need Barbara.

SAM watched Olivia hoist her own weapon, then got out the oil-sensitive paper he'd used at her house. After determining which numbers on the keypad had been pushed on a regular basis, he attached the computer and asked for the correct sequence of numbers to push.

Time seemed to stand still as he waited for the computer to finish its calculation. He had to force himself not to tap his foot as each red number appeared in the horizontal bar on the screen.

When the sequence of numbers was finally displayed, he felt goose bumps rise on his skin. The OFF button was number one. Then four digits followed—1027. It was a birthday. Not Ethridge's but Olivia's.

Her face had turned pale as she stared at the numbers. Sam took a deep breath, then pressed the five keys. The red light winked off and the green came on. But the security system at the top of the stairs wasn't the only thing they had to worry about.

Ethridge had a special surprise for anyone who got this far and didn't punch in an additional code two steps from the bottom—a hail of bullets to the midsection.

The mechanism was triggered by a photoelectric cell, not by pressure on the stair treads. Which meant that Sam could lie on the steps and slide down. At least he hoped that was going to work—because he couldn't punch in the combination until he performed the decoding procedure.

"Stay back until I give you the all clear," he whispered to Olivia. She gripped his arm, and he turned back to her. "Are you okay?"

"Yes. Be careful."

He nodded, grabbed his pack, and gave it a push. It slid down the steps and bounced at the bottom. So was that because of its small size? Or because of the low profile? He guessed he'd find out in another minute.

Fear made Olivia's heart pound as she watched Sam working his way toward the bottom of the steps, his body as flat as he could get it against the stairs. She was feeling light-headed from terror, but she knew that wasn't the only reason. Another attack was coming on. She could sense its steely fingers closing around her throat.

She needed to lie down. She needed to catch her breath. But there was no time for that.

Hold it together. Just hold it together, she chanted inside her head.

But what if she couldn't hold out until she reached the Astravor? What if she fainted?

When her legs threatened to give out, she sat down on the floor at the top of the steps and breathed from the oxygen tank Sam had set there. Her eyes never left him as he slithered down the steps. He had said this would work. And she had desperately wanted to believe him when they had been making their plans. But what if something went wrong now?

What if Ethridge came charging down the stairs to the first floor?

If he did, she'd shoot him, she thought, even as most of her attention was focused on Sam.

Oh God, let him be all right. Let him be all right.

It seemed to take forever, but he finally made it to the bottom of the steps, where the rug softened his landing.

Taking the computer from his pack, he pressed close to the wall as he reached up the stairs again to attach the cables to the second keypad. Then he began the procedure that he'd used before.

As she watched, her vision blurred, and she took another hit of oxygen.

Again, centuries passed while Sam got the combination. Finally, he looked up at her, and gave the thumbs-up. Still, they had agreed that she wouldn't walk down the stairs, just in case there was some additional secret to disarming the guns. She looked at the oxygen tank. She didn't want Sam to think she was in trouble, but the time for saving face was over. So she clasped the small tank in one hand and tucked her gun into her belt, then did what he had, sprawled on the steps and pushed herself downward. It wasn't elegant, but she had gravity on her side. And if it kept her from getting shot, that was fine with her.

She reached the bottom of the stairs, and it felt like she had descended into an old mine tunnel. It was cold down here. And the walls were hewn from solid rock. But what looked like a priceless Oriental rug underfoot helped ward off the chill.

"Over to the wall," Sam ordered, and they both pressed their shoulders against the chilly stone. She wanted to sit down on the rug, but she forced herself to keep standing.

There was one more door to unlock. The vault. Sam got out a different piece of equipment, something that would help him pinpoint the combination as he began to slowly turn the knob.

Olivia turned toward the stairs, gun in hand, guarding their back. It was almost over. Just a few more moments, and they would be inside.

Sam turned the knob, stopping on some number she couldn't see. Then he gradually turned it the other way. On the fourth turn, the combination clicked.

But at the same time, an alarm bell began to ring in their ears, and a hissing noise told her that some kind of gas was flooding the room.

* * *

UP in the tower, Luther was still trying to figure out what to do when he heard the alarm. He had been thinking that going into Barbara's room was a bad idea. Now he knew it was.

"Son of a bitch," he growled. Someone was down in the vault. Someone who had come up with an elaborate plan to trick him—and gotten past the machine gun emplacement.

But they had wasted their energy. Because he'd trapped them like rats in a flooded sewer pipe.

He bolted down two flights of steps to the second level of the house, grabbed an Uzi from one of the wall cases, pulled on a gas mask, and pounded down the stairs to the first floor.

OLIVIA saw Sam's look of horror as the gas flooded the room outside the vault. They had gotten all this way and finally run into a trap that Colin hadn't figured out.

Suddenly, she was very glad she'd brought the oxygen tank. Lifting it to her nose, she took a hit. Then handed it to Sam, who did the same.

His eyes fierce, he pulled the door a few inches open.

Olivia slipped inside. Sam followed, then slammed the barrier closed behind them.

The door had cut off the gas, and she dared to take a gulp of air. But now, as she looked around, she saw that they were closed inside a small metal room. And as she listened in dread, she heard the dial spin on the heavy door.

Luther was out there, undoubtedly wearing a gas mask. And he had trapped them in the vault.

She turned to Sam and terror leaped inside her chest as she saw him sag against the wall.

"Sam!"

"The gas," he wheezed.

She had breathed some, too, and her head felt muzzy. But she knew that chemicals affected him more strongly than they would a normal man. To her dismay, Sam slowly slid down the wall until he was lying limply on the floor.

30

SETTING down the gun, Olivia knelt beside Sam. He was breathing, and his pulse felt strong. But he was unresponsive when she called his name. When she dug her fingers into his arm, the reaction was the same.

The oxygen tank lay beside him. She gave him a whiff, and he made a groaning sound. But that was his only response.

"Sam, wake up," she ordered, shaking him, desperation making her movements sharp and rough. He had gotten her down here. And she needed him beside her, but she couldn't wake him.

She dragged in a deep breath, then imagined the walls closing in around her and the air thickening. All at once, a frightening thought wormed its way into her brain.

The sensation of the air turning viscous wasn't her imagination. They were in an unventilated vault. At least she thought so. And eventually they would suffocate.

Her head jerked up, and she made a quick inspection of the room. When she saw a camera perched near the top of the high wall, she struggled to hold back a moan.

A camera! Ethridge was watching them. He didn't have to take a chance on getting shot. All he had to do was wait for them to use up the air in here.

The camera was too high for her to reach. Turning her back to the device, she grabbed the oxygen tank and checked the gauge. It was less than half full, and they would certainly need it later. With a shaky hand, she made sure the valve was off.

Could Sam hear her? She wanted to explain that she was going to get the elixir. But she didn't know if Ethridge could eavesdrop if she spoke.

She was on her own, she realized with a sick feeling in her chest. In a way, she had understood that all along. But she had counted on Sam's moral support.

Now she had no choice but to fulfill her destiny, whatever that would be.

First she gave Sam one more hit of oxygen. Then she leaned down and kissed his cheek.

"I love you," she whispered. Then she looked at the camera and said it louder. "I love him. I belong to him—heart and soul. No matter what you do to us, we belong to each other. And, in case you don't know it, you brought us together."

After taking a little more oxygen, she propped the tank against Sam's chest in case he woke up and needed it, then she pushed herself to a standing position.

She was light-headed now. Shaking on her feet. Squaring her shoulders, she struggled to remain erect as she walked toward the box that sat on the ornate table.

It felt like the camera was boring into the back of her head. With a harsh sound in her throat, she fought to put it out of her mind. She had to focus on the task at hand. And she couldn't let Luther Ethridge interfere.

Before Sam had walked into her life, she'd felt doomed. He had given her hope that she could command her own destiny.

Yet now that she was here, she still feared the ultimate test.

Her father had warned her to go slowly with the elixir. But she had no time left. No time at all.

Lifting the lid of the box, she felt her throat constrict as she stared into the blood-red liquid shimmering inside like something alive. It could be poison. Or the wine of life. Or, she thought with a shudder, this might not even be the real thing. She had never seen the elixir. Ethridge might have secreted it somewhere else and set out this stuff as a decoy to lure her into a trap.

Lord, what if that were true?

It didn't matter. She had to try. How long should she stay in contact with it? Maybe someone who'd never had it before and who was sick should start slowly. Or maybe not. On a deep breath, she plunged her fingers into the viscous fluid.

Immediately, she felt a flow of energy into her body. The sickness vanished as though someone had lifted a heavy, wet cloak from her shoulders, and she realized for the first time how ill she had been—for months.

Suddenly, she was well, and she started to cry out in triumph. She had done it. She had gotten to the elixir and cured herself. But the jubilation was short-lived. In the next moment, her hand turned to ice. Hot ice that burned her flesh all the way to the bone. Then her muscles went rigid, and she toppled to the floor as her mind spun out of her control. Out of her body. Out of the universe, flashing across a dark field of stars. She had left the earth far behind. Left this plane of existence. And she knew with terrible certainty that there was no way to find her way back.

She tried to scream, but no sound came to her lips. She tried to breathe, but she had left her physical form too far behind. She had plunged her fingers into the elixir of life, but she was going to die because maybe she had taken too much, and now she had no idea how to control her reaction to the magic substance.

Time had no meaning. It seemed that centuries of agony flashed past in mere seconds. Olivia struggled to hold herself together. Yet she could sense her essence spreading thin, turning as insubstantial as vapor, molecule by molecule.

She would drift away into nothingness. But at least the pain would stop. Then, from far away she became aware of a voice. Someone was calling her name.

"Olivia, come back to me. *Olivia.*"

It was Sam. The man she loved. Her mate. Calling out to her. But she couldn't respond.

Then something crushed her fingers. Flesh and bone. A hand. Sam's hand.

"Olivia. Don't you dare leave me, Olivia! We haven't come this far for you to cop out."

The anger and the agony in his voice sent a shock wave through her mind. A shock wave that rippled and clanged inside her head.

She felt the pain reverberate through her body. It helped to center her being. Helped her feel the cold floor of the vault under her hips and shoulders. But not her head. Because it was cradled in Sam's lap.

And somehow she fought her way back—toward the sound of his voice, toward the warmth of his flesh clasping hers. Toward her need to be with him—and his with her.

Slowly, slowly she felt her mind taking possession of her body again. Then she managed to draw a breath into her lungs, and knew Sam was giving her pure oxygen.

When her eyes blinked open, she saw him leaning over, staring down at her, his face drawn and anxious

"Thank God," he whispered. "How are you?"

"I don't know." She tried to push herself up, but he kept a gentle arm across her chest, keeping her head pillowed in his lap. Turning her head, she saw his gun was in his other hand.

"Rest. Don't use up air trying to explain where you went."

So he knew she had left her body. She gave a small nod.

"Talk about that later." He was blocking the camera with his body. Now he lowered his mouth to her ear and spoke in a whisper. "Bastard's out there. We have to assume he's listening."

"Yes," she mouthed. Then asked, "Why didn't he rush in here?"

"Coward."

She nodded, not wanting to use up their life's breath by talking. But there were things she needed to know.

"Call Ross?"

"Tried. Phone won't work from here."

She didn't waste her breath on a curse. "How do we get out of this?" she whispered.

He was silent for a long moment. "Did the elixir give you . . . special powers?"

"I . . . don't know."

They stared at each other.

"Tell him you'll cooperate," Sam mouthed.

"Never."

"Trick him."

"Too late, I think."

She knew he was scrambling for a plan. She tried to do the same. But something was distracting her. Voices in her head. Was she going crazy, like her uncle?"

Again, fear leaped inside her. Then pain stabbed through her skull.

"What?" Sam asked urgently. "Are you sick?"

"Let me listen," she whispered.

"To what?" he asked.

"Voices."

Sam answered with a curse.

"Real voices," she mouthed and pressed a finger to her lips.

*   *   *

ROSS looked at his watch for the hundredth time. "It's been over forty-five minutes. We should have heard from them." His phone was in his hand. He was waiting for Sam's call. But all he could hear was the insects buzzing around him, and he was starting to think that something had gone terribly wrong in Luther Ethridge's house.

Barbara distracted him with a question. "They couldn't get to the elixir?"

"How do you know about that?" he asked sharply.

"Ethridge used to talk to me about it. After he . . . after he gave me that damn gas." Her features grew fierce, and Ross put a hand on her arm.

"I know you've been through a horrible experience. More than most people could survive."

"I owe you a lot for getting me out of there. But I don't want your pity."

"Good. Because we don't have time for pity. I'm frankly thankful that you're not a basket case."

"I'm strong. Or I'd be dead."

"I think that's right."

Her hands clenched. "I want to kill the bastard. He . . ." Her words stopped abruptly, and her expression changed. It looked like she was listening to someone speaking. Only nobody else was here. "I know," she whispered. "It's not your fault. I never thought it was."

Ross stared at her, wondering if she'd finally flipped out. "What are you talking about?"

She stood without moving for several seconds, then raised her eyes to him. "Olivia. She's talking to me."

He looked around, confused. "Where? I don't see her. Are you saying they got away? How do you know?"

"She's talking in my head. She said she's sorry Ethridge held me captive. I didn't ever think it was her fault. I felt sorry for her. Because Luther wanted her. I was just a substitute." She stopped speaking again, and sucked in a sharp breath. "Oh, Lord . . ."

He gripped her arm. "What's wrong? Where is she?"

"In the vault. They're running out of air. And Ethridge is waiting outside."

Ross made a low, angry sound. "Tell her I'm coming."

"I'm coming with you!"

He gave her a long look. Was she in any shape to help them? Or was she going to be a loose cannon? He didn't know. But the determination in her eyes told him he'd have to tie her up to keep her away—and he didn't have time for that.

"BASTARDS. Fucking bastards."

Luther stared at the television monitor. Morgan had been unconscious. Then Olivia had gone for the elixir. It had hurt her. He'd heard her gasp, seen her face contort before she slipped to the floor. He'd waited a few minutes to make sure it was safe.

And just as he'd been about to go in, Morgan sat up, snatched up his weapon, and turned to face the door. He was still holding the gun. Now they were both awake again, thanks to that oxygen tank they had brought along. Otherwise the action would be all over.

"Fuck!" He wanted to fling open the door and charge in there. But it was too dangerous. They had a gun, and he could get hurt.

"ROSS and Barbara are coming," Olivia mouthed.

"Shit," Sam growled, then remembered to lower his voice. "Tell them to go back."

"I did. They won't."

"I want them safe!"

"I know."

"We have to get out of here." He looked from her to the door, then spoke in a whisper, "Colin said you might have multiple powers. You heard Ross and Barbara. Can you do anything else?"

"I don't know! My father said I couldn't do it all at once," she said, sounding scared.

He squeezed her hand in his, trying to give her his strength. "I can't unlock that door. But maybe you can. Like your uncle who could move objects with his mind."

"I can't just do it. Not without practice."

Leaning closer, he began talking rapidly in her ear.

*   *   *

LUTHER kept his eyes glued on the monitor. They were still conscious, but everything would change soon enough. All he had to do was wait for the air to fill with carbon dioxide.

Olivia was lying on the floor. Morgan was crouched over her, blocking his view of her face. They were talking. Even with the volume turned up, he couldn't hear what they were saying.

Making plans. Well, it wouldn't do them any good. He had them trapped. It was only a matter of time before they ran out of air. Even with that oxygen tank. It couldn't last forever.

Olivia sat up, and he tensed. She scooted back, leaning against the wall while Morgan gave her more oxygen. Then he took a hit himself. Good. Great. They'd just use up their supply faster.

The fucker helped her stand up. Now what? Were they planning something? What the hell could they do from inside the vault?

She swayed on her feet, then braced her shoulders against the wall, her face turned toward the door. And then something strange happened.

Morgan moved away from her and started taking off his clothing. Jesus, what was he going to do? Make love to her for the last time?

Luther reared back, letting out a bark of laughter.

In the next second, he felt his blood run cold, when Morgan, naked as a jaybird, started moving his arms with little flourishes, like he was going to perform an important magic ceremony. That got Luther's attention, all right. As he listened, the guy started saying some weird chant. Loud. Nonsense syllables, as far as Luther could tell.

IT had been a long time since Sam had felt so defenseless—standing naked in a vault with a TV camera focused on him. But he would do what he had to for Olivia. For both of them.

He saw her from the corner of his eye. She stood tall and straight, her vision focused on something he couldn't see. She had started discovering her powers. She'd been able to speak to Barbara. And now she had to try something else. Under terrible pressure, with pitifully little time to perfect any of her new skills, she was going to try and open the lock on the vault door. But Ethridge was out there, watching everything they were doing.

So he was going to pull Ethridge's attention away from Olivia by putting on a very dynamic show.

They had both taken another whiff of oxygen, but his lungs were already burning again. The air in the little room was getting soupy. They needed the damn door open.

Nude, exposed to Ethridge's gaze, he chanted the ancient words of transformation. This wasn't the way he wanted to give Olivia a first-hand view of the change. But he had no choice. So he kept speaking.

"Taranis, Epona, Cerridwen," he repeated through parched lips. *"Ga. Feart. Cleas. Duais. Aithriocht. Go gcumhdai is dtreorai na deithe thu."*

He had always said the words at deliberate speed. Not too quickly—or too slowly. Now he dragged out the syllables, dragged out the process, moving his hands in strange, meaningless gestures as he spoke, drawing attention to himself.

He kept his eyes away from the camera, but he would bet he had Ethridge's full attention. The guy had to wonder what the hell he was doing.

The first threads of transformation wound themselves around him. He wanted to hurry the process—the measured pace exaggerated the pain—but he forced himself to do it slowly, forced himself to give Olivia the chance she needed.

OLIVIA stood quietly on the other side of the room. She had made contact with Barbara. She had told her to stay away. But she knew that Ross and Ethridge's former captive were driving around the mountain—to the front of the house. She knew what Barbara wanted to do.

One part of her mind kept tabs on them—kept in contact with Barbara. But that was only a side issue. Most of her attention was focused on the door lock. She had watched Sam rely on burglar's skills to open the door. He had brought along tools to do it. She had no tools. She must employ the newfound powers of her mind. Untried powers.

She didn't really understand what process she was using. She only knew that failure was not an option. She had to free Sam because he had come here to save her life and ended up trapped like a rat in a hole. Free herself, so the love that had bloomed between them could grow and mature. And free her family from the curse of Luther Ethridge.

All those obligations weighed her down, even as they gave her the strength she needed to reach with her mind toward the door, toward the locking mechanism. Sam had told her how it worked. He had given her the combination. But she had to make the tumblers move. In the right sequence.

She thought of Brice's homemade magic ceremonies. She thought of his steadfast belief in magic. Even when the Woodlocks had lost their powers, Brice had kept the faith with his totems and his ceremonies. He had called on ancient gods. And his rituals had helped keep her hope alive, even when she had mocked him because she was afraid to let herself believe.

Locked in Ethridge's vault, she took her own leap of faith, because she had to rely on more than her own untested powers.

The legend said that long ago a powerful goddess had given the elixir to her family. As a teenager, she had tried to figure out who that might be. It could be Isis. Or Venus. Gaia. Frigga. Uma. She had studied all of them and others, looking for clues. Now she called their names in turn. Asking for their help. Desperate words spoken only in her mind.

From the corner of her eye, she could see her mate. See him changing with agonizing slowness. She knew the pain must be terrible. But he was doing what he had to do.

And so was she.

LUTHER couldn't take his eyes off the man standing isolated and naked—doing something strange.

The man.

No, not a man.

Luther's pulse pounded in his ears while he watched in horrified disbelief. He saw Sam Morgan's jaw elongate, his teeth sharpen, his body jerk as limbs and muscles transformed themselves into a different shape, a shape that no man should ever claim for his own.

"God, no. No."

Earlier this evening, he had seen two wolves outside, staring at his house. And here, before his very eyes, was a wolf dragging itself into existence. Gray hair formed along Morgan's flanks, covering his body in a thick, silver-tipped pelt. The color of his eyes glowed yellow.

And as Luther stared at the animal, at last he understood what had happened in that storage room in Carmel.

A gurgling sound rose in his throat. It changed to a scream when

MOON SWEPT

the door to the vault burst open as though a bomb had gone off inside. But there was no bomb. He could see through the open door that the wolf and Olivia were unhurt.

"Jesus, no."

All at once, he understood what had happened. While he'd been focused on the man-wolf, Olivia had been using her power. The power she had gotten from the elixir. Late at night, Irene had heard the family talking about the Astravor. She'd told him that the powers wouldn't develop right away, even if she'd had no idea of what the term "power" meant.

Well, she had been wrong about that. And wrong about Morgan.

The wolf leaped through the door like an image in a 3-D horror movie. But this was no movie. It was real.

With a scream, Luther scrambled for the machine gun he'd laid on the floor. He would kill the wolf. And he would kill Olivia, too. She was dangerous. How had he ever thought he could control her?

What happened next seemed to take place in slow motion.

He raised the weapon, but a deep, menacing growl from behind made him stop.

He whirled to see the other wolf at the top of the steps. The two of them had him trapped.

Then Olivia's voice rang out from behind the new wolf.

"I'm up here. Not in the vault."

Two wolves. Two Olivias. Dressed in sweatpants and T-shirts— neither wearing Barbara's robe.

His hand closed convulsively on the trigger, sending a spray of bullets into the steps.

Olivia was behind him. The other Olivia.

"I'm here."

"No, here."

He raised the gun toward the stairs again. But the woman and the wolf had disappeared around the edge of the doorway.

"No. You're Barbara," he shouted.

"Wrong. I'm Barbara. In back of you," the woman in the vault called out.

"I opened the door for her, from the outside," the Olivia at the top of the stairs shouted. "With my mind."

His brain felt like it was spinning inside his head as he struggled to hold on to his sanity. He whirled again, intending to fire.

"Don't bother," the Olivia from the vault called to him, her voice cold and calm. "It's frozen."

Frantically, he pulled the trigger, but now it wouldn't move.

"No! No!" he screamed as the closer wolf leaped. Luther swung the gun like a club, and the wolf yelped. But still it landed heavily against his body, knocking him to the ground, jaws closing over his throat. Ripping through flesh and bone.

He tried to scream again, but the sound was only a gurgle of blood in his ruined throat.

He felt a terrible weight press down on his chest. Not the wolf— some massive outside force. And he knew Olivia was using her psychic power to aid the animal.

The last thing he saw was the image of two women standing over him. Olivia. And the twin he had made.

Which one was Olivia? He didn't know.

His lips moved. But no sound came out.

He wanted them to tell him which was which. But it was already too late. The light faded away. Faded to nothing.

31

THE wolf lifted his head, his mouth dripping with blood. Unable to face the women standing in back of him, he raced up the stairs and almost ran into the other wolf—Ross.

Together they turned the corner where a pile of clothing was waiting. Two pairs of sweatpants. Two T-shirts. Shoes.

Quickly, they both sped through the transformation. Once he had returned to human form, Sam picked up a silk pillow from the couch and wiped the blood from his mouth.

As he pulled on the sweatpants, he flashed his brother an angry look. "You said I was running the show. And I told you to stay away from the house after you got Barbara."

"I couldn't leave you to face Ethridge alone. If you want to make something of that, go ahead," Ross shot back.

For a charged moment, Sam thought they might leap on each other, the way he'd seen Ross and his father go at it.

Ross lowered his arms to his sides and bowed his head. "Hit me if it makes you feel better."

His brother's posture and his words brought Sam back to sanity. "No," he whispered. "What the hell am I thinking?"

"Knee-jerk wolf reaction," Ross answered. "I know I promised to stay out of it. But Olivia told Barbara what was happening. I wasn't in on that mental conversation, but when she told me you were trapped, I had to come back. And Barbara insisted on coming along to help."

"So she was working with Olivia just then?"

"Right. And I decided a wolf would add to the shock value."

"Um . . . what the hell did Barbara think about your changing in front of her?"

"I didn't do it in front of her." His brother gave Sam a direct look. "I tried to get Barbara to back off. But she wouldn't budge. She wanted to get Ethridge, at any cost. So I told her we had trained dogs working with us and not to be afraid of them. Then I left her at the top of the steps, ducked away, and changed. It was the best I could think of at the time. And I'm pretty sure Olivia told her the dogs were okay."

Sam nodded, thinking about continuing the conversation but knowing he was stalling. Instead of talking to Ross, he had to face Olivia.

When he reached the top of the stairs, she was at the bottom landing, looking upward, her expression riddled with anxiety.

They met in the middle of the staircase, and he was helpless to do anything but clasp her to him. His voice shook as he said, "You saw me kill."

She raised her head and met his troubled gaze. "You didn't do it alone. I stamped down on his lungs—with my mind."

He stared at her in shock. "You did?"

She gave him a fierce look. "I did. In the heat of the moment, I couldn't control my savage impulses any better than you could."

"I'm sorry," he murmured. "I know that's hard to deal with."

"It would be with anyone else. But not with Luther Ethridge. I know all the things he did to Barbara. I know what he was planning to do. He was going to kill Barbara on video, so my family would think I was dead."

"Christ!"

"Let me finish so I don't have to keep thinking about it. It gets worse. All along, he was going to hold me captive and let everyone else in my family die. He was only going to let me have a little of the elixir. But he was going to force me to have his children—who would be tied to me and tied to him."

"How do you know all that?"

"From his twisted mind. All in a rush of sick thoughts when the door burst open. He'd figured out he couldn't tame me, so he'd changed his plans. He was going to kill both of us."

Sam looked over her shoulder, seeing the woman who was Olivia's pseudo-twin sitting on the floor with her knees drawn up and her head resting on them. "What about Barbara and the wolves?"

Olivia kept her own voice low as she answered. "Well, I know Ross told her a story about trained dogs. But I decided it would be better if she just forgot about the whole animal thing. She just remembers you and me facing Ethridge—and her yelling down the steps."

"You have the power to alter her thoughts?" he asked carefully.

She dragged in a breath and let it out. "Not exactly. The wolves frightened her. I was able to push them to the status of 'bad dream.'"

"How much can you do?"

"I don't know yet." She stepped back so she could meet his gaze. "Will you think I'm crazy if I tell you I felt the energy of half a dozen ancient goddesses flowing through me?"

"Not if that's what happened."

"Maybe it did. Or maybe I made it up. I don't honestly know."

He was aware of Ross helping Barbara to her feet, but he stayed beside Olivia as she went back into the vault to where the box of Astravor sat.

He watched her pull out a small knife that looked like it was part of the side of the container. Quickly she opened the lid, then cut her finger, letting some of her blood drip into the red liquid shimmering inside.

"What are you doing?" he asked in a hoarse voice, as the red drops mingled with the liquid in the box.

"Renewing the Astravor. Colin told me how to do it. I didn't have time before, but I have to do it now."

"Yes," he managed. The ceremony had made his throat constrict.

After closing the lid and replacing the knife, she picked up the box and cradled it tenderly in her arms.

"I have to get this back to my family," she said in a voice that was heavy with emotion yet at the same time filled with a strength he didn't recognize.

He had walked through fire to save his mate. The woman he loved. And now he wasn't sure he knew her anymore.

"We still have things to do," she said.

He should have been the one to point that out. But she had taken the lead.

Upstairs, she set the Astravor on a side table and used his cell phone to call home and tell Colin that "the mission was a success."

"Thank God," he answered.

They kept the conversation short. When Olivia clicked off, Sam looked at Ross, who obviously wanted to say something.

"What?" he asked.

"We have to get rid of evidence."

"Yes," Olivia answered. "Tell us what to do."

"Start with fingerprints."

OLIVIA, Sam, and Ross retraced the path from the front door to the vault. After they had wiped away their presence and removed the silk pillow with Ethridge's blood, they joined Barbara in the tower room, where they did their best to remove the traces of her life there.

When a car pulled up in front, they all tensed.

"Who the hell is that?" Sam growled.

The door opened, and Thurston got out.

"What are you doing here?" Sam asked.

"I figured you could use some help about now." The security man swallowed. "And I'd like to be in on the end of this since Ethridge had a spy right under my nose."

"I understand," Olivia answered.

Thurston gave her a grateful look, then asked, "What about Irene's body?"

"She's in a well around back," Barbara answered.

"I don't want Ethridge's body there, too," Ross said.

As they all stood looking at the dead man lying on the small rug at the bottom of the stairs, Olivia said, "It's better if he just disappears."

"You stabbed him?" Barbara asked.

"Something like that," she murmured.

"We'll get rid of him," Ross said. "And let it be a missing person case."

Sam gave a sardonic laugh. "Convenient of him to bleed onto his own carpet. All we have to do is package him up and carry him away."

After rolling up Ethridge and wrapping the parcel in plastic, the three men carried it to the trunk of Ross's rental car.

When he'd closed the trunk, Ross gestured toward the hills. "Before I caught the plane out here, I did some research on local wildlife, which includes mountain lions. I'll take him up there, then meet you back at the Woodlock house."

"I'll go with you," Thurston said.

"And I will, too," Barbara added.

"You should get some rest," Ross told her.

"No. I need to go." She looked at the plastic-wrapped bundle. "I met Ethridge in a chat room. He was flattering and exciting. But he was scary, too. I should have run in the other direction."

"You couldn't know his twisted mind," Olivia told her. "He was very good at hiding his true self. Thank God you're free of him now."

"Thanks to you. But I need closure now."

"Yes," Olivia agreed, marveling at how coldly she could regard Luther Ethridge. But he had come close to consigning everyone in her family to a horrible death. Only Sam and Ross had prevented the ultimate disaster.

"We'll meet you back at the house," Ross said.

"And you'll stay with us as long as you want," Olivia told Barbara. "Let us help you get back on your feet."

"As long as I don't have to see another packet of lobster bisque."

"Why?"

"It's your favorite. He made me eat a lot of it."

Olivia swore under her breath. She would have continued the conversation, but Ross broke in.

"Let's finish this up," he clipped out, and she knew he was right.

Barbara climbed into the SUV. Thurston climbed into his own car.

Olivia watched Ross hesitate for a moment, then walk toward his brother.

Sam held out his arms, and they embraced.

"Sorry I got bent out of shape," Sam murmured.

"I understand. Believe me, I do."

"And I know I couldn't have done this without you. Thank you," he said, his voice gritty.

"I was glad I could be here, glad you contacted me," Ross answered.

Olivia stepped up and held out her arms, and Ross hugged her. "Thank you," she murmured. "Thank you so much."

"Family sticks together," he said, obviously trying to damp down his emotions.

He clasped her tighter, then stepped back. "We'll see you later."

Olivia stood beside Sam as the two cars drove away.

Now she was alone with her mate, and she knew that the two of them had to talk about what had happened and about the future. But she found she didn't know how to start such an important conversation, so she drove home with him, feeling the pressure of the silence between them.

It was a relief to step into the front hall where Colin and Brice were waiting.

"Dad's bad," her brother said. "I'd better give him the Astravor."

"Yes. Then you take a dose."

"No. Uncle D first, then me," Colin answered. She would have gone up with her brother, but she caught the look on Sam's face.

"You go on up. Sam and I need to talk about something."

Still, there was one more thing she had to do. Jefferies was hovering in the hall, and she stopped for a minute to receive his congratulations and personally thank him for everything he had done.

Then she turned to Sam. "Let's go out on the patio."

He nodded silently.

They stepped outside, and she carefully closed the door.

Finally she made herself ask the question that had been locked in her throat during the ride home. "Are you staying?"

ALL the way home, Sam had been dreading what they might say to each other. Now her question took him by surprise. Guilt made him ask, "Why do you think I wouldn't?"

"Since the vault . . . you've been . . . different."

"I'm sorry," he answered automatically, sorry that she had sensed the conflicts seething inside him. He didn't know exactly what he was feeling. And he didn't want to talk about it yet. Unfortunately, she was asking for answers from him.

Before he could speak, she did it for him. "You're having trouble dealing with a mate who . . . has changed . . ." she said.

"I'm sorry," he said again, feeling helpless and angry and—yes—frightened all at once.

"Don't be sorry. You saved my life."

He made a snorting sound. "I got you in there so that you could do the rest." He kept his gaze fixed on her, then forced himself to state the obvious. "You have amazing powers. You haven't even tapped into them all, I think."

"I wouldn't call them amazing."

"How would you put it?"

"That I have a heavy responsibility to carry."

He could only nod.

She kept her unwavering gaze fixed on him. "And you're worried about a couple of things. Like whether I still need you, since the crisis is over. And whether the powers I acquired will get in the way of our relationship."

"Are you reading my mind?" he asked sharply.

"No. I've been reading the expression on your face. I'm not walking around dipping into people's minds. It happened with Barbara because we were so tuned to each other, and we were in the middle of a crisis. Ethridge had done his best to turn her into Olivia Woodlock. That made her very open to me."

"Yeah, but what about with him?"

"That was a five billion megawatt blast of pure hatred hitting me between the eyes. Spewing out all the evil thoughts he'd ever had about me and my family."

"I felt it, too," he admitted. "But for me, it wasn't in words."

"You were lucky."

He raked a shaky hand through his hair, hearing the roughness in his voice as he spoke. "It's a little unnerving, being with a woman who can peek into your mind if she wants to."

"I know." She looked up at him. "I would never eavesdrop on you. Unless we wanted it. Or . . . in an emergency."

"I guess I'll have to take your word for that."

She stretched her arm toward him, then let it fall back. "We both did what we had to," she whispered.

"And you're not the same woman you were before you took the Astravor," he said, knowing it sounded like an accusation.

"I'm still trying to figure out who I am," she said in a soft voice.

"And how I fit into your life now?" he asked bluntly. The pressure to say things that had been haunting him for weeks finally broke through his reluctance to speak frankly. "As a matter of fact, I never felt comfortable with the Woodlock family."

"Because we're so dysfunctional?"

He laughed. "No. That doesn't change the basic fact that you come from privilege. I come from . . . nothing. You went to the right schools. Took the right lessons while I was scraping together enough money to buy lunch in the school cafeteria."

"You think I care about that?" she asked.

"*I* care about it."

She wedged her hands on her hips. "So you can't handle a mate with a social position that makes you uncomfortable. And you can't handle a mate who has psychic powers that are greater than your own. Is that it?"

Her bluntness struck right at the core of the problem.

"I'm who I am," he muttered.

She kept her relentless focus on him. "I'd like an answer to my question—about us."

Sam ached to take her in his arms the way he had that first time out here on the patio. He ached to bring his mouth down on hers and feel the magic between them kindle again.

But his own inner doubts kept his feet rooted to the ground. "I can't answer you. Not yet."

When he didn't say anything more, she filled the silence. "Okay. I guess you're exhausted and confused, the way I am. We both need to rest." She sighed. "I feel like I've used up a month's worth of psychic energy in a couple of minutes."

"But you don't know," he clarified.

"What do you want me to do about that? Make the whole thing go away?" she snapped.

When she said it, he knew it *was* what he wanted. But he wasn't going to admit that. Not when they were both so close to the edge.

He took a step back. "I need time to think."

She couldn't leave it at that. "You're walking away from me because your middle-class values won't let you imagine a mate who is your equal—or maybe more? Is that it?"

"Lower class. Make that lower-class values," he shot back.

Before she could say anything else, he turned away. Instead of walking through the house, he hurried around the vast structure. When he reached the driveway, he strode deliberately toward his car, all the time expecting some kind of mental bolt of energy from her. Some kind of angry denunciation. But he heard only the buzzing of blood in his own ears.

He started the car with jerky movements, then lurched out of the drive. He remembered the first time he'd come here. He remembered thinking that he'd changed a lot. He'd congratulated himself that he wasn't the angry, scared kid who had fled Baltimore. Apparently he'd been wrong. He was still Vic Marshall's son. He might have polished up his exterior, but inside he was Johnny Marshall. And that kid couldn't deal with Olivia Woodlock. Not when she had powers beyond his imagining, powers that could bring him to his knees with the touch of her mind.

He tightened his hands on the wheel, knowing he had to get away, even when the ache in his heart felt as though it might kill him. He'd said he had to think even when he knew he was fleeing the unknown. The question was—could he ever come back?

OLIVIA felt as though someone had cut through the wall of her chest with a dull knife and pierced her heart. Too shaky to stand, on her own, she reached back and braced herself against the balustrade.

She had been afraid of what she felt for Sam Morgan. She'd fought her attraction to him. Then, at the Reese house, he'd given her an excellent reason to run away from him. But the wolf had made no difference to her feelings. She'd fallen in love with him. And there was nothing she could do about it.

She'd thought the two of them would spend the rest of their lives together. Then, this evening, when she'd dipped her fingers into the Astravor, everything had changed.

She was still Olivia Woodlock, the woman who loved Sam Morgan. Yet she was more, and she couldn't lie about that—to herself or to Sam. As if lying to him would do any good.

Deep down, she had been afraid of what would happen when she claimed her family heritage. Now she had come into her powers and lost her mate.

She had taken the risk of loving, and she was left with ashes.

"Sam," she whispered. "Sam, don't turn away from me."

He couldn't hear her, and she wanted to reach out to him with her mind. Maybe she still had enough psychic energy left to do that. She didn't know. But she understood that it would be the worst thing she could do.

She looked toward the house. Probably Colin had given her father the Astravor. But she couldn't face either one of them now. She didn't want to hear anyone tell her she'd made a mess of her life. Tears stung her eyes as she pushed herself upright. Stepping off the patio, she walked into the garden, not even sure where she was headed. The cold air raised goose bumps on her skin, and she wrapped her arms around her shoulders, rubbing.

"It's too bad I'm not carrying your child," she whispered into the darkness. "You'd have to stick with me then."

Even as she said the words, she denied them. She didn't want Sam on those terms. She wanted him with her because he loved her, because the two of them could make a life together. Because she was his mate and he was hers.

And if he never returned?

She would have to find a way to live alone.

Without Sam, she would have no children. And that would be so sad. There were other things she could do with her life, though, starting with re-forming Woodlock Industries. But that would be a hollow existence.

"Come back. Just come back, and we'll work it out," she whispered into the darkness.

Only silence met her.

WILSON lay in the rumpled bed where he'd been confined for days. His heart was racing. He wanted to leap up. But he stayed where he was, his voice deliberately calm. "If you have the Astravor, then Ethridge must be dead."

"Yes."

"What happened?"

"I don't know for sure," Colin answered. "I wasn't there."

"But you know Olivia fought him," Wilson insisted.

"I think so," Colin admitted.

They were both silent for several moments, both lost in their own thoughts. He had taken the magic elixir a few minutes ago, and everything had changed.

"Are you feeling better?" Colin finally asked.

"Yes. Thank you. But I've been sick for a long time, and I need to rest," he lied.

"I understand," his son, the wimp, answered. He'd been raised to be the head of family. But he was willing to give that honor to his sister.

Wilson made his voice low and wispy. "Let me sleep for a while."

"Yes. Of course. I'll go take care of Uncle D. Then I'll come back and see how you're doing."

Colin finally cleared out, and Wilson sat up. The moment his fingers had dipped into the Astravor, he'd felt a surge of energy, wiping away the sick feeling that had hung over him for so long. He was himself again. Back in control.

The horrible muzzy feeling was gone from his mind, and he understood what his children had been doing. Going behind his back. Defying him.

Well, they had gotten away with it while he was sick. But he was better now. And it was time to test his psychic power—the power to see the future.

With a burst of joy, he called the old skill to him. There was a moment of fear when he felt nothing. Then the flickering of awareness crept into his mind.

A picture formed in his thoughts, gray and indistinct. But he knew how to bring up the color, sharpen the focus.

Cherished abilities came back. With a satisfying jolt of pleasure, the image was *there*. But as he stared into the future, the pleasure evaporated in a surge of fear and anger.

"No!" He wouldn't have it! Not after everything he'd been through. Not when he'd worked so hard to secure the future he wanted for his children and grandchildren.

He pushed himself out of bed, then cursed because it took a moment to get his balance.

When he was steady on his feet, he strode toward the door, knowing he was going to have to act quickly if he was going to have any chance at all of setting things right.

* * *

SAM sped north, feeling worse the farther he got from Montecito. He was doing the unthinkable. Leaving his mate.

Olivia.

And not Olivia. Because the woman he had left standing on the patio wasn't the woman he had first met at Wilson Woodlock's party. She was something more. Something astonishing, and he didn't know how to cope with what she had become.

Before he'd met her, when he'd thought of marriage at all, he'd thought of it in terms of his parents. He'd loved his mother, but she had been a woman who deferred in all things to Vic Marshall.

He'd known Olivia would never be like that. Still, he'd hoped his special talents gave him an edge that would make up for the Wood-lock position of power.

Now he knew there was no way he could ever be her equal. Not in this lifetime. And he understood on some deep, emotional level that his ego was rebelling against the role reversal. So he was crawling back into his cave and shutting the door behind him.

Some part of himself stood back, telling Sam Morgan he was a fool to let Johnny Marshall rule his life. But he couldn't stop himself from driving away.

He was almost at the turnoff to San Marcos Pass when a jolt of psychic pain and fear hit him like a million megawatt bolt of lightning, sizzling along his nerve endings.

Sam. Oh God, Sam, help me.

The physical and mental anguish were so searing that he almost skidded into the car in the next lane.

32

THE sound of the other driver's horn blared in Sam's ear as he fought to stay on the road.

"Olivia?" he shouted.

But she couldn't hear him because she wasn't there. After that one frightening call for help, he heard only a terrible silence.

All his self-serving thoughts of escape fled his mind. Fear for Olivia clawed at him as he sped to the next exit, took the off-ramp, and turned back in the other direction.

"Olivia. Love, I'm coming. Just hang on," he raged into the empty confines of the car.

He didn't know what had happened. He didn't know if she could hear him. But it helped to keep talking to her.

"Love, I'm so sorry. Forgive me. I never should have left you. Just hang on. Do that for me."

Then another jolt of pain hit him, worse than before. In that moment, the car skidded out of control, onto the shoulder, gravel crunching under the wheels, and he knew that disaster was less than a second away.

OLIVIA lay on the cold ground. In the illumination from the flood-lights, she stared up at the man who towered over her.

She blinked, trying to make her mind work, trying to understand what her eyes saw when every cell of her body shrieked in pain.

"Don't . . . please," she managed to get out before he bent down and pressed the weapon against her shoulder, hitting her again with a blast of electricity that vibrated through every cell of her body. She knew what it was. A stun gun. Her father had kept it in a locked cabinet, along with his other weapons. Now he stood over her, hold-ing it.

For days, he had been too sick to get out of bed, and she had been afraid he was going to die.

But the Astravor must have worked, and now he was on his feet again. His body was under his control, but his mind was still . . . sick.

She wanted to ask why he was doing this to her. But she couldn't make her voice work. She couldn't move. And the burst of pure terror she had sent to Sam had drained the last of her psychic abilities. But she could hear her father raging at her.

"I won't let him have you, not that lowlife Sam Morgan. Darwin called him a demon. He was right all along. The demon Morgan came to steal my daughter from me."

If she could have spoken, she would have told him Sam had left. But communication was beyond her.

Her father's voice rose as he stood over her, gun in hand. "You and Colin hired him to do a job. But you ended up in his bed. How could you? After the way you were raised."

Words formed in her mind, but she couldn't move her lips.

"I know he left. I heard the bastard drive away like he was leaving you. I wish to hell it were true. But he's coming back. Or you're going to throw yourself on his mercy. You. A Woodlock, groveling at the feet of a man who isn't fit to shine your shoes. Don't bother to tell me differently. I have my power back. I can see your future. I can see you and him and your brood of little bastard demon thieves. But I won't let it happen. I'll fry your brains with this thing before I let that happen."

No. Oh, God, no. Please.

Her father reached toward her with the weapon again, but the sound of running feet made him stop and whir.

Sam.

"No!"

She heard her brother's voice. "Dad! What are you doing?"

His question rang out into the awful stillness of the night, as still as the eye of a hurricane.

Her father swung away from her. "Stay away from me."

"Dad, put down the gun."

"I'm the head of this family. I make the decisions. You were all working behind my back. Taking over. And you think you can still defy me."

"We weren't working behind your back. We kept you informed. We had to do it, because you were too sick to take charge."

"I was never too sick to make decisions. I did what needed to be done. I let Darwin out of his room, so he could help Irene escape."

"Why?" Colin gasped.

"So she'd go back to Ethridge. I knew he'd kill her. I let him do the dirty work. But now I'm back in charge. So I'm warning you. Stay away from me."

"Dad . . ."

Colin leaped forward. The gun made a sizzling noise. Her brother screamed and fell to the ground.

Her father bent over him, and the gun hissed again. She knew, in some twisted way, he was doing what he had to. In his mind, he was preserving his family values.

Every scrap of her concentration now was on fighting her father. She had to get away. She had to save herself. And save her brother.

But she couldn't do it. Dad had disabled her body and disabled her psychic ability with the blasts from the stun gun.

As a silent scream welled inside her, a breeze sprang up, ruffling her hair. It picked up force, making the branches of a nearby tree shake with astonishing violence.

"Darwin?" her father called. "Is that you? Are you with me or against me?" The wind answered with a howl.

SAM roared into the driveway, pulled up in front of the house, and slammed on the brake.

He knew where Olivia was. She hadn't told him, but somehow he knew she was still out in back of the house, where he had left her.

He raced around the mansion, stopping in the shadows, because he realized that leaping into danger before he understood what was going on could be fatal, both to himself and Olivia.

The night had been calm. Out here, the wind roared, and lightning crackled in the dark sky.

In the illumination from the floodlights, he saw Olivia lying on the grass. Colin was sprawled nearby. Both of them looked limp and lifeless. And their father crouched over them. Had he hurt them? Or had Darwin knocked them to the ground?

Wilson bent toward his daughter again, his hand extended, and Sam felt his heart leap into his throat as he saw the weapon in his hand. The sick reality of what he was seeing snapped into focus. All along, he had thought Wilson might attack him. Instead, he had gone after Olivia.

"No!" he shouted. "Get the hell away from her."

The older man whirled, the weapon pointed toward the interloper. Sam's considerable training told him what he was seeing. A stun gun.

His mind made a quick assessment. There were several versions of the weapon. One used an air charge to fire two bolts over a fifteen-foot range. But it only had two shots before the whole system had to be reset.

The other kind fired electrical charges directly into a person or animal, but only with direct contact.

Either Wilson had reset the weapon, or he had to be on top of the victim.

A flash of movement made him swing his head to the right. Jefferies stood outside the French doors, holding a pistol, and Sam fought a new spurt of panic.

"Don't shoot," Sam called out, pitching his voice to carry only as far as the doorway. "You could hit Olivia or Colin."

When Jefferies nodded, Sam switched his focus back to Wilson and raised his voice. "Over here. Come and get me, you bastard. Or are you a coward?"

"You! Stay away from my daughter."

"Make me," Sam challenged. He thought about the night he'd started to change in front of Darwin. He thought about the trick he'd pulled on Ethridge. Every fiber of his being urged him to change into a wolf. But if he followed his instincts now, he wouldn't be able to speak to Wilson. And he needed to lure the man away from Olivia.

Heart-stopping moments dragged by before the head of the Woodlock family started moving toward him, looking a lot more fit than the last time Sam had seen him. He was old, Sam told himself. He was no match for a thirty-year-old. Yet Sam felt his muscles clench. He had underestimated Darwin that night in the sunroom. He could be just as wrong now. He plowed ahead.

"Come and get me," he shouted again. "Hurry up."

When Wilson charged toward him, he felt a spurt of triumph. Every step toward Sam Morgan was a step away from Olivia.

But the wind impeded the man's progress, whipping at his shirt and pants.

Wilson stopped, and Sam shouted a curse into the night. "Come on, you bastard."

The head of the Woodlock clan wasn't focused on his daughter's lover now. He was looking quickly around, then up at the sky.

"Darwin?" he shouted as the wind tore at him. "What the hell are you doing, Darwin?"

There was no answer. Not with words. But a shower of hail fell from the sky, not over the whole lawn but just on Wilson Woodlock's head and shoulders.

He screamed, raising the weapon, turning in a circle, looking for an enemy he couldn't see.

"Stay away from me," he cried out. "Stay the fuck away."

Sam watched as a bolt of lightning cut like a jagged knife across the dark sky.

The wind howled with a man's voice. And Sam realized there were words shrieking in the air. "Wilson, put down the gun."

"No! Leave me alone, you old fool. You don't know anything."

In answer, a savage gust of air raked across the lawn, catching Wilson and spinning him around.

Sam saw the stun gun discharge as another lightning bolt formed in the heavens, then speared down like the wrath of Zeus.

It hit Wilson in the chest. His scream rang out, followed by the smell of burning flesh. And then absolute quiet filled the night.

SAM sat rigidly in the chair beside Olivia's bed.

A blast from a stun gun wasn't fatal. He kept telling that to himself. But how many times had her father shot her?

The moment she stirred, every muscle in his body tensed and he leaned over her. "Olivia? Thank God."

"Sam," she breathed.

"How do you feel?"

"A lot . . . better."

A choking sound rose in his throat. "Forgive me."

"For what?"

"Leaving you."

"I called you back. And you came."

He told her what he had ached to say. "Yes. I heard you, love. And I would have walked barefoot across broken glass to get to you when you needed me."

"Oh, Lord, Sam." She tried to push herself up, and he put a gentle palm on her shoulder. When she reached to cover his fingers, he felt himself relax a fraction.

His vision blurring, he turned his hand and clasped hers, and a little sigh breathed out of her.

She tugged at his hand. "Come here."

He came down on the bed, gathering her in his arms, holding tight, and for a long moment cradling her against himself was the only thing that mattered.

Then he felt her swallow. "Is my father . . . dead?"

"Yes." Sam heard his own voice hitch. "Killed by a thunderstorm that looked like it blew up out of nowhere."

"That's what Jefferies thinks?"

"Yes."

"What about my Uncle Darwin?" she whispered.

"He's . . . resting."

"Does he know about my father?"

"I think so. But he's not quite himself."

"What's going to happen to him?"

"That depends on what kind of recovery he makes."

They were talking in a kind of code.

Finally, she spoke directly. "I wish Dad had . . . made it."

Sam couldn't hold back his outrage. "He hurt you! Why would he do that to his daughter?"

She tightened her hold on him. "Have you ever heard the phrase power corrupts? And absolute power corrupts absolutely."

"Yeah."

"Well, that was his big problem. His parents treated him like a king. He thought he was entitled to anything he wanted. And he wanted things the way they were."

"But he . . . attacked his own family."

"I just told you, he was raised to expect the world to turn at his command. And he didn't know how to cope any other way." She sighed. "He knew you and I were going to take his place."

"How could we . . . when I left?"

"You left today. But he could see the future. He told me he saw us together."

"Jesus. He hurt you because of me . . . because of us?"

"It wasn't just seeing the future. He knew you had already rescued me from him."

"I was too late for that," he reminded her, his tone gritty.

"No," she said softly, "you already saved me."

"When?"

"It started the night of the party. I saw you, and I knew my life was never going to be the same."

"Olivia." He gathered her closer, allowing himself a moment to clasp her tightly before easing away so he could look into her eyes. "While we're being brutally honest, you know I would have done *anything* I had to do to stop him from hurting you."

"Yes. I know that," she said, her tone very serious. "But I'm glad you didn't have to be the one." She dragged in a breath and let it out. "How did you handle the cover-up?"

"Jefferies called nine-one-one and reported that lightning had struck your father. Before they arrived, we took you and Colin inside."

Just then, the door opened a crack.

They both looked up and saw Colin's anxious face. "I heard you talking. Are you all right?"

"Yes," Olivia answered. "What about you?"

"Not too bad, considering." He gave them an assessing look. "I just wanted to make sure everything was okay. I'll leave you alone."

"Wait. What about Barbara—and Ross and Thurston?" Olivia asked.

"They came back a while ago. Ross said he'd like some downtime. So he's at the Biltmore."

Sam nodded. "He knows when to stay out of the way." He laughed. "At the best hotel in town."

"Yes," Colin agreed. "And Barbara is going to stay here for a while. She and Brice are out on the sun porch comparing notes on Mozart operas."

"I think you and Brice will be good for her," Olivia murmured.

"Right. We're two non-threatening males. I believe we can tell people she's our cousin. If anybody asks what she's doing here."

"Yes."

He looked at Sam. "I haven't thanked you . . . for everything. We'd still be sick, if it weren't for you."

"I'm glad it worked out. Very glad," he added.

"I'll go tell Barbara and Thurston you're okay."

"And call Ross," Sam added.

"Yes." Colin stepped back into the hall, leaving them alone again.

They lay on the bed in silence for several moments, Sam cherishing the chance to be close again. Then Olivia cleared her throat, and he tensed.

"What about us?" she asked. "I mean the rest of our lives."

He felt his face contort. "If you mean, am I going to cut and run again, I think I acquired a big dose of maturity in the past few hours. I mean, I would have eventually figured out I was acting like a jerk. But I had some incentive to hurry up the process."

"So you've decided you can live with a woman who . . ."

"A woman who called out to me—and nobody else—when she needed help," he finished, his voice gritty.

"When I was in danger, I reached out to you." Before he could respond, she went on quickly, "But I want to be clear. You know I'm . . . different from the Olivia Woodlock who hired you a couple of months ago."

"I see you don't want any misunderstandings," he answered.

"No. I don't."

"Well, then, let me put it this way. You're the woman I love. My mate. The mother of the children we're going to have together."

"And you can accept my . . . talents?" she murmured.

"I think so. I'm going to work hard at trying not to be a lower-class male chauvinist wolf." He laughed. "You can kick me when I forget that we're partners."

She reached for him again, and he gathered her to him.

"Oh, Sam. I want what we've made together. So much."

"Yes." He swallowed. "While you were sleeping, I was sitting here, daring to think about our future."

"Good."

"I was thinking about where we'd live."

"It doesn't have to be in this house."

"We don't have to decide yet. But we should talk about my profession."

She cocked her head to one side. "What about it?"

"It was suitable for a lone wolf. It's not so great for a family man."

"I wouldn't ask you to give up the job you love."

He laughed, feeling better by the moment. "I did get considerable pleasure from it. But I think I can reduce it to the status of hobby. I can support you very well on my investments. But maybe I can get a job with one of the environmental groups."

"Or maybe you'd like to help bring Woodlock Industries into the twenty-first century. Maybe you'd like to turn a major polluter into a model company."

He knew he must look startled. "You'd trust me with the family business?"

"I trust you with my life."

"Would it be okay with Colin for me to stick my paws in Woodlock Industries?"

"Colin and I already talked about your joining the company. He likes the idea. He didn't approve of what Dad was doing. But he particularly appreciates the notion of letting someone else take the responsibility of fixing it."

Sam laughed. "Convenient for him, to have a tree hugger for a brother-in-law."

"Yes. And a brother-in-law who can give him nieces and nephews to spoil." She cleared her throat. "Which brings up an important point. It would be nice if we got married before I get pregnant."

He felt like his heart would burst, but he managed to say, "Not a bad idea."

"Do you mind a quiet ceremony? I mean . . . because of my father."

"Just so the world knows you're mine."

"Oh, I am. Body and soul. And . . ."

"What?"

"How would you feel if I wanted to try having you use the Astravor?"

He blinked. "How could I? I'm not a member of your family."

"I think I have the power to . . . condition you. A tiny bit at a time. I think we might be able to do it."

"You'd want to share that with me?"

She wrapped her arms around him again. "Yes. I want to share everything with you that I can. Starting with . . . I'd like to find out what making love with you is like, now that I'm well again."

"Oh yeah." He struggled to rein in his enthusiasm. "But you just took a couple of bad jolts from a stun gun. You need to rest."

"I think I know what medicine I need. Let me show you."

Under the covers she slid her hand down his body, making him instantly hard.

"Maybe I'd better lock the door first," he murmured.

He got up and quickly turned the lever, then came back to the bed.

Even as he stretched out beside her, her lips touched down on his, settled, melded into a long, hot kiss—a kiss that told him they could work through their problems because they had a bond too strong for anyone or anything to break.